THE GREY KNIGHTS OMNIBUS

SERVANTS OF THE Ordo Malleus, the Grey Knights are imperious and incorruptible warriors. Their purpose is to seek out and destroy the most dangerous foes that humanity will ever face: daemons. Armed and armoured with the trappings of the daemonhunter, they bring death and destruction to the immortal denizens of the warp. Girded by faith, wielders of the nemesis force halberd, the Grey Knights step where others will not tread. Risking their immortal souls, they pursue the hungry entities of Chaos, the Imperium's most arch foes. Their epic struggles and heroic battles are collected in this omnibus of the novels *Grey Knights*, *Dark Adeptus* and *Hammer of Daemons*.

A WARHAMMER 40,000 OMNIBUS

THE GREY KNIGHTS OMNIBUS

Ben Counter

A Black Library Publication

Grey Knights copyright © 2004, Games Workshop Ltd.
Dark Adeptus copyright © 2006, Games Workshop Ltd.
Hammer of Daemons copyright © 2008, Games Workshop Ltd.
All rights reserved.

This omnibus edition published in Great Britain in 2009 by
BL Publishing,
Games Workshop Ltd.,
Willow Road,
Nottingham, NG7 2WS, UK.

10 9 8 7 6 5 4 3 2 1

Cover illustration by Clint Langley.

A CIP record for this book is available from the British Library.

ISBN 13: 978 1 84416 696 1
ISBN 10: 1 84416 696 1

Distributed in the US by Simon & Schuster
1230 Avenue of the Americas, New York, NY 10020, US.

See the Black Library on the Internet at
www.blacklibrary.com

Find out more about Games Workshop
and the world of Warhammer 40,000 at
www.games-workshop.com

Printed and bound in the US.

IT IS THE 41st millennium. For more than a hundred centuries
the Emperor has sat immobile on the Golden Throne of Earth.
He is the master of mankind by the will of the gods, and master
of a million worlds by the might of his inexhaustible armies. He
is a rotting carcass writhing invisibly with power from the Dark
Age of Technology. He is the Carrion Lord of the Imperium
for whom a thousand souls are sacrificed every day, so
that he may never truly die.

YET EVEN IN his deathless state, the Emperor continues his
eternal vigilance. Mighty battlefleets cross the daemon-infested
miasma of the warp, the only route between distant stars, their
way lit by the Astronomican, the psychic manifestation of the
Emperor's will. Vast armies give battle in his name on uncounted
worlds. Greatest amongst His soldiers are the Adeptus Astartes,
the Space Marines, bio-engineered super-warriors. Their comrades
in arms are legion: the Imperial Guard and countless planetary
defence forces, the ever-vigilant Inquisition and the tech-priests of
the Adeptus Mechanicus to name only a few. But for all their
multitudes, they are barely enough to hold off the ever-present
threat from aliens, heretics, mutants – and worse.

TO BE A man in such times is to be one amongst untold
billions. It is to live in the cruellest and most bloody
regime imaginable. These are the tales of those times
Forget the power of technology and science, for so much has
been forgotten, never to be re-learned. Forget the promise of
progress and understanding, for in the grim dark future
there is only war. There is no peace amongst the stars,
only an eternity of carnage and slaughter, and the
laughter of thirsting gods.

CONTENTS

AUTHOR'S INTRODUCTION

THE CHANCE TO tackle the subject of the Grey Knights came about when *Codex: Daemonhunters* was released for Warhammer 40,000. They cried out for a novel to be written about them and as the fates would have it, I got the job. Grey Knights have been a part of the Warhammer 40,000 background since the days of the atmospheric and completely insane *The Lost and the Damned* rulebook. In this book, ostensibly devoted to the minions of Chaos, the Grey Knights represented the elite forces facing the daemons that wanted to devour humanity. When the Grey Knights received an overhaul and regained their place in the 41st millennium, I knew I had to write about them.

One of the challenges with the Grey Knights is that they aren't just Space Marines. A Space Marine is enough of a challenge already: he started out a human being but he has been transformed both physically and mentally. He knows no fear, or at least he doesn't feel it in the same way we do. And he isn't a machine either. In fact he's the opposite, because his emotions – anger, grief at the loss of a battle-brother, the obligation to fulfil his duties – are stronger than a mere human's. A Grey Knight has all these qualities but more so, because he has to face not only the enemies besetting humanity but also, in the form of the daemon, the most dangerous and corruptive foe imaginable. He's stronger, more intense, more aware of the peril the human race is facing, and more adorned with the gothic, almost medieval, imagery in which so much of the 41st millennium is steeped.

All these challenges, however, were outweighed by the fact that the Grey Knights are just so *cool*. I had the chance to explore one of the most intriguing and clandestine corners of the Warhammer 40,000 background: the Inquisition's use of the moons of Saturn, the prayers the Grey Knights intoned before battle, their myths and principles, and the way they went about facing their impossible task. I made the Grey Knights grim and straightforward, but quick to anger and relentless once they have an enemy in their sights, perhaps even too stubborn and vengeful for their own good. They were proud, too, a trait typical of a superhuman Space Marine, and not without reason given their history. The chance to examine all of this was too good to pass up and eventually I started to really understand who the Grey Knights were and why they did what they did – not because they were ordered to, or because the Inquisition made them, but because every Grey Knight knows that if he doesn't take responsibility for saving the human race from daemons – then no one else will.

With *Grey Knights*, I wanted to show the Chapter's stock in trade – a battle against a cunning daemon prince manipulating a huge conspiracy to bring him back into reality. Justicar Alaric was the Grey Knight who found himself in the centre of all this. I wanted him to be a tough, devout warrior, one whose sense of duty meant he could never back down from his obligation to destroy daemons wherever he found them. In fact, this sense of duty forms a part of the Daemon Prince Ghargatuloth's plan, since he knows full well that the Grey Knights will come after him. As the conspiracy unfolded, I wanted to illustrate that a Grey Knight's most powerful weapon isn't his Nemesis halberd or his ornate power armour, but his strength of will. Alaric does more than his share of decapitating, maiming and destroying, but when the real struggle kicks in, it's his strength of mind that counts.

For *Dark Adeptus*, the set-up demanded a unique kind of villain. Ghargatuloth was a daemon in the classic Warhammer vein, a Lovecraftian horror of blasphemy and cunning, but his successor needed to be something different. The villain was taken from the Imperium's own past, corrupted by the warp but very much a product of the Imperial way of thinking. Alaric had relied to some extent on his fellow guardians of the Imperium in *Grey Knights*, so I cut him off for most of *Dark Adeptus* by dropping him onto an overwhelmingly hostile planet with some dubious allies and no way of getting help. Alaric also continued the change in his character that had begun at the end of *Grey Knights*. Alaric's human side was more pronounced than in his fellow Grey Knights, and he had the capacity for imagination and even doubt that his Chapter's leaders would see as a weakness. To help bring this aspect of him to the fore, Alaric's foe in *Dark Adeptus* is one who can only be faced with a combination of imagination and brute strength.

But daemons and the taint of the warp are all par for the course for a Grey Knight. The events of Alaric's first two adventures are typical of dire happenings all over the Imperium, and Alaric himself, in spite of his unusual outlook, is still a tooled-up daemon hunter familiar to anyone who knows the background of the 41st millennium. For Alaric's third outing in *Hammer of Daemons*, I wanted to really put him through the wringer. Daemons and conspiracies didn't cut it any more – Grey Knights deal with that kind of thing every day. This time, Alaric would be in unfamiliar territory. I decided to put him almost literally through hell, strip him of his weapons and cut him off from his allies. I wanted to see how far he would go to fulfil his duty, even at the risk of becoming something less like a Grey Knight and more like the foes he is sworn to destroy. I didn't know how far Alaric could bend before he broke, or what would happen if he plunged too deeply into the mind-set of his enemy.

At the end of the trilogy, I'm not sure what Alaric has become. Perhaps he can't even call himself a Grey Knight, at least not in the same way as he did at the beginning of the first book. He has changed a great deal, lost many allies, dispatched a lot more enemies and come to understand some truths about the galaxy cruel enough to shake even a Space Marine's faith. The Inquisition, in the form of Alaric's ally Nyxos, seems to have plans for Alaric, and no doubt he won't be hanging up his Nemesis halberd as long as there are daemons to be killed. But what does the galaxy hold for him next? That remains to be seen, but it will certainly involve heroism, the minions of Chaos and a lot of violence.

Ben Counter
September 2008

GREY KNIGHTS

ONE
KHORION IX

IT WAS A heaving sea of hatred, an ocean of pure evil.

Far below, the surface of Khorion IX was covered in a seething forest of torture racks, crosses and squares and stars of bloodstained wood on which were broken hundreds of thousands of bodies, mangled and wound around the wood like vines around a cane. It was like a huge and horrible vineyard, with rows and rows of crucified bodies spilling a terrible vintage of blood into the earth. The victims were trapped between life and death, their bodies exsanguinated but their minds just lucid enough to understand their agony. They were the servants of the Prince of a Thousand Faces, the cultists and demagogues summoned to their master's planet in the hope of an eternal reward that was all too real. Their bodies were merged with the wood that had grown as the seasons passed, twisting their limbs into canopies of fleshy branches and deforming them until there was barely anything human in them save for their suffering.

They said the screams could be heard from orbit. They were right.

At an unheard signal, the ground began to seethe. The crucified of Khorion IX began to wail even louder, their agony supplanted by fear, as the sodden earth burst into fountains of bloodstained soil and a hideous gibbering rose up from beneath. Iridescent, shifting creatures crawled up to the surface, some with long reaching fingers and torsos dominated by leering, huge-mawed faces, others with bloated fungoid bodies that belched multicoloured flame. There were ravenous swarms of tiny, misshapen things that gnawed at the roots of the crucified forest and immense winged monsters like huge deformed vultures that spat magic fire. Every one was a shining multicoloured vision of hell, and each was just a pale reflection of their master. The Prince of a Thousand Faces, the Forger of Hells, the Whisperer in the Darkness – Ghargatuloth the Daemon Lord, chosen of the God of Change.

A tide of daemons burst like an ocean from the ground and flooded through the crucified forest, shrieking in anticipation and hunger, the greater daemons marshalling the lesser and the lowest of them, forming a mantle of daemon flesh that covered the ground in a sea of iridescence.

The daemonic tide poured onto the surface until from far above it looked like an ocean of daemonskin, the lesser daemons sweeping between the rows of the crucified and the greater crushing Ghargatuloth's slave-victims beneath clawed feet. The will of Ghargatuloth resonated through the very crust of Khorion IX; every single one of the Tzeentch's servants felt it.

The next turning point will be here, it said. Thousands of the Change God's plots were coming to a head in this battle, a tangled nexus of fates that would set the path for the future. It was fate that formed the medium through which Tzeentch mutated the universe to his will, and so this was a holy battle where fate was the weapon, the prize and the battleground.

The cackling of the daemon army mixed with the screams of the crucified and the air vibrated with the din. For light years in all directions the insane babbling and screams of desperation gnawed at every mind, whispering darkly and shrieking insanely. Though the space around Khorion IX was largely devoid of human habitation, many of those few who heard the call of the daemon lost their minds in the prelude to the battle.

But the minds that mattered, the minds of those who would face the horde of Ghargatuloth, were unwavering. They had trained since before they could remember in resisting the trickery of Tzeentch himself and the creeping corruption that had brought so many to the fold of Ghargatuloth. They were armed with the best weapons the Ordo Malleus could give them, protected by consecrated power armour hundreds if not thousands of years old, shielded from sorcery by hexagrammic and pentagrammic wards tattooed onto their skin by the sages of the Inquisitorial archives.

They were ready. Their very purpose was to be ready, because when the time came to fight something like Ghargatuloth, who else could do it? They were the Grey Knights, the daemon hunters of the Adeptus Astartes, tasked by the Ordo Malleus of the Inquisition and hence the Emperor Himself to fight the daemon in all its forms. They were just a handful in number compared to the trillions of citizens making up the Imperium but when a threat like Ghargatuloth was finally brought to bear, the Grey Knights were literally the Imperium's only hope.

There were three hundred of them bearing down on Khorion IX to have their say in the confluence of fates. And Khorion IX was waiting for them.

THE FIRST THINGS Grand Master Mandulis saw of Khorion IX were the thick bands of cloud, white and streaked with red, as they rushed past the viewport of the drop-pod that plummeted through the planet's lower atmosphere. The screams from below sounded even through the din of the descent and the pod's lander engines, a million voices raised in praise and anticipation, calling out for blood and for new spirits to break on the anvil of Ghargatuloth's sorcery.

The Grey Knights' briefing sermon had told them that an ancient pre-Imperial barrows complex was their landing zone, but the plans they had to go by were from exploratory records three hundred years old. There could be anything on Khorion IX. It had taken more than a century to track Ghargatuloth to the planet, and the daemon prince would know the Grey Knights were coming. It would be savage. Very probably, nothing would survive. Grand Master Mandulis knew this and accepted it, for he had sworn long ago that the destruction of the daemonic was of greater importance than his life. He had decades of experience in the ranks of the Grey Knights, he had fought across a hundred worlds in the unending hidden war against the horrors of the warp, but if he had to die to see Ghargatuloth banished from real space then he would gladly die.

But it wouldn't be that simple.

The drop-pod's proximity alarms kicked in and filled the cramped interior with deep red light. It picked out the face of Justicar Chemuel, whose squad Mandulis was accompanying in the assault. Chemuel was as good a soldier as the Grey Knights had, and Mandulis had seen how he led his Purgation squad. His Marines carried psycannon and flamers and Chemuel had drilled them until they could lay down massive pinpoint fire. It would be Chemuel's task to help clear the path through Ghargatuloth's servants so the veteran Terminator assault squads could close with the greater daemons and even with the Prince of a Thousand Faces himself.

That was the plan, but plans never lasted. The Grey Knights could fight the battles they did precisely because every one of them was trained and psycho-doctrinated to survive in the forge of battle alone if needs be; Chemuel like his battle-brothers would fight alone when the battle broke down into a slaughter.

That was when, not if. That was the way of daemons. They wrought bloodshed and confusion because they enjoyed it. Ghargatuloth had surrounded himself with an immense army of such creatures, and if the Grey Knight had to fight them all at once, then they would.

The restraints holding Mandulis and Squad Chemuel into their grav-couches wound in suddenly for the impact. Blood-streaked clouds rushed past the viewport and then they were gone. The pod's lander engines fired and again the pod decelerated suddenly, swooping as it came in to land. For a moment Mandulis was looking out on the twisted nightmare that was Khorion IX – the landscape shattered as if struck by a giant hammer, row upon row of tormented bodies staked out or nailed to crosses and arranged in terraced fields stretching between horizons. A waterfall of blood poured into a churning red sea in the distance.

A network of pre-Imperial barrows, the only recognisable landmark from the ancient maps of the planet, was ringed with banner poles from which hung innumerable flags of flayed skin. And worst of all, the daemon army seethed, hundreds of thousands strong, surrounding the closest barrow in an unbroken sea of daemon flesh.

Mandulis had been a Grey Knight since before he could remember. He had fought the Chaotic and daemonic from the heart of the Segmentum Solar to far-flung daemon worlds, from the halls of planetary governors to the endless slums of hive cities. Mandulis had seen so much that volumes of his battlefield reports filled shelves of the Archivum Titanis, and yet still in all his days he had never seen anything like the horde of Ghargatuloth.

He was not afraid. The Emperor himself had decreed that a Space Marine shall know no fear. But Grand Master Mandulis's soul still recoiled at the sheer magnitude of evil.

'I am the hammer,' he intoned as the landing jets pushed even harder against the drop-pod's descent. 'I am the right hand of my Emperor, the instrument of His will, the gauntlet about His fist, the tip of His spear, the edge of His sword...'

The Marines of Squad Chemuel followed Mandulis as he led them in the final battlefield prayer, intoning the sacred words even though they could barely hear them above the scream of the drop-pod's final braking jets.

The impact was immense, like slamming into a wall. The grav-couch restraints jolted back as the pods ploughed through the branches of wood and bone, into the middle of the daemon throng. A great scream rose above the din of the impact as daemons were vaporised by the impact, and the viewport was suddenly covered in their many-coloured blood.

'Pod down!' yelled Justicar Chemuel. 'Blow the restraints!'

The servitor-pilot controlling the pod's systems responded to the pre-programmed order and the bolts holding the pod's sides together burst with a series of sharp reports. The sides of the pod burst open and Mandulis's restraints fell away. Baleful reddish light and a truly appalling stench of decay flooded in, so thick it was like plunging into a sea of blood. The screams of the engines were replaced by the unearthly and hideous keening of thousands of daemons, like an atonal choir howling out a wall of sound. The weeping sky was scratched by the reaching branches of crucified limbs, the forest swarmed with daemons, the pure hatred of Ghargatuloth's army was like a wave of pain pouring into the drop-pod.

Mandulis had a split second before the daemons closed in again. The pod had blasted a crater, thick with daemon gore, ringed by broken crucifix-trees. Blood spurted from tears in the ground as if from severed arteries. The stench that got through Mandulis's helmet filters was of burning and blood, and the howling of the daemons hit him like a gale.

'Squad, suppression fire!' called Chemuel and his Marines, their psy-cannons already loaded and primed, thudded off a single, huge volley that blasted apart the daemons scrambling over the ridge of the crater.

Mandulis saw another pod hitting home close by, throwing up a foul rain of blood and daemon body parts. 'That's Martel!' voxed Mandulis. 'Chemuel, give him cover and link up!'

Two Space Marines ran up the crater ridge and their incinerator-pattern flamers poured gouts of blue-hot flame into the tide of daemons pouring towards them through the woods. Mandulis stomped after them, the servos of his ancient Terminator suit whirring, his wrist-mounted storm bolter barking as he sent blessed bolter shots streaking into leering daemon faces. He reached the lip of the crater and saw the army for the first time from ground level – gnarled limbs of iridescent pink and blue, bloated creatures that belched flame, the lopsided shapes of avian greater daemons lurching towards the drop zone.

Mandulis drew his Nemesis sword from its scabbard on his back. The blade leapt into life, its power field calibrated to disrupt the psychic matter of daemons' flesh, the stylised golden lightning bolt set into its silver blade glowing hot with power. He lunged forward and cut a wide arc through the daemons clambering through the burning remains of their brothers; he felt three unholy bodies come apart under the blade's edge.

It was a good blade. One of the Chapter's best, given to Mandulis when he first attained the rank of master. But it would have to drink more daemon's blood than it had ever done before if he was to succeed in his mission now.

Psycannon fire from Chemuel was shrieking past, the modified bolter shells exploding in spectacular starbursts of silver that shredded the attacking daemons. The flamer troops moved up and were beside Mandulis, pouring more fire into the attacking daemons as Mandulis's Nemesis sword carved through any that got within range.

Martel's Terminator squad cut their way towards Mandulis, the huge tactical dreadnought armour battering aside the crucifix-trees as volleys of storm bolter fire cut through the forest.

'Brother Martel,' voxed Mandulis. 'Chemuel will cover you. We are close to the first barrow, follow me.'

'Well met, grand master,' replied Captain Martel as he speared a daemon with his Nemesis halberd. 'Justinian is close behind us. I think we are cut off from any of the others.'

'Then we will carry the attack ourselves,' voxed Mandulis. 'We knew it would come to this. Give grace to the Emperor for our part in this fight and keep moving.'

'In position!' came the vox from Justicar Chemuel. Mandulis turned to see the Purgation squad lined up on the lip of the crater, surrounded by the dissolving remains of charred daemons, ready to send volley after disciplined volley from the psycannon into Ghargatuloth's horde.

Grand Master Mandulis could feel, thrumming through the blood-soaked earth and cutting through the screams of the crucified, the deep angry growl of something waking. Below the ground, huge and malevolent, making ready to play its hand if the time came. The pre-battle guesswork had been correct – it was beneath the barrows and would be surrounded by the deadliest of its servants.

Mandulis mouthed a silent prayer to the Emperor as the daemon tide came again, gibbering and screeching as they swung through the trees and loped along the ground, shining with flame and foul sorcery.

Mandulis pressed down on the firing stud in his gauntlet and sent a stream of bolter shells ripping into the advancing daemons. He hefted his Nemesis sword ready to strike and, with Martel's Terminators at his side, he charged.

* * *

THE GREY KNIGHTS' strikeforce that attacked Khorion IX was the strongest the Ordo Malleus could assemble. Compact, fast, led by three grand masters of the Grey Knights and composed of the best daemon-hunting warriors the Imperium had, it was nonetheless far from certain that the force would succeed. It had taken a century to hunt down Ghargatuloth, the power which, through dozens of avatars and aspects, directed thousands of Chaos cults in acts of depravity and terror.

Ghargatuloth's purpose was to spread chaos and carnage in the name of its god Tzeentch, following an infinitely obscure plan that was all but impossible to trace. The Ordo Malleus had fought long and hard to find out that it lived on Khorion IX, an uninhabited and largely unexplored world deep into the Halo Zone of the Segmentum Obscurus where the beacon of the Astronomican barely reached. All that time Ghargatuloth had prepared and the Ordo Malleus had no choice but to send their troops into his trap, because they might never get another chance. Khorion IX was too isolated for a planet-scouring Imperial Navy assault and normal troops would last a matter of seconds on the planet. Even the Exterminatus, the ultimate Inquisitorial sanction, would not be enough – someone had to see Ghargatuloth die and, even with a devastating strike from orbit, the Ordo Malleus could not be sure.

It had to be the Grey Knights. Because if anyone could survive long enough to face Ghargatuloth in battle, it would be them.

The fast strike cruisers *Valour Saturnum* and *Vengeful* carried over two hundred and fifty Grey Knights, as large a force as could be moved quickly enough through the vastness of the Segmentum Obscurus. Lord Inquisitor Lakonios of the Ordo Malleus was in ultimate command but once the drop-pods were launched and the atmosphere of Khorion IX was breached, it was the Grey Knights themselves who gave the orders.

Grand Master Ganelon, who had personally killed the Vermin King of Kalentia when still a justicar, landed well off-centre in the thick of the daemon army. With nearly a hundred Grey Knights under his command he fought a valiant battle of survival against wave upon wave of daemons, back-to-back and completely surrounded. Marine after Marine died under sorcerous lightning or the talons of rampaging greater daemons and Ganelon himself began the Prayer of Purification, readying the souls of his men for the inevitable journey after death to join the Emperor in the final battle against Chaos.

The Marines under Grand Master Malquiant smashed into the edge of the crucified forest and formed a fearsome spearhead of seventy Grey Knights, tipped with the Terminator-armoured assault squads and ultimately the sanctified lightning claws of Malquiant himself. Huge portions of the horde swarmed to blunt the attack but those who bypassed the Malquiant's Terminators were cut to pieces by the massive, well-ordered crossfires from the Purgation and Tactical squads that followed. Malquiant's assault drained vast numbers of daemons from the forest, bleeding Ghargatuloth's horde dry in an awesome display of sheer bloody-minded aggression. But the horde was too vast and the broken terrain slowed the assault – Malquiant knew he would not reach the objective, and could only do what he could for his battle-brothers by forcing the bulk of the horde away from the barrows. As the assault ground to a halt Malquiant turned it into a killing zone, overlapping fields of fire and launching counter-assaults into anything that got through.

Grand Master Mandulis had landed closest to the barrows. Along with Squad Chemuel and Squad Martel, and Squad Justinian's tactical team who arrived in time to help cover the advance, Mandulis made the first strike into Ghargatuloth's lair. Over the static-filled vox he learned of Ganelon's sacrifice and Malquiant's relentless but bogged-down assault, and knew as he had somehow always known that it was up to him. Those who could told him that the strength within him was the Emperor's and that with His will he would prevail. Then Mandulis led the charge up the slopes of the barrows and all contact was lost, as sorcery flickered like lightning in the clouds ahead and the daemon horde began to sing the praises of their master.

THE CREST OF the barrow was lined with bodies whose skeletons had been deformed into tall spears of flesh and bone from which hung pennants of skin rippling in the hot, blood-damp breeze. The pennants were emblazoned with symbols that would have burned the eyes of lesser men – Mandulis recognised the same sigils that had been carved into the skin of Ghargatuloth's cultists and written in blood on the floors of their temples.

Beyond the crest of the barrow, something huge roared. Mandulis, his gunmetal armour now black with blood and smoke coiling from the charred twin barrels of his storm bolter, turned to see the Grey Knights who had followed him. One Terminator from Squad Martel was down, along with several from Squad Justinian who had followed in the path blazed by Mandulis. Justinian himself had lost an arm and his helmet had been wrenched off by the gnarled hands of a daemon – his face was streaked with grime and his breathing was ragged and bloody.

Further back, Chemuel was forming a cordon to protect Mandulis's men from a counterattack. Mandulis had no doubt that Justicar

Chemuel would sell his life at the foot of the barrow, holding back the daemonic tide with flamers and psycannon. It was a good and honourable way to die, but it would mean nothing if Mandulis could not press home the attack now.

'Martel! With me!' voxed Mandulis. The captain ran up the slick earth of the barrow, his Terminators following. 'Grace be with you, brother. Over the top.'

Under cover from Justinian, Mandulis and Squad Martel charged over the crest of the barrow. Before them stretched the whole barrows complex, a series of concentric circular mounds surrounding a ruined stone tower like the stump of a huge tree. Twisted trees, once Ghargatuloth's most loyal cult leaders, grew in tormented tangles everywhere, forming knots of screaming, blackened flesh. In the depressions between the mounds, blood had drained into deep moats, blood that churned as something massive writhed beneath the ground.

As Mandulis watched, the ground seethed and he saw pale shapes clawing their way from the earth. Stone coffins broke the surface and spilled mouldering bones and grave goods onto the ground. So massive was the evil beneath the barrows that those who had originally been buried there, thousands of years ago before Khorion IX had ever been discovered by the Imperium, were clawing their way from their graves to get away from it.

Mandulis led the charge. As he ran full pelt down the reverse slope of the first barrow there was a titanic eruption of earth nearby and something pale, towering and monstrous burst from the surface. A wave of daemonic sorcery washed over everything and the wards tattooed onto Mandulis's skin burned white-hot as they fought off the daemon's magic. He saw a hunched, twisted body, with a foul distended stomach, rotting skin sprouting feathers, and a long neck from which hung a wickedly grinning beaked head. Wings of blue fire spread from its back as it lunged and stamped down on Brother Gaius, shattering the Grey Knight's leg with a taloned foot. Storm bolter fire streaked up at it and Brother Jokul's psycannon punched holes into its decaying chest, but it just shrieked with joy as it picked up Gaius and tore him in two with its beak.

'Press on!' yelled Mandulis into the vox. 'Brother Knights, with me! Chemuel, Justinian, move up and give cover!'

Mandulis heard Gaius die over the vox, the Grey Knight's last breaths gurgling prayers of hate as he hacked at the greater daemon with his Nemesis weapon. Brother Thieln, Justinian's flamer Marine, died a moment later, cut in two by a huge rusted metal glaive wielded by a second greater daemon that tore itself out of the slope of the barrow.

Ghargatuloth's inner circle of daemons – Lords of Change, the cultists called them, generals of the Change God's armies – were bursting from the barrows to slaughter the Grey Knights who dared attack the Prince of a Thousand Faces. This was the heart of Ghargatuloth's trap. Mandulis had known it would end like this – a mad charge in the faint hope that the Grey Knights would reach Ghargatuloth in enough numbers to stand a chance of defeating him.

A daemon erupted from the ground close by, showering Mandulis with blood and earth. Captain Martel lunged in with his halberd, spearing the avian daemon through the thigh. Mandulis ducked the staff it swung, sorcerous lightning arcing off his armour and pushing his antipsychic wards to the limit. He swung his sword into the heart of the iridescence and the daemon's head was sheared clean off, the severed neck spewing viscous, glowing blue gore onto the ground.

Mandulis strode on as bolter fire and lightning streaked everywhere. He waded through the waist-deep gore of the moat and scrambled up the crumbling earth of the next barrow, crunching through ancient graves.

He could hear voices whispering and screaming inside his skull, a babble of madness that would have swamped a lesser man's mind. But the mind of a Grey Knight was built around a hard core of pure, depthless faith. Where other men had fear, the Grey Knights had resolve. Where others had doubt, Mandulis had faith. An Imperial guardsman, no matter how courageous or pious, still had that unprotected hollow of despair, greed, and terror at the heart of his soul. A Grey Knight did not. Ghargatuloth's mind tricks broke against Mandulis's mind like waves against rocks.

That was why it had to be the Grey Knights assaulting Khorion IX. The Lords Militant could assemble armies hundreds of millions strong, but not one of those Guardsmen would have kept his mind for a minute under the gaze of Ghargatuloth. So it was up to the Grey Knights, and now it was up to Mandulis.

Glowing hands were reaching from beneath the soil, large enough to pick up Brother Trentius and hurl him so hard that his body smashed into the stone tower at the centre of the barrows. One of the daemons held a staff of bloodstained black wood, pink lightning spilling from the bundle of skulls nailed to its top, arcing off power armour, blasting Space Marines off their feet where the other greater daemons could move in for the kill.

Squad Chemuel were buying time with their lives. They were surrounded, the towering avian daemons ablaze with blessed burning fuel and smoking from holes blasted by psycannon rounds. Chemuel himself had drawn his Nemesis weapon, which the artificers on Titan had fashioned into a spear, and was stabbing at the nearest daemon even as it tore off his other arm.

Squad Justinian had tried to keep pace with Mandulis and Martel but their charge had faltered. Justinian himself died in a sea of pink fire that boiled up from below, dragged down by daemon talons and torn apart. His battle-brothers were scattered by the daemon that rose from the fire, wielding a great spiked metal block on a long chain that scythed through two Marines before their battle-brothers could turn and riddle the daemon with storm bolter fire.

Mandulis scrambled up the slope of the final barrow. Martel's Terminators, only a handful of them left now, turned to cover Martel and Mandulis. The swarm of lesser daemons broke over the far barrow and poured into the complex to join their master in a waterfall of daemons' flesh. The last sight Mandulis had of Justicar Chemuel was of his body being thrown by a greater daemon into the advancing tide, to be played with and torn apart like prey.

Mandulis pressed on. The ground itself was fighting him, collapsing beneath his feet into great fissures. The tower loomed overhead, ancient stones spilling off its ruined walls, and beneath him the pure hatred reached a screaming pitch as Ghargatuloth tried to force his way into Mandulis's mind.

The daemon prince would not succeed. That meant he would have to stoop to defending himself personally. And that was Mandulis's only chance.

The tower was shattered and thrown into the air in a shower of stone. The ground tore open and Mandulis dug his feet into the crumbling earth as the storm tore over him.

The sky rotted and turned black. A shockwave of corruption ripped outwards and turned the landscape of Khorion IX into tortured, screaming flesh. Mandulis glimpsed Captain Martel being picked up by the howling wind and thrown into the sky and out of sight, fire still spitting from his storm bolter.

In the centre of the storm a huge, dark column shot up from the site of the tower, so tall it punched through the black clouds overhead. It was a spear of twisted flesh, something living but never alive, and it was accompanied by a seething chorus of pure madness that tore at the barriers of Mandulis's mind with such frenzy that Mandulis, for the first time in his long life, felt a spark of doubt that he would hold out against the assault.

He crushed that doubt and held his Nemesis sword in both hands, storm bolter forgotten because not even holy bullets could harm something like this.

The eyes of the storm swept over Grand Master Mandulis and suddenly the air was calm, the cacophony of screams clear and horrible, the assault on Mandulis's mind a pure keening.

The true face of the Prince of a Thousand Faces looked down on Mandulis. The grand master of the Grey Knights mouthed a final, silent prayer, and charged.

TWO
TETHYS

ONE THOUSAND YEARS passed. The Imperium endured – men and women died in uncountable numbers to ensure that. Armageddon was lost to the orks. The Damocles Gulf was conquered and strange new species were encountered. The Sabbat Worlds were overrun by Chaos and an immense crusade launched to reclaim them.

Stratix died in screaming plague, Stalinvast in the fiery extremes of the Exterminatus. The Eye of Terror opened and hell poured out through the Cadian Gate. The Inquisition continued to torture itself for the good of mankind, the Adeptus Terra tried to unpick laws and declarations from the will of the Emperor. The warp created new hells outside real space. Whole systems were lost in madness and new ones settled in their hundreds.

There were only two constants in the galaxy. The first was the Imperium's bloody-minded refusal to die beneath the weight of heresy, secession, alien aggression and daemonancy. The second was war – an unending, merciless, and all-consuming tide of warfare that formed the Imperium's bane, function, and salvation.

One thousand years of hatred, one thousand years of war. Enough time for a great many new horrors to rise, and for old ones to be all but forgotten.

* * *

WHEN THE FIRST shot had hit, Justicar Alaric had thought of the final days – the days when the Emperor would be whole again, when the heroes of the Imperium and the soldiers of its present would be led into war as one, and the final reckoning would come.

With the second shot, the one that punched through his leg and tore up into his abdomen, he had realised that he was not dead and that the final days would not come for him yet. He remembered red runes winking maddeningly on the back of his eye, telling him that his blood pressure was falling and both his hearts were beating erratically, that two of his lungs had been punctured by the shot to the chest and his abdomen was filling up with blood. He remembered dragging himself into cover as overcharged las-shots ripped into the stone floor beside him.

He remembered the shame as his consciousness drained into a dim grey oblivion, willing his limbs to move so he could loose a last volley of shots against the cultists who had wounded him so badly.

That was what Alaric felt as he awoke again. Shame. It reminded him of how young he was compared to some of the grand masters who had walked the halls of Titan. He had the crystal-pure mental core of a Grey Knight, that was certain, but wrapped around it was a mind that still had much to learn. Not about fighting – that knowledge had been sleep-taught to him so deeply that it had displaced any memory of Alaric's childhood – but about the great discipline that meant not even shame, rage, or honour could get in the way of a grand master's sense of duty to his Emperor.

Alaric was all but submerged in a vat of clear fluid, a concoction of Titan's apothecaries that helped flesh heal and kept infections at bay. He felt tubes snaking all around him, feeding medicines into his veins and sending information back to the cogitators he could hear thrumming and clicking away around him. He was bathed in light coming from lumoglobes arranged in a circle on the stone ceiling above him. The whole of the Grey Knight fortress-monastery was carved from the same dark grey living stone of Titan, snaking deep beneath the moon's surface in layer upon layer of cells, chapels, training and instruction halls, medical facilities, parade grounds, armouries and, deepest of all, the tombs of every Grey Knight who had fallen in battle during the Chapter's ten thousand year history.

Alaric turned his head to see the brass-cased cogitators quietly spewing sheet after sheet of paper onto which were scribbled the long, jagged ribbons of his life signs. The medical facility was one he had been to before – it was here that he had received the hexagrammic wards that

formed a thin lattice of blessed silver beneath his skin. Medical orderlies were moving quietly between other recovery tanks and autosurgeon
tables, checking on the patients – some were troops or other personnel
from the Ordo Malleus. Others were the inhumanly tall and muscular
forms of Alaric's fellow Grey Knights. The facility was like a vaulted cel-
lar, the ceiling low and oppressive, the stone cold and sweating. The
lumoglobes casting pools of light around the patients, surrounded by
shadow where cogitators and hygiene servitors hummed gently.

Alaric recognised Brother Tathelon, one arm blown off at the elbow
and his body covered in tiny shrapnel scars. Interrogator Iatonn, who
had accompanied Inquisitor Nyxos in the assault, lay with his entrails
exposed as the dextrous metallic fingers of the autosurgeon worked to
knit his innards back together. Alaric had seen Iatonn fall, a blade
plunged through his gut. Nyxos, as far as Alaric knew, had made it out
unharmed, but of course Alaric had not seen the final stages of the
assault.

One of the orderlies, one of the blank-faced, mind-scrubbed men and
women the Ordo Malleus used for menial work, saw Alaric was awake
and came to inspect the life signs streaming from the cogitators. Alaric
stood up in the tank, pulling electrodes from his skin and needles from
his veins. The black carapace, a hard layer beneath the skin of his chest
and abdomen, had a large ragged hole in it where the first shot had broken through his armour and Alaric could see through the crystallised
wound to the surface of the bony breastplate that had grown together
from his ribs. There was another hole, larger, in the meat of his thigh,
with a tight channel of internal scar leading up into his abdomen. He
could feel the wounds inside him but they were almost healed thanks
to his internal augmentations and the Chapter apothecarion. He was
covered in smaller scars, burns from where his armour had become red-
hot from the weight of las-fire slamming into it, cuts and gouges from
shards of ceramite, newly lain over the old scars from previous battle
wounds and surgical procedures.

Apothecary Glaivan was hurrying over from the far end of the facility. Glaivan was ancient, one of the few Grey Knights currently in the
Chapter who had reached the extended old age a Space Marine's
enhancements could grant him. Glaivan's hands had been replaced
long ago with bionic armatures that gave him a surgical touch far finer
than human hands, with splayed fingers tipped with scalpels and pincers. Grey Knights usually wore their power armour when outside their
cells or at worship, but Glaivan had long since left his battlegear
behind. Beneath the long white apothecary's robes his body was braced

with steel and brass, and his redundant organs had been removed to leave Glaivan a shell of a Space Marine. His face was long and so heavily lined it was hard to believe there had once been a younger man in there. Glaivan was more than four hundred years old, all but the first handful of those having been spent in service to the Grey Knights and the Ordo Malleus.

'Ah, young justicar,' said Glaivan in a voice lent a faint buzz by his reconstructed throat. 'You heal well. A good thing, borne of willpower. They were high-powered las-burns, justicar, very deep. I am surprised that you are awake so soon, and very little surprises me.'

'I didn't see how it ended,' said Alaric. 'Did we...'

'Seven dead,' said Glaivan with a hint of melancholy. 'Twelve were brought to me here, most will be made well. But yes, Nyxos was successful. Valinov was taken alive, they have him on Mimas.'

Alaric climbed out of the tank, feeling the tightness in his muscles. Alaric had seen Valinov, just as the storm of las-fire had ripped out of the underground temple from the cultists under Valinov's command. He had seen a tall slim man with a sharp face and shaven, tattooed head, barking orders in a foul warp-taught language. His cultists – the mission briefing had suggested several hundred of them in the underground temple complex – were hunched and pallid-skinned, wearing tattered robes of grimy yellow, but they had been well-armed and perfectly willing to die beneath the storm bolters and Nemesis weapons of the Grey Knights. Alaric had been one of the first in, leading the squad he had recently come to command.

Now the assault was over and the survivors were back on Titan.

'How long?' asked Alaric. The orderly handed him a towel and Alaric began to wipe off the fluid – the healing fluid was cold and sticky, and pooled on the cold stone floor around his feet.

'Three months,' replied Glaivan. 'The *Rubicon* made good speed back. They wanted to make sure Valinov was placed in Mimas as soon as possible. That man is pure corruption.' Glaivan spat on the stone floor, and a tiny hygiene servitor scuttled over to clean up the spittle. 'To think. An inquisitor. Radicalism grows ever stronger, I fear.'

It was a measure of the respect in which Glaivan was held that he could voice such concerns freely. The Grey Knights were technically autonomous, but the Ordo Malleus were in practice their masters, and they certainly didn't want the Grey Knights harbouring seditious opinions about the Inquisition. Radicalism was, officially, a non-existent threat, and that was all the Malleus would officially say to the Grey Knights about it.

Alaric sifted through his last memories of the raid – gunfire streaking through grimy underground tunnels, battle-brothers charging in a storm of explosions. If the *Rubicon* had indeed made good speed then Alaric had probably been in Glaivan's care for a couple of weeks. 'Who was lost?'

'Interrogator Iatonn will not survive.' Glaivan glanced sadly at the interrogator's body, opened up beneath the autosurgeon. 'LeMal, Encalion and Baligant died in the assault. Gaignun and Justicar Naimon died on the *Rubicon*, Tolas and Evain in my care.'

'Encalion and Tolas were my men.' Alaric had attained the rank of justicar three years before, and he had lost men before – but he had seen them die. It was part of the bond between Alaric and his squad that they had all shared in the deaths of their battle-brothers, but this time Alaric had not been there.

'I know, justicar. There is a place for them in the vaults. Grand Master Tencendur has decreed they will be interred after your debriefing. I shall tell him you are fit.' Glaivan picked up one of the long sheets of parchment and passed it through his metallic hands, reading the patterns in Alaric's heartbeats and blood pressure. 'I should not say much until Tencendur has had his say, but from Nyxos I hear that your battle-brothers did you proud. When you fell they pressed the attack for revenge instead of faltering in despair. I have seen many leaders in this Chapter and what marks them out is that whatever they do, even falling to the Enemy, they inspire the men who follow them. Your Space Marines thought you were dead, and they fought on all the harder. Remember that, young justicar, for I feel you shall not remain a mere justicar for much longer.'

Alaric pulled out the last of the needles from his skin. 'I need to get back to my cell,' he said. 'There are rites of contrition for my armour before the artificers can repair it. And I must have missed out on much prayer.'

'Do as you see fit. Soon you will be ready to fight again. Chaplain Durendin is receiving confessions in the Mandulian Chapel and it sounds as if you could use his counsel before debriefing. I shall have the servitors bring you a habit.'

Glaivan waved an order and two of the menial servitors rolled off through the cellars of the apothecarion on their tracks to fetch Alaric some clothing so he could walk through the corridors of Titan with suitable humility. There was a great deal Alaric had to do after any battle, let alone one where he had been both severely wounded and been exposed to potential corruption. He would have to confess, receive purification, have his battlegear repaired and reconsecrated, see his name entered in the immense tomes recording the deeds of the Grey Knights, and be debriefed by Grand Master Tencendur and the inquisitors who had been ultimately responsible for the attack.

The life of a Grey Knight was ritual and purification punctuated by savage combat against the foulest of foes – just a few days of it would break a lesser man, and sometimes Alaric was grateful he could not remember anything else. But this was not the time to skirt the edges of heretical doubt. Valinov was captured and his cult shattered. There was a victory to celebrate, and there were fallen brothers to remember.

INQUISITOR GHOLIC REN-SAR Valinov had been a member of the Ordo Malleus since his recruitment as an interrogator by the late Lord Inquisitor Barbillus. Barbillus was an old-school inquisitor, the kind of man sculpted into the friezes of Malleus temples and used as exemplars of righteous valour in sermons. Barbillus had worn armour covered in gold filigree depicting daemons crushed beneath the Emperor's feet and wielded a power hammer with a head carved from meteoric iron. He had ridden his war pulpit into the deepest pits of daemonic horror. He was a soldier, a fighter, a smiter of the foul and a scourge of the heretic. When the citizens of the Imperium heard rumours of the Imperium's secret defenders in the Inquisition, they imagined men like Barbillus.

Barbillus had an extensive staff, mostly of warriors who rode with him into battle, recruited from martial cultures all over the Imperium. But he also needed people to get him to the battlefield. Investigators. Interviewers. Scientists. Some of Barbillus's rear echelon staff went deep undercover for him, infiltrating noble houses suspected of daemonancy or vicious hive-scum gangs sponsored by hidden cultist cells. They were disposable and exposed, both to the violence that would follow discovery and the madness that could result from seeing too much of the Enemy. They did what they did because it was their way to join the fight against Chaos.

Very few of them survived to advance in Barbillus's private army. One of them was Gholic Ren-Sar Valinov.

The Ordo Malleus's records of Valinov's origins were patchy, mainly because he erased or altered most of the information held about him in Inquisition archives. He came from the Segmentum Solar, that was certain, from one of the massively industrialised worlds of the Imperium's heartland where only the sharpest and most ruthless could hope to gain recognition from off-world. His birthplace was not recorded but Barbillus recruited him during a spectacular purge of the debauched naval aristocracy on Rhanna.

There were some suggestions that Valinov's position in the Administratum on Rhanna gave him access to the statistical information that, in the right hands, led Barbillus to cells of sorcerers and pleasure-seekers in the planet's nobility. Other inquisitors had been adamant that Valinov's skills could only have been honed in the Adeptus Arbites, or the Planetary Defence Force, or even the criminal gangs that ruled huge swathes of Rhanna's underhive. But Valinov's most useful skills were clear from the start – he was an arch manipulator of people, capable of flattery and coercion alike. He could draw the most sensitive information out of the wariest suspects.

Valinov was just the man for Barbillus's rear echelon staff, joining noble families or wealthy guilds or criminal cartels to hunt down sources of heresy and forbidden magic. Over six years, Valinov's work led Barbillus to the heart of K'Sharr the Butcher's criminal empire, the hidden cults that had seeded the dockyard world of Talshen III with heretics, the savage pre-Imperial human tribes of Gerentulan Minor, and a dozen other pits of corruption. He was good. Barbillus saw promise in Valinov and marked him out as senior interrogator. It was expected that Valinov would become Barbillus's advisor, coming out of the Imperium's underworld to ride at Barbillus's side.

Then came Agnarsson's Hold. If Barbillus did not die fighting the Daemon Prince Malygrymm the Bloodstained on that planet then he certainly died when the Exterminatus was brought to bear. It was not the first time Barbillus had ordered the death of a world. This time it was his personal staff who launched the cyclonic torpedoes from Barbillus's fleet of warships, having been ordered by Barbillus to destroy Agnarsson's Hold if he didn't return from the daemon-infested surface. Senior Interrogator Valinov had watched from Barbillus's flagship as the verdant agri-world was swallowed up by the magma welling up from its ruptured crust. Malygrymm was destroyed, but Barbillus never returned to his ship.

Temples were built in the name of Lord Inquisitor Barbillus. Statues of him, grim-faced and battered, invariably smiting some indistinct horror with his ensorcelled hammer, adorned Inquisitorial fortresses throughout the Segmentum Solar and beyond. His name was inscribed on the wall of the Hall of Heroes in the Imperial palace and written in the pages of Imperial history.

The Inquisition's files were clear on how Barbillus's staff and resources passed into the control of the Grand Conclave of the Ordo Malleus, and how Valinov served a second apprenticeship with a dozen inquisitors. No records remained, however, to indicate under what circumstances Valinov was recognised by the Ordo Malleus as an inquisitor in his own right, though doubtless it happened. He was active somewhere near Thracian Primaris during the brutal campaigns around the Eye of Terror, and probably played a part in the subjugation of Chaos-infected species discovered during the tail-end of the Damocles Crusade. But there were no details. Valinov had been thorough. Probably he had turned by then, and would have covered his tracks as he went in case another inquisitor found clues of his changing allegiances.

There was almost no information at all about Valinov's biggest mission. He went to the hive world of V'Run with a division of storm troopers from the Lastrati 79th, a coven of sanctioned psykers from the Scholastica Psykana and a squadron of Sword class escort starships. He was officially following up reports of a devolution cult that ruled large swathes of V'Run's underhive and ash wastelands, but afterwards it was concluded that Valinov had created the threat to give him an excuse to intercede.

All that was known about the V'Run mission was that two weeks after Valinov arrived the planet was swallowed up by a boiling, lightning-scattered veil of incandescent stellar cloud, a warp storm so localised and complete that it could only have been deliberately created. The hive world was drowned in the nightmare dimension of the warp. The storm was impenetrable and no one could be sure what happened to the nineteen billion men, women and children who made up the population of V'Run, but astropaths reported hearing screams emanating from the planet for light years around.

Valinov left a trail of atrocity across the Segmentum Solar. He immolated the capital of Port St Indra by overloading the city's heatsinks. Chaos-worshipping pirate ships wiped out a pilgrim convoy off the Nememean Cloud and named Valinov as their leader. As if desperate to commit depredations in the name of Chaos, Valinov wreaked indiscriminate havoc. The Ordo Malleus had by now deployed several inquisitors to trail him and anticipate his next moves, and they tracked him to the plague-stricken communities of the Gaolven Belt. Valinov had joined up with a cult formed from plague survivors who believed they owed their survival to the pantheon of Chaos, and welded them in a matter of weeks into a well-armed and fanatically motivated army manning a fortified asteroid.

The Ordo Malleus concluded that Valinov was preparing for a last stand. If that was what he wanted, then that was what they would give him. The Conclave approached Grand Master Tencendur, and he agreed to send a force of Grey Knights to spearhead the assault on Valinov's fortress.

The first man out of the boarding torpedoes and into the breach had been Justicar Alaric.

THE MANDULIAN CHAPEL was a long gallery with a dizzyingly high ceiling, thick with columns and with statues in niches running along the walls. To reach the huge, three-panelled altar at the front of the chapel, a Grey Knight had to walk past the unwavering stone eyes of hundreds of Imperial heroes. Some of them were legends, some had been forgotten, and they represented every part of the web of organisations that kept the Imperium together. Closest to the altar was the statue of Grand Master Mandulis himself, who had died a thousand years before – his figure was carved into one of the pillars as if he were holding up the chapel's ceiling.

The message was clear. Mandulis, like every Grey Knight, kept the Imperium from collapsing.

Alaric walked down the centre aisle, the filters built into his nose and throat picking out particles of incense that billowed from censers high up in the shadows by the ceiling. Flickering candles ringed the columns and were tended by a tiny servitor that hummed through the nave lighting extinguished wicks. The faltering light glinted off the gold on the altar, wrought by Chapter artisans three hundred years before. The centre image depicted the Emperor in the days before the Horus Heresy, his face turned away as if in recognition of his near-death in the closing days of the Heresy. The scene was flanked by scenes of Grey Knights – not crushing daemons or heretics but kneeling, their arms laid down. It was an image of humility that formed the centrepiece of the Chapel to remind the Grey Knights that no matter how strong they were, they could only prevail with the will of the Emperor.

Alaric had not yet had his battle-gear returned by the artificers and so he wore a simple black and grey habit. He felt naked in that place of worship, his bare feet against stone worn smooth by centuries of armoured boots. His wounds still hurt and he could feel the channel of rapidly healing scar tissue where the las-bolt had burned through his abdomen. His skin felt raw from the healing tank. But worse, the idea of helplessness was hot and angry in his mind. He had not been there when his battle-brothers died.

Chaplain Durendin was waiting in the otherwise empty chapel. The Chaplain wore his enormous suit of Terminator armour as he always did when he was seeing to the Chapter's spiritual health. One arm was painted a glossy black to signify his office as Chaplain and the rest was the traditional gunmetal grey. Durendin wore the same pair of ornate lightning claws that had been passed down since the Chapter's earliest days.

Alaric reached the altar where Durendin stood, and quickly kneeled before the Chaplain. Then both men kneeled to the Emperor's image on the altar.

'Tencendur told me you would wish to see me,' said Durendin as they stood again. The Chaplain's face was mostly obscured by the cowl he wore, and like any good Chaplain he was a difficult man to read.

'You know what happened, Chaplain. I was wounded and unconscious. Encalion and Tolas died. I have lost men before, but I was always at their side. I wasn't there this time.'

'I will not absolve you of those deaths, justicar. Every one of us must accept responsibility for the deaths of our battle-brothers. You have not been a justicar long, Alaric. You clearly have capacity to lead but you have only taken a few steps on the path.'

'That is what worries me, Chaplain. I have never felt this doubt. Everything I have learned as a Grey Knight has told me that once the core of faith is breached then I am worth nothing as a warrior.'

'And you think that if you cannot forget that feeling of helplessness you felt when Valinov's men shot you down, you cannot trust the purity of your soul?' Durendin turned and somewhere under that cowl he stared deep into Alaric's spirit. 'Remember it, Alaric. Remember what it means to be broken and laid low. The mark of a leader is not whether you can avoid such misfortune, but whether you can take it and turn it into something that makes you stronger. Your battle-brothers are dead, but you can ensure their lives had meaning. That is what it means to lead.'

'I knew it would not be easy, Chaplain,' said Alaric, 'but the size of the task has never been more obvious. I know that this will not be the first test, and certainly not the hardest. I am only just beginning to really understand the sacrifices the grand masters must have made for the Knights to follow them. Their faith must be absolute. I do not think there is a higher aim in the Imperium than to be trusted as a grand master by the Grey Knights.'

'But you can do it?'

Alaric paused. He looked at the slices of polished red gemstones that made up the armour of the gilded Emperor, at the shadows covering the ceiling far above, and at the figure of Mandulis holding up the Imperium on his own. 'Yes. Yes I can.'

'That is the difference, Alaric. You cannot believe anything else. What you call doubt is the pain of learning a hard lesson. That you learned it at all proves what the Chapter has always thought about you. You have curiosity and intelligence, and at the same time the trust of your men. You represent a rare combination of qualities that means you will never be satisfied until you see your duty done at the highest level.'

Alaric stood and bowed quickly to the gilded Emperor. 'Tencendur will be waiting for me, Chaplain. I will think about what you have told me.'

'You may not have that luxury, justicar,' said Durendin as Alaric turned to leave. 'Given what was found at the Gaolven Belt, catching Valinov may have been just the first step.'

THE ORDO MALLEUS had taken the rings of Saturn shortly after the inception of the Inquisition, and had turned them into its own unofficial domain. The lord inquisitors of the Ordo Malleus ruled Saturn's moons absolutely, because that was the only way they could ensure the security of their facilities. The Malleus controlled some of the most dangerous artefacts, texts, and people in the galaxy. The immensely complicated geometry of Saturn's rings means it was all but impossible for any enemy force to penetrate the thousands of turbo-laser defences that bristled from asteroids captured by Saturn's gravity. The ordo controlled the only reliable way in and out of the rings, the naval fortress on the outermost major moon Iapetus.

Mimas, the closest major moon to the vast swirling mass of Saturn, was disfigured by an immense impact scar covering a quarter of the surface. Built into that crater was the Inquisitorial prison where the worst of the worst were held in complexes of isolated cells with psychic wards woven into the walls, guarded by gun-servitors and a regiment of Ordo Malleus storm troopers.

Encaladus, the next moon out from Mimas, housed the Inquisitorial citadel, a vast and imposing palace where the lord inquisitors of the Ordo Malleus held court and the most senior of the ordo's inquisitors maintained personal estates.

Tethys was the location of the Librarium Daemonicum, the repository of dangerous knowledge gathered over thousands of years of fighting the darkness. The Librarium was completely hidden from the surface – thousands of void-safe cells and galleries of crammed bookshelves filled a sphere hollowed out of the moon's core. Untold millions of tomes, data-slates, scrolls and pict-recordings were refrigerated to preserve delicate pages and unstable datacores. Access to them was given only on the authority of the lord inquisitors themselves, and the more restricted sectors formed some of the most sensitive locations in the galaxy.

Titan, the largest moon, concealed beneath its thick orange atmosphere the immense fortress-monastery of the Grey Knights, covering the surface as if the whole moon had been carved with a pattern of towers and battlements.

The docks of Iapetus, the furthermost major moon, extended kilometres out into space and were always hosts to whole roosts of cruisers, escorts and battleships, including the strike fleet of the Grey Knights and enormous Imperator class battleships requisitioned from the Battlefleet Solar.

It was only by controlling this miniature empire that the Ordo Malleus could ensure the safety of the terrible knowledge it collected and the dangerous individuals it captured and imprisoned. It was this security that meant Valinov's possessions could be isolated and contained. It was here that Inquisitor Briseis Ligeia could examine them properly.

A THIN, PALE blue-grey light filled the research floor, weakly illuminating the reams of books and data-slates that filled shelves lining walls one hundred metres high. Spider-like archiver servitors scurried up the walls on thin metal legs, the fleshy once-human parts scanning book spines and labels for the Malleus research staff who spent their lives poring over ancient texts for their Inquisitorial masters. Many higher-ranking Malleus inquisitors had a personal researcher or two on Tethys, whose sole purpose in life was to find obscure and potentially vital information on the enemies of the Emperor.

The many floors suspended between the immense cliffs of bookshelves were mostly empty. A few pale, large-eyed researchers were hunched over crumbling tomes, gun-servitors hovering over their shoulders in case the knowledge they were exposed to overcame their minds. Their breath coiled in the air and they all wore close-fitting thermosuits; the temperature was kept too low for a human to survive more than a few minutes.

Inquisitor Ligeia preferred it when it was quiet. It gave her more room to think. A tiny guide-servitor droned on ahead of her, weaving through the various workstations and down a couple of flights of steps to where Valinov's possessions had been assembled for her. Ligeia wore bulky furs and an overcloak trimmed in ermine – she affected the clothing of an extravagant Imperial noble because that was who she was, or at least had been. She wore rings outside her tharrhide gloves and her boots were of the finest pygmy grox leather. She had been pretty once, but that was a long time ago and life had hardened her soul enough for it to show on her face. She was still imposing, and she liked the fact that people would react to her appearance first. It meant that she would be underestimated – a fact that had saved her many times.

Ligeia was not a born fighter, although she had seen her fair share of scrapes. She was an investigator, a scholar, schooled by the best institutions noble money could afford. The Ordo Hereticus had taken her directly from the nobility of Gathalamor, finding that her skills with information overcame the unease some of them felt at her growing psychic abilities. The Ordo Malleus had headhunted her because of her facility with ancient or cryptic texts. She had stayed, becoming a more and more valued assistant to various Malleus inquisitors until she had attained the rank herself, all the time honing her psychic power. The Ordo Malleus were mostly typically bull-headed deamonhunters with weapons and armour to rival the Grey Knights themselves, charging into battle with the unholy, but Ligeia's weapon was knowledge. A psychic Malleus inquisitor was supposed to hurl bolts of lightning or banish daemons with a word, but Ligeia's powers were geared towards understanding and perception.

Without Ligeia, untold atrocities would have unfolded without the Ordo Malleus even suspecting them. Perhaps Valinov was planning something that would not be stopped with his capture.

Ligeia took a seat and the guide-servitor flitted off again. No gun-servitor approached, because one of the privileges of Ligeia's office was the trust the lord inquisitors placed in her willpower. A suppressor field she carried switched off the defences in her immediate vicinity, so the signature of her psychic abilities would not bring sentry guns out of the walls. In front of her were lain the items found in Valinov's personal chambers and upon his person when he was captured, much of it still bloodstained or scorched by bolter rounds. Valinov's clothes, deep red robes extravagantly trimmed with silver, had a large ragged hole in one arm. Ligeia remembered from the briefing that Valinov had been wounded. It was a measure of his strength that he had survived the shock of a bolter round against unarmoured flesh. All these items had been assembled by the research staff at her request, in the condition that they had been found on Valinov's asteroid.

Valinov had been armed with a custom hunting las, a holdover from when he worked within the auspices of the Ordo Malleus. It was a beautiful weapon, the casings and barrel enamelled in deep blood red with the details picked out in gold. The power pack was similarly custom-built and was heavily overcharged going by the scorching on the barrel. Valinov had carried a wrackblade, too, a sneaky little weapon that looked like a combat knife but hid a neurowhip processor. The same blade had turned Interrogator Iatonn's entrails to mush. All very expensive and very rare.

Ligeia ignored the weapons. They had been checked by psyker séance and were free of any taint. What interested Ligeia were the documents. There were a couple of data-slates, a handful of scrolls tied with what looked like lengths of sinew, and a large book. The data-slates were schedules and inventories for the fortress – they indicated how well Valinov had organised what amounted to a benighted band of fanatics, but little else.

The scrolls looked more interesting. They were covered in cryptic messages in cramped handwriting, complex diagrams of pantheons or magic spells, transcriptions of chants and descriptions of ceremonies. Ligeia held her hand over the tattered parchment and let her perception bleed out of the inside of her head and down into the paper, weaving around not just the shape of the letters and diagrams but the meaning that infused them. She had discovered the power while in the schola back on Gathalamor when she was still a child, and though the Sisters who taught her had told her it was witchery she had been lucky to be recognised not as a threat but as a strong and useful psyker. It was one of the paradoxes at the heart of the Imperium: the Imperium was terrified of psykers, men and women whose powers touched the warp and formed a bridge for dark things to come through into real space; but it also depended on psykers, like the astropaths who transmitted telepathic messages or psychic inquisitors like herself who did with their minds what no man could do with weapons.

The meaning on the scrolls was a faint, flitting thing, vague and frustrating. Ligeia suspected it might be some complicated code but the deeper she reached the more she came across a barrier of meaninglessness. The scrolls meant nothing. Their only purpose was to look impressive. True rituals of the Chaos gods would have lit up her psychic perception like fireworks.

Though Ligeia spent some time examining them to be sure, she quickly came to the conclusion that the scrolls were meaningless. Valinov had probably faked them up to give to his cultists and make them think they were doing the work of the dark gods. It meant they were not ready for Valinov to introduce them to the true worship of Chaos. Probably he never would have taken them that far – they were just bolter fodder, men he could manipulate into dying instead of him. And they had died, every one of them.

Ligeia left the scrolls and pulled the book towards her. It was old and all but ruined with damp and mould. The pages were thick parchment but the bindings were ragged – Ligeia guessed that the volume had been rebound several times. There was no title. If there had been one previously, it had disappeared as the original binding peeled off.

Ligeia carefully opened the book. Even with her perception withdrawn it tingled her fingers when she touched it, as if its meaning was struggling to get out and be understood. Archaic High Gothic covered the page in front of her.

Codicium Aeternum.

Beneath the title were written lines in an elegant hand by some transcriber-servitor hundreds of years ago.

Being a full and faithful account of the deaths of Daemons, Monstrous Prodigies and the Lords of Darkness, and accompanying extrapolations of their return from Banishment.

The seal of the Ordo Malleus was emblazoned underneath.

Ligeia caught her breath. This was something she genuinely had not expected. She leafed through a few of the pages. Monstrous names looked back at her. She recognised the name of Angron, the Daemon Primarch who had once been banished from the material realm in the first Battle for Armageddon. She saw Cherubael and Doombreed, N'Kari and hundreds of others, with the dates and predicted durations of their banishments noted beside. Some of those names alone would have corrupted lesser minds.

The *Codicium Aeternum*. By the Throne, if it was real…

It had last been seen in these very halls decades before. It had been thought simply lost, hidden somewhere in the bowels of Tethys where it had become a victim of the secrecy supposed to keep it secret. Many volumes had slipped through the gaps like that, and the Malleus had specialised knowledge hunter squads who roamed the lower recesses finding vital texts that had previously been forgotten. But that had not happened to this book – Valinov must have stolen it from the Ordo Malleus's collection when he was still in the employ of Inquisitor Barbillus, earlier than any of the signs of his corruption. He must have been working towards some terrible plan for longer than the Malleus suspected. The *Codicium Aeternum* was one of the most valuable reference works the Malleus possessed, listing thousands of daemons banished by the Grey Knights or the Inquisition. Emperor only knew what Valinov had meant to do with it.

Ligeia stood and waved over the guide servitor, which was hovering at a polite distance.

'Ligeia to Librarium command. We have a sensitive text, possible moral threat. Send down a containment team and let the Conclave know it's the *Codicium Aeternum*. Ligeia out.'

The servitor thrummed off carrying Ligeia's message to the Librarium's overseers. They would know how to contain and secure a book of such power and value. As Ligeia turned back to the table she noticed that the book had fallen open at a seemingly random page, stained with age and damp, and barely legible. One word, one name, jumped out at her, scratched in red ink by an elegant, looping hand.

Ghargatuloth.

THREE
TITAN

THE GATHERING WAS called in the Fallen Dagger Hall where Grand Master Kolgano, centuries before, challenged the Grey Knights under his command to an unarmoured dagger duel and promised his jewel-encrusted Terminator armour to anyone who could beat him. Kolgano was long gone, buried with his fighting dagger deep in the heart of Titan's catacombs, but the hall remained lofty and echoing.

It was used for drills, close combat training for newer recruits and sometimes, as now, for meetings between the Ordo Malleus and the Grey Knights.

A large round table of dark hardwood stood in the centre of the hall, flanked by rings of Malleus storm troopers in parade dress, their faces hidden by silvered masks. Inquisitor Nyxos attended most official functions with this silent, sinister honour guard, their faces never shown. He sat at the table flanked by two standing advisors, one an astropath of almost impossible age, the other a brilliant young woman rumoured to have been poached from the finest officer academy of the Imperial Navy. Nyxos himself was an old leathery warrior, wearing simple black that served to flaunt the silver-plated brackets and servo mounts that lent his frail old body immense strength and speed. His bald, liver-spotted head jutted forward like a hawk's, sharp little eyes always scanning for prey.

At Nyxos's side sat Inquisitor Ligeia in impressive noble regalia, looking more like an elegant family matriarch at a society ball than a hunter of daemons. She carried the mouldering *Codicium Aeternum* in a small portable void-safe to keep its delicate pages from crumbling.

Grand Master Tencendur entered, wearing his customised Terminator armour. He had removed his helmet, revealing a face with a broad, strong jaw and plenty of frown lines. He was accompanied by his own squad of Terminators and by Justicar Alaric, reunited with his repaired wargear and walking behind the squad.

Alaric had been fully debriefed by Tencendur and had briefly spoken with his squad. They had begun the process of mourning for their fallen battle-brothers. Encalion and Tolas had been allotted niches in the catacombs of Titan where their bodies would rest, shrouded until the time came for the Emperor's servants to join him once more. Brother Lykkos was undergoing intensive training with the psycannon that Tolas had once carried. The other Space Marines would carry their battle-brothers in the funeral parade, and Alaric would have to speak in their remembrance. He had spoken for fallen brothers before, but this time would be harder than the others.

In time, new recruits would be picked to join Alaric's squad, and eventually they would replace the fallen. But that would not happen soon. Until then Squad Alaric would be two men short as a reminder of the threats they had always to face.

'Grand master,' said Nyxos, rising from his seat in respect. His servos whirred slightly. 'My apologies for the short notice. Many protocols had to be waived.'

'I understand that sensitive material was recovered from Valinov's possessions,' said Tencendur, his voice inhumanly deep and gravelly thanks to the ruinous throat wound that had nearly killed him back when he had been a justicar. 'Were it not suitably important I am sure you would not have asked to meet me here at all.'

Nyxos indicated Ligeia, who placed the book on the table and pushed it towards Tencendur. She ran her thumb along the gene-lock and the void-safe snapped open, revealing the mould-blotched cover of the *Codicium Aeternum*. The grand master walked up to the table and reached over, picking up the book in his surprisingly dextrous gauntlets and turning over the cover carefully. He read the title off the first page.

'We believe Valinov stole it before his treachery became obvious,' said Nyxos as Tencendur leafed through the stained pages. 'In itself it is not dangerous, hence we can remove it from the protections of the Librarium. But the information it contains is of a most disturbing nature considering it was possessed by a Radical.'

'Do you know why he stole it?'

'Valinov has not yet told our interrogators anything,' said Nyxos. 'Mimas has the best excruciators in the ordo and he may crack in time, but that will not happen overnight. We can make some guesses, however. Ligeia?'

'The *Codicium*,' began Ligeia in a knowing, upper-class voice that contrasted with the hard-bitten growls of her fellow daemonhunters, 'contains the names of many thousands of daemons along with descriptions and dates of their banishments. As beings of pure energy many of them cannot be permanently destroyed, only sent back to the warp until they can re-form; we believe the *Codicium* was first compiled in an attempt to systematically monitor their returns. Of course, the ways of Chaos are anything but systematic but the authors were thorough, at first. Many of the entries are incomplete or damaged but there is one in particular that I have determined was of particular interest to Valinov.'

Ligeia had placed a marker between two of the pages. Tencendur opened the book to the right page and stopped.

'Ghargatuloth,' he said simply.

'Ghargatuloth,' repeated Ligeia, 'was banished from the material realm a thousand years ago on Khorion IX by Grand Master Mandulis.'

'And he was banished,' said Tencendur as he read, 'for a thousand years.'

'You understand why we thought this was of such importance,' said Nyxos.

Tencendur closed the book and placed it back on the table. 'What do you need?'

Nyxos consulted a data-slate handed to him by his advisor. 'We all know what is happening at Cadia, Grand Master. The Eye of Terror has opened and Cadia could fall. The ordo needs me there to conduct interrogators still operating on Chaos-controlled territory, so I cannot lead a response myself. Inquisitor Ligeia will have authority over this operation. On her behalf I am requesting that you assemble a Grey Knights strike force with all possible haste for her to use as she sees fit in investigating the possibilities this information suggests.'

Tencendur did not look impressed. He glanced at Ligeia. 'The galaxy is a large place, inquisitor. Do you know where Ghargatuloth will return? Khorion IX was destroyed by exterminatus.'

'We have an idea,' said Ligeia. 'The Emperor's Tarot consulted at the time along with visions suffered by astropaths in the vicinity of Khorion IX suggested that Ghargatuloth would return somewhere in the Trail of Saint Evisser.'

'How certain are these predictions?'

'They were recorded in the *Codicium* at the time. They are the most certain we have.' Ligeia's voice was admirably level as she indicated the final paragraphs of Ghargatuloth's entry in the book. The Trail of Saint Evisser was a set of systems to the galactic east of the Segmentum Solar, linked by association with an Imperial saint. Tencendur didn't recognise the name – the Imperium was a vast place and it had more than enough near-forgotten corners for Chaos to hide.

Tencendur shook his head and pushed the book back across the table. 'Not good enough, not if this is all you have to go on. You have said so yourself, Nyxos, the Eye has opened and we may all be called upon to stem the tide. We have companies on their way to Cadia already and I will soon be among them. I cannot conscience ignoring such a duty to follow your guesswork. Valinov could have taken the book for any reason. He could have stolen it out of spite, to test our defences, for the challenge. And even if he was hoping to bring Ghargatuloth back, we have him locked up on Mimas where he will be tried, broken and executed.'

'Do you know,' said Ligeia calmly, 'what Ghargatuloth was?'

Tencendur bristled. Alaric imagined he was not used to being talked back to, even by an inquisitor. 'Of course. A daemon prince.'

'It took the Ordo Malleus more than a hundred years to find out its name. Not even its truename, just the name it used to create cults all over the Imperium. Then it took decades to track it to Khorion IX and when they finally cornered it, they sent three hundred Grey Knights to banish it. Not one of them came back. Mandulis was the only one we were even able to bury. If Ghargatuloth is to return, he will need help. He could still influence the weak-willed from the warp but until they can bring him fully into real space he will be comparatively vulnerable. It will be the only chance we have to strike at him before he becomes too great for us to deal with. The ordo tried to count how many citizens died as a result of Ghargatuloth's cults but the even the logistitian's corps couldn't come up with a number. If there is a way we can stop that then we must take it. I will go alone if I have to, but I have a duty to the Imperium and it will be fulfilled.'

Tencendur paused. 'I cannot lead them. The other grand masters are needed elsewhere, as are our force commanders. I can spare you a small taskforce but officers…'

'That is why I asked for Justicar Alaric to attend,' said Ligeia, looking suddenly at Alaric. 'I understand you cannot spare battle-leaders. Justicar Alaric has distinguished himself and, as the first into Valinov's fortress, was there from the beginning. Alaric and his squad, a

Terminator assault unit, two more tactical squads and the *Rubicon*. I know it is still a great deal to ask when the Enemy is pouring from the Eye, but you understand that the possibility of Ghargatuloth's return means I cannot ask for anything less.'

'If Valinov's interrogations reveal…'

'Grand master, Ghargatuloth will already be calling to his followers. In four months he will have been banished for a full thousand years and he will be able to create new cults and instruct them in drawing him into real space. Valinov will take too long to break. We must go now.'

Tencendur turned to Alaric. 'Justicar?'

Alaric had not expected this. He still had the feeling he had failed at the Gaolven Belt, and he could still feel the wounds that had nearly killed him. Durendin had told him how far he had to go before he could be trusted to be a leader of the Grey Knights, and now he was being asked to join Ligeia on a mission she evidently believed was vastly important. For a moment, he floundered. Should he refuse? A servant of the Emperor should show honesty where he had doubts about being able to fulfil his duty. But if he didn't go, who else would? What Tencendur said was true – the Eye of Terror would soon be using most of the Grey Knights' resources and all of the senior brother-captains and grand masters would need to be there.

Alaric walked over to the table and picked up the *Codicium Aeternum*. It was heavy and decaying. Daemon's names marched across its pages, foul and terrible names along with descriptions of their atrocities and the circumstances of their banishment. Ghargatuloth's entry took up several pages – the Prince of a Thousand Faces created benighted cults all over the Imperium, each distinct and ignorant of the others, each working towards grand plans of atrocity that only became visible as their final horrific moments were played out.

A daemon's banishment was a complicated concept. The strength of the daemon, the method of banishment and sheer luck determined how long the daemon would have to languish in the warp. Mandulis must have dealt Ghargatuloth a fell blow indeed to banish the daemon for a thousand years. The *Codicium Aeternum* had been written in an attempt to catalogue all those factors and predict accurately when and where daemons would return, but Chaos by its very nature refused to be categorised so neatly and the book had been left half-finished – but not before Ghargatuloth's return had been predicted.

If Cadia fell, a spearhead of pure Chaos could punch deep into the Segmentum Solar. The Grey Knights, the only soldiers who could face Warmaster Abaddon's daemonic allies, would be needed there. But if the Grey Knights were all deployed at the Eye, and something terrible arose to strike at the Imperium's undefended underbelly...

It was Valinov who had taken the book. Valinov had openly rebelled against the ordo after taking the book from the Librarium. Had Ghargatuloth been the source of all his depravities? Was Valinov laughing at them from Mimas, knowing he had already set something in motion at the Trail of Saint Evisser that could strike when the Imperium was at is weakest?

'You have my squad,' said Alaric. 'Valinov has caused them to mourn. Tancred was there, too. For the other squads I would recommend Justicars Genhain and Santoro, they were both in the force that hit the fortress from the sunward side.'

'You will be on your own, justicar,' said Tencendur. 'I can vouch for your command but in battle there will be no one else.'

'I trust the judgement of the Inquisition.'

Tencendur nodded at his command squad to leave with him. 'You have the *Rubicon*. It will be made ready for launch at Iapetus within twelve hours. I release you into the authority of Inquisitor Ligeia. For the Throne, justicar.'

'For the Throne, grand master,' said Alaric with a bow of the head.

Tencendur left, his boots and the boots of his squad ringing off the stone floor and echoing grandly around the Fallen Dagger Hall. Inquisitor Nyxos left in the opposite direction, followed by his silent advisors and honour guard, the servos of his body bracings sighing as he walked.

'You are psychic,' said Alaric as Ligeia gathered up the book and stood up from her chair. 'The wards react to it.'

Ligeia smiled. 'I have seen my fellow inquisitors throw lightning bolts. I am afraid I can manage nothing so grand as that. I deal in knowledge, I am a scholar. And yourself?'

'All Grey Knights have some psychic capacity. I am strong enough for it to be a part of my conditioning but not to focus it. You knew that already, inquisitor.'

'Of course. I also know you are curious and intelligent, and you have an imagination. Those are qualities I value. You are also a born leader, even if the grand masters would rather watch you earn your stripes for a decade or two. You can lead your Marines when we need to fight and defer to me when we need to learn. We will have to do both, I fear, if I am right about Ghargatuloth.'

Ligeia turned elegantly and walked away, her long ermine-trimmed dress sweeping along behind her.

She had known he would agree to lead her strikeforce. She must have realised Alaric would want another go at Valinov, even if only to thwart whatever plan he had set in motion. Alaric had learned that was how inquisitors thought – people, whether Grey Knights or Imperial citizens or even other inquisitors, were weapons to be manoeuvred into position and let loose on whatever enemy it would be most expedient to destroy. He understood that was the only way the complex, monolithic Imperium could be manipulated into providing what an inquisitor needed to fight the enemies of humanity. But that didn't mean he had to enjoy being a part of it.

GHOLIC REN-SAR VALINOV was naked and bound, with shackles around his wrists and ankles. There was a metal collar around his neck packed with explosives that would neatly blow his head off if he left the interrogation cell, attempted to use psychic powers (although Valinov had never shown any measurable psychic capacity) or simply angered the supervising interrogator enough for the collar's detonator to be pushed. The cell around him was of plain obsidian flecked with white, smooth and unforgiving in the harsh light stabbing down from the bright lumosphere set into the ceiling. He sat on a metal chair in the middle of the otherwise unfurnished room. In spite of it all, he still looked dangerous. His body was hard-muscled, not big but strong. His skin was covered in scars too regular to be solely the result of the many wounds he had received in his career. Abstract tattoos covered the sides of his abdomen, curving up in thick dark blue bands over his back and shoulders to form a broad collar over his throat and lower chest like the clasp of a cloak, snaking over his scalp.

His face was sharp and alert. He had expressive, knowing eyes set into a thin hatchet of a face. His hair was shaved back brutally and his ears had been so full of rings that with all the decoration taken out they looked ragged and chewed.

Alaric waited from the monitoring station on the other side of the stone wall, watching images relayed from pict-stealers in the corners of the cell. The room was lit only by the light from the screens, casting a silvery light on the faces of the supervising interrogation staff. The prison on Mimas was staffed by men and women who had been totally mind-scrubbed and then given an education consisting of nothing but security protocols, interrogation techniques and utter hatred of the inmates. They were at a reduced risk of corruption because there was less of a mind to be corrupted.

The supervisor leaned over to a microphone jutting from the console in front of her. 'Confirm secure. You may begin, inquisitor.'

The stone door of the cell ground open. A servitor trundled in and placed a chair opposite Valinov, then left the room. Inquisitor Ligeia walked in and sat in the chair. Alaric saw she had toned down her clothing from her full regalia. Now she looked like a military officer in a dark and severe uniform, with just enough ornamentation to convey high rank.

Valinov looked up at her. Alaric could just detect a slight smile in his eyes. The same expression he had seen when Valinov stabbed Iatonn through the gut. Ligeia was carrying a thick file of papers and she opened it out on her lap, making a show of reading from one of the many files the Inquisition had on Valinov.

'Gholic Ren-Sar Valinov,' began Ligeia curtly, 'you are charged with heresy first class, grand treachery, daemonancy, warpcraft and association with persons identified as a moral threat. You will be aware that each of these charges is of such severity that no possibility of innocence can be accepted, and that each is punishable with death.'

'So,' said Valinov in that slick, smooth voice. 'You're going to kill me five times?'

Ligeia looked up at him. 'That was the plan, yes.'

Valinov said nothing.

'You have been away for some time, Valinov. You probably don't know the changes to our procedure. It's complicated, but ultimately, the office of executions has acquired a psyker who can keep you alive, even though you are dead. The Adeptus Astra Telepathica trained him up and they owed the ordo a favour, hence your impending five death sentences. I must confess, I find it difficult to imagine what it will be like for you to remain conscious while your body begins to rot.' This time Ligeia smiled faintly. 'But then I suppose you have a better imagination than I.'

At first, Ligeia was nothing but official. She stated simply the particulars of Valinov's various crimes and the authority by which he was condemned. Alaric knew them all already – the Conclave of the Ordo Malleus on Enceladus had already decided what Valinov was guilty of and what would be done to him. Every now and then Ligeia would try to flatter Valinov, such as pretending to be surprised at the speed with which he organised the cultists on the Gaolven Belt. Other times she would try to goad him into boasting about what he had done, by expressing ill-disguised disgust at his ability to kill from a distance without remorse. Valinov saw past these ruses easily – but Alaric imagined that was the point. It was a game. Valinov had played with all his interrogators, and Ligeia was playing along in the hope that Valinov would get comfortable enough running rings around her to let something important slip.

Ligeia was good, Alaric thought. But he still suspected that Valinov was better.

'I remember you,' said Valinov suddenly in a low, dangerous voice, cutting off Ligeia in mid-sentence. Alaric saw the interrogator nodding slightly to one of her underlings, whose finger hovered over the collar detonator.

'They brought you over from the Ordo Hereticus,' continued Valinov. 'That doesn't happen very often. They must have thought you had some steel in you, but it looks like they were short-changed. Do these threats work on petty witches and governors who don't pay up? Do you think an inquisitor of the Ordo Malleus will break so easily? I have seen Chaos, little girl, from both sides. You can do nothing to me.'

Ligeia didn't waver. 'Perhaps I have not made myself clear. We will make you suffer, Valinov. You have never had access to the most sensitive of the ordo's procedures. If you resist we can show you if you wish.'

'And what do you want in return for giving me a single death?' Valinov's tone was mocking. 'Information?'

'I am glad we understand one another.'

'There is not enough room in your head to understand what I could tell you. I have seen the forces that really hold this universe together, and it isn't your Emperor. All you Imperial vermin devote your lives to crushing the spirits of mankind until not one man or woman could survive knowing the truth.' Valinov sat back. 'You don't know, do you? They haven't told you. You're a messenger, Ligeia. A lackey. You think you have a future because you can do more than just smash a daemon's skull with a force hammer but you're the most pathetic of them all. They're lying to you. The ones who know, they lie.'

Ligeia leafed through the files in the folder again, as if Valinov's words just slid off her. 'While in the employ of Inquisitor Barbillus you had access to the Librarium...'

'The purpose of the Inquisition,' said Valinov suddenly, 'is to ensure that the Adeptus Terra retains power. It does this by covering up the truth with tales of your dead Emperor and fictions you call histories. Chaos is the essence of existence. It is power given form. It can be shaped, it can be used. Chaos could free mankind. Do you know what freedom is? I mean real freedom, releasing the shackles of your mind.'

'Your impending deaths,' said Ligeia levelly, 'now number six.'

'Have you ever killed a world, Ligeia? I mean, killed every single person on a planet, wiped out everything they are and everything they will ever be.'

'You did. You killed V'Run.'

'V'Run is a free world now. But I have destroyed worlds before. Under Barbillus I did everything except press the button. Whole civilisations, dead in hours. Do you know what he did to Jurn? They had to bring in freighters full of refugees to repopulate it. They're still finding unexploded virus torpedoes in the underhive to this day.' Valinov's eyes were alive. 'You have to be there, not just see it. I'm not a psyker, but I could feel them dying. I always told myself that I was doing the right thing, but when I finally began to understand and I made sure Barbillus couldn't get off Agnarsson's Hold, that was truly right. He burned, just like the billions he had burned. That's when I understood.

'The things the Imperium does to itself to crush the freedoms it calls heresy – that is the true heresy. You know nothing of the true glory of Chaos. If you did, you would see that the freedom and power it gives would be a better fate for the galaxy than the suffering the Imperium must dole out to keep that truth from existing.'

'Chaos is suffering,' said Ligeia. 'I have seen as much of that as you have.'

Valinov shook his head. 'Perspective, inquisitor. Some must always suffer. But Chaos gives so much more to those who do not. Under the Imperium, everyone suffers.'

'You have one chance,' said Ligeia. 'It is more than you ever gave anyone. Tell us about Ghargatuloth and the Trail of Saint Evisser. What were you going to do to raise him? Who did you instruct to carry on your work?'

Valinov sat back and sighed. 'You almost had me worried, inquisitor. For a moment it looked like you really knew something.'

Ligeia shut the file and stood up. She gave Valinov the kind of superior, officious look she did so well. Valinov's eyes glinted as if he were hiding a smirk. Beside Alaric, the interrogator staff worked the cell commands and the door ground open again. Ligeia walked smartly out, the servitor removed the chair and the door shut again.

The lights in the cell went out, leaving Valinov in pitch blackness. Alaric could hear the rogue inquisitor's breathing. He knew from the interrogator's previous reports that he wouldn't break by conventional means – Ligeia had been the last realistic chance they had of cracking Valinov open.

Ligeia's voice came over Alaric's vox-receiver. 'Justicar, we have done all we can here. Assemble your force on the *Rubicon*, we are running out of time.'

FOUR
THE TRAIL OF
SAINT EVISSER

THE TRAIL OF Saint Evisser was a grimy little skein of space towards the galactic west, on the edge of the Segmentum Solar near the Ecclesiarchy heartland around Gathalamor and Chiros. The Trail consisted of a couple of dozen settled worlds forming a long, gruelling journey that twisted around nebulae and asteroid fields to describe the lengthy pilgrimage of Saint Evisser himself.

Ligeia had acquired reference works on the Trail before embarking and Alaric spent some of the journey reading up on it. The Trail, it seemed, had once been a centrepiece of the Imperial cult. It was a shining example of piety, with cathedrals and shrines dotting every settled world, a rich vein of charismatic senior clergy and a brand of lavish exultation that covered cathedral spires in gold. Each world competed in works of devotion until the festivals of the Adeptus Ministorum became week-long celebrations with processions that snaked around continents. It rivalled the relic-trail of Sebastian Thor for ostentatious piety and material celebration of the Emperor.

But that had been some centuries ago. The Imperium was a vast and constantly changing place and cycles of poverty and wealth, fame and obscurity, churned between the stars. The Trail of Saint Evisser was all but forgotten now, just another band of worlds where billions of Imperial citizens lived out their lives. The population, Alaric saw, had fallen to about a quarter of its high point. The hive world of Volcanis Ultor was half-empty and whole agri-worlds were lying fallow. It seemed that religious fervour had at last waned and allowed warp routes to be forged that bypassed the Trail entirely. Shipping through the Trail was a fraction of what it had once been and Saint Evisser himself was little more than a name.

The Grey Knights strike cruiser *Rubicon* was a fast ship. Even so, it would take weeks to reach the Trail. Ligeia had sent an astropathic message to the Inquisition fortress which had jurisdiction over the Trail, but for now there was little to do but pray, train, and wait.

ALARIC AND LIGEIA met regularly in the *Rubicon*'s state rooms, a complex of lavish hardwood panelled suites that could have come from inside a governor's mansion were it not for the lack of windows and the constant deep thrum of the strike cruiser's warp engines.

'What do you remember,' asked Ligeia one evening after Alaric had seen to the Grey Knights' training rites, 'of what you were before?'

Alaric, his armour removed, sat opposite Ligeia wearing his dark grey habit. Ligeia had set out her customary evening meal of exotic delicacies from worlds on the other side of the Imperium, but Alaric as usual ate little. 'Nothing,' he said.

'Nothing?' Ligeia raised an eyebrow. 'I find that difficult to believe. It is what I did before I ever heard of the Inquisition that made me the inquisitor I am now.'

'A Grey Knight must have a core of faith that cannot be broken.' Alaric picked at the daemonfish fillets on the silver plate in front of him – truth be told, he was uncomfortable amongst the luxury with which Ligeia surrounded herself. 'Like a rock in an ocean. That's the first thing we learn, although none of us remember learning it. You understand, we cannot know what it is like not to have that shield of faith. If we could remember it, that core would be flawed. There would be a way in. There is no room to remember for us.'

Ligeia leaned forward, a faint smile on her face. She looked almost girlish, like a child swapping secrets with a friend. 'But you used to be someone else, Alaric. Do you know who?'

Alaric shook his head. 'That was a different person. The Ordo Malleus has the most advanced psycho-doctrination in the Imperium. It leaves nothing behind. I could have been a hive ganger or some tribal hunter, or anything else. The Chapter recruits from hundreds of planets of all kinds. Whoever I was, I was taken before adolescence and made into someone else.'

Ligeia took a sip of wine. 'It sounds like a high price to pay.'

Alaric looked at her. He knew she was playing with him. She had an insatiable curiosity and the Grey Knights were one more area of study. 'There is no price too high,' he said. 'If we don't do it, then no one will. Chaos is always a hair's breadth away from swallowing us all and losing a flawed mind is no hardship compared to the consequences if we fail.'

'I must confess,' said Ligeia, 'we fight in very different ways.'

'I understand you were not originally recruited by the Ordo Malleus,' said Alaric, satisfying some of his own curiosity. 'From what I know of the Inquisition, that is not common.'

'I was recruited into the staff of the Ordo Hereticus fortress on Gathalamor.' Ligeia dissected her own daemonfish expertly as she spoke, and Alaric imagined the education she must have received to make it such a reflex. He was mildly surprised that such a free-minded woman could emerge from the stifling nobility of Gathalamor. 'I was more useful than they realised. As a psyker I can discern information in whatever form it is written. The Ordo Malleus... made me an offer, and I accepted. There was some resistance, but the Malleus has its ways.' She gave him an odd, sideways smile.

'Resistance? I know even less about the Inquisition than I suspected.'

'Probably deliberately, justicar. Our politics can be very complicated and you are not a politician, you are a weapon. You don't need to know about our various factions and infighting – they are all mostly matters of pride and dogma, but believe me that men like Valinov are more common than any of us would admit.'

'You are very open,' said Alaric. Out of politeness he swallowed a slice of the daemonfish – it tasted rich and spicy, a world away from the balanced but tasteless sludge synthesised for the Grey Knights on Titan. He didn't like it. Eating like this was an affectation, a show of pride. Enough Space Marines had fallen to pride for Alaric to find the whole idea distasteful.

'I trust you, justicar,' Ligeia replied. 'We rely on one another. You cannot negotiate an investigation and I certainly cannot fight, so what can we do but trust each other?'

Ligeia had brought her death cultist bodyguards with her – they stood there now, in the shadowy corners of Ligeia's suite, wearing shiny black bodygloves and masks and carrying dozens of blades between them. They were highly-trained and bound somehow to Ligeia personally; with their help Alaric doubted very much that Ligeia could not hold her own when the bullets started to fly.

A chime sounded over the *Rubicon*'s vox-casters, indicating the arrival of an astropathic message. The astropaths used by the Grey Knights were little more than ciphers, men and women mind-wiped after each mission so they could recall no sensitive information. The voice that spoke was dim and grey.

'Astropathic duct established. Inquisition fortress Trepytos asserts jurisdiction, requests itinerary, manifest and mission.'

Ligeia stood up, smoothed her long dark blue dress and snapped her fingers, calling a trundling valet-servitor forward to clean away the remains of the feast. She wiped her fingers clean on a napkin, another affectation since she had used only silver cutlery. 'We have almost arrived. I'm afraid some of those politics I mentioned come into play now, justicar. The Ordo Hereticus inquisitors watching over the Trail of Saint Evisser are based at the fortress on Trepytos and there are protocols to be followed if I am to act freely within their jurisdiction.'

'I will tell my men we will arrive shortly.'

'Good. Have them spick and span, justicar, a force of gleaming Grey Knights will do no harm in getting us a free rein here.'

Alaric gave her a look. 'My battle-brothers observe their wargear rites constantly, inquisitor.'

Ligeia smiled back at him. 'Of course. Now if you will excuse me, they will need me on the bridge.'

Another snap of the fingers, and Ligeia's death cultists prowled out of the shadows to follow her as an honour guard, six black-clad assassins who moved with feline precision and always had one hand on the pommel of a blade. Their faces were covered with masks, featureless except for eyeholes. Alaric could appreciate the intimidating effect they could have. Not for the first time he wondered where Ligeia had got them – they were hardly the affectation of an aristocratic lady.

For the briefest moment, Alaric found himself wondering who he had once been. There had been a child once, who had been taken away by a Chaplain of the Grey Knights or a Black Ship of the Inquisition, and who was erased from existence by endless sessions of psycho-doctrination. What could he have been, if not a Grey Knight?

He would have been nothing compared to Alaric now. That was what he had been told, and what he had always believed. He chased the thought from his mind and headed back to the training decks to muster his battle-brothers.

THE RUBICON WAS the finest ship to dock at the planet Trepytos for several hundred years. It was a shining gunmetal grey with protective prayers wrought into the hull in gold. It was a heavily modified version of the strike cruisers used by the Space Marines of the Adeptus Astartes, with an enlarged drop-pod bay, heavily reinforced quarters for Inquisition personnel and a comprehensive hexagrammic ward network built into every strut and bulkhead.

The fortress on Trepytos, on the other hand, had seen far better days. It was an impressive dark granite castle, with its fearsome battlements concealing planetary defence lasers and orbital missile bays. Beneath it was the Inquisition stronghold from which the Ordo Hereticus watched over the Trail of Saint Evisser. Around it were massed the decaying suburbs of what had once been the wealthy and exclusive fortress city from which the aristocracy of the Trail had watched over the officer classes of the guard and Navy and the ranks of the Ecclesiarchy.

Trepytos had been the seat of authority for much of the Trail, but now it was in decay. The decline of Saint Evisser's worship had hit the planet worse than most. Elegant countryside, preserved for the benefit of noble houses who liked to hunt and adventure, now ran wild and encroached on the rotting cities. The population survived in enclaves, and the Ordo Hereticus presence was like a ghost in the lofty, half-abandoned fortress.

The *Rubicon* dropped into low orbit where the fortress's docking spire punched through the planet's grimy grey clouds. Docking clamps sealed and, as the cruiser refuelled, Inquisitor Ligeia, her bodyguards, and Justicar Alaric descended by dignitary shuttle to see what state the Trail of Saint Evisser was in after hundreds of years of decay.

INQUISITOR LAMERRIAN KLAES waited for them in the draughty, cavernous assembly hall in the heart of the Trepytos fortress. The hall had once seated audiences of hundreds in banks of seats but there was no one else there now. A giant pict-screen was folded up against the ceiling, wrapped in black fabric and gathering dust. Once the hall had been used to assemble the elite of the Trail to hear their concerns or issue Inquisitorial edicts – now it was so frequently quiet and empty that it was as good a place as any in the fortress to discuss sensitive matters. The only part of the hall that was lit was the very centre, where a semi-circle of databanks and cogitators stood shedding a pale greenish light. This was where Inquisitor Klaes worked, and in spite of the small staff and garrison that ran the fortress he effectively worked alone.

Klaes was a thin, angular, harried man who looked more like an Administratum adept than an inquisitor. Were it not for the engraved power sword at his waist and the Inquisition seal around his neck, he could have been just another one of the billions of pen pushers that kept the Imperium wrapped up in red tape.

Alaric and Ligeia were led in by the Hereticus storm troopers of the fortress's garrison. Klaes, surrounded by monitor screens and reams of printouts in the centre of the hall, looked up in annoyance at their entrance. When he saw Alaric, he straightened in surprise. Ligeia had been right, of course – Alaric, nearly three metres tall in his massive polished power armour, was a usefully impressive sight.

'Inquisitor Ligeia,' he said in a sharp and surprisingly strong voice, standing to greet her. 'I have been expecting you.' He nodded at Alaric, 'Justicar.' Alaric nodded back. Klaes had not been expecting the Grey Knights.

'I fear we have arrived at a time when you are overwhelmed.' Ligeia indicated the screens and the printouts. The screens were displaying pict-stealer recordings, columns of statistics, and reams of texts. The printouts were spooling onto the floor.

'Information is our lifeblood, inquisitor,' said Klaes. 'Even these days the Trail of Saint Evisser creates a lot of it. I am the only one here with the authority to do anything about what he sees, so I have to see it all.'

'Then we will need to work closely, Inquisitor Klaes,' said Ligeia. She walked over to Klaes's nest of screens and cogitators and ran one of the spooling printouts through her fingers. 'We have reason to believe there is a daemonic threat emerging or due to emerge somewhere on the Trail. It is my job to find it and, with the help of Justicar Alaric and his men, to destroy it.'

Klaes walked up to Alaric. Alaric saw a heraldic crest on Klaes's sword and wondered which noble house had owed Klaes so much they had given him one of their heirlooms.

Klaes held out a hand to shake, and Alaric took it. 'Justicar, a rare pleasure. I have heard of the Grey Knights but here in the Hereticus details are scarce. Welcome to the Trail of Saint Evisser, for what that is worth.'

'There isn't much to tell, inquisitor,' said Alaric, slightly uncomfortable with diplomacy. 'Our purpose is simple. We are soldiers, and we need support just like any soldier.'

'Of course. But you understand...' here Klaes turned to Ligeia, 'the Trail has fallen a very long way. I am the sole permanent Inquisitorial presence for the whole of the Trail and the resources of this fortress are limited. I can call upon the Adeptus Arbites, who are far more numerous than the Hereticus troops, but they are quite embattled themselves. They effectively rule several of the planets after the nobility took flight. There are no Space Marines who would answer my call when Abaddon is killing his way through the Cadian Gate. I will give you what help I can, but the Trail is very much on the wane and if it is to rise again, I fear you will have to wait a very long time.'

'Time is exactly what we don't have,' said Ligeia. 'I will need access to all your reports of cult or otherwise suspect activity. I need details. Interviews with the investigators if possible. I am afraid I need complete access, too. Total jurisdiction.'

'Many of my interrogators are in deep cover and I cannot withdraw them at such short notice. Most of the rest I could make available but I will be undoing many Hereticus protocols and I will have to answer to the sector Conclave. I would need to know what threat you are investigating.'

'Hmm,' Ligeia thought for a moment. 'If you are willing to ignore protocol then so am I. The creature we are hunting is known to some as Ghargatuloth. Justicar Alaric will be able to tell the story better than I. Justicar, if you will?'

Alaric was not expecting to turn storyteller. But he supposed Ligeia was right – to the Grey Knights the story of Grand Master Mandulis and the Prince of a Thousand Faces was almost a religious parable, an exemplar of the Grey Knights' sacrifice and the supernatural evil they were sworn to face.

Alaric told Inquisitor Klaes the story of the death of Mandulis and the banishment of Ghargatuloth, telling it the same way the Chaplains had told it to him when he was a novice still in awe of what he would become.

When he had finished, Inquisitor Klaes sat down in front of his screen and watched them for a few moments, columns of figures streaming past his eyes.

'Our records are in a sorry state,' he began. 'The Adeptus Mechanicus withdrew lexmechanic support two hundred years ago. I have had interrogators try to disentangle it but we have only made limited headway.'

'If you'd had me, inquisitor, there would not have been a problem. Information is my speciality.'

'Good, then you will know everything we know. I will put you in touch with Provost Marechal, he's the highest level Arbites contact. He won't thank me for making him available to you but make sure he understands the authority you carry and he'll give you all the help he can. I can offer you berthings for your ship here and anywhere else on the Trail with the facilities to handle a strike cruiser, not that there are many. I'll have the fortress staff prepare rooms for you, and the justicar can have access to the barracks, they're half empty anyway.'

Ligeia smiled graciously, something Alaric saw she was good at. 'I am glad you understand the importance of our mission here, inquisitor. I shall need to begin immediately, I shall bring my staff down from the *Rubicon* and start work in your records.'

'I'll assign you a guide,' said Klaes. 'I'm afraid, given the state of the fortress, you'll need it.'

INQUISITOR KLAES HAD two hundred staff at the fortress, mostly drawn from the Administratum and the Adeptus Arbites, as well as the three hundred Hereticus storm troopers in the garrison. The fortress archives were administered by a small cadre of ex-Administratum archivists and researchers, whose skill with the immensely complex bureaucracy of the Imperium meant they were better than most at dealing with the vast collection of information the Trail had generated.

Inquisitor Ligeia saw the archives were in severe disrepair. The dwindling staff had been unable to store all the ledgers, data-slates and written reports properly and many of them were uncatalogued, filling sagging, rotting shelves that in turn filled the dank vaulted catacombs beneath the draughty fortress. Each mottled yellow lumoglobe offered little more light than a candle, and the peeling gilded spines of thousands of books glinted weakly.

'The Adeptus Mechanicus maintained it at first,' the archivist was saying. She was a young, harried-looking woman with skin pale from too little sunlight and a drab Administratum uniform. 'But without their lexmechanics it was impossible to collate it all properly. We have Arbites' reports, astropathic monitoring, interrogation transcripts, everything from the Trail. We try to sort out the important information from the rest and archive it properly, but so much slips through that might be important and as you know, inquisitor...'

'...our work lies in the details,' said Ligeia. 'How many rooms like this are there?' Ligeia indicated the vault they were standing in, where dozens of ceiling-high bookshelves exuded the musty smell of decaying paper.

'Seventeen,' said the archivist. 'We think. The intact ones go back to the prime of the Trail. There are some vaults that were lost to flooding and twenty years ago a nest of rats ate their way through hundreds of books. And we're always finding new places where records were kept because the archive rooms became too full.'

'I shall need to look at your organised records,' said Ligeia, removing her velvet gloves and feeling the word-heavy air tingling against her skin. 'I shall require any information you have on active or defunct heretic cults. Give particular priority to apocalyptic sects. Find out if there are any survivors imprisoned on the Trail. I shall start here.'

'Of course, inquisitor,' said the archivist, unable to completely hide the bemusement from her voice.

Ligeia held out her hands as the archivist left. She could feel the weight of meaning in the vault, most of it stodgy and grey with irrelevance. But there were seams of violence and heresy running through it like veins in marble. The faint echo of the Trail's fallen splendour reached her – though the Trail was still home to billions of Imperial citizens it had in truth been dying for some time, and it mourned the loss of its celebrated piety and wealth. War had touched the Trail where nations or planets tried to gain independence from the Imperial yoke, and when legions of men and women had left to fight in the wars that constantly raged around the Imperium.

She started with the world she stood on, its details illuminated by the inventories and maintenance records of the fortress itself – she let the information flow into her. She could see that Trepytos's society had been almost laid bare, leaving only the cold, diamond-hard core of the Inquisition, dwindling smaller and smaller but still desperately trying to hold the Trail together.

She let Trepytos slip out of her mind and moved on to the Trail's most important world. Volcanis Ultor was a slow, irascible old world, now decrepit but still with potential for one last fight. Some of its hives were all but empty, others were full to their considerable capacity as if citizens were huddling together for safety. The handsome velvet sheen of the Ecclesiarchy lay over Volcanis Ultor – the authority the cardinals had over the planet was a relic of the Trail's religious prominence.

The forge world of Magnos Omicron throbbed with factories churning out weapons for the armies now heading for the Eye of Terror, but the Adeptus Mechanicus were insular in the extreme and the cargo ships that visited the world brought no benefit to the rest of the Trail. The planet was cloaked and dark to Ligeia, only the odd flashes of technical information – new marks of tanks or lasgun pouring out of the forges, abortive diplomatic moves to bring Magnos Omicron into the fold of the Trail's authorities. The Mechanicus had kept their world insulated from the workings of the Trail and, as far as Ligeia could tell, it was one of the few places on the Trail not trapped in a spiral of decay and obscurity.

Half-settled or depopulated worlds cast shadows of ignorance where the information stopped flowing. The garden world of Farfallen was a small bright spark, too underpopulated to ever be important but famed

for its beauty. The drab grey canvases of agri-worlds spoke only of production quotas and tithing rates. A few mechanical glints betrayed the
presence of monitoring stations on the outskirts of more important systems, their existence composed solely of blind numbers spooling from
various sensors.

Ligeia's psychic power let her draw meaning from any medium. The
whole of the Trail was there beneath the fortress at Trepytos. She could
see the planets hanging in space and feel the currents of their histories
churning through her. The cults she saw were dark wells of malice and
debauchery. The Imperium's responses were sharp wounds that bled
recrimination. But it was not enough – she needed details.

Ligeia walked up to the closest shelf, the hem of her travelling dress
becoming grimy with the thick gathering of dust. She pulled one volume off the shelf – it was a collection of annual reports from the Officio
Medicae on the agri-world Villendion on the edge of the Trail, going
back thirty years. Disease and antiseptic desperation bled from its pages.

Ligeia placed her hands on the cover, letting the knowledge seep into
her mind.

Silently, using the skills that had so scandalised the noble circles in
which she had been brought up, Ligeia began.

ALARIC ROSE UP almost onto his toes, his hands moving slightly from
side to side as he tensed up, ready to strike at any moment. He moved
as he had been taught, ready with every enhanced muscle to go in any
direction at split-second notice, to dodge or parry or strike.

Tancred was taller and so he ducked down lower, ready to use his
greater reach. All Space Marines were tall, Grey Knights no exception,
and Tancred was especially huge – not just tall but broad, with huge slab-
like pectorals lying beneath the implanted black carapace and wide
hands reaching to grab and throw. Tancred's head was a battered knot of
scars and around his neck hung the Crux Terminatus on a silver chain.

Alaric ducked forward and kicked out at Tancred's knee. Tancred
saw it coming and did what Alaric hoped he would – he turned to one
side and half-stepped away from Alaric's kick. Alaric swung behind
Tancred and drove an elbow into his back, knocking him forward off-
balance.

Alaric pounced, throwing his body weight onto the bigger man. Tancred fell forward but turned as he did so with dexterity that was always
so alarming in such a huge man, bringing a foot up into Alaric's stomach. Tancred slammed into the riveted steel floor and kicked out,
throwing Alaric solidly over his head to land hard.

Alaric turned over as quickly as he could, ready to dive forward and pin Tancred down. Suddenly there was a weight on the back of his neck – Tancred's foot pressed down on him. Like a hunter with a kill, Tancred stood over him.

'You're dead, justicar,' said Tancred in his customary growl.

Tancred took his foot off Alaric's neck, and the smaller man pulled himself to his feet. The sparring had left him breathless but Tancred seemed to be barely breaking a sweat.

'Good,' continued Tancred. 'What have you learned?'

'Not to try to beat you on the ground.'

'Apart from that.' Tancred was a true veteran, with an extraordinary panoply of scars and a place amongst the Terminator-armoured assault troops to prove it. He was older than Alaric and he had fought for longer – there was little he couldn't teach about combat of the up close and personal kind.

'Not to face a stronger opponent on his terms.'

'Wrong.' Tancred walked towards the edge of the training circle where an age-blackened steel arch led through to the cells. The *Rubicon* had been built with a deck set aside for the monastic cells in which the battle-brothers slept and spent their few moments of spare time, along with training areas, a chapel, an armaments workshop, a scaled-down apothecarion and all the facilities they needed to keep healthy in body and mind. The Grey Knights were segregated from the rest of the *Rubicon*'s crew, which consisted of well-drilled engine and weapon gangs wholly owned by the Ordo Malleus.

'The lesson,' continued Tancred as the two Space Marines walked through the shadowy corridors of the ship, 'is to play to your strengths. I am stronger and heavier. You are smaller and quicker. I used what advantage I had and you did not use yours.'

Alaric shook his head. 'Have you ever lost?' he asked.

'To Brother-Captain Stern,' replied Tancred. 'He did me the honour of breaking my nose.'

Brother-Captain Stern was one of the most respected warriors the Grey Knights possessed. Alaric was not surprised that it had taken such a man to best Tancred.

'What are your men saying?' asked Alaric. Tancred was not considered a leader with Alaric's potential, which meant he had stayed a justicar for far longer than most and had forged a bond with his Terminator squad that meant he was well worth listening to when it came to the morale of his men.

'I feel they would rather be at the Eye,' said Tancred, almost sadly. 'They have said nothing, but I can feel their doubt. They do not think Ligeia is a warrior.'

'She is not,' said Alaric. 'She does not pretend to be. And I trust her.'

'Then so will they. But it will not be helped if we are kept here without acting against the Enemy.' Tancred did not speak the name of Ghargatuloth. It was out of habit rather than Alaric's orders – the very names of daemons were unclean.

'We don't even know if he's on the Trail. Even if he is not, this place has been spared the Emperor's gaze for too long. I feel we will be called upon soon.'

They reached Tancred's cell, a simple, small room with texts from the *Liber Daemonicum* pinned to the walls. The stern words of the Rites of Detestation were the first thing Tancred saw when he woke and the last thing he saw before he entered half-sleep. Tancred's Terminator armour was laid out in one corner, the baroque polished armour plates shining dully in the dim light. The shield-shaped plaque of the Insignium Valoris mounted on one shoulder bore Tancred's personal heraldry – one half was glossy black representing space and the other was red with a field of white starbursts. One star for each boarding action.

'Take your men through the Catechisms of Intolerance,' said Alaric. 'I think it is an appropriate prayer for the Trail. I will lead Squad Santoro's firing rites, we will need them when the time comes.'

'Santoro is a good man,' said Tancred as he entered his cell and took his copy of the *Liber Daemonicum* from where it lay beside his armour. 'Tough. And Genhain lost a battle-brother at the Gaolven Belt, he will want revenge, too. I think you have chosen your justicars well.'

'This isn't about revenge, Tancred. This is about stopping Ghargatuloth.'

'Maybe,' Tancred leafed through the pages of the *Liber Daemonicum* until he found the well-thumbed page with the Catechisms of Intolerance. 'But revenge helps.'

Interrogation Chamber IX was stained black with blood.

The Ordo Malleus possessed the best interrogation personnel and equipment in the Imperium, and each interrogation chamber had seen generations of psychological theories turned into practice.

Psychic surgery that placed a new, compliant personality inside a prisoner's head. Complex stress cascade scenarios that could convince a man the universe had ended and that his interrogators were gods. Total personality destruction that removed every facet of a person's mind except for the part that contained whatever the Malleus wanted to know.

Usually, the interrogators started with some of the more old-fashioned techniques. Which accounted for the blood.

All the conventional techniques had been tried on Gholic Ren-Sar Valinov in Interrogation Chamber IX. He had been worked on for weeks, but he had not broken. Careful examination of his body would reveal near-invisible surgical scars where the damage done to him had been repaired, because the Ordo Malleus did not do anything so crude as to cripple their enemies out of spite.

It was almost a matter of procedure when dealing with a man like Valinov. As an inquisitor his training, indoctrination and hard-won experience would all but ensure he would not break under conventional measures. The staff on Mimas had gone through the motions with grim efficiency, pausing only to ask the questions. Who was Valinov working for? What was his connection to Ghargatuloth? Why had he been in possession of the *Codicium Aeternum*?

The time came, eventually and inevitably, to move to the next stages, for which the lord inquisitors themselves had to give permission.

Explicator Riggensen was one of a small staff of psykers apprenticed to Ordo Malleus inquisitors whose minds had proven strong enough to allow for their powers to be developed and expanded. Riggensen was a telepath who had studied under Lord Inquisitor Coteaz and had learned to use his power to lever open recalcitrant minds. Riggensen and a handful of men and women like him were permanently seconded to Mimas, to eke vital information from the minds of the toughest prisoners the Malleus brought in.

The interrogation chamber was monitored from a tiny adjoining room. A large window looked in on Valinov sitting naked in the corner of the unfurnished chamber. Screens on the walls showed the same image in various wavelengths, and several monitors displayed Valinov's life signs. Psychic and anti-daemonic wards hung on the walls of the monitoring room in the forms of devotional texts and purity seals. Gun servitors flanked Riggensen as he sat watching his latest charge, because more than one such explicator had been compromised by a psychic prisoner.

Two of the interrogation staff watched Valinov's life signs and provided communications with staff headquarters and the Inquisitorial fortress on Encaladus. The Ordo Malleus's brightest lights were mostly on their way to the Eye of Terror or were already behind enemy lines, but there was still a heady wealth of authority on Encaladus and many inquisitors were listening in.

'Wards down,' said Riggensen, as the interrogator beside him deactivated the psychic wards woven into the walls of the chamber.
Riggensen closed his eyes and reached out with his mind. The chamber
was dull and throbbing with the pain that had been inflicted there and
the blood that covered its walls. Valinov was a complex knot of life in
the corner, a tiny diamond-hard centre of resolve behind his eyes.
Riggensen had felt the iron will of an inquisitor before; he had always
known that one day he would have to try to crack one open. He was
also certain that he would fail. But every attempt had to be made to
find out as much information as possible before Valinov was executed,
and Riggensen was probably the last chance the Malleus had of breaking Valinov.

'Open it up,' said Riggensen, standing up.

The front wall of the monitoring room ground slowly open, and
Riggensen walked through into the chamber. The smoothed layers of
dried blood were like slick stone beneath his feet. The chamber stank of
stale sweat.

Valinov looked up at him. The rogue inquisitor had been deprived of
sleep and food but he seemed to take pride in not letting his health
degenerate.

'Explicator? Then you are finally getting desperate. I was wondering
how long it would take.'

'This does not have to happen, inquisitor,' said Riggensen.

'Yes it does. That's the way it works, isn't it? You do everything you can
to bleed me dry and then you kill me. So get it over and done with.'

Riggensen held out his hand in front of Valinov's face, focusing his
energy through it so that it poured out and flowed through Valinov's
mind.

Valinov resisted, and he was strong. Riggensen could feel landscapes
of hatred in the man's mind, a seething storm of arrogance. He was driven by the same conviction that drove every inquisitor, an absolute faith
that could not be broken. But Valinov's faith was in darkness. The stink
of Chaos filled him. The names of gods that Riggensen had been forbidden to speak echoed through the parts of Valinov's memory that the
rogue inquisitor let the explicator feel.

Valinov was taunting him. Riggensen had never felt such strength of
mind. Valinov couldn't hide his corruption but he could pick and
choose which details Riggensen pried out of him, and he wasn't giving
anything away. That diamond core of willpower shielded everything –
there were no records that suggested Valinov was psychic, but his sheer
resolve was superhuman.

Without warning, Valinov pushed back. Psychic feedback flooded into Riggensen's mind and he was hurled across the chamber, crashing through into the monitoring room. The two interrogator staff were thrown to the ground and the gun-servitors whirred angrily as they trained their guns on both Riggensen and Valinov.

Riggensen pulled back from Valinov's mind before the feedback knocked him unconscious. The wrecked monitoring room swam back into view, with shattered machines sparking.

'Abort!' yelled one of the interrogators, reaching for the control that would send the psychic wards leaping up around the chamber again.

'No,' said Riggensen, grabbing the man's wrist.

Valinov stood up and walked slowly across the chamber. 'I kill millions of vermin in the plain sight of your Inquisition, and they send me a boy,' he sneered. 'This mind will never crack. Don't you see? There is nothing left for me to fear.'

Riggensen sent a white-hot psychic spike into Valinov's mind, visibly leaping from the monitoring room into the chamber and spearing into Valinov's forehead. Valinov spasmed as the motor control portions of his brain were overloaded but the spike shattered like a glass arrow against the core of his resolve.

Riggensen's mind flowed around Valinov's psyche, finding only deserts of boiling hatred. Valinov spat wordless filth back at him. *Traitor*, he called him. *Scum. Failure. Child. Less than nothing*.

Riggensen screamed prayers straight into Valinov's mind. Words that would draw tears from daemons scoured through storms of anger. Valinov grabbed hold of Riggensen's psychic probe and the two men wrestled, Valinov's willpower against Riggensen's psychic strength. Valinov was on his knees and grinning wildly through bloodied teeth, but his mind was undamaged.

'Life signs fluctuating,' said one of the interrogators at the edge of Riggensen's perception. He could just hear the screams of the medical cogitator as it told him that Valinov was going into cardiac and respiratory arrest. But Valinov kept fighting.

Sharp flashes of pain washed through the mental battleground as Valinov's body reached the edge of its limits. Riggensen could taste Valinov's heart as it beat wildly out of time and the agonising grind of his lungs as they tried to draw breath.

Riggensen limped into the chamber, staggering against Valinov's resistance like a man walking against a hurricane. Valinov lashed out with a bolt of sheer malice and Riggensen was thrown against one of the chamber's walls, then yanked the other way and slammed against the opposite wall. Riggensen kept hold of Valinov's mind, clinging on grimly as the most powerful psyche he had ever faced clawed at him like a wild animal.

'Signs critical! Get the apothecarion crew in here!' someone shouted. Riggensen didn't listen. Everything he despised was staring at him like a single huge burning eye of hate. Corruption. Treachery. Surrender to the great Enemy. Valinov had hatred, but so did Riggensen.

Riggensen reached out with the last ounce of his willpower and wrapped a mental fist around the diamond at the heart of Valinov's mind. As his sight greyed out he put more willpower that he knew he had into crushing that diamond.

The dried blood was flaking off the walls. The white tiles beneath were cracking, falling like sharp flurries of snow. Klaxons were blaring on the gun-servitors that were demanding the order to fire. Life sign indicators were bleating that Valinov was about to die. The interrogators were shouting orders. The cacophony grew louder and louder, merging with the din spouting from Valinov's mind.

As the storm rose to a crescendo and Riggensen knew he was about to black out, Valinov cracked.

The diamond of resolve shattered and the shards ripped through Valinov's mind. Valinov himself was thrown backwards to land flat on his back, blood pumping from his ears and nose, his breath gasping hopelessly through a blood-flecked grimace.

'Speak,' said Riggensen breathlessly.

Valinov's mind was blown wide open. Riggensen could see atrocity and corruption in hideous vistas of memory. Faces screamed. Blood flowed. Whole worlds died before Riggensen's psychic eye.

'The Prince will rise,' said Valinov weakly. 'The Thousand Faces will look on the galaxy and make it ours. The Prince will give mankind to the Lord of Change and the galaxy will turn to Chaos under his eye.'

'More.'

'The… the tides of fate are his to control, the ways of men are weapons in his hands, the course of time runs as he wishes, everything that makes you and decides your fate is the tool he uses to rule…'

'More. Tell me everything. Everything.'

Valinov coughed and thick blood flowed down his chin. 'My Prince Ghargatuloth will never die. Only the lightning bolt will cleanse this reality of Ghargatuloth's presence, and the bolt is buried so deep… there is no time, no space, no fate, no will, there is only Chaos… for the bolt is buried so deep…'

Valinov convulsed and couldn't speak further. Riggensen felt blind horror emanating from Valinov's mind, and he knew that the man had spoken the truth. He was horrified that he had broken, that he had given away so much. That meant his words represented a great and terrible secret he had sworn to keep.

Riggensen turned to the interrogators in the monitoring station behind him. They were covered in cuts from shattered monitor screens, but they were still at their stations.

'Did Enceladus get that?' said Riggensen.

'Everything,' replied one of the interrogators. 'Recorded and sent. Comms never went down.'

'Good. We'll need to get a transcript to the astropaths for transmission to Inquisitor Ligeia.' Riggensen looked down at Valinov, who barely had the strength left to breath. 'And get the apothecary crew in here. We want him healthy for his execution.'

FIVE
VICTRIX SONORA

THE DIRTY TURQUOISE sky of Victrix Sonora was darkening as late evening rolled by and the siege entered its eighth hour. A cordon of steel had been thrown around the Administratum complex in the heart of Theograd, the second-largest of the agri-world's settlements, where barricades of spiked steel had been set up covering every angle of fire and rows of Arbites riot-control APCs sheltered assault groups as they edged towards the sinister black-windowed building.

Several of the windows were broken. Here and there bodies lay broken on the paving outside the building where they had been thrown from the upper floors or gunned down as they ran. The remains of Squad 12, the Adeptus Arbites unit that had tried to force entry to the building, were piled around the door where high-powered las-weapons and sniper-fitted autorifles had cut them down from within the expansive entrance lobby.

Arbites officers had been called in from all over Victrix Sonora, and some from off-planet. The Arbites were the ultimate law enforcement of the Imperium – they answered not to local authority but to their own higher echelons, forming a galaxy-wide body that enforced Imperial law. Arbites officers had commandeered the best riot and assault troopers from law enforcement throughout the Victrix system, armed them with their best equipment, and organised them into units for the operation against Theograd's Administratum complex. When the darkness was this deep it had to be the Emperor's Justice that was served, and the Arbites were the instruments of that justice.

Whatever heresy and treachery festered within the Theograd Administratum complex, it had finally shown its hand and there was no reason left not to take the building by force and enact justice upon anything they found. Squad 12 had been prepared to do things with civility, to serve notice of the inquiry in extremis – Provost Marechal himself had put his name to this action. But the heretics had been waiting and had cut down Squad 12 where they stood, eight officers compelled to give their lives in service to the Imperial law, and so every Arbites on the planet had been brought in to ensure justice was done.

Provost Marechal himself arrived in the sixth hour of the siege, shuttled down from visiting Victrix Sonora's orbital dockyards. By the time he arrived at the mobile command post the officers surrounding the buildings had been fired at several times from the building's upper floors. Arbites sharpshooters trained their long-las rifles on the blacked-out windows but still the information about the hostiles was sketchy in the extreme. The heretics were numerous and well-armed. They knew the complex and they were well-led and organised. The two survivors of Squad 12 reported men and women masked in scarlet, yelling horrible high-pitched war cries. They were wearing the floor-length black greatcoats typical of Administratum dress uniforms. Other than that, the Arbites were working blind.

No one knew if the heretics had hostages. They probably did, but hostages were not a priority for the Arbites. Something foul had taken root in Theograd, and justice must be done.

Shortly after Provost Marechal took over on the ground, local defence monitoring reported with shock the two Thunderhawk gunships descending from close orbit towards Theograd. At the same time a strike cruiser made itself known to the small planetary defence installation orbiting Victrix Sonora, identifying itself as the *Rubicon*.

ALARIC COULD SEE the weight of duty etched on the faces of the officers around him. They had known they would have to assault the Administratum building eventually, and that some of them would end up like Squad 12. The fact that they had been joined by Space Marines – half-mythical warriors from children's stories and preachers' parables – had shaken them up even more. The Adeptus Astartes had not been deployed in the Trail for eight hundred years, and the fact that thirty of them were here, now, meant that the enemy they faced must be far fouler than they had suspected.

Some of them were more scared of the Space Marines than they were of the coming assault, Alaric guessed. They would not speak when they were within earshot of the Marines, whispering to one another as though in reverence. They didn't understand why Space Marines were here – it was bad enough that the Arbites had come down and taken over command of the assault, but Marines! That was unheard of. Even the Arbites who led the squads were shocked by their presence, radioing in to the command post to get sketchy explanations from Marechal's staff.

Alaric hoped the officers would not be put off by the giants fighting beside them. But everything Ligeia had told him suggested that Theograd's cult was more than an isolated Chaos sect. He didn't know how she had managed to absorb and quantify the astounding amounts of information on Trepytos, but she had collated details of thousands of the Trail's cults and found that some of them had things in common. The debasement of sacred objects, the worship of a being who had many forms, the idea of playing a part in an immense plan far too vast for human minds to understand. They were nihilistic cults who believed they were nothing compared to their half-glimpsed masters, mere vermin to be used and crushed at the unknowable whims of Chaos. They wanted to serve. They wanted to die. The Trail's overstretched Adeptus Arbites had shown admirable dedication in ensuring the latter wish came true.

'Santoro in position,' came Justicar Santoro's voice over the vox. Santoro's squad were best up close, right in the thick of the action where Santoro's own Nemesis mace would extract a toll of blood from anyone who got too close. Tancred's Terminators and Genhain's retributor squad were on the other side of the plaza, moving into position with the Arbites tasked with storming the service entrances at the building's rear.

'Brother Arbites, officers of the law,' came Provost Marechal's grim tones on the Arbites vox-channel. 'The time has come for this heresy to end. We all knew it would come to this. Something foul has taken root on this world, for most of you your own world, and we are the only force for justice on Victrix Sonora. Battle-brothers from the Adeptus Astartes, the Space Marines themselves, are with us. That alone should tell you what is at stake.'

Provost Marechal had heard there was a Space Marine force under Inquisitorial auspices on the Trail. If he had been unnerved at Alaric's sudden appearance, or offended that they were going to spearhead an assault that belonged to his Arbites, he had not shown it. Alaric had been impressed by the Provost who now sat in the mobile command APC coordinating the two hundred officers and Arbites arranged around the plaza. He was a huge man with skin the colour of old leather, wearing full ceremonial armour and carrying a power maul in one hand. He had been professional and curt – Alaric and Santoro were to take their place in the charge into the lobby, through the fire fields that had cut Squad 12 to pieces. Tancred's peerless assault troops were to batter their way into the back of the building where a nightmarish warren of offices, corridors and labyrinthine networks of chapels and workshops would reward sheer up-front momentum. Genhain would form a fire base duelling with the heretics who would be sure to use the large loading yards to the building's rear as a killing zone.

The Arbites would be with them. Fifty officers were behind the same barricade as Alaric, glancing with disguised awe at the giant silver-armoured warriors who had joined them without warning. They were armed with shotguns and autoguns, with the Arbites to the front wielding power mauls and riot shields. In total the law enforcement troops and Arbites numbered more than two hundred, representing the whole squad strength of Victrix Sonora. The assault was the culmination of an effort against the planet's cult that had cost them much in manpower and resources. If they failed here, the whole Trail would suffer.

'In position, lord provost,' voxed Alaric. Santoro, Genhain and Tancred sounded off in similar fashion. Alaric glanced back at his Marines, who were sheltering behind the massive sloping plasteel barricade. 'Lykkos, stay with me. Dvorn, you're up front. Break the doors down if you have to.' Dvorn nodded. Of all Alaric's squad he had the highest muscle mass and raw physical strength – his Nemesis weapon was a hammer, a rare form that had almost died out amongst the Chapter artificers but was perfectly suited to Dvorn. 'The rest of you, keep firing and keep moving. The Arbites will do the fighting, we must get into the heart of the place and crack open whatever lies in the centre. Tancred will be doing the same. Remember, we do not know what the enemy is capable of. We cannot guarantee that we can hold our own if we get bogged down. We have lost too many brothers to the Prince's followers already.'

Lykkos gripped the psycannon. Dvorn, Vien, Haulvarn and Clostus placed hands to the compartment in their breastplates that held their copies of the *Liber Daemonicum*, letting its sacred knowledge guide their hands.

'I am the hammer,' began Alaric.

'I am the hammer,' replied his squad. 'I am the hate. I am the woes of daemonkind…'

It was an old pre-battle prayer, one of the oldest. One of Alaric's roles as justicar was to prepare the minds of his men before battle, just as they prepared their bodies and their battle-gear. Over the vox he could hear Tancred leading his squad in a similar prayer, as Santoro joined in with Alaric. The officers nearby watched them warily, intimidated by having to witness this ancient battle-rite.

'…from the frenzy, temptation, corruption and deceit, deliver us, our Emperor, that the enemy might face us in Your wrath…'

'Marechal to all units,' came the provost's strident voice. 'Assault plan primary! All units advance!'

The front plates of the barricade were rammed outward, and the plaza opened up before Alaric. Almost instantly bright streaks of fire spattered down from the upper floors of the ugly, black-windowed Administratum building. Return fire from Arbites sharpshooters coughed up in reply, kicking showers of broken glass from the sides of the building.

The riot-equipped Arbites were in front, their shields held up to protect the officers behind them. Alaric refused such protection and strode out in front of Arbites as the line broke into a jog, Dvorn ahead of him. Alaric could see Santoro doing the same, leading his Space Marines at a run. They would hit the doors first, charging onto one side of the cavernous lobby while Alaric took the other side – the side where the men of Squad 12 had died.

Shots punched into the smooth ferrocrete of the plaza. Muffled cries marked where officers were hit and wounded, metallic thuds where shots impacted on riot shields. An autogun shot spanged off Vien's shoulder pad, and another hit Alaric's foot. The age-old power armour turned both shots aside easily.

'Clostus, give me range!' called Alaric as the building loomed closer – he could see where upper windows had been blown out, where the shapes of heretics could just be seen taking up firing position. Clostus, the best shot in Alaric's squad, fired a roaring volley of shots from his wrist-mounted storm bolter, firing at a run when the recoil of the bolter might break the arm of a normal man. Explosive shells ripped around the frame of one of the windows – the heretic sheltering there broke cover and ran, only to jerk suddenly as a sharpshooter's long-las round punched through his throat.

'Haulvarn, Vien, keep their heads down!' called Alaric and bolter fire ripped up from his squad, slamming into the building. The fire coming down at them in return was thicker now – they had a rapid-firing lasweapon, probably a multilaser, that stitched glowing red spears of fire through the advancing officers. Men tumbled to the floor. Haulvarn stumbled as las-shots spattered up one leg, leaving glowing dents in his armour.

Santoro was at the door. He had kicked in one door and brother Mykros was pouring a gout of flame from his incinerator into the lobby.

'Dvorn!' called Alaric. 'Take the doors!'

The squad broke into a headlong run as heavier fire spattered down from above. Dvorn reached the doors and without breaking stride swung his Nemesis hammer in a wide arc, shattering the flak-glass of the doors in a shimmering crescent of shards.

Alaric was next in. His auto-senses adjusted instantly to the shadowy interior of the lobby and in a heartbeat he took in his surroundings – several floors rose around him, hung with banners bearing litanies of obedience and diligence, the mantras of the Administratum. A fountain in the form of a statue of the current High Lord of the Administratum dominated the lobby, its hands sheared off and its stone eyes gouged out. The water was black and foul, pouring from the base of the statue into a fountain pool choked with bodies. Gunfire ripped down from the first and second floors – Alaric saw faces wrapped in scarlet, Administratum uniforms worn like a badge of treachery. The bodies were Administratum, too, workers in drab fatigues or foremen's greatcoats, except for the black-armoured bodies of officers by the doors.

Alaric opened fire, bolter rounds streaking upwards. The fire blew the arm off one heretic and he tumbled raggedly over the railing around the first floor, but there were still dozens more of them up there. They had upturned desks to use as cover and, though they would offer scant protection against storm bolters, the Grey Knights could not fight it out here; enough fire could be brought to bear to pin them down.

Santoro was already moving into the building, vaulting over the scattered furniture of the lobby into the networks of offices.

Alaric made a sharp, stabbing hand signal to the chapel entrance leading off from the lobby's near side as the rest of his squad charged in through the broken doors and heavy fire suddenly stitched down from above. Chunks of marble were ripped from the floor and stray shots blew half the head off the stone High Lord.

'They've got an autocannon up there!' voxed Dvorn.

'Suppress fire and move!' shouted Alaric. An autocannon was a loud, inefficient, old-fashioned weapon that fired shells of sufficient size to crack even power armour. Alaric's squad fired streaks of rapid storm bolter fire up at the source of the autocannon fire as they ran through the arch leading to the chapel.

The chapel was a long narrow room of black marble crowded with pews, with an altarpiece depicting diligent Imperial citizens locked in lives of holy obedience. The body of an Administratum under-consul lay draped over the lectern, where he had apparently been killed while lecturing the adepts.

Alaric knew they were in here – it was little more than an instinct, a sound, a flicker of movement. Even as he turned they screamed and charged out from between the pews, a dozen cultists, tattered blood-stained cloth covering their whole faces except for their hate-filled eyes.

One of them dived onto Alaric, a knife flashing down. Alaric threw the man aside and heard him slam into the wall, ribs crumpling. Alaric's Nemesis halberd flashed out and beheaded another before he stabbed the butt-end of the halberd into the stomach of yet another, pitched him into the air, and brought him smashing down through a pew that splintered under the impact. Storm bolter fire streaked past Alaric, punching through the wood of the pews and through the bodies of the cultists trying to shelter there. They screamed as they died, not with pain but with hate.

Laspistol fire rattled up from the survivors – Alaric grabbed the nearest and fired the storm bolter mounted on his wrist, blasting the cultist out of his hand to spatter against the far wall. Dvorn charged right through the pews and knocked two more flying with a single swipe of his hammer while Haulvarn impaled another with his sword.

The squad ran forward to secure the chapel, sweeping the shadows between the pews with the barrels of their guns. Alaric bent down and turned over the closest body. The scarlet cloth wrapped around the cultist's head fell away and Alaric saw the face of a young adept, the same as billions of men and women who ran the endless bureaucracy of the Imperium. But this man's skin was altered. Scales, like scabs over burnt skin, surrounded the dead staring eyes and ran under the cultist's throat down into the redolent remains of his adept's uniform. Those truly marked by Chaos carried a mark on their bodies as well as on their soul, and the cult on Victrix Sonora had sunk deep indeed.

Gunfire rattled from the lobby where the Arbites and officers were swapping volleys of fire with the cultists. Alaric knew that if the momentum of the assault was lost, the Arbites could be surrounded and massacred. The Grey Knights had to keep moving.

'Dvorn!' said Alaric nodding to the closest wall of the chapel. 'Get us moving.'

Dvorn nodded and sprinted at the stone of the wall, hitting it with all his running strength. The thin covering of marble shattered and Dvorn's armoured body ripped through further into the building, crashing through wood and plaster.

Haulvarn followed, sword flashing. Alaric went next, charging through the ragged hole. He saw rows of glowstrips up above, networks of workdesks in front of him in a wide, low-ceilinged room. Cogitators were surrounded by reams of paper. Supervisors' pulpits broke the sea of partitioned workstations like columns, and above them slogans of obedience looked down sternly from the beams of the ceiling. 'Diligence is salvation,' read one. 'The Emperor's eye is upon you.'

Las-fire spattered out at Alaric even as his eyes took all this in. He dropped low, behind the flimsy partition of the closest workstation, as lasblasts rang off his armour. Cultists were shouting and Dvorn was bellowing as he charged through the workstations to get to grips with the closest cultists. Dvorn understood very well one of the tenets of any Space Marine – when you fight, fight up close, where your strengths count for so much more.

Alaric ran forward, using the workstations for what little cover they provided. He could see the cultists sheltering behind the wooden partitions as they fired – two of them died as Haulvarn's return fire chewed up their flimsy cover and ripped through their bodies. Dvorn was at the centre of a storm of splintered wood as he charged into the closest knot of cultists, hammer swinging, storm bolter blazing at point-blank range. More fire streaked past as the rest of the squad entered.

Alaric heard the voice as clearly as if it were in his own head. It cut through his auto-senses and right into his very soul. It was a language Alaric had heard before on a benighted forest world where Chaotic witch-cults haunted the woods, a language taught to the cultists through communion with the dark power they had sworn themselves to. It was understood only by high priests and champions of Chaos, and what Alaric knew of it told him the speaker was ordering his men to charge.

Dozens of men and women charged in a storm of las-fire. They had been waiting in the offices of the Administratum building, waiting for the first assault to break through so they could counter-attack. They were adepts and menials, supervisors and even one in the uniform of an under-consul, armed with lasguns and autoguns looted from Departmento Munitorum shipments. They had bayonets and swords, pistols and bare hands, and as they charged they screamed foul curses in the tongues of Chaos.

'Hold!' yelled Alaric and, in the seconds it took for the charge to hit, his squad gathered around him, Nemesis weapons ready to receive the weight of the assault, las-blasts spattering against their armour and shredding the air around them. Alaric could feel the faint hum in the back of his head as the anti-daemonic wards woven into his armour overlapped, their feedback echoing in his psychic perception.

He could feel the hatred, too, pouring off the cultists like a stink.

The wave of forty or fifty cultists broke against the Grey Knights. Their priest kept yelling his orders as Alaric and his battle-brothers slashed and bludgeoned around them, every stroke severing a limb or a head. Dvorn's hammer carved great red crescents from the throng. Alaric saw mad eyes rolling between folds of red cloth, men and women, old and young. The din was appalling as the living howled curses and the dying screamed in pain.

Alaric reached forward and hauled himself out of the mass of bodies, throwing attackers aside. The priest was on the far side of the workroom – it was an under-consul, the highest adept rank likely to be found on a world like Victrix Sonora, resplendent in a black greatcoat trimmed with silver braids and the golden sash of his office. His face was covered in layers of scabby scales, so thick that his features were just ugly lumps.

He held out a hand as Alaric clambered over the workstations towards him. A lance of lightning spat out and a blue-white flash burst around Alaric, but his wards kept his body safe and the rock-solid wall of faith shielded his mind. Alaric's storm bolter barked out a dozen rounds but they shattered in purple starbursts in the air just in front of the priest.

The sorcerer turned and ran, and Alaric followed. From the noise of the fight behind him he knew his squad were wading through the cultists to follow him but Alaric had to give chase. The sorcerer ran through the workstations and through a narrow exit deeper into the building. Alaric charged through the wooden partitions and smashed through the narrow doorway, his auto-senses adjusting to the darkness beyond it.

At one time the main Administratum workhouse had filled the centre of the building, where the most menial adepts slaved at long wooden benches, stamping forms and marking timesheets in their hundreds. They had been surrounded by icons of diligence and berated by the building's under-consuls, who constantly sermonised them on the meaninglessness of any labour save that in the Emperor's name.

The workhouse was gone now. The floor and ceiling had been ripped away to form a cavernous space filling most of the inside of the building. Below was a tangled mess of smouldering wreckage. From the bared rafters above hung scores of banners, foul symbols and heretic words daubed in blood and filth.

In the centre of the room, three storeys high, was a monstrous cogitator. Like a massive mechanical church organ, teetering stacks of datacores jutted from the top and fumes belched from the grotesque furnace-like body. Every working cogitator from the workhouse must have been combined into one huge calculating engine, and the whole mass sat in a nest of printouts. Its tarnished black surface writhed with dull red runes and it groaned menacingly as it worked, valves and armatures chattering like a swarm of insects.

The sorcerer was running in the air above the mass of wreckage, sorcerous energy crackling around his feet. He turned, saw Alaric following him, and began to wail a hideous high-pitched chant as he flew towards the monstrous cogitator.

Flashes of blackness began to burst around the cogitator and it rumbled hungrily. Alaric's wards flared hot as the wall between realities was pulled thin and began to fracture. Horrible cackling laughter echoed around the chamber. Leering faces and gnarled limbs reached from the black gashes in the air.

'Daemons!' yelled Alaric over the vox. 'Squad Alaric, Squad Santoro, to me now!'

Daemons were Chaotic will made flesh, at once a part of the dark gods and their servants. They were the tempters of foolish humans and the foot soldiers in the armies of darkness. Daemons were a threat both moral and physical, capable of corrupting the human armies sent against them. That was why the Grey Knights had been created. To them, the words of daemons were not temptations but just another sign of their evil.

It looked like Ligeia was right, thought Alaric as he leapt into the pit. He could hear his squad close behind him. Alaric landed on his feet and carried on running as the shimmering, reaching shapes coalesced from the darkness.

He reached the closest daemons at a sprint and he could feel them recoil from the shield of faith around his soul – a dozen of them formed a wall of iridescent flesh around him and Alaric used their revulsion to get in the first blow. He carved through one with a stroke of his halberd, but suddenly he was surrounded by them. The sorcerer must have been more powerful than even Ligeia had suspected, because he was pulling a veritable horde of daemons from the warp.

Alaric stabbed and hacked at the unbroken mass of daemon's flesh around him. Deformed hands grabbed at him, howling mouths vomited flame over his armour, mad eyes spat hate. Alaric's battle-brothers were trying to pull the daemons off him as storm bolter fire ripped overhead from Squad Santoro, arriving at the edge of the pit.

Alaric plunged both hands into the mass, dragged a daemon above his head and ripped it in two. He forged through the gap, storm bolter ripping shells into the daemons behind him. Over him loomed the cogitator, deep red fires burning inside and steam billowing from malignant vents. Alaric saw that there was a ring of crude wooden statues surrounding the machine's base, and black lightning was playing around them. The sorcerer himself was standing on top of the machine, lit by the silver fire surrounding his hands. Alaric took aim, hoping to knock him off-balance and prevent him from completing the sorcery he was working. The Grey Knights were proof against direct attack from sorcery or psychic powers, but that did not mean the sorcerer could not summon yet more daemons or collapse the building around them.

'I am the hammer!' yelled a voice over the vox, and Alaric saw the enormous form of Justicar Tancred clamber up beside the sorcerer. The sorcerer turned and silver fire streamed from his hands over Tancred, framing the Terminator armour with a blazing halo. Tancred swung his Nemesis sword and, with a single stroke, carved through the sorcerer's body, the blade passing into the heretic's shoulder and slicing down through his body to come out at his waist. The upper half tumbled off down the casing of the monstrous cogitator and silver fire sprayed from the lower half, which blazed and guttered as it disintegrated with the force of the power released.

There was a terrible, high-pitched scream as the sorcerer's soul was immolated in the power gushing out of his ruptured body. The runes on the giant cogitator flared white as if they were drinking the energies of the sorcerer's death, before the two halves of the corpse thudded wetly to the floor and the runes faded.

'Well met, Brother Tancred!' voxed Alaric. 'You made good time.'

'Had to go through a few of them to get here,' replied Tancred as his fellow Terminator Marines took up firing positions on the machine beside him.

A scream went up from the daemons. Justicar Santoro directed his Marines to fire a savage volley of fire through their ranks, and squad Genhain on the far lip of the pit did the same. Daemon flesh dissolved in the crossfire. Tancred led his men down the side of the cogitator, charging past Alaric and into the broken mass of daemons. The screams as the daemons discorporated were hideous and they rose higher as Tancred's Marines trampled their bodies and impaled them on their Nemesis weapons. Alaric saw Brother Locath strike off a head, Brother deVarne cut one in two. Alaric's squad helped them and Dvorn drove another daemon into the ground with his hammer. In a few moments, all the daemons had dissolved into gory stains of many-coloured blood, leaving only the echoes of their dying screams.

Squads of officers were starting to emerge around the pit, and shotgun blasts echoed from elsewhere in the building as the rest of the heretics were hunted and cut down. Provost Marechal's voice was barking orders over the Arbites vox, organising squads to dissect the Administratum building and cut their heretic defence into pieces, using the pandemonium wrought by the Grey Knights to press home the attack. Arbites were leading the officers in kill-sweeps, partitioning the building into zones where each squad killed anything that moved. The Victrix Sonora cult was dying, with their under-consul leader dead and the cogitator at the heart of their worship in Imperial hands.

Alaric walked through the wreckage and picked up one of the looping strips of paper that spooled from the cogitator. The giant machine was still billowing smoke but its rumbling was becoming quieter.

'...and when the Prince rises, so shall the galaxy become His plaything, and mankind will become His lieutenants in the ways of the Change just as shall the stars themselves be blotted out by the Alterer of Ways with the Prince of a Thousand Faces at His right hand...'

Rantings covered every sheet of paper. The cogitator had evidently been the means by which Ghargatuloth communicated with the cult. The fires in the heart of the machine were dying now and, without the cult leader's magic to keep it going, ugly grinding noises came from within as its workings tore apart.

Alaric dropped the paper and walked to one of the statues that surrounded the machine. It was a crude wooden figure hacked from the trunk of a tree, the dark wood charred black. The figure was vaguely humanoid but it had dozens of hands and a face covered with eyes, staring out from around a wide leering mouth. The statue was carved in a harsh, angular fashion that made it even more grotesque.

'Alaric to Marechal,' voxed Alaric, 'We're done here. We'll take what we need and leave the rest to you. I suggest you burn everything here.'

'Understood,' replied Marechal. 'I hear what you have found there. Is it true?'

'Too true, lord provost. Do not let your men tarry here. Destroy it all.'

'Of course, justicar... my men are honoured that they could fight alongside you. I do not think any of them thought they would see they day when the Astartes joined them.'

Marechal was just like the officers in a way – he had been shocked by the Space Marines, and he couldn't entirely keep it out of his voice. 'We all have the same enemies, lord provost,' said Alaric. 'Your Arbites led well here. Just be sure to finish the job and make sure nothing of this cult remains.'

'Of course, Emperor be with you, commander.'

'Emperor be with you, lord provost.'

Alaric picked up the statue and a handful of the printouts. The statue was heavier than it should be, as if it didn't want to be picked up. 'Alaric to all squads, get back to the Thunderhawks. We have what we need. Santoro, cover us over the front plaza. Genhain, we'll meet you at the landing zone. Tancred, with me.'

Alaric waved his squad back through the wreckage of the pit. They passed back through the body-strewn offices and chapel, and through the lobby where a massive firefight had erupted between the Arbites and the heretics on the upper levels. The Arbites were counting the dead and helping their wounded, and the floor was smeared maroon with blood.

The Grey Knights crossed the bullet-scarred plaza back towards where their Thunderhawks were waiting. Alaric glanced back and saw smoke billowing from the top floors. Marechal had followed his advice. Already, the Administratum building was starting to burn.

SIX
RUBICON

The cult on Victrix Sonora had found itself an excellent hiding place. The Administratum, as the largest and most notoriously hidebound Imperial organisation, could have deflected less urgent enquiries indefinitely. It took Provost Marechal himself to cut through the red tape and authorise an intervention from the Arbites.

No one knew how long the cult had been there. Victrix Sonora had been a prosperous agri-world with several large cities in the Trail's heyday, but with the decline of Saint Evisser's worship those cities had kept their populations and lost their income. Crime became one of the most viable routes to survival. The planet's law enforcement had left Victrix Sonora to its own devices since the decline of the Trail, maintaining order around the properties of the Imperium and leaving the rest of the world to rot. They hadn't possessed the resources to police the rest of the planet and no leadership emerged from the civilian population to restore any form of order. There was no telling what had festered in the slums of Victrix Sonora before the cult came to Theograd and found its way into the Administratum.

Perhaps it had even started with the under-consul. The possibility was frightening but very real.

The cult's activities were mostly hidden but from the scattered reports in the archives of Trepytos, Ligeia had built them up into a vivid picture. What few holy places there were on Victrix Sonora had been systematically raided for the past fifty years and relics were stolen. A cargo freighter was intercepted twenty years before and an illegal cargo of looted relics stolen. It was assumed to have been little more than cutthroat smugglers feuding, but now it seemed the cult had wanted the relics and had used its influence in Victrix Sonora's criminal world to get them.

There were killings, for there were few cults that did not vent their rage or exalt their masters with violence. The cult slew apparently random victims all across Victrix Sonora, always taking body parts back with them. All these individual crimes had meant little in the planet's decaying cities, but each one had shone like a jewel in Ligeia's perception. She had known the cult that the Arbites had traced to the Administratum building was the same cult that had been doing the work of Ghargatuloth for decades, just as she had known that Ghargatuloth was somewhere on the Trail, pulling the strings that would bring it back into real space.

The Prince of a Thousand Faces, in its reign before Mandulis banished it, had directed cults in long-term plots that they themselves rarely understood. The cult on Victrix Sonora was engaged in the same sort of inscrutable, slow-burning plan Ghargatuloth favoured. To most it would be a tenuous link, but to Ligeia it was the mark of certainty. That was why she had been recruited by the Inquisition, and why the Ordo Malleus had worked so hard to take her from the Hereticus. She could be certain when others could not – she could sift meaning from the most disparate of facts. Ghargatuloth was on the Trail, Victrix Sonora had been tainted by his will, and the evidence Alaric had brought back from the planet had confirmed it.

LIGEIA HAD SET the staff at Trepytos to furnishing her a set of quarters fit for a lady. They had been busy in the three weeks since she had begun her hunt for meaning. Her suite of rooms was lavish, panelled with dark hardwood and hung with tapestries. A large fire burned in an open hearth and antique furniture salvaged from the derelict portions of the fortress was now gleaming and restored. Mouldering rugs had been cleaned up and now lay on the polished wood floor. Pict-screens set into burnished gold frames hung on the walls and a vox array was set into a wide hardwood desk in one corner. An intricate crystal chandelier hung from the ceiling. One of Ligeia's death cultists stood in the corner of each room, silent and immobile, all but invisible against the finery that Ligeia affected everywhere she went.

Ligeia knew that the Grey Knights would not approve. They slept on hard beds in monastic cells free of luxury. Ligeia had detected slight unease in Justicar Alaric when he was forced to confront the finery Ligeia brought with her – it was almost amusing to see. Probably he saw lavish expense as one of the forerunners of weak-mindedness and corruption. For Ligeia, it was a way to cloak herself in the image of a noblewoman, so her real talents would be hidden.

Against this backdrop, then, the statue in the middle of the room was incongruously horrible. Ligeia didn't want to guess what it was supposed to depict, but that was her job. It was something daemonic, certainly. Its every angle screamed insanity. Ligeia felt it hurting the psychic corners of her mind just looking at it. Unbidden, hints of its meaning filtered into her consciousness – it was a celebration of something foul, an imperfect rendition of something the sculptor had seen and wanted to emulate in his art.

Ligeia flicked a switch on her vox-array and the device began recording her voice onto a data-slate. Many inquisitors travelled with a savant or a lexmechanic to keep their records and collate findings, but Ligeia preferred to do her own bookkeeping, accompanied only by her silent death cultists. 'The… item,' began Ligeia, unwilling to assign the repulsive sculpture a name, 'is of hardwood not native to Victrix Sonora. It must have been made off-world and imported by the cult, which means it is of ritual significance.' She paused. Half the thing's many eyes seemed to be staring at her through hard wooden pupils, the rest of them scanning the room as if looking for a way out.

'The texts recovered from the cult's cogitator, coupled with the obvious heretical references in the carving's shape, suggest that the sculpture depicts one of the Thousand Faces of Ghargatuloth.'

Ligeia stared at the sculpture for a good few minutes. She reached out gingerly with her psychic perception, feeling oceans of meaning wrapped up in the carvings which might be too much for her consciousness to cope with. She tasted metal in her mouth and heard something laughing, or perhaps screaming, far away.

She could hear a name – very, very faint, too distant for her to make out. She listened harder, reached closer. The eyes were windows onto a perfect galaxy, a place devoted to the architecture of Chaos. The leering mouth spoke the unending spell that would remake the universe for the Lord of Change. The grain of the wood was the swirling pattern of fate that wrapped around everything, dragging it inexorably towards the final end – ultimate Chaos, the totality of the Change, the unending magnificence and pure horror of which Ghargatuloth was the herald.

Ligeia saw the galaxy, saturated with the power of the Change. She saw stars weeping and dying. She saw worlds crushed into crystal shards of hate. She saw the galaxy uncoiling and spilling all creation out into nothingness, down the throat of the ringmaster of Chaos, Ghargatuloth's master, the Change God Tzeentch.

Ligeia snapped her mind away just in time. She was on her knees, gasping, sweating. A lock of her carefully dressed hair lay lank across her face. She brushed it away with a shaking hand.

The death cultist in the corner, Taici, inclined his head almost imperceptibly forward. The subtle, silent code Ligeia and her bodyguards used was clear – did she need help? Medical assistance?

Ligeia shook her head, clambered shakily to her feet and tottered over to a table, where there were several crystal glasses and a decanter of syrupy, vintage amasec. She poured herself a good bolt and swallowed it down – she knew it did her no good but her mind told her differently, relaxing its grip on her and shedding some of the after-image of a galaxy gone mad.

'The… the item,' she continued, 'is now under absolute quarantine, with access available only to myself. Should I be lost, access shall be granted only on the permission of the Conclave of the High Lords of the Ordo Malleus.' She opened a draw of the desk and took out a slim wooden case, flipped it open, and withdrew a surgeon's scalpel. Carefully she sliced a sliver of wood off the sculpture, placing the sliver in a specimen bottle. 'A sample from the item is to be tested under my authority as soon as possible.'

Ligeia took another bolt of amasec and composed herself. If she had needed proof, it was here. That only she could see it – her power was extremely rare and she had never heard of another inquisitor possessing it – was frustrating. She would probably have to provide proof eventually that did not rely on her ability to draw meaning from any form of communication. But for her, this was enough. She could still taste in her mind the after-image of Ghargatuloth draped across the stars, an endless ocean of seething Change. A lesser mind, untrained by the rigours of an interrogator's apprenticeship and the demands of the inquisitor lords, might have snapped. If that madness came out from the warp back to real space, how many minds would be lost?

ALARIC WAS CLEAN at last. Twelve hours of prayers, seeking deliverance from the corruption he had come so close to, had scoured his soul of the sorcery that had blasted against it. Ritual decontamination had left his skin raw and tingling beneath armour gleaming from a ceremonial bath of mild acids and incense. The *Rubicon* echoed to the rituals that followed battle, slower and more reflective, as the battle-brothers sought to understand what they had experienced without letting it corrupt them. Alaric had seen terrible things before, from the sky turning red and bleeding over Soligor IV to the legions of the Lust God marching across the plains of Alazon. Each of them had left its mark, but observance of the prayers and rituals of the Grey Knights had washed those marks away. Other men were driven mad, but a Grey Knight was made clean and became stronger.

In the dim light of his cell, Alaric read from his copy of the *Liber Daemonicum*. The Rituals of Conclusion told of the soul being wrapped in faith like a planet is wrapped in an atmosphere, like a warrior is clothed in armour. Faith is a shield, a badge of the righteous, and is required for the very survival of the Emperor's soldiers. They were words Alaric had read thousands of times, but each time it gave him comfort as it did now. He was not alone. If the Emperor was not watching, then faith would mean nothing – but Alaric's soul was intact, and so faith must be a shield against corruption, and so the Emperor must have His eyes upon the Grey Knights.

In the infinite, cold, hostile universe, where the futures of so many trillions hung by the slimmest of threads and the tendrils of Chaos reached everywhere, it was only the Emperor who could show the way. To know He was there gave Alaric all the strength he needed.

The rituals were done. Alaric was safe from the depredations of the enemy until the next battle. But he knew, as always, that would not be very long.

Alaric put on his armour in time for Justicar Santoro's arrival. Santoro was a quiet and intense man who rarely let any emotion surface. That did not mean he had no presence, however, because his men followed him as if his every word was that of the Emperor. If he further proved his prowess as a justicar, Santoro would have a place in the Chaplain's seminary under Durendin if he wanted it, and Alaric knew he would take it.

Santoro stood outside Alaric's cell. He was in full armour – as a justicar he could display his own heraldry on the stylised shield attached to one shoulder. Santoro's heraldry consisted of a single white starburst on a black field – the light in the darkness, the cleansing flame of the Emperor, the wrath of the Knights piercing the black heart of the enemy.

'Justicar,' said Alaric. 'How are your men?'

'The rites are done,' replied Santoro. 'Jaeknos suffered a lasgun shot to the back of the knee but it will be healed in a day or two. Their spirits are good, but they do not feel they know enough about our enemy here.'

'Have they told you this?'

'It is what I feel. My men always feel the same.'

'It cannot be helped. Knowing too much is as dangerous as knowing nothing when it comes to the Enemy.'

'Too true. But that was not why I needed to speak with you. Inquisitor Ligeia contacted the bridge a few minutes ago with new orders. She needs us to go to a world named Sophano Secundus.'

Alaric though for a moment, then went back into the cell and found the data-slate onto which he had downloaded the basic information about the Trail. Sophano Secundus, he read, was a backwater, a feudal world that hadn't yet reached blackpowder-level technology, where the sole Imperial authority was a preacher of the Missonaria Galaxia. The world had been bypassed by the Trail's prosperity because it had no resources of any note and had been lost in the bureaucracy surrounding the settling and development of new worlds.

'It does not sound promising,' said Alaric. 'The population would normally be too small to hide a cult of any size.'

'The inquisitor believes the statue you recovered from Victrix Sonora originated from there,' continued Santoro. 'She thinks there could be a link between the cults of the Trail and that she could find it on Sophano Secundus. We are to remain in orbit and back her up. She does not seem to think it would be wise for us to accompany her.'

'And you disagree?'

'The inquisitor is in command of this mission. There is nothing to disagree with.'

Alaric knew the men under his command. Santoro was not so inscrutable that he could hide his lack of enthusiasm. 'Inquisitor Ligeia will have a lot in common with the nobles she will need to deal with,' said Alaric. 'It would hardly help her cause if she had to go everywhere surrounded by armoured superhumans. She's better off on her own in this case.'

'Of course. I will tell my squad.'

'Let Genhain and Tancred know, too,' said Alaric. 'I need to read up on our destination.'

As Santoro left, Alaric began to search the *Rubicon*'s databanks for information on Sophano Secundus, using the data-slate terminal in his cell. He had certainly not expected to end up on an undeveloped backwater of the Trail when there were still so many population centres where, he knew from experience, a cunning leader could hide whole armies of cultists. The Missonaria Galaxia, the organisation through which the Adeptus Ministorum sent preachers and confessors to benighted worlds throughout the galaxy, was notoriously quick to call in the Sisters of Battle or even the Ordo Hereticus when they suspected something evil had taken root in their flock. If there really was a connection to Ghargatuloth on Sophano Secundus, it would have to be subtle. And subtle, Alaric suspected, was something Ligeia did well.

Once again, however, he had to trust her. All the prowess of the Grey Knights would mean nothing if Inquisitor Ligeia's hunches proved wrong. She was a psyker, yes, a powerful one, and a determined woman devoted to the eradication of the Enemy – but she was still human, and even her most precise divinations were ultimately guesswork.

Alaric had learned long ago to put his trust in the Emperor, for he was engaged in a fight against such odds that only through the Emperor could he prevail. But he was still not completely certain that he should have the same level of trust in Inquisitor Ligeia.

SOPHANO SECUNDUS HAD been discovered so long ago that it was all but impossible to trace its whole history under nominal Imperial rule. In the latter years of the Great Crusade, when the Emperor was already worshipped as a god, missionaries from his fledgling church had sent one of their number to Sophano Secundus to preach the word. They found a world mostly barren and drab with only one habitable continent that could only support a handful of feudal kingdoms around a few cities. Such rediscovered worlds were common, because the scattered human worlds had been torn apart in the Age of Strife and during the Crusade many were found that had been forgotten since the first waves of colonisation.

The Missionaria Galaxia maintained a presence on Sophano Secundus, which was why there were any records of it at all. The first missionary to be named in the records, Crucien, described primitive but broadly harmless kingdoms that bowed before an Allking and occasionally settled disputes with pitched battles. At some point the planet was forgotten by the Administratum and so a formal settlement order was never drawn up for Sophano Secundus – it became, by default, the responsibility of the Adeptus Ministorum, who were unwilling to waste any more resources on the backwater than the personnel required to keep a mission on the planet.

There were many such planets in the Imperium, most of them on the outer reaches of settled space or scattered through the Halo Zone, but more than a few surrounded by more developed systems. The Imperium's official policy was to 'civilise' such worlds and open them up for settlement, but even at the best of times there were more than enough wars and rebellions to keep Imperial efforts elsewhere. And times were never the best.

Sophano Secundus, according to the reports that had filtered back to the Trail authorities from the missionaries, was almost deliberately bad at accepting new technology and ideas. In any case, the Ecclesiarchy knew better than to cause a perfectly good Imperial flock to decimate itself by giving them lasguns. The Allking had therefore ruled over a feudal nation for as long as the records stretched back, knowing nothing of the Imperium other than that the missionary was holy and untouchable and that fire would rain from the sky if heresy ever showed its head. The missionaries considered the population's faith to be relatively stable, albeit prone to the sorts of misunderstandings inevitable when existing beliefs came into contact with the Imperial faith. There was no suggestion that the Ecclesiarchy had been forced to quell any rebellions or cult activity (although the Ecclesiarchy kept such things to itself) and other Imperial authorities seemed not to have even visited the world for several thousand years. Aside from the missionaries and perhaps a few curious wealthy visitors keen to observe how humans survived outside the hive cities, Inquisitor Ligeia would be the first 'outsider' to set foot on Sophano Secundus for all that time.

Alaric reviewed this information on a data-slate as he waited on the bridge of the *Rubicon* for Ligeia's shuttle to drop out of orbit and start its descent. He tapped the slate mounted on the rail around the captain's pulpit, trying to work out why Ghargatuloth might want to make his presence felt on such a world. He had certainly inspired cults on feudal and feral worlds before his banishment – Khorion IX itself was such a backwater. But was there any real benefit for him in doing so, or was it just another feint? Alaric knew that the Prince of a Thousand Faces would not let anything lead the Grey Knights to him as directly as the statue on Victrix Sonora, but perhaps there would be a link somewhere on the planet below them, and perhaps Ligeia would be able to find it. Much would lie in how she negotiated with the current Allking Rashemha the Stout, and with the current missionary, a hardy confessor named Polonias.

The bridge was a huge space, all highly polished metal wrought into elaborate scrollwork on every surface, swirling and organic, forming a grand series of murals around the huge viewscreen on the sloping ceiling like an ornate frame around a picture. Command pulpits stood around the walls, each with a grim, silent Ordo Hereticus crew member manning the controls. The Hereticus raised its own fleets and provided most of the crews for the Grey Knights – each had a complex psycho-trigger, built into their minds by sleep-doctrination, that would wipe out their higher brain functions if the order was given from a Grey

Knight. That way, if the taint of Chaos ever touched the crew they could all be reduced to drooling idiots before they took control of the *Rubicon*. The crew knew it, too, and they were generally a grim and humourless lot. They never associated with the Grey Knights, and were replaced regularly. The *Rubicon* itself, a heavily modified Space Marine strike cruiser, was a fine enough ship to fight above its weight even with such a fatalistic crew.

The viewscreen was showing an image of Sophano Secundus, half-lit by its sun. Most of it was grey-brown slabs of land rearing up from dark blue oceans, but towards the equator one continent bloomed with life, a burst of green against the drabness. Somewhere in the middle of it was Hadjisheim, named after a legendary Allking, the capital of Sophano Secundus. It contained the Allking's palace and the temple built around Crucien's original mission, and it was where Inquisitor Ligeia was headed.

Alaric wished he could be down there. Though he had not heard anything so vulgar as a complaint from his battle-brothers, he knew that they would rather know where the enemy was and have the chance to fight it than wait in orbit while Ligeia navigated through unfamiliar politics a Grey Knight had no time for. Tancred, in particular, was bristling – the old warhorse was most at home in the thick of the fight, and he must have felt like every moment out of it was a moment of unforgivable dereliction of duty. Alaric had felt that same impatience himself, many times, when the forces of Chaos had run rings around Imperial intelligence and forced the Grey Knights to wait for the next atrocity to happen. As a justicar and as the leading military officer on this mission, though, he knew how such distractions could take the edge off a fighter's instincts. The Grey Knights were some of the most dangerous troops in the Imperium, but that did not mean they could afford to lose their edge. He hoped he could keep his Marines sharp enough to face Ghargatuloth, because he still had to keep faith that Ligeia would lead them to it.

'Seventh stage,' came the flat, monotonous voice of the crewman at the shuttle control pulpit. 'Atmospheric controls on-line.'

'Descending,' said the shuttle pilot in reply, voice crackling over the vox. Ligeia's shuttle pierced the atmospheric envelope around Sophano Secundus.

'Wish me luck, justicar,' said Ligeia cheerfully over the bridge's vox-casters.

'You don't need it, inquisitor,' replied Alaric. 'Just find out what they're hiding down there.'

An inset image showed the faint orange streak as the shuttle entered the atmosphere, and then it was gone. It was time, thought Alaric, for Ligeia to do with words what the Grey Knights could not do with strength.

THE FIRST TASTE Inquisitor Ligeia had of Sophano Secundus was from the warm, slightly damp air that filled the passenger cabin of the shuttle as the rear ramp slid down. It was faintly spicy, faintly dusty, with a slight taste of the forests that rolled out across the continent. The light that streamed in was bright and yellowish, a stark contrast to the cool harsh lumostrips of the *Rubicon* and the feeble illumination in the archives of Trepytos.

She hoped the change would do her good. She had been suffering headaches and painful joints, and she had been woken by sudden sharp nightmares where invisible hands clawed at her while she slept. She had rarely used her powers as intensively as she had done scouring the Trepytos archives for information on primitive sculpture and the trade in artwork through the Trail, and it had taken its toll. She was reminded that she was not a young woman any more.

'Taici,' she said to the leader of her death cultists, who surrounded her in a silent, sinister honour guard. 'Follow.' The death cultists slunk out of their grav-couch restraints to surround her. Xiang, a deceptively slightly-built young woman whose death cult mask showed only a pair of exotically-shaped eyes, carried a plain black case containing Ligeia's effects.

Ligeia left the Hereticus crew on the shuttle and walked elegantly down the ramp to see what she had to work with.

The buildings of Hadjisheim were of pale stone and plaster, with marble tiled roofs that shone in the strong light. The roads were paved light grey. Brightly coloured curtains, banners and signs hung everywhere in contrast to the pale tones of the buildings, announcing shopfronts and street names in a language that used elaborate loops and whorls as an alphabet. Ligeia's shuttle, on advice from Polonias's Mission, had landed in a broad round space at the head of Hadjisheim's longest road, the broad avenue leading up to the Allking's palace.

It was along this road that the reception had been set. Ligeia had let Polonias know of her visit in time for the Allking to receive her as befitted a visiting dignitary, and he had not disappointed her. The road was lined with ranks of soldiers, men in polished armour over bright crimson uniforms, all carrying spears and shields with the twin crescent design of Allking Rashemha. Behind them, thousands of chattering men, women and children had gathered to watch – word had evidently spread, probably against Polonias's wishes, that a stranger from the sky was coming to visit, and they all wanted to see her. Ligeia saw the people of Sophano Secundus had an odd blend of dark skin and pale hair, giving them a faintly unearthly look when coupled with the bright colours they seemed to wear habitually.

The soldier-lined avenue ran up toward the Allking's palace, a creation of massive white stone that reared up to overlook Hadjisheim from a rise in the centre of the city, festooned with banners and pennants in dozens of colours.

The honour guard were riding from the direction of the palace. A hundred of the Allking's own cavalry, ribbons fluttering from their lances and the powerful sunlight gleaming off their highly polished armour, trotted towards Ligeia. As they came closer, Ligeia saw that most of them were riding tharr rather than horses – tharr were odd hunched creatures with dark, scabbed scaly skin and powerful hind legs that, according to the sketchy histories of Sophano Secundus, could be ridden into fearsome cavalry charges. A few of the officers in the front, their ranks denoted by golden trims to their armour, rode more familiar Terran-style horses, a symbol of prestige since so few breeding animals were ever brought to the planet.

A single rider galloped out of the cavalry ranks. Ligeia sensed her death cultists tensing slightly, their hands ready to fly to the hilts of their swords or throwing knives, but with a motion of her finger Ligeia had them stand down. The rider carried a long curved horn instead of a lance and pulled up suddenly a short distance away, blowing a long rasping blast from his horn. The riders behind him halted at the sound.

'In the nineteenth year of the reign of Allking Rashemha,' he called out in strongly-accented Low Gothic. 'His overhighness made it be known that his home is home to the representative of the realms above, that his soldiers are hers to protect her and that his people are her people to exalt her. In the name of the Emperor and of the kings long dead! So has the Allking decreed!'

There was another blast of the horn and the herald rode back into the ranks of the Allking's cavalry, which trotted forward to surround Ligeia and escort her to the palace. A squire rode forward on a tharr to offer her a Terran horse and, with a nod of appreciation, she mounted it sidesaddle. She had ridden once or twice in her youth but she thought it wisest to let the squire take the reins as the cavalry clattered their way back towards the palace.

The death cultists walked alongside, barely breaking into a jog to keep up with the brisk pace of the escort. Ligeia glanced at the people behind the soldiers lining the road, and the death cultists drew rather more attention than she did. Sophano Secundus had probably never seen anything like them – half a dozen perfectly muscled men and women in skin-tight black bodygloves, three or four weapons apiece, moving with such elegance and grace it was hard to believe they were human. Their sinister, near-featureless masks enhanced the impression that there were not normal faces underneath.

Allking Rashemha met Ligeia at the gates to his palace grounds, a broad belt of lavish lawns, flower beds and stands of exotic trees that surrounded the imposing white walls. Rashemha was a huge man with nut-coloured skin and shockingly pale blond hair and beard, wearing layers of bright flowing silks. Behind him stood a small army of courtiers and advisors, all competing in the brightness and elaboration of their dress but all dwarfed by the presence of their Allking. A small delegation of plainly-dressed young men and women, representing Polonias's mission, stood to one side.

Ligeia rode up to the Alking and dismounted. The Allking strode forward with a practiced beaming smile of welcome and grabbed Ligeia's hand in his two massive paws.

'Our people are your people,' he rumbled impressively. 'Greetings.'

Ligeia smiled back. The Allking smelled strongly of spices. 'Greetings from the Imperium, your overhighness. I am glad you have received me so readily, I have urgent business with Missionary Polonias.'

'Of course. Come inside, Outworlder Ligeia. I would not have the kingdoms of the sky believe the Allking's hospitality is lacking.'

The delegation headed across the grounds towards the palace. Ligeia saw that the representatives from the mission had a sickly greyish cast to their skin, and she imagined that endless hours of prayer inside the mission temple meant they rarely saw the sun. They wore simple habits of undyed cloth, evidently to show their humility before the Emperor – they would probably be most alarmed to see the extravagance of the Ecclesiarchy in the Imperium proper.

'Our lands are fertile and broad,' the Allking was rumbling, to be echoed by the agreements of his courtiers. 'Our people adore their king and the spirits of the kings long dead. They do well in the worship of your Emperor.'

Ligeia wasn't really listening. She knew that the centre of Hadjisheim was impressive but that the rest of the city, and the rest of the Allking's domain, was poor and backwards, and the underkings and barons had little ability to properly monitor the population. The Allking's blustering was less interesting than the palace itself – inside, shaded from the unforgiving sun, the cavernous spaces were cool and the inlaid marble floors formed complicated murals of the deeds of past Allkings. The double eagle of the Imperium crowned every pillar and devotional High Gothic texts were inscribed alongside prayers to the long-dead kings of Sophano Secundus. Gaggles of courtiers gathered around the columns, watching the Allking and his dignitaries as they passed, occasionally applauding as he expounded the glories of his world.

Ligeia saw how fragile Sophano Secundus was in those few minutes. The Allking held his underkings and barons together by the force of his personality. His household troops numbered a few hundred tharrback cavalry, never enough to properly rule even Sophano Secundus's single continent. A rebel underking could forge havoc, and Ligeia knew this had happened in the past. The Allking's rule was personal, not by strength but by unspoken agreement. It was weak. It was the way mankind had once ruled itself before the Age of Strife had shown how dangerous it was to rule by anything other than strength and vigilance.

Polonias was waiting in a side chapel, which had been decorated with dark marble and a plethora of incense burners more typical of Imperial architecture. Ligeia made her excuses to the Allking, promised to join him in an extravagant feast that evening, and took her death cultists into the chapel. The courtiers followed their Allking into the heart of the palace, towards the audience chamber where Rashemha the Stout would continue the long task of holding his planet together.

Polonias was an old, old man, stooped and gnarled. His long robes hid a body that moved achingly slowly through the incense-drenched interior of the chapel like a ghost. His head was covered by the heavy cowl of his habit and a golden double eagle hung from around his neck, giving the impression that he was bending under its weight.

Ligeia waved her death cultists back to a respectable distance. Polonias was surrounded by piles of papers and books, spread across the stone floor or lying on the front pews.

'Missionary,' said Ligeia. 'I bear the authority of the Emperor's Inquisition, and I require your co-operation.'

Polonias smiled, and the visible lower half of his face creased up unpleasantly. 'Inquisitor Ligeia. I trust the Allking gave you an appropriate welcome.'

'He made sure I was thoroughly impressed. I was more concerned with what you might tell me.' Ligeia walked to the front of the chapel and sat down on the front pew, surrounded by Polonias's books.

'As you can see,' said Polonias, waving a liver-spotted hand to indicate the spilled parchment and piled books, 'I have been preparing for your visit. There is only one reason why the Ordo Malleus would visit my world. You think I have not been thorough enough in preparing the minds of the people for the inevitable designs of the Enemy.'

'I am not here to accuse,' replied Ligeia calmly, picking up the closest book and turning it over in her hands. 'I am here to investigate. Someone or something on Sophano Secundus is connected to the imminent rebirth of a very powerful daemon.'

Polonias looked up at her and for the first time Ligeia saw his eyes – large and pale like the eyes of a sea creature. 'Daemons? The Throne preserve us.'

'The inquisitors responsible for the Trail have very little information on Sophano Secundus, and that makes you my best source.' Ligeia spoke almost conversationally, inspecting the cover of the book as she did so. It was heavy and old, sealed with an elaborate brass lock mechanism. 'I am looking for any signs of cult activity on your world.'

Polonias shook his head. 'The people here are devout in their worship. There are few rivals to the Imperial cult, just a few ancestor-worshipping sects. I have felt no trace of the Enemy amongst them and I would have let the cardinals know if I had. Of course, there are tribes scattered through the forests that the Allking can do little about, but they are bandits, not fanatics.'

Ligeia snapped her fingers and Xiang strode forward lithely, holding Ligeia's case. The death cultist snapped the clasps and the case opened. Ligeia took out the ugly wood sculpture from Victrix Sonora. 'What can you tell me about this?'

Polonias shuffled forward and bent over to peer at the sculpture. Ligeia noted that he smelled strongly of incense and chemicals, as if he was pumped full of preservatives to keep his ancient body from deteriorating. 'A hideous thing. Degenerates of the nobility used to collect such things, I believe, back when Saint Evisser's worship was at its height. Traders would come to buy them off the forest peoples. There has been no such trade for many years. This planet's art is a curiosity now, nothing more.'

'When were the last ones taken off-planet?'

Polonias shrugged. 'Fifty years. Seventy. The Allking will have some historical advisor who could tell you. I think such heathen images are hideous, myself. I preach against such things.' Polonias straightened and Ligeia placed the statue back in the case – gratefully, because she could feel it squirming in her hands. 'My world has many problems,' continued Polonias, 'but the grasp of the Enemy is not one of them. The people are poor and benighted and the land provides little, but there is no corruption here. I have preached from Hadjisheim to the Callianan Flow on the northern coast and all the wickedness I have seen is wrought by human hands.'

'I am glad to hear it,' said Ligeia. 'But that makes my work here rather less promising.'

'I am sorry I could not help you more. The Emperor's Inquisition will have to look elsewhere for its ghosts and its heretics.' Ligeia thought Polonias was smiling as he spoke, but she could not be sure.

'Well, then, it seems I have little more to do here.' Ligeia stood, straightening her long skirts. 'I will go through the motions, see what I can get from the Allking and his advisors, but I doubt they know anything meaningful that you do not. You are well-read,' she added, holding up the book she had found. 'I haven't seen a volume of Myrmandos's *Lamentations* for a long time.'

'My predecessor left it for me,' said Polonias. 'I have always felt Myrmandos lacking, but his parables are simple enough to use in my sermons.'

'The cardinals on the Trail have made it a standard text for seminary study,' said Ligeia. 'They would be disappointed to hear your lack of appreciation.'

'Well, the cardinals are entitled to disagree with a crude old missionary,' said Polonias.

'The *Lamentations*,' said Ligeia simply, 'have been lost for twelve hundred years. No member of the Ecclesiarchy would have a copy unless they had been alive since then, not even the cardinals.'

The death cultists strode forward from the back of the chapel, swords and throwing blades in their hands. Ligeia's hand was held flat on the cover of the *Lamentations*, absorbing the flow of information confirming the book was the same volume believed lost by all the authorities she knew, including Trepytos.

'I do not believe you are Polonias,' continued Ligeia. 'By the authority of the Holy Orders of the Emperor's Inquisition I demand you submit yourself to moral examination. You will accept all grades of interrogation and your every word will be true at the expense of your life and your soul.' Her voice was suddenly cold, and the muscles of her death cultists were so taut she could almost hear them humming.

'Stupid girl,' spat the missionary. 'Stupid, stubborn, weak little girl!' Something flared under his cowl and his eyes were suddenly burning with violet fire, illuminating a face so hollow and aged that no human could have naturally lived all the years that weighed down on it.

The air turned thick as Missionary Crucien, his identity revealed for the first time in millennia, was suddenly ablaze with sorcerous fire.

A HANDFUL OF seconds later, the *Rubicon* lost all contact with the surface of Sophano Secundus.

SEVEN
SOPHANO SECUNDUS

'Nothing,' said the crewman at the comms helm. 'We've lost it all. Life signs, the shuttle beacon, everything.'

Alaric jumped down from the command pulpit. 'How?'

'I'm not...'

'On screen!'

The image of Sophano Secundus on the viewscreen disappeared to be replaced with shifting static. The crewmen in the sensor pit in the floor of the bridge, surrounded by monitors and chattering cogitator banks, scrambled to find some meaningful signal from the surface. There was a flash as something shorted and sparked.

'Tancred, Genhain, get your squads onto your Thunderhawk and launch, await landing coordinates. Santoro, wait for me. I'll be there as soon as I know more.'

'Trouble, justicar?' came Tancred's gruff voice.

'Nothing but,' replied Alaric, as something appeared on the viewscreen.

The image was of the hinterland of Hadjisheim, dominated by a steep valley surrounded by rolling forests. Where Hadjisheim itself should have been was a purple-black circle of interference, boiling evilly.

'Are they jamming us?'

'If they are it's nothing we've seen before,' shouted someone from the sensor pit.

Alaric paused, looking at the horrible stormy blot on the surface of Sophano Secundus. 'I think they've seen plenty of it,' replied Alaric. 'That's sorcery.'

Even from orbit he could feel it, fingers of magic spattering against his armoured soul like cold rain.

There was no time for the wargear rites or for the ritual purification of the soul that a Grey Knight should undergo before battle. Ligeia was down there, and if she was not dead already then she very soon would be. The Grey Knights were her only chance.

'Navigation, take the pulpit!' called Alaric as he ran towards the doors leading out of the bridge. 'Get us into a launch position. Flight control, get me a landing course before I get to the flight decks!'

Alaric mumbled quickly through the Seven Prayers of Detestation as he ran through the decks towards the *Rubicon*'s flight hangar, the ship's engines rumbling angrily somewhere below him. Ordo Malleus crewmen and servitors hurried through the corridors around him and the ship lurched suddenly as it made a sharp turn to bring its flight doors around to face the planet's surface.

'…and fill my soul with righteous hate to steel my arm the stronger…'

'The astropaths are reporting something in the warp,' came a voice from the bridge, cutting through the vox-traffic. 'They say it's screaming.'

Alaric wrenched open the bulkhead leading to the flight deck. Two of the *Rubicon*'s three Thunderhawks were fuelled up and ready for flight, the deck servitors even now unhooking the promethium lines from the hulls. Tancred and Genhain's gunship was ready for takeoff, while Alaric and Santoro's still had its ramp down. The rest of Alaric's squad were already waiting for him.

'…and guide my aim, bless my gun, make my hate your hate and through me let it scorch the flesh of the Great Enemy…'

'We've got a signal!' came a vox from the comms helm.

'Ligeia?'

'Taici.'

'Good enough. What does he say?'

'It's just a string of coordinates. But it's definitely him.'

'Where?'

'The valley outside the city, just beyond the zone of interference.'

'Then that's our landing spot.' Alaric ran up the ramp into the passenger compartment of the Thunderhawk, the familiar faces of his squad nodding in silent salute at him before they put on their helmets and fixed their grav-restraints. 'Nav helm?'

'Landing solutions already loaded.'

The exit ramp slid up into place behind Alaric. 'Then open the hangar doors and launch.'

The pitch of the Thunderhawk engines kicked in and rose as the pre-launch countdown flicked the gunship's systems on. The air in the hangar boomed out as the doors ground open and there was a lurch as the ship bolted forwards on its primary thrust engines, jamming the occupants back into their grav-couches. Alaric glanced out of the gunship's porthole as it roared out of the *Rubicon* – the strike cruiser's hull ripped past and the glowing crescent of Sophano Secundus slid into view, barren and grim, the sole streak of fertile green now blackening purple.

Alaric could taste the sorcery, dark and mocking. But sorcery was what the Grey Knights had been trained to fight.

THE FORESTS STREAKED by beneath a darkening sky slashed with purple lightning, the valleys deep in shadows like rivers of ink, the distant barren mountains like broken teeth around the horizon. The Thunderhawk engines screamed as the deceleration thrusters resisted the pull of gravity on the falling gunship.

The valley yawned blackly below the Thunderhawk as it dipped into its approach. The Thunderhawk's sensors were barely functioning thanks to the interference flowing from Hadjisheim and the Malleus pilots in the cockpit were flying mostly by eye. The dark grassy sides of the valley swept upwards and the Thunderhawk slewed into a wide crescent, landing gear grinding down from the hull. With a jolt the runners hit the ground and the main engines cut out.

The valley was deep and shadowy. The forest that rolled up to the crests on either side was deep and very dark, the greenery like a solid mass. The valley was covered in coarse grasses and shrubs. In the distance, some way along the valley, the sorcery could be seen like a solid blackish dome. The sky above was almost the same colour as the sorcery – black streaked with purple, the stars like silver dust. The runners of the Thunderhawks carved deep furrows in the thick earth as they came to a halt.

'Deploy!' called Alaric and, as the ramp descended, Squad Alaric and Squad Santoro were out of the gunship in seconds, storm bolters raised. Alaric hit the ground and at once felt the echoes the astropaths had reported – a seething in the warp, an agitation just beyond the veil of reality.

Alaric's auto-senses cut through the gloom. The vegetation of Sophano Secundus was dark and wretched, clinging feebly to the banks

of the valley until it became a thick tangled row of trees at the crest.
'Tancred?' voxed Alaric on the all-squad channel.

'Coming down now. Do you have him?'

'Negative. We're searching.'

Tancred's Thunderhawk curved around, its landing thrusters leaving
glowing blue streaks in the air, to settle behind Alaric's. The ramp was
down and Tancred's squad was out before the thrusters cut out, massive Terminator-armoured bodies dropping to thump onto the damp
grass.

'Got something,' came a sudden vox from Brother Marl, one of Santoro's Marines. 'I think it's him.'

Santoro waved his squad forward in the direction Marl was indicating.
'Squad, get their back,' said Alaric, and his own Space Marines turned to
keep an eye on the perimeter.

'Confirmed,' voxed Santoro. 'It's one of hers.'

'Taici?'

'It's hard to tell.'

'Squad, hold,' voxed Alaric to his squad and hurried over to where
Santoro was standing over a dark shape sprawled on the ground.

It was one of Ligeia's death cultists, that was certain, wearing a glossy
black bodysuit now torn and shredded. The hood had been torn off and
Alaric realised it was the first time he had seen the face of one of Ligeia's
cultists.

He recognised the sword still held in the man's hand as belonging to
Taici – if the death cultists had a leader other than Ligeia, it was Taici.
And if there was anyone she would send to summon the Grey Knights
to a safe landing site, it was him.

Alaric knelt down beside Taici. He was still breathing, but he had
taken a severe beating. His skin was torn and tattered. One leg was
clearly broken and his chest was lopsided so much that Alaric was surprised he could manage even the shallow breaths he was taking. A sleek,
handsome face was now bloody and broken, glossy black hair, bloodied golden skin, the jaw now broken and shattered. Slivers of teeth were
mixed in with the blood running down his chin.

'He's alive,' said Alaric. 'Can you speak?'

Taici's eyes opened. But they were not eyes.

Like fat, pink worms, two tendrils poked from Taici's eye sockets,
writhing obscenely like pointing fingers, tiny ravenous maws opening in
the tips. Taici's face disintegrated and a nest of worms gnawed out
through the bones, chewing the death cultist's head into a foul mess of
bubbling gore.

'Mykros!' called Santoro, and his squad's flamer bearer stepped up. Alaric stood back and Mykros immolated the writhing mess with a heavy gout of blessed flame. Harsh, spicy incense mixed with the stink of charred flesh and soon the corpse was gone.

'That was–' began Santoro.

'Tancred, Genhain,' voxed Alaric, and he saw that both squads were now on the ground. 'Taici was being controlled. They've got her. Give me a...'

Tancred saw them first and Alaric knew something was wrong by the way his squad's aim suddenly snapped upwards, to the ridge along the top of the valley slope. Alaric followed their gaze and saw the ridge bristling, as if the forest itself were marching down towards them. There were suddenly spearpoints and banners, the bright colours of the Allking's barons muted in the gathering gloom, the jangling of armour and the grunt of the tharr filtering down over the sound of the cold wind through the trees.

Alaric looked around. There were men on both sides of the valleys, probably thousands of them. Waiting for the Grey Knights. The creature in Taici's head had controlled him, tricking him into leading the Grey Knights into the trap.

'Soldiers from the sky,' called down a herald's voice from the Allking's men. 'Our Emperor abhors the heretics who hunt His people. The spirits of the kings long dead spit on infidel invaders who befoul the Allking's lands. The Emperor, the Lord of Change, and the Prince of a Thousand Faces rot your hearts. Your deaths are our lives.'

'Close up,' voxed Alaric, and the Grey Knights gathered in a tight circle between the Thunderhawks. Then to his own squad, 'They'll charge. Vien, Clostus, in the front with me. Lykkos, in the centre with Squad Glaivan. Let them come to us. Cleanse your souls and have faith.'

A hunting horn brayed above and the army's leaders yelled a final order in the language of their dead kings. As one, in a spiky black mass, the tharr cavalry charged forward and the valley thundered. Alaric saw the massively muscled legs of the tharr powering them forward, the flashing armour of the knights on top and the streaming coloured pennants of a dozen feudal barons.

Justicar Genhain, in the centre of the Grey Knights, bellowed an order and storm bolter fire streaked out. Every Grey Knight's gun spat bright white streaks into the charging mass of soldiers, kicking up bursts of blood. Bodies wheeled as tharr hit the ground and threw their riders. Men were blasted backwards in flailing broken bursts of blood. But more came, trampling the bodies of their dead and, as the killing zone around the Grey Knights was piled deeper with the dead, the rear ranks of the cavalry galloped over the heaps of corpses and bore down on Alaric's Marines. The too-familiar stink of death flooded forward as the charge slammed home.

The first of them hit. Alaric saw gritted teeth beneath the noseguard, banded armour over bright flowing cloth, dark skin and white hair. Alaric turned the lance aimed at his head with the blade of his Nemesis halberd and punched his other hand into the grisly maw of the tharr beneath the rider. His fist smashed through ranks of teeth and Alaric squeezed the firing stud, sending a volley of bolt shells from the wrist-mounted storm bolter ripping through the beast.

Alaric impaled the rider on his halberd and, without throwing the body off his blade, hacked clean through the rider behind him. Beside Alaric, Brother Vien had sheared the head off a tharr and clambered over its fallen body, swinging his halberd like a mace and knocking men aside. Haulvarn reached over Alaric's shoulder and plunged his sword through yet another rider while Dvorn waded in, his hammer sweeping the squad's flank clear to leave a wide semicircle of shattered bodies.

Alaric felt, more than heard, the charge hit Tancred's squad, and saw a tharr sailing through the air no doubt flung by one of Tancred's Terminators. He heard Santoro's voice yelling a prayer of steadfastness as the ringing of steel showed Santoro's Marines were already duelling with the swordsmen on foot.

Under the guns and blades of the Grey Knights the charge had been reduced to bloody tatters but the mass of the Allking's army was on foot, swordsmen and spearmen swarming forward. This was how the Grey Knights could be lost – swamped and smothered, trapped between a mountain of men where, eventually, their power armour would fail them, their bolters would run out of shells, their sword arms would be pinned and they would die.

Alaric spotted the Thunderhawks swarming with men who were clambering over them, trying to lever the hatches open and smash the windows. He caught sight of movement inside one cockpit where the Malleus pilots were evidently fighting soldiers who had got inside. They would fight to the death, but die they would. The Thunderhawks wouldn't survive, either.

The mass of men pressed home. Swords stabbed out at Alaric, clanging off his armour, a wall of steel in front of a sea of hate-filled faces. One of them ducked Dvorn's hammer and leapt on the Marine, knocking him back a step to be followed by a dozen more who dragged Dvorn to the ground. Clostus cut one swordsman from throat to groin and threw off another, but they were pouring in through the breach, fearless, fanatical.

'Tancred! Break us out, there are too many!' voxed Alaric. He spotted Santoro clambering over the sea of soldiers, striking left and right with his Nemesis mace. Storm bolter fire was still streaking from Genhain's squad, and Lykkos's psycannon threw shining blasts into the rear ranks, but there were too many to thin out.

Tancred, Alaric knew, was probably their only way out.

'Brothers!' Tancred was yelling. 'For vengeance! For purity! In hatred be strong, in valour be sure!'

'In vengeance be foremost!' echoed his men, and Alaric could feel the buzzing in that part of his mind that possessed enough psychic talent to accept the training of a Grey Knight.

'In suffering! In glory!' lead Tancred, slicing two men in half with a sweep of his Nemesis sword as the crescendo rose, a deafening choir, and white blades of light flickered around Squad Tancred.

Finally, like a bomb detonating, like a meteor hitting, a titanic burst of light ripped through the surging throng in front of Tancred, sending a shockwave tearing through the Allking's ranks. In the flash Alaric saw men blasted clean of their flesh, tharr disintegrating, a wide space scoured of the enemy who were sent flying through the air and thrown backwards onto the men behind them.

The inquisitors of the Ordo Malleus had nicknamed it the holocaust, but it was something far more complicated than that. Only those of the Grey Knights with the strongest psychic signature could do it, and even then not alone – it took a full squad, led by a psyker, to channel the hatred placed in them by years of training and prayer into a devastating physical form.

The holocaust had blasted a space clear in front of Tancred, the earth scoured white. With a roar Tancred charged into the broken ranks and Squad Genhain followed, spraying gunfire into the mass. Tancred's Terminators excelled on the offensive and they carved through the Secundan swordsmen, Nemesis weapons flashing, gunfire blazing.

Alaric and Santoro followed, hacking all around them to keep back the press, following the trail of carnage that Tancred bored into the army. The ranks were fleeing now, dropping their weapons and running back up the side of the valley as Tancred chased them. The battle had turned into a rout and more and more swordsmen followed. Officers, noblemen on tharrback or even on horses, yelled at their men to keep fighting, but the banners of the barons were down now.

That was how to break an army. Show them what the Grey Knights could do, make sure every man saw it, and convince them that if they stayed then they would be next.

Alaric checked the runes projected by his auto-senses back onto his retina. Dvorn's rune was flickering, he must be wounded. 'Any men lost?' voxed Alaric.

'Caanos is dead,' said Santoro simply. 'Mykros is carrying him.'

Alaric felt a flare of anger. Sophano Secundus had betrayed the Grey Knights and now it had taken the life of a Marine. Alaric remembered a Marine in Santoro's own mould, quiet, devout, devoted. Now Caanos would never pray for anything again.

It was the worst of omens to leave a Grey Knight's body on the battlefield. The gene-seed that regulated Caanos's metabolism and his vat-grown organs would be removed and taken back to Titan, so they could be implanted in a novice just beginning the path of the Grey Knight. But that would only happen if any of them got off Sophano Secundus.

'Take cover in the treeline and keep moving,' voxed Alaric. 'They'll have men following us.' He switched to squad frequency. 'Dvorn?'

'Broken arm,' said Dvorn. It was all the answer Alaric needed – a Marine's metabolism would quickly heal a broken bone, but Dvorn would be fighting below his best until then.

The Allking's army was disintegrating below the Grey Knights. Nobles tried to organise the swarming mob to pursue the Grey Knights but it was bedlam down there, all order lost. Tancred was already in the forest, his Space Marines snapping storm bolter shots off at the few men trying to follow them.

Alaric glanced down and saw orange flames burning in the engines of the two Thunderhawk gunships where the Allking's men – either with great prescience or, more likely, under orders – had cut the fuel lines and set the promethium alight. If the Grey Knights were going to escape Sophano Secundus, it would not be by gunship.

IN THE MIDDLE of the night, in the heart of the forest, they buried Caanos. Stripped of his armour, the gene-seed organ in his throat cut out by Justicar Santoro, Brother Caanos was lowered into the makeshift grave.

Santoro made a short speech about duty and sacrifice and an honourable death before the gaze of the Emperor, the sort of thing Caanos might have said himself.

Alaric understood, as he heard again the same words he had listened to in every sermon and hero's funeral he had ever heard, why Ligeia had wanted him to lead. He could think outside the constraints that bound most Grey Knights, but at the same time, he was strong enough to always remember the truly important things – strength against the corruption of the Enemy, devotion to a fight that could not be won, faith in the strength the Emperor had given him.

Santoro could not lead, not really. Not when he understood his place in the universe as rigid and unchangeable. Neither could Genhain or Tancred, good men though they were. They were the soldiers that could hold back the darkness, but to lead them, they needed men like Alaric. He would be able to change the rules they lived by when the Enemy's designs meant they had to adapt. That was why Durendin had shown such faith in him, and why Ligeia had seen something in him that even grand masters did not possess.

Alaric was not sure if he was grateful. It would be so much easier just to fight and to obey. Leadership over men like the Grey Knights needed so much more than he could offer now, he had so much to learn and so many trials to endure before he could prove he was worthy.

Santoro had finished. Caanos's battle-brothers were heaping earth into the shallow grave. Alaric noted down the grave's coordinates on his data-slate to make sure that, if possible, Malleus interrogators could return and recover Caanos's body for burial in the vaults of Titan. They would recover Caanos's armour and weapons, too, which had been buried at his feet once Santoro's squad had shared out his ammunition. Alaric realised that, if they were trapped on the planet without support, they might find themselves running low.

Before they moved off Alaric sent a secure communication to the *Rubicon* telling the Malleus crew that the Thunderhawks were lost, but that shuttles could not come down to the planet. He ordered the crew not to accept any communication from anyone but him, even Ligeia herself, and told them he would contact them if those orders changed.

He received a terse acknowledgement code in reply.

Justicar Genhain walked over from Caanos's grave. 'Justicar?' he said, his bionic eye glinting in the faint moonlight. 'Where next?'

'Where else is there?' said Alaric, putting away his data-slate and unholstering his Nemesis halberd. 'Hadjisheim.'

THE ALLKING'S PALACE was a huge labyrinth, extending underground where the huge vaulted chambers became long, low galleries, plunging white stone staircases, complexes of rooms and narrow hallways, all covered in holy texts chiselled into the stone. The deeper the palace went, the more the Imperial prayers were replaced by profane texts glorifying the Secundan people's service to the Lord of Change and to a many-faced servant god that could only be Ghargatuloth. The air was close and smelled of burned flesh, the lanterns guttered and whole floors were plunged into darkness at random. The sound of angry men filtered down from every direction at once, and the whole place was like the stone warren of a hunted animal.

That animal was Inquisitor Ligeia. Five of her death cultists still lived – Taici had given his life so the rest could escape down the staircase from the grand ground floor – but there were scores of men closing in on her. She could hear prayers and curses, soldier's songs, orders yelled, the clank of armoured feet on stone, the hiss of swords unsheathed.

'Xiang, Shan, go ahead. We have to go deeper,' said Ligeia as she hurried along a long, low corridor lined with statues. Each statue's face had been eaten away as if by acid. The two death cultists loped ahead in long, graceful strides, slipped around the corner like ghosts. The others stuck close by their mistress – Ligeia could smell the spices of the artificial hormones now coursing through their veins.

The death cultists owed Ligeia lifelong fealty, even to the death, and they were literally bred to kill. The cult was a curious offshoot of the Imperial church, developing away from the monitoring of the Ecclesiarchy. It offered the deaths of their enemies as a sacrifice to the Emperor. The cultists offered their services to anyone who did the Emperor's work, and since Ligeia had saved the cult from a parasitic daemon in their midst the cult had given six of its best to guard Ligeia permanently. Each one had a complement of artificial tendons, neuro-activated hormone injectors, muscular enhancements, and digestive alterations to allow them to live off the blood they drew from their victims.

Now, they were down to five. And Ligeia knew the Allking's forces were too many for even her death cultists to face on their own. She would be trapped down beneath the palace and killed, and there was nothing she could do except fight her best and put off the inevitable.

Torch lights danced from around the corner behind Ligeia. 'Lo! Gao!' she called, but the two cultists were already sprinting back down the gallery.

Gao jumped and planted a foot on the head of the closest statue, pushing off to somersault across the corridors. A blade flashed down and the head of the first attacker to round the corner was sheared clean off. Lo dived along the floor, twin daggers flashing upwards to gut the next attacker. The attackers were members of the Allking's own guard, the same men that had escorted Ligeia to the palace on tharrback – their heads were hidden by helms with a dozen eyeholes cut into each, and they carried swords of what looked like pale bone.

Something screamed as the men hit the ground, something just beyond the wall of reality between real space and the warp. Ligeia held out a hand and let the meaning of the inscriptions on the wall bleed into her – somewhere she had passed a barrier and headed into a place where the creatures of the 'Emperor' – the Lord of Change, the Prince of a Thousand Faces, the horrible mingling of Imperial and Chaotic religion the Secundans worshipped – could walk freely. Ligeia could feel the walls of reality wearing thin.

Ligeia reached the next corner. Shan was crouched beside it, pointing forward to indicate the way was safe. 'The Enemy holds sway here,' said Ligeia to her death cultists as Gao and Lo sprinted back towards her. 'This is their territory, I can feel it. Your strength may not be enough here. I do not think we will survive, so you should know that you have always served me well, my brothers and sisters.'

The death cultists did not answer – they never spoke. But Ligeia knew they understood her.

Gao flipped out of the way as a shower of arrows broke against the wall. Someone was yelling back there – Ligeia let the meaning of the words through into her mind and she translated hatred and the joy of the hunt.

Ligeia ran on. She heard blades clashing ahead and by the time she reached the next junction, Xiang was standing between four dismembered bodies, knives slick with blood.

'They are closing in?'

Xiang nodded. Ligeia looked down at the bodies. One corpse sported three arms, and the dislodged helmet revealed a third eye in the middle of its forehead, blood-red and staring. Mutants. The touch of Chaos was hidden even in the Allking's own guard. Emperor alone knew how far the Allking himself had fallen.

Ligeia could feel hate seeping from the walls, the ceiling, the floor. With a yell, more attackers flooded forward – Ligeia saw tentacles reaching and a horribly distended jaw bristling with teeth as a score of men attacked from three directions.

Xiang ran up the wall and along the ceiling, cutting through two men's necks before she hit the ground. Lo dived headfirst, spinning, into a mass of men, daggers rotating with her, slicing limbs from bodies. Three attackers clambered over Lo and charged towards Ligeia herself – she pointed and willed the neuro-receptor in her large amethyst ring to fire. The digital weapon, rare xenos tech that had cost more than her father's palace, spat a blue-hot lance of laser through a man's throat and killed the charge before Xiahou flipped over her and killed the other two as they stumbled.

Ligeia felt the power before it was unleashed, a deep roar just below the range of hearing, building up to a psychic crescendo as a bolt of black fire ripped down one corridor. Darkness flooded the area and pincer-strong hands grabbed Ligeia from behind, throwing her across the corridor and hard into the wall. Light washed back and Ligeia saw Gao, the cultist who had saved her, blasted to bits by the psychic explosion. Gao's blood spattered over her and so loaded with hormones and stimulants was it that it burned her eyes.

The burning chunks of Gao's body thumped into the walls and floor. Ligeia shook the gore form her eyes and through her tears she saw the sorcerer, naked to the waist, his legs wrapped in a kilt made of dozens of pieces of brightly coloured cloth, the symbols of the Change God cut deep into his scrawny torso. The blood that ran from the wounds was deep blue. His face was completely featureless, a smooth globe of pale skin, but his shoulders and upper chest were covered in eyes. Black fire rippled around his hands and he launched another blast at where Xiang was holding off six swordsmen. Xiang jumped out of the way but was thrown hard against the ceiling by the force of the blast.

With each explosion the voices from the warp gibbered louder. Ligeia knew they were close to the source of the corruption that saturated Sophano Secundus.

Xiang and Shan grabbed Ligeia and dragged her through the smoke-choked corridor, away from the sorcerer and the soldiers charging past him.

Ligeia tried to read the very stones around her, divine the intricate pattern of the palace's sub-levels. She could taste the tangled knot of corridors and anterooms around her, and feel them radiating from a dark central heart.

'This way,' she gasped, indicating where the corridor turned sharply. Lo and Xaihou ran ahead while Xiang and Shan carried her as they ran, darkness swarming around her and black flames flickering.

There was a large wooden door stained dark red up ahead. Xaihou kicked it open and it splintered, red light and unearthly screams flooding out.

Ligeia was bundled inside. The room was blood-warm, the stone floor buzzing. It had many sides, but Ligeia couldn't count them; every time she looked the angles altered and the room changed size, the dimensions squirming before her eyes.

The wall hangings were covered with writing in the flowing Secundan language, the letters wriggling like worms. Piles of books and scrolls choked the edges of the room and in the centre was a shallow pit blackened by fire and redolent with burnt spices and flesh. The symbols of Chaos were everywhere, the eight-pointed star and the arcane stylised comet of the Lord of Change, fleeing from Ligeia's vision as if they were afraid to be read. The walls pulsed with power, and a blood-red glow oozed from them.

There were three doors. The shattered door behind her was already breached, Xaihou's sword flashing out to sever the sword-arms reaching through. The other two burst open and through one stormed a swarm of the Allking's soldiers. There was no doubt about their allegiance now – every one sported grotesque mutations, claws and insectoid limbs, multi-faceted eyes rolling in their chests, mouths screaming from their stomachs. Some had dropped their swords to fight with spines and pincers.

Through the other door came the sorcerer. He was powerful, Ligeia could taste it. He burned his way through the door with the black fire that covered the upper half of his body. Ligeia could see his skeleton through his burning skin, glowing with power, his dozens of eyes like bright pearls jutting from his body.

'Don't touch him!' yelled Ligeia over the noise in her head. She knew that the very presence of the sorcerer was toxic – without their minds shielded, the death cultists could be killed just by touching the sorcerer. Ligeia could not move as quickly or kill as cleanly as they could, but as a Malleus-trained psyker her mind was stronger than their bodies.

Shan was sprinting around the walls, hurling knives as fast as bullets, the blades thunking into throats and stomachs. Xiang was surrounded and holding a dozen men at bay on her own, twin daggers ripping mutants open and spilling ropy entrails onto the ground. Xiahou and Lo were by Ligeia, lashing out with their swords against anyone who approached, but there were just too many of them to kill and they were getting closer.

The sorcerer stepped into the air. The room – the temple, for that was what it must be – elongated around him and suddenly he had space to rise into the air, black lightning fountaining off him. Ligeia could hear the crescendo rising again. For her and her death cultists the room was shrinking, too small to contain the psychic blast that was coming – it would incinerate everyone in the temple.

She was dead. She could not match that power in combat. Her power was to do with meaning, not destruction. But the meaning in the temple, the corruption, the hate…

Ligeia opened up her mind and it flooded in, words of hatred that covered the pages of the books, prayers of corruption from the hangings on the wall, suffering and death from the very stones beneath her feet. She rose into the air with the power of it all, she could feel it filling her. She had never felt that magnitude of hatred before, not with the Hereticus or the Malleus. It was like a living thing inside her, welling up and taking form, hot and angry, too huge for her to contain.

The Prince of a Thousand faces would rise. The Lord of Change would follow in the path Ghargatuloth carved through the stars. Chaos was the natural state of all things, and the feeble resistance of the blind would fall before the rising tide. Tzeentch would rule, and there would be no law but Chaos.

Ligeia crushed all those thoughts and images into a tiny hard ball of hate in the pit of her stomach, every word, every syllable. With a scream she tore them out of her mind and spat them out into the outside world.

A white-hot stream of pure hatred tore out of her open mouth and punched right through the chest of the sorcerer. Its power filled him up and he burst in a shower of white flame, black lightning, charred bones and shattered jewel-hard eyes. The flame coursed around the temple like a whirlpool; her death cultists somersaulted into the air over the tide of hatred as it smothered the Allking's men and stripped their deformed bodies to the bone.

The books and hangings were untouched. This was hatred so pure it could only touch living things. Then the last of it was gone and Ligeia was exhausted. Her body spasmed and fell – one of her death cultists darted forwards and caught her before she hit the hard stone floor.

She was gasping for air. She had never felt that magnitude of power before, never. She had never understood that she could contain such sheer strength of emotion – the Hereticus had never trained her to her full potential, and the Malleus after them had only wanted to ensure that her kind was proof against the Enemy. By the Throne, she could be magnificent.

Shan helped Ligeia to her feet. The death cultist inclined her head very slightly – a question. What now? Where do we go?

Ligeia looked around her. The charred bones of the Allking's men lay mingled with the books and papers piled up against the walls. She could hear no more orders yelled or feet ringing on the stone floor. She had incinerated the whole of the force sent down to corner her.

'We go back up,' said Ligeia.

EIGHT
THE MISSION

THE GREY KNIGHTS' attack came just before dawn. The storm surrounding the city formed a dome that began beyond the city walls and curved right overhead in a shield of near-opaque dark cloud and lightning, so the sun's light barely pushed through. The storm cut out all communications, electronic or psychic, but a man could walk right through it to reach the edge of the forest just beyond the high walls.

The walls were of hardwood with stone foundations and watchtowers. The Allking had put the city on a war footing – his household cavalry were in the palace, hunting down Ligeia and her death cultists, but the rest of Hadjisheim's standing army was on the walls. There were thousands of them patrolling the battlements and manning the gates that led into courtyards which would be turned into killing zones by archers and spearmen. Beyond that the lower city of Hadjisheim was a warren of poor crumbling houses, where a small body of men could mount a defence that might last for weeks. The upper city, surrounding the Allking's palace and the imposing black marble temple of the mission, was more open ground where the streets would funnel attackers into crossfires from archers on the roofs.

The Allking, however, had only ever had to fend off attacks from jealous barons or forest bandits. He didn't even know that such men as Space Marines existed.

Squad Genhain led the attack, shredding the wooden battlements and men behind them before Tancred's Terminators charged straight through the wall, splintering through into the cavity at the centre of the wall before tearing through into the city itself. Alaric and Santoro followed him through the breach, stitching storm bolter fire through the men pouring down off the walls to stop them.

Tancred kept going. The flimsy mud brick walls collapsed into powder under the boots of his Terminator armour. Townspeople fled in terror as Tancred led the charge deeper and deeper, Alaric and Santoro keeping counter-attacks off him. The Allking's soldiers were not fanatics like the household troops and they found themselves hopelessly tangled in the same streets that were supposed to fox invading enemies. When they saw the eight-foot armour-clad monsters that battered their way through the city, most of them fled. Those that fought on died beneath the guns and Nemesis blades of Alaric and Santoro.

The first archers to sight the spearhead gathered hastily on the rooftops of the upper city where the Allking's nobles cowered in the cellars below. They loosed volleys of arrows at the invaders, but every shot bounced off their armour. They set rivers of burning oil running down into the old city, but the attackers just charged straight through as if they couldn't feel pain at all.

Sprays of bolter fire sent archers fleeing from the rooftops. By the time the Grey Knights reached the avenue that led to the Allking's palace, black swarms of arrows lashed down at them like rain. Tharr were corralled into the road and lashed until they charged madly at the attackers, only to be hacked apart by the Grey Knights' blades. Squad Tancred crushed hastily-erected barricades beneath their feet, ripped apart a formation of pikemen stretched across the avenue, and pressed onwards. Squad Genhain in the rearguard sent volley after volley of bolts into the swordsmen and spearmen trying to surround the spearhead, until their weapons were dry and they had to share ammunition from Alaric and Santoro.

More and more men were drawn into the carnage. Barons eager to earn the Allking's favour charged their contingents into the upper city, forming huge swelling crowds of men who were herded like cattle into Genhain's fire zones. Dozens were trampled and crushed as they tried to flee. Archers ducked rattling volleys of bolter fire and ran when they saw the slaughter the Grey Knights wreaked on their fellow soldiers.

The last hundred men of the Allking's household army massed in the grand entrance to the palace, ready to meet the Grey Knights with claws and tentacles, the banner of the Lord of Change above them. The

Allking stood ready to face the invaders personally, and his retainers were ready to collapse the roof of the entrance hall on the invaders if they broke the line.

But the Grey Knights didn't attack the palace. Tancred led them through the villa of a baron in the shadow of the palace, bypassing the palace defences. Alaric and Santoro fended off a frenzied charge from the Allking's men while Tancred bashed through the stone walls and crunched through carved black wood furniture.

The Grey Knights went out through the back wall and their objective became clear. Alaric had ordered his Marines to head for the most likely source of the darkness on Sophano Secundus: the mission temple.

TANCRED TORE THE tall black-stained wooden doors off the front of the mission, his gauntleted hands splintering through the wood. Tancred was covered in dust from pulverised mud brick houses and battered from where he had charged straight through solid marble walls, but there was no sign of his slowing down. His Terminators charged in through the breach with him, their massive frames splintering the stone steps that led up to the doorway.

'Genhain, cover us!' voxed Alaric. 'Santoro, with me!' Alaric led his squad and Santoro's in the wake of Squad Tancred. Arrows were lancing down from the nearby palace and Alaric could hear the chattering of Squad Genhain's storm bolters as they returned fire. Genhain would be responsible for keeping the battle for Hadjisheim outside the entrance to the mission, allowing the rest of the Grey Knights to deal with whatever they found inside.

Thick, heavy air rolled out as Alaric followed Tancred through the doorway: incense and burnt flesh stank. A hoarse, dim roaring, like a distant hurricane, keened from the heart of the temple.

Alaric's auto-senses automatically yanked his pupils open in response to the dark but still it was like charging into a sandstorm. Heavy, solid darkness crowded Alaric. He could just see the shadowy shapes of the Terminators ahead, muted muzzle flashes marking the gunfire they were sending ripping through the interior of the temple.

Static flooded the vox. 'Santoro, back us up!' yelled Alaric above the roar, and plunged into the darkness after Tancred.

The screams of daemons rang out like a peal of bells, discordant and terrible, flooding Alaric's senses. For a moment he thought he would black out – and then he saw the pink and blue flames billowing up from the marble floor, bright in the shadows, reaching up like fingers to surround Squad Tancred.

A blast of light burned straight up from the floor like a spotlight, illuminating the ceiling of the temple. Alaric saw it was impossibly high – the dimensions of the Mission had warped horribly, far too large to be contained within the building itself. This was a place not fully within real space – it was saturated by the warp, taking on the strange properties of the immaterium. The ceiling was like an unnatural sky far above, ugly bulbous shapes of stone looming down from the distant walls. It was like being inside the belly of a titanic stone creature, and the mission's structure flexed and bowed as if that creature were taking breath. Lightning crackled far overhead. The walls groaned.

Daemons were boiling up through the glowing floor, long-limbed, shining, flame-spewing creatures. Alaric dived into the fray to cut through the circle of daemons surrounding Tancred.

The daemons screamed as they touched the sacred wards woven into the Grey Knights' armour. Tancred beheaded one, spilling globules of glowing blood that fell upwards towards the distant ceiling. Alaric glimpsed surreal, individual combats through the darkness, illuminated in shafts of light from below. He saw Justicar Tancred slashing at the daemons, Brother Locath fending off reaching hands that grabbed at him with charred fingers, Brother Karlin aiming his incinerator into the monsters rising around his feet and pumping a gout of flame straight downwards until it looked like he was standing in a volcano.

Alaric cut downwards and felt daemon's flesh coming apart under the blade of his halberd. A crack rang out as Dvorn, at Alaric's side, drove the head of his Nemesis hammer down into the body of a gibbering daemon. Alaric saw that Tancred was surrounded – the Grey Knights were trained and equipped to fight the daemonic, but there was a prodigious tide of them erupting now, just like on Victrix Sonora, just like on Khorion IX a thousand years before.

A shrill scream cut through the din of battle and shapes speared down, flying creatures with bladed wings that swooped low and tore through Squad Tancred. Alaric jabbed upwards and gouged off the wing of one screamer, sending it cartwheeling away, spraying burning blood. Alaric saw Brother Krae, one of Tancred's oldest battle-brothers, beheaded by a swooping daemon that caught fire as it touched him. Krae's Terminator-armoured body fell to the ground and his body sunk into the deeper darkness that opened beneath him.

'Krae!' bellowed Tancred. He grabbed one of the swooping daemons with his bolter hand, dragging it downwards and slicing it clean in half with his sword. But there were more of them, whole squadrons of them dropping from far above to shriek through the shadows. Brother Vien, just behind Alaric, brought one screamer down with a volley of bolt shells, and Haulvarn spitted another on the point of his sword.

But Squad Tancred were in the centre of it all. Tancred himself almost lost an arm to one that ripped its blades deep into his shoulder pad. Alaric plunged deeper into the fray and the daemons below parted as he waded through them, his wards burning bright-hot, reflected in the burns that covered the daemons' skin. But there were so many of them.

A white light shone down suddenly as they fended off the daemons around them, and Alaric saw that someone was rising from the flood in the middle of Squad Tancred, directing the screamers – a bent and wizened figure dressed in a long flowing cloak, a mockery of Ecclesiarchical robes. The hood fell back and Alaric saw an emaciated face, thin as a corpse's, with huge, white, pupilless eyes that dripped purple lightning.

Polonias, the missionary – but Alaric felt such age and malice emanating from the figure that it must be someone far older than Polonias was supposed to be, perhaps even the first missionary, Crucien. If that was the case then Ghargatuloth had planted his plan on Sophano Secundus even before he was first banished by Mandulis.

Tancred strode towards the elevated figure but the missionary drew a long, gnarled wooden club from thin air and met Tancred's Nemesis sword in a flash of sparks. The missionary struck back with inhuman speed and Tancred only just parried the blow, forced onto the back foot.

Alaric tried to close with Tancred and the missionary but the hands reaching up from the floor slowed him down, and for every one he and his squad severed three more seemed to reach up in their place. Tancred fought on, cutting deep into the missionary's body only for the wound to heal up with a ripple of purple fire.

Tancred was almost on his knees, the missionary's staff striking again and again, the storm bolter fire from his Terminators spattering against a shield of purple-black lightning that the missionary span around himself. Tancred was as physically strong a man as Alaric had ever fought with, but the missionary was a fearsome champion of Chaos and his blows kept raining down.

There was a flash of light from a discharging Nemesis blade and the head of a halberd punched out through the front of the missionary's chest. Behind the missionary, Alaric saw Justicar Santoro flanked by his squad, covered from head to feet in smoking daemon's blood, determination behind the glinting glass of his helmet's eyepieces. Santoro twisted the blade of his halberd and opened up the missionary's torso, spilling burning organs onto the floor. Tancred rose to his knees and sliced off one of the missionary's arms, then as Santoro held the missionary wriggling like a worm on a hook Tancred cut down with his sword and clove the missionary's head clean in two down to the collar bone.

Pink fire blossomed up from the missionary's ruined skull and spurted from his massive chest wound. The screaming of daemons rose higher and with a thunderclap the missionary exploded, throwing Terminators and power-armoured Grey Knights to the floor. Chunks of flaming flesh flew everywhere.

The discharge of sorcerous energy rippled through the stones and Alaric felt them shift beneath his feet. Not trusting the vox, he ripped off his helmet and took in a searing breath of hot incense, blood, and flamer chemicals.

'Out! Everyone, now!' he yelled at the top of his voice as the floor pitched suddenly, huge chunks of black marble falling. A pillar gave way and crashed to the ground like a falling tree. Falling sheets of crumbling marble reduced the visibility even more, and even through his autosenses Alaric felt as if he were blundering through pitch darkness.

The shards of fire that leapt past him were bolts of covering fire from Squad Genhain, and Alaric knew he was heading the right way. He stumbled, but Brother Clostus grabbed his shoulder pad and dragged him forward, through the doorway and into the comparative brightness outside.

Alaric saw the steps up to the mission temple were littered with bodies, many of them mutants in the livery of the Allking's household troops. Squad Genhain had held off a spirited counter-attack on the steps, and by the wounds on the bodies had used hand-to-hand combat when their ammunition ran low.

'Good work, justicar,' said Alaric, his helmet still off.

'What was in there?' asked Genhain.

'The missionary. He's dead but the whole place is coming down. Get us into cover.'

Genhain nodded and pointed towards a single-storey complex, the villa of some feudal lord a short sprint away from the temple. Tharn and Horst, Genhain's two psycannon Marines, led the way, hunting for targets as they ran towards the building. Alaric ordered his squad to follow and hung back to see Santoro lead Squad Tancred out. Both squads were badly beaten up, their armour covered in claw marks and spattered with smouldering gore. The smell was appalling. Brother Mykros and Brother Marl from Squad Santoro carried Brother Krae's massive body between them, Tancred himself close behind with his Terminators.

Alaric jammed his helmet back on his head in time for Brother Tharn's vox. 'We've got hostiles at the palace's rear gates,' he said.

'Heading this way?' asked Alaric, looking towards the imposing rear wall of the palace where an ornate archway led into the Allking's gardens.

'I don't think so. Looks like they're fleeing... one's huge, a mutant maybe...'

Alaric saw Allking Rashemha the Stout storm through the archway leading from the white stone palace, a ragged band of his retainers and courtiers around him. The Allking carried a huge mace and was swinging it indiscriminately, knocking his own troops off their feet to keep some unseen enemy away from him. He was yelling orders and curses, and blood streamed down his face.

Alaric hadn't seen the Allking before but the man's massive girth and authority over the hapless stragglers around him left him in little doubt.

Dark shapes flitted around him. One of them stopped for a split-second, spinning in the air, and Alaric recognised it as one of Ligeia's death cultists. Twin swords flashed and two retainers fell dead, their heads neatly removed. Another death cultist ran up the inside of the arch, flipped over, and took off the Allking's hand. His hand and mace clattered to the ground and the Allking roared as thick, writhing worms spurted from the stump of his wrist instead of blood.

Both death cultists slashed at the Allking, opening up dozens of wounds that all bled fountains of hideous worms. With a final bellow of defiance the Allking's body disintegrated into a foul squirming heap of wriggling vermin.

The death cultists landed and gave the heap a wide berth, neatly despatching the few surviving courtiers as they skirted around it. Then, two more death cultists stepped through the arch and around the bubbling mess – these two were carrying Inquisitor Ligeia between them, who somehow managed to look stately and unflustered as the death cultists placed her back on the ground.

The death cultists and Ligeia hurried towards Alaric, the cultists swatting away the few arrows that were still being fired their way from the upper levels of the palace. Ligeia's face was stained with smoke and blood and her hair was messy and singed, but she didn't seem hurt. In fact, to Alaric she looked rather more dangerous than he had seen her before.

'Justicar,' said Ligeia as her death cultists accompanied her to the threshold of the mansion Genhain had indicated. 'I am glad you could join us.' She glanced back at the mission – the roof had just fallen in and a cloud of noisome black dust spewed from the open entrance. 'I think we have found ample evidence of Ghargatuloth here.' Alaric saw that both Ligeia and the two death culstists who had carried her were also carrying several large leatherbound books and rolled-up scrolls and banners.

'The missionary is dead,' said Alaric. 'We have lost two men and several injured.'

'The missionary was Crucien,' said Ligeia. 'Ghargatuloth has had this planet marked since before the Imperium discovered it.'

'It must be important to it,' said Alaric, leading Ligeia into the shelter of the mansion. It was all white marble and hanging tapestries, relatively untouched by the fighting. 'Crucien had daemons and sorcery at his command. He almost overwhelmed us. It takes a very powerful man to do that and Ghargatuloth must have taken a great risk to give him such power.'

Ligeia indicated the books she was carrying. 'Perhaps there is something here that will tell us why. We need to get back to the *Rubicon*.'

'We lost the Thunderhawks,' said Alaric, 'but I can get a message to the *Rubicon* once we're out of the city and they can send shuttles down for us.'

'Good. Once we're out of here we can drop a few torpedoes on this place. What do you think?'

Alaric nodded. 'It would be my pleasure.'

Ligeia smiled. The expression was stark contrast to the blood on her face. 'We'd better get moving, then.'

NINE
THALASSOCRES

Two THOUSAND YEARS before the outpost on Sophano Secundus was lost, a great compact was signed.

The Prince of a Thousand faces withdrew from his real space lair on Khorion IX into the warp, where the Lord of Change himself had cried out – a terrible keening loaded with unholy knowledge, the tolling of a great bell at the heart of the warp. The other powers of the warp – sometimes allies, usually accursed – shrunk away, the daemons said, cowering from the incandescent might of Tzeentch. The god himself sent ripples through the warp, calling his servants to him.

The Prince heeded the call. The Prince could do this because he was much, much more than his daemonic body – he was knowledge, pure information, revelations of darkness hidden in the hearts of millions of men. He could be in real space and the warp at the same time, pulling puppet strings in both universes, doing the work of the Change. For the Prince of a Thousand Faces was one of the most powerful of its kind.

The Conclave gathered at Thalassocres, a benighted world trapped screaming in the warp like a madman in a cell. Every hour its continents changed, melting into the seas of liquid nitrogen and spewing great mountains into the sky. The Change God's faithful gathered and soon those awestruck by their fellow daemons fled in terror, leaving only the most powerful sons of Tzeentch.

Their followers ran out across the melting plains of Thalassocres, settling old scores and marking up new ones in idle battle while their masters brooded. The Princes competed in the might of their armies and the magnificence of their displays. Tzeentch ignored the best and awarded the least with gifts that, in centuries to come, would rot their souls and lead to their downfall, for this was the favoured vengeance of the Lord of Change.

Ghargatuloth was in the foremost group, along with Bokor the Wildsman who turned whole species to the cause of the Change, and Maleficos of the Burning Hands who struck like a thunderbolt to plunge star systems into war. Master Darkeye, who hid amongst mankind and tormented it invisibly, and Themiscyron the Star-Dragon held court on Thalassocres, too, magnificent and savage. A hundred other Lords of the Change took their places on the melting plains, and courts of daemons cavorted around them, gibbering and monstrous, until the whole planet rang with the praises of the Change.

Thalassocres was a great beacon of worship, a lynchpin of the Change, and the Conclave caused much mayhem in the minds of humankind. Although mankind's sages searched long for the reasons behind rashes of madness throughout their galaxy, to them Thalassocres remained hidden.

When Tzeentch spoke, the planet shook. Its crust and mantle were torn off and to this day, they say, Thalassocres is not one planet but a shoal of drifting continents surrounding a single core. Those not strong enough to hear the words of Tzeentch were thrown off into the warp, but the strongest stayed, their courts remaining glorious on the floating shelves of melting stone.

Tzeentch spoke to them of impossible things, of the tangled threads of fate that ran through the universe like threads of a tapestry, of the immense shifting components of reality – time, space, the massed minds of humanity and the dozens of alien species that had yet to play their parts, the mindless hordes of predators teeming in the warp, the powers of Chaos themselves. The greatest of Tzeentch's followers could divine meaning from the stream of concepts the voice of Tzeentch conveyed. Some found intricate plots for them to enact on reality. Others saw glimpses of a future they could alter, or bring to pass. Some saw only desolation and hatred, and revelled in it, for they were the most savage agents of the Change.

Some were destroyed, unable to comprehend the majesty of the Change God's vision.

Ghargatuloth was not destroyed. Nor did he skim some plan from the surface of Tzeentch's words. Instead, the Prince of a Thousand Faces immersed himself in his god's message. Knowledge streamed around him, and straight through him until he was wallowing in a raging torrent of information like a white river of flame that coursed through the broken heart of Thallasocres.

For days on end, measured in the strange timescale of the warp, Ghargatuloth received the revelation of Tzeentch. The other daemon princes looked on in awe, hatred and jealousy. Some were certain that Ghargatuloth would be destroyed. The daemons at his feet were swept aside by the tide of revelations. The substance of Thalassocres was further fractured by the sheer power of Tzeentch. There was a permanent scar left on the warp, a dark barren shadow, but Ghargatuloth remained.

In real space, Ghargatuloth's daemonic body shuddered with the effort of receiving the revelation. Some say this caused the sages of mankind to first realise that the Prince of a Thousand Faces was in their midst. The indigenous life of Khorion IX was extinguished, and space was tormented for light years around.

Then, at last, it was over. The white river of knowledge stopped. Thalassocres fell silent.

And when Ghargatuloth arose again, a thousand new faces looked out upon the warp.

LIGEIA SNAPPED HER head back in her seat, trying to shake out the images that filled it. She pulled her hands away from the book on her writing desk, the skin on her fingers and palms burning with the unholiness of the knowledge covering the pages.

The dark wood panelling and lustrous furnishings of her quarters filtered back into view. She was back on Trepytos, in the quarters Inquisitor Klaes's staff had supplied – but the images in her head were still ghosted over her vision. Ghargatuloth, a formless chaotic monster, bowing beneath a raging river of obscene knowledge. The words of Tzeentch – the god of change, trickery and sorcery, one of the foremost of the Chaos powers – echoing around the warp and shattering a world with their power.

The contents of the book were even more invasive than the brief flashes of blasphemy she had received from the wooden sculpture. The passage she had just experienced – pulled directly from the pages by her psychic sight – was just a tiny fragment of the revelations the book contained. The meaning was so pure and undiluted that it had to have been dictated directly to the author by Ghargatuloth himself, and Ligeia was sure she could taste the old human malice of Crucien behind the words.

Dictated by a daemon prince, written down by a thousand-year-old Chaos sorcerer; Ligeia was shocked at their sheer intensity.

The book in front of her was just one of more than a dozen recovered from the temple beneath the Allking's palace. In addition there were more than thirty scrolls, each one holding a complex prayer or spell, and the banners from the walls. Many of them were written in the Secundan language which Ligeia was having to learn very quickly from the sketchiest of references, and most referred to 'the Emperor' as a euphemism for the Prince of a Thousand Faces. Without Ligeia's powers, they would take years to translate. Ligeia wished that she had years to do it in, instead of receiving the concentrated meaning straight into the centre of her mind.

She closed the book and placed it on the floor of her chambers. Even wearing her nightdress she was sweating with the effort of understanding, and straggles of her hair were clinging to her cold, damp face.

She heard footsteps on the carpet behind her. When not actively defending her, the death cultists were courteous enough to make some noise when they moved around so she knew where they were.

Ligeia turned to see Xiang standing behind her. The death cultist's quizzical stance reminded Ligeia that she had summoned the death cultists – Xiang had probably been standing there some time before letting Ligeia know she was there.

'Ah. Xiang, yes. Please excuse me.' Ligeia managed a faltering smile. 'I need you to perform an errand for me. It is rather menial but I need to know it will be done. Here.'

Ligeia took a folded piece of parchment from her desk, on which she had written her orders in her elegant, sloping hand. Xiang plucked it from her hand, and read it.

'I know,' said Ligeia. 'One of the justicars would probably be more efficient. But… you are mine, you four. They do not belong to me like you do. I have arranged for Inquisitor Klaes to supply a ship – it is small and lightly armed but it is very fast. You should be there within two weeks, if you leave immediately.'

Xiang bowed her head and, without turning around, backed swiftly out of the room. Ligeia had never worked out how the death cultists communicated with one another – she could sense the meanings of their conversations without seeing any movement or hearing any sound – but Xiang would be going to tell her fellow death cultists what Ligeia wanted of them.

There were only four left now. Death cultists, almost by definition, did not grieve – death was a welcome end for them, as long as it came in such a way that their own lives were offered to the Emperor in sacred combat. But they had lost two of their number on Sophano Secundus, and Ligeia was saddened to see two such highly trained and devoted servants of the Emperor lose their lives. They protected Ligeia but, even more, Ligeia was responsible for them. She owned them, and she was their reason to exist. Their deaths were echoes of her own death.

There had been no funeral rites – they had left Taici and Gao on Sophano Secundus. Their deaths alone were sacred, and what happened to the bodies was irrelevant. Ligeia found their lack of pretensions quite refreshing but she would still not want to be left, decaying and forgotten where she had died. She hoped that someone would feel responsible for her when the time came.

Ligeia poured herself another glass of amasec, letting its strong fruity smell chase some of the horrors out of her head before taking a swallow to calm her shaking hands.

Then, she took one of the other books from the floor, put it on the desk, and placed her hands on the cover. She took a deep breath, and dived back into the revelations of Ghargatuloth.

JUSTICAR GENHAIN TOOK careful aim and waited for a moment, as the lenses of his bionic eye snapped into focus. Then he fired a single bolt through the forehead of the human-shaped target at the far end of the gallery.

The shooting gallery on the *Rubicon* was a long, low room, windowless like an underground chamber, with walls carved deeply with scenes of battle and victory intended to focus the mind on diligence and improvement. The columns separating the firing positions were carved into the likenesses of Imperial saints – Genhain at that moment was flanked by a glowering Saint Praxides and Saint Jason of Huale, who were both trampling hapless heretics beneath their feet. Several servitors patrolled the shooters' area, waiting for the Grey Knight to require more ammunition, while the firing range itself was empty save for targets hanging from the ceiling as they trundled along.

'Good?' asked Alaric, standing just behind Genhain.

'Doesn't feel right,' replied Genhain, lowering Alaric's storm bolter. 'Leave it with me for a few hours. I'll have it better than new.'

Genhain had a feel for guns that rivalled any Grey Knight in the Chapter. He was one of the best shots the Grey Knights could field and, even with the existing wargear rites, many of the Grey Knights who knew him would ask him to check their guns for flaws they could not detect. A storm bolter might be working perfectly as far as other Marines were concerned, but Genhain would know if it was too likely to jam, to buck in the hand on full auto, to lose its accuracy in certain conditions.

'Do not neglect your own men on my account,' said Alaric.

'My squad are doing well,' said Genhain. 'They are observant and in good spirits. I'd rather not lead them too closely when it comes to prayers and suchlike. It always feels better to lead yourself in such things.'

'And their guns?'

Genhain smiled and took aim at the same target again. 'Their guns are good.' He fired again, the bullet hole appearing just above the first.

'They fought well on Sophano Secundus.'

'They did. I am proud.' Another shot, this one wide. Genhain bit down a curse and began to inspect the bolter's firing mechanism. 'I was worried about the inquisitor.'

'Ligeia?'

'I don't think she is a fighter. She looked rattled.'

'Ligeia is a strong woman, justicar. You're right though, she'd rather leave all the fighting to us.' Alaric thought for a moment. Genhain led his men very differently from Santoro or Tancred, and Alaric knew Genhain's judgement was sound. 'What do you think of her?'

Genhain looked up from Alaric's bolter. 'Me? I think she is very good at her job, just not as good at ours.'

'Well, she won't be fighting any time soon. They broke Valinov back on Mimas and he let slip that Ghargatuloth can only be killed by a "lightning bolt". The Nemesis sword Mandulis used was fashioned into a lightning bolt, so Ligeia has sent her death cultists to get it from the catacombs on Titan.'

'They could have trouble,' said Genhain. 'It is difficult even for inquisitors to get into Titan, let alone have one of the grand masters disinterred.' Genhain tightened the firing mechanism and took aim again. 'But at least it shows Ligeia understands us.'

'How so?'

'She asks us only to fight and doesn't expect anything else. She could have sent you to Titan, and you could have retrieved Mandulis's sword far more effectively, but she didn't. She respects us. Some of the Ordo Malleus think the Grey Knights were created to serve them, but we are a sovereign and independent Chapter, as much as the Space Wolves or Dark Angels or anyone else.'

Genhain had deliberately named two of the more unpredictable Space Marine Chapters. 'Few Grey Knights would speak that way,' said Alaric.

'It is only the truth.' Genhain fired again, this time on full auto, and a cluster of holes blossomed in the centre of the target's head. 'If the Grey

Knights did not think for themselves, they would be far weaker soldiers. That is the core of what a Space Marine is. We work with the Ordo Malleus because it is the most effective way to do what we have to do, but we were not founded for their benefit. We were founded to do the will of the Emperor, just like the Inquisition. I think Ligeia understands that.'

'I am glad you trust me well enough to tell me this,' said Alaric. Many of the more traditionally-minded Grey Knights would think that Genhain had strayed dangerously close to insubordination. Alaric, on the other hand, was quite glad that the Space Marines he had chosen to accompany him on this mission were able to think for themselves. If there was one danger in the way Grey Knights were trained and indoctrinated, it was that their own spirits would be so crushed beneath the weight of dogma and duty and they would not be able to form their own judgement.

'If I cannot trust my commander, Alaric,' replied Genhain, handing Alaric his bolter, 'then who can I trust? This gun could have lost accuracy in a protracted firefight, but its machine-spirit has been persuaded to be more co-operative.'

Alaric took the gun and fitted it back onto his gauntlet. It felt subtly different, as if it belonged there. 'Thank you, justicar. It always helps to shoot straighter.'

'You have to trust your gun,' said Genhain with a smile. 'Otherwise, where would we be?'

WHEN SOPHANO SECUNDUS fell, a silent call went out across the Trail.

On Volcanis Ultor, a sect hidden deep in the underhive of Hive Tertius overloaded the city's geothermal heatsinks and caused several layers of hive city to be swallowed up in nuclear fire.

Even as ships sent by Inquisitor Klaes pounded Hadjisheim into smouldering ash from orbit, a mutiny in the small sector battlefleet caused three cruisers to be scuttled with all hands.

A prophet appeared on the forge world Magnos Omicron preaching the new word of the Machine God, demanding innovation and creativity over the worship of the Omnissiah and the endless search for perfection. Before he was found and killed, he had rallied three forge cities to his cause and it took a minor civil war amongst the tech-guard to stop his crusade.

Provost Marechal lost thousands of Arbites as he shuttled them from world to world to douse the flashpoints where heretics suddenly played their hands. From an orbital command station around Victrix Sonora, Marechal co-ordinated hundreds of Precincts as they battled riots and rebellion across the Trail.

On the garden world of Farfallen, once a playground for the Trail's rich, a previously unknown tribe of feral humans crept out of the overgrown botanical gardens to slaughter the planet's isolated Imperial communities.

The governor's villa on Solshen XIX, an agri-world whose wide oceans teemed with fish that fed the Trail's hives, was transformed overnight into a charnel house overrun with daemons. A cult led by the governor's own son had summoned creatures of the warp in response to visions from the Prince of a Thousand Faces, and the governor had been hanged in a noose of his own skin from the cliffs surrounding his villa. Many thousands on the Trail's downtrodden hive worlds would starve with the planet lost to Chaos and anarchy.

A hundred cults broke their cover and engaged in wanton, apparently purposeless destruction. Places of worship were looted, hundreds in one night in a seemingly co-ordinated strike against the Ecclesiarchy and the Imperial Church.

It could not last long. The cults could only do so much before the combined efforts of the Arbites, the Imperial Navy and the horrified population stamped them out. And in a way, that was the worst thing about the uprisings on the Trail of Saint Evisser – they had all the hallmarks of an endgame. It was the final setting of the stage for something vast and terrible, where cults hidden for centuries gave their lives away to enact plots dictated to them by sinister voices in their heads.

The Ecclesiarchy responded with uncharacteristic speed. The Order of the Bloody Rose sent a Preceptory of Sisters of Battle to be co-ordinated by Cardinal Recoba on Volcanis Ultor, and their request for additional manpower was met by the Imperial Guard, namely the Methalor 12th Scout Regiment and the Balurian Heavy Infantry. Even the Imperial Navy diverted a force of subsector battlefleet size from the long journey up to Cadia. Someone powerful in the Ecclesiarchy was clearly rattled by what was happening on the Trail – but though the Sisters and Guardsmen were deployed to guard religious sites throughout the Trail, they could do little to stop the steadily rising tide of heresy.

Ghargatuloth had spoken. And to those who knew how to listen, everything he said indicated that it would not be long now before the Trail was drowned in horror.

TEN
MIMAS

THERE WAS A place on Mimas, just outside the great crater, where the earth was torn and scarred. It had been dug up thousands of times by servitor labourers and covered over again. Here and there seismic activity had caused broken bones, even the odd grinning skull, to break the surface, only to be re-buried by roving patrol servitors. In the centre of the broken land was a single building in the High Gothic style, its every surface tooled deeply with images of punishment and retribution – sinners burning in the many indistinct hells of the Imperial cult, vengeance crashing down on the heads of the heretic, the eyes of the Emperor seeing every sin and the servants of the Emperor exacting revenge. Men were killed in scores of ways, from hanging to dismemberment to exposure in the toxic Miman atmosphere, all recorded in sculpture on the building's pillars and pediments.

Dozens of gun-servitors guarded each door. A garrison of Ordo Malleus mind-scrubbed troops stood permanently at attention in their quarters below the building, ready to react to any threat. The building itself was formed around a central chamber with many galleries looking onto it, where a single raised platform stood surrounded by seating for dignitaries, technicians and archivists, like the slab at the centre of an anatomist's theatre.

Gholic Ren-Sar Valinov was brought to the execution chamber on Mimas seven weeks after he had been broken by Explicator Riggensen.

Valinov had not said one more word since that day. If anything he appeared more sullen and uncooperative than before, as if cursing himself silently for letting Riggensen's interrogation crack his mask of infallibility. And so the interrogation staff on Mimas had advised the lord inquisitors of the Ordo Malleus that Valinov was of no further intelligence value.

The Conclave of the lord inquisitors unanimously approved the execution of Valinov. It transpired that Ligeia had indeed been bluffing when she had first questioned Valinov – there would be no elaborate psychic half-death, just an old-fashioned execution. Valinov had been convicted of several capital charges but it was as punishment for grand heresy that he was brought from the prison to the execution chamber just outside Mimas's crater, and Imperial law required that the punishment for grand heresy was death by dismemberment.

IT WAS A solemn occasion. There was no sadness that Valinov was about to die – there was, however, a shame-tinged regret that a fellow inquisitor, once a greatly respected and valuable man, should have fallen so low. The Ordo Malleus had lost inquisitors before to Radicalism and worse fates, but every time it happened the wound was as deep. The Malleus was proud of what it did, and every traitor amongst them was an affront to that pride.

Explicator Riggensen was there to take down any deathbed confessions Valinov might make. He had witnessed executions before but the antiseptic smell of the execution chamber and the gleaming insectoid shape of the servitor-mangler suspended from the ceiling still made him uneasy – which was saying something, considering his occupation.

An official clerk sat at a lectern in front of Riggensen, a pale and heavily augmented woman who scritched details of the execution with quills mounted on metal armatures she had instead of arms. The clerk's head darted from side to side as she noticed who entered the darkened, circular chamber – several more clerks and archivists observing particular aspects of the execution entered, shuffling along in their long robes.

Inquisitor Nyxos entered next, wearing ceremonial crimson robes over his whirring exoskeleton. His two advisors were with him, the ancient astropath and the young tactical officer in her undecorated Naval officer's uniform.

Medical technicians were next, the chief medicae manning the controls for the servitor-mangler and the others checking the lifesign monitors attached to the table in the raised centre of the room. There had been occasions in the past where the executed criminal had not died in spite of the comprehensive nature of the servitor-mangler, and so the chief medicae would be required to assert that lifesigns had ceased.

The next individuals to enter were a surprise to Riggensen. Four death cultists walked in, lithe and athletic figures in glossy bodygloves festooned with daggers and swords. Riggensen glanced over the clerk's shoulder as she wrote down that the death cultists were representing Inquisitor Ligeia. It seemed right to Riggensen that Ligeia would want someone she trusted to witness Valinov die with their own eyes. Otherwise she might never have believed he was truly dead.

The various dignitaries and adepts filled the seats around the pedestal. The lumoglobes dimmed until only the pedestal was lit, bathed in a pool of pale unforgiving light. Then a set of mechanical security doors slid open and Valinov was brought in.

Stripped to the waist, with his hands and feet shackled, Valinov was still an imposing figure. His heavy dark tattoos gave him an almost feral look, accentuated by his sharp, intelligent face and the cords of muscle wrapped around his arms and torso. His head was high and he showed no fear – but then true heretics never did, not until their souls were removed from their body and thrust before the vengeful gaze of the Emperor.

Just by looking at the prisoner, every witness to the execution could tell the ex-inquisitor was a dangerous man. Not even the rigorous work of Mimas's interrogators and explicators had broken him, save for Riggensen's sole moment of fleeting triumph. Death, most of them would agree, was too good for Valinov – but when someone this dangerous was still alive, there could be no guarantee he was safe.

An old preacher stood in the front row, his heavy crimson and white robes dark in the dim light. He read from a battered leather prayer book, giving Valinov the Cursed Rites that would mark his diseased soul as an enemy of the Emperor.

'Though your spirit is rotten and your deeds most heinous, we call upon the Emperor to look upon that spirit in pure and just judgement...'

The preacher's voice droned on through the familiar lines. The chief medicae made a last few checks of the mangler apparatus while his orderlies affixed various electrodes and sensors to Valinov's shaven skin. The clerk seated in front of Riggensen wrote constantly, noting every correct procedure as it was completed. The blood drains were opened in the chamber's floor. Riggensen himself was handed a data-slate and quill, so he could sign that he had witnessed Valinov's death. The servitor-mangler unfolded and each of its six bladed manipulators were tested quickly in turn as the preacher's assistants made the sign of the aquila over Valinov's chest.

The orderly carrying the organ bucket stood ready. The various parts of Valinov's body – head, torso, viscera – would be buried separately in the plain of unmarked graves around the execution building, to prevent some dark power from bringing the corpse back to life. It was a lesson that had been learned the hard way.

The death cultists observed keenly, their eyes expressionless, their bodies motionless save for the occasional twitch of their drum-taut muscles.

The preacher was finishing. The two Malleus troopers flanking Valinov manhandled the prisoner onto the pedestal, where his manacles slotted neatly into the locks at the base and above the head.

The mangler descended, the chief medicae working the controls. The clerk scribbled with greater rapidity. The front rows would be spattered with blood, but it was worth the indignity to ensure that another foe of the Emperor was dead.

'...and so, Lord Emperor, we place this wretched soul before you and remove it from this body whose hands have committed such foulness. May there be redemption for this soul in the eyes of the God-Emperor, and when there can be no redemption, may the hatred of the God-Emperor destroy it for ever.'

There was a pause before the mangler did its work. It was traditional, like so much of the execution – the prisoner to be executed could, if there was some possibility of redemption, cry out for mercy from the Emperor. No one expected Valinov to speak.

'So it has come to this,' he said in a low, quiet voice, as if speaking to himself. 'The threads are drawing taut. This death is the death of galaxies. You may begin.'

As if in response, the hand of the chief medicae reached for the switch that would begin the dismemberment. His hand never got that far.

There was a flash of silver, like a tiny sliver of lightning arcing across the room, and suddenly a long bright blade was stuck quivering into the seat behind the medicae and his severed hand thudded onto the floor beneath him.

Riggensen saw the chief medicae look up at his attacker and stare into the unblinking, unforgiving eyes behind the mask of a death cultist.

The mind-wiped troops standing by the pedestal reacted first. The las-blasts from the hellguns they carried spattered across the room but the death cultist had read their movements perfectly and she twisted like a gymnast, the blasts ripping through the air centimetres from her skin. A split second later both troopers were dead, sliced in two across the waist by the twin curved short swords of the second cultist.

Inquisitor Nyxos bellowed and took a silver-plated plasma pistol from beneath his robes, his servos screaming as they forced his limbs to move with supernatural speed. The young tactical officer beside him hit the ground, her Naval officer's cap flying.

The two remaining death cultists leapt from their seats, one heading for Nyxos, the other for the pedestal where Valinov lay. The preacher threw his old, frail body between the cultists and the pedestal, but he didn't even slow the cultist down as he was neatly bisected by the cultist's sword.

Riggensen carried an autopistol as a sidearm, and he took it out from beneath his plain explicator's uniform as he stood up. He snapped off a shot at the cultist who had just cut off the medicae's hand, but the cultist jinked to the side faster than the bullet.

The cultist by the pedestal flashed his sword down twice, and Valinov was out of his restraints. He rolled off the pedestal and Nyxos, quickly realising that Valinov was the biggest threat in the room, fired. The cultist threw himself in front of Nyxos and the plasma pistol's blast ripped through the cultist, the power of the shot dissipating as it vaporised his midriff.

Gunfire shattered down from everywhere, from adepts' sidearms, from Nyxos, from Riggensen. The cultist whom Riggensen had so nearly killed flipped over the head of the adept in front of him. Riggensen felt sure the cold steel would slice through him but instead the cultist flipped over the heads of the audience and ran impossibly along the wall behind them, sprinting halfway round the circular room to slash her sword through the Malleus troopers.

Riggensen fired again at her but, as the autopistol kicked in his hand, he could see the cultist ducking the shots or stepping to the side, moving faster than anyone should.

Valinov was taking shelter by the slab he should have died on. He was showered in the blood of the cultist who had died for him, and his hard dark eyes were glancing back and forth as he evaluated all the many threats to his life that were unfolding. Nyxos with his plasma pistol, who would at least have to wait a few seconds while the weapon recharged. Nyxos's assistant, the tactical officer who would surely have a sidearm of her own. The mind-wiped troopers who would shoot him without hesitation if any of them survived long enough. The servitor-mangler which was still writhing lethally less than a metre over his head.

Riggensen, whose autopistol shots seemed to be moving slower than if he had thrown them.

The cultist heading for Nyxos leapt across the room, slamming into the ageing inquisitor. Mechanised limbs clattered to the ground. A blade shot out and rang against the bracing around his pistol arm. A second plasma bolt ripped out, scouring the black glossy mask off half the cultist's face.

The tactical officer leapt to her feet, plunging a glowing power knife (a beautiful weapon, something that would be awarded to an outstanding cadet at one of the Imperial Navy's finest academies) into the cultist's calf. A flick of the wrist and the cultist threw her across the room to slam into the front row of seats with a gruesome crack.

The third surviving cultist, the one who had cut up Valinov's guards, finished the job of killing the chief medicae with a thrown knife that thudded into his throat and pinned him to his seat. Riggensen fired again, three shots streaking towards the last cultist. The cultist ducked low and ran towards Riggensen – Riggensen was a well-built man, young compared to many of the aged adepts and veterans of the Ordo Malleus. He was a prime target, a definite threat.

The cultist crossed the room in a flash. A second flash and the cultist fell, the tactical officer's power knife still stuck through his ankle.

The cultist landed on top of the clerk in front of Riggensen. Riggensen flicked the shot selector and fired the whole magazine of his autopistol into the cultist's back, the cultist jerking as finally there was no more room to dodge and the bullets tore through him.

Riggensen had probably killed the clerk, too. The fact was a bleak, dark veil at the back of his mind. He couldn't let it stop him, slow him down. He would do penance later. Now, he had to survive.

One of the cultists had thrown Valinov a hellgun and he had it on full auto – a fan of glittering crimson blasts ripped across the chamber. By now everyone was in cover or firing back, yelling, screaming. Nyxos was struggling with the cultist on top of him, blades slicing into him time and time again, threatening to shut down even his multiple augmetic systems.

Riggensen pulled the power knife out of the cultist's calf. He scrambled over the mess, his eyes fixed on Valinov. Riggensen was a servant of the Emperor. Riggensen would not run. He would not cower. He had shown no fear in the interrogation room, when he faced Valinov not knowing fully what he was. He would show no fear now.

Valinov was firing at the troopers now coming in. They were returning fire, shots spattering against the pedestal. Valinov hadn't seen Riggensen.

Time was going by in slow, tortured heartbeats. Riggensen was not a trained killer like Valinov, but he was strong and capable. He just needed one good shot – Valinov was tough and had many augmetics that would help him resist injury, but he could not go through a wound from a power knife and carry on defending himself.

Valinov span round and quick as lightning he brought the butt of the hellgun slamming into Riggensen's ribs. Riggensen fell, the hard cold metal of the pedestal cracking into the side of his head.

Valinov was kneeling, looming over the sprawling Riggensen. But Riggensen was not dead yet.

He had one last weapon. Something no one else had. It was the death of Nyxos's astropath that reminded him – Riggensen felt the psychic feedback of the astropath's mind flitting out of existence, the psychic spark going out.

He had broken Valinov once. He could do it again.

Riggensen reached through the fog of pain and shock, into the part of his mind where he kept the weapon that had made him an explicator. The eye inside him opened and looked out at Valinov's mind, reaching a lance of perception into the ex-inquisitor's soul. He could crack him open again, lever open Valinov's mind, blind him, deafen him, fill his head with noise and insanity.

Riggensen let everything he had flood out of his mind to crack that diamond at the heart of Valinov's soul. He dug into his half-remembered childhood amongst the dregs of Hydraphur, the even murkier months of testing and conditioning on the Black Ship that had picked him up, the pain, the humiliation, the fear of the power that grew inside his head that might see him executed at any moment.

He found it all and compressed it into a crystal-hard mental spear. With all the strength the Malleus had taught him, he hurled it at Valinov.

There was nothing for it to hit. There was nothing, nowhere, no one.

Riggensen's mind flailed hopelessly at nothing, because Gholic Ren-Sar Valinov had no soul.

That abyss, where Valinov's soul should be, was the last thing Riggensen saw. He couldn't even see beyond it to the writhing arms of the servitor-mangler as Valinov hauled his body up into its grip and it started the quick, slippery work of cutting Explicator Riggensen apart.

WHEN GHARGATULOTH WAS young – relatively speaking, for a true daemon suffered neither birth nor death – it was said that he walked like a mortal man, sometimes striding through from the warp when there was a mind of sufficient psychic power for him to possess.

He did what so many daemons did. He gloried in the feeling of flesh wrapped around him. He danced with his new feet. He told stories with his new tongue, stories that the small-minded human beings called insanity. Everyone who met him knew that he was not human – whatever body he wore, power dripped like tears of blue fire from his eyes and he spoke in riddles that drove men mad. But Ghargatuloth was fortunate, for he made his first forays into real space in a time of unfettered destruction and war. They called it the Age of Strife and, for one of the rare times in the history of mankind, the name they gave their era was completely appropriate.

He saw whole cultures stripped away until only plains of charred bones remained. He saw madmen made kings, brutal warlords who burned whole worlds as fuel to generate their personal power. Mankind lost the means to travel the stars in the slaughter, and retreated to their planets like vermin into their burrows, to consume one another in their wars.

He saw them rediscover space flight, too, and mankind was suddenly divided into a million bloodstained factions thrust into the same melting pot. Ghargatuloth, in a series of madmen's bodies, was a hero. Billions worshipped him. He was the prince who wore a cloak of many faces, each cut from the head of a traitor. He was the woman who swam in an ocean of blood every morning, so the strength of her exsanguinated foes would leach into her. He was the pirate king who united a dozen star systems, only to set them on one another to see which one would survive.

The Age of Strife lasted for longer than human history could properly record. In those days, Ghargatuloth lived out several lifetimes of warfare, suffering and mayhem. He had striven and triumphed, he had been defeated, he had died. Every moment fed the lust for knowledge that infected every servant of Tzeentch.

But Ghargatuloth slowly came to understand the truth. He was just a child, and the Age of Strife was his playground. The more he understood mankind, the more he began to understand the will of the Chaos powers. For every victory he achieved while amusing himself with war, there was a defeat. For every empire that rose, there would be a fall.

Mankind was fundamentally weak. It was incapable of true victory – it would always fail. Always. In the warp, there were gods, beings that had gathered such power that they would be gods forever. But mankind could not emulate them. When Ghargatuloth realised this, he came to despise the species he had played with for so long.

He became bored. He would sometimes make forays into real space and cause wanton havoc, but it was empty and meaningless. There was no knowledge to be found there. No secrets to learn. Mankind was a crude and ignorant animal, incapable of gathering true, meaningful power.

Until the crusade.

A man calling himself the Emperor conquered the cradle of mankind, holy Terra, the homeworld. He led a crusade across the stars, conquering the space mankind had settled, reuniting the species into the Imperium. Every human being in the galaxy was declared an automatic citizen of the Imperium, whether they knew it or not. The crusade had never truly ended, for the Imperium throughout its entire history had striven to bring every human world into its oppressive embrace.

And suddenly, the galaxy was interesting again. For the first time mankind had secured enduring power for itself, a dominion over the known galaxy that had remained for well over ten thousand years. It had survived even the death of the Emperor himself at the hands of the Chaos-blessed Warmaster Horus, civil wars and invasions, everything the universe could throw at it. The Imperium endured, in spite of the dimness of the human intellect and the tiny scope of their minds.

And as Ghargatuloth had seen, every victory was followed by defeat. Every empire built, must fall.

Ghargatuloth's existence had meaning again. One day, the Imperium would fall. And Ghargatuloth would be there when it happened...

LIGEIA THREW HERSELF against the far wall of her bedchamber, her clothes drenched in sweat, her mouth dry and her breath hot and painful. She was shaking. On the table across the room, the book lay crackling the antique patina with its evil. It was a small, slim volume, small enough to hide in the palm of one hand, but written onto its pages were the revelations of Ghargatuloth, pure and undiluted, an unabridged tirade of madness. Ligeia had to forcibly shut down her mind to stop its meaning from seeping into her.

Her chambers were a mess. Clothes were strewn around and half-eaten meals curdled on silver plates balanced on every surface. There had been too much in Ligeia's head for her to keep up the appearance of a noblewoman – such things didn't seem to matter anymore, not when she had seen some of the full horror of the forces that were tearing at the fabric of reality.

Ghargatuloth was speaking to her. Ghargatuloth was not just a daemonic body – he was knowledge. He was all the knowledge that he had gathered in his immensely long lifetime. That was why he could not be killed, only banished – he left that knowledge in the hearts and minds of his cultists, so that even if he were banished from real space enough of him would remain written in books or madmen's minds to bring him back.

Ligeia couldn't beat him. She couldn't face something like that. The most basic understanding of Ghargatuloth was simply too vast and complex to fit into her mind.

She wished she had her death cultists still, so she could explain to them what she felt. They never answered, of course, but even just talking helped. She could not talk to the Grey Knights, not even Alaric, not about something like this. The Malleus crew who skulked through the guts of the *Rubicon* were no better, nor was Inquisitor Klaes or the rest of the Inquisition. Ligeia was completely alone, with no one but the afterimage of Ghargatuloth in her head for company.

But her death cultists were gone. They would not be coming back.

There was a loud bang from elsewhere in her chambers, as an explosive charge blew the door in. Ligeia heard someone yelling an order and armoured feet crunched through the antique furniture in the next room.

Ligeia straightened up. She still had her digital weapon disguised as a large ornate ring on her finger, and there was a needle pistol somewhere in her luggage that she could use competently. But she knew that neither of them would do any good. Tzeentch was going to swallow the galaxy. What good was any weapon?

The door to her bedchamber was kicked in. Splintered wood flew everywhere. Ligeia stepped back from the door, shaking, knowing what a pathetic figure she would cut – bedraggled, exhausted, ill, looking all her many years and more.

She recognised Justicar Santoro, the most straight-laced Grey Knight, barging his way into the room. He was just the person they would bring down from the *Rubicon* to face her. No imagination. No chance of listening to her pleas.

Santoro levelled his storm bolter at Ligeia's head. If she moved, if she spoke, he would kill her.

Somehow, she had known it would come to this. Even before she had ever heard of Ghargatuloth, as a junior investigator for the Ordo Hereticus before the Malleus had even found her, she had known she would end her days at the point of gun a held by someone who was supposed to be her ally. That was the way the Inquisition worked, how the whole Imperium worked – mankind always killed its own in the end.

Three more members of Squad Santoro moved into the room, their weapons trained at Ligeia, their huge armoured bodies filing the room. Ligeia shivered in a sudden cold.

'Clear,' said Santoro.

Inquisitor Klaes followed the Grey Knights into the room. He held a data-slate in one hand – the other hand was on the hilt of his power sword.

'Inquisitor Briseis Ligeia,' said Klaes carefully. 'We have received a communication from the Ordo Malleus Conclave on Encaladus demanding your immediate arrest. As the principal Inquisitorial authority in this area I am required to carry out that order. The rules of your situation are now very simple, Ligeia: surrender or Justicar Santoro will kill you.'

Ligeia held her shaking hands up. At a hand signal from Santoro, a Marine Ligeia recognised as Brother Traevan stepped forward, grabbed her hand and pulled the ring off her finger, grinding its precious miniaturised technology beneath his boot.

'Do you have any other weapons?' said Santoro grimly.

Ligeia shook her head.

'Restrain her.'

Traevan pulled Ligeia's arms behind her and she felt manacles being clamped around her wrists. It was only professional courtesy from Klaes, she knew, that kept her from being strip-searched and put in chains.

'Inquisitor Ligeia,' said Klaes, reading now from the data-slate, 'the orders of the Emperor's Holy Inquisition are placing you under arrest for the crimes of grand heresy, association with enemies of the Emperor, corruption of the Emperor's servants, and other charges pending a full hearing. You will be taken to the facilities on Mimas where the truth will be drawn from you and your fate decided by the Conclave of the Ordo Malleus. You will be afforded no freedom that might lead to the furtherance of your crimes. Your authority as an inquisitor is revoked.

'These charges relate to the assistance received by the condemned enemy of the Emperor, Gholic Ren-Sar Valinov, and the deaths of Imperial servants in the commission of this heresy. By the decree of the Ordo Malleus there can be no innocence of your crimes, only degrees of guilt, which shall be decided upon in due time. Until then you are no longer a citizen of the Imperium but a creature owned and disposed of by the Ordo Malleus. May the Emperor have mercy on you, for we will not.'

Klaes switched off the data-slate. Ligeia could see the sadness in his eyes. No inquisitor could enjoy persecuting one of their colleagues – it reminded them of how close they themselves were to falling. 'Tell me why, Ligeia, and I'll see that they treat you well.'

'Why?' A hot tear ran down Ligeia's face. 'What else is there? The galaxy will die. The Change will swallow everything. No matter how hard we fight, we are all lost in the end. I have seen it happen. There can be no victory against fate, inquisitor. Valinov's freedom is a part of that fate, just like my arrest, just like the fact that you will all die, and all your triumphs will crumble to dust.'

'Enough,' said Santoro. He stepped forward and hit Ligeia with a backhanded strike across the face that sent her reeling to the floor.

As unconsciousness took Ligeia, she could still see Ghargatuloth smothering the stars and the Lord of Change marching in step behind him, infecting the very fabric of the universe with the stain of Chaos.

ALARIC HAD LOST a colleague he trusted. He had also lost a friend. When Ligeia was brought onto the *Rubicon* and shut into the ship's psyker-warded brig, Alaric had seen a broken woman, not much more than a shadow of the insightful noblewoman he had come to trust.

Inquisitor Klaes, Alaric could tell from looking at his face, felt the same. To think that Ghargatuloth could rob such a woman of her reason, without her even having to come close to him, was terrifying. No one was safe. For the first time, Alaric seriously wondered if Ghargatuloth could do the same thing to a Grey Knight if one of them got near enough. Not one single Grey Knight had ever fallen to Chaos – would Alaric, or one of the men under his command, be the first? The thought all but made him sick.

Ligeia had not sent her death cultists to retrieve the sword of Mandulis. She had sent them to Mimas where, acting on her orders, they had helped Valinov escape his execution. The last anyone heard of Valinov, he was fleeing on a stolen gunship out of Saturn's rings, followed by a host of Ordo Malleus ships from Iapetus which lost him in the gas giant's outer ring.

Valinov would have been well out of the solar system by the time Ligeia was arrested. There was a possibility that one of the death cultists was still alive and accompanying him. It was treachery on a grand scale – Ligeia, who knew more than most about the many atrocities Valinov had committed against the Imperial citizenry, had conspired with him to help him escape his punishment.

Quite how Valinov had got his claws into her, Alaric couldn't be certain. But he was certain of one thing – Ghargatuloth had helped him do it. Probably it had started with the *Codicium Aeternum* itself, and with Ligeia's first interrogation of Valinov on Mimas. Alaric himself had read the pages of the *Codicium Aeternum* – had Ghargatuloth tried to lever open his mind, too, and plant his orders inside?

Ghargatuloth had acted through the statue from Victrix Sonora and the texts recovered from Sophano Secundus, maybe even the archives on Trepytos in which Ligeia had immersed herself, planting hidden information in her head that had eaten away at her sanity without her knowing it until it was too late. She had been used. The Grey Knights had also been used to play their part in an unravelling plot Ghargatuloth had woven into the Trail of Saint Evisser since before the first time he was banished.

And now, with Ligeia gone, Alaric had to face it alone.

Ghargatuloth was not just the monster Mandulis had killed. He was knowledge planted in the minds of his followers, the same knowledge that could infect the minds of his pawns and force them to do insane things. Alaric had fought daemons and cultists in the past many times on the road to becoming a justicar, but they had always ultimately been enemies he could see and touch and kill. Ghargatuloth, on the other hand, was a power that did not have to fight the Ordo Malleus to win.

AFTER THE *Rubicon* had left Trepytos for Mimas, Alaric set about picking up the pieces of Ligeia's investigation. He had to have her chambers stripped and the contents burned; there was no way of knowing how many of the notes she left behind were tainted. But it was the only chance Alaric had. And if there was anyone in the Imperium who could follow up her investigation without falling prey to the call of Ghargatuloth, it was a Grey Knight.

Inquisitor Klaes had put all the resources of the Trepytos fortress at Alaric's command. Klaes's best ship, the one Ligeia's death cultists had used, was still impounded at the Naval fortress on Iapetus, but Klaes called in some favours. Within days Alaric had two armed merchantmen, the fastest ships on the Trail with veteran ex-Naval crews.

Alaric had sent Genhain on the *Rubicon* to escort Ligeia to Mimas. Genhain was to travel to Titan afterwards and, on Alaric's authority as acting brother-captain and commander of the strikeforce, recover the sword of Mandulis. If this really was the 'lightning bolt' Valinov had spoken of, then perhaps it was the only chance the Grey Knights had in the coming reckoning with Ghargatuloth.

Squad Santoro and Squad Tancred were now quartered in the fortress, taking up the training floor in makeshift cells and practising their combat drills in the duelling arena. The fortress had once been impressive but Alaric was acutely aware, as he prepared to take up the investigation that had cost Ligeia her mind, that the Trail of Saint Evisser had few resources he could commandeer compared to the millennia-old cult network of Ghargatuloth. The upsurge in cult activity had seen the Naval ships and Guardsmen stationed on the Trail increase in number, but it was still too small a force to cover the whole Trail.

Even if the Ecclesiarchy could be persuaded to put their Sisters of Battle – tough and motivated troops who demanded respect – at Alaric's disposal, there would never be enough manpower for anything other than one solid strike.

Most of the Grey Knights were at the Eye of Terror, fighting a tide of daemons pouring out of that huge warp storm into realpsace. The rest were stretched far too thinly, holding down the many daemonic blackspots across the Imperium – the Maelstrom, the Gates of Varl, Diocletian Nebula, a dozen other weeping sores in real space. There would be no reinforcements from Titan.

Alaric knew now why so many qualities were needed for a leader, qualities he was still not sure he had. He had to fight, win, never waver in his faith in the Emperor and lead his fellow Grey Knights in all these things. But more than that – he had to be able to do all this when he knew he was utterly alone.

ELEVEN
PECUNIAM OMNIS

THE PECUNIAM OMNIS dragged its cargo painfully across the Segmentum Solar, its engines flaring badly where the exhaust vents had become caked in deposits, its ageing nav-cogitator wasting fuel by constantly correcting its course. The run between Jurn and Epsion Octarius was a hard one, too competitive to allow for capital to be wasted on maintaining a decaying cargo ship, nowhere near lucrative enough to be able to replace it.

Captain Yambe knew that he would probably die with the *Pecuniam Omnis*. He was forty-seven years old. It was a good age for a cargo crewman – most died in accidents or dockyard brawls long before then. Yambe had survived two major wrecks and Emperor knew how many rough nights at harbour, but having finally made captain of his own ship he knew he would never be able to break out. He owed too much to too many people to be able to walk away, and he would never amass enough credits to upgrade his corroded ship.

Yambes's crew, at least, knew what they were doing – thirty men manning the few habitable areas surrounding the ship's bloated metal abdomen. The huge airless cargo holds carried vast quantities of Jurnian industrial product, from pre-moulded STC habitats to crates of mass-produced lasguns. The crew were hard-bitten and tough, most of them probably criminals treating the *Pecuniam Omnis* as a place to hide. Yambe didn't care as long as they gave the tech-rituals at least some passing respect and knew one end of a hyperspanner from the other.

The bridge of the *Pecuniam* was cramped and hot, stinking of sweat and engine oil. Yambe himself was running to fat, filling the command chair and slowly saturating its tattered upholstery with sweat. A half-empty bottle of Jurnian Second Best, a foul but highly effective spirit that Yambe could no longer sleep without, teetered on the arm of the chair. In front of Yambe a transparent plasteel hemisphere was blistered out of the front of the *Pecuniam* like the bulbous eye of an insect, looking out onto the cold, hateful space in which Yambe had spent most of his life.

The *Pecuniam* had dropped out of the warp so the ship's second-rate Navigator, a skinny, twitchy guy from one of the Lower Houses, could meditate for a few days on the right path to take on the next warp jump. The Navigator was a joke, but his House's fee wasn't. The astropath, Gell, wasn't much cheaper but at least she had some idea of what she was doing.

Yambe hated space. That was why he couldn't stop looking at it. He knew that one day it would rear up and kill him, and that would be the day he had let his guard down. He had been centimetres away from hard vacuum, once, and had seen friends turned inside-out in a hull breach back when he still let himself have friends. Space had killed more men than women had, and that was saying something.

The crammed banks of comm-consoles and instrument cogitators beeped and hummed behind Yambe, occasionally belching plumes of steam from coolant leaks. He could hear the engines groaning as they pushed the *Pecuniam* slowly through overlapping gravity fields from an asteroid belt looping around ahead of it; his ship wouldn't last much longer.

Maybe when he got to Epsion Octarius he would just leave the *Pecuniam* to rot and jump planet, try to find some other way to live out a lifetime he didn't deserve. Screw the docking fees. Screw the creditors.

But he knew full well he would just load up with food and luxuries from Epsion Octarius and start hauling them back to Jurn.

'Boss,' came a vox, warped and distorted from the stern of the ship. It was Lestin, the head of the engine crew and the only man Yambe trusted to keep the *Pecuniam* moving. 'Got a problem.'

Yambe spat. 'What kind?'

'Impact. Looks like something took out the fourth cluster.'

'"Took it out" like you can fix it or "took it out" like it's gone for good?'

'Kerrel went to take a look. Hasn't come back.'

Yambe didn't need to lose a man. The margin on this cargo would be low enough without having to hire someone new. 'I'm coming down. Don't anyone die till I get there.'

Yambe struggled out of his captain's chair, knocking the bottle of Second Best down into the guts of the cogitator array around him where the alcohol fizzed and popped against a hot coolant pipe. He swore liberally as he clambered over the chair and through the door in the bulkhead, feeling the ship thrumming painfully through the stained metal under his hand. A previous owner had carved machine-litanies into the girders and pipes, High Gothic pleadings to the Machine God to keep the ship safe and working. They didn't seem to be doing much good.

Through portholes in the corridor Yambe could see the cargo nets cradling massive volumes of building materials, tools, and weaponry, things Epsion Octarius couldn't make for itself. He jogged towards the stern along the long, arching dorsal corridor, feeling all his years and all his weight.

Once, on an armed merchantman out of Balur, he had been there when a plasma reactor vented into three decks, and heard two thousand men boiled in liquid fire. As a captain he had lost seven men when an airlock seal gave way. With each death you see, he believed, a little part of you turns dark and cold, which was why born spacers were all such hard-hearted sons of grox.

The corridor narrowed and split again and again, forming a lattice like a net which held in the bulbous forms of the plasma reactors, engine vents and warp generators.

Yambe forced a vox-bead into one ear. 'Lestin?'

'Found him, boss,' came Lestin's reply. He didn't sound as if this was a good thing.

'Where was he?'

'In about twenty pieces. Someone got him at the airlock, looks like he was running from something.'

'Like what?'

'We're not hanging around to find out. I'm closing the bulkheads around the fourth vent cluster.'

Yambe reached the ship's armoury, a dark little room where the crew's motley collection of weapons were racked up against the walls. Yambe pulled a naval shotgun from the rack and hurriedly snapped six rounds into the weapon's magazine. Shotguns were the weapon of choice of spacecraft where firefights were at close range and guns with greater penetrating power could punch through a wall and damage some vital system. Yambe paused to drag a tattered mesh armour jacket out of a cupboard and pull it over his shoulders. He headed back out into the corridor – the mesh jacket didn't cover much of his bulging stomach but it was better than nothing.

'Lestin, make sure the boys in the reactor crew are pulled back,' voxed Yambe. 'There's enough coolant channels from the vents to the reactors that anything could climb through.'

There was no reply.

'Lestin?'

Static filtered through the vox-bead. The vox-net on the *Pecuniam Omnis* was on its last legs, and seemed to go on the blink whenever it was most needed. This was what Yambe told himself as he racked the slide on his shotgun and hurried forward.

He heard footsteps approaching, weak and arhythmical. A shadow flickered in the weak glowstrip light and Yambe nearly blew the head off the figure that stumbled towards him.

It was the ship's Navigator. All Navigators were a strain of human – it was impolite to call them mutants, but that's what they were – who could look on the warp and guide a ship through it, and who were universally spindly and weak. The Navigator on the *Pecuniam Omnis* was no exception, but he was more than just weak – he was wounded. His dark blue Lower House uniform was black with blood, pumping from a wound in his chest, dribbling from his mouth and spattered on the pale skin of his face.

The Navigator, whose name was Krevakalic, fell forward into his arms and nearly knocked him flat on his back.

'What is it?' said Yambe, breathing hard. 'Where?'

Krevakalic slumped to the ground and looked up at Yambe from beneath the headband covering the third eye in his forehead, the warp eye. '…it… she was in… she came for me and Gell first…'

'Gell's dead?'

Krevakalic nodded.

That was bad news. Gell, as ship's astropath, was the only person who could transmit a psychic distress signal.

Krevakalic coughed and sprayed a gout of warm blood over Yambe. Yambe had to leave him – in a few moments he would die. Yambe had seen it before. His lungs and guts were laid open. It would be crueller to try to save him than to just leave him.

Yambe, meanwhile, had to press on. Not just because he had to find Lestin or any of the other crew, but because the ship's only working saviour pod was towards the stern and Yambe knew he could well have to get off the ship in a hurry.

He left the Navigator sprawled and dying on the floor of the corridor. If Krevakalic begged for Yambe to stay, the words were lost in the froth of blood bubbling from his lips.

The corridor opened up ahead into a wide circle that surrounded one of the plasma reactors, a bulbous cylindrical chamber five storeys high where the ship's energy was generated. The plasma core growled deeply as it provided power to the ship's systems, and white clouds of coolant vapour spurted from the pipes running along the floor and up the curving walls.

There was a body slumped over the closest control console. It was Ranl, a kid the *Pecuniam Omnis* had picked up at their last maintenance stop. Ranl was young and stupid and probably a criminal on the run, but he did what he was told and kept his head down. He hadn't deserved to have his head sliced off and his torso cut clean open, but that was what someone had done to him.

Yambe had never seen a man dead like that, killed and bisected as cleanly as if a good butcher had gone to work on him. Yambe looked around and saw Ranl wasn't the only one – there was another body draped over the railings around the upper level of walkways surrounding the plasma generator core. Yambe couldn't recognise him but his arms had been cut off and a rust-coloured streak of blood ran down the wall beneath him.

Something moved near the ceiling, scurrying too quickly for Yambe to make out, sweeping up and down as if it were actually running along the curved outer wall instead of along the walkways. Yambe tried to train his shotgun on it but it was gone before he could bring the barrel up.

His men were dying. Something had come onto his ship with the intent of killing everyone they found. They had gone for the astropath and Navigator first – that meant no distress signal and no escape.

Pirates? Yambe had had his brushes with them. Maybe even xenos – every spacer had heard more than enough tales of heathen aliens preying on Imperial shipping, from the callous and degenerate eldar to the murderous greenskins.

Maybe a more primitive life form. They said that the tyranid hordes that had swarmed over whole planets used fast, deadly creatures with multiple arms as scouts and spies, which could hitch a ride on ships on transit and kill everything on board. There were things that could possess crew members and creatures that could claw their way through the hull, all illustrated in lurid detail in tales told in bars, brothels and holding cells in ports all over the Imperium.

It moved again. Closer this time, further down, scurrying through Yambe's peripheral vision. He knew he couldn't hit it – it had to be something alien, something deadly. He wouldn't end up like Ranl. Damn the ship. Gak the cargo. He wasn't going to die out here.

Yambe ran out of the core, ducking his head to get through the low door leading towards the ship's stern. There was one saviour pod that he trusted to work – if no one had taken it already and if a ship passed close enough to pick up the distress signal, it might enable him to survive.

The further into the engine section Yambe got, the more cramped and filthy the ship became. Coolant vapour swirled around his feet. The stinking, oily air clogged up his nose and made his head throb. His breathing was so heavy it hurt – he was too old for this.

There was something over the vox. The film of thin static broke up and a man's voice came through, low and strong, resonant, confident.

'Captain Yambe,' it said. 'How much fuel does your ship hold?'

Yambe stopped. Lestin had the vox-bead. That meant the speaker had Lestin, and Lestin had been heading for the stern. Whoever had killed Lestin was between Yambe and the saviour pod.

Yambe turned and ran back the way he had come, ducking into a service tunnel that branched off and was barely high enough to run down. He needed somewhere to hide. The shotgun in his hands felt heavy and useless. There had to be somewhere to go. The *Pecuniam Omnis* was an old and filthy ship, with cavernous cargo spaces you could get lost in. Yambe had once picked up a stowaway who had given the crew the run-around for seven months. He had to hide. He had to survive.

Yambe blundered out into the ship's shuttle bay. The bay was a large, flat cavity between two of the reactors, and held the ship's single battered shuttle that was used for skipping between ships while in orbital dock. The shuttle was squat, tarnished and ugly, but if Ranl had remembered to refuel it as he had been told, Yambe should be able to start it and get the bay doors open in time to take off.

It was useless as a way out. It had air for about seven hours, no food, no water, and the energy cells were shot so it had to burn promethium just to heat the cabin. Its comm-link had such a limited range that it would never be found.

But it would let Yambe choose how he died. He could hide in the ship and try to outwit the invaders, or he could flee on the shuttle and pick a death from cold, suffocation, or just walking out of the airlock.

Yambe was about to head for the shuttle when a man walked out from behind it. Yambe began to raise his shotgun but out of nowhere a silver slash punched through his hand, slicing through to pin both the gun and the hand to his thigh. The shotgun's barrel pointed uselessly at the ground. White shock rushed through Yambe, followed by a red tide of pain. He sunk to his knees. The tip of the blade ground against the bone of his leg but refused to come free.

The man walking towards him was tall and well-built, wearing a battered, stained voidsuit and somehow still looking noble. His face was harsh and angular, his head shaven, and the skin of his face and scalp were covered in thick, blocky tattoos. His eyes looked straight through Yambe, so piercing that for a moment the captain forgot the pain in his hand and leg, and the hot blood spattering onto the floor.

'How much fuel,' repeated the man in that same thick deep voice that had come over the vox, 'does your ship hold?'

'Gak you, groxbanger,' snarled Yambe. Defiance was the only thing keeping him conscious. He would not die here. He would not. He was supposed to jump ship at Epsion Octarius and start a new life, away from space. He would not die.

The man threw something at Yambe, something warm and horribly wet that smacked into the side of his head and knocked him to the greasy metal floor. Pain rifled through him, and when the spots cleared from in front of his eyes Yambe saw Lestin's severed head lying on the floor beside him, jaw hanging off, eyes still open.

'How much fuel is there on this ship? Your man said he did not know.'

Yambe looked up. The intruder had absolutely nothing behind his eyes. For a second, it was like looking out into the warp, the endless Chaos that drove men mad.

'Enough…' stammered Yambe. 'Enough to get to Epsion Octarius from here. You could push the reactors for more.'

'Good,' said the man. He glanced to a point above and behind where Yambe lay. 'Kill him.'

Yambe looked around. There was someone standing over him – he hadn't heard them sneak up behind him. It was woman wearing a glossy black bodyglove, her face masked, her clothing tight over muscles like snakes coiled around her limbs. Gold-flecked eyes looked down at him, filled with disgust.

'I can't die here…' said Yambe, but that didn't stop her from drawing a long, gleaming sword and cutting him clean in two.

ALARIC COULD NOT feel the state of the Trail, as Ligeia had done, but it was clear enough from the reports coming into the fortress on Trepytos. The forge world of Magnos Omicron was in open civil war, where regiments of tech-guard loyal to the Imperium fought the titan legions that followed the world's blasphemous prophet. Volcanis Ultor was in a state of martial law, with Cardinal Recoba using the Balurian heavy infantry to patrol the streets and seal off the wealthy upper levels from the cultist hordes sure to emerge from the underhives.

The Trail's small battlefleet began harassing shipping between the worlds, destroying any freighter that could not give a satisfactory account of its crew and cargo.

An apocalyptic malaise fell over many worlds. Imperial citizens flocked to the cathedrals as rumours spread. Preachers led massed prayers for deliverance and forgiveness for the sins of the people against the Emperor, and in places it was impossible to tell the cults of Ghargatuloth and the Imperium apart.

Alaric was beginning to realise just how powerful Ghargatuloth must be. He could cause suffering and horror simply by the rumour of his existence.

PERHAPS ALL THE information Alaric needed was locked up in the archives on Trepytos. But he couldn't root through the endless vaults of decaying ledgers to find what he needed. Inquisitor Klaes's entire staff had tried many times before, and they had failed. All Alaric had to work with were the reports coming in from the rest of the Trail, and a handful of properly catalogued works on the Trail's history.

The room at the head of the archives was high and draughty, with watery shafts of light seeping through the tall, thin arched windows to pierce the gloom. A few of the fortress staff were working at the bookshelves that lined the room, bringing down reference works that Alaric had requested. He knew he would not be able to find anything that Ligeia had not already examined and dismissed, but he had to cover all the possibilities. There was too much at stake to assume anything.

In front of Alaric were hundreds of report sheets, each detailing some atrocity committed by the cults of Ghargatuloth. Bomb blasts, assassinations, uprisings, and more sinister things – heretical broadcasts over vid-nets, raids on Imperial cathedrals, mass kidnappings.

Inquisitor Ligeia had delved straight into the heart of darkness, into the beliefs and insanities that drowned the minds of Ghargatuloth's followers. Alaric could not do the same – compared to Ligeia's, Alaric's mind was a closed room.

'Brother-Captain,' said a familiar, deep voice. Alaric looked up from the stack of papers to see Tancred walking towards him through the archive room. A couple of the fortress staff looked round in surprise at Tancred's sheer size – he wore his Terminator armour, and in it he stood almost twice as tall as some normal men. 'Fortress astropaths have received the message that Genhain has reached Titan.'

'Good.' Alaric still hadn't got used to being addressed as 'brother-captain'. 'I want us ready to head out as soon as the *Rubicon* returns. We don't have any time left. Ghargatuloth is already rising.'

Tancred nodded at the piles of papers. 'How bad is it?'

'Bad. There isn't a world free of corruption. Even Magnos Omicron is suffering. The Planetary Defence Forces are completely overwhelmed. Local law enforcement is the same. The Arbites are doing what they can but there are just too many cults to pin down.' Alaric shook his head. 'How long have they been there? Sophano Secundus was one thing, it's an isolated world, one tainted individual could last for centuries there. But we're talking millions of men and women, in hundreds of cults across almost every single world of the Trail. And they've all lain dormant until now.'

'The Navy could quarantine the place. Declare a crusade.' Tancred was serious – whole sectors of space had been purged before. The Sabbat Worlds, the Asclepian Gap, a handful of others, each cleansed in a great crusade of Imperial armies and battlefleets.

'If the Trail was in open rebellion,' replied Alaric, 'and if the Eye of Terror wasn't tying up half of the Imperium's forces, then maybe the Malleus could do it. But not now. Ghargatuloth won't play his hand overtly enough to bring the whole of the Imperium down on him. It's up to us.'

'You sound as if you despair.' There was a dangerous note of steel in Tancred's voice.

'There is no despair, justicar,' replied Alaric. 'Not while one of us still lives. I am simply aware of how cunning our enemy is. Ghargatuloth has been planning this for some time, probably from before Mandulis banished him the first time. It might not even be an accident that he is returning at the same time the Eye of Terror is opening. And we have one advantage.'

Alaric picked up a handful of the reports, some of the worst. 'He's out in the open. All this is distraction, Tancred. He's trying to blind us, and as far as the Arbites and the PDFs are concerned it's working. But we are different. We know that until his cultists bring him fully back into real space, he will be vulnerable. Once he gets dug in like on Khorion IX it will take nothing short of a crusade to get to him, if we even keep track of him. But now he is vulnerable. He knows we are here, and he is afraid of us.'

'But how do we find him, brother-captain? We cannot fight what we cannot see.'

Alaric held out his arms, indicating the whole of the archives. 'It's here somewhere. Ghargatuloth's cultists have to make the preparations for the rituals that will bring him back, and most of the cults on the Trail are rising up just to distract the Imperium from those few who are making those preparations. Ligeia could have filtered out the real cult activity from the distractions, but she is not here, and so we must do it instead.'

'I should let you work, then. My men must stay sharp.'

'Of course. Emperor guide you, justicar.'

'Emperor guide you, brother-captain.'

Alaric watched Tancred leave. As far as Tancred was concerned, the Grey Knights should be fighting the vermin who were setting the Trail alight, not hunting through the archives for clues that probably weren't there. Tancred would never voice such doubts openly – he was too much a soldier, too aware of how he slotted in to the vital chain of command. But he could not hide his concerns from Alaric.

Alaric knew he could only ask obedience from his Grey Knights, and not control everything they thought. But he hoped that he could keep their trust for long enough to find a lead on Ghargatuloth, because Alaric could only fight one enemy.

TWELVE
THE VAULTS

THEY SAID YOU could feel the years on Titan, layers of history weighing you down. The truth was that Titan's gravity was slightly heavier than Terran standard due to the superdense core that had been injected into the moon some time during the lost Dark Age of Technology. But there was some truth to the saying – history was literally etched into the rock of Titan, faces of forgotten heroes, inscribed litanies of deeds once famous, murals depicting terrible battles against the forces of Chaos. The whole surface of Titan was inscribed as if by a huge chisel, forming a network of battlements and citadels, and it had been carved layer upon layer since before the dawn of the Imperium. There was so much history there that it would overfill all the libraries of the Inquisition, if only it could be unlocked.

Justicar Genhain wondered how much the Imperium could learn if its scholars could properly read all the images and messages that covered the walls of Titan's vaults. Beneath the upper levels of Titan, where the Grey Knights lived and prayed, were the catacombs where their dead were buried. Down here, there were vaults and tunnels carved by artisans from before the Ordo Malleus had even been formed from the fires of the Horus Heresy. As Genhain followed the procession down to the vault where his battle-brothers would be buried, he saw faces of Grey Knights in archaic marks of power armour, locked in endless combat with leering stone daemons. A column was wrought to represent an

157

unnamed saint of the Imperium. The names of battle-brothers covered
the vaulted ceiling; Grey Knights who had died in action but whose
bodies had never been recovered for burial.

Genhain walked behind Chaplain Durendin. In full black power armour,
the face of his helmet a skull of gunmetal grey, Durendin had walked these
tunnels many times before. As a Chaplain, he was the guardian of the dead
just as he guarded the spiritual health of the living brothers.

Behind Genhain, the battle-brothers of his squad carried the biers on
which lay the body of Brother Krae, the dead Grey Knight from Squad
Tancred that Genhain had brought back to Titan on the *Rubicon*. Brother
Caanos had died on Sophano Secundus, too, but his body had been left
on the planet. Genhain knew that if the Grey Knights were to close in
on Ghargatuloth, there would be many more to bury beneath Titan
before it was over.

Krae was covered in a white death caul, draped over the huge plates of
his Terminator armour. The shape of his Nemesis halberd was visible,
placed on his chest with his gauntleted hands folded over the hilt.
Behind Krae's bier, several novices walked. They were young trainees
who had only just begun the transformation into Grey Knights – they
carried the censers that filled the close air of the catacombs with the
dark, spicy smell of sacred incense. Genhain remembered the time,
almost hidden in the fog of psycho-doctrination and endless medical
procedures, when he had walked behind the funeral procession of a
dead Grey Knight and wondered how long it would be until it was his
body on the bier, draped in white.

The procession moved in silence through the catacombs. Here and
there the walls opened up into cells cut into the stone, each holding the
mouldering bones of a centuries-dead Grey Knight. Here and there were
inscriptions on the floor, almost obliterated by the marching feet of
countless funeral processions, detailing the names and histories of the
battle-brothers lying nearby. Genhain read fragments of names as he
passed. Some of the dead down here would not even be recorded in the
histories of the Grey Knights, having fought and died in times skipped
over by the earlier records.

Durendin reached the chamber where Krae was to be buried, and led
Squad Genhain and the novices in. Several stone coffins lay on
pedestals, perhaps fifty of them, ranged through the chamber. Three of
the pedestals had no coffin, and it was onto one of these that Krae was
placed.

Krae would lie there until Squad Tancred returned from the Trail,
when Tancred and Krae's battle-brothers would remove Krae's armour

and Nemesis weapon, ritually cleanse his body, and oversee the Chapter artificers as they built the coffin around the body.

In the earliest days, great heroes of the Grey Knights would be buried with their weapons and armour. But the valuable Terminator armour could not be spared, and soon it would be worn by a Space Marine newly inducted into one of the Chapter's Terminator squads. Krae's gene-seed, harvested from the body just after his death by Tancred himself, would be implanted into a novice and a new Grey Knight would take shape. His weapon would be handed to a Marine just receiving his first sacred blade, his bolter ammunition would be redistributed amongst the Chapter. In this way Krae would continue to fight the Great Enemy, and have his revenge against the foul forces that killed him.

'Before the sight of the Emperor most high, in the face of the Adversary, did Brother Krae fall in combat with the forces of corruption.' Durendin's voice was low and grim, and seemed to fill the whole catacomb. The *Liber Daemonicum* contained dozens of different funeral prayers, and Durendin had spoken each of them hundreds of times. Brother Krae had chosen one of the simplest to be spoken at his death – Genhain remembered Krae as a humble man, one who followed Justicar Tancred's orders absolutely, seeing himself as nothing more than an instrument of the Emperor's will.

Genhain and his Space Marines bowed their heads as Durendin continued. Behind them, the young novices hung on the Chaplain's every word, seeking meaning for themselves in the eulogy for the fallen Krae. 'The Enemy found no purchase in his mind, and no mercy from his arm. In the Emperor's sight did he fall, and at the Emperor's side will he fight to destroy the Adversary at the end of time. In the name of the Golden Throne and the Lord of all Mankind, let our Brother Krae live on through our fight.'

Durendin's prayer finished, the young novices filed out silently. They would return to their cells and meditate on all the battle-brothers like Krae who had fallen before, and whose gene-seed organs were now implanted in the novices to regulate their transformation into Grey Knights.

Genhain turned to Brother Ondurin, the Marine who carried his squad's incinerator and acted as unofficial second-in-command. 'Ondurin, take the squad back to the *Rubicon* and have the crew prepare to take off. I shall be with you shortly.'

Ondurin nodded and silently led the Space Marines of Squad Genhain back out of the chamber. It would take them two hours to reach the entrance to the catacombs.

Justicar Genhain was left alone in the chamber with Durendin.

'Brother-Captain Alaric did Brother Krae a great honour in delivering his body to Titan,' said Durendin. 'But he did not send you and the *Rubicon* just for that.'

'You're right, Chaplain. He has sent me to make a request.'

Durendin nodded. 'I received your astropath's message. It is a rare request. I do not know of a similar request being made for many centuries. It is even rarer for such things to be granted. Alaric explained all of this?'

'He did. He also explained that he has the authority of an acting brother-captain and that he can demonstrate an urgent need for the item I am here to collect.'

Somewhere within the skull helmet, Durendin smiled. 'Of course, justicar. But you understand the meaning of what you ask. As one of the guardians of our dead, I must consider such things very carefully. Follow me, justicar.'

Durendin walked off between the pedestals. Genhain glanced down and saw stone faces looking back up at him. They were stern faces covered in scars, and Genhain knew that the spirits of these Grey Knights were not at peace – they were still fighting, battling the Adversary as the Emperor did from the Golden Throne, and they would carry on fighting until the end of everything.

An arched doorway led off into a corridor, and Durendin led the way down it. Genhain followed into the gloom. Lumoglobes down here were spaced far apart and many had failed. The niches in the walls held bodies that had been there for centuries.

The tunnel curved downwards, describing a tight spiral that corkscrewed into the crust of Titan. Sculptures so old the details had been ground away by time lined the walls. Durendin's armoured footsteps echoed against the smooth stone floor.

The air got warmer. Genhain saw glimpses of carved Grey Knights wearing long-obsolete marks of power armour, of which a handful of examples survived on display in the Chapter's chapels and scriptoria. Exposed skeletons were all but handfuls of dust and gleaming white teeth.

Some way down, the tunnel opened up into a huge underground chamber. It was so wide that the far wall was like a horizon, the roof like a sky of stone. Large, elaborate structures filled the chamber like the buildings of a wealthy, sombre city of marble and granite.

'Our dead were not always buried side by side as brothers,' said Durendin, his voice low in the silence. 'Few realise it, but the Chapter does change. These levels survive from a time when the Grey Knights were buried like heroes in these cities of the dead.'

'How long ago?' said Genhain, almost unwilling to speak. Like every Grey Knight he had fought truly terrible things and witnessed sights that would drive lesser men mad, but still the oppressive, silent necropolis struck him with awe.

'The last was just over nine hundred years ago,' replied Durendin. 'Follow, justicar.'

Durendin walked out beneath the stone sky, down a broad avenue tiled with gleaming granite. Tombs rose on either side, many several storeys high, each different. Carved reliefs of battles adorned some, others bore monumental carved symbols – the stylised 'I' of the Inquisition alongside the sword-and-book symbol of the Grey Knights. Genhain saw a painted mural, the colours faded, of a Grey Knight in archaic Terminator armour fending off a tremendous horde of pestilent, tentacled daemons. Another tomb was topped by a massive marble Thunderhawk gunship, poised as if to ascend at any moment carrying the soul of the Marine buried beneath it.

Durendin turned a corner and Genhain saw, at the far end of the avenue, a building shaped like an amphitheatre. Arches in the circular walls looked in onto an area where hundreds of stone figures sat silently watching the raised obsidian block in the centre.

Durendin entered the amphitheatre. It was huge, the size of one of the grand gladiatorial arenas that could be found in the Imperium's more brutal hive cities. The watching figures were hooded and cowled, and wore the symbols of the various Imperial organisations – the Inquisition, Adeptus Mechanicus, Ecclesiarchy, Administratum, even the Adeptus Terra. The symbolism was powerful – every man and woman of the Imperium, whether they knew it or not, owed an impossible debt to the Grey Knights.

'You see why we bury our dead as brothers now,' said Durendin. 'Not kings.'

Genhain was momentarily lost for words. Saying such things had seen more than one novice chastised for impiety.

'The Grey Knights have made their own mistakes, justicar,' said Durendin. 'Alaric trusted you enough to send here, so I trust you to understand. Whole Chapters of Space Marines have fallen to pride before. No Grey Knight has ever fallen from grace, partly because the Chaplains have seen such sins as pride and tried to guide our brothers away from them. That is why we no longer bury our dead here.'

Durendin carried on down the steep steps, into the shadow of the obsidian tomb. Words in High Gothic were inscribed into the glossy black stone – names of worlds and crusades where the entombed Space Marine had fought, allusions to daemonic enemies he had vanquished, the honours bestowed on him by the lord inquisitors of the Ordo Malleus.

The last battle honour listed was Khorion IX.

Durendin spoke a whispered prayer. He passed a hand over a panel set into the sarcophagus and slowly, with a deep grinding noise from within, the obsidian lid slid open. The stone around the sarcophagus rose up to form marble steps leading up, and as the steps formed Durendin walked up them to stand over the head end of the sarcophagus. There was a strong smell of spices and chemicals, the resins and incense with which Grey Knight bodies were once prepared before burial.

Genhain followed Durendin up the steps. When he got to a level where he could see into the sarcophagus, he bowed his head with almost instinctive reverence.

Grand Master Mandulis had been buried without his armour, for he had died in a time when all precious suits of Terminator armour were passed on to Grey Knights who had just been granted Terminator honours. His shroud was old and yellowed and it clung tightly to the skeleton beneath, so the bones and the features of the skull were clearly visible. Genhain could see the surgical scars around the eye sockets and on the cranium, the breastplate of fused ribs, the holes where lifesign probes and nerve-fibre contacts had once connected to the body. Mandulis's warding, the anti-daemonic patterns woven into his armour, had burned so brightly in his final moments that they were still traced onto his bones in intricate spiralling paths.

Mandulis's skeletal hands were folded across his chest, and in them he still held his Nemesis sword. The lightning bolt design, wrought in gold, started at the crossbar and ran halfway up the blade. The gold and silver still glinted. The blade was so bright it reflected the distant stone sky, brighter and clearer, as if the weapon was so holy its very reflection was pure.

The more Genhain looked down at the grand master's body the more he could see what terrible damage had been wrought on it. Something corrosive had eaten away at the inside of the rib-plate, spilling over the clavicle to leave a scabrous honeycombed scar on the bones. Hairline cracks covered the limbs where they had been broken and then re-set by the apothecaries tending the body. The back of the skull was a web of fractures. Mandulis had died in the death throes of Ghargatuloth, and the daemon prince's malice was so great that he had shattered the body of a Grey Knight as if it were nothing.

'Were this anyone else,' said Durendin, 'Alaric's request would have been refused, brother-captain or not. But Mandulis died to banish Ghargatuloth. None of us could deny that he would make any sacrifice to help us do it again.'

Durendin reached down and unfolded Mandulis's fingers from around the hilt of the Nemesis sword, careful not to damage the old bones. He lifted the weapon, and handed it to Genhain. The blade was still as sharp as the day Mandulis had last drawn it.

It felt heavy in Genhain's hands. It had been made in an era when Nemesis weapons were handled differently – the blade was heavy, for chopping through armour and bone, while the Nemesis swords used by Genhain's battle-brothers were lighter and thinner for slashing and stabbing.

'It has been four hundred years since a tomb in the city of the dead was opened,' said Durendin. 'The Chapter wishes it could render Alaric more support, with Ligeia now gone. But Alaric knows as well as any of us that the Chapter is stretched woefully thin at the best of times, and with the Eye opening no Grey Knight can be spared. We know now that the threat of Ghargatuloth has been proven to be real, and we hope that the sword of Mandulis will help Alaric when his brothers at the Eye cannot. I wish I could impress this upon Alaric himself, but I trust you will convey my words.'

Genhain knew that Durendin could have spoken to Alaric himself, through astropathic relay. The fact that Durendin would not told Genhain that Durendin was not going to be on Titan for very much longer.

'Emperor be with you in the Eye, Chaplain,' said Genhain.

'May his light guide you on the Trail, justicar,' replied Durendin.

They walked down from the sarcophagus, which ground closed again over the body of Mandulis. Silently, the two Grey Knights began the long walk back towards the surface of Titan.

THERE WERE NO chances taken with Ligeia.

As soon as the *Rubicon* had arrived at Iapetus, Ligeia had been sedated and kept in a stupor until the interrogator command on Mimas had locked her up in the most secure holding cells they had. Normally reserved for prisoners in the throes of full-blown daemonic possession, Ligeia's cell floated in close orbit above the dark side of Mimas, anchored to the surface by a long metal cable. The only way to get to the grim, pitted metallic cube was to take a servitor-transporter that crawled like some parasitic insect up the cable to dock with the underside of the cell. The cube contained the cell and an observation room, a supply of enough oxygen and heating fuel to keep the occupant alive (both of which could be switched off instantly), and a fully-furnished interrogation array that would allow for intensive questioning assisted by both physical and psychic pressure of anything up to the ninth degree of intensity. The cell had not been deemed a resource suitable for Valinov, since he had never shown any psychic ability. But considering the circumstances of his escape, the Conclave on Encaladus had insisted that Ligeia be kept in the most secure location Mimas had.

Inquisitor Nyxos knew Ligeia. For normal men, that would make him a poor choice to interrogate her. An inquisitor, however, accepted that those he knew the best could still fall from grace and become a danger to the Imperium. Nyxos had been called in to break friends before – there were still such colleagues, even fellow inquisitors, rotting in the depths of Mimas. The only tragedy worse than an Imperial servant fallen to the Enemy, was one who fell and was not brought to justice. Nyxos was the automatic choice to conduct Ligeia's interrogation.

The servitor-transporter only had room for two passengers. Nyxos could taste the fear and desperation left in this place, from all those inquisitors and interrogators who had made this journey to converse with daemons bound in human flesh. The portholes looked out across Mimas's barren, broken surface, and in the black sky above hung the huge multicoloured orb of Saturn.

'Mimas command have given the word, inquisitor,' said Hawkespur beside him. Hawkespur was a brilliant young woman, headhunted for Nyxos's staff from the Collegia Tactica on St Jowen's Dock. Her face, normally youthful and flawless, was darkened by several livid bruises and she now walked with a cane. She had only narrowly avoided dying in the slaughter at Valinov's botched execution. Augmetic correction at Nyxos's expense would render her wounds invisible, but Hawkespur would be marked far more deeply by witnessing the cunning of the Enemy at first hand.

Nyxos had nearly died, too. Were it not for several redundant internal organs the death cultist's knife would have killed him in a moment. Nyxos banished the thought. There was no point in pondering how close you are to death, otherwise you live all your life in fear.

'Take us up,' said Nyxos. Hawkespur pressed the control stud and the transporter began to climb the cable, swaying as it went. Nyxos's servos whirred as they compensated for the movement. He had not been able to move under his own power for more than thirty years, not since he had been all but dismembered by cultists who had offered him up as a sacrifice to their gods. The experience had left his body broken, but his mind far sharper. He had seen what went on inside their heads. He had seen what the taint of Chaos did to a man, and glimpsed the sights they saw beyond the veil. Only an inquisitor had the strength of mind to understand such things and live.

The transporter reached the top of the cable and metallic grinding sounds indicated that it was docking with the cell.

'We're there,' Hawkespur voxed to Mimas interrogator command. There was a pause, and then the side of the passenger compartment slid open.

Through the door was a small monitoring room full of lifesign read-outs and cogitator consoles, with a window looking out into the cell itself. The air was cold and heavily recycled – it tasted metallic and almost hurt to breathe. A single door led into the cell, so an interrogator could enter the cell and talk to the prisoner face to face.

The prisoner was Inquisitor Ligeia. She was curled up in one corner of the white-tiled cell, dressed in the plain bone-coloured coveralls that the Mimas interrogators issued to isolated prisoners. Her hair, which Nyxos remembered as always being elaborately fashionable, was long and straggly, clinging to her face in greying rats' tails. Nyxos had never seen her looking so old.

She was shaking. It was cold in the cell, and at Nyxos's request she hadn't been fed for some time. She was kept almost permanently sedated, but she was just aware enough of her situation to be uncomfortable.

Nyxos settled his augmented body into the observation chair. He could feel the wounds deep inside him, like dull knives still stabbing.

Ligeia's lifesigns were stable. Her heartbeat flickered on one of the cogitator screens. Other monitors showed blood sugar and temperature. She was cold, hungry and tired.

Good, thought Nyxos.

'Wake her up, Hawkespur,' said Nyxos coldly.

Hawkespur took an injector gun from a cabinet beside the door, then punched a code into the door lock and headed through into the cell. Nyxos watched as Hawkespur injected a dose of stimulants into Ligeia's throat. Ligeia spasmed, then gasped and rolled onto her back, eyes suddenly wide, mouth gaping.

'Get her up,' said Nyxos into the vox receiver in front of him.

Hawkespur grabbed Ligeia by the scruff of the neck and hauled her into a sitting position against the back of the cell, using her cane for extra balance. Ligeia shook her head, then stopped shaking and looked around her, lucid again.

Hawkespur returned to the monitoring room, locking the door behind her.

'Ligeia,' said Nyxos carefully. 'Do you know where you are?'

The window was one-way. Ligeia would see only her own reflection looking back at her.

'No,' she said faintly.

'Good. The only facts relevant to you are that you will suffer if you do not answer our questions.'

'I'll... I'll suffer anyway...'

'Once you tell us what we need we can dispose of you and all this will end. Until then, we own you and will do with you as we see fit. You are an object now. You are a receptacle for knowledge that we will wring out of you. That process will be easier if you co-operate. You ceased to be a human being when you betrayed your species and your Emperor, the only way out for you is death. I can make it quick but those who come after me will not be so generous.'

Nyxos let her wait for a while, He wanted her to be the one who spoke next.

'It's Nyxos, isn't it?' she said at last. 'You knew me. They think you'll open me up quicker.'

Ligeia was sharp, always had been. That was one of the reasons the Malleus had headhunted her from the Ordo Hereticus. 'That's right. And we both know they made a mistake. I can't do to you the things they want me to, Ligeia, not to a fellow inquisitor. So this is your only chance.'

Ligeia put her hand over her eyes and shook. Silently, she was laughing. 'No, no, Nyxos. You're not my friend. I don't have any friends.'

'Your cultists were your friends. They died for you.'

'Do you know why they served me? I should have had them executed! They were heretics, they should have burned and they knew it. They just wanted to kill and so they killed for me.'

Nyxos paused. There was a chance that Ligeia was doing to him what Valinov did to her. If that was the case he had ordered Hawkespur to kill him at the first sign of deviance, an order he was certain she would be capable of carrying out.

'What did he tell you to do?' asked Nyxos bluntly.

Ligeia was shaking her head mournfully. 'No one told me to do anything, Nyxos. Don't you even understand that much yet? I saw what would happen. I saw what I had to do. There was no one controlling me, I didn't make any decisions to be influenced.'

'What did you see?'

'I saw that Ghargatuloth would rise and that Valinov would bring him forth. It wasn't bad, it wasn't good, it just was. Once I saw beyond the veil and forced myself to understand, it was all clear.' Ligeia looked up suddenly. Her red-rimmed eyes were fierce. Though she could only be staring at her own reflection, her gaze seemed to reach out and punch right through Nyxos's soul. 'Nothing you do, inquisitor, nothing anyone does, has the least bit to do with what you want. You do not control any action you take, you simply react to the changes around you. You are a puppet of the universe. The only thing that has any power in this galaxy or any other, the only thing worth seeking or worshipping or even giving a moment's thought, is that change that controls you.'

'The Lord of Change,' said Nyxos. 'Tzeentch.' Nyxos saw out of the corner of his eye as Hawkespur flinched at the name. The officer was so straight-laced the forbidden names still sounded wrong to her coming from the mouth of an Imperial servant

'Men give it a name,' said Ligeia, sadness in her voice. 'But it doesn't need one. Nothing any of us do will make a difference. Change had decreed that Ghargatuloth will rise and Valinov will make it happen. I was the only one who could free Valinov, and so I did it. I didn't make a choice. The act was completed before I began it.'

Nyxos sat back in his chair, watching Ligeia's movements as she slumped against the wall and stared at the ceiling. That was how she had been broken, then. She had been convinced that all human actions were governed by fate instead of free will, and that nothing she did was of her own volition. She had been absolved of all responsibility for her actions and turned into a puppet of whatever had been talking to her. Possibly Ghargatuloth itself, maybe Valinov through some unknown means, maybe another intermediary no one had detected yet. In any case, the undermining of Ligeia's spirit had been complete. Nyxos had seen it before, and he knew how hard it would be to break her now.

'Where is Valinov, Ligeia? What is he planning? Is he still in contact with you?'

Ligeia said nothing.

'You will tell us. You know that. You know that we will break you eventually and you will answer all the questions I have just put to you. You might say that you have already broken down, it's just a matter of time. Isn't that how the universe works, Ligeia?'

'Her heart rate's going up, sir,' said Hawkespur.

Panic always accompanied doubt. Doubt was an inquisitor's weapon.

'It will happen, Ligeia,' continued Nyxos. 'We broke Valinov. Do you really think you will hold out when he could not?'

'We don't choose,' said Ligeia quietly, as if to herself. 'We only serve.'

'Where is Valinov? What will he do? How will we stop him? You have to tell us, but you do not have to suffer. You can see that, can't you? You know how all this will end.'

'We only serve!' said Ligeia again, loudly this time. 'We serve the Change and the Change is our fate! Hear its words! Kneel in the darkness and obey the light!'

'Heart rate rising. Anomalous brainwaves.' Hawkespur's face was lit sickly green by the monitor screens. 'Much more and we may have to revive her.'

'Fate has already broken you, Ligeia!' shouted Nyxos as Ligeia began to whimper pathetically. 'Fate wanted us to arrest you and bring you here. It wanted you tried and executed, and it wanted you to tell us everything you know. Otherwise, why are you here? Fate brought you to this cell so I could give you the chance to talk before the explicators started working on you. What else could fate want, if not for you to talk?'

'She's going,' said Hawkespur as the cogitator interpreting her lifesigns suddenly started beeping alarmingly. 'Her heart's stopped.'

Ligeia spasmed again and suddenly sat bolt upright.

'Tras'kleya'thallgryaa!' she screeched, in a hideous atonal voice that seemed to break through the walls of the cell and straight to the inside of Nyxos's head. 'Iakthe'landra'klaa...'

Nyxos smashed a fist down on the emergency shutter controls and a steel curtain fell down in front of the observation window. Ligeia's voice was cut off. Nyxos had felt something monstrous in the words, something old and terrible. Ligeia was speaking in tongues, and it was one of the worst signs – her head was so full of forbidden knowledge that it was flooding out of her. Emperor only knew what damage her words could do to an unprotected mind.

'She's gone,' said Hawkespur. Ligeia's vital signs were flat green lines running across the cogitator screens.

'Bring her back,' said Nyxos. 'We have to give the explicators something to work with.'

Hawkespur pulled a medicae pack from beside the door, punched in the code, and hurried into the cell, where Ligeia lay sprawled on the tiled floor, twitching.

Nyxos watched Hawkespur take out a narthecium unit and pump Ligeia full of chemicals to get her blood flowing. Both Hawkespur and Nyxos would have to undergo a thorough mind-cleansing to ensure that Ligeia had left no trace on them of whatever was in her head. Ligeia would be quarantined even more completely – interrogation would be performed by remote control, with only pain-servitors allowed to go near the prisoner.

Ligeia coughed once and drew a long, sputtering breath.

'Leave her, Hawkespur,' said Nyxos, and rose from his chair. 'She was lost to us a long time ago.'

There was nothing left now but to lock Ligeia's cell, call a servitor-medic to stabilise her, and head back to Enceladus. The woman Nyxos had known was gone, her personality swallowed up by a mind full of blasphemies.

She would suffer much. But that was Mimas's problem now.

THE RUBICON MADE good speed back to Trepytos, carrying Squad Genhain and the sword of Mandulis. It docked above the Trepytos fortress just as the last of Inquisitor Klaes's few small ships left to keep a closer eye on the Trail. Klaes had a handful of interrogators, mostly drawn from the Trail's Arbites and the brighter of the fortress personnel, and now they were all but immersed in the slow madness engulfing the Trail of Saint Evisser. Alaric had impressed on Klaes the importance of high-quality information about the cult activity rising everywhere, and so all the men Klaes had at his disposal were scattered throughout the Trail. Klaes himself left on the last ship, heading for Magnos Omicron where civil unrest was threatening to tear the forge world's great cities apart. Klaes's priority had to be the citizens of the Trail – the Grey Knights on the other hand were no use on the front lines, where their small numbers would ultimately mean nothing. Alaric had to concentrate on Ghargatuloth, and hope the authorities on the Trail of Saint Evisser could keep the systems in check long enough for the Grey Knights to make a difference.

Genhain found Alaric still in the archives, surrounded by spilling heaps of books and papers. Alaric had removed his armour and worked by candlelight – it was night on Trepytos and the lumoglobes high in the ceiling did nothing but tint the darkness yellow.

Alaric was absorbed in his work. Several data-slates lay on the table in front of him, amongst scores of open books and sheafs of loose papers. Numerous plates and empty cups were piled up, too – Alaric was spending so much time in the library he had ordered the remaining fortress staff to bring his food to him there. He was scribbling notes with an autoquill, the candlelight glinting in his eyes. A Space Marine could stay awake for more than a hundred hours without negative effects, but even so it looked like Alaric had gone without sleep for some time. It had taken more than three weeks for the *Rubicon* to make the return journey to Saturn, and it seemed to Genhain that Alaric had been awake almost the whole time.

'Brother-Captain,' said Genhain carefully.

Alaric paused a moment, then looked up. 'Justicar. It is good to see you.'

Genhain held up the sword of Mandulis. Its heavy, razor-sharp blade felt as if it were alive. The bright blade seemed to make the whole room slightly brighter, reflecting and magnifying the dim light. 'Durendin said Mandulis would have wanted you to wield this.'

'I won't wield it, not if I can help it. Tancred is better with a sword than I am.' Alaric put down his quill and sat back in his chair. 'Forgive me, justicar. You have done well. There was no guarantee the Chapter would grant us this, thank you.'

Genhain walked up to Alaric and laid the sword on the table. 'Brother Krae was lain out.'

'Good. I will let Tancred know. I only wish we could have brought Brother Caanos back with us.'

The Grey Knights had left Brother Caanos behind on Sophano Secundus, burying him after harvesting his gene-seed.

Genhain looked around at the piles of books surrounding Alaric. 'Are we any closer?'

'Maybe,' said Alaric wearily. 'Ghargatuloth uses his cultists to hide his true intentions. All this is misinformation.' He waved a hand over the piles of reports, each one detailing some new atrocity. Persons unknown had sabotaged the geothermal heatsinks on Magnos Omicron, destroying several layers of the forge world's capital hive. A group calling themselves the Nascent Fate had taken control of the media transmitters on an orbital station and filled the airwaves for several systems around with non-stop broadcasts of blasphemous sermons. 'Ghargatuloth is talking to his followers, and they are doing everything they can to raise hell on the Trail so those who are doing his true work will go unnoticed.'

'Can we be sure what the Prince is doing?'

Alaric looked up at Genhain. 'Right now Ghargatuloth is weak, and he has to fight to survive. Ultimately, everyone fights the same. You hide your strengths, move them into position, and strike. Ghargatuloth might herald the Lord of Change but for the moment he's scrapping for survival just like all of us.'

Genhain leafed through a couple more of the reports. There was a rash of mutated births on Volcanis Ultor, and shipping throughout the

Trail was reporting crewman driven suddenly insane for no reason. 'There is so much here. Ghargatuloth could be doing anything. That's why Ghargatuloth drove Ligeia mad – he knew she could sort through it all and find what really counted.'

Alaric sighed. For the first time, Genhain saw Alaric somewhere close to defeat. 'Mimas transmitted her interrogation logs. She's insane. Speaking in tongues. Klaes is helping, but it's all his staff can do to keep bringing the information in. I had wanted to leave as soon as you brought the *Rubicon* back but until we make some sense of this there is nowhere for us to go.' Alaric stood suddenly, and took hold of Mandulis's sword. Like every Space Marine, Alaric was a huge man, but even so the sword's long, broad blade made him look small. Emperor only knew what Mandulis must have looked like, wielding it in battle. Alaric held the blade, turned it in his hand, looked at his face staring back at him. The reflection picked out the hollows around his eyes, the lines in his face. The sword reflected more than just light – it was so pure that it saw the truth. After a thousand years buried on Titan, it was still as sacred as the day it had been forged. 'Inquisitor Klaes has given us the run of the fortress,' said Alaric with sudden determination. 'Levels seven through twelve are derelict – Tancred is running urban combat drills there with his squad. Have your men join him, I need them battle-fit. My men will join you later.'

'Yes, brother-captain. Where will you be?'

'Praying,' replied Alaric. 'I need to think without all this… this noise.' He indicated the piles of books and papers. 'Ghargatuloth does not have to corrupt us directly to fuddle our minds.'

'Durendin told me some truths I believe he would rather you heard directly,' said Genhain. 'It is not my place to repeat them, but… brother-captain, I feel Ligeia was right to choose you.'

'That remains to be seen, justicar. Now attend to your men, I hope I shall be able to call on them soon.'

'Yes, brother-captain.' Genhain turned to leave. 'Emperor guide you.'

'I hope he does, justicar,' replied Alaric. 'Without him we are lost.'

THIRTEEN
HIVE SUPERIOR

CARDINAL RECOBA'S OFFICES were alive with activity. The liaison officer from the Adeptus Arbites had taken over a side chapel and was yelling impassioned orders into a vox-relay as he moved Arbites units to support local law enforcement all over Volcanis Ultor. The three adepts who made up the chief Departmento Munitorum presence sat surrounded by reams of printouts and requisition forms, dozens of lesser adepts running messages to and from them as they tried to organise supply lines for the forces still arriving at the hive world. Representatives from various noble houses, including that of Volcanis Ultor's Imperial Governor, wandered the lower corridors and the anterooms trying to get someone to listen to them.

Cardinal Francendo Recoba had seen the crisis growing and had ensured that he would be in charge. Governor Livrianis was under effective house arrest, to prevent his potential corruption. He was a slow and cowardly man at heart – it took Recoba to manage a potential catastrophe like this. Volcanis Ultor was the primary hive world on the Trail, its population accounting for a good proportion of all the citizens of the Trail, and it had to be held against the hidden tide of heresy at all costs. Recoba was the only man with the respect and natural authority to lock the planet down, and organise a military defence for when the crisis truly broke and the legions of the Enemy rose from amongst them.

Recoba had long preached to his fellow clergy that the Ecclesiarchy could only enforce the true meaning of the Imperial cult if it had temporal as well as spiritual authority. Here was his proof – the Trail of Saint Evisser needed faith now more than anything, and its chief hive world had chosen Cardinal Recoba to lead its defence. This would be a battle for the spiritual survival of Volcanis Ultor and of the whole Trail, even more than it would be a physical conflict, and Recoba was determined to be in control.

Recoba's offices occupied several layers of Hive Superior, the capital hive of Volcanis Ultor. It was located in the secondary spire – the primary spire, where the governor's family and sub-families lived, was locked down completely with the troops of the hive's Municipal Order Regiment guarding every entrance. Recoba's private chambers occupied three layers, which he maintained as his personal realm where only trusted advisors and invited representatives could tread. The rest were divided into grand areas for receiving dignitaries and private chapels where Recoba normally ministered to the spiritual needs of Volcanis Ultor's elite, and it was in these layers that leaders from all the authorities active in Volcanis Ultor's defence had set up headquarters. Recoba had just received the canoness of the Order of the Bloody Rose, whose Battle Sisters were now reinforcing the defensive lines around Lake Rapax just outside Hive Superior. Several Imperial Guard officers were also trying to get a foothold in Recoba's realm, to coordinate the Guard regiments now policing the planet's hotspots and forming defensive positions.

At that moment, the crisis seemed some distance away. Recoba sat in his state room, reviewing some of the field reports coming in. The state room was furnished as a lavish bedchamber, though Recoba never slept here, only received his most trusted advisors. It did him good, he knew, to retire to his state rooms when everything around him was at its most hectic. He, above all, had to keep a clear head. It would be too easy to get drawn into the details – a hundred lives here, a hundred lives there. He took a sip of imported Dravian wine – a good vintage, something he had been saving for a crisis – and went back to reviewing the overall state of Volcanis Ultor.

Recoba saw that almost half the levels in Hive Tertius were still out of contact, having been overrun by factory workers under the influence of some kind of popular messianic movement. Recoba shook his head and tutted. He had hoped the sealing of the main exit routes would be the end of the troubles in the hive, but now it looked like the survivors were in danger of losing their minds to the tide of heresy. He would have to send the scout platoons of the Methalor 12th Regiment into the hive to keep the madness from spreading.

The next report he picked up from his writing desk was a communiqué from the colonel of the Salthenian 7th Infantry Regiment. He regretted that he was unable to commit his regiment to the defence of Volcanis Ultor, citing garrison duties on Salthen itself. Recoba sighed. He would have to call in a few favours from the clergy on Salthen, and show the colonel how a few well-chosen words from the regimental preachers could make his commission look very shaky indeed.

There was a knock on the chamber's hardwood door. Recoba looked up in annoyance. 'Enter,' he said sharply.

A valet servitor opened the door with a polished chrome hand. Deacon Oionias walked in, a young but eager man who Recoba trusted as a messenger and aide. 'Your blessedness,' said Oionias. 'There is someone who most urgently needs to speak with you.'

'Remind this someone that my office has protocols. My time is valuable. Have him go through Abbot Thorello if it's important.'

'That's just the thing, your blessedness,' said Oionias. His plump face was slightly red. 'He says he has the authority to address you directly.'

'I do not have the time to–'

'You have the time for *me*, cardinal,' said a resonant voice from behind Oionias. A man walked in, breezing past the young deacon – he was tall and well-built, with a sharp, noble face and intelligent eyes. He wore a splendid traveller's cloak of flakweave trimmed in ermine over a dark green officer's uniform with several sheathed knives worn across the breast. His synth-leather boots shone like glass.

'Forgive my intrusion, your blessedness,' he began graciously with slight bow, 'but we are better served by dealing with one another directly. I bring news critical to the defence of Volcanis Ultor, and to the survival of the whole Trail.'

Recoba felt slightly less aggrieved. 'What authority do you represent?'

'I am honoured to bring the tidings of the Holy Orders of the Emperor's Inquisition,' said the visitor, taking a small Inquisitorial rosette from inside his cloak. 'I am Inquisitor Gholic Ren-Sar Valinov, and I fear our Enemy may be even more dangerous that you suppose.'

THE BATTLEMENTS OF the Trepytos fortress were bleak and cold. The dark granite blocks of the fortress formed grim, blunt teeth along the edge of the battlements and the dismal half-decrepit city around the fortress spread out towards a barren grey-brown plain. Trepytos used to be beautiful. Now, it was drained and dying. The fortress was still formidable, with sheer unscaleable walls and a massive set of gates protected by watchtowers and scores of gun emplacements – but the emplacements had rusted solid and the garrison that once permanently manned the walls was long gone. The fortress had been there since before the Ordo Hereticus chose it as the Inquisition headquarters for the Trail, but it was difficult to imagine anything for it now but slow, grim decay.

Alaric stood on the battlements, his augmented eyesight picking out the faint glimmer of the planet's weak sun on the edge of the ocean some distance away. The *Rubicon* was a sliver of silver in the sky directly overhead, and there were lights scattered throughout the inhabited parts of the city. The winds sheared across the battlements and most men would be chilled to the bone. Alaric barely noticed it.

He was so close. He knew it. He had an advantage Ghargatuloth had not expected the Grey Knights to get – he had faced one of Ghargatuloth's chosen champions on Sophano Secundus, someone he was not supposed to find. That meant that the place that had led the Grey Knights there – the cult temple in the Administratum building on Victrix Sonora – was important, too.

'Brother-Captain!' called Justicar Tancred over the driving wind. He was walking towards Alaric in full armour, and he was taller even than the megalithic teeth of the battlements. 'The staff found what you needed.' There was a data-slate in Tancred's gauntlet.

'Good,' said Alaric, taking the slate. 'We may have to leave very soon. Are you ready?'

'Always, brother-captain.' Alaric saw Tancred was sweating and the sheen was off his armour – he had only recently finished training rites with his squad. Tancred had been training gradually harder and harder, Alaric had noticed, turning derelict floors of the fortress into warrens of kill-zones for the Grey Knights to battle through. Justicar Santoro had been driving his Space Marines hard, too, taking them on endless squad drills along the walls and through the fortress's upper levels. The Grey Knights needed to fight. The Trail was going insane around them, and to them it was blasphemy to just sit by and watch it happen.

'Do you know where to look?' asked Tancred.

'I know where to start,' said Alaric. 'I know why Ghargatuloth drove Ligeia mad. It is information that is his weakness. If we have too much of it, we can use it against him. Think about it. We hurt him on Sophano Secundus, because we found a part of his plan that had been there since before he was banished. That's where the link is.'

'The link?'

Alaric began flicking through the files on the data-slate. 'We know the cult on Victrix Sonora raided Ecclesiarchy sites and stole relics. They had been doing so for a long time, since before they were detected at all. The Arbites thought it was just spite, and with everything else the cultists did no one thought it was important.' Alaric paused. 'And... and on Sophano Secundus Missionary Crucien based his cult in the Imperial Mission. He could have hidden it anywhere in the forests, in the mountains – there was a whole planet to hide it in. But he stayed in the most obvious location there was, a place sanctified by the Imperial Church. Why?'

'The Enemy is perverse,' said Tancred simply. 'They need no logic.'

'But it's not just Sophano Secundus. Why here at all?' Alaric held his arms out wide, indicating everything around him. 'The last time Ghargatuloth reigned, he laired on Khorion IX. That was on the far edge of the Segmentum Pacificus, it took us a hundred years to find him. Why the Trail? There are backwaters more decrepit than the Trail, there are whole sectors of empty space where he could hide. What makes the Trail of Saint Evisser special?'

'Saint Evisser?' said Tancred.

'Saint Evisser. Ghargatuloth has his cults collecting Imperial relics. He needs the biggest relic of all to complete the ritual that will bring him back.' Alaric held up the data-slate. It was showing a set of planetary coordinates. 'The Hall of Remembrance on Farfallen was the biggest Ecclesiarchical archive on the Trail. As far as we know it's still there. We are going to find out where the body of Saint Evisser is buried, because that is where Ghargatuloth will rise.'

THE PRIMARY DEFENCES of Volcanis Ultor described a semicircle around the base of Hive Superior, several hundred kilometres of hastily-dug trenches, prefabricated bunkers and command posts, endless rolls of barbed wire, emplacements for Basilisk self-propelled guns and even an immense Ordinatus artillery piece manned by Volcanis Ultor's class of tech-priests. Hundreds of supply trenches zig-zagged back through the pollution-bleached ground into the outer reaches of the hive, crawling with thousands of men from the Balurian heavy infantry, Methalor 12th Scout Regiment, 197th Jhannian Assault Regiment and Volcanis Ultor's own PDF. Rearward positions were held by men and women drafted from Hive Superior's underhive gangers, who had answered the call of the Departmento Munitorum and joined the defence in return for being allowed to keep the weapons they were issued with. The strongpoint at the northern end of the line, where the broken plain met the shore of

Lake Rapax, was held by the Sisters of the Order of the Bloody Rose, and Cardinal Recoba had personally sent hundreds of preachers and confessors to the front lines so spiritual leadership would never be far away from the troops.

The attack, when it surely came, would come from the plains in front of the defences. The jagged mountain ranges on the far side of Hive Superior meant that the plains were the only place an arriving army could gather, and the defences would be ready for them. Recoba knew that if Hive Superior was overrun, Volcanis Ultor would fall, and with it the keystone that held the whole Trail intact. He had drawn troops and resources from all over the planet and even off-world, sacrificing the smaller hives and inter-hive settlements to ensure that Hive Superior would survive.

The northern half of the line was served by a rearward command centre, a massive plasticrete arena of bunkers and parade grounds built along standard template lines and dropped from orbit by a Mechanicus transport just a few days before. Rings of overlapping gun emplacements surrounded it and Hydra anti-aircraft quad autocannon were mounted to cover central parade ground. Transport and staff shuttles zipped overhead, and the sky was patrolled by an occasional Thunderbolt fighter of which three squadrons had been scrambled to the surface. A pulpit and lectern had been set up in the centre of the parade ground, linked to vox-casters and to the comm-net that covered the entire hinterland of Hive Superior.

As the sun's murky morning light filtered through the clouds of pollution overhead, troops began filing into the parade ground. Several platoons of Balurian heavy infantry were first, smart and well-drilled. The Methalorian scouts were less polished in their parade ground skills, and they had a ragtag appearance with each carrying non-issue weapons and gear, from camo-cloaks to orkish combat knives. The Guardsmen were from units who were still waiting to be assigned to a section of the defences – every one of them would be heading to the front line within a few hours. There were even some of the conscripted hive gangers milling around towards the back of the parade ground, almost feral figures in clashing gang colours who carried trophies from gang-scraps in the depths of Hive Superior.

Officers yelled at the men to redress ranks and smarten up. A couple of commissars prowled, and everywhere they looked Guardsmen stiffened at attention. They all knew they could soon be in the thick of fighting against Emperor knew what kind of enemy. Even the gangers mostly fell silent.

Finally, Cardinal Recoba's staff arrived to take their places beside the pulpit. Recoba himself wore his full cardinal's regalia, the crimson and white standing out amongst the drab fatigues of the soldiers, the gold of his mitre glinting in the murky light of the rising sun. There were several deacons and preachers with him, along with the lexmechanics and protocol officers who followed senior officers everywhere.

Finally, alone, Inquisitor Valinov entered the parade ground, and ascended to the pulpit. Vox-casters would send his voice booming across the parade ground, and across the comm-link so that thousands of soldiers could hear his every word. Cardinal Recoba had required all officers to ensure their men were listening. The media of Hive Superior were broadcasting, too, because Recoba knew how important Valinov's words would be.

Valinov looked out over the thousands of men assembled on the parade ground. The eyes looking back at him didn't know who he was. That meant he could be whoever he wanted to be. It was something he had learned a long time ago, as an interrogator in the service of Inquisitor Barbillus. He wore polished carapace armour and an antique power sword, taken from the armoury of the Governor's household – today, Gholic Ren-Sar Valinov was a hero.

'Men and women of Volcanis Ultor,' he began. 'Soldiers, Sisters and citizens. All of you know that a dark time has come to the Trail of Saint Evisser, and that darker times still are yet to come. The Enemy, who we must now speak of freely, has come to the Trail. I have seen this Enemy, and fought it, and believe me when I tell you it can be beaten. You will see things that may make you despair, things that you cannot understand, but you must fight. The Enemy fights with lies, and will use confusion and dissent to break your resolve. It cannot succeed. No matter what, you must fight, and carry on fighting until the Trail is free. That is the order I give you that supersedes all others, by the authority of the Holy Orders of the Emperor's Inquisition.'

Valinov paused. The existence of the Inquisition was officially suppressed, but rumours were the most universal currency of the Imperium. Guardsmen talked over bottles of bootleg spirits about the figures who could kill planets with a word and purge entire populations to root out the taint of corruption. Valinov would be one such figure – a legend come to life, a story made real. The soldiers had flinched when they realised that an inquisitor was in command – a real, genuine inquisitor! Even the lexmechanic scribbling down a record of his words had paused.

'But there is a far darker truth that I must tell you. You have all heard of the Adeptus Astartes, heroes of the Imperium. The defenders of mankind.' Valinov knew well that they had – the Balurians had fought alongside the White Consuls at the Rhanna Crisis, and the chapels of Hive Superior had stained glass windows depicting the Ultramarines who destroyed the rebels of Hive Oceanis centuries before. If inquisitors were figures in dark stories told on long nights, Space Marines were the heroes of wide-eyed children's tales. 'And you have all been told of the Horus Heresy, when the Enemy stole away the minds of billions and waged a civil war against the Emperor-fearing people of the Imperium. It is my duty to tell you that the Space Marines were at the heart of this conflict. Fully half their number fell to the Enemy and marched with Horus.'

Valinov let that sink in, too. Imperial histories – as told to the ordinary citizens who needed to know no more – glossed over the details of the Horus Heresy, and of the Traitor Legions of Space Marines who fell to Chaos.

Valinov let his voice rise. He could see the eyes of the soldiers growing wide. For one of them to say these things would be heresy – for an inquisitor to say them was a revelation.

'For ten thousand years those Traitor Marines have held their grudge. Now they are returning, for the Eye of Terror has opened and the eyes of the Enemy fall again on the galaxy. The Traitor Marines think that the Trail is the weak underbelly of the Imperium. They think that with so many of our forces at the Eye, they can do what they want with our worlds and our homes. If we stop them here, they will be thrown back into the darkness, and the touch of the Enemy that curses the Trail will go with them.

'I tell you this because the Traitor Marines are coming here, to Volcanis Ultor. I have been sent ahead of them by the daemon hunters of the Inquisition to ensure that you understand what you are fighting. In a few days they will be here. They were once the Imperium's finest soldiers, now corrupted beyond redemption, but they are expecting to meet no resistance. We have the advantage of surprise. That is why the battle will be here, and that is why it must be won.

'Recognition documents are being circulated to every officer now. Understand the form and markings of this enemy! In their arrogance they proudly display the marks of their heresy. The sword and the book is their symbol. To parody the nobility of what they once were, they call themselves the Grey Knights. They bring with them daemons and foul sorcery, but we have the hearts of Imperial citizens and the steel of the Emperor's will!'

Valinov could taste the heady mix of emotions. Fear, because every Guardsman had heard of Space Marines but never expected to see one, let alone have to go against their legendary strength in battle. Pride, because they were the ones trusted to stop them. Awe, because suddenly the defence of a single hive city had become a crusade against darkness, led by a hero of the Imperium.

'Take your positions, obey your commands, have faith in the Throne of Terra and show the Enemy no quarter! For here will the Enemy's will be broken, and here will be forged your future.'

Everyone had heard of Space Marines. Some had heard of the Inquisition. No one had heard of the Grey Knights. The Inquisition's own obsessive secrecy was its greatest failing, an irony Valinov enjoyed as he stepped down off the pulpit and turned his thoughts to the coming battle.

LIGEIA HAD ASKED for Valinov's execution to be stayed. There was no one left to ask for Ligeia.

Ligeia was still in her cell, anchored just above Mimas's upper atmosphere. All interrogations had elicited only the same garbled stream of syllables she had uttered when Nyxos had broken her. She was all but useless as an intelligence source, and her freeing of Valinov marked her as an enemy of the Imperium and an immediate moral threat.

The lord inquisitors came to the only conclusion they could. Ligeia had to die.

Inquisitor Nyxos stood in the interrogator command control room at the heart of the Mimas facility, waiting patiently as the interrogators, explicators and chief medicae staff made the last few checks on Ligeia. In the past, particularly corrupt prisoners had waited until the moment of their execution to display Chaos sorcery they had managed to hide until then. Ligeia, however, had not changed – she was still in a constant state of physical shock, her heart rate fluctuating, her brainwaves fractured and haphazard. Several pict-stealers watched her from many angles, but all she did was curl up in the corner of her cell and shiver. She had nearly died when Nyxos had interrogated her, and since then had been just a few steps from death.

'No lifesign change,' said one of the medicae as the final checks were completed.

'Negative brainwave change,' said another.

The chief medicae, an elderly, portly man who had taken on the role after the death of his predecessor at Valinov's botched execution, turned to Nyxos. 'Medical go.'

'Good,' said Nyxos. 'Explicator command?'

The chief explicator's voice was voxed from elsewhere in the facility. 'Psychic activity residual only. No change.'

Nyxos stepped up to the comm-pulpit, which was connected to Ligeia's cell via several warded filters that lessened the likelihood of her words corrupting the listener.

Nyxos opened the channel. His voice was fed directly into the cell.

'Ligeia,' began Nyxos, 'this is the end. I promised you it would be over and now it is. There is one last chance before you die. Tell us where Valinov is, tell us what he is doing. Do this and the Emperor may show you mercy where men cannot.'

Ligeia stirred. She lifted her head and looked up at one of the pict-stealers, and on the screen Nyxos could make out her deathly pale, almost translucent skin, her sunken red eyes, grey hair clinging to her damp skin. She shook and seemed to be choking on something, her fingers curling into claws, her jaw clenching and unclenching.

'Tras'kleya'thallgryaa!' she yelled suddenly, as if vomiting the words up from somewhere deep inside her. 'Iakthe'landra'klaa! Saphe'-drekall'kry'aa!'

Nyxos snapped the sound feed off, leaving Ligeia screaming silently out of the monitor.

'She is lost. In the sight of the Emperor, witness her excommunication from the human race and the extinguishing of her corruption.'

Nyxos slammed his fist down on a large control stud on the pulpit. Soundlessly, the back wall of the cell blew out and the image shook violently as the air was torn away. Ligeia grabbed instinctively, digging thin fingers between the tiles, hanging on as suddenly the blackness of space was shockingly close. The cell was open to space, the barren frozen rock of Mimas below, the glowing banded disk of Saturn above, the blackness streaked with stars and the smears of dust that made up Saturn's rings.

Ligeia looked with horror at the void in front of her. For a few moments she tried to crawl towards the front of the cell, her eyes fixed on the endless darkness. But then something inside her finally realised it really was the end. She lay helpless on her back as the freezing cold seized up her limbs and the vacuum paralysed her lungs. Her eyes flooded red as blood vessels burst. She gasped silently for air that wasn't there. Then, she stopped moving altogether, red eyes wide, mouth frozen open.

Nyxos watched her for some minutes, trying to detect the slightest movement. There was nothing.

'Monitor her for three days,' he said eventually to the interrogator command staff. 'Then destroy the body.'

An inquisitor was due a proper burial, below the fortress on Enceladus if possible. But Ligeia wasn't an inquisitor any more. Aside from a warning footnote, she would be better off forgotten completely.

FOURTEEN
FARFALLEN

FARFALLEN WAS A dying world. It had once been a garden world, one of those rare breed of planets kept pristine as rewards and playgrounds for the Imperium's nobility. Retirement on a garden world tempted the most ambitious of planetary governors and rogue traders to toe the Imperial line. At the height of the Trail, when the mass pilgrimages had given plenty the opportunity to leach fortunes from the faithful, Farfallen had been a wondrous mixture of lush virgin forests and carefully manicured landscape gardens. White marble villas had nestled in the fronds of towering rainforests. Elaborate turreted castles of coral had looked out on an endless azure sea. Sky yachts plied the clouds and elderly nobles hunted imported big game on the vast rolling plains.

The Ecclesiarchy, who could claim the greatest credit for the Trail's prominence, maintained a great estate on Farfallen, and used it as the seat for the Hall of Remembrance where the Trail's religious legacy would be collected and compiled for posterity. The Administratum took a tithe of land from the garden world, so Consuls Majoris of the Administratum could themselves retire in splendour.

With a stable ecosystem, hardly any predators, a predictable temperate climate and the protection of the Adeptus Terra, Farfallen had been a rare paradise in the grimness of the Imperium. But that had been a long time ago.

Much of Farfallen was untended and overgrown. Landscaped gardens fell into disrepair and tree roots broke up the marble buildings. With fewer fortunes to be made on the Trail only a handful of noble families remained, ageing and cut off, retreating into their estates as Farfallen became wilder. Imported game predators could no longer be controlled by hunting and they turned the jungles into savage places. And somewhere, somehow, the uninvited had come to Farfallen – feral humans who infested the deepest jungles. For centuries no one noticed them, and they remained hidden from Farfallen's dwindling Imperial population.

Then Ghargatuloth's call went out across the Trail, and suddenly hundreds of thousands of savages poured from the forests to do the work of the Change God.

THE GREY KNIGHTS had lost two Thunderhawks on Sophano Secundus and so Alaric took only as many Marines as would fit into the remaining gunship – he chose his own unit and Squad Genhain. He might discover something unpalatable, and he trusted Genhain to cope with it best of all.

Alaric watched the surface of Farfallen from the Thunderhawk as it made its approach. It was late evening and the thick carpet of forest was dark green, the curling fronds of the trees like the bristles on an animal's hide. It was easy to see how the dense forests had hidden the feral tribes, and how they could be corrupted away from Imperial eyes.

The forest sped past beneath the Thunderhawk and on the horizon Alaric could see the Hall of Remembrance. It was built into a cliff that soared above the forest canopy, a massive blocky shape carved from the rock face. High arched windows like dead eyes looked out from beneath a deeply carved pediment depicting the heroic figures of past Ecclesiarchs, trampling the minions of Chaos beneath their feet.

As the Thunderhawk swooped lower for the final approach Alaric could pick out signs of the chaos on Farfallen. Lights from fires burning at ground level flickered on the stone. Charred tatters marked the places banners had once hung. The edges of the roof were scarred where crude catapults had slung stones and balls of fire at defenders firing down. The jungle on the top of the cliff just above the hall's roof was chewed and trampled – early on the ferals had tried to climb down the cliff, only to be shot off the rocks as they made the descent. Some broken, desiccated bodies were still wedged into cracks in the cliff face, a testament to the first moments of the attack. The Hall of Remembrance, the most visible Imperial bastion to remain on Farfallen, was under siege.

'The hall has responded to our comms,' said the Ordo Malleus pilot in the Thunderhawk's cockpit. If the Malleus crew on the *Rubicon* had mourned the loss of two of their pilots on Sophano Secundus, they hadn't shown it. 'We can land on the roof.'

'Do it,' said Alaric.

The Malleus-trained crews were a strange breed. All of them had emotional repression doctrination and Alaric knew some of them even had cortical detonators that would activate in extremes of terror or elation, so that even if some Chaos power corrupted them the experience would kill them before they did any harm. They were little more than servitors, denied the chance to ever develop a fully-fledged human personality. It seemed to Alaric that countless lives had to be wasted or destroyed just to make the fight against Chaos possible. Of course, that in itself was a victory for the Enemy.

The Thunderhawk passed over the roof of the hall and the top of the cliff, slewing round as it decelerated. Alaric could see the siege lines of the ferals – they had dug trenches in concentric circles and piles of spoil marked the places were they were undoubtedly digging tunnels in the hope of finding a way in through the foundations. There would be enough vaults and cellars beneath the Hall of Remembrance to make it more likely than not that they would succeed. To the rear of their lines huge bonfires burned, with wild-haired, paint-daubed figures dancing around them. Alaric was sure he made out mutations and flickers of sorcery among them as the Thunderhawk descended.

The ferals couldn't trouble the Thunderhawk. For ranged weaponry they had only catapults and bows. The Thunderhawk's landing gear lowered and the gunship touched down on the roof of the Hall of Remembrance, its engines leaving great scorch marks on the cliff face.

The exit ramp lowered, letting in the smell of old stone and burning forest. Squad Alaric and Squad Genhain dropped down onto the pockmarked marble tiles of the roof.

An old, barrel-chested, battle-scarred deacon ran over from a lookout position on the edge of the pediment. He carried a battered autogun and wore grimy, tattered Ecclesiarchical robes. A few young novice preachers and archivists with haunted eyes manned the walls, now looking in undisguised awe at the huge armoured warriors emerging from the Thunderhawk.

The deacon was the only one there who looked like he was worth a damn in a fight. The days of the Hall of Remembrance were numbered.

'Throne be praised!' bellowed the deacon as he approached the disembarking Marines. 'Long have we prayed for deliverance. We had begun to doubt that reinforcements would ever arrive. And yet we have been sent Space Marines in our plight! Truly the Emperor has heard our pleadings!'

'We're not reinforcements,' said Alaric bluntly. 'Are you in charge here?'

The deacon's shoulders dropped. If he had been hanging on to the possibility of the hall's survival, that hope was now gone. But servants of the Emperor did not bemoan their lot, and he did his best not to let it show. 'I am in command on the roof,' said the deacon.

'And below?'

The deacon sighed. 'No one is commanding the defence. We are not soldiers – I was, once, but I can't command a siege. With Confessor Arhelghast dead Senior Archivist Serevic has rank but he's just a scholar.'

'Good. I need to see him as soon as possible.'

'I'll have one of the novices show you down. But… brother… if one of you could stay. Just one of you. Think what could be lost here, think what the Enemy could do to us. One Space Marine could do the fighting of a hundred men, everyone knows it.'

'Farfallen stands or dies alone, deacon. I need all my battle-brothers for when we take the fight to the enemy. Do what you can to survive, but my Marines will not die here for you.'

The deacon looked like he was about to argue, but he bit back the words. He had not chosen to lead, but he was the only one here who could – now hope of survival was gone, perhaps he would be able to face death on its own terms and realise the only fight he had to win was against despair.

THE HALL OF Remembrance was cut deeply into the rock, a dense warren of vaulted corridors and high-ceilinged chapels that seemed to have been designed with no reason or purpose. Piles of ledgers and scrolls were crammed into every available room and alcove, and some corridors were lined with them. The hall, if it had been designed as anything, had not been designed as a library. Alaric picked one volume up as he passed – its cover identified it as a record of the tithes paid to one of the sub-chapels on Volcanis Ultor. The last entry was three hundred years old.

The whole place stank of rotting paper. The novice who led them down into the Hall – a gangly, hollow-eyed novice preacher carrying an antique lasgun he clearly didn't know how to use properly – took the Grey Knights lower and lower until the chanting of the ferals outside could be heard through the walls. The boy was terrified of the Grey

Knights – very few Imperial citizens indeed ever saw a Space Marine, let alone got this close to them. It must have been like a dream lain over the nightmare of the siege.

'How is all this organised?' Genhain asked, echoing Alaric's own thoughts.

'It's… it's not, really, sir,' answered the novice. 'The archivists keep it all in order, in their heads. They don't write it down. The word of the Emperor is in the hearts and minds of His subjects, not written down where heretics might twist it for their own use.'

Alaric sighed inwardly. Like all Imperial organisations the Ecclesiarchy matched its immense size with its enormous variety. Every preacher and confessor did things differently, and in spite of the zealously conservative synods on Earth and Ophelia VII, matters of dogma and interpretation sometimes made one branch of the Imperial cult look like a whole different religion to the next. The traditions by which the Hall of Remembrance did its sacred work evidently had more to do with the prominence Farfallen once had than with the Emperor's own will – the senior archivists had protected their own coveted position on the garden world by making sure only they understood the hall's archives.

The central levels of the hall contained the archivist's offices. Most were empty – the hall had by then lost most of its staff. Novices' cells led off from one wall, with exhausted novices recuperating in a couple of them. One hard bed contained a body, the bedclothes pulled up over the head, a well-thumbed copy of the *Hymnal Imperator* placed reverentially on the chest.

'Senior Archivist Serevic,' said the guide meekly, indicating a carved door of dark wood and standing aside. Alaric opened the door and a cloud of heavy purplish incense flowed out. The novice stifled a cough as Alaric entered.

Alaric's enhancements meant the incense and darkness didn't bother him. It was still a dispiriting sight – Serevic, an unassuming, scholarly man in late middle age, bent over a lectern as he pored over a huge illuminated tome, had evidently shut himself up in the room some time ago.

Serevic looked around at the intrusion, evidently about to remonstrate with whichever novice had dared to disturb him. When he saw Alaric filling the doorway his watery eyes widened in shock and he half-fell off his chair, stumbling back against the far wall and dislodging tottering piles of papers and books.

'Who…? Throne preserve us!'

Alaric stepped into the room. He noticed an unmade bed in the corners, scraps of paper everywhere, books heaped against the walls. 'Archivist Serevic?'

'Senior… Senior Archivist. Machas Lavanian Serevic.'

'Good. Acting Brother-Captain Alaric of the Grey Knights, in the service of the Emperor's Inquisition.'

'The Inquisition? We… we are Emperor-fearing servants here, there is no need…'

Alaric held up a hand. 'We are not here to judge you. Something dark has come to the Trail and we need information from you if we are to fight it.'

Serevic tried to compose himself, but his voice still wavered. 'I have heard them singing at night, even here. They say their Prince is here.'

'They are right. It is rising somewhere on the Trail, but if we are to fight it we must find out where. The violence here is happening all over the Trail and there is not much time left.'

'The other archivists are dead. There is so much that has been lost to us.'

'This will not be lost. The Prince of a Thousand Faces will rise at the burial place of Saint Evisser.'

There was a long pause. 'There is no burial place.'

Alaric stepped closer so he was looming right over Serevic. 'The Prince needs Evisser's body to come back. That is the only reason he is on the Trail at all.'

'Brother-Captain, there is no burial place. There is no Saint. That the Trail will soon die proves this. We were forsaken a long time ago.'

Serevic was steeling himself. This was a moment he had prepared for, which meant it was important to him since he was clearly not prepared to lead the defence of the Hall.

'What happened here?' asked Alaric.

'The Emperor's Inquisition cannot save us, brother-captain. The Emperor's Church must keep its own counsel.'

'Very well.' Alaric turned to Justicar Genhain, who waited just outside the door. 'Burn all this.'

Serevic gasped. 'Burn? But… this is sacred, this is our…'

'The Hall of Remembrance will fall. This knowledge will fall into the hands of the Enemy. If it is of no use to the Emperor, then it is nothing more than a weapon for his foes.'

'There is no reason! No reason! This is… this is sacrilege! The sacred word must remain! To destroy all this is no more than heresy!'

'I first thought,' said Alaric carefully, 'that the archivists only wanted to maintain their own positions here. But that's not why you keep all this knowledge organised only in your own memories. Is it, Serevic?'

Brother Ondurin had unslung his incinerator and a blue flame was flickering at its nozzle.

'You are here to guard this knowledge. You are here because the Ecclesiarchy knows something about the Trail, and Saint Evisser, and Ghargatuloth, and they want it kept secret. But we are offering to destroy it all, so that once the ferals tear you apart there will be no secrets left to find. So why shouldn't we burn it all? We would be helping you. Why do you care about saving any of this?'

Serevic's voice was a whimper. 'Because... I'm not finished...'

Alaric held up a hand. Ondurin lowered the barrel of his incinerator, which had been poised to send a gout of flame into the books piled up in the nearest cell. 'The Ecclesiarchy should have appointed a stronger-willed man to keep their secrets. Tell us what we need to know or it will all burn, and you will watch it.'

A fat tear rolled down Serevic's face. 'I can't tell you. Throne of Earth, they took me here as a child, and even when I didn't know anything they told me it is a mortal sin to tell...' Serevic looked up. His lip trembled. 'But... I can show you.'

KELKANNIS EVISSER WAS nobody. He was a novice adept sent to the tiny Administratum offices on Solshen XIX back when it was a newly-settled planet earmarked for use as an agri-world. He was no more than a name on a roster, just like trillions of men and women who would never amount to anything more.

It was late in Evisser's life when Solshen XIX found itself in the path of greenskin raiders. The orks belonged to just one of thousands of warbands who marauded through the frontiers of the Imperium, and their periodic bouts of carnage amongst scattered Imperial settlements were as much a part of an Imperial citizen's life as prayer, work and obedience.

Nothing remained when they left Solshen XIX. Nothing but burning ruins.

And Kelkannis Evisser.

Evisser was not the only sole survivor in the Imperium. Whole mythologies had grown up around them – to some they were unlucky, having used up the good luck of everyone around them. To others they were lucky charms, protected by the Emperor's grace. To the Administratum a sole survivor was just another adept, to be moved sideways while the settlement on Solshen XIX was rebuilt.

But Kelkannis Evisser would not be drawn back into the vast machine of the Administratum. He had seen the will of the Emperor as the greenskins butchered his colleagues. He had seen how even the orks were, in their own way, instruments of the Emperor's hand – they had been sent to show Evisser the Emperor's infinite mercy and strength, the blinding heat of His wrath, the endless depth of His belief in mankind's destiny to rule the stars. Kelkannis had been chosen to survive precisely because he was nobody, just like the trillions who made up the Emperor's flock, and it was Kelkannis's duty to show them all how the Emperor's message applied to the lowly and the exalted alike.

They thought him mad. He refused to prove them right. Those sent to denounce him listened, and in turn came to believe that it was something more than blind fortune that had saved him from the rampaging greenskins. The mere fact that the Administratum could not make him another part of their machine made him special. Even the faceless, endless bureaucracy of the Imperium could not crush his spirit.

He was more than just a man with divinely inspired grace who spread the word of the Emperor. He was hope itself – hope that the lowly men and women of the Imperium could play a meaningful part in the Emperor's plan for humanity, hope that a single soul could mean something to the Imperium.

If there was one thing the people of the Imperium needed, it was hope. Worlds clamoured for Evisser to visit them, and when he came the governors and Arbites were powerless to stop immense crowds flocking to hear him speak. It was not long before some started speaking of future sainthood.

Then came the miracles. A savage plague was decimating the lower city of one of Trepytos's port hives. Evisser went to the heart of the quarantined zone and stayed there for six months, easing the dying hours of thousands, giving to millions the comfort of knowing they died in the Emperor's grace. That was miracle enough, but in spite of spending every waking moment at the bedsides of the dying Evisser was untouched by the plague.

An uprising of mutant slaves on Magnos Omicron threatened to tip the forge world into anarchy. Evisser walked miraculously through the gunfire to speak with the rebellion's leaders and convince them, through nothing but the clarity of the Emperor's word as it was spoken through him, to lay down their arms and return beneath the Imperial yoke.

In the void between the star systems starships followed Evisser everywhere he went, for as he passed he left the warp cold and still. Not one ship was lost to warp storms or madness so long as they followed. In this way the Trail was first marked out, systems linked by the journeys of Evisser as he ministered to the despairing and the downtrodden.

He brought the Emperor's grace to deaths that would otherwise mean nothing. He left a wake of renewed faith and diligence everywhere he went. The citizens of the Trail adored him and began to celebrate him vociferously – within a year of his miracle at Trepytos there were festivals and parades in his name. Chapels were dedicated to his spirit. Soon, the speculations of sainthood were forgotten and people began to refer to Saint Evisser as a matter of course – for what else was a saint, but an individual made graceful and miraculous by the Emperor's will, an embodiment of His mastery over humanity?

And so as a living saint, Kelkannis Evisser did wonders that came to bear his name. He spent decades travelling to almost every system in the Trail, and wherever he trod shrines and chapels were built in celebration. The Hall of Remembrance itself was built where he first landed on Farfallen, for when he stepped off the exit ramp of his shuttle it was said that every flower on the planet suddenly bloomed in exaltation. He blessed the dark towers of Volcanis Ultor and the subterranean geothermal forges of Magnos Omicron, the fields of Victrix Sonora and the teeming oceans of Solshen XIX, the very stars that shone down on the Trail.

It was due to Saint Evisser that a tract of frontier space had become a populous and wealthy cluster of worlds. Pilgrims came and brought prosperity with them, and in thanks the wealthy and powerful built monuments to Saint Evisser. They refused any overtures of humility from the Ecclesiarchy and built gold-domed cathedrals, jewel-studded statues, museums of priceless art in Evisser's name.

A saint had been born to the Trail to show how the Emperor looked out as lord over all humanity – the wealthy and the poor, the powerful and the meaningless, those ministered by his church and those who toiled ignorant in the hives and the forges.

And while the Trail of Evisser endured, Evisser himself would never truly die.

ALARIC SNAPPED THE book shut crossly. Serevic had shown him to a locked vault beneath the hall, where books and scrolls lay strewn seemingly at random across the floor. But Serevic had known exactly what each one contained, and had picked out for Alaric only those that were relevant – the true and corroborated history of Saint Evisser.

And when the eulogising and myth-making were taken out, there was very little truth indeed. All Alaric had was a skeleton of a saint's life. No details. No description of Evisser's family, his companions, even what he looked like. Of course, the history of the Imperium had never been written down in its entirety – such a thing was impossible – and events of the distant past were coloured by interpretation and bias if they survived at all. But there had to be something more. Why else would the Hall of Remembrance have trained its archivists to maintain such secrecy over Saint Evisser?

Alaric was almost alone in the darkness of the vaults. A terrified novice waited by the door, attending on Alaric to show that the hall, though besieged, still observed the protocols that one Imperial servant deserved to receive from another. Genhain and Brother Ondurin, his incinerator still held ready, waited just outside the door. Genhain and Alaric's Space Marines were in a defensive cordon around the vault, and they were not just there for show – Alaric was sure he could hear scratching beneath the vault where the ferals were tunnelling under the Hall. It was only a matter of time before they got in.

'Justicar Genhain,' said Alaric. Genhain walked in, leaving Ondurin at the door. 'What do you make of this?'

Genhain walked over to the table Alaric sat at, and looked at the pages lying open. They were from a sketchy, official history of the Trail, and Serevic had assured Alaric that this description of Saint Evisser, along with a few documents confirming some of his miracles, constituted the body of information the Ecclesiarchy had wanted to protect.

'It's not much,' said Genhain as he scanned it.

'It's all the truth we have.'

'Perhaps that's the point.'

Alaric thought for a moment. What did he know? There had been a man named Evisser who claimed inspiration from the Emperor and was proclaimed a saint. That was it.

And of course, that was the point.

Alaric stood up, grabbed the book, and strode out of the room, pausing only to glare at the novice who stood shivering just inside the door.

'Where is Serevic?'

The boy pointed nervously. Alaric headed in the indicated direction, walking into a long, low gallery where the walls and ceiling were covered in pages torn from books, pinned to wooden supports or stuck in a ragged patchwork to the stone. Serevic was standing in the middle of the gallery, gazing at the thousands of words as if he was looking out of a window at Farfallen's landscape in its prime.

'There never was a Saint Evisser,' said Alaric simply, throwing the book down at Serevic's feet. 'The Ecclesiarchy never confirmed his ascension. He was proclaimed by the people and the Ecclesiarchy had to accept it, but to them he was nothing more than just another man.'

Serevic seemed to deflate, if anything looking even less imposing than before. He shook his head sadly. 'That so much good can come from a man we could never accept. It was shame that kept our secret.' He looked up at Alaric, and he seemed on the verge of tears. 'Can you think what harm would have come to the Trail, if the cardinals had denounced him? There would have been terrible strife. Hatred would be turned not on the Emperor's enemies but upon his faithful.'

'But he had miracles. He forged the Trail out of frontier space. He should have been a prime candidate for canonisation. What did they find?'

'It was too late then, you see,' continued Serevic. The knowledge had been bottled up inside him for so long that now he had committed the sin of revealing it, he had to get it all out. 'Evisser had been a saint to the people for decades before the Inquiry Beatificum was even begun. By the time it reported to the Holy Synod it was too late. Our own cardinals preached in cathedrals built to his spirit. Men spoke his name in prayers. You cannot root out that kind of belief, not when it holds a place like the Trail together.'

Alaric knew now that Ghargatuloth had not just chosen the Trail. He had very probably made it in the first place. 'So the cardinals had their clergy cease his worship until the Trail decayed and Evisser could be forgotten. But why was he never a saint? What did they know about him?'

Serevic choked back a sob. Outside, the sound of foul chanting filtered through the walls as the ferals made ready for another attack.

'All this,' said Serevic in a near-whisper, 'all this will burn...'

Alaric picked up Serevic by the throat and slammed him up against the wall of the gallery, head against the ceiling. Alaric only had to will it and his gauntlet would crush the archivist.

Serevic forced his eyes to meet Alaric's. 'His... his home world. There was a taint there. If... if the cardinals had ignored it, and it was discovered, there could be even worse strife... Evisser a traitor, holy war, another Plague of Unbelief...'

Alaric let go and Serevic slipped down to the floor in an undignified heap.

'It's what you didn't write that betrays you,' said Alaric, kicking the book at Serevic. 'No home world. No burial place. No canonisation. Because the Ecclesiarchy knew that Evisser could be tainted, and that he could have been warped by some dark power. And they were right. But they would rather let it take root amongst Imperial worlds than admit they could not control this new prophet. Where was he born? Where is he buried?'

Serevic whimpered.

'Now! Or it all burns, and you will go with it!'

Serevic buried his head in his hands. He was broken. Since he was a novice, a child, he had been trained to keep the sacred knowledge of the Trail, remember and protect it in the Emperor's name. Now he had nothing left. Nothing at all. And knowing that no matter what, all that knowledge would burn eventually, he gave up.

'He was born on Sophano Secundus,' said Serevic weakly. 'But we buried him on Volcanis Ultor.'

FIFTEEN
VOLCANIS FAUSTUS

THREE DAYS AFTER Valinov escaped his execution on Mimas, the Conclave on Encaladus sent a fast messenger ship to the Trail. The information it carried was too sensitive to be transmitted by astropath – every Imperial organisation on the Trail was considered compromised by the hidden cults rising up on every system, and corrupted astropaths had leaked vital Inquisitorial intelligence before. A messenger was the only option.

Its message was simple. Valinov was probably heading for the Trail, and he was a man considered so dangerous merely speaking with him carried an intolerable risk of corruption. Killing him on sight was the only acceptable response.

The message was entrusted to Interrogator DuGrae, an ace pilot and trusted agent of Lord Inquisitor Coteaz, and she had been given multiple cortical enhancements that allowed her to convey sensitive information in her head without the possibility of anyone retrieving it by psychic means. DuGrae was once a fighter pilot who had thrown a Thunderbolt across the skies of Armageddon, racking up scores of kills against the flying contraptions the greenskins used. The craft she now flew through space was as responsive as a fighter. It was a sleek, glossy black dart of a ship, the smallest and quickest warp-capable ship the Ordo Malleus could scramble at such short notice. It hit the warp like a knife, the sole crew members DuGrae and her Navigator.

The ship cut through the immaterium quickly at first, but three days out warp storms blew up without warning: a sudden flare of black madness in the warp that rippled in a wide crescent across the Segmentum Solar from Rhanna to V'Run. A clumsier craft would have been cut off completely but DuGrae, flying blindfold while her Navigator talked her through the warp currents, flung the sleek messenger ship through roiling banks of hatred towards the Trail.

But it used up time. Too much time – if Valinov got a big enough head start they might not catch him now.

DuGrae, without an astropath to contact Encaladus, had no way of reporting back or receiving news of the Trail. She had to trust that the Emperor would foil the Enemy's plans for a few hours more, and that she would fly fast enough.

DuGrae sliced out of the warp just beyond the edge of the Volcanis system, the light of the livid red star flooding the cockpit. Volcanis Ultor was the seat of authority on the Trail – once the cardinal and governor there had been warned, the next stop was the Inquisitorial headquarters on Trepytos.

Straight away it was obvious the state of the Trail had worsened. There were Imperial Naval ships in the system, doubtless drawn there by the rising tide of Chaotic activity. The Mars-class battlecruiser *Unmerciful*, an old craft left over from when fighter-carrying warships were the weapons of choice, sent patrols of fighter-bombers out to sweep for marauding enemy ships. The Lunar class cruiser *Holy Flame* and the three Sword class escorts of Absolution Squadron kept close orbit around Volcanis Ultor itself.

With no astropath, DuGrae couldn't contact them until she flew in closer. But she was still uneasy. Were there Chaos ships prowling the system that would make short work of her lightly-armed ship if they found her? She held off approaching Volcanis Ultor until she could get more information from the ship-to-ship traffic picked up by her close-range comms. She sent her craft in a slingshot around Volcanis Faustus, the barren, baked rock planet closest to the star Volcanis. The scraps of information she picked up suggested very nervous captains waiting for an inevitable conflict, as if the chaos on the Trail was rising to critical mass that would explode into open warfare. Crews were pulling multiple maintenance shifts to get older craft battle-ready. Ordnance was at a premium and the Departmento Munitorum couldn't provide enough fuel for the fighters.

From out of the shadow of Volcanis Faustus drifted the battered, proud shape of the old warhorse *Unmerciful*. The proximity of the star warped communications and the carrier deployed three wings of fighter craft to get closer. When they were in range, they scanned DuGrae's ship and transmitted a simple message – the Volcanis system was not safe. The *Unmerciful's* fighter wings would escort DuGrae into the spaceport on Volcanis Ultor's principal hive.

DuGrae thanked the squadron leader and shut down her engines while the fighters approached her to take up escort formation.

While she was hanging helpless in orbit, the captain of the *Unmerciful* gave the order and the fighter wings fired every missile they had, turning DuGrae's ship into an expanding cloud of plasma. And with her died the message she carried, that the man calling himself Inquisitor Valinov was in reality a servant of Chaos.

GHOLIC REN-SAR VALINOV watched the blinking triangle representing the messenger craft wink out. The blue squares representing the *Unmerciful's* fighters whirled around for a couple of minutes, skirting around the debris field. The large orbital command display mounted in the suite Valinov had commandeered was set to depict the area around Volcanis Faustus, and as Valinov watched, the fighters scattered back to join their parent ship on the other side of the barren world. Recoba had thrown out two noble hangers-on to give Valinov free rein of an entire floor, and he had set himself up with cogitators, pict-consoles, several holomats and the orbital command display to ensure he knew as much about what was going on in the system as possible.

'Kill confirmed,' came the static-masked voice of the squadron leader.

'Good hunt, Squadron Theta,' was the captain's reply. The large blue rectangle of the *Unmerciful* began to bring its ponderous bulk around for the short journey back to the outer orbits of Volcanis Ultor. The fighters followed it, like pups hurrying back to their mother.

There was a commotion at the door and Cardinal Recoba entered, shrugging himself into his voluminous official robes, followed by a gaggle of lesser clergy.

'Inquisitor!' called Recoba. 'I just heard. Was it an intruder?'

'It was good we found them when we did,' said Valinov. 'If I had not been informed they might have been escorted straight here. The ways of the Enemy are many and foul, Emperor only knows what they could have done had they reached us.'

Recoba swallowed. 'It was an agent of the Dark Powers?'

Valinov nodded. 'As soon as the *Unmerciful's* fighters scanned it, I knew. It was a sorcerer, I am sure. It was good the fighters could destroy it quickly, otherwise their crews might have been corrupted.'

Recoba shook his head. 'Then they were so close. Thank the Ever-Living that they were stopped. Indeed, the Throne protects.'

'The Throne protects, your blessedness,' said Valinov humbly.

They really had been close. Valinov wondered who had been sent – probably one of their best. Maybe Nyxos had sent someone, since he had probably survived Mimas and wanted to have a personal hand in stopping Valinov. No, more likely it was one of the lord inquisitors on Encaladus, taking matters into their own hands to cover up the mistakes they had made. Probably that showman Coteaz, preaching blood and thunder and sending off one of his star pilots to die. Valinov allowed himself a small smile – it was crusaders like Coteaz who could be the easiest to use. Of course they would send a messenger ship. And of course Valinov would use it to heighten the fears of the Trail's defenders.

It was as if the rest of the galaxy knew its role in the grand dance of Chaos, and obeyed its tune without complaint. And what was more pleasing to the Lord of Change, than letting his enemies forge the chains of their own slavery?

'Should I have the captains increase our patrols?' Recoba was asking. 'We have promised a dozen fighter wings to Magnos Omicron, but we could fly them out to the far orbit watch stations…'

Valinov held up a hand. 'No. Bring the captains into close orbit. But bring the extra fighters in, too. The rest of the Trail will have to fight their own battle, Volcanis Ultor itself is the keystone that must not fall. Put a wall of steel around our world, cardinal. It will not be long before it will be the only protection we have.'

'Of course, inquisitor,' said Recoba, sounding almost obedient. This pleased Valinov, as Recoba began snapping off orders to his hangers-on.

Gholic Ren-Sar Valinov glanced back at the orbital command display before he switched it off, knowing that the empty space where the messenger ship had been represented the death of the Trail's last hope.

CANONESS LUDMILLA OF the Order of the Bloody Rose looked through the magnoculars at the place the battle would be fought. Her Battle Sisters, the soldiers of the Ecclesiarchy, held a strongpoint of bunkers and trenches surrounding a chemical reclamation plant on the shores of Lake Rapax.

On her left flank were trenches held by the Balurian heavy infantry, well-armoured and well-drilled Guardsmen who could be trusted not to break and leave her Sisters vulnerable. On her right flank was Lake Rapax itself, an expanse of liquid so befouled by pollution that it couldn't be called water any more. Ludmilla commanded the extreme right flank of the defensive line in front of the capital hive, and she had hundreds of Battle Sisters to help her do it. Many considered the Sisters of the Adepta Sororitas to be the most effective troops the Imperium had save for the Space Marines themselves, and with power armour and disciplined bolter fire there were few who could fend off the hordes of Chaos any better.

The plains in front of the capital hive were barren and broken, stained the colour of livid wounds by centuries of pollution, drained and battered until fractured stony desert and dunes of ash were all that remained. In the dim distance foothills rose, framing the much smaller Hive Verdanus, but behind Ludmilla rose the true prize of Volcanis Ultor – Hive Superior, the seat of government for the planet, the system and the Trail.

The battle could be over in moments if the Ordinatus stationed amongst wasteland fringing the hive could home in on the landing enemy forces and send pinpoint salvoes of multiple warheads on top of them. Ludmilla, however, knew it would not happen that way. The attack would be spearheaded by Chaos Marines, the heretics of the Traitor Legions, who would use the speed and strength of all Space Marines to get amongst the defenders before most knew they had even landed. This battle would be won not on the plains but at the range of a bayonet, the attack dragged down and stifled by the ranks of defenders.

Ludmilla looked over her own defences, which had been built in admirable time by drafted hive citizen labourer gangs. The squat, ugly plascrete processing plant formed a bastion that went right up to the edge of the lake itself, and Ludmilla had placed several Retributor support squads on the plant's roof to cover it with heavy bolters and multi-meltas. Two Excorcist missile tanks guarded the sealed gates of the plant and several Sisters squads were in cover around rockcrete defences. They could not enter the plant itself because of the volatile open vats of chemicals, but nothing would get that far.

Around the plant looped long lines of trenches, bristling with razorwire. Rockcrete blocks studded the broken plains in front of the trenches to break up tank assaults, and there were points on the line where these defences had been removed to channel armoured assaults into crossfires from Retributor squads and anti-tank teams supplied by the Balurians. The Sisters who manned the front trenches could easily fall back into bunkers behind them that still sat in shallow craters where they had been dropped, pre-fabricated, from low orbit when the defences were first being marked out.

To break through, the attackers would have to push through several trenches, then bypass dozens of bunkers. The Balurians had a large body of reserves who could sweep from their own rear lines to meet any assault that got that far, pinning them down so the Sisters could emerge from their bunkers and charge into the attackers from behind.

That was the plan. Plans, as Ludmilla knew as well as anyone, only lasted as long as it took for the first trigger to be pulled. But it would take a massive assault indeed to shatter the line at this, probably its best-held point, where the resolute Sisters formed as impassable a barrier as the toxic waters of Lake Rapax.

Ludmilla watched the Balurians down the line presenting themselves for inspection to their regimental commissar, a black-uniformed figure who had the authority to execute anyone – man or officer – who was suspected of failing in his duty to the Emperor. Ludmilla could just catch his voice as he barked short speeches at each platoon he inspected. The enemy was coming, he was saying. It would try to take their minds even as it broke their bodies. Any man found wanting when his faith was put to the test would be lucky to get a bullet from his own squad-mates. This was a war of the soul, not just of physical conflict.

Ludmilla closed up the magnoculars and climbed back down the short ladder into the interior of her command bunker. Two of her Celestians, elite Sisters who served as her command squad, stood to attention by the door and Sister Superior Lachryma was waiting to speak with the canoness.

'Canoness,' said Lachryma with a bow of the head. 'The Seraphim are in position.' Lachryma led the Seraphim squads, units of Sisters skilled in hand-to-hand combat who wore jump packs to charge into the thick of the fighting. They would be used as a rapid counterattacking force to charge any enemy getting past the first line of trenches.

'I want priority given to the join in the lines. The Balurians are good but the enemy will exploit the gap.'

'Of course. My Sisters positioned with the Balurians say the Guardsmen are getting nervous.'

'As well they might. Make sure you lead the battle-hymns personally in that sector. The Balurians must hear our example.'

'And… Canoness, may I speak freely?'

'Go on.'

'Inquisitor Valinov's speech has caused some doubt amongst the Guardsmen and, I believe, in the Sisters too. Very few of us have met the Traitor Legions in battle before. The schola progenia taught us they didn't exist.'

'Pray that one day, that will be true.' Ludmilla thought for a moment. 'If any of the Balurians ask, let them pray with you. If they break we could be lost.'

'Understood.'

'And Sister?'

'Canoness?'

'The Traitor Legions fell because the Enemy exploited their sins of pride and arrogance. Those are sins we will not commit. Do not let the Enemy break your spirit before the battle has even begun.'

Lachryma saluted and left the bunker to join her Battle-Sisters. Ludmilla watched her go – Lachryma was a tall woman, given greater bulk by her power armour and the flaring jump pack mounted on her back. The black sleeves covering her glossy blood-red armour bore the bleeding rose symbol of the Order. In the days before the Horus Heresy, Space Marines had painted kill marks on their armour to proclaim their battle-prowess – the Sisters of Battle did nothing so vulgar.

One of Ludmilla's command staff, a Sister Dialogous manning the Sisters' communications, appeared from the lower level of the bunker. 'Canoness, Cardinal Recoba's staff have contacted us. Inquisitor Valinov wishes to review our defences in person.'

'Tell him we are honoured,' said Ludmilla, 'and that I trust our preparations will match his standards.'

The Sister hurried back down to relay the message.

Valinov is a born leader, thought Ludmilla. He had taken to commanding the defences without seeming to even try. The Guardsmen hung on his every word ever since he had told them the Traitor Legions were real, and Ludmilla imagined that some of her Sisters felt the same. Ludmilla was a fighter, not a politician, but even she had to admire the way Valinov could take such complete control so quickly, when the stakes were so high.

And the presence of Valinov meant more than just decent leadership. The Sisters often worked with the Ordo Hereticus rather than the Ordo Malleus, but Ludmilla knew Valinov was probably a member of the Malleus – for him to be involved, it meant that the threat to Volcanis Ultor was daemonic in nature.

Traitor Marines and daemons. There were few more potent forces in the Enemy's arsenal. She understood why Valinov wanted to inspect the Sisters' preparations – it was not just political showmanship, but a genuine concern. The daemons would strike here, on the very edge of the line in the hope of gaining a foothold and then rolling up the defences before turning in towards the hive. The Sisters had to hold.

And hold they would.

THE RUBICON HAD left the Hall of Remembrance to burn. The ferals would tunnel into the lower vaults soon and when they did, the defenders would die alongside their books. Serevic would probably be one of the last, cowering amongst his burning tomes. Alaric knew all this and left anyway – he could spare no Grey Knights to help the defenders fight a hopeless battle. He was a leader, and leaders could not waste the lives of their men on lost causes.

The bridge of the *Rubicon* was silent save for the distant thrumming of the engines and the clicking of the bridge cogitators. The coordinates had been plotted and in a few moments the short warp jump would begin. It would take only a few more hours to make the jump to the Volcanis system, and the Malleus Navigator was good enough to put the *Rubicon* well within system space.

Alaric watched the quiet preparations for the jump from his command pulpit. The bridge doors hissed open and Justicar Santoro walked in.

'Brother-Captain? I had the crew bring up all the information they had on Volcanis Ultor.'

'And?'

'Nothing much we didn't know already. A hive world, controlled by the Ecclesiarchy with a nominal governorship. We looked up the location Serevic gave us – Lake Rapax is just outside the capital hive. It doesn't look like there's much there.'

'But we know different. Have they given us landing coordinates?'

'That's the problem. The astropaths say there is no one receiving messages.'

'Quarantine?'

'Possibly. Volcanis Ultor had some of the worst of the cult activity, a psychic quarantine would be a logical step.'

'Not very convenient for us, though. We'll just have to arrive unannounced. I want us on a battle footing just in case – if Volcanis Ultor has gone the way of Farfallen we might not have a friendly reception.'

'Understood. I'll brief my men.'

Alaric stepped down from the pulpit so he was on the same level as Santoro. The justicar's face, as always, betrayed little. 'Justicar, I know you are frustrated at not being able to fight. Ghargatuloth wants to use that as a weapon.'

'The Enemy will find no weapon in me, brother-captain.'

'I know, but he will try to find one. This fight will not be on our terms.'

'They never are. Not for Mandulis, not for us.'

'Make sure your men understand.'

Santoro saluted and walked out. Alaric knew the justicar didn't trust him completely as a leader yet – Alaric himself knew that the grand masters wouldn't have chosen him as brother-captain on his own merits, and it had taken the madness of Ligeia to put him in command. Ghargatuloth would be the sternest test of leadership possible, and no matter what else happened Alaric would find out if his core of faith would ever have been strong enough.

But of course, this battle was not about him. It was about billions of Imperial servants who would die, or worse, if the dark star of Ghargatuloth rose again.

'Navigation is go for warp jump,' said one of the crewmen at the nav helm.

'Engineering go,' was the vox from deep in the *Rubicon*'s stern.

The ship's commands counted off. The ship was ready.

'Take us in,' ordered Alaric, and the *Rubicon* dived headlong into the warp.

THE NAVAL DEFENCES around Volcanis Ultor were the strongest the system – the whole Trail – had seen in centuries. The *Unmerciful* was an old ship but a proven one, its multiple fighter decks crammed with Starhawk bombers and Avenger torpedo craft flown by battle-hardened pilots who had been expecting their next action to be around the Eye of Terror. The *Holy Flame* was newer and tougher, with a proud crew whose rapid gunnery could throw out broadsides massive enough to turn huge swathes of space into a shrapnel-filled killing zone. Absolution Squadron, comprising three Sword-class escort craft, was almost brand new, paintwork gleaming as bright as the day they had first been launched from the dockyards of Hydraphur.

Drawn around Volcanis Ultor, the two warships and three escorts could cover the whole of the planet with ease, sensor fields overlapping over population centres, information from out-system monitoring stations flowing in constantly. All commercial shipping in the Volcanis system had been halted, and anything that moved was to be considered a threat.

Inquisitor Valinov's orders had been very clear. The enemy were coming. Everything else was secondary. They would try to make landfall, and the best way of destroying them was to engage their ships in high orbit where they would be vulnerable as they delivered their payloads.

Captain Grakinko of the *Unmerciful* liked the odds. Of the oldest Lastratan stock, Grakinko had seen dozens of engagements through a born officer's analytical eyes. The new-fangled tacticians said battleship broadsides were the ultimate weapon but Grakinko knew better – wave upon wave of fighters and bombers could achieve what no one battleship could, and in the close quarters of this coming engagement they would be as deadly and swift as a swarm of spitewings.

Grakinko waited in his gilded captain's throne, the bridge of his old proud ship so richly decorated and furnished it was more like the ball-room of a palace spire on his home hive than the functional heart of a warship. He waited in the satisfying knowledge that Volcanis Ultor was now the safest place on the Trail.

The *Holy Flame*, in contrast, was crewed by a well-drilled core of officers almost all of whom were graduates from the Imperial Navy Academy on Hydraphur, and were near-fanatical adherents to the belief that superior gunnery and discipline could overcome any enemy. Pryncos Gurveylan, ninth-year valedictorian and highest-scoring graduate for a decade, was the captain, but the whole officer corps on the *Holy Flame* functioned as one decision-making machine trained to analyse every situation and apply strict Naval doctrine. The fighter swarms of the *Unmerciful* would doubtless serve as a useful distraction but it was the guns of the *Holy Flame* that would win the day.

The captain of the *Holy Flame* shared a second cousin with the vice admiral who had commissioned the building of Absolution Squadron and so a quick private communication with the squadron's captains had ensured that they and the *Holy Flame* would fight as one. With the guns of the *Flame* firing at full rate and the escorts of Absolution Squadron to herd the enemy into range, nothing could approach Volcanis Ultor without being forced through a withering curtain of disciplined fire.

Pryncos Gurveylan was confident, as a captain must be, that every eventuality had been covered. The bridge of the *Holy Flame* was all wood panelling and upholstery, mirroring the old halls and lecture theatres of the Academy – the ship itself was an extension of the Academy, a repository for the best received wisdom the Navy had to offer. Gurveylan's fellow officers bustled efficiently, poring over large parchment system maps with compasses and rulers, relaying orders to engineering and ordnance, manning the constantly chattering communications helms.

It was just then that an urgent communication arrived from the outer system monitoring stations. A ship had just entered the Volcanis system unannounced, apparently at full battle-readiness. To all intents and purposes it was a Space Marine strike cruiser but its speed and ornate design were of unknown origin.

Both the *Unmerciful* and the *Holy Flame* received the message at the same time, and both knew there was only one explanation. Just as Valinov had said, the Traitor Legions had arrived.

SIXTEEN
HOLY FLAME

'INCOMING!' YELLED SOMEONE from the nav helm as scores of angry red hostile blips appeared on the bridge viewscreen.

'What have you got, comms?' ordered Alaric.

The crewman on the comms helm looked up. 'We sent an acknowledgement message to Volcanis Ultor but there was no reply.'

Alaric gripped the sides of the pulpit. It didn't make sense. They had been in the Volcanis system less than an hour and suddenly, without even challenging the *Rubicon* over the comms, a carrier warship was steaming towards them and sending out waves of fighter-bombers, armed up and aggressive.

'Archivum, I want the class and designation of that ship. Any others in-system. Someone told them we were coming and they said we weren't friendly.'

The other justicars were listening in to the situation over the vox. 'Has the system fleet been compromised?' voxed Justicar Tancred.

'I don't know,' replied Alaric. It was a possibility. If Ghargatuloth had corrupted the crews of the warships in the Volcanis system, it would explain their aggression. But at the last count Volcanis Ultor was standing relatively firm, its defenders rallying around Cardinal Recoba – if the whole system had been corrupted then it had happened with impossible speed. 'More likely misinformation. If they think Ghargatuloth sent us then they'd attack on sight. Nothing we said would make a difference.'

How many Imperial citizens had heard of the Grey Knights? Very few. Even if the command crews on the warships could see the design and livery of the *Rubicon*, would they be able to recognise it?

Alaric felt that Ghargatuloth would like nothing better than for the Inquisition's own secrecy to be used against it. Whether the ships heading to engage the *Rubicon* were controlled by Chaos or not, the Grey Knights would have to fight this one through.

'How long do we have?' asked Alaric. Gradually the noise and bustle on the bridge was increasing as warning alarms sounded and the various command helms sent messengers to other parts of the ship.

'Less than twenty minutes,' came the reply from the navigation helm. 'Then the first wave will hit.'

'I want every defence we have in space. Chaff, ordnance, everything. Then we punch through them into upper atmosphere. We're not here to engage them, we're here to get a force onto Volcanis Ultor.'

Ordnance helm started barking orders and several Malleus crewmen and women began running as messengers off the bridge, heading down to the gunnery decks where torpedoes and anti-ordnance charges would be loaded and ready to fire. Short-fused torpedoes would fill space with enough debris to throw off the first fighter waves, but the *Rubicon* would be short of armaments if it had to tangle with another warship.

'All justicars, get to the launch bays now. I'll take the Thunderhawk. Tancred, you'll be with me. Genhain and Santoro, you'll have to go in by drop-pod. I want you loaded up before the fighters reach us.'

The justicars sounded off. They were already armoured up – the Grey Knights would take just minutes to reach the launch deck. Alaric would need to be with them soon.

Alaric spoke through the bridge vox-caster so the whole crew could hear him. 'Crew of the *Rubicon*, your objectives are clear. Your goal is to reach the upper atmosphere of Volcanis Ultor and allow for deployment. All other concerns are secondary. This includes the survival of this ship and yourselves. Sacrifice the *Rubicon* if you have to. You may also have to sacrifice yourselves. I know the Ordo Malleus has prepared you for this but you cannot know if you are truly prepared for death until you face it. The Emperor trusts that you will do your duty in this. I trust you, too. Helm commands, you have the bridge – use whatever means you deem fit but get us close to that planet.

'You do not need to know what is at stake. It is enough that I must ask you to do this. Go with the Emperor, as He goes with you.'

There was a brief moment of silence, a reaction of considerable emotion considering the mind-scrubbed and psycho-doctrinated nature of the crew. Then the bridge bustle kicked in again as the blips on the viewscreen display crept closer to the position of the *Rubicon*.

Alaric stepped down off the command pulpit. An officer from the navigation helm gave Alaric a quick salute as he took over the pulpit controls. Alaric watched as a messenger was sent to engineering to make sure the engines were primed ready for evasive action. The ordnance helm began counting off all the various stores of ammunition that would be expended when the first wave was upon them. Officers at navigation were plotting the positions of the other ships in-system – three escorts and a cruiser, lying in wait around Volcanis Ultor, ready to pounce on whatever the carrier left for them.

The archive helm, with a small crew of scholars surrounded by membanks, had identified the closest ship as the *Unmerciful*, a veteran of Port Maw in the Gothic War. That was good. It meant the ship was old, and old ships were usually slow. The *Rubicon* could skirt around her and her fighter swarms. Then the real battle would begin, where the air of Volcanis Ultor met the void.

Alaric had rarely even noticed the crew of the *Rubicon*, composed as they were of efficient but almost invisible men and women. Some had been literally bred for anonymity, the product of breeding programs that produced easily-doctrinated individuals. But Alaric was glad of them now. They were efficient and unshakeable. They could never have the leadership to take a ship through war on their own but now they didn't need it – they just had to do things by the numbers, keep the *Rubicon* going long enough for the Grey Knights to get onto the planet.

They didn't need Alaric now. He hurried off through the bridge doors to join his battle-brothers, and left the crew of the *Rubicon* to their work.

CAPTAIN GRAKINKO ON the bridge of the *Unmerciful* watched the huge holographic tactical display where the fighter blips swarmed towards the Chaos ship. To think, the enemy had even tried to claim they were Imperials, and asked to be allowed to land at Volcanis Ultor! Inquisitor Valinov had predicted their every move. If they thought an old ship like the *Unmerciful* was easy pickings, then they were woefully wrong.

'Fighter command! I want the torpedo ships to the front. Pull the Starhawks and the assault boats back, we'll soften them up first!'

'Aye, captain!' came the enthusiastic reply from the fighter command helm, manned by several dozen petty officers most of whom had been born on the ship during its long service history. The pitch of activity on the bridge was rising as the *Unmerciful* worked itself up to full battle-readiness. The medicae crew were manning triage stations near the engines and fighter decks where casualties were always highest, and the chapel staff were scattered throughout the ship leading prayers. Refuelling crews waited nervously on the decks, ready to re-fit and bomb up the first wave of fighters and bombers when they returned.

'It's beautiful, isn't it?' said Grakinko, beaming proudly. 'Damned beautiful.' He turned his considerable bulk in his seat and opened up a panel in the arm of his throne, pulling out a bottle of finest sparkling Chirosian wine. With a fleshy thumb he popped the cork out and held up the bottle in salute. 'To war!' he bellowed.

Several of the bridge crew returned the toast enthusiastically. A chatter rose from the fighter command crew as they gave final approach orders to the attack craft.

As the first orders to open fire were given, Captain Grakinko took a good swig to mark the beginning of the battle.

Good wine, he thought.

THE FIRST WAVE of torpedoes was met by a return salvo from the *Rubicon*. Short-fused ordnance from the Space Marine cruiser burst in a shower of debris, bright blossoms of flame imploding in the vacuum leaving storms of silver metal shards like a glittering curtain.

The first wave of attack craft, maybe thirty craft strong, launched their own torpedoes and banked sharply to avoid deterrent fire spattering from the *Rubicon*'s turrets. Most of the torpedoes were detonated by the wall of debris and massive pulses of exploding munitions ripped silently through space, sending ripples through the debris like stones thrown into water. Some torpedoes, inevitably, made it through, and great black flashes played over the hull of the strike cruiser as the ship's shielding absorbed the blasts.

The real damage was done. As the damage crews on the *Rubicon* fought to restore the shields to full strength the next waves approached, Starhawk fighter-bombers this time, sweeping in through the debris field. Many were lost as their engines were clogged by debris but most of them made it through, for the fighter pilots of the *Unmerciful* were veterans who had mostly done this many times before. Instead, the debris shielded them from the *Rubicon*'s turret fire and they emerged in formation, close enough to make their attack runs.

They banked into long swooping strafing runs and with nose-mounted turbolasers began spattering the gunmetal hull of the *Rubicon* with fire.

In the gun decks and maintenance runs of the strike cruiser, men and women began to die.

* * *

ALARIC HEARD THE strafing runs hitting home, dull chains of explosions rippling along the outside of the hull. He was inside the Grey Knights' remaining Thunderhawk, strapped into a grav-couch ready to launch, alongside his squad and Squad Tancred.

With Krae lying dead in Titan's vaults, Squad Tancred now numbered just Tancred himself and his remaining three Terminator brothers. Tancred cradled his Nemesis sword, Locath and Golven held halberds, and Karlin carried the squad's heavy incinerator. The Terminator Marines were much like Tancred himself – uncompromising assault troopers who lived to do the Emperor's work up close where their massive armour and Nemesis weapons would bring them the greatest advantage.

Karlin was a regular student in the Chaplain's seminary, where his incandescent brand of faith echoed the blessed burning fuel he sprayed over enemies. Locath was as strong as Tancred himself, and the Nemesis halberd he carried was a powerful relic given to him by a brother-captain he had once attended on as a novice. Golven was a skilled halberd fighter who had earned his Crux Terminatus boarding abandoned spaceships and fighting Chaos-tainted genestealer cults.

Alaric carried the Nemesis sword of Mandulis under one arm.

'This is yours, justicar,' he said, handing the weapon to Tancred.

Tancred took the weapon and looked up at Alaric in surprise. 'Brother-Captain, I do not feel I have earned the...'

'You are our best soldier, Tancred,' said Alaric. 'It took Captain Stern to beat you. We need you to carry the Lightning Bolt. It's what you do the best of all of us.'

Tancred put his own Nemesis sword to one side and held the sword of Mandulis. It was an abnormally large weapon but it fitted Tancred perfectly – it was made more for strength than for finesse but in combat Tancred had plenty of both, and it looked as firm and balanced in his hand as it must have done when Mandulis held it. The inside of the Thunderhawk was lit by the gleam of its blade – Tancred seemed to loom even larger in the reflection from its blade, darker and stronger, a reflection of the spirit inside Tancred. 'The sword that banished Ghargatuloth,' said Tancred, almost to himself. 'I can believe it.'

He turned the blade, weighing its point of balance, checking the razor sharpness of its edge and the flawless surface of the blade. It seemed like an extension of Tancred, a weapon he had been born to hold. To Alaric it was a sacred relic, but to Tancred it was a sword the Emperor wielded through him.

Another sequence of dull ripping explosions echoed overhead, so close the strafing run must have scored hits along the side of the launch deck itself. Secondary explosions sounded somewhere in the ship. Alaric could hear the vibrations running through the deck as the *Rubicon*'s manoeuvring engines were fired up.

'Pray to the Emperor that you will get the chance to use it,' said Alaric, as the high resonant vibrations of failing shields thrummed through the hull.

THE ENGINES OF the *Rubicon* kicked in even as strafing runs tore ruby explosions from its hull. The strike cruiser, using its superior mobility, darted forward suddenly, ploughing forward through its own debris field and right into the upcoming fighter wings. Many pilots were forced to adopt new formations as the ship bore down on them, launching runs that impacted only against the *Rubicon*'s thick prow armour. Attacks down the side of the hull were shortened as the craft flashed by and those fighters who banked for a second run were targeted by the turrets now free of debris interference and reaping a harvest of burning fighter hulls. More than seventy craft were destroyed or disabled, their valuable pilots killed or stranded with little hope of rescue, munitions detonating in firing tubes before they could be fired, attacks scattered as the huge silver beak of the *Rubicon* ripped through space.

The strike cruiser's ordnance was depleted, and it was bleeding fire from scores of wounds. The Avengers and Starhawks had done their work, but they had not finished the *Rubicon* off.

Leaving shoals of attack craft whirling in its wake, and with the follow-up squadrons of attack boats and boarding torpedoes fleeing before it, the *Rubicon* headed at full speed towards Volcanis Ultor.

CAPTAIN GRAKINKO, ON the bridge of the *Unmerciful*, listened in to the sounds of his fighter assault breaking up. Crackling screams as cockpits filled with fire. Static-filled chains of explosions as ammunition cooked off. Transmissions cut short as power plants detonated. The crewmen operating the fighter command helm were used to hearing such long-range death and Grakinko had lost thousands of men in naval engagements before, but it was still disheartening.

'Navigation!' bellowed Grakinko above the growing din on the bridge. 'Why are we standing still? Where are they going?'

'Heading for the planet, sir!' came the reply from somewhere in navigation, where dozens of junior officers were wrestling with system charts and compasses while the cogitators smoked with the effort of calculations.

Grakinko let out a barking, triumphant laugh. 'Then we'll get in front of 'em and give 'em a broadside! Let's see the gakkers run away from that!' He slammed his hand down on the arm of his throne. 'Gunnery! What are our rates?'

The gunnery officer – seventh-generation Naval man, Grakinko remembered playing three-board regicide with his father – stood up smartly. 'Fresh gangs and fully loaded, captain. At their speed I can give her three full volleys to the prow.'

'And if we hang about to get them in the backside?'

The gunnery officer thought. 'A good two half-volleys to the stern.'

'I've got a bottle of dry amasec older than I am. Give me three half-volleys to her stern and it's yours, you hear?'

'Yes, captain!'

The *Unmerciful* wasn't a pure gunnery ship, but it had been refitted (against Grakinko's wishes, he admitted) with plenty of guns after the Gothic War and by the Emperor it could give a decent volley when it had to. Three full volleys, and then three half-volleys from the depleted gun gangs, should be enough to cripple any ship at point blank range. Then it was a matter of bringing the surviving fighters in and bombing the gak out of the strike cruiser until it came apart.

Grakinko thought he might let the escorts of Absolution Squadron get a sniff of the kill, too. It was the done thing, a gesture of courtesy to fellow captains.

Those upstarts on the *Holy Flame* could go gak themselves, though.

'Navigation, get us side-on to them now!' ordered Grakinko. He felt the *Unmerciful* lurching as its engines turned its old creaking hull round and hauled it into the path of the strike cruiser.

The holographic tactical display on the viewscreen zoomed in, leaving the scattered attack craft out of its field of vision. Instead it concentrated on two blips – the shining blue symbol denoting the *Unmerciful*, and the red triangle of the Chaos strike cruiser, streaming burning fuel and debris as it hurtled towards Volcanis Ultor.

ALARIC WAS STRAPPING himself into the grav-restraints when he heard klaxons going off all over the *Rubicon*.

'Collision warnings,' he said to himself, as the ship's engines roared louder.

THE UNMERCIFUL OPENED up with a few straggling shots, range finders that streaked past the oncoming prow of the *Rubicon*. The gunnery sergeants denoted the target in range and closing, the officer at the gunnery helm concurred. With that order, every gun on the port side of the *Unmerciful* let loose.

Against a ship with full shields and the ability to return fire, the effect would have been damaging but ultimately unspectacular. Against a ship with few shields and in no position to return fire, the guns could pour volley after unanswered volley into the strike cruiser's prow. The massive armoured beak of the strike cruiser, shielded with layers of adamantium and covered in engraved prayers of warding, was first battered and then pierced by the munitions fired by the massive guns. Plates of armour were ripped off, flung spiralling through space, trailing fire. Secondary explosions sent walls of flame spurting from between the seams of hull plates. With a single titanic eruption the whole prow was blasted off, a rushing cowl of flame billowing out from the front of the *Rubicon*. The void swallowed the fire and an ugly, blackened ruin of metal was all that remained of the ship's prow.

The ship didn't slow but it did veer dangerously, systems without number damaged, fires coursing along maintenance ways and corridors, bulkheads bursting into hard vacuum. The bridge was rocked, and had it been set a few metres further forward it would have been torn apart, too. Thousands of Malleus crew died, immolated, blown apart or sucked out into space. The wrecked prow shed armour sections, plumes of debris, and broken, frozen bodies.

THE THUNDERHAWK WAS thrown sideways, slamming against its moorings as the *Rubicon* rocked.

'Injuries?' voxed Alaric.

'None,' said Genhain, whose men were loaded into one drop-pod alongside the Thunderhawk.

'None here,' echoed Santoro.

Alaric checked the Space Marines in the Thunderhawk with him – his Marines were unhurt and it took more than that to injure one of Tancred's Terminators.

Alaric voxed the bridge. 'What was that?'

'Took the prow off,' came the reply, warped by the damaged vox systems. 'All forward locations lost.'

'And the bridge?'

'Minor damage. Nav is correcting our course. We'll hit the atmosphere in twenty-two minutes.'

From the tone of the crewman's voice and the background noise on the bridge, Alaric knew he wasn't alone in thinking that was too long.

THE RUBICON PASSED close underneath the *Unmerciful*, close enough for the wreckage raining off it to spatter like iron rain against the *Unmerciful*'s underside.

Gun gangs on the starboard side of the *Unmerciful* were under-manned and under-munitioned compared to those on the opposite gun deck, but they had their part to play, too. As the stern of the *Rubicon* emerged from under them the ship tilted to give them a better firing angle before they poured everything they had into the aft section of the strike cruiser.

The massive engine exhausts were punctured again and again as red lances of fire fell in a burning hail. Jets of superheated gas kilometres long shot from the ruptured engines. One plasma reactor was cracked open and boiling plasma flooded out, forming a ragged smouldering ribbon where it hit the cold of space. The secondary explosions tore a hole in the upper hull four decks deep, exposing the primary engineering command centre to the void. The chief engineering officers stared up at the yawning hole above them where the ceiling of their aft bridge had once been, their breath stolen from their bodies, their blood frozen, the *Unmerciful* rolling slowly and pouring fire into them from above.

The bridge's primary link with the engine section of the *Rubicon* was gone. As far as the state of the engines went, the ship was flying blind.

The starboard guns of the *Unmerciful* ran dry. The *Rubicon* passed underneath it, prow gone, stern badly chewed, spewing air, plasma and wreckage. But it was not dead yet. The fleet records on Iapetus would witness that it had survived worse.

Plasma reactors thrumming with the strain, the *Rubicon* plummeted on towards the pale disc of Volcanis Ultor.

CAPTAIN GRAKINKO LOOKED up to see the gunnery officer standing on front of him, the buttons of his neat starched uniform gleaming.

'That was a few shots short of four half-volleys from the starboard guns,' said the officer.

Cocky little prig, Grakinko thought, taking the bottle of amasec from within the arm of his command throne. Never taking his eyes of the officer he smashed the neck of the bottle on the edge of the arm and poured the whole bottle down his throat, letting it spill down his chin and the front of his uniform. When it was empty he threw the bottle to smash on the bridge floor.

Heretics or not, those gakkers knew how to build themselves a damn spaceship.

CAPTAIN PRYNCOS GURVEYLAN, seated behind one of the many banks of cogitators that made up the bridge of the *Holy Flame*, watched the *Rubicon* trailing wreckage as it ploughed through the curtain of fire from the

Unmerciful's starboard batteries. The *Unmerciful* was not a ship known for its guns, but it had opened fire on a closing opponent at point-blank range, with everything it had. It was a testament to the toughness of the enemy strike cruiser that it was still going.

Gurveylan was not a ship captain in the old sense. His word was not law on his ship – he left that privilege to Security Officer Lorn and Ship Commissar Gravic. He did not rule his bridge with an iron fist, since he could rely on his officers to do their duty. He was, instead, the executive arm of the *Holy Flame*'s officer corps. That was how they had done things at the Academy – teamwork, responsibility, obedience.

The giant holoprojection unit filled the bridge with the image of the enemy strike cruiser, its prow chewed off, ribbons of congealing plasma coiling from its engine section. The projection of the *Unmerciful* drifted through the ceiling of the bridge as the strike cruiser carried on, tracked by the *Holy Flame*'s sensors. It was headed directly for Volcanis Ultor – not taking any evasive action, just streaking towards the planet.

'I want a damage report on that ship,' said Gurveylan.

One of the several dozen engineering officers took the bridge vox-caster. 'The ship's an unknown marque, captain. It's a Space Marine strike cruiser. We don't have the specifications for it.'

'Give me your best guess.'

'Extensive prow damage, non-essential systems only. Command structures probably intact. One major plasma breach, engines down to seventy per cent. Crew casualties thirty to fifty per cent.'

'Gunnery and logistics!' snapped Gurveylan. 'If we match her speed and hit her with rolling broadside volleys, what is the probability she'll be crippled?'

There was a long pause as gunnery officers and lexmechanics scrabbled and calculated. 'Eighty per cent,' came the reply.

'Good. Comms, contact Absolution Squadron and have them take up high orbit in case the enemy gets through. Everyone else, I want us alongside the enemy ready to open fire in seven minutes. I think after this is done I shall shake Captain Grakinko's hand for softening her up for us. All stations, to your duties.'

At the order the hundred-strong officer corps of the *Holy Flame* snapped into action. The wood-panelled theatre of the bridge was full of activity. Navigation had to plan complex vectors. Gunnery and ordnance had to flood the gun decks with gangs to work the enormous broadside cannons. Engineering had to place damage control teams at strategic points because even the depleted firepower of the enemy strike cruiser could, with bad luck, cripple key systems of the *Holy Flame*.

A warship was a beautiful thing: every part and crewman directed at the same goal, bound by the same duty. From the short-lived labourers of the engine gangs to the command crew and Gurveylan himself, the whole of the *Holy Flame* was united towards a common purpose.

If all the Imperium were run like the *Holy Flame*, the Enemy would be thrown back into the darkness forever. But for now, Gurveylan was content to see the Chaos Marine strike cruiser reduced to flaming wreckage.

VALINOV COULD SEE, through a break in clouds of pollution, the white streaks of fire in the sky as the *Holy Flame* opened up on the *Rubicon*. He knew how much firepower the *Holy Flame* could bring to bear. If Valinov had pulled the right strings, if the threads all came together as they should, then the end was almost here.

Valinov was in an open-topped groundcar driving through the final dregs of ruins and shanty towns that marked the western edge of Hive Superior. In front of him the dry broken earth was cut through with lines of trenches edged with razorwire, and studded with large plasticrete bunkers. Even from some way behind the rear lines Valinov could see men hurrying to their positions, and hear the klaxons and vox-casters ordering them to full battle alert. Recoba had managed to put together a fairly cohesive defence and the word had spread quickly down the command chains that the enemy was in-system and, just as Valinov had predicted, were heading straight for Volcanis Ultor and Hive Superior.

The groundcar, driven by a liaison officer from the Balurian heavy infantry, rounded a rear supply post where pallets of lasgun power packs were being stacked, ready to go out to wherever the fighting required. Standing in the back of the car, Valinov watched as tiny crimson explosions blossomed in the sky as the battle in space raged on. The last of Ligeia's death cultists sat beside Valinov, her ever-taut muscles twitching now and then. Valinov had made sure the death cultist was hidden while he went about his business in Recoba's spire – she looked sinister and dangerous, and she could have compromised his attempts to be trusted. Out in the field, he didn't need to hide her any more. Valinov had to look like a warrior, and the death cultist certainly helped generate an air of lethality.

The groundcar turned north and Valinov saw they were driving just behind the Balurian lines. The Balurian heavy infantry were noted for their discipline, which was as much an asset to Valinov as the heavy half-carapace armour the Guardsmen wore or the lasguns they carried which were configured for high power and short range. The Balurians would do what they were told. That was all he needed of them.

Their officers were barking orders, shuffling units into position. Fields of fire were overlapping, counterattacks were placed, key weak points were reinforced with heavy weapons posts. The regimental commissar prowled the ranks, bolt pistol in hand, but Valinov knew he wouldn't have to use it on his disciplined, faithful men.

Except perhaps towards the end. But by then it wouldn't matter.

The groundcar headed towards the northern end of the line, the processing plant and the bleached shore of Lake Rapax. The glossy red armour of the Sisters of the Bloody Rose glinted in the murky greyness that passed for the morning sun on Volcanis Ultor. Valinov spotted Sisters on the roof of the plant itself, Retributor squads with heavy bolters. Seraphim units, with their distinctive winged jump packs, were kneeling in prayer as their Sisters Superior prepared them to act as counter-attacking units when the enemy broke through. Canoness Ludmilla had brought a whole commandery of more than two hundred Sisters of Battle. It was them that Valinov was going to review, to thank the canoness personally for answering Volcanis Ultor's call, and to warn her further about the nature of the Enemy. Their leader, he would tell her, carried a powerful daemon weapon that must be captured so the Inquisition could have it destroyed. And she would believe him, of course, because in high orbit the blazing sheets of broadside fire were proving him right.

Valinov had already won. The Lord of Change himself had promised him that – all he had to do was to go through the motions and let the threads of fate twist into shape around him. He could feel it even now, the weight of fate lying on Volcanis Ultor, crushing the freedom out of it. Chaos was pure freedom, the glory of the soul's full potential, the realisation of what mankind could be under the tutelage of the Lord of Change – but for Chaos to rule, first the minds of the mortal had to be squeezed dry of their freedom so they could receive the full wisdom of Tzeentch. Mankind had to be enslaved to the will of Tzeentch, so it could eventually become free. The masses would never understand, even though it was the only possible truth, and so it fell to men like Valinov to act as instruments of the coming Chaos.

The shape of the *Rubicon* could just be made out now in the sky, a twisted splinter of silver trailing debris and vented plasma like a comet.

The groundcar arrived at the rear of the Sisters' lines. The Balurian driver stepped smartly out and held open the door for Valinov and the death cultist.

Valinov stepped onto the parched, dusty ground, gathering his long blastcoat around him, shoulders back and hand on the pommel of his power sword like a true gentleman. The death cultist stood just behind him, and Valinov wondered if she had any idea of what she was involved in. She didn't speak, and Valinov didn't even know her name, but he knew she would follow him to the death just as she had her previous mistress, Ligeia.

Which was just as well, because whatever fate Tzeentch had in store for Volcanis Ultor, it would involve a great deal of death.

'BRIDGE!' YELLED ALARIC into the vox, almost unable to hear his own voice over the din of the *Rubicon* coming apart under the vast waves of punishment. Shells were still crashing into the hull, screaming as they detonated, hull plates were howling as they were ripped off the ship, air was booming out into the vacuum.

Voices sounded through the static. '...damage reports in... thirty per cent...'

'Can we get to low orbit?' shouted Alaric.

'...systems down, engines... down to twenty...' Alaric couldn't tell which one of the Malleus crew was speaking. It sounded like the bridge itself had sustained damage. How many of the command crew were dead? How many would it take before the *Rubicon* was left blind and crippled?

The Thunderhawk shook violently in its moorings, as if it was flying through heavy turbulence. The Grey Knights were held fast by their grav-restraints as explosions groaned through the ship.

Suddenly the static on the vox was gone and a clear voice was layered over the sounds of the dying strike cruiser. 'Brother-Captain Alaric, we've lost the bridge. We've set the *Rubicon* on a final deployment run but control systems are gone so there's no one to correct if the approach is wrong.' Alaric recognised the voice of the officer who held the comms helm, a man Alaric couldn't name. 'We will hit high atmosphere in six minutes if the engines hold. We're heading down to your decks now to make sure the hangar doors open.'

'Good work, officer,' said Alaric as the vox filled back up with static. 'What's your name?'

'None of us have names,' came the faint reply. 'Deployment in six minutes, brother-captain. The Emperor protects.'

THE STRIKE CRUISERS used by the Chapters of the Adeptus Astartes weren't built for gunnery. They were built for speed and resilience, since their primary purpose was to move Space Marines quickly and safely and to take part in boarding actions. They could take a hell of a lot of punishment, the equivalent of Imperial Navy ships of far larger classes, and so the *Holy Flame* had calculated that it would take almost its whole stock of munitions for its starboard guns to destroy the *Rubicon*.

The *Rubicon*, however, was not just a Space Marine strike cruiser, as rare and remarkable as those were. It had been commissioned by the Ordo Malleus whose resources dwarfed those of the highest Naval admiral. The *Rubicon* had been built using alloys and construction techniques so advanced the Adeptus Mechanicus could no longer replicate them. The Ordo Malleus demanded the best of their Chamber Militant, the Grey Knights, and they provided the best as well. The *Rubicon* was as solid a ship as had flown since the Dark Age of Technology.

The slow dance of the *Holy Flame* and the *Rubicon* twirled into the first wisps of Volcanis Ultor's atmosphere, the thin air ignited into long bright ribbons by the shells that pumped from the *Holy Flame*'s starboard guns. The *Rubicon* blossomed into flame as it entered the atmosphere, fire rippling like liquid up its sides, pouring from the ruined prow and billowing in huge fluid plumes from its shattered engines. A second plasma generator exploded and sent superheated plasma flashing through the whole engineering section. A section of hull blew out so huge that the *Rubicon* was split down half its length, spilling wreckage and bodies like a gutted fish. When the ordnance magazine detonated, the explosion was like an afterthought compared to the shrieks and eruptions as the *Rubicon* began to come apart.

The *Holy Flame* disengaged, forced out of the dance by the thickening atmosphere that threatened to melt the underside of the hull. But the *Rubicon* was tougher, and the remaining engines kept it on course to enter the atmosphere shallow enough to deploy its payload.

To hit the *Rubicon* with another broadside, the *Holy Flame* would have to loop around, adopt a shallower trajectory to enter the atmosphere, and slide into step with the enemy strike cruiser. But that manoeuvre would take almost twenty minutes to achieve, and by then it would be too late. Captain Gurveylan ordered it anyway.

In the end it was Absolution Squadron, who had waited just inside the atmospheric envelope, who killed the *Rubicon*. The three Sword Class escorts had enough firepower between them to see off the crippled *Rubicon* – with a bit of luck just one of them could have done it. But there was not enough time. Any second the *Rubicon* would send down its drop-pods full of Traitor Marines and then it wouldn't matter what happened to the crippled ship.

To the captain of Absolution Beta, the lead ship in the escorts' formation, his duty was clear. Captain Masren Thal was a pious man who had been born into the Navy and earned his place on the bridge with a service record as long as his lifetime. Thal knew that one day he would have to die doing the Emperor's work, and he had given his vow to the Emperor (who always listened, always watched) that when that time came he would not be found wanting.

He knew that his officers and crew, had he had the time to explain it to them, would have agreed. So it was with no hesitation that Captain Thal ordered Absolution Beta to ramming speed.

THE THUNDERHAWK ENGINES opened up, barely audible over the near-deafening roar of Volcanis Ultor's atmosphere burning against the underside of the *Rubicon*'s hull. Alaric would have voxed his battle-brothers to be strong and have faith, but he didn't think they could hear him. It was better to leave them to their own prayers.

The Thunderhawk lurched forwards as its engines thrust it against its docking clamps, ready to shoot the ship forward when the clamps were released. The inside of the passenger compartment was bathed red as warning lights came on – Alaric could see the grim face of Justicar Tancred as he mouthed the Rites of Detestation, one hand touched to the copy of the *Liber Daemonicum* that was always locked in a compartment in his chest armour.

There was no way of contacting Santoro or Genhain. The vox was a screaming mess of interference. He couldn't even signal the Malleus crewman in the Thunderhawk's cockpit. Alaric realised the pilot was probably one of the few crewmen left alive on the *Rubicon*.

So many had to die just so the fight could continue. So many had to suffer so the Grey Knights could do their duty. It was as if Chaos had already won – but then that was the same thinking that drove men into the arms of Chaos in the first place. Alaric spat out a prayer of contrition.

An impossibly loud explosion ripped through the ship behind the Thunderhawk, an appalling crescendo of tortured metal. Something was tearing through the ship, something massive. Or perhaps the ship was finally splitting in two, the strain of entering the atmosphere too much for the shattered hull.

The Thunderhawk and the drop-pods wouldn't make it. The engines would send the gunship smashing into the flight deck doors because there was no one left alive to make sure they opened. The drop-pods would stay fixed in their clamps until they shattered when the *Rubicon* crashed into Volcanis Ultor. The Grey Knights would die, and Ghargatuloth had known all along it would end this way.

Alaric put a hand to his copy of the *Liber Daemonicum* locked in his breastplate, and prayed that someone would avenge him.

Alaric was slammed back into his grav-couch as the Thunderhawk shot forward. The viewport next to Alaric snapped open and he could see the flight deck rushing by – promethium tanks spewed flame, charred bodies lay in pieces, holes gaped into space streaked with fire.

Then the screams of the dying ship were gone, replaced by the pure roar of the Thunderhawk's engines. Alaric craned his neck to see the *Rubicon* shrinking behind the ship, a plume of flame gushing from the flight decks where the Thunderhawk had waited a moment before. The prow of another ship punched suddenly through the tortured hull of the *Rubicon*, cutting through the strike cruiser like a knife, massive explosions erupting behind it as its own hull was sheared in two by the force of the impact.

Alaric didn't see the *Rubicon* explode, but he felt it, the shockwave thudding through the gunship as it descended in its landing course. He knew that the final plasma reactors had gone critical, and that the chain reaction would have turned both ships into a ball of expanding flame like a new star in the sky of Volcanis Ultor.

'...pod down...' came a crackling vox from either Santoro or Genhain. One of them had made it at least, maybe both if the surviving Malleus crew had been quick enough. Not that any of the crew survived now, of course.

'Battle-brothers,' shouted Alaric over the noise of the engines. His Grey Knights were all brought out of their private prayers and looked to him. 'Ghargatuloth will think we are probably dead. I have every intention of showing him that we are not. And though we yet live there is little chance that many of us will survive. Pray now, then, as if this is your last word to the Emperor.'

The Grey Knights bowed their heads.

'I am the hammer,' began Alaric. 'I am the sword in His hand...'

SEVENTEEN
LAKE RAPAX

CANONESS LUDMILLA HURRIED through the twisting, cramped trench towards the front line. She passed squads of Battle Sisters, and offered them a quick blessing as she passed. The hush over the front lines was chilling – Ludmilla had seen enough battles to associate it with the sudden unleashing of violence that was sure to follow.

She turned a corner and saw the front-line trench stretching before her, its forward edge snarled with razorwire. Ludmilla had almost a hundred Sisters in the front trench; they were the rock against which the attack would break. The Sisters were excellent troops for fighting off a massed assault – their power armour and bolters kept them alive long enough for the Seraphim counter-attacks.

The sound of murmured prayers was a quiet backdrop to the silence. Each Sister had endless pages of prayers memorised, and many had those sacred words sewn into the cloth sleeves or tabards over their armour. Their faith was a shield, a weapon, a way of life.

Sisters were sheltering beneath the front wall of the trench. Trench junctions were held by isolated heavy weapons Sisters, carrying heavy bolters or multi-melta guns to turn enemy breakthroughs into killing zones. Several tanks were dug in to act as anti-tank bunkers – an Excorcist tank was positioned where it could send its payload of rockets streaking down the broad trench should the enemy take it.

Sisters Superior, quietly leading their units' final ministrations, saluted discreetly as the canoness walked down the trench to take her own position on the front line. Ludmilla switched onto the vox-channel that let her communicate with the whole commandery of more than two hundred Sisters, most of them soldiers about to join the fight.

'The Emperor is our father and our guardian,' began Ludmilla, quoting the Ecclesiastical Fundamentals of the revered Saint Mina herself, in whose name the Order of the Bloody Rose had been founded millennia before. 'But we must also guard the Emperor. For He is all humankind, and humankind is no more than its faith and diligence in the Emperor's name. An injury to that faith is an injury to the Emperor and to every citizen of the Imperium. It is through affirmation of that faith that our greatest duty lies, but sometimes mere affirmation does not suffice and we must act against those who would harm the faith of humanity through heresy. For we are engaged in an unending war for the soul of the Imperium. Though it may seem the fight will never end, there is victory even in the defeat we see threatening all around.

'There is no greater proclamation of faith than to offer up our very lives to guard the soul of humankind. In this we win a victory greater in magnitude than the harm that any heretic can inflict, and so every battle is a shining triumph that the traitor and the apostate can never take away from us.'

Ludmilla let her words hang in the air, the final words dictated by Saint Mina on her death-bed. Every Sister had heard them before. Now, in the calm before the slaughter, every Sister heard the words more clearly than ever before.

Then, in a low, mournful voice, Canoness Ludmilla began to sing.

'*A spiritus dominatus, domine, libra nos…*'

Recognising the High Gothic opening lines, the Sisters Superior joined their canoness in the invocation of the Fede Imperialis.

'*From the lightning and the tempest, our Emperor, deliver us…*'

The Fede Imperialis began to echo around the front line as the Battle Sisters took up the hymn.

'*From plague, deceit, temptation and war, our Emperor, deliver us…*'

The Sisters of the Seraphim squads behind the front line and the Retributor units stationed around the industrial plant joined in the hymn. The crews of the tanks and the Sisters Hospitaller setting up casualty stations along the rear lines sang, too, their voices ringing through the vox. Even the Sisters Famulous back in Cardinal Recoba's spire sang, steeling their hearts so their faith would be equal to the task.

'*From the scourge of the Kraken, our Emperor, Deliver us…*'

Those Guardsmen who knew the Fede Imperialis, the battle-hymn of the Ecclesiarchy, joined in. The singing rang out from the northern end of the line, hundreds of voices raised in affirmation forming a choir that filled the polluted air with faith and hope.

They were still singing when the remains of the *Rubicon* crashed into the Balurian line.

THE THUNDERHAWK WAS sweeping low over the broken plains of Volcanis Ultor to keep below the sensors of anti-aircraft guns. Alaric could see the plain streaking past below a murky sky, dirty pale earth drained of all its life, bleached by chemical pollutants, dried and cracked by aeons of merciless industry. It was barren and bleak, a place where men could not survive long amongst the ash dunes and toxic dribbles that passed for rivers.

Alaric checked the runes displayed on his forearm readout. The drop-pods' beacons were working – the pods of Santoro and Genhain had both made it down, landing close enough to one another for the point between them to serve as a rendezvous. The Thunderhawk could not get close to the defences and the Grey Knights had no armour to transport them – they would have to reach Lake Rapax on foot. What little Alaric had seen of the defences from the *Rubicon*'s bridge indicated that the end of the line was very well-defended. It would not be easy. Ghargatuloth had seen to that.

All Alaric knew about the resting place of Saint Evisser was that it was on the shore of Lake Rapax. That much Serevic had told him. Everything else he would have to find out the hard way.

'How long?' yelled Alaric over the engines.

'Thirty seconds!' shouted the Malleus pilot in reply. Alaric tried to imagine what the man must be thinking, knowing that all his colleagues had died in the fireball the Thunderhawk had only just escaped. But who could know what such a man was thinking when he didn't even have a name to call his own, when he had been stripped of everything that made him human so he could better serve the Ordo Malleus?

The Thunderhawk ramp rolled down and Alaric saw the ground speeding past beneath it, the Thunderhawk's wake kicking up spirals of ash. They were going in fast – there would be more than enough artillery, perhaps even Ordinatus, to destroy the Grey Knights before they could even launch their attack. They had to move fast, for every moment until they got to Lake Rapax was a moment they were intolerably exposed.

The *Rubicon* had tried to contact Volcanis Ultor to claim the Grey Knights were on Imperial business, but after the first few exchanges, all communications were cut. The defenders were convinced the Grey Knights were the heralds of a Chaos attack, and had sealed their vox-nets and other communications in case the imaginary enemy tried to infect their minds. The only way to get through the defences would be to fight through them, and Alaric could feel the Imperial blood on his hands already.

'We're going in hot, prepare to deploy!' shouted Alaric, the acrid chemical smell of Volcanis Ultor filling the Thunderhawk. Squad Alaric and Squad Tancred snapped off their grav-restraints. The Thunderhawk slewed around and decelerated, the Grey Knights inside holding on tight as the ground loomed close.

Alaric jumped first, followed by the men of his squad. Squad Tancred was next, their armoured bodies smashing craters in the ground as they landed. Justicar Tancred himself held the sword of Mandulis, its mirror-polished blade shining incongruously in the swirling dust and murky light.

'Get away from here,' voxed Alaric to the Malleus pilot, possibly the last survivor of the *Rubicon*. 'Head west.'

The pilot didn't answer. The Thunderhawk swooped down as it turned, then its engines gunned and it shot off leaving the swirling trail of ash.

Alaric glanced at the runes on his readout. They pulsed brightly – the drop-pods were a short jog away.

'Genhain, Santoro, we're down,' voxed Alaric.

'Genhain down,' came one justicar's voice. 'Ready to move out.'

'Santoro down,' said the other.

'We're heading your way. Stay defensive and be ready to…'

Alaric was cut off as he saw a rose-red light burning through the gauze of dust. Something had punched through Volcanis Ultor's mantle of bruise-coloured cloud, burning red. It seemed to be falling incredibly slowly, its underside white-hot, huge sheets of fire trailing behind. Alaric could hear a roar like a hurricane and he recognised, stripped bare and melting, the shape of one of the *Rubicon*'s engines.

'All Space Marines take cover!' yelled Alaric into the vox, and dropped down to the fractured ground.

A great white flash of heat burst like a wave. A roar followed, a shock-wave running through the earth like the blast from a huge bomb, a hot blast of air washing across the plain. The sound was appalling, like an army of daemons howling. Suddenly the fire in the sky was gone and a mantle of ash and pulverised rock was drawn across the plain like a thick black blanket, turning Volcanis Ultor as dark as night. The hot, dry storm ripped over Alaric's Grey Knights as they took cover, the shock-waves rippling back and forth. The vox was a wall of interference, the feeble sun was shut out, the sky replaced by a grimy swirling mass of dust and ash

Alaric yelled at the top of his lungs. 'To me, Grey Knights! Press on! Stay close!'

The Grey Knights could not stay where they were. They were vulnerable – man-to-man they were some of the best soldiers in the galaxy, but trapped in the open they were just so many targets.

Tancred lumbered out of the darkness, the sword of Mandulis shining so bright it seemed to be on fire. His Terminator-armoured battle-brothers followed him. 'At your side, brother-captain,' he shouted grimly.

Alaric gathered his men and plunged on into the storm, heading for Squads Santoro and Genhain, and Lake Rapax.

AN INTACT STRIKE cruiser at full speed would have been like a meteor hitting Volcanis Ultor, forging a winter decades long, exterminating whole ecosystems. The falling section of the *Rubicon* represented a fraction of its weight and it had decelerated dramatically to deploy its payload, and so it did not annihilate most of Hive Superior and a fair chunk of the plains surrounding it.

To the city's defenders, that was little consolation. The engine section landed towards the southern end of the line held by the Balurian heavy infantry and it hit with a force larger than a shell from one of the huge Ordinatus artillery pieces built by the Adeptus Mechanicus. A full orbital strike from a battleship would scarcely have done more damage.

The heat and shockwave released by the impact vaporised a good portion of the Balurian regiment, and hundreds of men drowned in the flood of ash and dust that coursed through their trenches. Three kilometres of trench were destroyed, from the front line to the rearward assembly areas. The command post was wiped out, killing the Balurian colonel Gortz and almost his entire staff. Sisters Hospitaller perished at their medical posts. Supply posts full of equipment and munitions were crushed, exploding into flat sheets of fire and shrapnel.

The Ordinatus deployed behind the Balurian lines was destroyed, its immense cannon barrel and titanic loader systems ripped apart by the flood of wreckage that spewed from the engine section as it disintegrated.

The engines did not explode, for the plasma reactors had bled their contents into the upper atmosphere when the Absolution Beta had torn the strike cruiser apart. Instead there was a terrible eruption of darkness, a pall of black ash and earth that boiled up almost as high as Hive Superior's outer spires and billowed out across the plain. It swept out over the no-man's-land beyond the front lines, down through the sections south of the Balurians and north to halfway across Lake Rapax. It boiled into Hive Superior's outer reaches. Some were buried, others suffocated, while others dug themselves out of drifts of ash that gathered everywhere.

The whole north end of the defences was buried under a blanket of blackness, as if night had fallen. Further south disruption was immense – communications cut, bunkers undermined by the shockwave, eardrums burst, unstable munitions and fuel dumps detonated. Confusion paralysed the defences, and only the most well-equipped and disciplined troops could hope to fight with anything approaching full effectiveness.

Those troops were the Battle Sisters of the Adepta Sororitas.

ALARIC SAW JUSTICAR Santoro through the gloom, crouched with his storm bolter ready to fire. The other four Space Marines of his squad were in a tight formation around the drop-pod site, hunkered down behind the opened steel petals of the pod.

Alaric clapped Santoro on the back. 'Good to see you got down.'

Santoro nodded grimly. 'Night has fallen early. It looks like we're in the right place.'

Genhain loomed out of the darkness. Were it not for Alaric's enhanced vision he would not have been able to see the justicar at all. 'Lachis is hurt,' he said – the vox was still down so vocal communication was the only option.

'How bad?'

'Mangled a leg in the landing. He'll lose it.'

Alaric saw Brother Grenn and Ondurin helping Lachis along – the lower part of his right leg was severely mangled, bone jutting from the sundered armour plates. Anyone other than a Space Marine would have been unconscious.

'Brother, can you fight?' said Alaric.

'Always,' said Lachis. He was a relatively young Grey Knight, having been promoted from a novice into Genhain's squad just over two years before. 'But not run.'

'Your brothers will help you until we reach the front line. After that you move under your own power. We'll need your covering fire.'

'Understood, brother-captain.'

'We'll leave you behind. You won't survive.'

'Understood.'

Alaric looked through the dust storm. He couldn't make out the processing plant that marked the end of the line and the shore of Lake Rapax but he could sense it there, the centre of a web spun by Ghargatuloth, drawing them near.

'The vox is out and we won't be getting it back, so we stay close and stay in communication. The defences are manned by Imperial citizens but while Ghargatuloth lives they are the enemy. When we reach the Prince of a Thousand Faces, we will have our revenge for their deaths.'

With that Alaric ran into the darkness, his Grey Knights following him, every thought turned towards how many would have had to die before this fight was done, and how every death would be visited on Ghargatuloth.

CANONESS LUDMILLA CROUCHED down in the front line, feeling her filtration implants grinding in her throat as they cleaned out the dust and ash that would otherwise flood her lungs. Several Sisters had put on their Sabbat-pattern helms, keeping the storm out of their eyes; Ludmilla rarely wore hers, preferring to see the enemy as plainly as possible the better to hate them.

Sister Lachryma, the leader of Ludmilla's Seraphim, hurried down the trench towards the canoness.

'It hit the Balurians!' Lachryma called out. 'They're in disarray. Gortz's staff is gone. It's just us now.'

'Did you see what it was?'

Lachryma was standing right beside Ludmilla now. The veteran Seraphim's face was streaked with sweat and grime, and the glossy red of her armour was dull with ash. 'It fell from the sky. Some Sisters think the Ordinatus crew has betrayed us. It looked more like a meteor. Some foul weapon of the Enemy.'

'With the Emperor's grace the Enemy will have died beneath it, too.'

'His plan is rarely so simple,' said Lachryma grimly.

'I have heard few words truer,' replied Ludmilla, drawing her inferno pistol.

Somewhere down the trench, ranging shots snapped from a heavy bolter, sharp gunshots stitching through the dim roar of the storm.

'Enemy sighted!' came the call down the trench.

'Give me range!' yelled back Ludmilla at the Sisters.

'Close! Visibility's nothing, but they're Space Marines!'

Chaos Marines. And with the visibility so bad, the Sisters would have to fight them toe-to-toe, without fields of fire from the Retributor squads at the plant.

'Lachryma, bring your Sisters forward. We can't fall back, the fight will be here.'

'Yes, canoness.'

Sisters Superior were calling out final battle-rites. Ludmilla could feel the tension, perceived not by her senses but by her years of battlefield experience – the tension before every battle, now about to break in a shower of blood beneath the darkness that had fallen over Volcanis Ultor.

Space Marine bolter fire erupted and heavy bolters opened up in return, snapping back at half-glimpsed targets. Space Marines had full auto-senses that would give them a crucial advantage here, when the Sisters couldn't make out targets at long bolter range.

'Sisters!' yelled Ludmilla. 'For the Throne and the end of time! Charge!'

ALARIC SAW THE first defenders rising out of the trench in front of him, trampling through the razorwire, heavy bolter fire snapping in red-white tracers from behind them. He saw red armour and black cloth, an Imagifer's banner depicting the symbol of the Bloody Rose.

Sisters. Ghargatuloth had put them up against the Sisters of Battle. The foulness of the daemon prince's plan just got deeper – the Sisters were dedicated, faithful, noble, soldiers of the Imperial church who had fought under Inquisitorial command innumerable times.

There was no room for doubt. No mercy, not even here. Here, they were the enemy.

When the first bolter shells rang off his armour, Alaric broke into a sprint, charging headlong for the front line. Bolter fire opened up all around him and his armour was battered terribly, waves of shells ripping through the air. Alaric dived into the fray, Nemesis halberd swinging, smashing one Sister back and slicing off the arm of another. Hate-filled eyes looked through the darkness, and Alaric could hear prayers to the Emperor yelled over the howling of the storm and the drumming of the gunfire. Dvorn was beside Alaric and there was a flash like a lightning strike as his hammer swatted one Sister backwards.

Tancred battered his way through the Sisters who charged against him, swatting them aside. Brother Karlin's Incinerator sent a gout of flame out to clear a path and a Sister's flamer roared in reply, illuminating Squad Tancred in a sea of fire so they seemed to be battling the Sisters across the surface of hell.

Alaric's Space Marines were charging forward with him now. Brother Clostus was fighting, halberd to power sword, with a Sister Superior who yelled the Catechisms of Righteous Loathing as she fought.

She sliced down and cut deep into Clostus's chest, punching her free hand hard into his face and barging him back into the swirling ash.

Alaric couldn't stop now. He had to press on.

Fire was streaking from all sides. Heavy psycannon rounds punched through the air from Genhain's squad who were following Alaric in. Somewhere back there the wounded Brother Lachis was left by Squad Genhain, to cover his battle-brothers with storm bolter fire while he crouched down for cover on his shattered leg.

Squad Santoro, beyond Tancred, reached the lines first, leaping into a trench junction that would have been covered by heavy weapons Sisters had they been able to see him. Alaric saw the clusters of bolter fire like chains of firecrackers where a short-range firefight developed. Alaric himself was still out in the open and exposed, trying to follow the trail literally blazed by Squad Tancred. Alaric ran towards the glow of flamers and saw Tancred, wading knee-deep in burning promethium streaking from several flamer-armed Sisters firing from the trench itself.

Clostus's rune was gone from Alaric's retinal display – either the Marine was dead or he was too far away for his armour's life sign readings to get through the interference. Either way he was lost to them now.

Alaric saw one of Squad Santoro, probably Brother Jaeknos, on his knees, his armour pocked and smoking by a dozen bolter wounds. He was still firing but his Nemesis halberd was on the ground – Alaric saw the hand he normally used to wield it was reduced to useless bloody rags. The ash closed in on him as vengeful Sisters bore down on him, bolters blazing.

'Forward, Knights!' yelled Alaric. 'Forward!'

Shells ripped into his shoulder pad and hot pain blossomed there. Tancred, silhouetted in the blazing fire, kicked his way through a bank of razorwire and dropped into the trench, bellowing war-prayers as he did so. Alaric shook off the pain and followed – a Sister charged from behind the cover of the razorwire and ducked Alaric's first blow, grabbing one shoulder pad and smashing him in the face with the butt of her bolter.

Alaric grabbed the collar of her power armour, lifted her up, and pitched her into the fire at his feet. She scrambled to her knees, blazing horribly from head to toe, and Alaric swiped her head off with his halberd as she moved to fire.

Lesser men would break. Not a Grey Knight. For if Alaric gave in to despair at killing Sisters, then Ghargatuloth would win yet again.

He clawed through the razorwire and dropped into the trench. Bodies were already choking the trench section, battered with bolter fire or cut open by Nemesis weapons. Tancred was still fighting, the sword of Mandulis mirror-bright in spite of the dust, sprays of blood frozen in the strobing gunfire as Brother Locath plunged his halberd blade through the chest of a Sister Superior.

The trench was their best chance, away from the gunfire of the Sisters charging forward from the rear lines, where the Grey Knights' superior armour and close combat skills would help them the most.

'North!' yelled Alaric. 'North! Now!'

Heavy bolter fire streaked down from ahead. Santoro yelled for his Marines to take cover in alcoves and dugouts as Tancred stomped forward to take the brunt of the fire on his Terminator's superior armour. Alaric, even with his enhanced senses, could barely see what was going on ahead – his superior hearing picked out the different sounds of storm bolter shells smacking through the air and heavy bolter fire thudding into the sides of the trench. Ceramite armour cracked. The sword of Mandulis cut the air and the low roar of burning promethium swirled from somewhere ahead.

A new sound suddenly cut through the din – engines shrieking in an arc overhead, plunging down towards Squads Alaric and Genhain to the rear of the Grey Knights' spearhead.

Alaric knew jump packs when he heard them. He knew the Seraphim would hit home before he saw them plunging through the black ceiling of ash, he knew their twin bolt pistols would fill the confined trench with a wall of shrapnel. He knew that the elite close combat Sisters were the hardest-hitting shock troops the Ecclesiarchy had, and that the Grey Knights would have to kill these brave, zealous servants of the Emperor if they were to survive.

The Seraphim Superior dived, power sword-first, streaking through the darkness. Alaric turned the point of her sword but the Seraphim slammed into him, her face against his, her breath hot through gritted teeth. Alaric stumbled and fell onto his back, the thrust of the Seraphim's jump pack driving him into the mud. He pinned the Sister's blade under his halberd arm but she got a knee down on his storm bolter hand. Her free hand pistoned up and slammed down an elbow into Alaric's jaw – the blow made him reel but he held on, trying to break the Sister's hold, throw her off him before the other Seraphim now battling Squad Genhain could come to her aid and riddle Alaric with bolt pistol fire.

'From the blasphemy of the fallen...' she snarled as she struck again and again.

'...our Emperor, deliver us...' gasped Alaric.

The Seraphim Superior paused for a split-second as Alaric spoke the words of the Fede Imperialis. In that moment Alaric wrenched his hand free and punched the Seraphim so hard she was flung against the side of the trench. He felt her jaw give way – had it not broken the blow would probably have snapped her neck.

Dvorn shattered a Seraphim's hand but the pistol in her other hand stitched heavy bolts into his breastplate, raising showers of sparks as he was battered backwards. Brother Lykkos, hampered at close quarters by his psycannon, kicked a Seraphim's legs out from under her only for her to squirm away from under his aim, so he blasted a crater of glowing mud out of the trench floor. Sisters were firing blindly into the trench from above, and gunfire was spitting in from everywhere. Squad Genhain was holding off another Seraphim squad – explosions sounded from the north as Tancred and Santoro faced heavy weapons from Retributor squads and dug-in tanks.

The air stank of blood, propellant and sweat. Ash was everywhere, the darkness lit from beneath by flame and muzzle flashes like the heart of a hellish thunderstorm.

The Seraphim Superior was dragging herself to her feet, blood running from her mouth.

'From the begetting of daemons!' shouted Alaric above the gunfire, his storm bolter levelled at the Sister. 'Our Emperor, deliver us!'

There was a commotion behind Alaric and he saw a figure vaulting over the razorwire into the middle of the Grey Knights – Vien tried to fend her off but the Sister was quicker, blocking Vien's halberd with a forearm and swinging him behind her to close with Alaric. Alaric swung his aim around but suddenly he himself was staring into the barrel of an inferno pistol.

'From the curse of the mutant...' said Alaric levelly. He saw the Sister's armour was detailed in gold with the symbols of the Ecclesiarchy. High Gothic words were embroidered into the cloth of her sleeves and the red rose of her Order was tattooed onto her cheek. Her face was lined and bore several faint scars, left over from reconstruction by a good medicae, he guessed.

'Grey Knight,' said the canoness. 'Show me the book.'

Alaric let his aim fall and he opened up the small compartment in his chest armour. He took out the small volume of the *Liber Daemonicum*. 'Read from it.'

Alaric opened the book at a well-thumbed page. 'The nature of the daemon is such that righteous men may not know it, and yet know it we must to fight it...' read Alaric hurriedly, feeling the death around him, the storm bolters of his Grey Knights firing, the clash of blades on ceramite, the explosions from up ahead. 'And so the Enemy must be known not through direct discourse and study but through allegory and parable…'

'Sisters!' shouted the canoness, and Alaric knew she was talking over the vox – the Sisters must have had a robust vox-relay station somewhere in the rear lines, that kept their vox-net intact. 'Cease fire! Now, all of you!'

'Grey Knights cease fire!' echoed Alaric. An explosion sounded from Tancred's spearhead down the trench. 'Now, Tancred! Cease fire and fall back to me!'

Alaric glanced around. The Seraphim were standing back, bolt pistols aimed. Several Sisters appeared at the edge of the trench training their bolters on Alaric. The Grey Knights moved warily towards Alaric, storm bolters levelled, Nemesis weapons held ready. Alaric saw Lykkos was bleeding from several rents in his armour and Dvorn's chestplate was pockmarked and smoking. Squad Genhain had fared better but every Marine was looking the worse for wear, covered in wounds and bullet scars. Several Sisters lay wounded or dead, and the mud of the trench was soaked with blood.

The Seraphim Superior was helped to her feet by one of her Sisters. Her skin was pallid with shock but there was no hiding the hate in her eyes.

'Justicar?' said the canoness.

'Brother-Captain,' replied Alaric. 'Acting.'

'I fear there has been a terrible error of judgement.' The canoness looked down at the Sororitas bodies in the trench. She could rein in her emotions when so much was at stake, but she could not completely hide her sorrow.

'There was no error,' said Alaric. 'The source of the suffering on the Trail is here on Volcanis Ultor. The Enemy has used Imperial troops to guard it. The same Enemy was counting on none of the defenders having heard of the Grey Knights, in which respect I am assuming he was wrong.'

'My Order served with Lord Inquisitor Karamazov at the Tigurian Flow. The Grey Knights were there, too, though I never fought with them. You were fortunate I recognised you at all.' The canoness lowered her inferno pistol. 'Canoness Carmina Ludmilla, Order of the Bloody Rose.'

'Brother-Captain Alaric. Are your Sisters defending Lake Rapax?'

'It hardly seems worth defending. We are holding the end of the line, the only thing here is the processing plant.'

'Is there anything else on the lake?'

'No, just the plant.'

'Have you been inside?'

Ludmilla shook her head. 'Valinov warned us the chemicals inside were volatile.'

Alaric started. 'Inquisitor Valinov?'

'Yes. Did he send you?'

Alaric paused. How could he begin to explain? But seeing the noble canoness waiting for an answer, he knew the only choice was to tell her the truth. 'Valinov is the enemy. He was sentenced to death by the Ordo Malleus and escaped. The confusion is his doing. He ordered you to defend the plant because it conceals the place where his master will rise.'

'Valinov is an inquisitor.' Ludmilla's voice was stern – Alaric could tell he hadn't yet completely earned her trust. 'He has the blessing of Cardinal Recoba and everyone else on Volcanis Ultor. You, however, have killed my Sisters and very nearly killed me. Grey Knight or not you are asking me to believe a great deal in a very short time.'

'We are not aggressors here,' said Alaric. 'Your Sisters fired the first shot.'

Ludmilla glanced to the south, where the inferno of the blast site glowed dully through the ash. 'The Balurian heavy infantry would argue otherwise, brother-captain.'

Tancred stomped through the trench towards Alaric. Smoke was pouring off him – the servos of his Terminator armour were working hard and the ceramite plates were charred and stank of promethium. 'Canoness,' he said darkly. 'Your Sisters fight well. I wish I had found out another way.'

Ludmilla glared at him.

'Where is Valinov now?' asked Alaric.

'He has offices in Cardinal Recoba's spire,' replied Ludmilla. 'But he was due to review our positions when the crash happened.'

'Then he's here already.' Alaric looked down at the dead Sisters, brave soldiers and servants the Imperium could not afford to replace. Sisters Hospitaller were hurrying from the rearward lines to tend to the wounded and take away the dead. 'I am sick of being too late. canoness, I need you and your Sisters. Valinov is raising something terrible on the shore of Lake Rapax and he has created our conflict to cover his tracks. He assumed that we would fight each other to a standstill, but he was wrong. I intend to prove him wrong with or without you, Sister, but I fear we cannot prevail on our own.'

'I cannot help you if I do not know what we are fighting, brother-captain.'

Alaric took a breath. How could he articulate something like this, an evil composed of pure knowledge that used insanity and corruption as its weapon, that could not be fought or killed or understood, that once risen would ingrain itself into the fabric of the Imperium until it would take another thousand years to find?

'Sister,' began Alaric carefully, 'There is no time, so I cannot make you begin to truly understand. But it calls itself Ghargatuloth...'

EIGHTEEN
THE STATUE GARDEN

THE BALURIAN HEAVY infantry had lost a third of its men, wiped out by a crash that turned them into dust that swirled over the mantle of ash and mud. Colonel Gortz was dead and communications were gone, so another third were cut off and helpless, stranded blind and out of contact, forced to hunker down and hold their defences against an enemy they could not see.

The rest of the Balurians, more than seven hundred troops, gathered towards the northern end of the Imperial lines. The Balurians were exceptionally disciplined troops but with so many officers dead there was no one to lead them against the enemy that would surely attack in the wake of the catastrophe.

But the Imperial Guard could fight on without officers. Because when officers could not lead – whether through incompetence, corruption, lack of willpower or, as at Volcanis Ultor, sheer magnitude of casualties, the Guard had another command structure that took over.

A commissar was not a tactician. He was not a strategist. He could not fine-tune an assault or design the perfect defence. But when the Guard needed leadership, such things were irrelevant. Commissars led when the Guardsmen needed to be led from the front into the teeth of a foe a colonel and his officers could not face. When there was no room for tactics or skill or anything but sheer bloody-minded, fanatical bravery, the commissars took the lead.

Commissar Thanatal had always known he might have to take the Balurians into combat when there was no one else to do it. It was what he had been trained for since he first came to the schola progenium, an orphan of one of innumerable Imperial wars. In many years of harsh tutelage he had learned that duty was a sword that would kill you as surely as it could be wielded against the enemy, a sword it was his destiny to wield. He did not care about the lives of his men or the cleanness of the victory, or even his own wellbeing. He cared about punishing the enemies of the Emperor for the sin of daring to exist in His sight, in bringing the souls of his Guardsmen to the embrace of the Emperor in the holy light of war.

He believed in culling the cowardly and the weak-willed, so the Balurians could count only true Imperial spirits in their number when the time came to die for the Emperor's glory.

The hem of Thanatal's long black leather coat dragged in the clotted mud of the trenches and his mesh armour was heavy as he struggled northwards through the blinding ash. He heard men yelling their comrades' names, screaming in pain, praying out loud. He stumbled over choking bodies. The commissar took off his peaked cap and pulled his rebreather over his head, breathing deeply as the filter screened out the worst of the ash.

The clouds parted and Thanatal could see, just, as if in the dead of night. Torchlight cut through the swirling gloom. Men, dim struggling shapes, were scrambling over the ruined defences, heading back in the direction of Volcanis Ultor.

Thanatal saw a sergeant directing a gaggle of men. 'Sergeant!' he yelled. 'Where are you going?'

'They're coming at us through the Sisters' lines. We're gathering at the rearward trenches. We're going to hold the supply trenches, set up another line…'

Thanatal drew his bolt pistol and shot the sergeant through the throat. The soldiers nearby stopped dead.

'The regiment!' yelled Thanatal as if he were bawling orders on the parade ground, 'Will advance to the north! The enemy has assaulted us to cut us off from his objective, but he has failed! While Balurians still live, the enemy will be punished!'

Men tried to scramble through the darkness away from Thanatal. Two more shots barked out and a Guardsmen fell, draped over the razorwire. No one else ran.

'The enemy is to the north! The regiment will advance!'

Men were gathering around him. Thanatal strode as best he could through the bodies and mud, clambering over the crumbling edge of the trench so all the men could see him. He grabbed a torch off one of the men and held it high, casting a finger of light that pointed upwards through the ash.

'The enemy is trying to surround us and cut us off! Even now he butchers our brothers and plots our deaths! Even now he thinks he has won! But if he wants victory then by the Emperor, he will have to kill us all! While one Balurian lives the Emperor will suffer no defeat!' Thanatal fired again, at random this time into the murk. More Balurians were scrambling towards him. He walked north, through the wreckage and razorwire, and gradually the pull of the crowd drew more and more with him.

'To the north!' men were shouting. 'They're gonna get behind us! Follow me!'

Out of the chaos was forged a growing crowd of men, stumbling through the darkness, Thanatal never letting up as he commanded their attention. He told them of the revenge they were seeking. He fired at men who tried to crawl away as he approached. He took the anger of the Balurians and turned it into something that drowned out their fear, and his heart swelled as he thought of all those loyal minds turned upon him when they could have been seeking refuge in despair.

He was their salvation. He was walking the path that led them away from the sin of cowardice and into the blinding light of the Emperor.

The enemy was here. They had to be. The devastating crash was the first gambit in an all-out attack, and Thanatal would not let his Balurian charges lose the chance to be in the heart of it.

'Commissar!' came a voice from up ahead. Thanatal saw the shape of an armoured car through the ash. A figure jumped down from it and hurried over the mud. It was a tall, lean figure in a long flak-coat, holding a power sword. As the blade leapt to life it shone a pale blue and Thanatal could make out a proud, noble face, eyes burning with determination.

'Commissar, praise the Emperor! I had thought the Balurians were lost!'

'Not while one still breathes,' said Thanatal, making sure his men could hear. 'Not when we can still make the enemy suffer!'

'Then your men will be my honour guard, commissar. The enemy is here and they are foul indeed, but with you I can bring them the justice they crave.' The man saluted with the blade of his sword. 'Inquisitor Gholic Ren-Sar Valinov, commissar, honoured to serve alongside the men of Balur.'

Thanatal gripped Valinov's hand in a firm leader's handshake. 'What do you want of us, inquisitor?'

'Steel and guts, commissar. It's the only way.' Valinov held up his sword so the men could see it, a sparkling beacon like harnessed lightning. 'For the Throne and the Balurian dead! Vengeance and justice, sons of the Emperor! Vengeance!'

'Vengeance!' men yelled back, and soon the men took it up as a chant led by Thanatal. 'Vengeance!'

Vengeance. Everyone knew it was the only thing worth fighting for. Commissar Thanatal knew his duty would be done, for under him the sons of Balur would have the chance to fight for it.

The processing plant loomed up through the darkness, squat and ugly, its sheer plasticrete sides streaked with grime. Alaric could just make out Retributor squads on the roof, trying to train their heavy bolters on the defences around the plant. Large rockcrete anti-tank blocks and several bunkers were ranged around the plant, offering plenty of cover to the Grey Knights and Sisters moving into position at the front of the plant.

The plant itself was on the very edge of Lake Rapax, the foul waters lapping at its rear wall. The squat blocky shapes that made up the plant were streaked with chemicals that had condensed on the walls. The whole plant looked filthy and neglected, like a prison – no windows, no markings, just the single rusted entrance serving the whole bloated building.

The stench of Lake Rapax cut through everything – harsh and metallic, a terrible chemical smell. The oily glint of the lake's surface was just visible, still rippling from the shock of the impact. Foul greasy mist rose off the lake, mingling with the ash to form a grim drizzle of corruption.

Alaric jogged through the defences towards the plant, his squad and Justicar Santoro's Space Marines around him, Ludmilla close behind.

Ludmilla had brought almost a hundred Sisters of Battle with her – she had seen many of the atrocities committed throughout the Trail, and now she knew that Ghargatuloth was behind them she understood why the Grey Knights were there.

She could now understand the web of lies and manipulation that had turned her Sisters into instruments of the Enemy, and Alaric thought it must have made her feel so unclean that only pure bloody revenge could get her soul clean.

'Sister Heloise,' ordered Ludmilla, her voice raised to get over the static still fouling all communications. 'Bring your multi-meltas to ground level, now!'

The rusted steel front doors of the plant wouldn't have opened even if the Sisters could have unlocked them. The Excorcist tanks stationed at the front of the plant could have blasted through them but the Sisters and Grey Knights would have had to hang back to avoid the explosion – the multi-meltas could cut through the metal and let them charge in much more quickly.

Ghargatuloth would know they were coming. Whatever they found, the Sisters and the Grey Knights had to strike before it could fight back.

The Seraphim Superior, Sister Lachryma, brought her Seraphim to the front. Two squads had lost so many Sisters that they now fought as one, seven Seraphim under Lachryma whose jaw was now a large purple bruise.

She nodded once in salute as she led her Sisters behind a buttress on the plant wall for cover. Tancred stomped forward to the other side of the doors. These two squads, without having to be ordered, would be the first in.

The Retributor squad of Sister Heloise were down off the walls, lugging their multi-meltas and massive heavy bolters with their chains of explosive ammunition. Alaric saw Heloise had a bionic arm and her shaven scalp was half-covered in an ugly burn scar.

'Anything from inside?' asked Ludmilla.

'Nothing,' said Heloise.

'Open it up,' ordered Ludmilla. 'Sisters, ready! Lachryma and the Knights will lead. Steel your souls, for the Enemy will try to take you first.' Ludmilla turned to Alaric. 'I know the Grey Knights have never had a brother lose their mind to Chaos. But the Adepta Sororitas have lost Sisters to the Enemy before. It is rare, and no one will admit to it, but…'

'It is bad enough that Ghargatuloth has used you,' said Alaric. 'I would not let any of you live on with your minds violated.'

Ludmilla nodded in thanks. Then, she turned back to Heloise. 'Fire!'

The melta beams cut through the steel, sending showers of sparks that cast huge, sinister shadows through the mantle of ash. A section of the doors fell away, and even to Alaric's superior sight there was only blackness inside.

Lachryma hurried out of cover and charged into the darkness, sword drawn. Her Seraphim followed, pistols out, and Tancred's squad followed. Their Terminator armour barely fit through the gap.

'Clear,' voxed Tancred after a few seconds.

'Move in!' called Alaric and ran for the gap, halberd ready. Santoro and Genhain followed him in. Ludmilla was next along with several squads of Battle Sisters, leaving Heloise outside to back them up.

It was pure blackness inside, not just an absence of light but a veil of obscuring darkness. Alaric couldn't make out the walls or the ceiling. The floor was ancient broken marble, once covered in exquisite mosaics but now fragmented and crumbling. There were no chemical vats or processing turbines – the plant was silent and cold, and the air smelled only of age. The place had been completely sealed against the corrosion from Lake Rapax.

Alaric advanced carefully, the faint shaft of pallid light from the doorway his only point of reference. He spotted Lachryma's Seraphim up ahead, Tancred's Terminators holding a loose line in front of them. The sword of Mandulis glowed faintly in Tancred's hand, gleaming bright and clean in spite of the blood and ash that covered it – casting a faint pool of pale light around the justicar.

Alaric approached Tancred and saw why they had stopped. Looming through the darkness, stretching as far as Alaric could see, was a sinister forest of immense statues. They seemed to grow from the marble floor like trees, many times the height of a man, each one cracked and ancient. Many leaned at awkward angles. They were figures carved in sweeping robes or elaborate finery, turned by darkness and age into indistinct half-glimpsed shapes. Alaric jogged up behind Tancred and saw the face of the nearest statue was gone, eaten away as if by corrosion, blank pits where eyes should have been, the faint outlines of bare teeth instead of a mouth. The figure had once been a cardinal or a deacon in long robes, but now it leaned precariously as if about to topple down on whoever approached.

'Forward,' said Alaric. 'Spread out but stay in sight'

He passed the faceless cardinal and saw there were dozens of statues, forming a field of monuments that seemed to fill the shell of the processing plant. Here there was a dashing figure in a naval uniform whose head had crumbled into a featureless twist of stone. An astropath reached out to make the sign of the aquila, but his hand was a pile of broken stone on the floor beneath him.

There was even a Space Marine, the titanic stone form toppled completely to the floor and half-shattered. Lachryma's Seraphims skirted around the fallen Marine, using its broken forearms as cover, picking their way through the debris that remained of its torso and backpack.

Alaric could make out tarnished blackened gold inlaid into the floor, marking out elaborate patterns of mosaic that were broken and obliterated by age.

'I have something,' voxed Lachryma, her voice thickened by her injury. Ludmilla and Alaric had ordered their troops to use the same vox-channel, so the Sisters and the Grey Knights could fight as one force. 'Up ahead.'

'Tancred, check it out. We're behind you,' said Alaric. He heard Ludmilla order Battle Sisters squads to move forward on either flank, surrounding any potential enemy.

Alaric followed Tancred past a giant stone Sister Hospitaller, mostly intact except for her missing hands. Ahead, the floor of the statue forest rose into a pyramid of steps leading upwards towards what looked like a temple, bathed in a very faint pale glow from above. Alaric peered through the gloom and made out columns holding up a pediment whose sculptures had long since crumbled, an inscribed frieze with a few remaining letters of High Gothic, the remains of smaller statues at the corner of every step. He saw these statues had completely eroded until they were just vaguely humanoid forms.

There was only one word still legible on the frieze below the pediment.

EVISSER.

'We've found it. It's the tomb,' said Alaric.

'Looks like we're the only ones who have been here in a long time,' replied Ludmilla. 'No one's here.'

'Valinov is on Volcanis Ultor. This has to be the reason.' Alaric was certain as he said it. It all made such perfect sense. The Trail of Saint Evisser was a puzzle created by Ghargatuloth, and this was the final piece.

'We can storm the place,' said Lachryma, waiting with her Sisters at the base of the steps. 'We'll take the rear, the Terminators go in the front.'

'Good,' said Alaric. 'Santoro, go with her. Genhain, follow us in and cover us if we need it. I need to see what's in there. I'll go in with Tancred.' He turned to Ludmilla, who was directing her Battle Sisters to skirt around the steps and surround the temple. 'Back us up, Sister. This is a multi-point assault on a location we have to assume is defended and there is no way to know what is inside. You may all have to think on your feet.'

'That's what we're good at, brother-captain. You and me both. Face the unknown when no one else can? Fight the darkness itself? It's what they made us for.'

The canoness was right. Sisters, like the Grey Knights, were in their own way created. Trained from childhood, saturated in the word of Imperial clerics just as Grey Knights were indoctrinated, very little remained of the woman every Sister might otherwise have become. They had, in many ways, already made the ultimate sacrifice – their lives were not their own, for they had been moulded into the only soldiers that could do the Emperor's work when it really mattered. The Grey Knights and the Sisters of Battle had more in common than a mutual enemy.

'For the Throne, Sister,' said Alaric as he went to join Tancred on the steps.

'The Emperor deliver us, brother,' said Ludmilla.

Squad Alaric and Squad Tancred moved up the steps towards the looming temple. Black threads of corruption had snaked up the columns and the top steps were riddled with dark oily veins. The whole building seemed diseased when he saw it close up, and it was huge – its colonnaded sides stretched out into the darkness where Lachryma was poised to charge into the rear of the building.

There were more rows of columns beyond the first, staggered so it was impossible to see into the inside. At the top of the steps the air was cold and wet, as if something had drawn the life out of it. Alaric could feel his senses heightened and his muscles tensed by the malice that saturated the air – his psychic core was thrumming with alarm, as forces he could not see surrounded him.

Something inside the temple screamed. It was the screaming of daemons.

'Go!' yelled Alaric, and began the charge into the Tomb of Saint Evisser.

COMMISSAR THANATAL SAW the broken bodies of dead Sisters lying in the trench and knew he was right. The enemy had come over the lip of the trench, fending off a spirited counter-attack from Sisters who now lay butchered on the blood-soaked ground in front of the first line. Bodies in the red power armour of the Order of the Bloody Rose lay draped on coils of razorwire or battered into the ground – the wounds were from bolters or power weapons, speaking of a murderous short-ranged struggle.

The Balurians were moving rapidly up the trenches once held by the Sisters, Thanatal and Valinov at their head. One of the regimental preachers had survived and now spoke the words of the Hymnal Odium Omnis, a High Gothic prayer of hate that most of the Balurians had learned as boys in the temples of their homeworld.

'Got one!' shouted a sergeant on the Balurian left. He was aiming his lasgun at the huge battered corpse of a Chaos Marine, its grey metal armour stained with blood, one leg folded and mangled beneath it. Thanatal could see the ornate patterning on its armour and the huge halberd it had fought with, lying spattered with Sisters' blood on the ground beside it.

'Stay back!' yelled Valinov. 'Their very bodies are corrupt!' The sergeant barked an order and his men skirted carefully around the body, the Balurian who followed giving it a wide berth.

It was just like the Enemy to threaten Imperial servants even after death, thought Thanatal bitterly. Death was too good for them – but death was what they would receive.

'Sir? Where are all the Sisters?' The question came from a young officer who was hurrying along just behind Thanatal.

Valinov interrupted. 'The Sisters are lost,' he said simply.

'Remember, son of Balur,' said Thanatal. 'Vengeance.'

The officer nodded briskly and turned to make sure his men were following.

Lost? What could wipe out so many Sisters of Battle? Many of the Balurians to the north of the line had joined the Sisters in their prayers, and all the Balurians were aware just how effective the Sisters could be. What could destroy them? And where were the rest of the bodies?

Those kinds of questions could unsettle the men. Thanatal could not let them be asked.

'By their sacrifice the Sisters of Battle have weakened the enemy!' he called out to anyone who could hear him, knowing the nervous soldiers would pass the message between them as quickly as a vox-cast. 'Through their deaths the foe has been left bloodied, and it is up to us to deliver the killing blow!'

'There!' shouted Valinov from the head of the column, pointing with his power sword. Up ahead, on the very shore of Lake Rapax, the processing plant loomed, its monstrous form a squat shadow through the clouds of ash. 'That is where they lie!'

Thanatal was thankful. The Balurians could have become too wrapped up in the idea of the missing Sisters to retain cohesion. Now they had something to charge at. 'See, sons of Balur! See how the enemy cowers! Now, strike when he is still weak! Strike for vengeance, for your comrades and for the Sisters! Vengeance, Balurians! Vengeance! Charge!'

'Charge!' yelled the old preacher, holding up his holy book and scrambling out of the trench as nimbly as a younger man to shame the soldiers who might lag behind.

'You heard the man!' shouted an officer in the mass. 'Double-time, loaded and ready to kill!'

The Balurians were alive again, filled with the fire. Thanatal broke into a run and he didn't need to lead them any more – he just had to be the first in, leading by example, Inquisitor Valinov alongside him. The Balurians surged forward, scrambling through the trenches and running along the bloodstained earth, charging towards the processing plant.

Whatever happens, Thanatal told himself, we have already won. When the time comes and they are given the chance to offer themselves up on the altar of war, the Balurians will thank me for leading them here, into the last fight.

A Chaos Marine was worth ten loyal Guardsmen, Thanatal knew that. But with enough spirit and no fear in their veins, the Balurians could even those odds. They would buy time for the rest of the defenders. They might even break the Enemy there on the shore of Lake Rapax. Either way, the Emperor's will would be done.

Valinov ran full-tilt, sword drawn, Thanatal following him. The Balurians yelled war-cries as they charged, and when the first heavy bolter shots rang out from the heretics holding the plant, there was nothing that could have stopped the Balurians from fighting back.

NINETEEN
THE TOMB OF SAINT EVISSER

THE SEVENTY-SEVEN SCREAMING masques of the Hidden One were born in the depths of Volcanis Ultor six hundred years before Ghargatuloth awoke. Amongst the gangs of the underhive, where a lucky man lived to twenty and guns were as valuable as food or clean water, a prophet arose who claimed he knew each of the seventy-seven faces of death and could promise any devoted follower of his that they would be immune to each form of death that stalked the underhive. For one face was the hot buzzing steel of bullets, another the cold red pain of a knife.

The thick strangling death of drowning, the pallid crushing face of starvation – each of the seventy-seven masques lusted for death, and only by understanding them and worshipping them could death be cheated. The prophet (his name forgotten, his face remembered) told them that death itself was the object of their devotion – a study, a religion, a way of life.

His followers formed the most formidable gang in the underhive, for each one was immune to many forms of death. Eventually there was only one option left. The gangs buried their enmities for one long night of slaughter, and the prophet's followers were butchered in the twisting streets below Volcanis Ultor. Few stories came from the gang war for few survived to tell them.

No one knew where the prophet went. That he survived is not in doubt because the seventy-seven masques reappeared, worshipped in secret by those who remembered the tales of men who knew death so well they could not be killed. Gradually, the masques were revealed to be just aspects of the one – the Hidden One, a force so powerful that death itself was just one facet of its being. The cult spread, taking in the embittered and the fearful, those crushed by the weight of revenge or tainted by madness. All were welcome. The most devoted few became servants of the Hidden One himself, and his voice spoke to them through the centuries-old prophet.

Eventually, they understood.

The final masque of death was the most complete. It was utter destruction, dissolution of the body, evisceration of the soul, crushing of breath, the very cessation of existence. Once this masque was understood the follower would become something beyond death, something to whom life and death were just shadows cast by the true light of existence. A purity, a glory beyond the grasp of the living or the dreams of the dead – this was what the Hidden One promised.

The final masque could be realised only in the place where the underhive's legends spoke of destruction and chaos – Lake Rapax, a seething pit of pure corruption where the sin and hatred of thousands of years had seeped into the earth. They said it was alive, and hungry. They said monsters roamed its depths and ghosts reached helplessly from its oily surface. Beneath Volcanis Ultor they said many things, and the followers of the seventy-seven masques knew that they were all correct.

One terrible night the followers left their hovels and gathered in the streets of the underhive, following the call of their prophet. No one tried to stop them – fear gripped every heart beneath the city and the underhivers could only watch, horrified, as the insane took over the streets.

They marched out through the city's broken hinterland right to the edge of Lake Rapax, where the skeletal form of the prophet waited, howling insanely the praises of the Hidden One and recounting the seventy-seven masques that had reaped such a bounty in the underhive. His followers rejoiced as they walked in a huge crowd into the lake, the corrosive waters stripping them clean of skin and muscle, sucking the breath from their lungs, worming its way through their eyes and eating out their minds.

The lake boiled and seethed as it swallowed them up, its thick shining waters closing over the heads of the faithful, its shore foaming pink with blood. Finally the prophet himself walked upon the lake's surface, right into its very centre where, slowly, always singing the litany of the masques, he sunk beneath the waters.

The underhivers gave their thanks that the insane and the benighted had left them. Had they known the truth, they would have despaired.

The seventy-seven screaming masques did not let their followers die for nothing. The cultists really did become something else beneath the surface of Lake Rapax – with bodies of corrosive pollution and minds rebuilt in the image of the masques, they were beings so pure the Hidden One could speak to their hearts directly from beyond the veil of the warp.

And as they reformed in the toxic silt of the lake bed, their new cause was made clear to them. They were the Hidden One's children, devout followers who had transcended the boundaries of life and death. They would be given the most important task the Hidden One had – they were to travel to the forgotten place on the lake's shore, make their home there, and stay vigilant for the day when the Hidden One would bring seventy-seven shades of suffering into the galaxy.

They went to guard the great forgotten tomb, wherein lay the bones of Saint Evisser.

ALARIC HAD NEVER felt such a wall of pure hatred, solid and terrible. It was like charging in slow motion, the weight of malice dragging him down. It was that, more than anything, which told him he was in the presence of Ghargatuloth. That purity of emotion could only be product of the warp, ripped from the minds of humanity and layered thick over this place where the sea of souls intersected with real space. He could feel it battering against his mind, and his psychic shield felt a precariously thin barrier. If his will broke, what would flood into his mind? Would he see the madness of warp and go insane? Would Ghargatuloth himself dig his talons in and turn Alaric into a servant of Chaos? For the first time, Alaric felt he could fall. A Grey Knight could become one of the Enemy, and the Grey Knights would never be forgiven for their failure.

Then Alaric banished the doubt. He would not fall. The Emperor was with him. He stumbled onwards and clawed himself through the wall of hate, feeling the veil pulled off him. The darkness peeled away and he saw what had happened to the resting place of Saint Evisser.

Past the columns of the entrance the space within the tomb warped horribly, forming a gigantic landscape with a sky of veined marble and a sun that hung in a giant censer, swinging backwards and forwards casting shadows across a hellish landscape. The tomb was several kilometres across, impossibly, like a warped mockery of a planet's surface, monstrous and wrong.

It could only be pure Chaos, the kind that had saturated Khorion IX. The land was of splintered stone, jagged plates of dark marble balancing between deep black chasms. Sprays of black water gushed upwards at random, like geysers, and large black creatures circled over the landscape like vultures. Alaric could hear screams that seemed to come from everywhere at once, and the air stank of a hundred things – sweat, blood, sulphur, burning meat, gunfire, decay, disease, pollution, incense.

Broken walls cut through the stone, becoming thicker towards the centre of the scene until they formed what looked like a skeletal city. The city clung like a parasite to a rise in the stone, as if something huge was forcing its way up from below. Empty shells of temples and basilica seemed to ooze from the mountain, forming a nightmarish labyrinth, dark and broken, a place of unalloyed death. The stone peak of the mountain pushed up through the buildings and terminated in a stark, white plateau forming the acropolis of the city. On a massive slab of the summit was a block of pure white marble, incongruous and shining, bathed in a pool of golden light. The marble sarcophagus was like the lynchpin that held everything in place, the heart of the tomb, the point to which all paths led.

Alaric tore his eyes away. He saw his battle-brothers following him, shaking the terrible veil of hatred from their shielded minds – Lykkos carrying his psycannon, Vien, Haulvarn, Clostus, Dvorn with his Nemesis hammer. Tancred and his Marines – Locath, Karlin and Golven – were close behind, their massive forms dwarfed by the scale of the evil in front of them.

Tancred made the sign of the aquila. It seemed a futile gesture here, a tiny drop of virtue in a sea of sin.

'I don't think the Sisters will make it,' said Alaric. There was regret in his voice, but they all knew it was true. 'It's up to us. Santoro and Genhain will follow, we keep moving.'

'What's our objective?' Tancred, like Alaric, knew they could not go back. Ghargatuloth knew they were there. It had to end now.

Alaric pointed to the sarcophagus, high up on the acropolis above the city. 'Throne be with us, for otherwise we are alone.'

Squad Tancred and Squad Alaric moved out, leaving the columns behind them and moving quickly onto the shattered landscape. Chasms gaped everywhere and the tortured ground formed insane angles and sharp gradients. There were a thousand places for ambushers to hide, a hundred ways to get lost. Were it not for the beacon of the sarcophagus shining up ahead, the maze of shattered marble could form a labyrinth no man would ever escape.

The screams were deeper the further in they went, like layers of suffering bearing down on them. Skeletal trees loomed between the jagged peaks of marble and somehow it didn't surprise Alaric that they had once been human beings, warped by corruption and deformed until their skeletons spread into branches and their faces screamed hopelessly from twisted trunks of skin and muscle. Sinister black shapes flapped overhead – Alaric could make out hollow rotted eye sockets tracking them through the rocks.

Alaric glanced back and saw Genhain following, hurrying to keep Alaric and Tancred in sight. Covering fire hadn't been needed yet but Alaric knew that very soon it probably would, and he would be relying on Genhain to keep enemies pinned down while the other Grey Knights pressed home the attack.

He wondered if Santoro would make it, far across on the other side of the tomb. He feared for Lachryma's Seraphim, and for Ludmilla's Sisters that would probably try to follow them in. Would they make it inside the tomb at all? Would they be warped by Ghargatuloth's presence and turn into another enemy the Grey Knights had to fight?

Whatever happened, happened. The Grey Knights were trained to be ready for any weapon the Enemy threw at them – and that included their own allies.

The vox, Alaric wasn't surprised to learn, didn't work in the tomb. 'Anything in sight?' he asked his Space Marines.

'They're watching us,' said Dvorn bleakly, gripping his Nemesis hammer in two hands. Lykkos was scanning rapidly for targets, sweeping the barrel of his psycannon through the shadows.

The ground was crunching underfoot. Alaric glanced down and saw finger bones mixed in with the gravelly surface of crumbled marble.

The Grey Knights could smell the enemy before they saw them – it was a cold, foul stink, as if all the corruption that saturated the tomb coagulated and solidified into a wall of repugnance that all but forced the Grey Knights back. It was the sharp odour of toxic pollution and the sickly taint of decay, a force bearing down on them from all directions.

'Genhain! Covering fire, now!' yelled Alaric and suddenly the shadows were alive, the traces of bolter and psycannon bullets picking out tall, loping shapes between the rocks. Gunfire streaked from Genhain and Tancred's Space Marines, and through the storm of gunfire forms leapt from the darkness to attack.

Alaric's first parry was more reflex than decision, the kind Tancred had taught him in long sparing sessions. It was just as well because even he might have faltered had he seen his enemy before he acted – it was only vaguely humanoid. Its skin was dark grey and translucent so organs could be seen squirming in its torso, writhing up its neck and down its arms and legs. A foul curtain of transparent slime coated it, and its arms ended in long whip-like tentacles, one spraying corrosive slime as Alaric batted it away with his halberd. The thing's face was barely a face at all – a high thin mouth lolled wildly open, blind pale smears passed for eyes, and it emitted a horrible low howling as it pounced.

Alaric fired wildly, spraying storm bolter shells around the creature and the other following it. The attacker moved with fluid speed, whipping its tentacle around the halberd and dragging it down, drawing itself up plastically to its full height and bearing down on Alaric with that mindless gaping mouth.

Alaric plunged his free arm down the creature's throat and rattled off a solid volley of shells, blasting the back of the creature's head into flying globs of stinking gore. The creature shrieked and powerful muscles closed around Alaric's arm, trying to suck him in. Through the stench Alaric could smell burning and knew the outer layers of his armour were being eaten away by the creature's corrosive substance. Alaric pulled hard and lifted the creature off its feet, swinging it into the attackers following it, batting one aside and firing another volley. The creature came apart in a spray of acidic gore, and Alaric was free to move.

His Marines were right behind him, forming a tight circle as the corrosive attackers leapt at them from every side. Alaric saw Clostus holding one up high on the point of his halberd so one of the psycannon Marines in Squad Genhain could blow its head clean off with a single shot. Dvorn swung his hammer down straight through the closest enemy, reducing the creature to a slime-filled crater in the marble ground.

Alaric turned and saw Tancred, easy to pick out because of the bright lightning flash of the sword of Mandulis as it lashed out time and time again. Writhing tendrils of slime fell oozing to the ground but the fluid creatures reformed even as Tancred sliced through their bodies. One leapt on Tancred, trying to wrestle him to the ground – Tancred flipped it over his head, turned deftly and stamped down on it so hard it burst apart in a welter of toxic filth.

'Blades won't work!' yelled Alaric over the unearthly howling. 'Dvorn! Take them apart!'

Squad Alaric turned, forming a wedge with Dvorn at the head, facing down the dozen more enemies charging from the darkness. Dvorn swung his hammer in wide arcs, battering the creatures back or ripping the hammer's head right through them, while Squad Alaric concentrated on blazing away with their storm bolters and holding the enemy back.

'In war and abandonment!' Tancred was bellowing, 'Be thou my shield and my steed! Be thou retribution, and I shall be your hand in the darkness! Light from the shadows! Death from the dying! Vengeance from the lost!'

Alaric could feel the buzzing in the back of his mind as Tancred's remaining Marines tried to focus their willpower.

It was the Holocaust – the expression of the Grey Knights' faith, focused through Tancred's mind and forged into a weapon worthy of the Emperor's finest. Alaric knew it was hard enough to do with a full squad – with only Tancred and three battle-brothers, the power would require almost everything they had.

'Vengeance from the lost!' echoed Alaric, giving Tancred all the help he could. 'And from the void shall rise only the pure!'

The sudden psychic crescendo nearly knocked Alaric off his feet – a pure white flame of faith, bursting out from the sword of Mandulis like a shockwave, rippling across the stone. Alaric saw the closest creatures blasted into ash, the after-images of their twisted forms ghosted against the light as they came apart.

The creatures facing Dvorn shrieked and whipped their tendrils around their faces as if trying to block out the light. Alaric's auto-senses were overloaded and he could see nothing, just pure whiteness, the sword of Mandulis at its centre like a shard of lightning.

'Down!' yelled a voice from behind Alaric and he instinctively dropped to the ground. He felt his battle-brothers doing the same an instant before heavy thudding impacts ripped overhead. Blessed bolts from Genhain's two psycannon Marines thudded into viscous flesh, their psychic detonations ripping through corrupted bodies.

Alaric's sight came back. He was face-down on the ground, which was spattered with stinking, steaming blood. He quickly got to his feet to see the area covered in smouldering patches of gore, and heard Squad Genhain walking down the slope behind Alaric snapping off shots at any enemy that still moved. Brother Ondurin poured gouts of holy promethium from his incinerator into the shadows, and Alaric heard the screams as he immolated the creatures lurking there.

The armour of Alaric's squad was smoking and corroded, its gunmetal covered in patches of smouldering black.

Tancred's Marines had fared worse. Tancred himself was on his knees, sagging with fatigue. The use of the Holocaust power had drained him terribly – even he had not expected the strength of his Marines' hatred to be that great. The sword of Mandulis still shone, smoke coiling off its blade.

Brother Golven, one of Tancred's Terminators, lay face-down and limp. Brother Karlin turned him over and saw the whole front of Golven's armour had been rotted away, exposing blackened, oozing flesh. Karlin dropped Golven back down. It was obvious the Grey Knight was dead – he must have been dragged down almost right away and had his armour corroded by the attackers. Even blessed Terminator armour wasn't proof against the guardians of Saint Evisser.

Tancred turned to Karlin, who was armed with the squad's incinerator.

'Burn our brother,' he said, and Karlin dutifully scoured Golven's body clean with a spray of flame. It took a few seconds for Golven's corpse to be reduced to a guttering shell of charred armour.

They wouldn't even be able to take his gene-seed for return to the Chapter. But Alaric, if he survived, would ensure that Golven would be remembered.

'Move on,' said Alaric. 'Stay tight. The Emperor is with us.'

As the Grey Knights moved on into the stunted outskirts of the skeletal city, Alaric could see the carrion beasts circling in greater and greater numbers overhead.

COMMISSAR THANATAL HAD almost given in to despair when he had seen what surrounded the processing plant on the shore of Lake Rapax. Creatures were writhing out of the ground all around the plant, faces and clawing limbs reaching from the earth, moaning and gibbering in a thousand tongues. There were hundreds and hundreds of them, foul things with massive mouths full of teeth, grasping hands with fingers that ended in razor-sharp talons, all dragging themselves from the earth to defend the plant.

Thanatal had felt then that the Emperor's duty lay not in death, that being torn apart by the maddening horde was too great a price to pay for duty. The sin of doubt had clawed at him, and he had felt his resolve eroded by the sight. The men around him stopped as the ash parted and the scene was laid out before them and the cries of daemons reached their ears.

But Inquisitor Valinov was not afraid. Thanatal's fears were banished as he watched awestruck – Valinov walked out into the boiling sea of daemons, sword held out, and they recoiled from his presence, shrieking in fear as he approached.

Valinov bellowed out words in a strange, sibilant language – a prayer, Thanatal guessed, an ancient rite dedicated to the Emperor – and the daemons parted before him. Valinov walked out into the very centre of them, calling out words of power as he did so, making sharp arcane signs with his free hand that sent daemons reeling back into the earth.

'Be thy cowed in the presence of your Master's work!' called Valinov in High Gothic. 'Fear His touch, be burned by His words! Back, back, servants of decay, back into the earth, back beneath the notice of the pure!'

The daemons were forced back beneath the ground by Valinov's words, his commanding presence spreading out in a ripple through the sea of daemons, forcing them down until a path was cleared between the Balurians and the tomb.

'See!' shouted Thanatal. 'See how the word of Emperor cows the Enemy! He is with us! Press on, servants of the Emperor, for the work of mankind has yet to be done!'

'The Enemy recoils!' echoed Valinov from up ahead as he began to lead the Balurians towards the processing plant. 'We are but the tip of the Emperor's spear. Feel His spirit as he drives us home, rejoice as we pierce the heart of corruption!'

Their faces alight with wonder, the Balurians moved across the sea of daemons who were now whimpering in defeat, their faces turned away, the shimmering iridescence of their skin now dull and defeated.

The ash was parting and a shaft of pure, bright sunlight, such as had not shone on Volcanis Ultor for centuries, illuminated the processing plant, turning its grey plasteel walls golden, lining it with a white light of purity.

The Emperor's eyes were on this place. The gates of the plant stood blasted open, as if entreating the Balurians to enter and purge it of corruption. Valinov strode boldly towards it with hundreds of Balurians behind him, Thanatal at their head.

Without prompting, the Balurians began to sing an old, popular marching-tune they had sung as boys on their first parade grounds on Balur. It was a song about duty, bravery, longing for home, yet adventuring through the stars. Their valour crushed the daemons down further until they were cloaked in shadow, weak and pathetic, cowed into helplessness by the light of the Emperor filling the Balurian hearts.

The doors of the plant were up ahead. The darkness within was pleading to be filled with light. Valinov didn't have to urge the men on any more – he just broke into a run and plunged through the burst doors. Thanatal followed and the Balurians poured after him, lasguns ready, not one man faltering in his step.

Light streamed in with them, illuminating a place of ancient stone. Statues of Imperial heroes looked down with approval on these servants of the Emperor. A temple was up ahead, covered in gold and shining like a beacon – this was the place the Balurians had to liberate from enemy hands.

And ranged in front of the temple were the enemies. They were shimmering and indistinct, their very existence threatened by the sudden appearance of the faithful Balurians. Their red-painted armour would not help them, neither would the guns in their hands. The Balurians had the Emperor, and his most faithful servant, Inquisitor Valinov. They would not fail.

Thanatal didn't even realise he was singing along with the Balurians as he drew his chainsword and, along with hundreds of his men, charged.

CANONESS LUDMILLA HAD expected the threat to come from the temple. The vox was cut off completely and she had no way of knowing what was happening inside the temple, but she knew the Grey Knights and Lachryma's Seraphim had gone in intending to secure the place rapidly, and no one had come out. She was about to order her Sisters in after the Grey Knights when Sister Heloise, the Superior of the Retributor squad holding the plant's gates, reported there was some sorcery afoot – the ground outside the plant was seething and creatures were trying to force their way up.

Heloise was halfway across the statue graveyard, heading for Ludmilla's position, when the enemy force burst in.

'Sisters! To the front of the temple, now! Heloise, get into cover and fire at will! The rest, rapid fire and prepare to engage!'

'Looks like Guardsmen, my canoness,' said Heloise over the static-filled vox. 'Maybe we should…'

Thousands of las-shots ripped through the air from hundreds of lasguns on full auto. Ludmilla watched in horror as the ruby-coloured lances of fire filled the air with crimson threads, riddling the statues until they crumbled and fell, scoring chunks out of the ground, whipping around the temple steps and spattering against Sisters' armour. Somewhere heavy bolters and multi-meltas opened up from Heloise but they were soon drowned out by the sound of las-fire and – obscenely – of singing, a parade-ground tune carried by hundreds of hoarse throats as the Guardsmen charged closer.

Ludmilla's inferno pistol was in her hand and she could see Battle Sister squads converging at the foot of the steps to form a firing line. About half of them were in position and just beginning to fire volleys when the Guardsmen hit.

Heavy chains of bolter fire punched through deep royal blue body armour, sending out sprays of blood frozen in the strobing las-fire. The lasgun fire blasting back riddled the marble steps and Ludmilla saw Sisters spasming as las-bolts found weak points in their armour. One shot burst against Ludmilla's lower leg and nearly knocked her flat on her face, another thudded into her breastplate, and she felt the sleeves over her armour fluttering as shots streaked through the material.

She saw a tide of men, teeth gritted. A commissar led them, bolt pistol in one hand and a chainsword in the other. The front rank of Guardsmen was chewed up before her eyes by the Sisters' bolter fire but there were hundreds of them, trampling their wounded as they charged. She heard their voices raised in anger and loathing.

And she saw Inquisitor Valinov, his face lit by the glow from his power sword, striding tall and heedless of danger in front of the horde.

The Guardsmen crashed into them and Ludmilla's world suddenly shrunk into a tiny painful place of pressed bodies, stabbing bayonets and swinging lasgun stocks. It was full of the smell of sweating bodies and smoking barrels. Ludmilla held firm as Guardsmen scrambled all around her, and she struck left and right. She fired her inferno pistol point-blank into the press and she was sure its superheated blast must have bored through three or four bodies – the weight lessened and she pushed bodies off her.

She couldn't lead her troops now, as a canoness should. It was every Sister for herself.

'In the name of the Throne!' someone was yelling in the thick of the fight, his voice carrying over the yells of anger and the screams of the wounded, the sound of blades against armour and bolter fire muffled by the press of bodies. 'For the saints! For vengeance!'

A Guardsmen reared up over the throng, his bayonet slashing down at Ludmilla. She grabbed the barrel of the gun and dragged the man over her head, wrapping an arm around his neck and wrenching it until his neck broke. She kicked out and felt bones break beneath her ceramite boot. She fired again and saw a Guardsman's torso come apart in front of her, his body collapsing in on the ragged burning hole bored through its centre.

Blood was slick on her face, thick in her hair. The din of the fight was becoming a wall of white noise, like a dream. Men and Sisters were dying – Sister Superior Annalise cut an officer's legs out from under him with her chainsword, sending out a crescent of blood and shredded flak armour. Sister Gloriana fell back clutching her face, blood spurting between her fingers. Sister squads were falling back up the steps unloading bolter clips into the tide, while others were in the thick of the fight trying to beat back the Balurians with combat knives and bolter stocks.

There was a flash of light and Ludmilla saw it was a power sword – the one carried by Valinov. A Sister's head flew through the air, teeth still gritted in defiance as the sword flashed by.

Valinov. Alaric had told her the inquisitor had betrayed them, and this was the proof. Inquisitor or not he had killed her Sisters and in the Emperor's name he would pay.

Ludmilla clambered through the throng, blasting a path with her inferno pistol, battering her way through. In the dark rabid mass of heaving bodies she could only see that power sword as it stabbed and slashed, its power field carving through ceramite in showers of white sparks. Valinov had a sneer on his face as he killed, a picture of utter arrogance. Ludmilla felt that same holy anger boiling up inside her that had filled her when she heard the tales of the Emperor's foes from the pulpit, that had driven her on her first missions as a Battle Sister and fuelled her ascent to the position of canoness.

It was hate that kept her going, even as a lasbolt burned right through her thigh and a bolter stock cracked against her forehead. She pressed on as her eye filled up with blood and the screams of dying Sisters cut through the din. She could hear the commissar urging his men on and it spurred her on, too, because it reminded her that the Balurians had been betrayed as well.

She could see Valinov now, cutting a space around him, forcing a squad of Battle Sisters back up the steps as Guardsmen died all around him. Ludmilla made one last charge, barrelling headlong through the Balurians, feeling them fall back as she threw them aside and trampled them under her feet.

Then she was free, and she launched herself right at Valinov, inferno pistol held out in front of her.

Ludmilla was an excellent markswoman. She would not miss, not now. Through her hate the Emperor guided her hand – she could feel His strength filling her, for He had listened to every prayer she had made throughout her whole life. Now He was rewarding His faithful with the honour of being the instrument of His vengeance.

The melta-coils burst into life. The barrel flared and a bolt of energy leapt from the weapon, carving through the air right towards the centre of Valinov's chest.

A sudden flash of white light burst and Ludmilla felt heat wash over her. The after-image of Valinov was burned into her retina, framed in light as the conversion field around him dissipated the energy of the shot and crowned him with an outline of white fire.

An energy field. Expensive, rare, coveted. Probably taken from the Imperial Governor's armoury in Hive Superior, like the power sword. Ludmilla should have guessed, and the awful cold knowledge of failure was so strong it was like a punch to her stomach.

Ludmilla hit the marble steps hard. Valinov slashed his sword in a wide arc as she fell and sliced her arm off at the elbow, her hand still gripping the pistol as it spiralled away.

Ludmilla tried to scramble to her feet but as she rose, the inquisitor reversed his grip and plunged his sword straight through her midriff. She felt the blade shearing through her spine – red electric pain flared and dragged the breath from her lungs, and she even forgot her severed arm as pure freezing agony flooded right through her, cold as the blade in her guts, sharp as its edge. For a single endless moment, all she could think of was the pain. Las-bolts froze in the air. The screams became a blank wall of noise. The Emperor, her Sisters, the galaxy she had sworn to protect, were all gone, all replaced by agony.

When Valinov twisted the blade Ludmilla felt a great blackness open up in her mind as her life spilled out onto the steps. Valinov withdrew the sword and turned his attention back to the Sisters in front of the temple.

He didn't even bother to check if Ludmilla was really dead. He didn't need to. Ludmilla crashed back down onto the steps and knew that she was dead already – her senses just hadn't realised yet. She saw flak-armoured Guardsmen swarming over her as they charged, feet stamping down on her, warm blood flooding out of her and leaving only a huge black coldness that grew and grew.

Then it grew so big it swallowed her whole, and the tomb of Saint Evisser was left behind as Canoness Ludmilla died.

TWENTY
ACROPOLIS

THE CITY SWARMED with cultists.

At least, they had once been cultists, followers of Ghargatuloth in one of his many forms. Now they were debased and devolved, infused with the filth of Lake Rapax and animated by the will of the Prince of a Thousand Faces. The city itself was just as much a servant of the Prince as they were – its walls were contorted into bloated biological shapes or wrought into daemonic faces, its streets treacherous slabs of shifting marble. It was outlined in the light from the sarcophagus and drowned in the deepest shadow.

Tentacles reached from between chunks of fallen masonry. Cultists leapt from gaping windows or sagging roofs, spewing corrosive venom, lashing out with tendrils to drag down and smother.

Tancred led the way, the sword of Mandulis cutting a cultist in half with every stroke, the massive bodies of his Terminators charging through the crumbling walls. Alaric's Space Marines followed, fending off the cultists that tried to force their way between the Grey Knights, trying to surround them and cut them off from one another. Alaric's halberd cut through slime-covered muscular bodies, sliced off foul gibbering heads. Dvorn's hammer smashed through walls and Genhain's psycannon Marines riddled fire through the cultists lurking behind them.

Somewhere in the slaughter Brother Vien died, dragged back down the slope by arms that snaked up from the ground and dissolved their way through his leg armour. Vien had been a part of Alaric's squad since Alaric had been chosen as a justicar – Alaric knew him as a Grey Knight whose personal prayers were brief and incisive, an intelligent and studious soldier who spent as much time immersed in Imperial history and philosophy as he did performing bolter and close combat drills. He would probably have become a justicar himself, and now, in a flash of shadow and a final bitter prayer spat through dying lips, he was gone.

The Grey Knights struggled up the slope, the city becoming a tight warren of stone with cultists around every corner. Faces began to leer from the walls. The marble sky overhead bowed and rippled as if reality itself only had a tenuous hold over the acropolis. Voices gibbered in the back of Alaric's mind, his psychic shield muffling them until he could not make out the words.

The wards woven into his armour were freezing cold against his skin, reacting to the malice that infused the tomb. His breath was cold in his throat, and even with his Space Marine's metabolism it hurt him to draw breath. The place was sucking the life out of him. There was pure death at it centre.

The acropolis was just above the Grey Knights, a final encrustation of parasitic buildings between the Knights and the summit. The roofs of the buildings were edged in gold but all around the Grey Knights was deepest shadow. There were no roads between the looming buildings – the Grey Knights would have to make their own path up. One more row of buildings, and they would be there. One last place of shelter before they reached the top.

Alaric led the way into a tattered basilica, a domed building that seemed to ooze out of the steepening slope. Its steps crumbled beneath his feet and once inside the shadows swallowed him, turning his vision dark and grey. High above, indistinct writhing figures were carved, covering the dome in an illusion of movement. Words in a language Alaric couldn't read were inlaid into the floor and walls, and they squirmed as he watched. The place was a drained shell, devoid of life, but the hatred suffusing the tomb kept it alive. Alaric felt the floor recoiling as he stepped on it, his wards flaring in a cold spiral around his body, the carved figures turning their heads away in disgust at his piety.

His depleted squad followed him in, Tancred close behind. Alaric saw Tancred's armour was battered and scraped, and blood was running from one shoulder joint. Tancred himself was breathing heavily like an exhausted animal. His Terminators had born the brunt of the charge, battering through walls and stumbling into nests of cultists – only Tancred, Locath and Karlin with his incinerator remained. The use of the

Holocaust had drained them, and Alaric knew they could not call on it again.

'We are close,' said Tancred. 'I can feel it. The sword knows it.' Impossibly, given how much toxic slime and gore it had carved through, the sword of Mandulis was still bright. Its mirror-polished surface reflected light where there should have been darkness.

'One more,' said Genhain, his Space Marines coming up the steps into the basilica. 'One more step.'

There was nowhere to hide in the basilica and for the moment the cultists were regrouping somewhere. The Grey Knights had a few seconds here to pause.

'If I were a proper brother-captain,' said Alaric as he caught his breath. 'I would know the prayer we are supposed to say. But I think you all know what we have to do. We do not know what our chances of survival are, so we fight as if they were zero. We do not know what we are facing, so we fight as if it was the dark gods themselves. No one will remember us now and we may never be buried beneath Titan, so we will build our own memorial here. The Chapter might lose us and the Imperium might never know we existed, but the Enemy – the Enemy will know. The Enemy will remember. We will hurt it so badly that it will never forget us until the stars burn out and the Emperor vanquishes it at the end of time. When Chaos is dying, its last thought will be of us. That is our memorial – carved into the heart of Chaos. We cannot lose, Grey Knights. We have already won.'

There was silence for a moment, broken only by the breathing of the Grey Knights, the psychic babble of the tomb far away beneath it.

Dvorn hefted his Nemesis hammer and walked across the basilica to the far wall, where faceless carved figures squirmed around each other to get away from him. Tancred followed, Locath and Karlin ready for one final charge. Dvorn mouthed a silent prayer and swung the hammer.

The back wall came apart beneath the impact and light flooded in, silhouetting Dvorn and Squad Tancred in shocking brightness.

'You'll make a leader yet, Alaric!' called Tancred, and charged into the glare. Alaric and Genhain followed, their auto-senses straining to keep from burning out.

Alaric ran through the back wall, up the steep marble slope, and out onto the acropolis.

The psychic din was replaced by a single, strident note, like a vast choir singing. Light streamed down from above. Alaric glimpsed cherubim, such as those depicted attending on Imperial saints, fluttering above a huge block of white marble that shone so brightly to look at it was like staring at the sun.

There were no cultists up here. The light would have taken them apart.

Tancred walked across the smooth stone, Genhain and Alaric covering him. The sarcophagus was so huge it even dwarfed Tancred.

Tancred waved forward Karlin and Locath, who stomped up to the sarcophagus itself. They reached high above their head, digging their fingers into the stone seam between the body of the sarcophagus and its lid.

Their enhanced musculature and the servo-assisted Terminator armour gave them even greater strength than a power-armoured Grey Knight. Slowly, as they heaved, the lid broke free.

Squad Tancred helped lift the lid and pushed it to one side. It fell with a crash onto the stone of the acropolis, shattering into fragments.

The light cut out instantly. The sound of the choir turned into a scream.

Something stirred within the open sarcophagus. Squad Tancred opened fire with storm bolters, Genhain followed suit. The bursts of bolter fire were drowned out by the howl blaring down from overhead. Alaric lifted up his arm to take aim and fire but he knew, deep within him, that bolter shells wouldn't make any difference.

A skeletal hand, each finger as long as a Space Marine's arm, reached blindly out of the sarcophagus. A huge dark shape shifted and the head of Saint Evisser emerged, huge and decayed, its face stretched, tattered skin over dark bone, the remains of its death shroud clinging to it in rot-coloured tatters. Blind, dripping orbs seethed in its eye sockets. Gnarled teeth grinned. The hand planted itself on the ground and Saint Evisser rose from the sarcophagus, an enormous, twisted monster, his once-human form saturated with corruption.

The mouth opened and Saint Evisser bellowed, the sound sending cracks through the marble sarcophagus. Bolter fire spattered off its face – teeth shattered, fragments of bone flew. Its other hand reached out and grabbed Brother Locath, picking up the Terminator and, with a screech, dashing him against the stone ground so hard he impacted in a shattered crater and his armour split open. Saint Evisser lifted what remained and threw it to the ground again, and this time blood spattered across the ground.

Tancred charged, as Alaric knew he would – Saint Evisser swung an arm and Tancred was sent flying. Alaric watched as the justicar was hurled through the air and straight through the wall of the basilica below. Karlin, the last member of Squad Tancred, drenched Saint Evisser with fire from his incinerator but the fallen saint ignored the flames.

Saint Evisser stepped out of the sarcophagus. At full height it was four of five times as tall as a Grey Knight. Its foot slammed down and a chasm ripped across the whole acropolis, the stone tipping inwards. Squad Alaric and Squad Genhain fought to keep their footing, scrambling as they slid towards the creature. It picked up a man-sized shard of marble and, with a bestial shriek, hurled it into Squad Genhain – Alaric saw Brother Grenn sliced in two and Brother Salkin's severed arm go cartwheeling away.

Alaric couldn't hear them yelling in defiance as they died. He couldn't hear Genhain ordering his Space Marines to fire, or even hear himself calling for vengeance and holy anger from his own squad. Alaric regained his footing and, his senses close to overloading, charged down the shifting slope at Saint Evisser. The saint swung a hand at him but Alaric ducked it, coming up swiftly to slash with the blade of his halberd.

The blade passed between mouldering ribs, glancing off bone, cutting through dried tattered organs and death robes. Alaric withdrew the halberd and stabbed, the blade passing through Saint Evisser's body and lodging in its spine.

Alaric twisted the halberd to get his blade free. Saint Evisser's enormous hand closed over his head and he felt himself lifted – he lashed out with the halberd, hoping to sever the skeletal wrist, but all he could see between Saint Evisser's fingers were those revolting liquid eyes, pale pools of malevolence, full of madness and Chaos.

His wards were overloading, blazing with cold fire inside his armour and cutting into his skin. It was only the pain that reminded him he was still alive. He squeezed down on the firing stud in his bolter hand, knowing that the volley would do no good, but knowing that he had to fight on as he died.

A flash burst just beyond Alaric's vision and Saint Evisser's head snapped to the side, bone shards flying. The hand let go and Alaric thudded onto the ground to see Saint Evisser throwing Justicar Santoro off its back, where the justicar had just landed a massive blow with his Nemesis mace. The side of Saint Evisser's skull was coming apart and Alaric could see the reddish fibrous mess inside that had once been the brain of an Imperial saint.

Fire rippled up Saint Evisser's torso – Sister Lachryma, her faced streaked with blood and grime, her jaw swollen and bleeding, was clambering through the shattered stone of the acropolis as her Seraphim attacked. One Sister with twin hand flamers was pouring fire up into the fallen saint, drawing his attention as bolt pistol fire from the other Seraphim thudded into its head.

Alaric dragged himself away from Saint Evisser. Brother Mykros, the Marine who carried Squad Santoro's incinerator, slammed into the ground beside him, one side of his armour caved in by the impact. Alaric rolled to the side as Santoro hit the ground beside him – Santoro was battered but alive, his mace smouldering with the unholy flesh that clung to it.

Alaric grabbed Santoro and the two helped each other to their feet, moving as quickly as they could up the broken slope as Saint Evisser lashed this way and that, trying to scatter the Sisters and Grey Knights. Sister Lachryma narrowly dodged a blow that shattered the arm of one of her Seraphim, and Brother Marl was trying to crawl away, his leg clearly broken.

Suddenly, the huge shape of Justicar Tancred appeared at the edge of the crater Saint Evisser had formed. His armour was battered and the ceramite plates were bent out of shape – sparks spat from ruptured servos and blood leaked from a dozen rents. The whites of his eyes were tiny glints in a mask of blood. The storm bolter on the back of his wrist had been wrecked by the impact as he smashed through the basilica wall but in his other hand was the sword of Mandulis.

Saint Evisser kicked out and another Seraphim went flying, her shattered jump pack spurting burning fuel. The fallen saint turned back towards Alaric and Santoro, and beyond them Squad Genhain was still trying to pin it down with a constant stream of fire.

Alaric knew what had to be done. Santoro, too.

Alaric ignored the pain and the screaming in his head and charged once again. Saint Evisser knocked the blade of his halberd aside and Alaric barely kept his footing, but Santoro was behind him, smashing Evisser's hand away with his mace. Alaric stabbed upwards again and felt monstrous ribs turning the blow away, but he wasn't trying to kill Saint Evisser this time.

Saint Evisser reached down and Alaric rolled out of the way of the gigantic fist that slammed into the rock behind him. He heard the impact of Santoro's mace against the saint's ribcage and knew the creature would be reeling – Alaric cut down at Evisser's leg and was rewarded with a shower of bone.

'I am the hammer…' intoned Tancred, his deep level voice somehow cutting through the din. 'I am the sword in His hand, I am the point of His spear…'

Tancred was walking carefully towards Saint Evisser, judging its every movement. Alaric and Santoro had to keep it busy. They had to stay alive for a few moments more, because Saint Evisser was the vessel through which Ghargatuloth would be born and only Tancred could kill it now.

Saint Evisser ripped a slab of marble up from the ground, straight and pointed like a blade. It swung it like a two-handed sword – Alaric pivoted to one side to avoid it and Santoro met the blade with his Nemesis mace, shattering the marble into a thousand stone splinters.

Evisser bent down to pick up Santoro and tear him apart, but Alaric was quicker – he dived at the fallen saint, both hands on the haft of his halberd, and planted the blade through one of Evisser's seething eyes.

Evisser shrieked so loudly Alaric thought his auto-senses would short out against the white wall of noise. Evisser flicked its head and Alaric was thrown hard against the broken marble slope, the bruised sky of the tomb reeling around him. The saint kicked out and Santoro hurtled through the air, cracking against the lip of the crater, his body cartwheeling brokenly out of sight.

'I am the gauntlet about His fist! I am the bane of His foes and the woes of the treacherous! I am the end!'

Tancred was the best swordsman Alaric had ever fought alongside. It had taken Brother-Captain Stern to best him. Saint Evisser was brimming with Chaotic strength but Tancred was a wily and merciless attacker. The sword of Mandulis flashed and Evisser's hand was sheared clean off its massive skeletal arm, falling to the ground in a spray of bone, light streamed from the wound. Tancred slashed again and the mirror-bright blade plunged into Evisser's torso, gouging again and again, hacking through ribs. Splinters of bone showered Tancred, chunks of vertebrae flew like bullets.

Saint Evisser was on its knees, Justicar Tancred battering it back with every strike. Evisser lifted its head to howl and the sword of Mandulis lashed out in a bright crescent, shearing right through the neck of the fallen saint.

Saint Evisser's head, its face twisted in the shock of a second death, toppled to the side. From the stump of the neck a shaft of pure light leap upwards, piercing the dark sky.

The screaming rose to a shriek almost too high-pitched to hear, spearing right down into Alaric's soul.

With a sound too loud to be heard, the acropolis exploded in a starburst of white light.

GHOLIC REN-SAR VALINOV reached the inside of the tomb in time to witness the rebirth of his lord.

Behind him, the Balurians stumbled and faltered in horror as they saw the sprawling, corrupt world that Chaos had built around Saint

Evisser's corpse. The rotted shell of a city that crawled with the seventy-seven masques, the heaving stone sky heavy with destiny, the shattered marble and hungry chasms, and the daemon carrion creatures that circled over the shining acropolis.

Many of the Balurians lost their minds there and then, even before the acropolis exploded. Valinov had already bent them to breaking point, using the subtleties of his words and actions to whip them into a frenzy and direct them to the tomb. Now they had served their purpose he didn't need them, so he let them go insane. Ghargatuloth had erected a shield of pure emotion around his tomb to keep out the unwary who might somehow find their way here, protecting his sacred site with madness – most of the Balurians quickly succumbed, but Valinov was not so weak.

Some Balurians saw only beauty and light as their minds were divorced from any sense of morality. They saw a world of glory and bounty, and ran open-armed into it only to fall down unseen chasms or be snatched into the shadows by the few cultists the Grey Knights had left behind. Others collapsed at the sight, their subconscious minds preferring to cut them off from their senses rather than risk the deeper madness that might follow. Some turned on their friends, convinced that anyone around them must be corrupt – lasguns barked and knife blades hissed through flesh.

The commissar stayed true to his duty to the last, accusing everyone near him of heresy and daemonancy in an attempt to explain where such corruption had come from. He fired at random into the Balurians, and those still composed enough to act leapt on him, dragging him to the ground so he disappeared beneath a heap of insane Guardsmen. Bolt pistol shots thudded out of the mass as the commissar enacted the Emperor's justice even as he was crushed and beaten to death against the fractured marble floor.

Valinov was untouched. The part of him that might have once gone insane had long since left him along with the weak spirit that could be levered open by psykers and the lake of despair that could boil over in lesser men's minds. Valinov had once prayed to anyone who would listen that those parts of him would shrivel and die, because they had caused him such torture when he did the grim, violent work of the Inquisition under Barbillus. Ghargatuloth had listened and stripped away Valinov's weaknesses until he was free of conscience and doubt. It was the greatest gift a man could receive. It was no hardship for Valinov to repay the Prince of a Thousand Faces with his servitude, and now he was going to join his master at last.

The explosion tore the acropolis apart in a tidal wave of white life, the birthing pains of Ghargatuloth shattering stone and wiping out the crumbling city, vaporising the seventy-seven masques in an instant, a shockwave coursed through the marble like a ripple through water. The whole tomb bulged outwards with the psychic force of the blast and the Balurians were thrown backwards, some smashing against the columns, others hurled right out back into the statue garden. Valinov was sure he saw the armoured body of a Grey Knight as it shot through the air like a bullet and slammed into the distant wall of the tomb.

Valinov was untouched. Ghargatuloth would protect him.

A massive crater like a giant gaping mouth was all that remained of the city.

And then, at long last, the Prince of a Thousand Faces was complete, and in an eruption of glory he was brought back into real space.

THE SHORE OF Lake Rapax rippled like water. That was all the warning there was, before the roof was ripped off the processing plant by a column of shimmering iridescent flesh several hundred metres across and a kilometre high, erupting like a volcano into the sky of Volcanis Ultor.

The outer spires of Hive Superior were dwarfed by the column as it tore up from the tomb of Saint Evisser, shimmering in colours that didn't exist outside of the warp. Reality twisted and folded around it as it forced itself into dimensions real space couldn't hold. As it poured upwards thunderheads of sorcery formed around it, shining nebulae that spat multicoloured lightning. Great writhing tentacles split off from its mass, spasming with new-found freedom, lashing out and demolishing the processing plant and the defences around it.

The ground in its shadow was boiling. The daemons that served as Ghargatuloth's heralds were following it out of the warp, dragging themselves up through the earth.

From the bleached empty plains to the depths of the underhive to the tips of the noble spires, fatal sorcery sparked into life. Many went mad. Others were struck down, hearts stopped by fear. A panic gripped everyone in Hive Superior – the Prince of a Thousand Faces brought fear with him, so pure that those who had never seen the sky of Volcanis Ultor were overcome with terror of the daemon prince manifesting outside the city.

Hatred became liquid and dripped down the walls. Suffering was a cold, lethal mist that rolled out across the plains. Deceit rained down in fingers of black malice over the remains of the trenches, and minds snapped all along the defences.

The column rippled and shifted, and on the end of each squirming tentacle monstrous, maddening features were formed from the flesh. A thousand new faces were looking down on Volcanis Ultor.

ALARIC HIT THE wall, and time stopped.

He watched as Ghargatuloth erupted from the ground, unfolding in horrifying slow motion, oceans of iridescent flesh moulded into a single daemon spear that punched up through the sky of the tomb and out into the air of Volcanis Ultor. The landscape of the tomb crumbled. The skeletal city and the foothills of marble were shattered into dust as the daemonic flesh ripped out from beneath them.

Alaric was falling, slowly. Broken bones were recoiling inside him. The tomb was being destroyed a stone at a time and the full hideous spectacle of Ghargatuloth was being played for him so he could experience every maddening moment of it.

Alaric was in awe of the sheer scale of it. He had faced daemons before, but nothing that spoke of such power. His mind was full of Ghargatuloth's horror, the mindless strength of the tentacles that tore out from its flesh, the enormity of its explosion into real space.

'How small your mind is,' said a voice, 'to be impressed by such a little show of my power.'

Alaric tried to look round but his muscles, locked in agonising slowness, couldn't respond. The voice was so familiar it started somewhere inside his head and worked its way out.

A figure coalesced from the air in front of Alaric, as a portion of Ghargatuloth's immense knowledge shifted into a physical form. The Prince of a Thousand Faces appeared as a tall, muscular, strong-featured man, wearing clothes of skins and hide. He had a hard-won physique that spoke of short, brutal lives, war, survival and the hunt. His long black hair was tied back with strings of finger bones and feathers, and he carried a spear with a head of flint.

Every cultist who worshipped Ghargatuloth saw a different face. This was the face that Alaric saw, taken from somewhere deep beneath him, ripped from the lowest levels of his mind to tell him how he was going to die.

'Is this how you appear to me?' said Alaric, for his lips were the only part of him that he could force to move. 'One of the thousand faces?'

'I have many more than a thousand.'

Alaric could not read the expression on the man's face – it kept slipping away from his sight, as if focusing on it made it change. 'On this world I was the Seventy-Seventh Masque, the death beyond death. On

Farfallen I was the God of the Last Hunt. To you, I am just the face you yourself see in me.'

Behind the Prince, his daemonic body was billowing up from the ground to form a lance of flesh now reaching up high into the sky through the shattered roof. Thick writhing tendrils were laying waste to the walls of the tomb, reaching in exultation towards the sky.

The Prince turned to watch it, seemingly in admiration or even nostalgia. 'The Changer of the Ways granted me that body. Holy Tzeentch himself. A vessel for what I am, which is knowledge, the most sacred weapon of the Change. Every man I kill, every secret I force a follower to divulge, every moment of suffering I cause, I learn more and I become more. I have learned a great deal in the last few months. I am more now than I have ever been. When Mandulis banished me I was like a child, and now I understand so much more. The galaxy needs me, Grey Knight. Time and space are prisons. The minds of mankind are the bars that keep everything inside. Break their souls, and they will become free, and freedom is the essence of Chaos.'

'Lie to me,' said Alaric. 'Go on. Lie. Prove to me that I am right.'

The Prince turned back to Alaric, his face still a vague swimming hint of an expression. 'You are very interesting to me, Alaric. You embody what I first tasted in Mandulis when he died. You run from the very elements that once made you human. You have become less than human – you have shut away the only parts of you that could ever be enlightened by the Changer of the Ways. You call it faith, but if you understood the true nature of what Tzeentch promises to the galaxy then you would realise how grave a crime it is to render a mind so inert.'

'We found you once, daemon. We will find you again.'

'And then what?' Ghargatuloth's voice was mocking. 'Where would I be if Mandulis had not found me? Here, Grey Knight, here and now, with my followers and the work of my Master well under way. Banishing me changed nothing. Why must you refuse to understand? Chaos cannot be defeated, you must know that.'

Clouds were gathering in the sky as Ghargatuloth's body shrieked up into Volcanis Ultor's upper atmosphere, and sparks of blue lightning reflected off the shining flesh. The face of the Prince in front of Alaric hung in the air ignoring the destruction behind it, as more and more of the tomb was sucked into the searing column of flesh.

'You just had to look around you, Grey Knight, and you'd have seen it. What is Chaos? Suffering, you might say. Oppression. Deceit. But could not all these things be said of your Imperium? You hunt down the talented and the strong-willed. You break them or sacrifice them. You lie to your citizens and wage war on those who dare speak out. The inquisitors you call masters assume guilt and execute millions on a whim. And why? Why do you do this? Because you know Chaos is there but you do not know how to fight it, so you crush your own citizens for fear that they might aid the Enemy. The Imperium suffers because of Chaos. No matter how hard you fight, that will never change. Chaos exists in a state of permanent victory over you – you dance to our tune, mortal one, you butcher and torture and repress one another because the gods of the warp require you to. The Imperium is founded on Chaos. My lord Tzeentch won your war a long, long time ago.'

Alaric could feel the blasphemous words hitting his shield of faith like broadsides from a battleship. The Prince's words cut more deeply that any sorcery ever had, worming their way through the layers of doctrination. He felt naked – he had never been this vulnerable, even when he had been surrounded and outgunned, even when Ligeia had been lost and Alaric had been left alone in the hunt for Ghargatuloth. He let his anger burn hotter, to drown out the fear.

'We killed, daemon!' spat Alaric furiously. 'We killed you with the sword of Mandulis! The lightning bolt!'

'"Only the lightning bolt will cleanse this reality of Ghargatuloth's presence",' said the Prince. 'Valinov told you that, I suppose? When you broke him on Mimas? Must I really explain to you that Valinov cannot be broken? I removed those weak parts from him when I made him my own. So pleasing it is, Grey Knight, to deceive by telling the truth. So ironic, so beloved of Tzeentch. You see, Valinov was right. I cannot be killed, I cannot be stopped. The only way I can be cleansed from the galaxy is if I finish Tzeentch's work and turn the galaxy into a thing of pure Chaos. Then I shall become one with my lord, and then will I cease to exist. The weapon that banished me was the one with the power to bring me back, so I could do this work of Chaos. Valinov was telling the truth – you simply chose to hear a different truth.'

Of course, it was true. Every daemon had a condition that had to be fulfilled before it could return – a particular date, a location, a specific sacrifice or spell. Ghargatuloth, a being of great power, had many. He had to be born through a corrupted Imperial relic, the body of Saint Evisser. It had to be on the Trail, and it had to be now. And the vessel through which he was reborn had to be killed with the weapon that had first banished him.

Gharghatuloth could create them all – the Saint, the Trail, the cultists to serve him and the plots to bring the threads into place. But he could not create the sword of Mandulis. That had to be brought to him, and the Grey Knights had done exactly that.

Alaric's mind burned with conflict. The Grey Knights had not been used. They had fought and killed and done their duty. They were not a part of this plan, they were not the instrument of the Enemy…

'It was the way it had to be,' he said, teeth gritted with anger. 'You did not use us like you used Ligeia. We had to fight you face to face, to do what Mandulis did… we freed you so you could be fought…'

'Desperation, Grey Knight. You were with me from the beginning. It had to be you, you see. I find you Grey Knights so fascinating, with your unbreakable souls. Such wonderful tools. Impossible to discourage, some of the best soldiers the Imperium can muster, completely devoted to whatever cause I can plant in you. I just have to point you in the right direction and I know you will do what I want. *You* brought the sword of Mandulis to me, *you* helped fuel the carnage on the Trail, *you* turned Volcanis Ultor into the kind of bloodbath I needed to hide my preparations until it was time for me to fully awaken. And the challenge of breaking you afterwards is more than I can resist.'

Alaric saw the Balurians dying, a tiny swarm of dark blue figures by the entrance to the tomb, seething as they killed one another in their madness. He saw Valinov, hands raised in praise.

'Like all humans you have your flaws,' continued Ghargatuloth, 'but you are so proud you cannot see them. Your fault is fear, Alaric. You know the Grey Knights have never lost one of their own to corruption by the Enemy, and somewhere deep inside you is the fear that you will be the first. It is this that makes you feel so helpless in your unguarded moments. It is why you could never have been a leader. Why else do you see this face of me?' Ghargatuloth indicated his current form, the fierce tribesman. 'I appear to you as what you could have been. I am what you fear – I appear as what you could have been, if this fragile reality had not delivered you into the Grey Knights. Beneath your conscious mind you remember your old life on that savage world, and it reminds you that you could change again – you could change into someone who worships me. And I shall make sure that fear comes true, Alaric. I shall spend a long time breaking you, and when you fall you will be one of my dearest trophies.'

Alaric was silent. He didn't have long to live. He might only have one chance, but it was more than he could have hoped for. He had to make it count. For his fallen brothers, and for Ligeia. For Mandulis, who had given more than his life a thousand years ago.

Ghargatuloth hadn't brought him here. Alaric had made all those decisions himself. The sword of Mandulis, battling the Sisters, hunting Ghargatuloth to Lake Rapax – it was all his own choice. He was following his plan, not Ghargatuloth's. And there was one last chance to prove it.

His shield of faith was failing. He had to act now, before it fell and Ghargatuloth saw what he kept hidden there.

'Then it really is the end,' he said. 'But a death defying the Enemy is a victory in itself. You cannot take that away.'

'Perhaps not,' replied Ghargatuloth. 'But after death, you will be mine. I will have an eternity to make you fall.'

'You had to use the whole Trail,' continued Alaric. 'Saint Evisser, the cardinals, every single citizen, you had to move them all into position to beat us. Remember that. You put your plan in motion before the Trail even existed, because you knew it would take nothing less. We made you work, daemon. You feared us so much you had to move star systems to make us dance to your tune.'

'Keep that pride, Alaric. It gives you so much more to lose.'

'Well then,' said Alaric resignedly. 'Let us go through the motions. A Grey Knight should have some heroic last words, that's what the stories tell us. A final denial of the Enemy.'

'Indeed. Something to remind you of how futile your death was.'

'Good.' Alaric forced himself to focus on the figure's face. He concentrated until Ghargatuloth's eyes were drawn into view – they were hard, expressive, determined. A lot like Alaric's.

'Tras'kleya'thallgryaa…' began Alaric, and suddenly the world shifted back to full speed as the face of Ghargatuloth shattered.

A TENTACLE OF daemon flesh reached out from the column, bending gracefully over the wreckage of the disintegrating tomb towards where Valinov stood, surrounded by dying Balurians. Hundreds of hands reached out from the shimmering skin and lifted Valinov up, drawing him face-first into the body of Ghargatuloth, bestowing on him the ultimate reward for his devotion to the Lord of Change and his herald.

Valinov felt the power all around him – the power of pure knowledge, a perception so intense it seeped through his skin and began to eat him away, reducing him, too, to the pure substance of the knowledge that made him. Ideas of skin and bone were freed from their prisons. Valinov's organs began to dissolve in the shining liquid mass of Ghargatuloth. Faces beyond human description were staring out of the tentacle now as Valinov was drawn into it, watching their master's greatest servant becoming one of them – a new Face for the Prince, an idol before which countless cultists would bow. When Tzeentch swallowed up the galaxy and all was Chaos, Valinov would be a god.

* * *

ABOVE VOLCANIS ULTOR the thousand faces of Ghargatuloth suddenly recoiled, slipping back into the column of flesh. Tentacles writhed, looping in tortured knots around the pulsing central column. The clouds flared with angry lightning, the daemon's pain made solid, arcing in brutal red streaks to the ground. The iridescent flesh rippled with mottled dark colours, like wounds beneath the skin.

Daemons shrieked and were thrown back, their flesh becoming unstable, one daemon flowing into another and dying as their burning blood and organs spilled out onto the bleached stone. The sound was awful, like a million death-rattles at once.

Against the shattered wall of the tomb, destruction all around him and Ghargatuloth towering over him, was Alaric of the Grey Knights. His body was battered and broken, his armour split and torn. But he was alive, and he was conscious. He was shouting out the same words that Inquisitor Ligeia had, over and over again, in the run-up to her execution.

The Inquisition had believed she was speaking in tongues, her mind ruined by Ghargatuloth's influence. But Alaric knew how strong her mind was, and he had found it in him to trust her one last time. He had taken the transcripts of her interrogations and memorised the phrase she repeated over and over again.

It was not a stream of meaningless syllables. It was Ligeia's last desperate message to her captors, her last attempt at getting revenge against the Prince of a Thousand Faces.

'Iakthe'landra'klaa...' shouted Alaric, and the flesh of Ghargatuloth was shocked into dullness, flakes of it shearing off and falling like grisly grey snow.

Every daemon was ultimately a servant. Every one had a master, even one as powerful as Ghargatuloth whose master was Tzeentch himself. But for daemons to serve unquestioningly, a master had to have power over them. And so every daemon had a name. Men might know them by any number of names, but only one was the True Name.

Inquisitor Ligeia had known her mind was being invaded by Ghargatuloth. She had known her fall was inevitable, and so she had left herself as open as she possibly could. Her psychic power drew information out of any source, and Ghargatuloth was pure information – she had let him course through her, giving up her sanity and ultimately her life, searching for the knowledge she needed. She had found it, and in her final moments she had stayed just lucid enough to communicate it to her captors.

Of all of them, only Alaric trusted her enough to listen.

Syllable by painful syllable, just as Ligeia had done even in her dying moments, Alaric recounted the True Name of Ghargatuloth.

THE SYLLABLES BURNED Alaric's lips. Had it not been for his faith, he could not have survived saying the True Name at all. It was hundreds of syllables long and Alaric knew that if he made the slightest mistake he would fail, and so he pushed through the pain flowing through him and carried on.

The immense form of Ghargatuloth was flashing black and sickly green, blotches of purplish decay rippling up it. The faces writhed beneath the skin, fighting to get to the core of Ghargatuloth's body and away from the words that were burning their way through the daemon prince's flesh. Skin was flaking off in great slabs now, falling to earth in a terrible hail of dead flesh. Tentacles became dry, grey arches of flesh that cracked and fell to crash against the ground far below.

Alaric forced the last syllable out of himself, a sound he thought he could never make, ripping up through his throat. He thought he would die with the effort – he fell forward and landed face-first in the drift of shattered marble at the base of the ruined wall

Unconsciousness pulled at him. Blackness flashed at the edge of his vision. The death cry of Ghargatuloth cut through the pain – it was a low, hideous keening, at once pathetic and full of rage. It was hatred and pain. It was a raging against the agony of death.

Alaric forced his eyes open. Over the shattered shell of the tomb, the column was showering dead flesh and leaning drunkenly. Tight masts of flesh near its base snapped and Ghargatuloth toppled sideways, towards the plains that lay to the east of the processing plant and the line once held by the Sisters of the Bloody Rose. Slowly, appallingly, Ghargatuloth fell with a terrible sound as thousands of tendons snapped in sequence.

Alaric forced himself to his feet. The air was thick with falling scraps of desiccated flesh like black snow. His Nemesis halberd lay nearby. He stumbled over to it and picked it up as he heard the massive crash of Ghargatuloth hitting the ground.

Alaric clambered up the wreckage until he could see out from the remains of the tomb, painkillers flooding through his system but failing to cut off the ache that came from everywhere at once. Ghargatuloth was a huge, dying drift of flesh. Daemons were dissolving back into the ground.

Justicar Genhain stumbled across the wreckage towards Alaric. A couple of other Grey Knights could also be seen – Alaric recognised one of the Terminators and realised it must be Brother Karlin, for Tancred must surely be dead.

There were perhaps ten Grey Knights left – Karlin, a couple of Genhain's men, a couple of Alaric's. Alaric couldn't see any of Squad Santoro – he wasn't even sure how many had made it to the acropolis at all. Lachryma and her Sisters were gone.

Alaric turned back to Ghargatuloth. The True Name had weakened it, for so soon after its birth the shock of having a new, mortal master had made its very fabric unstable. But the Prince of a Thousand Faces wasn't dead yet.

Alaric began to walk towards the fallen daemon prince, followed by the remains of his command. He still had work to do.

IN THE END, it wasn't the Grey Knights who killed Ghargatuloth. It was mostly the Balurian heavy infantry, who marched in a cloud of ash wheeling anti-tank guns to finish the job the Grey Knights had started. None of them knew what had happened or that the Grey Knights were even there – all they knew was that immense destruction had been unleashed on Volcanis Ultor, that many of their regiment were dead, and that the fallen beast was responsible. A couple of Leman Russ tanks were brought up and the few surviving officers began to direct their fire into Ghargatuloth.

Tank shells and heavy weapons fire ripped into the daemon's flesh. Many-coloured blood soaked the earth, turning the ash-choked ground into a foul swamp and running off into Lake Rapax.

The surviving Sisters of the Bloody Rose added their firepower, too, their one remaining Exorcist tank sending rockets streaking into Ghargatuloth. The Methalor 12th Scout Regiment made the long march up from their positions on the south of the line and added what little long-range firepower they had, too, until Ghargatuloth was a pulpy burning mess of oozing flesh.

The Balurians advanced, the Methalorians by their side. Lasgun fire flashed in a crimson storm, turning Ghargatuloth's blood into clouds of foul steam. Both regiments fixed bayonets and, filled with the hatred they had felt when Ghargatuloth first erupted from beneath the ground, set to hacking it to pieces. The Sisters joined in, intoning prayers of righteous wrath as they blasted Ghargatuloth to pulp with their bolter fire and the Sisters Superior laid into it with their chainswords.

Few noticed the Grey Knights. There were few of them, and everything was obscured by clouds of smoke and steam. Alaric and Genhain stood side by side as they hacked with their halberds, grimly and methodically reducing Ghargatuloth's daemonic body into a filthy viscous lake of daemon's blood.

* * *

THE SUN OF Volcanis Ultor was setting somewhere behind the ever-present clouds. Alaric could feel Ghargatuloth's life draining away and he stayed on the shore of Lake Rapax, waiting until his psychic core told him the daemon prince was gone.

He had several severe injuries – his storm bolter arm was broken somewhere, his rib-plate was fractured and shards of bone were loose inside his chest cavity. His third lung was the only thing keeping him breathing. Lesser men would have died. But the medicae facilities in Hive Superior could wait – Alaric would not go anywhere until he was sure Ghargatuloth was dead. And the faint throb of willpower was dying out. Alaric didn't have long to wait, leaning on the shaft of his halberd, feeling the night-time cold settle over the plain.

Justicar Genhain was trying to find all the surviving Grey Knights, and locate as many bodies of the fallen brethren as he could. He had found Santoro's body, broken almost beyond recognition by the explosion of the acropolis. He had been only metres away from Alaric – it could so easily have been Alaric who had died. Some of Santoro's Space Marines had died earlier without Alaric knowing anything about it, killed by Ghagratuloth's cultists on the way to the acropolis along with several of Lachryma's Seraphim. Tancred's body could not be found – Alaric knew that it never would be.

The sword of Mandulis had survived, glinting brightly at the bottom of the crater where the processing plant had once been. Genhain held it now, wrapped up so its blade would not reflect the drab destruction around it. It would be Genhain who returned with Durendin to the tomb of Mandulis, to re-inter the weapon beneath Titan. Until then the sword would be kept wrapped, its work now done.

The Sisters of the Bloody Rose were recovering their own dead, and Alaric had watched as they took away the body of their canoness from what remained of the steps up to the tomb. The whole of the processing plant was now just a crater filled with rubble, and it was impossible to see where the normal dimensions of the plant had ended and the abnormality of the tomb had begun. Balurian dead lay everywhere, and a Chimera troop transporter had been commandeered to carry loads of bodies back towards the rear lines.

So many had to die. So many that could not be replaced.

Something stirred in the dark stain of Ghargatuloth's blood. Alaric painfully walked over to it and saw, writhing in the filth, a human body.

Its skin was gone, eaten away as if by acid. It was covered in slime, its lidless eyes rolling madly, its hands wrapped around its entrails to keep them from spilling out.

At first Alaric thought it was a Balurian. But then he recognised the power sword that still hung on a tattered sword belt around the figure's waist, the same sword that Alaric had seen on Valinov as he welcomed Ghargatuloth into real space.

Alaric almost wished Valinov could still speak, so he could hear Valinov's taunts. But it didn't matter. As Alaric had recounted the True Name, Ghargatuloth had rejected his servant. Valinov had devoted his life – more than his life, his soul, his very existence – to Ghargatuloth, and it had been snatched away from him at the very last second. The pain of dying would mean nothing to Valinov, but the agony of failure when he had come so close was a torture of which Ghargatuloth himself would have been proud.

Perhaps it would have been fitting to let Valinov carry on despairing. But the Ordo Malleus had already executed Valinov once, and Alaric knew they would expect the job to be finished.

'By the authority of the Holy Orders of the Emperor's Inquisition,' said Alaric, 'and as a brother-captain of the Grey Knights, Chamber Militant of the Ordo Malleus, I enact the judgement of Encaladus and place your soul before the Emperor for judgement.' Alaric bent down and picked up Valinov by the scruff of the neck. Valinov stared wildly at him, shivering, vile slime oozing out of his red wet body.

'But then,' said Alaric, 'you don't have a soul. So this is the end of everything, Gholic Ren-Sar Valinov. This is oblivion.'

Alaric walked slowly away from Ghargatuloth's dissolved corpse, up to the edge of Lake Rapax, which shone a multitude of sickly colours in the faint pale moonlight that filtered through the clouds. He knelt down at the lake's edge and plunged Valinov into the polluted waters.

Valinov struggled weakly. Slowly he stopped kicking. Alaric waited long enough to be sure that Valinov was dead, and then waited some more, alone and silent on the shore of the lake.

DAY WAS BREAKING by the time Justicar Genhain came to find him. Genhain had taken a Chimera from the Methalor regiment and was using it to take the surviving Grey Knights back to Hive Superior, where along with the Sisters they would tend their wounded until transports came to take them to proper apothecarion facilities.

Karlin had survived – he still held his incinerator in spite of the shrapnel wounds that covered him. Justicar Genhain along with Tharn, Ondurin and Salkin (who had lost an arm, sheared clean off). Alaric's Marines Haulvarn, Dvorn and Lykkos. Alaric himself. No one from Squad Santoro.

As the Chimera trundled across the battlefield towards Hive Superior, Alaric looked back, once, at the huge dark stain that remained of Ghargatuloth.

It wasn't over, of course. Ghargatuloth couldn't be permanently killed. But the Grey Knights – and Mandulis, and Ligeia – had shown that he could be beaten. And it was the duty of the Ordo Malleus to make sure that he stayed beaten.

The sun broke through the clouds, but it only shone on death and pollution, the piles of wreckage, the heaps of the dead. Slowly, very slowly, the long and gruelling task began of purging Ghargatuloth's influence from the Trail of Saint Evisser.

ON A RIDGE deep into the plain, the death cultist Xiang watched Ghargatuloth dissolve. Xiang had finally completed the last orders of her mistress Inquisitor Ligeia, and ensured that the daemon prince was brought into real space so that the Grey Knights could have their chance to destroy it.

Xiang was in a situation she had never been before. She had no master. She had once served the sect of the Imperial church that demanded blood sacrifice for the Emperor, and after that had sworn allegiance to Ligeia. Xiang had never been without a master, and it was a strange feeling – her thoughts, her movements, her decisions were her own now. She was not an instrument of another's will. There was only her own will to obey.

Perhaps she would find a new master eventually, and suborn herself to his commands. But perhaps she would explore this feeling more. Volcanis Ultor was as good a place to start as any – bleak wilderness to explore, layers of lawless underhive in which to test her skills, all manner of Imperial citizens to learn from, to observe, perhaps to obey.

She turned away from the dead daemon prince and looked across the plain, towards Hive Verdanus just visible far to the east. Xiang wondered if she would ever find a master like Ligeia again. Then she wondered if she wanted to.

Her taut muscles barely registering the effort, Xiang began the long walk.

THE AIR WAS cold deep beneath Titan. The psych-warded chamber was small and bleak, lit only by a single guttering candle. The chamber had been excavated only a few days before to serve as a secret, secure repository for information that had to be kept secure – and more importantly, that should never be forgotten. It was hidden in the bowels of Titan's catacombs, guarded by the legions of dead Marines, where only the Chaplains of the Grey Knight would know where to find it.

A single large desk dominated the room, and a scribe-servitor sat hunched over a large open book. The book was new, only recently bound, its pages white and blank. The servitor's quill arm hovered over the page.

Chaplain Durendin and Inquisitor Nyxos stood towards the back wall of the room. Durendin had led Nyxos down to this place, because it was on Nyxos's insistence that the chamber had been built. Nyxos was recovering from the injuries he had suffered at Valinov's execution but he still looked weak and drawn, aged even beyond his advanced years, his every movement supplemented by the servos of his exoskeleton.

'You may begin,' said Nyxos, and the scribe-servitor began scratching a title onto the page.

Second Book of the Codicium Aeternum, it began in perfect flowing script. *Being a description and naming of Daemons, the Dates and Durations of the Banishments and Details thereof, that the Enemy might be known before his Machinations are complete...*

Inquisitor Nyxos began to dictate the details of the report Alaric had given in the apothecarion, about Ghargatuloth's elaborate plans to create a fallen saint to act as the centrepiece for the ritual that would revive him, to use the Grey Knights to deliver the weapon that had first banished him, and to suborn unnumbered cultists and demagogues to cover his tracks. Those same cultists were even now being purged from the Trail of Saint Evisser in an operation commanded by Inquisitor Klaes and Provost Marechal, and it would not be finished for decades, if ever.

He made sure to mention Inquisitor Ligeia, and how Alaric was the only one who trusted her in the end. He mentioned the many, many Imperial citizens that died, and the many that were still to die as Ghargatuloth's influence was scoured from the Trail.

Finally, the scribe-servitor noted down that Ordo Malleus research and readings of the Imperial tarot had suggested the duration of Ghargatuloth's banishment. He would be able enter real space again in one thousand years. But this time, the Malleus would not give him the chance to succeed.

'Note this exactly,' dictated Inquisitor Nyxos, 'for every syllable must be pronounced perfectly lest the banishment fail. Know that the True Name of the daemon Ghargatuloth is Tras'kleya'thallgryaa...'

For several minutes Inquisitor Nyxos forced the syllables out of his throat. When it was done, the servitor-scribe was taken away to be destroyed to ensure that hearing the True Name had not implanted some corruption in its biological brain.

Then Inquisitor Nyxos left Titan for Iapetus, to head for the Eye of Terror and continue the Emperor's fight. One chapter of Ghargatuloth's story was done, and by the time the next one began, Nyxos and all those who had fought the Prince would be long gone.

WHEN IT WAS done, when the bodies recovered had been buried beneath Titan, the reports had been made to the Ordo Malleus and the survivors had been thoroughly purified, Alaric was granted a few days of convalescence to himself while it was decided if he should retain his rank of brother-captain.

He was given permission to make the short journey to Mimas, and there he was guided by the interrogator staff to the place where Inquisitor Ligeia had died.

There was nothing left. The cell had been dismantled – only the clamp remained bored into the rock where the cable had once been fixed to the surface.

Ligeia's body had been cremated and scattered in orbit, to ensure there would be nothing left of her. All Alaric could do was say a prayer for her passing, but it was still more than anyone else had done – Ligeia had died a traitor, so no one had seen to it that her soul was commended to the Emperor's side. It wasn't much, just a few sacred words pitted against the horror of heresy. But it was enough.

So many had to die, thought Alaric as he looked out over the barren surface of Mimas, the huge glowing disc of Saturn overhead. So many had to suffer.

But sometimes, the fight was worth it. That was why the Grey Knights existed. The fight would never be over, but sometimes, it could be won.

DARK ADEPTUS

ONE

'I long for death, not because I seek peace, but because I seek the war eternal.'
— Cardinal Armandus Helfire,
'Reflections on the Long Death'

THE SKY OF Chaeroneia shuddered with static and changed, displaying a new channel of geometric patterns. Holy hexagons representing the six-fold genius of the Omnissiah merged with the circles representing the totality of knowledge that the tech-priesthood sought. Double helices, fractals born of sacred information-relics, litanies of machine code, all swirled against the sky of the forge world, casting the pale light of knowledge over the valley of datacores. The smokestacks of the titan works were silhouetted against the holy projections, ironwork bridges spanning gigantic factory towers, sky-piercing obelisks where tech-priests watched the heavens, radio masts where they listened for the voice of the Omnissiah in solar radiation. The valley itself, lined with towering cliffs of obsidian datacores, was a long deep slash of shadow.

Projected onto the thick layer of pollutants in the forge world's atmos-phere, the sacred arcs and angles were a visual representation of that evening's data-prayers being intoned by thrice-blessed worship-servitors in the Cathedrals of Knowledge. Beneath the titanium plated minarets rows of identical servitors would be standing, their vocal units emitting streams of digital information, singing the praises of the Omnissiah in the binary of pure lingua technis.

Magos Antigonus knew that meant a new solar cycle was starting. The pollutants over Chaeroneia were so thick there was no sun, so it was only the clockwork-regular services of the Cult Mechanicus that gave time any meaning on the forge world. That in turn meant he had been on the run for three Terran standard days. It was a long time to go with no food or sleep.

The datacore valley was a good place to hide out. Visual sensors were often confused by the pure blackness of the datacores themselves and the impenetrable shadows that flooded between them. The information in the cores was so pure that sensoria were dazzled by the intensity, while even augmented eyes could miss a single man in the darkness. But Antigonus knew he was still far from safe.

He turned to the servitor next to him. Like all servitors, this device was built around the frame of a once-living human being, the baser levels of its brain computing its functions and its nervous system relaying commands to its augmetic limbs. It was a basic manservant model, programmed to follow its owner and execute simple commands.

'Epsilon three-twelve,' said Antigonus and the servitor turned its face towards him, large round ocular implants whirring as they focused on the tech-priest. 'Journal additional.'

Epsilon three-twelve's hands clicked as the long articulated fingers reformed, reaching inside its hollowed chest cavity and bringing out a roll of parchment. A dextrous servo-arm reached out of its mouth, holding a quill.

'Third standard day,' said Antigonus. The servo-arm dipped the quill into an inkwell concealed in the servitor's left eye socket and wrote down Antigonus's words in a stilted, artificial hand. 'Investigation halted. The existence of a heretical cell has been confirmed. Primary goal executed.' Antigonus paused. He had thought that finding them would be the worst of it. He had been utterly wrong. Unforgivable.

'The heretics are between ten and thirty in number,' continued Antigonus, 'representing all Adepta of the Mechanicus, including genetors, lexmechanicus, xenobiologis, metallurgus, pecunius, digitalis and others unknown. Also include ranks from menial to archmagos and probably above. No upper limit to penetration of Chaeroneia's ruling caste.'

Antigonus stopped suddenly and flicked his ocular attachment upwards. Its large glass orb surveyed the sky above, still swarming with the sacred imagery. He was sure he had heard something. But he had been on the run for three days and had been unable to risk accepting maintenance on Chaeroneia for some time before that, so perhaps his aural receptors were failing him just as his motive and circulator units were wearing out.

Epsilon three-twelve waited patiently, quill poised over the scroll. Antigonus waited a few moments more, the ocular orb searching up and down the valley. The sheer sides of the chasm were glossy and black, drinking in the pallid light, while the floor was littered with rusting, unrecognisable chunks of machinery. Antigonus was sure he and his servitor were well-hidden behind one such massive slab that looked like the engine from a mass-lifter vehicle. However, he knew better than to think that made them safe – a heretic tech-priest with a powerful auspex scanner set to detect Antigonus's life signs could sniff them out.

'The nature of the heresy itself is not fully understood. Secondary objective incomplete.' Antigonus shook his head. The ways of the Machine-God were often argued over by the tech-priests of the Adeptus Mechanicus, but he still did not understand how any of them could turn to such base heresy as he had witnessed here. 'Sorcery and warpcraft are suspected but not proven beyond doubt. The heretics venerate the Omnissiah, but through an avatar or mouthpiece. The nature of this avatar is not known, but cross-reference previous entries on any pre-Imperial presence on Chaeroneia.'

A hot, dry wind swept down the valley, throwing a few pieces of rusting sheet metal around. A maintenance servitor drifted overhead on thrumming grav-units, its fat belly full of antioxidant foam to spew over any fire or corrosive spill that might threaten the precious datacores. Far above, the data-sermon was coming to an end, the sacred geometry fading. In its place, work rotas and diagrams of emergency procedures flickered by, ensuring that the forge world's menial population was constantly reminded of its duties to the Mechanicus. So many people lived utterly normal lives in the factories and mineshafts, never knowing the monstrous blasphemies festering in the ruling population of tech-priests.

'The origins of the heresy and the individuals responsible for its dissemination are unknown. Tertiary objective incomplete. But see note on pre-Imperial presence above.' That was the most frustrating of all. Antigonus's evidence was compelling but incomplete. He had read the debased datapsalms describing the Omnissiah as a force for destruction instead of knowledge. He had witnessed minor tech-priests, their bodies swollen with forbidden biomechanical augmetics, using base sorcery to escape the tech-guard commanded by Antigonus. He had seen those same tech-guard driven mad by warp magics that any tech-priest would abhor. But he knew so few details. He did not know what the heretics wanted, or who they were. He did not know how all this had started. He did not know how to stop it.

Now it was just him, fleeing through the underbelly of Chaeroneia with his servitor in tow, augmetics failing through lack of maintenance.

They were hunting him down. He was sure of it. The heretics were everywhere on the planet, at every level from the menial barracks to the
control towers.

'Personal note.' Antigonus heard the sounds of the scratching quill
change as the servitor dutifully altered its handwriting to something less
precise. 'The cell is not large but it is well organised, highly motivated
and thoroughly ingrained into the society of Chaeroneia. Its existence is
suspected only by those who are members or are otherwise under the
cell's control. There is no upper limit to the seniority of its members. I
can only hope it does not extend off-world. My primary objective completed, I believe the best course of action is for me to leave this planet
at the first opportunity and recommend a full purge of Chaeroneia by
the authority of the archmagos ultima. I also recommend that the Fabricator General be appraised of the situation on Chaeroneia given that
the nature of the heresy is such that...'

Antigonus paused again. He was aware of something huge and dark flitting over the valley, blotting out the projections overhead for a moment.

'There is no logic in fear,' he told himself. The servitor wrote the words
down automatically, but Antigonus ignored it.

Antigonus rose to his feet, mechadendrites snaking from below his
grimy rust-red robes. His augmentations were not designed for combat,
but he could still handle himself if it came down to it – each mechadendrite could extrude a monomolecular blade and he had enough
redundant organs to keep him alive through terrible injuries.

They were watching him.

Antigonus whirled around as another shadow passed over him. His
left hand – the non-bionic one – reached inside his robes and took out
a brass-cased autogun. The weapon was a good, solid Mars-pattern gun,
but Antigonus had never fired it in anger. He was a seeker of knowledge,
a metallurgist in service to the Priesthood of Mars – he had been sent to
Chaeroneia because he had a sharp and inquisitive mind, not because
he was a warrior able to face down vengeful heretics by himself. When
it came down to it, could he survive?

Antigonus sighted down the barrel at the shadows between the wreckage that littered the valley.

'Query,' said the thin, grating voice of Epsilon three-twelve. 'Procedure
terminate?'

'Yes, terminate,' said Antigonus, annoyed. The servitor's limbs folded
up as it stashed the scroll back in its chest.

The light levels changed, flooding the valley with a pale greenish glow.
Antigonus searched for the source, knowing it must be the searchlight

of a hunter-servitor or armed grav-platform, come to chase him down like an animal. But there was nothing.

Then Antigonus looked up to the sky.

Magos Antigonus, read hundred metre-long letters projected onto the clouds.

Join us.

The letters hung there for a few moments then disappeared, replaced by a new message.

You are ignorant and blind. You are like a child, like a menial. Blind to the light.

The Avatar of the Omnissiah is among us.

When you see it, you will know it is beautiful and pure. You can take this understanding back to Mars. You can be our prophet.

Antigonus shook his head, glancing around, panicking. His finger trembled on the trigger. He held out his bionic right arm and grabbed the gun with steel fingers, steadying his aim. 'No!' he shouted. 'I have seen what you are!'

We are the future.

We are the way.

All else is darkness and death.

Antigonus began to move, jogging through the hunks of wreckage, trying to find somewhere they couldn't see him. They must have a grav-platform watching him from somewhere above, perhaps even a vehicle in orbit with sensoria that could cut through the thick pollutant clouds. Epsilon three-twelve waddled after Antigonus on its ill maintained legs, its subhuman mind oblivious to the threats all around them.

You will never have a greater chance than this, Magos Antigonus. Your life does not have to continue as a statistical irrelevance.

Antigonus sped up. If they could track him through the valley then he was trapped. At one end of the valley was a massive cogitator housing where the contents of the datacores were searched and filtered. It was staffed mostly by tech-priest information specialists – the heretics would find him there. But the other end led into a tangle of workshops and factory floors, many half ruined. It was populated mostly by menials and roving servitors. Antigonus might be safe there. He broke into a run, servitor in tow, the servos on his withered legs grinding painfully as they took the strain.

One chance is more than the Adeptus Mechanicus will ever give you. Look upon the face of the Omnissiah, Antigonus, and understand!

Antigonus ran as fast as he could, the servitor somehow keeping up. He was ill-lubricated and low on power but he re-routed all his non-essential systems to keep him moving. His vision greyed out as his ocular implants switched down to minimal and his digestive system shut down temporarily. The multi-layered factory complex loomed up ahead – its warren-like structure and menial population would mask him from observation. It was his only chance.

Then it seems you are as small-minded and inflexible as all your kind. You are a disappointment.

You are obsolete.

WHO COULD ORCHESTRATE the hijacking of the projector units and the kind of surveillance technology needed to follow Antigonus here? The names were few. Scraecos, the archmagos veneratus who masterminded Chaeroneia's extensive data networks and commanded all the planet's formidable reserves of information. Archmagos Ultima Vengaur, responsible for liaising with the Imperial authorities about Chaeroneia's tithes and adherence to Imperial law. Another archmagos veneratus, named Thulharn, whose domain was Chaeroneia's orbital installations and space traffic. There were very few others with the necessary seniority and ability.

But could a small heretic cell really sway such men? Men who had risen so far in the hierarchy of the Adeptus Mechanicus that they could barely be called men at all any more?

Epsilon three-twelve.

Execute.

Antigonus turned just in time to see Epsilon three-twelve fold out its augmetic limbs, this time with the articulated tines bent into wicked claws. It lurched forward crazily and crashed into Antigonus, barrelling him to the floor. Antigonus's head smacked into the grime-slicked rockcrete.

The servitor's mechanical parts made it heavy and its rugged construction made it strong. Antigonus was trapped on his back and had to drop his gun to grab the servitor's wrists and stop it from clawing at him. He was face-to-face with Epsilon three-twelve – the servitor's eye sockets were polished bone, but the nose and mouth beneath them were grey, expressionless dead flesh.

Antigonus lashed out a mechadendrite and the tentacle-like appendage wrapped itself around the stock of his autogun. Antigonus whipped the mechadendrite back and clubbed the servitor in the head with the butt of the gun. Sparks spat off its brass-chased skull but the servitor didn't move its weight off Antiogonus and the tech-priest felt one of his ribs break in a flare of pain. Painkillers pumped out of his bionic heart and the red mist flowed away. Antigonus used the moment of clarity to wrap one mechadendrite around the servitor's throat, forcing its head back, fighting the servo motors in its spine. He reeled back another and thrust it forward, its tip tearing through the servitor's forehead and into the biological brain.

Epsilon three-twelve convulsed. Its hands broke free of Antigonus's grip and flailed madly. Its mouth opened and its vocal unit let out a grating, garbled scream. The mechadendrite in its head was ripped free by the strength of the servitor's spasms, whipping back and forward like a striking snake.

Antigonus forced a knee up under it and rolled over on top of the servitor, scrambling to grab his gun again. The servitor bucked and threw Antigonus onto the ground, pain rushing up at him again as silvered augmetics crunched against the hard ground.

The servitor was quickest to its feet, spraying gore from the massive pulsing wound between its hollow eyes. A mechanical hand clamped around Antigonus's throat and slammed him against the valley side, the black glass of the datacore material splintering into razors that sheared through Antigonus's thick robes into the pallid skin of his back.

The servitor's mouth lolled open and the tiny mechanical arm shot out, stabbing the gold-nibbed quill through Antigonus's bionic eye.

A white star burst in front of Antigonus's vision. White, knife-like pain rifled through his head. His back, his neck, his eye, so much of him was shrieking in pain at once that he couldn't tell where he was, or what he was doing.

He only just remembered that he still had the gun. Roaring through the pain, he stabbed the gun into the servitor's gut and fired. He fired again and again, until its grip went limp. Antigonus slid to the floor and realised he must have blown the servitor's spine out, severing the connection between its upper and lower body. The servitor stumbled a few steps, its arms and head hanging limp, before the dead weight of its upper half dragged it down to the ground.

Everything was suddenly silent. The only movement was the oily smoke sputtering from the servitor's ruined body. Antigonus's vision, already muted, was now somehow skewed, as if shifted sideways. Antigonus only had one eye left – his normal, unaugmented one, which meant he was limited to the visible spectrum and couldn't zoom in any more. He had lost a mechadendrite and his ribs were broken. He was bleeding somewhere inside, but his internal alterations were probably robust enough to cope with that. Already his bionic heart was forcing his pulse down to calm him. He was hurt, though and it would only get worse without maintenance – and no way in the Emperor's great creation would he ever let anyone on this tainted world repair him. He had to get off-world.

Antigonus struggled to his feet and began to run, the shadows of the industrial complex rolling over him. As black iron and red-brown rust closed over him the heretic projections flickered off overhead and were replaced with work rotas for the menials.

They couldn't watch him from overhead now. But they had hijacked the projection units, seduced the highest ranks of the tech-priesthood and sabotaged his personal servitor which had been sent with him from Mars. They didn't need eyes in the sky to watch him. They would find a way.

TWO

'You may say, it is impossible for a man to become like the Machine. And I would reply, that only the smallest mind strives to comprehend its limits.'
— Fabricator General Kane (attr.)

MAGOS ANTIGONUS WASN'T supposed to die like this.

Light was scarce beneath the complex. A single charred bulb cast a dull brownish glow over the abandoned workshop he had found. Old workbenches covered in rusted equipment were piled up against one wall and the low ceiling was hung with corroded cabling. Antigonus sat against the other wall, rivulets of rust-red water running down his back from the sweating metal behind him, trying to fix the failed servo in his motor units. His legs were withered and weak and without the servo-powered braces that encased them he could barely walk. He wasn't designed to fight. He was there because he had a facility with information systems and he could access Chaeroneia's data networks with ease. His purpose on Chaeroneia had been to debunk the apparently spurious rumours about heretical practices among the planet's tech-priests, then take that news back to Mars to satisfy the tech-priests there that their forge world was free from the taint of blasphemy.

'Primary objective failed,' he thought.

Antigonus sat bolt-upright. The voice had come from everywhere at once. He was alone in the workshop and yet there was something else in there with him. He pulled out his autogun again but he knew instinctively that it wouldn't do any good.

'Heretics!' shouted Antigonus, struggling to his feet. 'You can hide from me but the Mechanicus will find you! More will follow me! More from Mars!'

The only answer was Antigonus's own voice, echoing back through the empty workshops.

Antigonus crept through the darkness, wishing his servos were quieter. There was no one else in the workshop, but they must be near. He knew he couldn't put up much of a fight any more, but he wasn't going to go down easily. They would have to work for their kill.

More will follow. More will die. This is the way of our Machine-God.

The voice was too close, little more than a whisper directly into Antigonus's ear. It had to be someone in the room. Either that or someone controlling a machine in the room, like a servitor or machine-spirit, something complex, something that could speak. But Antigonus had secured the area before he stopped to rest. There was nothing like that in here.

Nothing, that is, apart from his own augmentations.

Clever boy.

Antigonus dropped the gun and grabbed the screwdriver he had been using to repair himself. The heretics were doing to him what they had done to Epsilon three-twelve, hijacking his more complex systems and taking control. Either they were controlling one of his augmentations directly or they had infected him with a machine-curse, an insidious self-replicating set of commands that could cause a system to self-destruct.

Which system? Like many tech-priests above the most junior rank, Magos Antigonus had several sophisticated augmentations, including datalinks that would provide a perfect point of infection. At least they hadn't got his bionic heart, otherwise he would be lying dead right now. His bionic eye was destroyed but the control circuits were still there, spiralling around his optic nerve. His mechadendrites? They were plugged directly into his nervous system through an impulse link. His bionic arm? The intelligent filtration systems in his throat and lungs?

Closer, closer. But not close enough. Know you the way of the Omnissiah, fellow traveller. The avatar speaks with us even now and it speaks to us of your death.

Antigonus jabbed the screwdriver under the housing of his bionic eye and levered the unit out of its socket, forcing himself to ignore the unnaturally dull, cold pain that throbbed from the ruined bionic. With a gristly sound the eye came out, taking a chunk of artificial flesh with it and landing on the floor with a blood-wet plop. Antigonus gasped as the shocking cold of the air hit the raw nerves in the wreckage now filling his eye socket.

Closer.

Antigonus scrabbled on the floor, dizzy and sickened by the awful raw throb spreading across his face. His natural hand grabbed the autogun on the floor and he put the barrel against the side of his head.

Don't let them take you, he told himself. They'll make you one of their own.

Even if you are dead, fellow traveller.

'Get out!' yelled Antigonus crazily. 'Out! The Machine-God commands you! By the light of understanding and the rule of Mars I cast this unclean thing from this machine!'

An enginseer sent by the Adeptus Mechanicus to maintain the war machines of the Imperial Guard would know the tech-exorcism rites off by heart. But such things were not often needed on Mars, the heartland of the priesthood where Antigonus had learned his role in the Cult Mechanicus. Antigonus knew he couldn't banish the thing with words alone, but right now they were all he had.

If it had his bionic arm, it would be using it by now to force the gun away from his head. No, it was something inside him, something it couldn't use to kill him straight away.

'I cast you out!' Antigonus put the gun barrel against his left knee and fired.

A thunderbolt of pain, the worst Antigonus had ever suffered, ripped right through him and knocked him unconscious as his left leg was blown clean off at the knee. Paralysing pain reached down and dragged him back to his senses, gripping hard and not letting go. Antigonus screamed, but somewhere inside him he heard the tech-infection scream too, as part of it was ripped away and the rest fled into the mechanisms of his right leg.

It was in the servos that powered his leg bracings, infesting the systems that carried commands from his nerve-impulses to the motors. Maybe it had got in when he had scoured Chaeroneia's information nets for suspicious power spikes early in his investigation, or when he had been forced to have his nerve impulse units repaired a few days ago. Maybe it had been in him since he arrived, waiting to see how much he would uncover before striking.

Either way, now he could kill it.

His heart was working overtime, leaching so much power from the rest of his augmetics that his bionic arm fell limp. It filled him full of enough painkillers to all but kill him and he dragged himself away from the twitching mess of charred flesh and metal that had been his left leg.

Mmmaake you sufferrrr...

'Don't like that, do you?' spat Antigonus, blood running down his face where he had bitten a chunk out of his lip. 'Did you think they would send just anyone? Someone you could defeat with a machine-curse? They teach us well on Mars, heretic tech-pox.'

Nnnot machinnne-cuuuurse... much worssse... much, much worssse...

Ice-cold fingers of information scraped up Antigonus's spine. The tech-priest writhed on the floor, the edges of his vision turning white, a high scream filling his ears. He fought the chill seeping up through him, forcing its way through his augmetics into his flesh, the whispering voice quivering with anger. It wanted revenge. It was supposed to just control him, but now it wanted to kill him instead.

Antigonus choked back the horror that had infected him and forced it, nerve by nerve, back down into the smouldering servo units in his remaining leg. He tried to pull himself upright but only got into a lop-sided crawl, dragging the tattered stump of his left leg behind him as he slithered out of the workshop. He had to get out of there – it was a dead end and he was trapped. Perhaps he could find a menial down here that could help him, or a better weapon. Anywhere was better than the workshop, because the infection, or whatever it was, must have been capable of transmitting his location to the heretics.

The resources required to acquire – or, Omnissiah forbid, even create – such a sophisticated machine-curse were massive. There were relatively few even on Mars who could have done it. Antigonus didn't even want to think about what the heretics must have had to do to get hold of it.

The voice was a low stutter now, hissing darkly from the depths of Antigonus's augmetics. Antigonus made his way painfully out into a long, low gallery, like a natural void formed between the strata of collapsed factory floors. The ceiling dripped rust-coloured water and pools of it gathered on the floor. From somewhere far below came the throb of an ancient, powerful machine, probably one of the geothermal heatsinks that provided so much of Chaeroneia's power. Antigonus dragged himself to where the ceiling had fallen in and a faint reddish light bled down from above.

No ussse, tech-priest... they willll find you, they always do... I am not the only one...

Antigonus ignored the voice and dragged himself up the incline of the fallen ceiling. The floor above was more intact, with knots of machinery and hissing steam pipes everywhere. Somewhere he heard men's voices shouting. As he moved the noises got louder – shouting, machinery, humming generators, the lifesigns of a forge world.

The painkillers dispensed by Antigonus's augmetic heart were killing most of the agony from his shattered leg, but they were flooding his body in such amounts that they made the world dull and distant. Every metre he moved drained him as if he had sprinted it and he kept trying to push himself forward with a left leg that wasn't there.

He was a mess. When they got him off this planet he would have to spend months being cleansed of the tech-curse and then getting all his wrecked augmetics replaced. He imagined the hospitals where servitors trundled the corridors keeping everything clean, the polished steel of the operating theatres and the spidery arms of the autosurgeon that flensed away weak flesh and grafted on strong metal. The bionics experts who would take him apart and put him back together again.

He shook the images out of his head. He was exhausted and starting to see things. If he lost his focus and started letting his mind wander the tech-infection would take a hold and rot him away from the inside.

He rounded a corner and saw he had come across a functioning factory floor – dilapidated and dangerous, but still working. Several massive stamping machines thudded on, forming metal components that were carted away by conveyor belts.

Antigonus tried to find a menial or a tech-priest who could help him. A bent-backed servitor stood hunched over a conveyor line leading from a broken stamping machine, its hands working away to perform some routine modification on parts that no longer moved past it. Antigonus ignored the servitor – even if it had been sophisticated enough to interrupt its programmed task and summon help, the machine-curse inside him could have leaped into the servitor and used it to cut Antigonus to ribbons.

Antigonus pulled himself up against the casing of the closest machine and used it to steady himself as he inched forward on his remaining leg. The machine-curse was hissing and spitting, whispering abuse at him. He had hurt it, but he also knew that such things were self-repairing and soon it would be strong enough to take him over again.

Antigonus rounded a corner and saw more servitors, but no menials. The menials were the lowest class on any forge world, men and women who were little more than living machines ordered and directed by the tech-priests. They were there simply because there were many tasks that servitors could not do, but their servitude was self-reinforcing because it was from the ranks of menials that many junior tech-priests were recruited. At the moment Antigonus could trust a menial rather more than he could a fellow tech-priest, which counted as a sort of heresy in itself.

The servitors ignored Antigonus as he forced himself to traverse the factory floor. A battered iron stairway led upwards – Antigonus didn't fancy his chances of getting up them in his current state but it was better than waiting in the deserted factory for the heretics to hunt him down.

Getting desperate? Now you realise. This whole planet is against you. It is only with the rats and dregs that you can hide. What life is that? Not life at all. So much of you wants to join usss, traveller. It is no great hardship for the rest to agree.

'Shut up,' spat Antigonus as he struggled up the spiral stairs. 'You know nothing. You do not even have the blessing of the Omnissiah, you should not even be.'

No Omnissiah dreamed me into being. No, not that god. Another one.

'There is no other.'

Really? What of your Corpse-Emperor?

'Two faces of the same being. The Omnissiah is to the machine as the Emperor is to His servants.'

What was Antigonus saying? Why was he debating with this thing?

So innocent to think such things. So easily led. My god is something else. My god is one of many, the many who serve the One, the End, the Future that is Chaos…

'Out!' Antigonus was yelling now. 'Stop these lies, heretic thing!'

The traveller starts to understand. Not a machine-curse, not a tech-pox. Something older, something stronger.

Daemon…

There was movement up ahead, footsteps and voices through the grinding of the machines. They were too urgent to just be more menials going about their business. Antigonus spotted the beams of powerful torches cutting through the shadows.

Daemon. It was a lie, just another way of rattling him. Antigonus had to concentrate on getting away. He looked around and saw a cargo elevator, rusted and old. Faded lights winked on the control panel and perhaps the machine still worked. Antigonus got across the factory floor to the elevator, trusting the noise of the machines would cover the sounds of his movement.

He let his mechadendrites haul the rusted gate open, keeping hold of his gun with one hand and steadying himself with the other. The socket in his back where Episilon three-twelve had torn out the mechadendrite was just one of a thousand points of dull raw pain forcing their way through the painkiller haze.

With an effort Antigonus shut the gate behind him and jabbed a mechadendrite at the control stud. The cargo elevator shuddered and moved grudgingly upwards. Antigonus heard someone shouting from below – they had guessed he might be escaping on the elevator but the factory complex down this far was a warren of dead ends and it was better to keep moving that to let them close him down.

He didn't even know what he was running from. Maybe they had hunter-servitors with scent-vanes that could track him through the filthiest corners of Chaeroneia's undercity, servo-skulls with auspex scanners that already had his lifesigns logged. But he had to hope. The grand machine of the universe moved according to the Omnissiah's will and he had to keep the faith that the machine would move to keep him safe.

Antigonus leaned against the back wall of the elevator. Crushed strata of factories and workshops marched past, reduced to claustrophobic voids in the mass of twisted metal. Gouts of steam burst from fractured pipes. Rivers of pollutants and fuel forced their way through fissures in the metal, feeding rainbow-slicked underground rivers. Thousands of years of industrial history were crusted on the surface of Chaeroneia – charred ruins, glimpses of faded finery, strange machines that perhaps represented some technology lost to the Mechanicus, hidden places where escaped menials or wild servitors had carved out a short existence, even abandoned chapels of the Cult Mechanicus long since replaced by magnificent cathedrals and temples far above.

And somewhere, something beneath the surface that had created a heresy worse than Antigonus had ever imagined.

The elevator juddered to a halt. The doors chattered open and freezing vapour rolled in. Antigonus crawled out warily, feeling the temperature dropping rapidly around him and letting his newly unaugmented vision adjust to the half-light. Antigonus saw that he was in a stratum that must have lain undisturbed for decades or even centuries. It was relatively clean and intact and lit by hundreds of tiny blue-white lights mounted on control panels and readouts. Data-engines, huge constructions of knotted cables and pipe work like slabs of compacted metal intestines, stood like monoliths in long rows. Heavy ribbed coolant pipes hung from the high ceiling and the deep chill in the air suggested that the coolant systems were still working. This was archaic technology, the kind that Antigonus had only seen on abandoned parts of Mars and which was obsolete on even the most traditionalist forge worlds. These engines had held information in crude digital forms, before the newer datacore technology was rediscovered and disseminated. Antigonus wasn't even sure how such things might work. There must have been thirty such engines, great rearing knots of obsolete technology, silent and untouched. The structure of this floor was intact and Antigonus couldn't even see the trails of vermin or stains of corrosion that touched everywhere else in Chaeroneia's undercity.

'Lord of Knowledge be praised,' whispered Antigonus instinctively, as it was appropriate to offer a prayer to the Omnissiah when confronted with such old and noble technology. But he couldn't stop and offer proper respects to the machine-spirits – there wasn't anyone to help him here and he had to get help or find safety.

He stumbled past a few of the data-engines, mechadendrites steadying him against the frost-cold metal. There didn't seem to be a way out other than the cargo elevator behind him. Such a facility would be well sealed against contaminants and the elevator itself had probably been protected originally, before its shielding was taken by menials and used somewhere else. At most he could hope for an access vent, but he wasn't confident about his ability to crawl through a small space with one leg missing and his head fuzzy with painkillers.

The data-engine closest to him shuddered. It coughed out a spray of super cooled air and some old mechanism inside it ticked over as it wound up to operate. Antigonus shrunk from the engine, reluctant even in his current state to disrespect a machine-spirit. More of the machines seemed to stir, lights flickering. The power coming into the room was fluctuating. Something was interfering with the power supply and Antigonus knew it wasn't a coincidence.

A sudden howling of metal tore from the far wall. Antigonus saw sparks showering and the readouts on the data-engines turned an angry red, their machine-spirits objecting to the rudeness of the intrusion. A whirring, screaming sound of tortured metal filled the floor. Antigonus took shelter behind the closest data-engine, wishing his bionic eye still worked so he could banish the shadows and see what was forcing itself into the room after him.

Had he really thought he could escape?

No escape.

'Shut up. You are no daemon.'

Lie to yourself. It makes me stronger.

A huge, dark form lumbered into view between the data-engines, sparks still spitting off the massive breacher drill that formed one of its forearms. It was a servitor, a heavy labour pattern designed for mining. One arm was a drill and the other was an enormous pneumatic ram. Its torso was broad and packed with synthetic muscle, controlled by the tiny shrunken head almost buried by the massive muscles of its shoulders. It was easily twice the height of a man. It blasted through the hole it had ripped in the wall on a track unit that belched greasy black smoke.

There were more figures behind it. Dark, robed. Tech-priests. Further back Antigonus could make out beams of torchlight – the gunlights of tech-guard, the standing armed forces of the Adeptus Mechanicus. No doubt these men and women were used as ignorant foot soldiers by the heretics.

Antigonus shrunk back, hoping to make it to the cargo elevator. His right knee servo locked and he fell backwards, hitting the freezing cold floor hard enough to send a bolt of pain punching through the painkillers. Antigonus yelled. The tech-priests would certainly have heard him.

Got you.

'Get out! Give me my body back! When I die, you die!'

Run, traveller! Run! My kind never dies, just moves on, always moving, always changing...

A deep, sibilant voice spoke a streak of zeroes and ones – pure Lingua Technis machine code. The huge breacher servitor paused, its drill still spinning, compressed air whistling from its ramming arm.

More Lingua Technis. Antigonus could have translated it instantly if his auto senses had been operating, but all auxiliary power was being diverted to his bionic heart to keep him alive. He was naked, ignorant, helpless and trapped by heretics in this holy place.

'Magos Antigonus,' said the voice again, this time in Low Gothic. 'You are a resourceful man. But a man is all you are. It is impressive that you found us at all and while there was never any chance of your doing us meaningful harm there was always the possibility that Mars would send someone more competent when you reported back to them of your failure. So this is the way it has to be.'

Antigonus gave up trying to get away. His body was half-paralysed. 'They will,' he spat, determined to spend his last few moments defiant in the face of heresy as the Omnissiah would demand. 'When I don't return. They'll send a whole Diagnostic Coven. Blockade the planet. Switch the cities off one by one. Hunt you down.'

'Will they really now?' The lead tech-priest walked into view. His robes were deep grey, made of some superfine mesh that flowed around him like water. His hood was thrown back and Antigonus saw that the upper part of his face was pulled so tight that it was barely more than two gleaming silver eyes in a skull. The lower jaw had been removed entirely and replaced with a nest of slender mechadendrites that hung down to the floor, writhing like tentacles. In place of his hands the tech-priest had nests of long, metallic filaments that waved like the fronds of an underwater plant, fine and dextrous. He moved with a strange sinuous grace, more like some living, boneless thing than a machine, even though the tech-priest was undoubtedly more heavily augmented than almost anyone Antigonus had ever seen.

'Scraecos,' breathed Antigonus. The leader of the tech-heretics was the archmagos veneratus who commanded Chaeroneia's data-reserves. He had probably tracked Antigonus all the way through security pict-stealers and sensor-equipped servitors. He had just been waiting to see how much Antigonus knew and what he would do next before moving in. He had known all along exactly where Antigonus was and what he had been doing. Antigonus had never had a chance, not from the moment he had set foot on Chaeroneia.

'And that,' said Scraecos, his synthesized voice thick like syrup, 'is why you have to die. So curious. And often correct. A dangerous combination.'

Antigonus grimaced with effort and closed his natural hand around the stock of his autogun. With strength he didn't think he had he pulled it out from underneath him and fired.

The shot thunked into Scraecos's midriff. Scraecos barely moved – he just parted his mechadendrites and glanced down at the small smoking hole in his robe. He shook his head slightly, as if with disappointment.

'Azaulathis,' he said.

Master.

'Kill him.'

The world went white and Antigonus's body spasmed with pain, as if there was an electric current running through him. His augmetics glowed white-hot, charring his skin, burning muscle. He couldn't see, couldn't hear, couldn't feel anything but the pain.

Sparks spat as Antigonus's bionic arm was forced out of the flesh of his shoulder, servos winding so tight the metal splintered. His mechadendrites stood on end, his bionic heart thudded arhythmically sending more bolts of pain through him. The remains of his bionic eye unscrewed from his face and shattered on the floor, leaving a fist-sized gap in his skull. The machine-curse was infecting all his augmetics, forcing them to self-destruct and when it got to his bionic heart it would kill him.

Antigonus prayed. Pain was a design weakness of the human body. All he had to do was fix it and he could move. He put every drop of strength into forcing his internal augmetics into obedience, keeping the machine-curse in check for a few split seconds more. He ordered one mechadendrite to work. Linked directly to his central nervous system, he had more precise control over the mechadendrites than any of his other bionics. And he only needed one.

Antigonus screamed and jabbed the tip of one mechadendrite into the closest data-engine, forcing its interface probe to stab into the ancient machine. Then, he let go.

The machine-curse, like electricity, flowed through the points of least resistance. It rippled through Antigonus's body, leaving trails of internal burning as it went, spiralling up into the mechadendrite and on into the data-engine.

Before it could turn back, Antigonus withdrew the mechadendrite. The data-engine shuddered, its lights winking blood-red as the machine-curse thrashed around inside its systems. The curse was trapped in the data-engine. Antigonus had bought himself a few more seconds.

Antigonus had committed a terrible sin by infecting the noble old machinery with such a foul thing. No matter what happened now, the Omnissiah would never forgive the machinery deep inside his soul. But Antigonus hadn't just committed the sin to stay alive – to a tech-priest life itself had no intrinsic value, only service to the Machine-God. Antigonus still had his duty to fulfil. The heretics still had to suffer.

A massive force ripped through him – the servitor's breacher drill, grinding through his body into the floor. Loops of organs were thrown about the room as the drill bored through Antigonus's abdomen. He didn't feel pain – he couldn't feel anything any more. He guessed his nervous system must be on the edge of shutting down. He was cold and numb. Helpless. He was probably physically dead already.

The servitor lifted Antigonus and threw him clean across the room. Antigonus's ruined body smacked into one of the data-engines, scattering bionic fragments and spatters of blood.

He compelled his mechadendrites to act. One last time, in the service of the Omnissiah. Once last chance to repent of all his sins – because he had failed and he was as bad as a sinner could be.

The metallic tentacles reached behind him into the body of the data-engine. He felt old, grim technology, lorded over by a melancholy machine-spirit, indignant at the destruction and angered by the machine-curse that had infected its brother. Antigonus begged the machine-spirit for forgiveness. He never got an answer.

The servitor's ram arm thudded down onto Antigonus's head and chest, crushing him instantly into the machinery of the data-engine, blood and bone driven deep into the machine's core.

Antigonus's mechadendrites dropped limp.

THE CREATURE ANTIGONUS had referred to as Archmagos Veneratus Scraecos drifted back towards the other tech-priests, similarly deformed and augmented figures who were nevertheless clearly subservient to him.

The breacher-servitor stood at rest over the hapless remains of Antigonus, which no longer resembled anything that might have once been human. The tech-guard, in their rust-red environmental suits wielding brass cased lasguns, fanned out into the room. But there was no one else.

Antigonus had been the only one who had known.

He had probably been right. There would be more from Mars, probably many more, an armed mission with the authority of the archmagos ultima, perhaps even of the Fabricator General. But by the time such a mission got through the warp to Chaeroneia it would be too late for anyone, even the Fabricator General, to do anything.

'Good,' said Scraecos. He turned to the tech-priests who had followed him, loyal to the Omnissiah as revealed to them through His avatar. 'Brothers. The loyal. The true. We have seen the face of the Machine-God. Everything he has told us has come to pass. So the time has come for us to begin at last.'

THREE

'And so fear you the Unknown, for every foe was once but a mystery.'
– 'A History of the Ultima Segmentum',
Lord Solar Macharius

'EMPEROR'S DOWN.'

'Frag you it is.'

Suruss pointed to the corner of the regicide board, where a single lone templar piece stood. 'The templar has it in check. He's got nowhere to go.'

Argel peered at the board. The young Suruss looked so pleased with himself he might just be right. 'You little groxwiper,' growled Argel. 'It scroffing has and all.' Argel frustratedly knocked his emperor piece on its side, signifying the end of the game and another victory for Suruss.

'Another game?' asked Suruss.

'Sure. Frag all else to do.' Argel was right. They were on Deep Orbit Monitoring Station Trinary Ninety-One, Borosis system, Gaugamela subsector, Ultima Segmentum. It was a corroded metal sphere about five hundred metres across, most of which was engineering and maintenance space and such stations were rarely equipped with entertainment facilities. Suruss and Argel were lucky they even had space to set up the regicide board. Three months into a nine month shift, Argel had come to the conclusion that Suruss was better at the game than he was, but he didn't have much choice but to play on and hope he got better.

The alternatives numbered two. Stare at the walls, or go and talk to Lachryma. Unfortunately Lachryma was an astropath, a tremendously powerful telepath who relayed psychic messages from one end of the Imperium to the other. Astropaths were all creepy, morose creatures who kept their shrivelled, blinded selves to themselves. Lachryma was worse than most. So regicide it was.

Something blared on one of the upper levels, loud and braying.

'Throne of Earth,' said Argel, 'that's the proximity warning.'

'Must be broken,' said Suruss, who was laying out the regicide pieces for another game. 'There's nothing out here.'

'Every time those things go off it's a mountain of bloody paperwork. I'll go and have a look.' Argel stood, careful not to scrape his head on the low ceiling of the station's cramped living compartment. He scratched the bad skin on his neck and shrugged the enviro-suit over his shoulders. They didn't heat the outer maintenance layers of the station and it was cold enough to kill you.

Another alarm went off, closer this time.

'Gravitational alarm,' said Suruss. 'Looks like they're all on the blink.'

'You gonna help?'

Suruss gestured at the regicide board, half set up for the next game. 'Can't you see I'm busy?'

Argel grumbled obscenities as he struggled through the narrow opening into the primary maintenance shaft. The alarms were blaring and there were more of them – meaning radiation or outer hull integrity, other ones he didn't recognise. Suruss was probably right. It was just the station's machine-spirit getting uppity again. Argel would have to delve into the thick book of tech-prayers and minister to the station's inner workings until the spirit was placated. The station needed a tech-priest of its own, but the Adeptus Astra Telepathica didn't think Deep Orbital Station Trinary Ninety-One was important enough so it was up to Argel and Suruss to keep it working.

Argel was about to start the climb up the primary shaft when he saw something moving down the corridor connecting the living space to the astropath's quarters. It was Lachryma, the astropath herself, shambling forward. Her hands were reaching blindly in front of her and the hood of her robes had fallen back, revealing her wrinkled, shaven head and the white band she wore across her eyes.

'Lachryma! It's nothing, Lachryma, just a glitch in the spirit.'

'No! No, I can see them… I can hear them, all around…' The astropath's voice was shrill and piercing, cutting through the sound of the alarms. She stumbled forward and Argel had to catch her. She was shivering and sweaty and smelled of incense.

'I… I sent a message,' she gasped. 'I don't know if they heard. We have to get out, now…'

It wasn't a fault. It was real. Astropaths were always the first to know when anything really, really bad was about to happen, every spacer knew that.

'What is it?'

Lachryma reached up and pulled the bandage down from her eyes. Except there weren't any eyes – just empty bone, the insides of the sockets inscribed with prayer-symbols that burned a faint orange as if a great heat was trying to escape from behind them.

'Chaos,' she said, voice quavering. 'The Castigator.'

The station shook as if something had hit it. The floor tilted as the gravity generator's gyroscope was knocked out of line and half the lights failed.

'We can get you to the saviour pod,' said Argel. 'Just… just stay calm. And put that thing back on.'

Argel dragged Lachryma back into the living quarters, where Suruss was frantically working the sensorium display among the wreckage of the regicide table.

'It's an asteroid hit!' shouted Suruss above the din of the alarms and further impacts. 'Never saw it coming!'

'We're getting out of here,' said Argel.

Suruss shook his head. 'Not yet we're not. The auxiliary power has to be warmed up. Get the generator ticking over and we can launch the saviour pod.'

'Why me?'

'Because you know what you're doing!'

Another hit, the biggest yet, slammed into the station. Gouts of steam shot through the living compartment and part of the ceiling fell in, spilling broken pipe work everywhere. Suruss fell forward and cracked his head against the sensorium console. The knock sparked one pict-screen back into life and it flickered on.

Suruss held his head and tried to sit up. Argel knelt down and pulled the fallen Lachyrma into a seating position – blood was running down her face from a long cut in her scalp. She was muttering darkly and the orange glow was bright enough to seep through the bandage over her eyes. Argel didn't know what they did to astropaths on their long pilgrimage to Terra, but it seriously messed them up.

Argel looked around the destruction in the room. The outer decks would be even more of a mess. It would be murder getting the auxiliary power up, but the saviour pod was their only chance. And Suruss was right – the only person Argel trusted to do it was Argel.

Argel saw the image on the pict-screen next to Suruss. It had finally switched itself on and was showing a view of space outside the station, relayed from pict-stealers in the station's sensorium array.

'What the frag is that?' he asked.

Suruss looked round. The pict-screen was showing a point of red light gathering in space a short distance away from the station. The stars around it seemed to smear as the light from them was bent around the anomaly and it was growing, flaring out a white-hot corona as it forced its way into real space.

Suruss looked at Lachryma. 'Tell me someone knows about this.'

Lachryma nodded weakly. 'Yes. Yes, I sent a message... all the symbols, everything I'd seen... the planet coming out of the warp, the... the cities made of hatred, the cannibal world... all of it... and the Daemon from the Imperial Tarot, the Beast, the Heretic, all the worst signs... the worst of the worst...'

Argel shook Lachryma. 'But who? Who's going to see it?' Astropathic communications were complex and semi-mystical and completely beyond Argel. Astropaths transmitted images from the Imperial Tarot and elsewhere in the hope that adepts in the Telepathica's relay stations would cross-reference them from immense books of augurs and work out what the message said and who it was supposed to go to. An astropathic distress signal would be no good if it took an adept six months to work out what it meant. 'The Telepathica?'

'No, no... there's nothing they can do, not now.'

'Then who?'

'Perhaps... the Adeptus Terra, so it gets back to Earth... or even the Ordos... yes, the portents will have them running... maybe even the Ordo Malleus...'

Argel frowned. 'Who?'

Then the primary power failed completely.

SEVENTY THOUSAND KILOMETRES from Deep Orbit Monitoring Station Trinary Ninety-One, asteroids streamed from a growing, burning hole in the fabric of real space. The hole grew as a truly immense form forced its way out. The asteroids streaked outwards, a few impacting on the disintegrating orbital station, most of them spinning out and looping back towards the emerging object in complex irregular orbits. More and more of them shot out until the breach was surrounded by a dizzying, shifting mass of asteroids, sorcerous fire licking across their surfaces.

Space puckered and tore as the rest of the object's mass forced its way out and the orbital station was finally destroyed in the shockwave that rippled through reality. Astropaths and other psykers for light years around felt it happen. The star of the Borosis system was turned an unhealthy black-streaked crimson by the unholy force spewing from the breach.

And there, outside the furthermost orbit of Borosis's reach, was a new planet where no planet had ever been before.

FOUR

'Many claim they wish to destroy their enemies. If this were true, most would be compelled to destroy themselves.'

– Abbess Helena the Virtuous,
'Discourses on the Faith'.

THE TRIBUNICIA WAS cold as a tomb. Outside it had the brutal lines of a warship but inside everything was dressed in marble and granite, worn smooth by generations of crewmen sworn to serve the Imperium. Many of them had been born on the ship and almost all of them would die on it, so the ship's architecture served as a constant reminder that this ship would literally be their tomb.

Justicar Alaric slipped out of half-sleep. He was sitting cross-legged on the freezing granite floor in the middle of his small cell. A Space Marine didn't have to sleep normally and could retain some awareness while in half-sleep and something had jolted him back into full wakefulness.

The engine pitch had changed. The *Tribunicia* was coming out of the warp.

Alaric stood up, murmuring the Seventeenth Prayer of Alertness as he turned to his power armour, stacked neatly in the corner of the cell along with his storm bolter and Nemesis halberd. For a moment he just looked at the wargear, ornate gunmetal armour plates with his personal heraldry over one shoulder. He had added a single bright yellow star to his heraldry to commemorate the soul of Briseis Ligeia, the bravest person Alaric had ever met, who had saved him and countless others even after a daemon had driven her mad. She was dead now, executed by the same Ordo Malleus that Alaric served.

Alaric knew he would die in that armour. Most people would never touch it if they knew that one fact as surely as he did.

Alaric intoned the Rites of Preparedness as he picked up the left greave of the power armour and began to put it on.

THE BRIDGE OF the *Tribunicia* was a magnificent cathedral deep inside the heavily armoured prow, with a massive vaulted ceiling and soaring columns of white marble. Scores of crewmen and tech-adepts crowded the pews, working communications consoles or sensorium displays. The command throne of Rear Admiral Horstgeld took up the front pew, just before the grand altar itself, a creation of marble and gold crowned with a golden image of the Emperor as Warmonger. Horstgeld was a religious man and so the ornate pulpit that looked out over the whole bridge was always reserved for the use of the ship's Confessor, who would take to it in times of crisis and bellow devotional texts to steel the souls of the bridge crew.

Horstgeld rose as Justicar Alaric entered. Horstgeld had served with Space Marines before, even if he had probably never quite got used to their presence. The man who sat on the command pew alongside him, however, had no such reservations. He was Inquisitor Nyxos of the Ordo Malleus, a daemonhunter and the man who had requisitioned Horstgeld's ship into the service of the Inquisition.

'Justicar,' grinned Hortsgeld. 'Well met!' Horstgeld strode down the bridge's nave and shook Alaric's hand. He was a huge and bearded man whose heavily brocaded uniform looked like it had been altered significantly to fit him. 'I must admit, I am accustomed to being the biggest man on my bridge. It will take some getting used to you.'

'Rear admiral. I've read of your victory over the *Killfrenzy* at the Battle of Subiaco Diablo. This is a tough ship with a tough captain, I hear.'

'Pshaw, there are plenty of brave men at the Eye of Terror. I was just fortunate enough to have the charge.'

'You would rather be there now?'

Horstgeld shrugged. 'In all honesty, justicar, yes I would. That's where all the Navy wants to be fighting, we're the only ones holding them back. But I don't run my ship according to what I happen to want and when the Inquisition comes calling one does well to answer.'

'Well said,' added Inquisitor Nyxos. He was an ancient, sepulchral man who wore long dark robes over a spindly exoskeleton that kept his withered body standing. Alaric knew that in spite of his immensely frail appearance, he was an exceptionally tough man thanks to the scores of internal augmentations and redundant organs the Inquisition had supplied him with. An encounter with the rogue Inquisitor Valinov would have killed almost anyone, but Nyxos had survived.

It had been Nyxos who had given the order to execute Ligeia. Alaric didn't resent the man for it, it was what had to be done. And now Nyxos was the Ordo Malleus inquisitor with whom Alaric worked most closely. Such were the mysterious ways of the Emperor.

'The reports from this area of space were alarming indeed,' continued Nyxos. 'While we must send everything we can to the Eye of Terror, the consequences will be grave if we take our eyes off the rest of the Imperium. It will do no good to throw the Despoiler back into the warp if the rest of the Emperor's work is undone behind our backs.'

'True, inquisitor, true,' said Horstgeld. 'But do we even know what we are dealing with here? Or if there is anything here at all? All the records the ship has on the Borosis system suggest it is a veritable backwater.'

Nyxos looked at the rear admiral. His large, filmy grey eyes seemed to look straight through him. 'Call it educated guesswork, captain.'

The engines changed pitch again and the whole ship shuddered. Warning klaxons sounded briefly somewhere on the bridge before someone shut them off.

'Entering real space!' came a call from one of the officers in engineering. 'Warp engines offline!'

'Geller field disengaging!' came another cry. The noise on the bridge rose as well-practiced commands were relayed and acknowledged. Down in the bowels of the *Tribunicia* a couple of thousand crewmen would all be labouring to ensure a safe end to the ship's warp jump – engine-gangs redirecting the plasma reactors to power the main engines, weapon crews manning the ready posts for their broadside guns and torpedo tubes, the ship's small complement of tech-adepts calculating the huge numbers involved in making the ship plunge from one reality into another.

The altar in front of Nyxos, Horstgeld and Alaric rose from the floor and Alaric saw that the sculptures of the altar actually crowned the ship's massive main pict-screen. The screen rose up from the floor until it dominated the whole bridge. It was flooded with grainy static until one of the communications officers powered up the ship's main sensorium and the image swam into view.

'Hmmm,' said Nyxos. 'It's bad, then.'

The pict-screen showed a view of the Borosis system from deep orbit, where the *Tribunicia* had emerged into real space. The star Borosis itself was a swollen, livid red, streaked with angry black sunspots, its corona bleeding off into a halo of sickly red light. Borosis should have been a healthy mid-cycle star, similar in type to Terra's own sun.

'Close in on the planets,' said Nyxos. Horstgeld quickly relayed the order to his comms crew and the pict-screen cycled through closer views of the planets that orbited the sickened star.

The light and heat coming from the sun had dropped massively. That meant Borosis Prime, the closest planet in the system to the star, was even bleaker than the burning globe of rock it had been before – it was dying. Borosis Secundus's atmosphere was gone entirely – once covered by a thick blanket of superheated gases, the planet was now naked, the sudden temperature change having thrown its atmosphere into such turmoil that its layers bled off the planet entirely.

There was a long gap to Borosis Cerulean, the most inhabited world, home to seven major colonies with a total population of about one and a half billion. It was cold and dark. The planet's cities were advanced enough to provide shelter from the eternal winter that had now fallen over the world, but their power and supplies would not last forever. Perhaps the world could be evacuated, perhaps not. That wasn't the Ordo Malleus's problem.

The lifeless world of Borosis Minor, almost completely covered in ice, was an inhospitable as ever, as was the gas giant Borosis Quintus where a few thousand workers were probably deciding how they were going to survive on their gas mining platforms when the solar collectors failed. The change in the star had barely affected the outermost planet, Borosis Ultima, a ball of frozen ammonia almost too small to qualify as a planet at all.

The viewscreen cycled to show the last object in the system.

'I cannot claim to be an expert,' said Alaric carefully, 'But I gather that is the reason we are here.'

There was no seventh planet in the Borosis system. There never had been. But there it was.

It was deep charcoal grey streaked with black and studded with thousands of tiny lights. Around the world were thousands upon thousands of asteroids, tiny speckles of light from this distance, like a swarm of insects protecting the planet.

All Grey Knights were psychic to a degree. They had to be for their minds to be so effectively shielded against corruption. Alaric's psychic powers were all internalised, focused around the wards that kept his mind safe – but he was still psychically sensitive and he could still feel the wrongness pulsating from the new world. It was like the echo of a scream, a smell of old death, a slick and unhealthy feeling against his skin.

'We've had astropaths going mad for light years around,' said Nyxos matter-of-factly. 'That would be the reason.'

'Guilliman's rump,' swore Horstgeld. 'I've been in space all my life and I've seen some things, but never a whole world where there shouldn't be.'

'Try not to get too overwhelmed, captain,' said Nyxos. 'I need a full data sermon on that planet, everything you've got. I'll send Interrogator Hawkespur to coordinate. Atmosphere, lifesigns, dimensions, everything the sensoria can find. And what is the arrival time of the rest of the fleet?'

'Within the day,' replied Horstgeld. 'If you could call it a fleet.'

'We'll need it. That's an inhabited world and if they've got ships of their own we might have to go through them to get down there. And we are going down there.'

'Of course, inquisitor.' Horstgeld turned to his crew and started barking orders, sending communications officers and messenger ratings scurrying.

'What do you think?' Nyxos asked Alaric quietly, as the bridge went about its noisy, barely controlled business.

'Me? I think they were right to send us.'

'I agree. What would you do?'

'I would defer to the wisdom of the Inquisition.'

'Come now, Alaric. You know why I had you accompany me, out of all the Grey Knights.'

'Because they are all at the Eye of Terror.'

'Wrong. You showed an unusual level of independence and creative leadership on the Trail of Saint Evisser. The Chapter made you relinquish your acting rank of brother-captain but they all know your qualities. Space Marines are all very well but even Grey Knights are just soldiers. Ligeia thought you could be something more and I am coming round to her point of view. So, think like one of us, just this once. What should we do?'

'Land an army,' said Alaric, without hesitation. 'Take all the Guard we have and send them down. Right away.'

'Risky.'

'Nothing is riskier than indecision, inquisitor.'

'Quite. And as it happens I agree with you. Is your squad ready?'

'Always.' Alaric's squad was under-strength following the costly defeat of the daemon Ghargatuloth on the Trail of Saint Evisser, but it still represented a concentration of firepower and fighting prowess that no Guard being transported by the fleet could hope to match.

'Good. I want you at the data sermon. You'll probably end up the leader on the ground, one way or another.'

'Understood. I shall pray with my men, inquisitor.'

Alaric left the bridge, knowing instinctively that they would find more on the seventh planet than any amount of prayer could really prepare them for.

'THE EQUATORIAL CIRCUMFERENCE of Borosis Septiam is just under thirty-eight thousand kilometres,' began Interrogator Hawkespur, indicating the pict-grab projected onto the screen behind her. 'Rather less than Earth standard. The mass, however, is the same, suggesting super-dense mineral deposits. As you can see, the thick atmosphere and surrounding asteroid field prevents us from probing the surface but we do suspect the planet is without polar caps, perhaps due to deliberate depletion. The atmosphere shows strong indicators of being breathable, but with severe levels of pollutants.'

The ship's auditorium was normally used for tactical sermons, or public dissections of interesting alien specimens and unusual mutations by the sick bay crew. Now it had been set up for Hawkespur's data sermon and the command crew, along with Nyxos and Alaric's squad, sat in rows around the central stage where Hawkespur was speaking. The pict-grab showed the ugly, weeping sore of a world, provisionally named Borosis Septiam, that had so completely mystified everyone on the bridge. Hawkespur's voice was clipped and professional – she was Naval Academy material from the finest aristocratic stock, a brilliant young woman employed by Nyxos who felt certain she would one day take up the mantle of inquisitor herself.

'The asteroids are in unusually low and stable orbits,' continued Hawkespur. 'It is unlikely that anything larger than a single light cruiser could navigate through them and multiple smaller ships would be out of the question. This precludes a large-scale landing.'

Alaric heard Horstgeld swear quietly. Thousands of Imperial Guard were being transported with the fleet – the initial plan to send them down to the planet had failed before it had even begun.

Hawkespur ignored the captain. 'The temperature readings are particularly anomalous. A planet at such a distant orbit from the sun, especially given the current state of the star Borosis, should be extremely cold. Borosis Septiam's climate suggests temperate conditions over almost the entire surface. This can result only from a massive thermal radiation source or climate control on a planetary scale. The indications we have of extremely high power outputs suggest the latter. Finally, there appear to be a great many orbital installations, apparently man-made. The interference from the asteroids means we cannot get a good look at them but they represent a major presence suitable for an orbital dock-yard.'

'What are your conclusions, Hawkespur?' asked Nyxos, sitting in the front row of the auditorium.

'Highly industrialised, with a large and long-standing population. All the data we have has been sent to the Adeptus Mechanicus sector librarium to see if any planet matches it.'

'Any idea how it got there?'

'None.'

'Ship's astropaths have done no better,' said Horstgeld. 'They say it's like a blind spot.'

Nyxos looked round to where Alaric and his battle-brothers were sitting. 'Justicar? Any thoughts?'

Alaric thought for a moment. The Imperium had lost planets through administrative error before – all it took was for one scholar to forget to mark down a world's tithes and that world could eventually disappear off the stellar maps, especially in an out of the way system like Borosis. But this world was suspicious enough to warrant Inquisitorial scrutiny, if only to be sure. There was something so wrong with the world that it would be a lapse of duty to leave it be.

'Since no major landing is possible, we should send a small well-equipped mission down to the surface. An investigative team.'

Nyxos smiled. 'Excellent. Hawkespur? How's your trigger finger?'

'Commendation Crimson in pistol marksmanship, sir. Third round winner at the Hydraphur nationals.'

'Then you'll take the team down. I'll co-ordinate from the *Tribunicia*. Alaric, your squad will support on the ground along with as many Imperial Guard special forces as we can get onto an armed insertion craft.'

'Commendation Crimson?' said Horstgeld approvingly. 'Good Throne, girl, is there anything you can't do?'

'I haven't found anything yet, sir,' replied Hawkespur, completely without humour.

THE IMPERIAL NAVY was the only thing holding back the Thirteenth Black Crusade and all the Imperial authorities knew it. Abaddon the Despoiler had shattered the attempt to pen his Chaos-worshipping forces up in the warp storm known as the Eye of Terror and it was only Imperial command of space that had kept his ground forces from taking planet after planet all the way into the Segmentum Solar. Every Imperial warship was on notice that it could be ordered into the Eye at any moment and thousands upon thousands of them had been, from mighty Emperor class battleships to squadrons of escorts and wings of fighter craft.

Rear Admiral Horstgeld, for all his experience and commendations, couldn't tear a handful of good ships away from the Eye for the mission to Borosis, even with the authority of Inquisitor Nyxos and the Ordo Malleus. His own ship, the veteran cruiser *Tribunicia*, was the only ship in the small investigative fleet that he considered ready for a battle. The escort squadron *Ptolemy*, under Captain Vanu, was brand new from the orbital docks of Hydraphur and consisted of three Python class ships of a completely untested configuration.

Nyxos had requisitioned an Imperial Guard regiment, the tough deathworld veterans of the Mortressan Highlanders, along with the transport *Calydon* to carry them. The *Calydon* was a corpulent and inefficient ship with barely enough guns to defend itself and Hortsgeld knew it would do nothing in a battle apart from get in the way.

Along with a handful of supply ships and shuttles, these craft comprised the fleet that exited the warp over the course of a few hours just outside the orbit of Borosis Septiam. Shortly afterwards another craft was detected in the warp which broke through into real space a short distance away, all its weapons powered down in a display of alliance. It was a large ship, easily the size of a cruiser, but of an ugly, blocky design painted a drab rust-red, covered in ornate cog-toothed battlements and training long flexible sensor-spines like the stingers of a sea creature.

The ship immediately hailed the *Tribunicia*. It identified itself as the Adeptus Mechanicus armed explorator ship *Exemplar* under the command of Archmagos Saphentis, who demanded complete jurisdiction over the entire Borosis system.

'I DON'T LIKE it,' said Alaric, looking at the landing craft. 'It's too fragile. This couldn't take half the punishment a Thunderhawk gunship could.'

The ship was being bombed-up and refuelled in the loading bay of the *Tribunicia*, a grimy, functional deck where the vaulted ceiling was stained black with oily fumes. The landing craft was bulbous and simple, with twin flaring engines and a thick black carapace over its nose to protect it from re-entry. It could probably seat thirty passengers plus crew.

'It's the best we have,' replied Hawkespur. She wore a heavy black spacer's voidsuit, ready for take off – she looked very different without her starched naval uniform. A marksman's autopistol was holstered at her waist. 'We're fortunate the *Tribunicia* has an armoured lander at all.'

'Then we have no choice,' said Alaric. He turned to the Marines of his squad. 'We take off in half an hour. Check your wargear and pray.'

A Grey Knights squad ideally consisted of between eight and ten Space Marines. Squad Alaric consisted of six Marines, having never recovered the losses it suffered during the battle against Ghargatuloth on Volcanis Ultor over a year before. Brother Dvorn was by far the biggest, packed with muscle. He carried a rare mark of Nemesis weapon, a hammer, which was all but unheard of now among the Chapter artificers but which was brutal and unsubtle enough to suit Dvorn perfectly. No one doubted that Dvorn would soon be trained in the use of Tactical Dreadnought Armour and join the ranks of the Grey Knights Terminator squads, the heaviest shock troops in the Chapter.

Brother Haulvarn and Brother Lykkos were the other two survivors of Volcanis Ultor. Lykkos carried the squad's psycannon, which fired ensorcelled bolter shells to tear through the bodies of daemonic or psychically active targets.

Brother Archis and Brother Cardios, who carried the squad's two Incinerators, had both heard the story of how Alaric, as acting brother-captain, had led the mission to the Trail of Saint Evisser to locate the daemon Ghargatuloth and help Imperial forces destroy it on Volcanis Ultor. But they had not been there. They had not seen it.

'Justicar,' said Dvorn as the other Grey Knights checked the storm bolters and armour seals according to the ancient Rites of Preparedness. 'Do we have any more news on what is down there?'

'I wish we did, Dvorn,' he said. 'But the squad knows as much as anyone in the fleet.'

'But they need us, don't they? Whatever is down there, it's corrupt. Can you feel it?'

'Yes, Dvorn, I can feel it. Anyone sensitive could. And they will need us down there, of that I am certain.'

Dvorn looked at the lander craft. There was a look of disdain on his battered face – Dvorn was not a gnarled old veteran but he was well on the way to looking the part. 'I wouldn't trust that thing to dust crops, let alone land thirty men on a hostile world.'

'I know, but it's the best the fleet has.'

'The main armament is twin lascannon. I could carry more firepower than that and still have a hand free.'

'You probably could, Dvorn, but the Emperor does not make us strong by making our duties easy. We will make do.'

'Justicar,' came Nyxos's voice over Alaric's vox-unit. 'Problem.'

'The stormtroopers?'

'Worse.'

A warning klaxon sounded and the docking doors of the adjacent landing bay slid open. Alaric could see a slice of the dirty purple disk of Borosis Septiam beyond it and space scattered with stars. The rest of the landing deck was protected from the void by a force field so Alaric couldn't hear the engines of the shuttle that slid into the *Tribunicia*. It was clad in heavy, ugly slabs of armaplas and its prow was a massive flat disk ringed with turbolasers. The cog-toothed symbol of the Adeptus Mechanicus was emblazoned on its side. The deck crew had evidently had no notice of its arrival but it didn't need the help of any deck hands or docking servitors as it settled onto the deck. The bay doors slid shut and the void-seal field boomed off.

A deck-officer strode towards the interloper craft, hand on his dress sword. 'You!' He yelled up at the ship. 'I don't see this damn thing on the docking manifests! Explain yourself!'

A dozen turbo-lasers trained themselves on the officer's head. He stopped in mid-flow and took a step backwards.

'I think this is our problem,' said Alaric. 'Follow me.'

As Alaric and his Marines walked towards the shuttle a ramp unfolded from its side. Thick, purplish incense billowed out, followed by a detail of twenty tech-guard, their faces hidden behind the reflective visors of their helmets. Alaric recognised the tech-guard uniforms and distinctive pattern lasguns – they were the standing army of the Adeptus Mechanicus, their regiments raised to defend the Mechanicus's forge worlds. Two tech-priests followed behind the soldiers – they were holding the censer-poles which were the source of the incense. The tech-priests seemed mostly human, suggesting they were lower-ranked members of the clergy. The priest behind them was clearly something totally different.

The delegation was led by a creature that could only be called human with a great deal of charity. He moved as if he wasn't walking at all but gliding, as if his long Mechnicus robes hid some strange motive attachment instead of legs. He had four arms, two with what looked like silvered and intricately engraved bionic hands and two ending in bunches of dataspines and interface units. His head was the most bizarre of all – he had large multi-faceted insectoid eyes and his mouth was hidden by a heavy metal collar with a series of slits cut into it through which he presumably spoke. There was not one scrap of biological flesh visible on him.

The tech-guard fanned out into a semicircle to let their master through. The lead tech-priest looked around for a moment and his inhuman eyes settled quickly on Alaric and his squad.

'Excellent,' said a clearly artificial voice. 'You are a representative of Inquisitor Nyxos?'

'I represent the Adeptus Astartes Chapter of the Grey Knights.'

'I see. By your heraldry I surmise you possess the rank of justicar.' The voice was programmed with a slightly aristocratic, supercilious accent. 'It is unlikely you are in command of Imperial forces here. Please direct me to someone who is.'

'I should like to know who you are, first.'

'Forgive my manners, I was unable to bring my protocol-servitor with me. I am Archmagos Saphentis of the Adeptus Mechanicus, commander of the *Exemplar* and senior tech-priest of the Librarium Primaris on Rhyza, appointed by the office of the Fabricator General to lead this reclamation mission.'

'Reclamation?' said Interrogator Hawkespur, looking almost ridiculously small next to the fully-armoured Alaric. She didn't seem in the least bit fazed by Saphentis's bizarre appearance. 'This is an Ordo Malleus investigation. The Holy Orders of The Emperor's Inquisition have authority over this planet and everything pertaining to it.'

'You misunderstand me.' Saphentis held out one of his more humanoid hands and an attendant tech-priest handed him a dataslate. The slate's screen glowed purplish with an image of Borosis Septiam. 'You are Interrogator Hawkespur, I believe. You yourself sent the specifications of this planet to the sector librarium requesting identification. That request has been fulfilled. The world you have inaccurately named Borosis Septiam is a forge world, a possession of the Adeptus Mechanicus according to the Treaty of Mars. I am therefore here to lead the mission reclaiming it according to the orders of the Fabricator General.'

'The Inquisitorial Mandate supersedes all other authority, including the Treaty of Mars,' said Hawkespur crossly.

'You may well be correct. While you debate the legalities, my men will be conducting an examination of the planet.'

'Forgetting the rules,' interrupted Alaric, 'anyone who goes down there may not come back. We're looking at a moral threat on that planet. The Mechanicus can't deal with something like that on its own.'

'Your concern is appreciated,' said Saphentis. 'But there is little a fully armed Explorator mission cannot cope with. Now, if you will excuse me, I had hoped to extend Inquisitor Nyxos the courtesy of explaining the authority under which I operate, but if that courtesy is not going to be reciprocated then I shall return to my ship.'

Hawkespur glared at the deck officer, who was still being tracked by all the craft's turbo-lasers.

'Not... not without deck clearance, sir,' he said. 'And I'm afraid I can't give it to you. So you'll have to explain yourself to the captain.'

'This craft and this planet belongs to the Adeptus Mechanicus,' said Saphentis sharply. 'If you cannot comprehend this then I certainly hope your captain will be less obtuse. You will take me to him and hope that he extends me the respect for my authority that is due.'

'This is ridiculous,' said Hawkespur as Saphentis drifted away escorted by his tech-guard retinue. 'Men have been executed for questioning Inquisitorial authority. We should launch as soon as the stormtroopers arrive.'

'It would be better to wait, interrogator,' said Alaric.

'Why? There is no point in being tangled up in a debate while we could be learning what is on that planet.'

'I know.' Alaric pointed at the Mechanicus shuttle. 'But if we're going down there, I'd far rather do it in a ship like this.'

THE COMMS CENTRE of the escort ship *Ptolemy Gamma* was, like the rest of the ship, brand new. It was well known within the Imperial Navy that the old ships were the best – construction techniques were lost faster than they were rediscovered, so newer ships were often thought of as flimsy copies of far superior veterans. The communications of the escort squadron had been characteristically petulant, the frequencies fluctuating, the machine-spirits of the comms cogitators sulking and bickering like children. Many libations of machine-oil and tech-rituals of adjustment were needed just to get the *Ptolemy Gamma* talking to the *Alpha* and *Beta*, the other two ships in the squadron. But there were no full tech-priests stationed with the squadron and the tech-rituals did not always work.

'Anything?' asked Communications Officer Tsallen. The comms centre was cramped and stifling, crammed into the heart of the ship between the gun-decks and engineering where it was supposed to be safest. Tsallen had been trying to get the *Gamma* speaking to Squadron Captain Vanu for three hours now and her heavy starched Naval uniform was not endearing her to the heat down here.

'Cogitator three isn't responding,' replied the rating in front of her. Stripped to the waist, he had levered the panel off the front of the massive cogitator and was trying to make sense of the half-clockwork machinery inside.

'There must be something,' said Tsallen. 'The squadron is supposed to be in tight formation protecting the *Tribunicia* and right now we can't even tell her where we are.'

'If it's broke it's broke,' said the rating.

Tsallen sighed. She was supposed to command her own ship one day and this wasn't the way to go moving up the ladder. 'You!' she said, pointing at another rating. 'Are we receiving yet?'

The second rating was a skinny man sweating heavily as he sat at a large receiver station shaped like a church organ. He was listening intently to the static streaming through his headset. 'Maybe.'

'Maybe?'

'It's not letting me isolate frequencies. I keep getting snatches of things.'

'Let me.' Tsallen pushed the rating away from the receiver station and bent over the hundreds of blinking lights and readouts. Most of them hadn't even been labelled yet. She pushed a couple of buttons and pulled a few levers experimentally.

The station shuddered. Its cogitator stacks, shaped like organ pipes, thrummed as they went into overdrive. A bewildering shimmer of indicator lights flowed over the console.

'Did it work?' she asked.

'Looks like it's cycling through all the frequencies, ma'am. Depends on whether it finds anything.'

Tsallen heard a horrible grinding sound and smoke spurted from beneath the console. At least if she'd broken the damn thing it wouldn't be her fault, she thought. That was what the ratings were for.

The rating screamed. His head was jerking, neck spasming and his eyes were rolled back and white. He was clawing at the headset – Tsallen grabbed it and tried to pry it off his head but it was red-hot, burning itself into the man's skull.

'Oh frag! Oh frag, we've lost the whole bloody lot!' shouted someone, probably the rating working on cogitator three. The rest of the comms crew, about thirty men and women crammed into the hot, dark space, started shouting for attention as the whole comms centre started overloading itself.

Tsallen pushed away the rating, who had by now stopped screaming and was exhaling stinking, oily smoke instead. 'Stay calm!' she yelled, drawing her laspistol. 'What is it?'

'Some signal's coming in,' shouted someone in reply. 'Something strong! It's overloading everything!'

'Where's it coming from?'

There was a moment of frantic commotion. Sparks flew as one of the cogitators blew, spraying shattered components everywhere.

'Point of origin is Borosis Septiam!'

'Isolate us from the rest of the ship,' ordered Tsallen.

'Primary controls are offline!'

'Then grab a bloody fire axe and cut the cables!'

There was an ear-splitting scream as all the cogitator circuits blew at once. All the lights went out.

Silence drowned the comms centre.

'Anyone hurt?' asked Tsallen carefully.

The sound that came from the main receiver console might have been described as a voice, but it spoke a language so horrible to hear that Tsallen froze. It was painful to listen to, so many dark, guttural sounds overlaid that it sounded like a million onlookers spitting curses at her.

'Moral threat...' said Tsallen weakly, hoping her own vox to the bridge still worked. 'We have a moral threat in comms. Isolate us and get a message to Horstgeld...'

A dark purple glow rippled up from the console, stippling the walls with deep swirling colour. The voice continued. And though Tsallen could not understand the language it spoke the meaning was impossibly clear – malice, anger, hatred, dripping from every syllable. Tsallen forced herself to look at the console readouts – the signal was massively powerful, streaming from somewhere on the surface of the mystery planet below, using a frequency that could barely be received but strong enough to tear through the filtration circuits and bleed, pure and evil, into the *Ptolemy Gamma*.

After a few more moments the physical structure failed and the whole comms centre imploded.

'I PROPOSE A compromise,' said Inquisitor Nyxos. Rear Admiral Horstgeld's personal quarters took up several rooms of cold, dressed stone, piously furnished with solid hardwood and adorned with icons of the Imperial Creed. Nyxos had called the meeting in Horstgeld's private chapel, well away from any of the crew. He had Hawkespur by his side, along with Hortsgeld and Alaric. Archmagos Saphentis and Tech-Priest Thalassa, a relatively unaugmented female tech-priest who attended him, represented the Adeptus Mechanicus.

If Nyxos was unnerved by seeing his hundredfold reflection in Saphentis's insectoid eyes, he did not show it. 'Arguing will get us nowhere.'

'Unusual words for an inquisitor,' said Saphentis. 'And in the circumstances probably the wisest.'

'I am glad we got off to a good start, then,' said Nyxos. 'But first, I need to know what you found at the sector librarium.'

'Am I to understand you are asking as an inquisitor and not as a curious individual?'

'You are.'

'Very well.' Saphentis, Alaric guessed, was well aware that refusing to answer an Inquisitorial interrogation could be met with whatever punishment the inquisitor could devise. 'The planet in question is named Chaeroneia. It disappeared a little over a century ago following an investigation into the potential of tech-heresy among the lower ranks of its tech-priests.'

'You are certain?'

'We are. Chaeroneia is a forge world according to the principles of the Treaty of Mars and is owned in its entirety by the Adeptus Mechanicus, hence our insistence that we are to conduct any investigations.'

'The Treaty of Mars is nowhere accepted as superseding Inquisitorial authority,' snapped Hawkespur.

'Perhaps this is true,' replied Saphentis, whose voice seemed programmed to sound condescending. 'But the time taken to ascertain this for certain is time none of us have.'

'Hence my proposal,' said Nyxos. 'A joint mission.'

'Under my command, of course,' said Saphentis.

'Unacceptable. Interrogator Hawkespur will represent me on the ground. Justicar Alaric will be in operational command.'

'The mission shall be attended by myself, Tech-priest Thalassa and a detachment of tech-guard troops.'

'Agreed.'

'And the *Exemplar* will be under my command as part of the fleet,' interjected Horstgeld.

'Very well. My flag-captain, Magos Korveylan, will accommodate you.' Saphentis's voice was as calm as ever but Alaric guessed that Saphentis realised he was getting about as good a result as he could have hoped – Nyxos was probably being generous letting such a high-ranking tech-priest accompany the mission at all.

In some ways, Alaric was glad the Mechanicus would be coming along. If Borosis Septiam really was the forge world Chaeroneia, someone knowledgeable in the Cult Mechanicus would be a real asset on the ground. He didn't like the idea of wrangling for control, though, and Saphentis seemed the kind of man who would refuse to budge once he had decided he was going to be in charge.

The doors to the chapel opened and a nervous-looking bridge officer entered, the pips on his dark blue uniform denoting him as a member of the comms crew. He hurried up to Captain Horstgeld, unable to help glancing at the bizarre form of Archmagos Saphentis and the no less otherworldly appearance of Alaric himself.

'Moral threat on the *Ptolemy Gamma*, sir.'

'Moral threat? What's the source?'

'A broadcast from the planet.'

'Hell and damnation,' said Horstgeld. 'Quarantine the *Gamma*, physical comms only. Have the fleet purge all communications. And have Fleet Commissar Leung informed.'

'Can the *Exemplar* set up a completely secure receiver?' Nyxos asked Saphentis.

'Indeed we can.'

'Good. Have Korveylan do so and start studying that broadcast and work out where it's coming from.' Saphentis didn't move. 'If you please.'

Saphentis nodded to Thalassa, who hurried off to relay the necessary orders to the *Exemplar*.

'It looks like our hand is being forced,' said Alaric.

'Quite right,' replied Nyxos. 'That is the annoying thing about the Enemy, he never gives us time to think. Are you ready to move, Alaric?'

'My men have observed their wargear rites and can deploy immediately.'

'That's what I like to hear. Saphentis?'

'The tech-guard accompanying me represent our most efficient combat unit. They are ready to go, as is our ship.'

'Excellent. Gentlemen, you carry the authority of the Emperor's Holy Orders of the Inquisition with you. Whatever you find down there, it falls under the aegis of the Emperor and must be claimed in His name or made pure according to His laws. His Will be with you.'

Alaric and Saphentis left the chapel for the launch deck. Alaric knew that once down on the planet, the balance of power would shifty dramatically without Nyxos to back up Hawkespur and Alaric – Alaric only hoped that whatever he found on Chaeroneia, he would only have one enemy to fight.

FIVE

'The words of the faithful are the mountains. But the deeds of the faithful are the world.'

– Final words of Ecclesiarch Deacis VII

ASTEROIDS SHOT BY the viewport, streaming trails of dust and gases. The upper layers of Chaeroneia's atmosphere were dirty wisps of pollution, lit by the feeble glow shining from the star Borosis and reflected off the planet's surface. Alaric's first close-up image of Chaeroneia was one of pollution, the filth that wrapped the planet bleeding off into space, infecting everything around it.

'Heat exchanger activated,' came an artificial voice voxed from the cockpit, probably a pre-recorded sample broadcast by a pilot-servitor. It meant the friction of the atmosphere was heating up the ship's hull.

The inside of the ship was cramped and functional. Everything was painted in the dark red of the Adeptus Mechanicus. The cog-and-skull symbol was raised in steel and brass on the low ceiling. Grav-couches lining the passenger compartment held the twenty-strong tech-guard unit, Alaric and his five Grey Knights, Interrogator Hawkespur, Tech-priest Thalassa and Archmagos Saphentis.

'Our readings from the *Exemplar* suggest the asteroids may not be entirely natural,' said Tech-priest Thalassa to Hawkespur. Thalassa's age was difficult to guess owing to the silvered circuitry embedded in her skin, describing complex patterns across her face, but she was evidently of a low rank since her simple dark red habit had few signs of status. 'The guns can keep the path clear but there may be resistance.'

'Resistance?' Hawkespur looked unimpressed. 'Orbital weaponry?'

'We don't know. But this craft is designed for atmospheric intrusion so we can take a lot of fire.'

Alaric looked across the passenger compartment to the tech-guard. They wore full-face helmets with polished brass visors and heavy rebreather units and they were armed with what looked like more complex versions of the standard Guard lasgun. Alaric couldn't see their faces – they seemed more like servitors than soldiers.

The craft shuddered as the turbulence of the upper atmosphere threw it around. Alaric could see the blackness of space overlaid by a gauze of pollution through the viewport, the ugly lumpen asteroids glowing orange where they plunged in and out of the atmosphere. The pallid light of Borosis shone through the crescent of atmosphere that Alaric could see clinging to the side of Chaeroneia's disc, making it glow a sickly purple-grey.

Alaric could feel the world beneath him, reflecting off the psychic core that kept his soul safe from corruption. He could feel it churning, pulsing – the heartbeat of a world. Dull, ancient pain throbbed far below, like the agony of something old and captive. The world was tortured.

'The heresy that Mars investigated here a hundred years ago,' said Alaric, looking at Saphentis. 'Were there any details?'

Saphentis shook his insectoid head. 'Very little. Rumours of improper practices. Unauthorised creation of techniques. Attempted instigation of machine-spirits. The investigation was not intended to prosecute any named individuals, just collate data on potential heresies against the Cult Mechanicus.'

'Do we know if they found anything?'

'No reports were received.'

'That's not the same thing, though, is it? If you know anything about what is down there, archmagos, we need to know it.'

'I have extensive details on the workings of the forge world prior to its disappearance.'

'And now?'

'If much has changed, then we shall learn of it as we must.'

Something slammed hard into the underside of the ship, sending it bucking like an animal as the directional thrusters forced it back into line.

'Impact,' came the annoyingly calm voice from the cockpit servitors.

The ship began to swing, slaloming its way between the asteroids. Alaric saw through the viewport that they were spearing thicker through the atmosphere, congregating on the craft as it plunged towards the surface. Flames rippled across the asteroids' surfaces as they ripped into the next thicker layer of atmosphere, forcing their way down through the air resistance to meet the ship.

'Grav-dampeners to maximum,' ordered Saphentis as the ship bucked again, several small impacts thudding against the underside like bullets.

'I am the Hammer,' said Brother Dvorn. 'I am the point of His sword. I am the tip of His spear.'

'I am the gauntlet about His fist,' said the other Grey Knights, intoning the prayer that had been heard by the Emperor when they had entered the Tomb of Saint Evisser to face Ghargatuloth.

A red glare crept up the edge of the viewport, the force of re-entry superheating the hull. Flames licked off the edges of the hull just visible outside the ship.

'I am His sword just as He is my armour, I am His wrath just as He is my zeal...' Alaric couldn't hear his own voice as the impacts rang louder and the howl of the atmosphere outside vibrated through the hull, the whole ship shaking.

The tech-guard were calm and unmoving no matter how they were shaken around. Saphentis had all four arms splayed against the wall behind him, holding him firm. Thalassa look less comfortable, thrown about in her grav-restraint. Hawkespur was pulling on the hood of her black voidsuit, always ready for the worst.

Alaric knew the low thudding sound from the prow was the noise of the forward guns, tracking and blasting apart asteroids that were thrown in the way of the ship. The fragments spattered on the hull like gunfire, streaking past the viewport as tiny burning sparks.

The view of space was gone, replaced by a purple-black sky streaked with filthy clouds. Strange geometric shapes were flashing in the sky, projected onto the clouds from far below. The lander was heading for the probable origin of the signal – the analyses on the *Exemplar* had located the transmission source to within seventy kilometres. It was a big margin of error, but it was the best information the Imperial fleet had about where to start looking for answers on the planet's surface.

With a horrible sound like a metallic thunderclap something huge struck the ship head-on. The pressure vessel that kept the passenger compartment at Earth-standard pressure was breached and wind howled through the compartment, flinging debris around. The door to the cockpit banged open and Alaric saw only the ground beyond it, a distant dark mass speckled with lights, framed by the remains of the cockpit. The broken metallic limbs straggling in the air were presumably the remains of the servitor-pilot.

'Autosystems engage!' came Saphentis's voice, amplified above the din. 'Landing pattern beta! Drag compensation maximum!'

Another impact sheared deep into the side of the vessel, stripping away hull plates. The viewport cracked. Alaric could see gouts of burning exhaust jets streaking down from the craft, trying to slow its descent. It was heading straight down, the massive damage done to its prow destroying any chance of even the ship's machine-spirit controlling it properly as it fell.

There was a city below them, like a huge dark spider straddling the scorched black landscape. It was the size of a hive city and the uppermost spires knifed up towards the craft as it fell.

Another impact flipped the craft over and it was tumbling now, completely out of control, the engines spurting to correct its trajectory.

'I am the Hammer! He is my Shield!'

The craft smashed into the first spires of the city and even a Space Marine's resilience couldn't keep Alaric conscious as the impact split the ship apart.

HORSTGELD WAS RAPIDLY losing his patience. Magos Korveylan was supposed to be under his command, but the Mechanicus captain had spun a web of red tape and protocols to prevent Horstgeld from sending any of his officers onto the *Exemplar* – not even Fleet Commissar Leung.

Horstgeld was therefore still on the bridge of the *Tribunicia*, waiting for Korveylan to contact him at the tech-priest's leisure.

The obvious moral threat on the planet below – now called Chaeroneia, apparently – was such that the ship's Confessor Talas was on permanent duty warding the souls of everyone on the bridge. Talas, a hellfire preacher with a scrawny build but undeniable presence, was on the pulpit at that moment uttering an uninterrupted stream of religious fervour. The Emperor's wrath featured strongly, as did the many places in the various hells of the Imperial Cult that sinners could find themselves in if they gave in to the whims of the Enemy. Horstgeld had employed a Confessor on the bridge for many years and to him the constant admonitions were just the music of the spheres – the rest of the bridge crew had to live with it.

'Transmission from the *Exemplar*,' said one of the comms officers.

'About gakking time,' said Horstgeld as the face of Magos Korveylan appeared on the viewscreen. If it could be called a face at all – half of Korveylan's skull was covered in a featureless cowl of gleaming silver and the other was covered in dead grey flesh.

'Rear Admiral,' said Korveylan. Rather disconcertingly, the voice that came from Korveylan's vocal synthesiser was female. 'Is there any news of our mission?'

'We lost vox-contact with them in the upper atmosphere,' replied Horstgeld. 'What about you? Have you found anything?'

'We have.'

There was a long pause. 'And?' asked Horstgeld tetchily.

'The transmission's source is the surface of Chaeroneia. It is extremely powerful, well beyond the capabilities of any one spacecraft or standard comms device the Imperium has. The navigational beacons within the Sol system are of comparable intensity.'

'Very good, captain. What does it actually say?'

'The signal cannot yet be deciphered.'

'You mean you don't know.'

'The signal cannot be yet deciphered.'

'Hmph. Anything else?'

'It is clear the information encoded into the signal has not been created using logic engine techniques known to the Adeptus Mechanicus. It includes patterns and energy types of a clearly non Terrestial origin.'

Horstgeld leaned forward on the command pew. 'Sorcery?'

'That is a crude but accurate summation, yes.'

'And do we know who the target is?'

'Aside from the fact that the signal is being broadcast towards the galactic north-west, no.'

'Since this is clearly a supernatural threat, I want Fleet Commissar Leung on the *Exemplar*. I don't want any of your men losing their minds over this.'

'Unnecessary. The Magi Psychologis can maintain mental wellbeing among the research crew.'

'Take Leung on board. That's an order. Your ship is a part of my fleet and you command it with my authority. Don't make me use it against you.'

Korveylan held up a hand – her hand, Horstgeld supposed – as if appealing for calm. 'The Adeptus Mechanicus maintains strict protocols regarding...'

'Frag your protocols,' said Horstgeld. 'Do as you're bloody well told or I'll haul you over here for a court martial. And I am not known for my lenience. Prepare to receive Leung's shuttle, Horstgeld out.'

Horstgeld snapped the viewscreen off and it reverted to an image of the Borosis system, the hateful purple-black stain of Chaeroneia in the foreground. He sat for a moment listening to Talas sermonising.

'…for is not the Emperor both your light and your fire? The light that guides you and the fire that waits below to burn the unbelievers? I say, yes! Yes He is! For if you believe, O faithful citizens, then you are His tool, a tool to break down the edifice of heresy and build His temples in its place…'

It comforted Horstgeld to know that one inspired by the Emperor was always there, tingeing everything on the bridge with the Emperor's own authority. And he needed that, because the hell-planet below him, screaming out a signal that only daemonancers and sorcerers could hear, wasn't very comforting at all.

THE TECH-GUARD was dead. He was lying on his back, the length of his spine opened up wet and red, fresh blood glossy in the faint but hard-edged light.

Another was hanging, impaled on one of the shards of metal that ringed the huge wound in the side of the lander craft. His lasgun was still gripped tightly to his chest, his hands constricted in death, refusing to let go of the weapon with which he defended the Adeptus Mechanicus.

Alaric was alive. He tried to move and found he could. Rapidly he worked through the Rite of Wounding, testing each of his muscle groups, searching for tears or broken bones – he was knocked about but there were no injuries he couldn't ignore. He turned his head and saw the rest of the wrecked ship's interior. A couple more tech-guard were clearly dead, one totally decapitated, still sitting strapped into his grav-couch. Other tech-guard were stirring. Hawkespur was unconscious but breathing – through the faceplate of her voidsuit's hood he could see there was blood on her face, but it looked superficial.

Dvorn, the Grey Knight strapped in next to Alaric, was moving.

'Dvorn?'

'Justicar. We made it?'

'This would make for a strange afterlife, so yes, I'd say we had.'

The Grey Knights squad was alive and its injuries seemed superficial. Dvorn was first out, hammer in hand as always, helping Alaric out of the crushed grav-restraint. Brother Haulvarn checked Hawkespur for injuries then unstrapped her and carried her out through the tear in the hull.

The air was heavy and thick, like strange-tasting smoke. Warning runes on Alaric's retinal display flickered on and the implants in his throat began filtering out the pollutants. Alaric clambered out of the wreckage, his enhanced eyes automatically adjusting to the twilight outside.

The lander had crashed in a valley with sides of twisted metal, layers of crushed buildings lying in hundreds of strata. Far above, the layers became thicker and less compressed until Alaric could just glimpse, at the very top, soaring spires studded with tiny lights, stabbing thin and sharp as syringe needles into the sky. The sky itself was ugly and bruise-coloured, the many layers of pollution tinting the pallid light from Borosis a strange cocktail of splotchy purples and greys. Shapes flickered, some geometric, some strange-shaped symbols like letters in an alien language, presumably projected from somewhere on the surface onto the underside of the cloud layer. The valley was a chasm cutting down through layers and layers of the forge world's buildings, the strata showing how the city had constantly been built on top of itself for the thousands of years the forge world had been in existence.

The valley was choked with wreckage that had fallen down from the top of the chasm – wrecked machinery, burned-out engines, spindly fragments of wrecked servitors. On top of a charred lump of what looked like an engine housing was Archmagos Saphentis, climbing nimbly with the help of his additional arms.

The surviving tech-guard were emerging from the lander's wreckage, along with Tech-Priest Thalassa. There were about a dozen of them still alive. One of them flipped up the visor of his helmet – his face was lined with age and experience beneath shaven dark brown hair and one of his eyes was a large but solid bionic.

'Pollutants fifteen per cent air volume!' he said to his men. 'Rebreathers at all times! Colsk, take the dead men's names and collect their power packs.'

Alaric recalled the tech-guard captain's name was Tharkk. He hadn't spoken to him before – the mission had been assembled and launched in a hurry. They wouldn't have the luxury of returning to the *Tribunicia* with the same kind of haste, that much was obvious.

Alaric clambered onto the engine housing where Saphentis had now stopped to survey his surroundings. The valley floor ahead of them sloped upwards until it met what looked like a plateau a couple of kilometres away.

'Archmagos!' called Alaric. 'Hawkespur looks unhurt, as does my squad. Many of your tech-guard are dead. Perhaps you should see to them.'

'They are unmoved by death,' replied Saphentis. 'They need no help.'

Alaric had dealt with members of the Adeptus Mechanicus on a few occasions – many were tied to the Ordo Malleus by ancient debts and served to maintain the Inquisitorial fleet anchored on Saturn's moon,

Iapetus, or attended inquisitors directly as lexmechanic archivists or augmetic chirurgeons. In Alaric's experience the more senior the tech-priest, the less human they were. Saphentis, with his rank of archmagos, wasn't doing anything to buck the trend.

'We will move to the head of the valley,' said Saphentis. 'We will get a better view of the city.'

'Do you have enough details on Chaeroneia to know where we are?'

'I have full topographic and urban maps of Chaeroneia. However, after a century they are unlikely to be accurate. Information is our first priority.'

'I agree, archmagos and as commander on the ground it is my decision. You are under Inquisitorial authority here, don't forget that.'

Saphentis turned his faceted eyes towards Alaric. 'Of course.'

'Squad, we're moving out,' voxed Alaric to his squad. 'Lykkos, get the psycannon up front. Cardios, keep the Incinerator in the centre in case of ambush. Haulvarn, is Hawkespur conscious?'

'Semi-conscious, justicar.'

'Keep her safe. I would like to get her back to Nyxos intact. Let's move out before something comes to investigate the wreck.'

Saphentis issued a stream of clicking sounds which Alaric guessed was binary machine code, filtered by the vox-receivers on the tech-guard and turned into recognisable language. Alaric would insist everyone on the mission use the same vox-channel once they were safe.

Alaric could hear distant machinery pumping away as the mission moved up the valley. Long and high-sided, the chasm cut out all but a sliver of sky as it wound through the darkness. It headed gradually upwards and Alaric hoped that it would reach a point where they could get a better look at their surroundings. There was something other than just the sounds and the darkness, too – the same psychic resonance he had felt in orbit, a sinister presence that seemed to be coming from everywhere at once, diffuse and all-pervading. It flashed through him as the images on the clouds above changed – complex occult wards and sigils, like the symbols cultists painted on their temple walls or etched out on the floor for their rituals. Occasionally shapes would flit across the clouds. Alaric hoped they were aircraft.

'Advanced machining,' Saphentis was saying as they moved past the burned-out heaps of wreckage. 'They have not regressed. They have progressed. Chaeroneia was a Gamma-level macro economy, but it now seems to be approaching Beta-level sophistication.'

'Is that normal?' asked Alaric.

'Not in a century,' said Saphentis.

Tech-priest Thalassa had recovered her wits and was quickly alongside Saphentis. She was mostly human so she stumbled as she fought her way across the uneven wreckage – Saphentis could help himself along with his extra arms. 'We should find somewhere we can interface with the planet's data repositories, archmagos,' she said. Alaric guessed from her circuitry-covered skin that she was Saphentis's data expert. 'I could extrapolate our location from Chaeroneia's last surveys.'

'Could you find out what has been happening for the last hundred years?' interrupted Alaric.

'Maybe,' said Thalassa, looking nervously at Alaric. Alaric remembered how people tended to react to Space Marines – with fear and awe. 'If the data vaults are similar to Mechanicus standard.'

'Contact!' came a shout from one of the tech-guard, barking out of Saphentis's vox-receiver. Alaric span around, Brother Lykkos beside him training the psycannon barrel over the dark valley floor. The tech-guard had hit cover, lying or crouched, squinting along the barrels of the lasguns to cover all the approaches.

'Tharkk?' voxed Saphentis quietly.

'Colsk reported movement,' came the reply.

'And yourself?'

'Can't see anything yet – wait!'

Alaric saw a slim, pallid shape stumble out of the gloom. It looked humanoid. Its pale body was naked except for tattered strips of parchment nailed to its torso and its bare feet shambled across the debris with only enough coordination to keep it upright. Its shaven head was a wreck – the lower jaw was gone and the one remaining eye was a rusting, weeping mechanical optic. It only had one hand, its other arm ending at the elbow in a fitting where the mechanical forearm had been removed.

Alaric overheard one of the tech-guard voxing. 'It's a servitor, sir. Scavenger.'

'Deactivate it,' was Tharkk's reply. One of the tech-guard drew a laspistol sidearm and put a las-bolt through the servitor's head. It shuddered, stiffened and fell to the ground. The tech-guard smashed its skull with the butt of his lasgun.

'Scavengers are dangerous,' said Saphentis. 'Others may be combat-capable. Stay on your guard and do not allow us to be caught out again.'

'Anything else I should be warned about?' asked Alaric as the troops got moving again.

'A forge world is not unlike any Imperial world in that respect,' replied Saphentis. 'It has its criminals and malcontents along with dispossessed menial scavengers and rogue servitors. But they are far less numerous than in a hive city or area of comparable population density.'

They were coming to the end of the valley, where the ground sloped up to meet what looked like a plateau level, spreading away from them. Alaric's retinal readouts were telling him that without his throat implants and superior ability to filter and absorb poisons, toxins from the polluted air would be building up in his body at an alarming rate. Thalassa was breathing heavily, but Saphentis wasn't showing the slightest discomfort.

'We need to be on the same vox-net,' said Alaric. 'If I can't co-ordinate the whole force at once then...'

They had reached the top of the valley slope, level with the small circular plateau that looked out on the cityscape beyond. And Alaric saw one of Chaeroneia's cities properly for the first time.

SIX

'It is good that we have seen such terrible things, for now death will be no great sorrow.'

– Commissar Yarrick
(attr., at the walls of Hades Hive)

THE CITY WAS an unholy fusion of black iron machinery and a pulsing biological mass, as if something vast and alive was reaching up from the bowels of the planet to strangle the steel city. Below them huge rounded masses of grey muscle bulged up from the city's black depths, ripped through with ribbed cabling and punctured by vents spewing evil-smelling steam. Deep shafts lipped with wet fleshy mouths belched black smoke. Strips of flickering lights suggested there were corridors and rooms hollowed out of the masses, that they were inhabited by whatever had done this to Chaeroneia. In some places slabs of muscle jutted out above the blackness, balconies or walkways, even launching pads for shuttle craft were painted in stained black and purples. Sensor-spines stuck out like poisoned barbs. Massive vertebrae reared up, weeping dark-coloured pus where they broke the skin, bent tortuously as if some massive creature had been chained and shackled under the city.

The forge world's towers soared out of the chasms below, masses of flesh like tentacles wrapped around them as if holding them upright. The towers were in the half-gothic, half-industrial style of the Adeptus Mechanicus but all similarity to an Imperial city ended there. The black steel spires were fused with the city's biological mass, so that some were like massive teeth sticking out from rancid gums or huge steel leg bones,

335

skinned and wrapped in greyish muscle. Bulbous growths fused obscenely with sheer-sided skyscrapers. Sensorium domes trailed waving fronds of tendrils. Pulsing veins snaked in and out between the girders of skeletal buildings, seemingly picked clean of their meat. Foul-coloured fluids leaked from wounds hundreds of metres long or sprayed from the mouths of iron gargoyles, gathering into waterfalls of ichor tumbling far down into the city's depths. Bridges of sticky tendrils, like spiders' webs, connected one spire to the next. In places the flesh was rotten and scabbed, covered in weeping sores the size of bomb craters and sagging under its own dying weight.

This had once been a forge world. The signs were there – massive cogs churning in the biological masses below, the thrum of generators over the reedy, stinking wind, the thousands of lights that burned in the spires. Here and there a balcony was edged with the cog-toothed pattern common to the Adeptus Mechanicus, or even a half-skull symbol almost buried in parasitic growths. Huge pistons pumped through the sides of a massive blocky building, but they looked more like the gills of an enormous sea creature than the workings of an engine. The machinery that had driven a world now resembled the organs of single creature, huge and monstrous, turned inside out and draped around a city of sweating black steel.

The tech-priests and Grey Knights had emerged from the valley onto a large circular platform, perhaps originally a landing pad, which jutted from a huge slab of city-layers that looked like it had been forced up from the prehistoric depths, like a tectonic plate driven up to form a mountain range.

'Throne of Earth,' breathed Brother Lykkos. 'Protect us from this corruption.'

'Pray that He does, brothers,' said Alaric. He turned to Saphentis. 'The truth, archmagos. Have you ever seen anything like this?'

'Never.' Saphentis was as inscrutable as before but Thalassa was looking at the sight in open horror, her hand over her mouth and her eyes wide.

'Did you know what we would find?'

'We knew there was something wrong.' Saphentis's voice was passionless. 'But not like this.'

Alaric looked up. As he had suspected, occult symbols were projected onto the clouds, graven images and writing in forbidden tongues spanning the sky on a truly vast scale. Tiny shapes – grav-platforms maybe, carrying cargo or passengers or patrolling the skies – skimmed just below the cloud layer. The sky was the final heresy, swirled with the colours of festering wounds, purples and greys as diseased as the city itself. This world was so steeped in corruption that even the sky was infected.

The tech-guard were joining the tech-priests and Grey Knights. They were showing little reaction to the horrible sight, just spreading out for the scattering of cover by the opening into the valley cleft. Hawkespur was on her feet by now and she saw the city too. Through the faceplate of her voidsuit's cowl Alaric saw even her eyes widen in shock.

'We're in the open here,' said Alaric. 'We have to get into cover. If they can see us here then they can trap us.'

'Tharkk,' voxed Saphentis. 'We require shelter. Fan your men out to find–'

Something large and wet slammed into the platform with a fleshy thud. A massive stain burst across the surface of the platform, dark and bubbling. 'Down!' yelled Alaric before the surface erupted into scores of spiny limbs, shooting up and out with a sound like thousands of breaking bones.

One of the tech-guard was speared by a spike-tipped tentacle, lifted off his feet and slammed against the jagged metal wall behind him. Las-blasts fired in return, severing thorny tentacles, impacting in bursts of foul greasy steam.

A tentacle snaked around Brother Haulvarn's leg but he hacked it off with his Nemesis sword. The other Grey Knights fell back, along with Saphentis and Thalassa. The tech-guard moved to surround Thalassa but Saphentis could evidently look after himself. Circular saw blades snapped into position on two of his limbs and he slashed around him with little apparent effort, sending twitching fragments of tentacle raining down around him.

'Cardios! Flame it!' ordered Alaric. Brother Cardios stepped past him and blasted a gout of blessed flame into the growing monstrosity, scorching wads of ichor off the metallic surface.

The tech-guard were falling back – one of them had seen there was a way into the neighbouring building, a monolith of sweating black iron that looked chewed and tunnelled as if by giant worms. The Grey Knights followed, cutting around them as the tentacles swarmed to surround them.

A dark, roughly circular shape buzzed into view, held aloft by a trio of flaring grav-engines on its underside. A jagged bone crown sat on top of the platform and Alaric just glimpsed a figure in the centre of it, held in place by dozens of thick ribbed tentacles. Half-machine, half-biological weapons crowded the platform's edge – Alaric guessed that one, a wide-mouthed mortar-like weapon squatting near the centre, had fired the bio-weapon at them. The other weapons opened up, stuttering down a rain of fire. Alaric returned fire, feeling the air around him split apart by the shells flitting past him, trusting in his power armour to keep him alive until he hit cover.

Brother Lykkos's psycannon put two fat holes through the base of the platform and black ichor sprayed out, the platform bucking as if in pain. The figure in the centre fought to keep it under control, working the vehicle's apparently biological brain like an organist at the keyboard. The break in fire let the Grey Knights hurry out of the range of the tentacles and into the rust-pitted hole that led into the neighbouring spire.

It was dark inside. Alaric's augmented vision could easily follow Tharkk's tech-guard as they spread out in the wide tunnel, wary of what they might find but intent on getting away from the attack outside. The place was dark and dank, the curved walls and floor slick with cold blackish liquid.

The gun-platform outside steadied and sent heavy chains of gunfire stammering around the tunnel entrance. Lykkos and Brother Archis returned fire for a few moments before heavy shots began slamming into the metal, hard shells of writhing parasites that burrowed quickly through the iron where they hit the wall.

'Get back!' shouted Alaric as he followed the tech-guard into the tunnel. 'Keep together, we don't know what's in here.' He quickly found Captain Tharkk in the darkness. The tech-guard officer's face was still covered in the opaque rebreather helm, lit a hard-edged green by the screen of the auspex scanner he was consulting.

'Up or down?' asked Tharkk.

Whoever now controlled Chaeroneia now knew where Alaric and the force were. If they went up they would run out of levels quickly – even though the upper levels were probably less likely to be inhabited they would be easier for the enemy to cut off, trapping the force inside. There was no telling what might be in the spire's depths where the black iron met the heaving biological masses below, but there would certainly be more places to hide.

'Down,' said Alaric. 'Grey Knights, to the fore,' he voxed. All Space Marines were trained – created, even – to fight up close and brutal and they excelled in enclosed spaces where their superior strength and weight of firepower counted for the most. If they were to forge their way to safety, the Grey Knights would be the ones to get them there.

There was more noise from outside. The grav-platform had stopped firing but Alaric could hear more, heavier lifters with deeper engines.

Full of reinforcements, maybe. And there was something else – something huge and heavy, travelling up the outside of the building with a sucking, scratching sound that reverberated through the narrow tunnel.

Alaric shouldered his way past the surviving tech-guard and led the way. The tunnels spilt and looped up and down, but the Larraman's ear implant meant Alaric had an excellent sense of balance and direction, picking the course that would take them into the centre of the spire and downwards. Faintly luminescent colonies of fungi clogged some tunnels, others were half-flooded with viscous grey gore. The sound of pumping pistons echoed from down below, the sound of the creaking, shifting iron from all around.

The tunnel opened up ahead. Alaric stopped and waved forward Cardios and Dvorn, who crouched down by the opening where the tunnel led into a much larger cavity in the iron. There was barely any light – while the Grey Knights could see perfectly well, presumably along with Saphentis, he didn't know if the tech-guard would be able to fight in the darkness.

There were too many things he did not know.

The tiny pilot flame on Cardios's Incinerator flickered as a warm, damp wind flooded down the tunnels. Dvorn's hammer was hefted as if he expected an enemy to be standing just past the corner, waiting to be beheaded.

'Large space,' voxed Dvorn. 'We're in an elevated position. Wait – movement.'

Alaric moved forward to crouch behind Dvorn. The tunnel led onto a balcony formed from the biological curves of the chamber beyond, a large cavity that looked like it had been eaten out of the iron. Scores of sub-tunnels led off in every direction and from one of these the figures Dvorn had spotted was emerging.

Menials. Alaric knew that the Adeptus Mechanicus included a massive underclass of menials, men and women bonded to perform the thankless tasks the Mechanicus required – labouring in the forges and mines, serving the needs of the tech-priests, crewing the Mechanicus's ships, even defending the forge worlds. It was from the ranks of the menials that the tech-guard were drawn and many tech-priests had been recruited from the most able.

But the menials he saw for the first time on Chaeroneia were different. Menials might be effectively controlled by the Adeptus Mechanicus but they were still ultimately free. Everything about these creatures told Alaric they were slaves. Bent postures, pallid skin covered in weeping sores, uniform jumpsuits so filthy Alaric couldn't tell what colour they were. Heavy dark blue tattoos disfigured their faces, broad barcode designs that wiped out any semblance of individual personalities. They had glass vials of strange-coloured liquids carried in harnesses around their waists or shoulders, with tubes leading off to the veins in their throats and wrists. A few were armed with battered autoguns and lasguns but if they were supposed to fight at all, most looked like they did it with bare hands and teeth.

There must have been thirty menials driven out of the tunnel into the gallery. Behind them was a figure standing a clear head taller than any of them, wearing long robes stained black. Its head was a nightmare, with a long, grinning equine skull wrapped round with tendrils of dark meat. One of its arms ended in long segmented whips instead of fingers, soldered directly into the blue-grey skin of its hand. As it lashed the menials forward in front of it, it chattered out a stuttering noise of dots and dashes.

'Machine-code,' said Archmagos Saphentis, who was crouching just behind Alaric.

In response to the code, two massive lumbering shapes followed the tech-priest into the gallery. The torso were those of bloated muscle-bound humanoids, the legs huge pneumatic pistons. One of the beasts had twin heavy bolters in place of its arms, while the other had a circular saw blade and a pair of massive shears. They belched hot vapour and sprays of oil as if they were steam-powered – Alaric guessed they were combat-servitors. That would mean they were physically powerful but extremely limited in their responses. In an open conflict they were at a severe disadvantage, unable to improvise like a good soldier had to, but in the close confines of the tunnels they would make for extremely efficient killing devices.

'They're hunting us,' said Dvorn.

The horse-skulled creature, who seemed to be in control, directed its menials to spread out while the two servitors stomped forwards to flank it. It beckoned one menial towards it with its whip hand – the menial in question had knee joints that bent the wrong way so it could move on all fours like a dog and its nose and mouth were gone, replaced by a bunch of knife-like sensor-spines.

The dog-menial listened to a burst of machine-code speak and darted forward, head jerking as it tasted the air, crawling up the walls as it rushed around trying to pick up a scent.

Before Alaric could have his men withdraw the dog-menial stopped, head arrowed right towards where Alaric crouched overlooking the balcony.

'Fall back,' hissed Alaric. 'Everyone back!'

The leader screamed a stream of machine-code, high and piercing. Heavy bolter fire streaked up from the gun-servitor and the menials bayed like animals at the sudden din. Alaric could hear sound from all around as the spire's inhabitants were alerted to the intruders in their midst – scrabbling, crawling, slithering, bestial howling and more bursts of machine-code.

Alaric found Saphentis as the force moved back through the tunnels. 'Are they Mechanicus?'

'Not any more,' said Saphentis simply.

Gunfire flared up ahead. In the flashes of the las-blasts Alaric could see tech-guard swapping fire with pallid, scrabbling menials. Brother Haulvarn returned fire and storm bolter shells tore down the tunnel, blasting a menial against the wall as Lykkos blew another one apart with a psycannon shot. But there wasn't enough space for the rest of the Grey Knights to get to grips with the enemy.

A hideous grinding sound tore up from below Alaric's feet. He dived to one side as the floor of the tunnel erupted in a storm of flying iron shards and something immense chewed its way through – a circular head like the mouth of a voracious metallic worm, ringed with grinders that ripped out lumps of metal and forced them into the bladed steel spiral of its throat. It roared as Alaric just swung his trailing leg away from its maw and Alaric felt his psychic wards flaming beneath his armour, describing a white-hot spiral around his skin.

The more powerful ward, the one woven around his mind, filled his head with a red scream as something very powerful and very angry expressed its psychic rage.

Witchcraft. The reason they were here.

The worm reared and Alaric realised it was mechanical, steam belching from its segmented body, whirling guts of clockwork deep inside its churning form. Alaric fired a spray of storm bolter fire down its throat and the worm spasmed in pain, vomiting acidic gore and broken cogs.

'Move!' yelled Alaric as he fired again but the monster surged forwards. Alaric paused only to grab Tech-Priest Thalassa and haul her clear as he dived into a side tunnel. The worm roared past and Alaric saw how thick greying muscles wrapped around its body until its tail was a long lash of biological sinew, whipping behind it.

'Witchcraft,' said Alaric. 'That thing was made with sorcery.' He flicked on the vox-channel. 'Grey Knights! Fall back!'

Alaric darted out of the side tunnel and lunged with his Nemesis halberd, hacking off a good length of the worm's tail. Gore sprayed from the wound as it lashed in pain and the thing's scream was truly terrible, vibrating through the iron like an earthquake. The worm's body contorted and its pain spasms forced it off course, chewing its way up through the ceiling of the tunnel.

'We've got hostiles up ahead!' came Brother Archis's voice, crackling over the vox. 'Heavy resistance! They're bottling us in!'

'Then fight!' replied Alaric, hauling Thalassa after him as he headed towards the sound of gunfire. Thalassa's eyes were wide in horror and her breathing was shallow – she was in shock. Data expert or no, Saphentis should never have brought her.

Alaric saw, up ahead, the Grey Knights and tech-guard fighting against the menials trying to force their way in through the side tunnels. Saphentis was in the thick of the fighting, his more normal bionic hands dragging enemies out of the throng while his blade-tipped arms cut them apart. One menial dived out onto a tech-guard and the vials at his waist emptied themselves into his veins. The menial's muscles swelled massively, bone cracking where the muscles on his arms and back pulled his spine apart. The menial roared and ripped off the tech-guard's arm, then pistoned a fist into his face with enough force to leave a dent in the tunnel floor.

Interrogator Hawkespur took aim and snapped an autopistol shot through the menial's head. It didn't drop and she loosed off several more, the shots slicing its head apart until it toppled onto the dying body of the tech-guard.

The Grey Knights were holding the front of the tunnel, storm bolters and Nemesis weapons keeping the way forward choked with bodies. A chain of heavy fire strobed down the tunnel and the Grey Knights took cover, using the menial bodies as a barricade. A couple of shots thudded off Alaric's power armour.

Alaric could hear noise from all around. Heavy battle-servitors stomped towards them. Something cackled a stream of zeroes and ones. They were completely surrounded.

Justicar Tancred and his Terminator squad could have pooled their psychic power and called up the cleansing fire the Chapter's Chaplains called the Holocaust. They could have forced their way through with their massive terminator armour and Tancred's own sheer strength. But Tancred and his squad were dead, annihilated so completely Alaric hadn't even been able to recover their bodies from Volcanis Ultor. Alaric's squad was on its own here, surrounded and exposed.

The wall near Alaric was being chewed away by breacher drills, screeching and showering sparks into the tunnel. A battle-servitor the size of a tank was lumbering into view at the far end of the tunnel, storm bolter fire ricocheting off it as it blasted at the Grey Knights. They had nowhere to go and a dozen ways to die.

'To me!' yelled Alaric. His squad broke cover and headed for Alaric, leaving the tech-guard to deal with the rampaging servitors. They ducked the chains of fire and reached Alaric just as the wall gave way, chunks of crumbling iron collapsing in a drift of metal.

Menials, crudely combat-fitted with drills and saws, clambered through the gap. Alaric met the first with the butt of his halberd, shattering its ribs even as he blocked a huge circular saw with the halberd's blade. The first menial reared up again, its ribcage collapsed and oozing gore. Nothing human could have gone on fighting. A breacher drill bored up into the collar of his armour, forcing him back as the tip ground through the ceramite in a shower of sparks, aiming for his throat.

'Perdition!' yelled Brother Dvorn as he smacked the drill-armed menial across the tunnel with his Nemesis hammer. 'Blasphemy!'

They were blasphemous, too. Muscles and nerve bundles slid over the menials' metallic parts in a way that Alaric had never seen in Mechanicus bionics, as if there was something else inside the menials, something independent and alive. That was blasphemy if ever he had seen it. Alaric reached up and grabbed the armature on which the second menial's saw was mounted, pulling and twisting. Tendrils of flesh wrapped around his wrist but the arm came away, the menial screaming bestially. Warm, foul-smelling blood spattered over Alaric. He hacked down into its body with his halberd and it died.

Brother Haulvarn spitted two menials at once on his sword and Dvorn struck again, his hammer's head smashing right through one menial and embedding itself in the nearest wall. Dvorn didn't miss a beat, filling another menial with storm bolter fire as he ripped the hammer head out again. Alaric looked around to see where Thalassa had got to – she was on the floor curled up, with her hands over her head. It was surprising she was still alive.

'Archis!' yelled Alaric but he needn't have bothered – Brother Archis was already ramming the nozzle of his Incinerator through the hole, pulling the firing lever and drenching the space beyond with burning promethium.

Alaric glanced through the hole. The menials had fallen back in confusion – Alaric guessed they were so corrupt they could understand a simple order to kill anything beyond the wall and now they had done so they needed someone to direct them to do anything more. The space beyond looked like a heavy engineering plant, with enormous pistons pumping into an oil-belching engine block.

'Fall back to me!' yelled Alaric over the din of gunfire. 'Saphentis! Tharkk! Back to me!'

The tech-guard broke from their own firefights and hurried towards the Grey Knights, who covered them with a spray of rapid storm bolter fire. Alaric led the way through onto the factory floor. The air was heavy and hot with steam and the machinery that surrounded them was on a huge scale, with massive hinged sections clanking as the masses of engineering reconfigured themselves.

There didn't seem an obvious way out. As the tech-guard got through the hole and reorganised themselves to cover it, Alaric waved over Interrogator Hawkespur.

'It's a dead end,' he said. 'We won't have time to find another way out.'

'What do you suggest?'

'Fight here. Hope they run out of troops.'

'Agreed. If they're only menials we can take on several waves of them. More battle-servitors and our chances will not be high, though.'

Las-fire from somewhere above interrupted them, spattering against the filthy metal floor. The tech-guard scattered, Tharkk yelling at them to take cover and return fire. The Grey Knights fired back instinctively, spraying shots up into the darkness overhead, then followed the tech-guard. Several slabs of machinery rose to shoulder height, like the teeth of a tank trap and behind them was an imposing bank of machinery that belched hot, choking fumes.

'Save it!' shouted Alaric and the Grey Knights stopped firing, getting into cover and peering into the darkness. Their ocular augmentations would help them see the threat before anyone else. Archmagos Saphentis drifted serenely back towards them, too, seemingly unconcerned about getting shot. Alaric had not imagined Saphentis would be a fighting man but now he was covered in blood and his blade-tipped arms were clogged with gore.

A shape drifted down overhead. It was like the gun-platform that had ambushed them outside but this one was more ornate and large enough to carry three figures, two of them far larger and flanking the third. A glistening corona surrounded the platform. Alaric guessed it was an energy field, which meant that most bullets would probably bounce off it. Lykkos's psycannon would be their best bet but it would have to be a damn good shot. The field was probably being generated by the pulsing, brain-like mass on the platform's underside. The platform extruded several biological looking guns, which trained themselves on the chunks of machinery that hid the Grey Knights and tech-guard.

The two larger figures were battle-servitors, bristling with guns. The third was the horse-skulled creature Alaric had seen earlier, now connected to both the platform and the servitors by a web of vein-like filaments running from his back. More smaller platforms were drifting down beside it. Some were simple gun platforms, others held parties of menials or what looked like more regular troops, hooded and crouched, with guns hardwired into their forearms. Maybe a hundred troops and those were only the ones Alaric could see.

The leader raised its arms, palms up, elongated face pointed upwards. It brayed a long, atonal sound and the guns on the platforms dipped slightly.

'It's a tech-priest,' whispered Brother Haulvarn, crouching down at Alaric's side. 'It's one of them.'

If it was a tech-priest, it was corrupted down to the core. It emitted a stream of dots and dashes, more machine-code, apparently directed at the tech-guard.

Archmagos Saphentis peered out of cover and replied, reeling off his own stream of machine-code.

The two exchanged machine-code a couple more times. Then the enemy tech-priest brayed and the guns were again trained on Alaric's force. The platforms began to descend, the menials and troops making ready to jump down onto the factory floor and attack.

'Whatever you said,' growled Alaric at Saphentis, 'it didn't work.'

The first shots fell, glowing black bolts of energy as powerful as lascannon shots shearing through the metal. One tech-guard was blown clean in half and the others hit the floor, the cover disintegrating around them.

With a massive grinding sound, the bank of machinery behind them began to open up. Hinged plates of corroded iron the size of tanks were reconfiguring to reveal a black and forbidding space beyond.

'Hawkespur!' shouted Alaric. 'We can't take them!'

'We don't know where it leads!' she replied, taking aim at the lowest platform. She loosed off a shot and a menial fell, knocked off the platform by a perfect hit. More fire was falling against them, tearing deep gouges in the floor, sending superheated shrapnel through the air.

'Move or die!' replied Alaric. 'Grey Knights! Tharkk! Covering volley, then retreat!'

The lowest platform was already disgorging its troops. Crimson and black bolts of energy were raining down now, scoring molten red scars everywhere. Another tech-guard fell, blown open by chattering automatic fire as his fellow soldiers withdrew through the storm of fire.

Alaric ran through the opening, turning to make sure Hawkespur made it. Brother Dvorn grabbed Tech-priest Thalassa as he ran, carrying her with one hand while he fired all but blind over his shoulder with the other. The inside of the machinery was tight and infernally hot, lit by a ruddy glow from furnaces deep within the machine. The machinery ground around them and the opening shrunk, fire thudding around the entrance. Saphentis was the last in, his robes flapping around him as gunfire punched through the fabric.

'Where now?' asked Hawkespur.

'Anywhere,' said Alaric.

The floor was sinking below and slabs of machinery closing over them. Alaric imagined them being crushed as the machinery closed, the ceramite fracturing, his bones splintering, dying in the furnace at the heart of the black iron spire.

'Close in!' barked Captain Tharkk. 'Form up around the archmagos! Fix bayonets!'

Something rumbled far ahead, massive and closing fast. The ceiling opened up above them again, this time in a spiral that bored rapidly straight upwards and the sound got louder. The floor began to open too, and the dull red glow subsided leaving only blackness.

Alaric could just see the troops around him clinging to anything they could find as the space became a sheer shaft, heading straight down into the lower levels of the spire.

The glimmer he saw above was a rush of foaming fluid pouring down towards them. Alaric hadn't seen much of Chaeroneia but it was enough to tell him it probably wasn't just water.

The flood hit and Alaric held on, the weight of industrial waste dragging him down. He gritted his teeth and held on but the metal beneath his gauntlet was giving way. With a yell of defiance he fell, sluiced downwards. He was battered against the sides of the shaft and the armoured bodies of his fellow Grey Knights. He had no control any more and whether he lived or died now was down to where the flow went and whether he could break the surface before he drowned. Everything was noise and motion, deafening, blinding, one hand gripping the haft of his Nemesis halberd and the other reaching out for a handhold.

He found none. The blackness rushed up around him and he willed himself to survive as everything, outside and inside him, went black.

SEVEN

'He that counselleth as does the Enemy, so shall he becometh that enemy, no matter that a friend he claimeth to be.'

– 'On Heresy', Chapter MMIV,
Lord Inquisitor Karamazov

'SHOW ME AGAIN.'

Horstgeld had not been in the tactical chancel for some time, ever since the *Tribunicia* had last been at war. Most of the intervening time the ship had run patrols or formed blockades and there had been no need for the complex holographic displays that could be projected into the centre of the circular room. The chancel was decorated with tasteful marble busts of past captains and Naval heroes and could hold several officers, but now it held just Rear Admiral Horstgeld and Chief Navigation Officer Stelkhanov.

Stelkanov pressed a sequence of control studs at the base of the central holomat and the grainy holo image appeared again – the equipment was old and should have been replaced decades ago.

'I grant it's not an excellent quality image,' said Stelkhanov, 'but it was enough to work with.' Stelkhanov's voice was slightly stilted thanks to the fact that he had been sleep-taught Imperial Gothic late in life, having been recruited from the engine-rooms where the press-ganged scum could barely speak Low Gothic at all.

Horstgeld watched the image roll by again. It was from a deep-space scan, picked up by the ship's sensoria in the ultra-orbital space beyond Chaeroneia. The swathe of space rippled, bulging and contracting in a dozen places, before flares of hazy energy indicated that something had broken through. Then, just as fleetingly, the images were gone.

'When was this picked up?' asked Horstgeld.

Stelkhanov consulted the dataslate he carried. The greenish glow of the holo picked out his refined, aquiline face – it was hard to believe the man had once been dragged out of the short-lived engine gangs. 'Seventy-nine minutes ago,' he said.

'And what do you think it is?'

'A fleet, captain. Newly arrived from the warp.'

'Quite an audacious conclusion, Stelkhanov. We haven't got any fellow hunters in this subsector, let alone this close into system space.'

'Then it is not Imperial.'

'Hmm.' Horstgeld stood back, running a hand unconsciously down his beard. 'Anything else?'

'It is substantial. And what little data we have suggests it is moving quite slowly, as would befit a large fleet remaining in formation. It is tempting, sir, to connect this with the anomalous signal detected by the *Ptolemy Gamma*.'

'I need more information before I decide, Stelkhanov. Have Navigation and the sensorium crew make this your second priority. First is still contacting Hawkespur and Alaric on the surface. We don't even know if they're alive.'

'Yes, sir. What preparations should the fleet make in case this is a hostile force?'

Horstgeld hadn't anticipated fighting a space battle here at all. Inquisitor Nyxos had been unable to acquire a fleet that was up to a major battle in any case. 'Reinforcements. Locate everything Imperial in space that's bigger than an orbital yacht and that can get to us within ninety-six hours. Prepare to send a fleet service order if we have to. If we're going to have a stand-off, then I want the numbers to do it. Understood?'

'Understood, sir. And Magos Korveylan?'

'She doesn't need to know just yet.'

'She?'

'Until I learn better, yes, 'she'. And make sure Commissar Leung knows, too, in case the *Exemplar* has seen the fleet already. I don't trust those freaks not to up and run at the first sign of getting their paintwork scratched.'

'Of course, sir.' Stelkhanov turned smartly and left the room.

Hortsgeld ran the image through again. Maybe ships, maybe some stellar phenomenon, maybe a shoal of rogue kraken or just yet another sensorium glitch. But if it was another fleet, it was definitely something he didn't need.

* * *

THE RAIN WAS toxic. It fell in thick, viscous globules, smacking down against the colossal wreckage and forming corrosive rivers of slime that wound through valleys formed by fallen spires. It stripped away dead flesh, so the enormous biological masses were reduced to forests of bleached ribs or banks of ragged gristle.

The rain probably wasn't rain at all but industrial and biological waste from above, maybe even the same flood that had poured down through the body of the black iron spire a couple of hours before. It fell down into a vast chasm, a wreckage-choked gap between the foundations of two spires, lit by sickly bioluminescence from algae colonies that clung to the pitted metal several storeys up. This was a place far, far below the city of spires, an undercity where anything that survived the fall did not live for very long. It was picked clean of life by time and corrosion, cold and dank and everywhere there was the chemical smell of death. The biomechanical masses that powered the city groaned and shifted far above and below there was the deep, sonorous sound of the rock beneath the city gradually giving way as it was compacted beneath the great weight of the iron spires.

Beneath a huge width of discarded engine cowling, there was shelter from the acid rain. The rain wouldn't have done anything more than strip some of the paint off the Grey Knights' armour, but Alaric knew that to the surviving tech-guard, Tech-priest Thalassa and Interrogator Hawkespur, it could have been lethal. So they had taken shelter here.

Somehow, they were still alive. The flood of waste had thrown them down through successive layers of the spire. The lower levels were industrial and Alaric had been sure, from the glimpses he caught of the massive machinery surrounding them, that they would be crushed or boiled at any moment. But sluice gates and purge valves had opened in front of them and they had kept going, finally being spat out into a large pool of festering waste a short distance away.

Chaeroneia hadn't wanted them dead, not yet, not like that. It wanted to make them suffer, first.

'Haulvarn, Archis, take watch,' said Alaric. The two Grey Knights saluted and went to take the first watch. The force couldn't stay there for long, but they needed a while to regroup and form a plan. They couldn't just blunder about hoping they would find something, otherwise they would be spotted and hunted down, and next time the planet wouldn't give them a stay of execution.

Hawkespur and the remaining tech-guard had started a small fire to keep themselves warm. There were only four of them left – Captain Tharkk and three tech-guard regulars. Their armour was battered and their fatigues were black with filth. As Alaric watched one of the tech-guard took his helmet off. His head was shaved and there were large, deep surgical scars in the back of his skull, where it looked like plate-sized sections had been removed and replaced. There was a barcode on the back of the man's neck.

Alaric walked over to where Archmagos Saphentis was sitting on a chunk of fallen wreckage, discussing something with Tech-priest Thalassa.

'Your tech-guard,' said Alaric. 'Emotional repressive surgery.'

Saphentis looked up at him. Alaric saw his face reflected a hundred times in the multi-faceted eyes. 'Quite right. I require it of the men performing retinue duties.'

'It would have been useful to know. Just like it would have been useful to know that your augmentations made you so combat-capable. And I would know what you said to that tech-priest.'

'He did not appreciate our presence,' replied Saphentis simply. 'I suggested he surrender to us and he did not accept it.'

Saphentis's artificial voice made it impossible for Alaric to tell if he was telling the truth or being sarcastic. 'I am in command here, archmagos,' said Alaric. 'Were you a Grey Knight you would do long months of penance for your reluctance to be led.'

'But I am not, justicar. And perhaps it would be better to discuss where we are and what we might do, rather than argue the point.'

'Do you know where we are?'

Tech-priest Thalassa, who had been viewing this exchange with some trepidation, showed Alaric the screen of her dataslate. 'The Mechanicus had detailed information on Chaeroneia before it was lost. The planet has changed much but from what little information we have it is most likely that we are here.' The screen of the dataslate showed a complex blueprint of a massive city, as dense as a hive on a heavily populated world, set among the blasted desert wastes that had covered much of Chaeroneia. The blueprint was labelled 'Primus Manufactorium Noctis'.

'Noctis was one of the largest forge cities on the planet,' continued Thalassa. Alaric noticed that her voice was wavering slightly, her eyes were ringed with red and her breathing was slightly ragged. It was easy to forget how frail normal humans were compared to a Space Marine like Alaric – she had ingested and inhaled enough pollutants to kill her given time. 'It was mostly dedicated to heavy manufacturing but it had some research and data facilities. Like this.'

The blueprint swung around and zoomed in on one structure, a large, smooth tower like a stack of massive cylinders, rising from the industrial tangle. 'The manufactorium's datafortress,' explained Thalassa. 'For the secure containment of information.'

'If it is still there,' said Saphentis, 'it could tell us what we need to know about where Chaeroneia has been and what has happened to it.'

'And you suggest we should go there?'

'No other course of action readily presents itself.'

'How far?'

'Not very far,' said Thalassa. 'Perhaps three days' march if there are no major obstacles. That is, if the datafortress is there at all and I am correct about our current location.'

'Could you make it?' asked Alaric.

Thalassa looked at the floor. 'I don't know.'

'Tech-priest Thalassa would be useful at the datafortress but not essential,' said Saphentis. 'I can perform similar functions.'

'I don't like it. There is too much about what lies ahead of us that we do not know. Nothing has killed more men on the battlefield than ignorance about what they are facing.'

'I do not see any other choice, justicar.'

'Neither do I. But I would be more prepared if I knew everything about the enemy here that you do. There is a reason you came down to this planet yourself. There are a great many tech-preists who are more capable in battle than you.'

'Thalassa,' said Saphentis, 'tell Captain Tharkk we will move out shortly.' Thalassa nodded and hurried over to the fire where Tharkk and his men were tending their wounds. For the moment, Alaric and Saphentis were out of their earshot.

'Go on,' said Alaric.

'They were Mechanicus,' began Saphentis. 'After a fashion. They have changed. Some tech-heresy has taken root. The fusion of the biological and the mechanical is permitted by the Cult Mechanicus only so that weak flesh may be replaced or improved, or that the otherwise useless might be made useful in the sight of the Omnissiah, such as is the case with servitors. The large-scale biomechanics we see here are forbidden, for they do not place machine and flesh at the command of tech-priests but create new forms of life entirely and such is not permitted by the tenets of the Priesthood of Mars. Successive Fabricators General have pronounced on this countless times.'

'So the enemy are tech-heretics?' asked Alaric. 'The same that were investigated here a hundred years ago?'

'Without doubt. And the heresy must reach to every level of Chaeroneia's priesthood. More importantly, what we have seen on

Chaeroneia represents a pace of innovation considered heretical. The Cult Mechanicus forbids designs and techniques not of the most ancient provenance. Many centuries must pass before quarantined knowledge is allowed beyond our research stations. But here there is innovation and creation. All around us! This world could never be created by the existing tenets of the Mechanicus. The pace of invention here must be astonishing.'

'You sound as if you admire them, archmagos.'

'That is not true, justicar. Heresy is heresy, as you yourself must know well. I would thank you not to make such suggestions again.'

'An ally who agrees with the enemy becomes that enemy, archmagos. I will be watching you.'

Brother Haulvarn stomped over hurriedly. 'Archis can see gun-platforms, justicar. They're moving like they're looking for us.'

Alaric looked round at him. The strike force was still in poor cover and vulnerable and they didn't need a fight right now. 'How far?'

'Two kilometres. Five plus platforms, at least two troop carriers. Sweep formation. They're about five hundred metres up, too.'

'Then they'll be on us soon. We need to move out.'

'We would be better hidden if we kept to derelict sections of the city,' said Saphentis. 'This planet will have fewer eyes on us.'

'That at least I agree on,' said Alaric. 'I'll work out a route with Thalassa. Get your tech-guard ready to move in five minutes. And in case there is any confusion left, you are under my command. As long as we are on this planet, you follow my orders.'

'Understood, justicar.'

'You don't have to understand. You just have to do it.'

The tech-guard were soon up and armed, their emotional repressive surgery meaning that they would not be affected by the trauma of the fight they had just gone through. Hawkespur was looking closer to exhaustion than she would ever admit and Thalassa was still half-numb with shock, moving like a woman in a dream. But they weren't the ones Alaric was worried about. The Grey Knights had taught him a great deal and the Chapter believed that one day they could call him a leader – but one lesson he had not learned was how to deal with an enemy that was supposed to be under your own command.

Alaric glanced at the shadows stretching above and saw tiny points of light darting about, the grav-platforms Archis's keen eyes had spotted. Chaeroneia had a lot of ways to kill intruders and Alaric knew they would discover a few more before they reached Thalassa's datafortress. But they had to go there because the datafortress meant information and once Alaric understood what he was up against on this world then he could finally turn around and fight it.

ONCE, WHEN THE Imperium was young and the Emperor was still a living being walking among His subjects, there had been hope. But that had been a long time ago indeed.

That hope had existed in the form of the Emperor's own creations – the primarchs, perfect humans each representing a facet of the strength mankind would need to fulfil its manifest destiny of possessing the galaxy. They had been such astonishing beings that even on the eve of their creation, their genetic material was being used to create a generation of superhuman warriors – the Space Marines of the First Founding, twenty immense Legions of them, made in the image of the primarch on which they had been modelled.

The primarchs were scattered across the galaxy. In the Age of Imperium no one knew how or why this had happened – whether agents of Chaos had snatched them away from holy Terra, or whether the Emperor had sent them forth as infants to be strewn around the galaxy and there learn the qualities they could never acquire living in the Emperor's shadow.

The Emperor, at the head of the Space Marine Legions, conquered the galaxy, gradually retrieving the scattered primarchs, who had grown into mighty leaders on their adopted worlds. In the Great Crusade the primarchs were reunited with their Legions and led them in the greatest military campaign mankind had ever seen, conquering the segmenta of space that would eventually form the backbone of Imperial territory, from the Segmentum Solar to the outlying Halo Zone and Veiled Region.

And the greatest of these primarchs was Horus.

Horus was the primarch of the Luna Wolves, the Legion that represented the most complete military machine in the Imperium. Resolute, valiant and commanded by Horus with a brilliance that rivalled the Emperor Himself, the Legion was such a finely-honed force that it was said that Horus wielded it with the precision of a master swordsman. There was nothing they could not do. When the Emperor acknowledged Horus as the Imperium's greatest warmaster the Luna Wolves became the Sons of Horus, their new designation reflecting the masterful command of their primarch.

But Horus was too brilliant. His star shone too brightly. As the Crusade reeled in more and more of the galaxy he came to see the arrogance and tyranny of the Emperor. The Emperor did not do what He did for mankind – He did it for Himself, to know that the human race lived and died under His dominion. Ultimate power had corrupted Him and no one, not even Horus the Magnificent, the Warmaster himself, could sway His belief that He was the master of mankind.

This was where the seeds of the Heresy were born. Horus, the greatest man who ever lived, came to surpass the Emperor and to understand as the Emperor never could that the true destiny of mankind lay beyond the stars, in the untamed, pure realm of the warp, where the only entities deserving of worship resided. They were the Chaos Gods, the beings who wished to see mankind elevated from corruptible, heavy flesh to pure, enlightened spirits. But the Emperor was filled with hate that Horus should pay fealty to anyone greater than the Emperor Himself. So Horus was forced to entreat the powers of the warp for aid and so became the first and greatest Champion of Chaos.

The Horus Heresy divided the galaxy. In a mere seven years of war Horus led a rebellion that reached Holy Terra and the walls of the Imperial Palace, marching with fully half of the Space Marine Legions whose primarchs he had convinced of the justice of their cause. The rest sided with the Emperor, cowed into obedience by their fear of the knowledge Horus promised to teach the galaxy.

Among the greatest of the Sons of Horus was Abaddon, Horus's right hand in battle, a force of destruction who blazed his way across the galaxy at the behest of his primarch, submitting his own life to the wishes of the Warmaster. Abaddon witnessed the final tragedy of the Heresy, when the Emperor and the Primarch Sanguinius ambushed Horus on his flagship. Horus slew them both but not before he was dealt a terrible wound by the Emperor's sword and with his last breath, entreated Abaddon to keep the Sons of Horus alive and not sacrifice them needlessly on the walls of Terra.

So Abaddon took the Legion and withdrew, masterfully evading the vengeful Legions of the Emperor and taking refuge among the daemon worlds of the Eye of Terror. With Horus dead, the surviving primarchs still loyal to the Emperor conspired to cheat the people of the Imperium into believing the Emperor was still alive, now a living god inhabiting his corpse.

The Sons of Horus renamed themselves the Black Legion in eternal mourning for the greatest man who had ever lived, the man who should have inherited the Imperium and led mankind to an era of enlightenment in the warp. Meanwhile, the Imperium sank beyond redemption, corrupt and worthless, its people slaving to uphold the worship of a traitor long dead, its institutions dedicated only to eradicating truth from the galaxy. There could be no redemption for it now.

Abaddon probed the defences of the Imperium. In twelve Black Crusades he found the gaps in the Imperium's armour through which the Black Legion and its allies could finally deliver the Imperium's death-blow. When the board was set and the pieces in place, Abaddon selected the finest of the Black Legion's heroes to lead their own armies in a grand, all-conquering campaign that would see the inheritors of the Imperium streaming from the Eye of Terror. The campaign would culminate in the destruction of Terra and the end of ten thousand years of resistance to Chaos.

Those chosen were the best of the best, leaders and warriors without peer, whose names would soon strike fear into anyone who had ever sworn fealty to the Corpse-Emperor. Among their number was Urkrathos, Chosen of Abaddon, Master of the *Hellforger*.

URKRATHOS STAMPED ONTO the bridge that led to the ritual chamber of the Grand Cruiser *Hellforger*. Above him was the chamber's ceiling like a distant black metal sky, hidden by clouds of sulphurous incense that rained a thin drizzle of black blood. Ghosts ran through the billowing clouds, spirits trapped by the sheer malice and power of the *Hellforger* and condemned to writhe around the ship's decks. Below was a churning sea of gore, swirling like a whirlpool, through which naked figures fought to reach the surface and were always dragged back down, punished for their insolence or failure with a permanent state of agony, always on the verge of drowning, never reaching the release of death. Their thin, pathetic screams wove together into a dark howling wind that blew across the bridge.

Suspended over the sea of sinners was a huge circular platform, with raised edges like the seats of an amphitheatre. This was the ritual ground, a place infused with unholy energy by the torment of those being punished below. It was covered in bloodstained sand into which complex designs had been drawn in dried blood and lengths of offal, the ritual carcasses discarded in a pile to one side. The sacrifices had been specially bred on a daemon world deep within the Eye of Terror, each one worth a lifetime's fealty to the Dark Gods. More incense billowed from burners made from the skulls of the *Hellforger's* less useful crewmen and more heads hung from spiked chains from the distant ceiling, weeping black rain onto the sacred ground.

'Feogrym!' called Urkrathos, reaching the ritual floor. Feogrym was a wizened, hunched figure sitting in the middle of the arena. He looked up as Urkrathos approached and slunk forward, crawling towards the *Hellforger's* captain. 'I need to know now. We have entered real space and it will not be long before we reach the world. Is it genuine?'

Feogrym scampered forwards on his hands, dragging his legs behind him until he was almost prostrate at Urkrathos's feet. 'Feogrym knows!' he spluttered. The sorcerer's face could have been mistaken for that of an extremely wrinkled, wizened old man from a distance. Up close it was clear it was actually a mass of tiny writhing tentacles that only formed human-like features out of a force of habit. 'Master, the Fell Gods speak, they speak... yes, they talk to Feogrym, tell him the truth, yes they do and old Feogrym can tell the truth from the lies...'

Urkrathos kicked Feogrym away from him, the boot of his power armour crunching through ribs Feogrym could heal easily enough. 'Don't try that nonsense with me, sorcerer,' he said impatiently. 'Abaddon warned me about you. You're no holy moron, you'd stab us all in the back the second you saw the chance. Take it from me you won't get that chance. Now, once again, sorcerer, is the signal real? I will not have this fleet wasting its time chasing echoes around the warp.'

Feogrym clambered to his feet and dusted the blood-caked sand off his tattered brown robes. 'Yes, the signs have been conclusive,' he said, rather more sanely. He looked nervously up at Urkrathos, who was twice the height of a normal man in his full Terminator armour. 'Lord Tzeentch speaks with me.'

'His daemons speak with you, old man and for every truth a daemon tells nine lies. You had better be right.'

'Of course. Have I not witnesses?' Feogrym pointed to the far side of the room and Urkrathos saw, through the billowing incense, the hundreds of desiccated corpses sitting in ranks around the amphitheatre like an audience. Urkrathos wondered for a moment where Feogrym had got them all and then realised he couldn't have cared less as long as the sorcerer discharged his duties to the Warmaster as he had agreed.

'So. What do you know?

'Listen.'

Feogrym spoke a few words, dark sounds that didn't belong to any register a human was supposed to hear. Urkrathos scowled as he recognised the dark tongue used by worshippers of Tzeentch, the Change God. Feogrym was one of those degenerates who worshipped one Chaos god over all the others, not realising that they were all part of the same many-faceted force that men called Chaos.

The blood rose in flakes off the floor, the flakes liquefying and running together like floating pools of quicksilver. The pools quivered and hundreds of crude, shifting faces were hanging in the air, their mouths working dumbly.

'Bridge,' commanded Urkrathos through the ship's vox-net. The vox-net whispered back at him as it transmitted his voice to the bridge crew. 'Play back the signal.'

The signal burst in a barrage of sound from the sky, bellowing through the ship's vox-casters. The blood faces began gibbering wildly, flowing into one another in agitation.

'Focus!' snapped Feogrym. 'Truth from the lies! The Changer of Ways commands you!'

The volume of the signal dropped and Urkrathos could make out the individual sounds, dots and dashes like some primitive code, wrought into a complex rhythm which he could tell had old, old magic pulsing at its centre.

The faces murmured a low babble of sounds, until words began forming in their speech, the words that formed the true message hidden so deep in the signal that only Feogrym's black magic could get to it.

'By the Fell Gods and the destiny of warp,' they began, 'By the death of the False Emperor and the dying of the stars, we bring to you, War-master Abaddon, Beloved of Chaos, Despised of Man, this tribute. For now these last days are the final fires burning, the black flames that consume a galaxy, the storms of the warp that drown out life, the End Times and the dawn of a galaxy of Chaos. We swear fealty to the Gods of Chaos and their herald, Abaddon the Despoiler, with this tribute that it might strike fear into the followers of the Corpse-Emperor and that through it they may see the true face of death...'

'Enough,' said Urkrathos. Feogrym waved a hand and the voices screamed silently as they dissolved into gobbets of blood that flowed up into the incense clouds. 'This is genuine?'

'Daemon-wrought,' said Feogrym. 'Most ancient. Yes, it is real.'

'Abaddon suspected rightly, then. It is an offer of tribute. Does it tell us what they are offering?'

Feogrym spread his hands. His tentacles writhed and for a moment Urkrathos saw the pulpy, grey mass that made up the sorcerer's real face. 'Would that I knew, Lord Urkrathos. Perhaps the exact tribute is so great they wish for you to know of it for the first time through your own eyes, magnificent as you are.'

'I warned you, Feogrym. I am less easily flattered than your acolytes.'

'Of course. Nevertheless, if they are new to our cause they may wish to impress us with their offering by not revealing it until we are there.'

'I have been around for ten thousand years. It will take a great deal to impress me.'

'And is it your intention, Lord Urkrathos, to give them the chance?'

Urkrathos glared at the sorcerer. The ways of Tzeentch, Changer of Ways, were by definition impossible to divine. Warp only knew what went on in the creature's head. Urkrathos didn't care. As long as he could serve Abaddon and the greater reign of Chaos then he would accept whatever the gods threw in his way.

He would still kill Feogrym, though, when the time came. A chosen of Abaddon was not to be mocked with impunity.

'I will keep my own counsel on that matter, sorcerer,' he said.

'So you will, then?'

Urkrathos scowled. Even without the enhanced strength of his terminator armour he could have pulled the sorcerer apart like a bored child might pull apart a fly. But he also knew that Feogrym was the type of creature that would not die just because you killed him. He would have to find some other way of destroying the man when he had outlived his usefulness.

Urkrathos turned and stomped off the ritual floor, leaving the madman to his divinations. Perhaps he would strip the soul from the sorcerer's body and cast it down into the pool of torments below them, so he would serve to fuel the spells of whatever sorcerer was sent by Abaddon as a replacement. The gods would be pleased by that.

But for now, Urkrathos had what he had come for. The Black Legion's fleet at the Eye of Terror had picked up the signal and Urkrathos had confirmed it was real. Now all that remained was to reach the planet and collect whatever was due to the Warmaster and perhaps bring the signal's author into the war effort. The Imperium was resisting with the tenacity of a hive of insects and the Black Crusade needed all the bodies it could throw into the fire. Urkrathos would be greatly rewarded if he could bring new allies in on the side of the Fell Gods.

Urkrathos reached the far end of the bridge and the deck elevator at the end, a shuddering, stained cage of steel that reeled up and down the throat-like shaft to give Urkrathos access to all levels of his ship. For now he was heading to the command deck, where he would give orders for the last stage of the journey to Chaeroneia.

EIGHT

'Beware in all things, lest the path forwards be the same path leading to hell.'
– Primarch Roboute Guilliman, Codex Astartes

ALARIC LED THE way with Archis at his side, the pilot light on the Grey Knight's Incinerator always lit, ready to douse anything they encountered with flame.

They were leading the strikeforce up a narrow, treacherous path formed from a huge serpentine skeleton. The skeleton was wrapped around a thin, endlessly tall spire of smooth black glass, its ribs forming the precarious steps of a spiral staircase.

Alaric glanced down. He couldn't see the floor of the city's underhive now, only a layer of pollutants trapped between the cold air below and the warmth pulsing off some mass of flesh living in the tower opposite. The snake's body was getting narrower towards the skull and Hawkespur and Thalassa were both roped to members of Alaric's squad. The Grey Knights might have been far larger and heavier but, paradoxically, their augmentations and training also made them far more dextrous.

'Entrance up above,' said Archis. 'See it?' The nozzle of his Incinerator was pointed at an opening just ahead, a large hole smashed in the black glass. The edges still looked sharp.

'We're going in,' said Alaric. 'Haulvarn, watch the rear. Everyone else follow us.'

They had been travelling along the hive floor for some time, always keeping in cover as best they could. Several times Alaric had been sure there were grav-platform patrols homing in on them, but each time the

Mechanicus had lost the strikeforce in the wreckage and gloom. Apart from a few rogue menials and stray servitors they hadn't seen anything else alive down there, not even vermin – just bones and waste fallen down from above. But they couldn't stay down there forever since the datafortress itself, assuming it was still there, was several layers above the hive floor. They had to head up and hope there were enough connections between the spires to take them there. The black glass spire was the first one they had found that looked like it provided a reliable way upwards.

Inside, the spire was quiet and cold, evidently riddled with irregular tunnels, like flaws in its crystalline structure. The tech-guard and Grey Knights clambered in, the tech-guard having to take great care not to cut themselves through their fatigues on the edges of broken glass. Saphentis glided through the gap, climbing effortlessly with his additional bionic limbs, hauling Thalassa behind him with a spare hand.

'Tech-priest, are you alright?' asked Alaric.

'I am fully functional,' replied Saphentis.

'I meant you,' said Alaric, looking at Thalassa.

'I'll be fine,' she said, though she looked far from it. 'I just don't like heights.'

'A fall from more than six metres is potentially fatal,' said Saphentis. 'Assigning any higher risk to greater heights is irrational.'

'Do you know where we are now?' continued Alaric, ignoring Saphentis.

Thalassa consulted her dataslate. 'We've been going steadily for a day. We're about half of the way there horizontally, but we still need to get much higher.'

Brother Haulvarn was last in. Haulvarn had been with Alaric for a long time, since before the capture of renegade Inquisitor Valinov that had started Alaric on the road to confronting Ghargatuloth, and he was the most level-headed of Alaric's men. Just the kind of man you wanted watching your back. 'The way's clear,' he said, making a final sweep of the outside with his storm bolter raised.

'Good. Archis, stay up front. We don't know what's in here.'

Saphentis ran a bionic hand over the faceted black surface of a wall. 'This looks like data medium,'

'You mean there's information in it?' asked Alaric. The Adeptus Mechanicus often used crystalline substances to store large amounts of data but they never let on just how they achieved such an advanced trick.

'Perhaps. Corrupted and incomplete, of course. Thalassa?'

Thalassa put a hand against the smooth surface. Small, drill-tipped probes emerged from her palm and bored a little way into the crystal. Pulses of light ran across the circuitry embedded in her skin, outlining her face and hands in the gloom.

'We don't really have time for this,' said Hawkespur quietly. She had taken off the hood of her voidsuit and Alaric saw there was a smudge of pollution around her nose and mouth.

'I know. But this mission is all about information. The more we have the better our chances.'

Thalassa gasped. She pulled her hand sharply away and breathed quickly for a few moments. 'There's hardly anything left,' she said. 'The damage is extensive. I could only find a few basics before the local data net collapsed.'

'Nothing that can help us?' asked Hawkespur.

'Well… there's the date.'

'And?'

'It doesn't make any sense. The corruption must be even worse than it looks. Even the datelines on the data are off. As far as this planet is concerned we're somewhere at the end of the forty-second millennium, that's more than nine hundred years out.'

'Let us hope the datafortress is more intact,' said Saphentis.

'And let's keep moving,' added Hawkespur.

The strikeforce moved upwards, through the flaws that spiralled up through the black glass. Here and there they found great silver probes drilled deep into the glass, like massive versions of Thalassa's own dataprobes. In other places crude faces had been hacked out of the crystal, faces with one eye or two mouths, or bestial features that blended with the fractured structure of the glass.

They clambered upwards for more than an hour, Thalassa always lagging behind, until eventually the flaw opened up into a massive glass-walled chamber, its walls sculpted into sweeping curves like crashing waves.

Alaric was first out with Archis. The chamber was the size of an aircraft hangar and pale blueish light shone from the walls, glinting off every curved edge so the room seemed like an arching skeleton of light.

Rows and rows of spindly machinery filled the floor, ancient and deactivated, their joints and moving parts sealed shut by a chalky patina of corrosion.

'Grey Knights, get up here and sweep. There's nothing moving but there are plenty of places to hide.'

Saphentis followed the Grey Knights out. He took in the sight with his faceted eyes, pausing to drink it in – the machines were spindly and elegant, a world away from the massive machinery more typical of the Adeptus Mechanicus. He knelt down by the closest machine. His insectoid eyes changed colour, thin lines of red light playing across the workings as Saphentis scanned their every detail.

'Fascinating,' he said to himself.

'Really?' said Alaric as he directed his Grey Knights to check the floor for hostiles. 'Enlighten us.'

'This appears to be an autosurgeon. Very sophisticated. But its function is unlike any I have seen before. It seems designed to only dissect, not to knit back together again.'

'Throne of Earth,' whispered Alaric, 'what were they doing here?'

Saphentis moved over to another machine, one with a large cylindrical tank of clouded glass and several armatures poised to reach into it. 'Here... here the parts were placed.' A probe extended from one bionic finger and emitted several rapid flashes of light. 'Yes. Yes, traces of biological matter. Here they were placed and broken down.' The next machine in line had a long conveyor belt that ran maybe a third the length of the room, passing through dozens of rings on which were mounted hundreds of tiny articulated arms. 'And then, the rendered substance was taken along here and woven together... into long strands... muscles, yes, that's it, ropes of muscle.' Saphentis straightened up and looked right at Alaric. 'Do you see? They took their unwanted menials and fed them in and they were rendered down and their proteins woven back into raw muscle. The living things they fuse with their machinery, this is where they began making them.'

'Just another tech-heresy,' said Alaric bitterly. 'It doesn't sound like anything to get excited about.'

'I forget, justicar, you are not one of us. To a tech-priest, this alone is a revelation. Do you not see? This world is self-sufficient! It makes perfect sense to me now. This is just one sign. How could a world live a century alone and yet build so much? How could they create what they have here, without raw materials from any other world? Chaeroneia had great mineral wealth but there is not one forge world in the Imperium that could survive in isolation – raw materials, manpower, food, it all had to be imported by the shipful. But not here. Here they took the one resource they had in abundance and made their whole city out of it.

'Their menials, justicar! Humans! It is so perfect. Humans breed, they grow, all of their own accord. They bred a surplus and took those they did not need, fed them in here and created the living things they fuse with their machines. There are magi pecuniae who have spent generations seeking a way to make a world entirely self-sufficient. Here, they solved that problem in a mere century. Amazing.'

Alaric rounded on Saphentis. 'Archmagos, you seem to admire this world more than you hate it. That is a very, very dangerous thing to suggest to me.'

Saphentis held out his arms, presumably in an attempt to look apologetic. 'This is pure heresy, justicar. Of course I realise that and I should not have to point it out to you. But the fact remains that their ways have suggested solutions to problems that have plagued the Mechanicus for thousands of years. The Omnissiah despises the man who has knowledge placed before him and yet refuses to understand it.'

'Well, the god I worship hates a man who lets himself be seduced by the ways of the Enemy. In any other situation I would have you arrested as a heretic, archmagos, and you could explain your admiration of this world to the Inquisition. And when we get off this world I will do just that. But if you do anything more to suggest you find Chaeroneia worthy of any kind of respect, I will have Hawkespur officiate at your execution here and now.'

A few strange colours flickered over the facets of Saphentis's eyes, too quick for Alaric to follow. 'Of course, justicar,' he said after a pause. 'My apologies. I forget how zealous a servant of the Emperor you really are. I will submit to the will of the Inquisition, as must we all.'

'Floor's clear,' voxed Brother Haulvarn.

Justicar glared at Saphentis, willing the archmagos to show some flicker of emotion. But Saphentis was completely inscrutable. 'Good,' he voxed. 'Let the tech-guard have a few minutes' rest. Then we're getting out of here.'

'Understood.'

Saphentis stalked away to continue examining the machinery. Alaric watched as Captain Tharkk's tech-guard sat down in a perfect circle on the floor, their heads bowed, letting a few minutes of rest chase away some of the fatigue. Their emotional repression surgery meant they wouldn't complain or despair, but they were still susceptible to exhaustion like any unaugmented human.

'You don't trust him,' said Hawkespur. She had sat down on the rusted-up conveyor belt next to Alaric.

'Do you?'

'An interrogator of the Ordo Malleus doesn't trust anybody, justicar.'

'I don't think Saphentis was sent down here just to find out what happened to this world,' continued Alaric. 'This is a forge world. There must be plenty of things here the Mechanicus would dearly want to get back. He's looking for something down here, something important enough to risk an archmagos for. Maybe it's even something to do with the tech-heresy that's taken hold here, he certainly seems interested enough in that.'

'Perhaps,' said Hawkespur, 'but Saphentis could still be useful. He could get us the information we're looking for, he knows the datasystems on this planet better than you or I. And your squad is the best chance he has of surviving down here. He's a tech-priest, justicar and they are logical people. He knows full well he can't cross you.'

Alaric peered across the room, to where Saphentis was calling Thalassa over to help him examine a complex piece of machinery. 'I could need Nyxos's authority to back me up if it comes to that. Down here that authority resides in you.'

'Of course. Saphentis will have to listen to reason in the end.' Hawkespur hacked out a rasping cough and held her throat again.

'You're ill,' said Alaric.

'Tumors,' replied Hawkespur. 'The air here is poison. Nyxos's medical staff will deal with it once we're off-planet. I'm more concerned about our immediate situation. Such as the date.'

'The date? Thalassa said that was just corrupt information.'

'Chaeroneia's systems seem to think the date is nine hundred years hence, correct? Well, that might not be an error. Time flows differently in the warp, justicar, and I think we both know where this planet must have been for the past century. But while it was a century from our point of view, in the warp a thousand years could have passed.'

'A thousand? Terra preserve us.'

'It would explain the comprehensive rebuilding that seems to have occurred. The corruption of the menial workforce. The pervasive nature of the tech-heresy.'

Alaric shook his head. 'A thousand years in the warp. No wonder this planet is sick. But it also begs the question, doesn't it? If the planet really is self-sufficient enough to survive for a thousand years completely cut off in the warp, then why return to real space now? Why return at all?'

'That's question number one,' said Hawkespur. 'Number two is, what pulled it into the warp in the first place?'

THE FORCE LEAVING the old flesh weaving spire was small. It made sense – only a tiny craft could have slipped past the asteroid field. The force consisted of six humans, one heavily augmented human (evidently a tech-priest, one of the unenlightened) and a squad of six Space Marines of the Adeptus Astartes. The livery on the Space Marines was unusual, with simple gunmetal grey as the Chapter colour and the twin symbols of a book pierced by a sword and the stylised 'I' of the Inquisition. There were no records of the Chapter in the historical files that remained from Chaeroneia's past as an outpost of the Imperium, but then many Chapters could come and go in a thousand years.

The cogitator-beasts that lived in the command spire of Manufactorium Noctis had lost the intruders soon after they arrived. The beasts, their brains massively swollen globes of pulsing fluid shimmering with cogitator circuits and calculator valves, had padded impatiently around their cells, scratching with metal claws at the walls in frustration. Then the intruders had been spotted again by one of the many flying biomechanical creatures that circled the city's upper spires. They roared in excitement, bounding around their cells in the pitch-black, bile-streaked menagerie floors of the command spire. Their brains, half-grown and half-built in the newer fleshweaving complexes elsewhere in the city, filtered the information into individual useful facts and assembled them into conclusions that they relayed in machine-code up to the very top of the command spire.

The cogitator-beasts had concluded the intruders were from the Adeptus Mechanicus with Astartes support, probably come to investigate Chaeroneia's re-entry into the physical universe. That meant the Imperium still existed, along with the old Adeptus Mechanicus whose beliefs would soon be replaced with the true revelations of the Omnissiah. For this information the cogitator-beasts were rewarded with gobbets of thick nutrient paste rendered from non-essential menials and piped into their cells where it was hungrily lapped from the filth-stained floor.

Far above in the isolated priests' chambers of the command spire, Archmagos Veneratus Scraecos reviewed this information. His thought processes had long ceased to resemble anything human and the cognitive functions of any human were insufficient to comprehend the revelations of the Omnissiah as revealed to Chaeroneia's tech-clergy a thousand years before. Streams of machine-code flowed through his mind, the images of the intruding enemies, their location relative to the other structures of Manufactorium Noctis, the many tech-priests, menial forces and combat-able servitors stationed nearby.

'We have regained contact with the intruders,' said the being called Scraecos, his words turned into packets of machine-code pulsed through the nerve endings that spun a data-network all over the command spire.

'Good,' came the reply, summarised from the thought impulses of the hundreds of tech-priests who resided in the spire. 'You, Scraecos, are responsible for the resolution of this event and are granted permission by the holy revelations of the Machine-God to assume individuality of consciousness for the duration of your task.'

'Praise be to the Omnissiah, I become one at His request,' replied Scraecos.

Suddenly the nerve endings around him were numbed into inaction by the will of the resident tech-priests and Scraecos was an individual creature again. His senses no longer comprehended the whole command spire, only the small womb-like cell where he lay, bathed in amniotic fluid in a large fleshy sac wound round with neuro-circuitry. The film of skin over his bionic eyes lifted and his vision swam back, showing him a world well beyond the visible spectrum. He felt his body now, too and it was heavy and crude around his mind. He flexed his mechadendrites and eased himself out of the fluid onto the slick, spongy floor.

He was no longer connected. He had to communicate with the other tech-priests by more mundane means. 'I have assumed individuality,' he said out loud, the nerve-endings in the walls absorbing the sound waves and turning them into data. His vox-unit was uncomfortable and unfamiliar. Memories – if they could be likened to something as human as memories – were coming back to him, the centuries in service to the Imperium, the dawn of his enlightenment when the Omnissiah's avatar had first been uncovered and the years of rebuilding in the warp as Chaeroneia was transformed into the Omnissiah's perfect vision.

'It is good,' came the reply. 'You possess the experience required to do the Machine-God's will. State your immediate intentions.'

'The standing declarations of the Omnissiah are clear,' said Scraecos. 'As given to me personally by the Castigator, there is one course of action compatible with the holiness of the planet's ground and the principles of the Adeptus.'

'State this course.'

'Kill them all.'

Scraecos let the weight of his physical form fall back onto him completely. He had been formidable in physical combat a long time ago and his body was still in efficient and uncorroded condition, which meant he was still a capable killer. He remembered the feeling of blood spattering on his few remaining areas of biological flesh, its warmth, its smell and felt a flicker of human emotions like bloodlust and exultation. Eventually, such crudeness would be gone from Scraecos and he would be a perfect being of logic in the sight of the Omnissiah.

Yes, Scraecos could kill. But there were far more effective murderers on Chaeroneia. Scraecos's first task, then, would be to summon those killers from the furthest corners of Chaeroneia's dataconstructs and give them the scent of their prey.

NINE

'Know the enemy not and the battle cannot be won. Know the enemy too much and the battle will be doubly lost.'

– Lord Admiral Ravensburg,
'Naval Maxims Vol. IX'

'ORDNANCE READY,' SAID the chief ordnance officer as Rear Admiral Horstgeld strode onto the bridge. 'We can fire at fifteen minutes' notice.'

'Excellent,' said Horstgeld. The bridge was buzzing. The *Tribunicia* had not fired a shot in anger for some time and Horstgeld had almost forgotten how it felt when danger was near. Now only the Emperor's guns and the Emperor's torpedoes stood between the good of the Imperium and the depredations of the Enemy.

It was a good feeling. It was why Horstgeld had been put in this galaxy.

'Preacher!' shouted Horstgeld heartily. 'What does the Emperor demand of us?'

'Obedience and zeal!' came the response from the raw throat of the confessor up on the pulpit. 'Defiance unto death!'

If the command crew disliked Horstgeld's habit of having the Confessor spouting prayers, they didn't show it. Navigation were assembling the rag-tag fleet into a battle line. Communications was relaying orders back and forth between the other ships under Horstgeld's command. Engineering was keeping the plasma reactors at full close orbit manoeuvring capacity and Ordnance was shepherding the ship's stock of torpedoes into the firing bays. The *Tribunicia* was old but she was tough, she had seen battle before and she was relishing it again.

But then, most of the crew hadn't seen what Horstgeld had seen – the full size of the approaching fleet.

Horstgeld paused briefly to kneel before the image of the Emperor that crowned the viewscreen. The screen was now showing a map of Chaeroneia's orbit, with the positions of the Imperial fleet and the complex maze of asteroids below. The Emperor's golden mask glowered down over the bridge as if admonishing the crew to work harder in His name – which of course He was, watching over them from the Golden Throne on Terra.

'Grant us the strength to forsake our weaknesses,' said Horstgeld. 'Our Emperor, preserve us.'

'Captain?' Stelkhanov stood over Horstgeld's shoulder. 'Ship's archive may have found a match.'

'So soon? I thought we'd have to ask Segmentum Command at Kar Duniash.'

'The archives found something in Ravensburg's histories of the Gothic War. The largest ship in the approaching fleet matches various energy signatures logged by the *Ius Bellum* at the Battle of Gethsemane.' Stelkhanov handed Horstgeld a sheet of complicated sensorium readings. 'The chances of a false match are very low.'

'Throne deliver us,' said Horstgeld. 'It's the *Hellforger*.'

'Sir?'

'Comms! Get me Fleet Commissar Leung. And put our reinforcements on screen.'

The viewscreen shifted to show the details and schematics of the ships that had answered Horstgeld's call to join the fleet at Chaeroneia.

'What in the hells is this?' he demanded, rounding on the Communications section. Several officers occupied the pews of the section, relaying streams of vox-commands and scanning ship-to-ship channels. 'I asked for warships! Subsector Command was supposed to send us everything they had!'

'These are all that were available,' replied Chief Communications Officer Kelmawr, a squat and powerful woman who had earned her stripes in boarding actions during the Rhanna crisis.

Horstgeld turned back to the screen. 'The *Pieta*... that's... that's a pilgrim ship for the love of Earth. It's barely even armed. And the *Epicurus* is a bloody yacht!'

'It's refitted,' said Kelmawr. 'The Administratum confiscated it and turned it into an armed merchantman...'

'Contact Kar Duniash. Tell them we have a crisis here. If Segmentum Command there can't help us then we're on our own.'

Horstgeld sat down on his command pew, shaking his head. It wasn't enough. They might have been able to hold off a grand cruiser, since that's what the *Hellforger* was. But not a whole fleet. Especially since the *Hellforger* had last been seen during the Gothic War in the service of the Chaos lord, Abaddon.

Chaos. The Enemy. Horstgeld couldn't tell the crew but the very soul of corruption was represented by ships like the *Hellforger*. Chaeroneia itself wasn't the only moral threat any more.

'Not good news then, Rear Admiral?'

In all the hubbub, Horstgeld hadn't even noticed Inquisitor Nyxos sitting quietly on the pew, almost hidden under the hood of his robes.

'The fleet is in the service of Chaos,' said Horstgeld. 'The flagship is the *Hellforger*. At Gethsemane it launched a boarding raid that killed...'

'I have read my Ravensburg, Horstgeld. They teach us rather more history in the Inquisition than I suspect they do in the Navy.'

'And we do not have enough ships to hold them off.'

'You are ready to abandon Chaeroneia?'

Horstgeld looked into the old man's eyes. He didn't like what he saw. He didn't believe the most outlandish stories they told of inquisitors – burning good Imperial servants at the stake, destroying whole planets – but he did know that an inquisitor's authority stood above all others and they did not take kindly to those who gave up in the face of the Emperor's enemies. 'Of course not,' he said. 'But there is little we can do.'

'You may not have to do all that much. Have you regained communications with Alaric and Hawkespur?'

Horstgeld shook his head. 'Comms are working on it but there is too much interference. At the best of times the pollution in the atmosphere is so thick it would be difficult to get any signal down. With the asteroid field it's all but impossible.'

'What about the *Exemplar*?'

'Magos Korveylan hasn't had any luck.'

'Hasn't she? I thought the Adeptus Mechanicus didn't believe in luck. I understand Commissar Leung is on the *Exemplar*?'

'He is.'

'Good. I am sure the combined efforts of Leung and myself will convince Korveylan to place contacting Alaric rather higher on their list of priorities. Can you live without me for a few hours?'

'Yes. But I might need your authority getting further reinforcements from Segmentum Command.'

'I will see what I can do on that account, but you must understand that my priority here is discovering what became of Chaeroneia. If we can get that information then you may not have to make a stand here at all.'

Horstgeld smiled bitterly. 'That won't happen, inquisitor. There's something on Chaeroneia the Enemy needs and they're going to go through us to get it. You're not going to just let them walk onto that planet.'

Nyxos stood up and smoothed down his robes. 'Quite right, of course. But I have my priorities. I shall require a fast shuttle and a couple of armsmen in case Korveylan proves recalcitrant.'

'Of course. And inquisitor… we can slow the enemy down. Perhaps force them out of formation and delay a landing, but not much more than that. I believe you represent the will of the Emperor and I will sacrifice this fleet if you feel it is necessary, but there is a limit to how much time we can buy for those men on the surface.'

'Unless I tell you otherwise, the Emperor requires you to reach that limit. There is nothing I will not do to seek out the foes of the Emperor and I will accept nothing less than the same from those under my authority. Now, if you please, my shuttle.'

Horstgeld stood and saluted – if this was the last time he would speak with Nyxos face-to-face, he wanted it to look formal. 'It will be ready by the time you get to the flight deck. Wish us all luck, inquisitor.'

'The Inquisition doesn't believe in luck either, Horstgeld. The Emperor protects.'

With that Nyxos swept off, looking imperious now rather than the hunched old man he normally appeared. Horstgeld knew then that Magos Korveylan would be on the same side as the rest of the fleet, whether she wanted it or not. That, at least, meant the Enemy would have to work a little harder to break through the fleet and reach Chaeroneia.

THERE WERE HUGE gliding things, like hollow-boned manta rays the size of fighter craft, that floated on industrial thermals in the lower reaches of the pollutant layer. Metallic snakes like animated cables, slithering through rainbow-sheened pools of caustic oil. Plumes of fungus made of living rust. Tiny bright insects made of metal, like intricate clockwork toys, scuttling like cockroaches looking for nuggets of iron to eat. Chaeroneia had once been typical of a forge world, with barely any indigenous flora or fauna able to survive the constant pollution – but the planet's thousand-year corruption had given rise to a unique bio-mechanical ecosystem where half-machine creatures flourished like living vermin.

Thalassa steered the strike force around the most obviously populated areas of the city. A dozen cities had been built on top of the original manufactorium and each one had seen areas fall into dereliction while others had prospered. The force moved through caverns formed from the fossilised remains of biomechanical factory-creatures, through twisting caves formed from their skulls and waist-deep seas of rancid coolant fluid that drizzled from some power plant far overhead. Aside from feral menials and wandering servitors they avoided the city's population successfully, though Alaric could feel a hundred artificial eyes on him and he knew that someone in the city knew exactly where they were. Gun platform patrols had been everywhere and Alaric had let his training take over his every movement, seeking out the best cover at every turn. His instinct had begun to rub off on the other troops, with even Archmagos Saphentis starting to move like a soldier.

And they had seen such things. Spires of glass. A slumbering monster with shiny grey skin that sweated a river of black blood. A creature like a corpulent tank-sized spider that writhed its way between the towers, exuding a stream of thick sticky strands which solidified into hardened bridges. Chaeroneia was becoming an exhausting parade of dark wonders, every turn bringing something new and terrible.

The journey had been arduous. Tharkk had called for more regular rest breaks to keep his tech-guard from collapsing from exhaustion and Tech-priest Thalassa had to be carried across the rougher ground. Something in Interrogator Hawkespur's metabolism had reacted badly to the pollutants, and tumours were breaking out in her throat and lungs so her breathing got more and more laboured and she had to stop to cough up lungfuls of foam. The Grey Knights were competent at battlefield first aid and Saphentis could have been an able surgeon, but Hawkespur was beyond help. Without a fully-functional medical suite, she would die within a week. Hawekspur herself hadn't commented on this at all – she was the finest naval stock, brilliant and brave enough to serve as interrogator to an inquisitor of the Ordo Malleus, and she didn't let anything as trivial as her own death get in the way of her duty.

'We should nearly be there,' said Hawkespur at the end of the third day. They were walking on the floor of a chasm between two multi-storey factory complexes, rearing up like tarnished steel skeletons. 'We should rest. The fortress will probably be guarded and we don't want the tech-guard going in exhausted.'

'You're not doing so well yourself,' said Alaric. Though the hood of Hawkespur's voidsuit was up he could see her reddened eyes through the visor.

'I could do with a rest, too,' she said grudgingly.

'You're no good to us dead, interrogator. I heard you were the best shot on Hydraphur.'

'Just a third-round winner, justicar.'

'Good enough.' Alaric looked around their immediate surroundings – the lower floors of the closer factory complex looked deserted and they would cover them from observers overhead. It was a good place to hole up before making the final slog down the datacore valley that led to the fortress. 'My Space Marines just need an hour of half-sleep. We'll take the watch, tell Tharkk to have his tech-guard rest. Thalassa, too.'

Hawkespur looked around. 'Where is Thalassa?'

Alaric followed her gaze. He could see the Space Marines of his squad, spread out through the formation with Lykkos taking up the rear. Tharkk and his remaining tech-guard were in the middle with Archmagos Saphentis. But not Thalassa.

The chasm floor was littered with debris and trash. There was plenty of room for Thalassa to be hidden if she had fallen. 'Damnation,' said Justicar. 'We need her.' He switched to the vox. 'Grey Knights, I need a visual on Tech-Priest Thalassa.'

The acknowledgement runes flickered back negative. 'I helped her over the broken ground two kilometres back,' replied Brother Cardios. 'I haven't seen her since.'

'Captain Tharkk!' called Alaric.

The tech-guard officer jogged up to Alaric. 'Justicar?'

'Was Thalassa with you?'

'No, justicar. No orders were given to assist her.'

'We can't spend time looking for her,' said Hawkespur.

'I know,' said Alaric. 'Tharkk, get your men into the cover of the factory. Hawkespur, go with them. Get some rest. Grey Knights, search by sections, half a kilometre range, then pull back and take the watch. I'll stay here.' He turned to where Archmagos Saphentis was sitting unruffled on a fallen slab of rusting machinery. 'Archmagos, you were responsible for Thalassa.'

'She was subordinate to me. I was not required to watch her. There was a difference.'

'Was? You sound like she's already dead.'

'And you believe she isn't?'

Alaric turned away from the archmagos and stomped into the shadow of the factory complex. Saphentis was probably right, that was the worst of it. Since the moment they had crash-landed he had known Chaeroneia would have ways of killing them without them even knowing, But they couldn't afford to lose Thalassa – Saphentis could perform some of the same functions but he wasn't a data-specialist like her.

Saphentis had been responsible for Thalassa and that was what worried Alaric the most. Thalassa had been horrified at Chaeroneia, as any right-thinking human would be, but Saphentis had not shown such revulsion. He seemed to be impressed by the way the planet had reinvented the Mechanicus creed. If Thalassa had suspected Saphentis wasn't on the planet for the benefit of the Imperium, but to fulfil some other agenda, would Saphentis have had any compunction about killing her? Probably not. The higher the rank, the less human the tech-priest and Saphentis was both high-ranking and soulless.

Alaric watched Saphentis idly pick up a chunk of rusted wreckage and incinerate it in a crucible formed from the palm of one bionic hand, watching the smouldering nugget giving way to a wisp of black smoke. The strikeforce now needed Saphentis more than ever, so Alaric couldn't just storm in accusing Saphentis of being a murderer and a traitor – Saphentis would just flee into the black heart of the city and the Grey Knights probably wouldn't be able to find him. Alaric wasn't even sure if he could take Saphentis in straight combat if it came to that, since Saphentis's combat augmentations were formidable and Alaric didn't know the full extent of what he could do.

And Saphentis knew it all, too. He knew full well Alaric couldn't do without him. If Alaric's worst suspicions were correct then Saphentis was just using the Grey Knights and tech-guard as a bodyguard while he searched for some tainted prize on Chaeroneia, and the wrench of it was that Alaric couldn't do anything but go along with Saphentis and hope he had the wits to know when Saphentis was about to betray them. This was what Alaric hated more than anything else – the politicking, the petty betrayals that seemed to seethe through everything the Inquisition ever did. There was a time when he had thought organisations like the Mechanicus and the Inquisition stood together in the service of the Emperor, but every day that went by seemed to show him some new way for humanity to fight itself instead of focusing on the Enemy.

At least the Grey Knights themselves stood apart. They were one, devoted, pure of purpose. That was the quality that would see them through this, traitors in their midst be damned.

'Haulvarn here,' came a vox from the squad. 'Nothing here. I'll bring the squad in on a final sweep.'

'Understood. I'll take first watch, make sure each of you gets some half-sleep. We're now a body short and the next stage will be harder.'

In Chaeroneia's gritty twilight, Alaric watched the bulky armoured silhouettes of his Space Marines as they moved back along the chasm
floor. The Grey Knights were some of the best warriors and yet they were
at the mercy of this planet, isolated, ignorant and alone. It gave Alaric a
glimmer of solace that they had been in just the same position fighting
Ghargatuloth and yet they had never once taken a backward step in
doing their duty. Even if Chaeroneia killed them, it would have to work
hard before they fell.

But the end was surely coming, even if the Grey Knights could hold it
off a little while. Thalassa was dead, there was little doubt. She had
fallen down one of the many sheer drops or been carried off by some
swift predator. And if it was the Enemy's greatest weapon to sow confusion and violence in the Emperor's own ranks, then the Enemy was
succeeding.

IMMERSED IN THE quicksilver slime of the datapool, the creature that
had once been Archmagos Veneratus Scraecos felt again the pathetic
weakness of his remaining fleshy parts. It was cold and painful in
there, the liquid metal crushing against him, the weaving filaments
cutting into the patches of skin that remained between his augmentations and attachments. Scraecos had long, long ago left behind useless
human fears like claustrophobia or the terror of drowning, so the datapool held no dread for him. But it was still shocking to be shown
how far he had to go before he was completely at one with the
Machine-God.

It was only the deeper, more human part of him that felt shock, of
course. That part was gradually being buried by the rest of Scraecos – the
haughty, pure logic that knew the Omnissiah's plan made no
allowances for concerns like fear or suffering.

The mechadendrites extending from Scraecos's face reached out into
the medium of the datapool, gathering bunches of the floating filaments. Dataprobes extended from the heads of the mechadendrites and
the information contained in the pool flowed into him. Scraecos saw
the structure of Manufactorium Noctis blooming in the logic architecture of his mind, spires and foundations riddled with chambers and
tunnels, webs of walkways stretching between the towers. Warm, enormous biomechanoids clinging to the underside of the city, flooding the
city with their bioelectric energy and the products harvested from their
bodies. He saw the works where menials were bred and birthed and
where they were brought back again into the city to form the raw materials for more biomechanical architecture.

Part of Scraecos glowed in admiration at what they had wrought over the last millennium. But that, of course, was only a tiny and insignificant emotion in the sea of logic. The rest of Scraecos simply absorbed it, discarded what he did not need to know and zoomed in on the rest.

The hunter-programs despatched by Scraecos had been exacting. They had demanded even more of the surplus menial stock than normal. Now there would be thousands more biological assets herded into the hunters' hidden places and given over to the hunters' strange ways. Self-aware data constructs, the hunters were relentless and voracious, surpassing even the immediate needs of logic in their pursuit of prey. But they had, of course, a weakness – though Chaeroneia was riddled with data media like the glassy black crystalline medium or the liquid metal of the datapool, there were still plenty of areas in Chaeroneia that were far away from any containment medium. That meant the hunter-programs could not go everywhere, only the places where a medium existed to hold them.

Scraecos illuminated Chaeroneia's data media in his mind. Whole towers of crystal glowed strongly, including the old menial reclamation spire the intruders had left only a short time before. Dataslates held by tech-priests overseeing work in the towers also glowed, tiny specks of moving light. A hunter-program could travel in such a medium if it had to. Many tech-priests themselves were lit up, as large data storage organs were a common augmentation among the overseers of Manufactorium Noctis.

On the horizon, between the city and the command spire complex, was a massive shining area where there were plenty of spaces for hunter-programs to hide. But that was an area the tech-priests of Chaeroneia wanted to keep the intruders away from. So that was no good.

Scraecos concentrated on the places in the city where the programs could hunt. Then he synchronised all the data feeds from tech-priests, sensorium-equipped servitors and all the semi-natural biomechanical creatures in Manufactorium Noctis. A single stream of perception coursed through the datapool, wrapping thousands of filaments into a long pulsing rope, writhing like a serpent.

Scraecos wrapped his mechadendrites around the filament rope as if they were the tentacles of a deep-sea predator, worming dataprobes into its length. The perception burst into him and he had to open up all his capacity to accept it, the datafeeds of millions of perceiving creatures and machines in one tangled burst.

Few tech-priests on Chaeroneia could have done it. Fewer still had the respect of the hunter-programs. That was why the tech-priests, Scraecos among them, had chosen him.

Because something, somewhere, knew where the intruders were.

Millions of images of Chaeroneia flickered through Scraecos's mind. He overclocked his augmented brain until they slowed down enough for him to sort them properly. Hordes of menials slaving over massive steaming engine-blocks. Sacred symbols projected onto the clouds, the endless holy litany of the Machine-God's revelations. Tech-priests gibbering the praises of the Omnissiah from spire-top temples, their machine-code prayers exalting the Great Comprehender who had given the priests of Chaeroneia His revelation through the avatar that had appeared to them long ago.

All magnificent, but not what Scraecos was looking for.

Scraecos concentrated on the wastelands between the spires, where intruders might think they could hide from the city's infinite eyes. Ruined and abandoned places, deep and forgotten. Layers of discarded history, wreckage and decay, swallowed up by the corrosion so daemonised by the literature of the old, ignorant Adeptus Mechanicus. But the God of Machines was also the God of Rust – Scraecos knew that now, and so did Chaeroneia and so these places were as a sacred to the Omnissiah as the most carefully anointed temple. Scraecos searched the alleyways and undercity sumps, the rotting graveyards of titanic biomechanical creatures and the windblown eyries of the flying animals that scoured the spire tops for prey.

There. One of them had seen something. Armoured humans in an unfamiliar gunmetal-grey, the unknown livery of the Space Marines who had infiltrated Manufactorium Noctis. The viewpoint was high and distant but there was no mistaking them. They were moving, spread out in formation, with unarmoured humans and what looked like a priest of the old Mechanicus in the centre.

Good. They were still moving like soldiers, still thinking their military minds could outwit the grand intelligence of Chaeroneia's priestly caste. Scraecos cross-referenced their location and direction.

It was clear where they were headed. And on Scraecos's mental map it was a place almost blinding with the level of data media it contained, a place where the hunters could grow strong and brutal, move like lightning and bear down on anything that would sate their hunger. And they would find prey now, that was for sure.

Somewhere deep, deep down beneath the desolate layers of his personality, Scraecos smiled. The rest of him, the logical majority, simply bade the hunter-programs to depart their logic-cages in the command spire's own data network and go hunting in Manufactorium Noctis.

TEN

'The daemon can exist in an infinity of forms, but all are identical in one respect. Every daemon is a lie given flesh, for only a creature made of deceit can take form in the truth of the universe.'

– Lord Inquisitor Coteaz at
the Conclave of Deliae

'This is it,' said Alaric as they reached the head of the valley.

'I don't like this,' said Haulvarn, who was taking point with Alaric. 'Anyone up there could cover us all the way in.'

He was right. The valley was a sheer-sided slash in the architecture of the city, dozens of storeys deep and walled with sheer black crystal like the substance in the crystal spire. Slabs of fallen crystal, like giant shards of obsidian, littered the valley floor. And if there was anything up on the crystal clifftops, they would have their pick of targets as the Grey Knights and tech-guard made their way towards the powerful, cylindrical shape of the datafortress itself at the far end of the valley.

'Then we'll have to be quick,' said Alaric. 'Lykkos, keep watching the clifftops, you're the only one with the range. Everyone else, stay close and keep moving. They'll see us coming.'

A thin, sharp wind whistled down the valley, cold and hard like the smooth glassy sides. The trash underfoot, Alaric realised with a jolt, was composed of ancient servitor parts – rusting craniums, metallic armatures, strands of tarnished steel that once wound round human limbs. Alaric had no doubt that the human parts of the servitors, probably harvested from the less-able menials, had in turn been removed and used to create the biomechanical monstrosities that powered much of the city. The mechanical remains, the servos and the exoskeletons, had ended up here.

The Imperium as a whole did not place great value on an individual human life, but at least humans were ultimately sacred to the Emperor and their deaths, no matter how numerous, were all unavoidable sacrifices. On Chaeroneia, human lives were no more than fuel.

'I am picking up contradictory readings,' said Saphentis, who was looking at the auspex mounted on one of his arms. 'There are unusual energy sources nearby.'

Alaric felt something prickling against his psychic core, the shield of faith that kept his mind safe from the predations of the Enemy. The feeling grew as the force moved down the valley. Something probing his defences, homing in on the beacon of his mind and scraping psychic nails against its surface.

The hexagrammic and pentagrammic wards woven into the ceramite of his armour were heating up. He heard something whispering, a low hissing sound that seemed to form his name, over and over again, just below the range of his hearing.

'Anyone else hear that?' he asked.

'Hear what?' said Hawkespur.

Something moved inside the black crystal of the cliff face, like a creature swimming under black ice. That was all the warning Alaric had.

His wards flared white-hot and he was thrown from his feet as something massive and yet somehow incorporeal ripped past him, hurling him against the opposite face. Crystal shattered and bit into the skin of Alaric's body, scraping deep gouges in his armour. He hit the ground hard, willing himself to keep a grip on his halberd. The screaming sound was so loud it was like a wall of white noise, shrieking right through him, filling his mind.

Gunfire stuttered. Bright crimson las-blasts streaked in every direction.

An ice-cold spectral hand reached out of the crystal Alaric had just slammed into, snaking around his throat and lifting him up. It was not physical, not flesh and blood or even metal. Alaric saw a glimpse of a face that was not a face beneath the crystal, formed of a jumble of geometric shapes that coalesced into snarling fangs and burning purple slashes for eyes.

'Domine, salve nos!' hissed Alaric and the psychic wall around his soul flared outwards, burning the creature's talons with the fire of his faith. The monster screamed and reeled back into the wall, dropping Alaric.

'Tharkk! Get your men in close! Grey Knights, surround them!'

Half-real creatures were leaping across the valley, streaking from one crystal wall to the other. One tech-guard was lifted off his feet as he went and the creature began to devour him. The tech-guard's emotional repression wasn't enough to cut out the pain as he was twisted around in the air, the maddening haze of shapes that made up the creature's body whirling about him. Piece by piece he was sliced apart, geometric scraps of skin flayed off, neat cores of bone bored out of him. The process took a handful of seconds before the creature reached the opposite wall but time seemed to slow down, as if Chaeroneia wanted the man to suffer as much as possible before it was done with him.

Tharkk hauled the remaining two tech-guard into the middle of the valley, Saphentis alongside him. The Grey Knights formed up around them, storm bolter fire chattering up as they tried to hit the creature streaking past them. They were lightning-quick and serpentine, clawed limbs extruding from their bodies at strange angles, their faces horrid slashes of deep burning light like broad strokes painted over reality. They were made of swirling shapes like some corrupt mathematics made real and the crystal of the valley walls seemed to conduct them, so that they arced across the valley like electricity.

Alaric's wards were absorbing the foul magic pulsing off them. The Grey Knights all had the same defences and the creatures hated it. They bent around the Grey Knights like refracting light, the force of the Marines' faith enough to warp the sub-reality they moved through.

The creatures screamed and contorted in torment, strange ugly colours rippling through them as they approached the Grey Knights. But it wouldn't be enough. Moment by moment they were getting closer, becoming quicker and more aggressive as if their first attack had been a mere warm-up.

'We can't stay!' shouted Hawkespur. She had her sidearm out and was sniping at the creatures, her bullets leaving rippling trails through them.

Alaric thought rapidly. She was right. They could hold out here but not forever – a few moments and the creatures could start injuring Grey Knights and carrying them away, getting among the tech-guard and finishing them off.

They had to move. To reach the datafortress.

'Brother Archis,' said Alaric levelly, his voice raised above the otherworldly screaming. 'I think our tech-guard companions could do with some inspiring words.'

'Justicar?' Archis paused between firing gouts of flame at the creatures to glance at Alaric.

'Tell them the Parable of Grand Master Ganelon. I hear you tell it well.'

Archis took aim again and bathed another creature in flame, the fire rippling purple-black where it flowed through the substance of the creature's body. 'There was once a man named Ganelon,' began Archis uncertainly. 'A Grand Master of our Chapter. He...'

'As related in the Index Beati of High Chaplain Greacris, Brother Archis. I taught it to you myself.'

'Of course.' Archis paused for a second, as if composing himself. '"... and so reflect, novice, on the works of Ganelon, who attained the rank of Grand Master two hundred and fifty-one years after taking on the mantle of the Knight. For the legions of the Lust God had done much evil through the Garon Nebula and the Holy Orders of the Emperor's Inquisition entreated the Grey Knights to make war upon the benighted peoples therein..."'

Archis had learned the parable by heart. Alaric had led the squad in prayers countless times and even the recent additions to the squad, Archis included, took equal responsibilities for their spiritual health. The parable was one Alaric had ensured Archis knew by heart so he could lead the squad in reflecting on its message, immortalised by High Chaplain Greacris eight centuries before.

Alaric waved the squad forward as Archis spoke, the Marine's voice getting stronger as the familiar parable unfolded. The Grey Knights and the tech-guard moved gradually down the valley, the creatures shrieking past them.

The strength of the Grey Knights was not in their wargear or their training, in their augmentations or in the patronage of the Ordo Malleus. Their strength was faith. That was how they would survive here. That was the one weapon the Enemy could never counter.

'And Ganelon saw the evils done by the Lust God,' continued Archis, raising his voice above the howling. 'But the minions of the Lust God were fell and many and Ganelon was surrounded by sorcerers and heretics and all who knew of it said he would surely die.'

The serpentine creatures flared red as the words of the parable burned them. They still reached out to test the Grey Knights' psychic defences, but their mental claws were burned and they squirmed away through the air, keening angrily. As they reeled the other Grey Knights could fire at them, storm bolter shells shredding the half-physical stuff of their bodies. Wounded creatures writhed behind the surface of the crystal cliffs, bleeding raw mathematics from the tears in their bodies.

'The datafortress is just ahead,' said Alaric. 'We're almost there.'

'If these things move through data media,' said Hawkespur as she stumbled through the underfoot wreckage to keep up with the tech-guard, 'then they'll be stronger there.'

'Let me worry about that. Just stay alive.'

'...And the Lord Sorcerer of the Lust God spake unto Ganelon,' said Archis, 'and offered him great things. The Lust God would give Ganelon anything he desired, no matter how base or beautiful, savage or tender, a lifetime of wonders in return for service. And the sorcerer's magic showed Ganelon all the things the Lust God could bring and they were wondrous indeed...'

Alaric glanced up and saw grav-platforms coming in to land over the datafortress. There would be resistance, then, but he knew there would be. Now he was ready. The Grey Knights were coming into their own – this was the kind of battle they were made for.

'But Ganelon spoke to the Lord Sorcerer. He spoke of the weight of duty he carried and the opportunity given to him by the grace of the Emperor to discharge that duty. And he said to the Lord Sorcerer, what else is there in this universe, or any other, that can compare to a warrior's duty done? What other gift can I receive, for the like of which I would give up what the Emperor has given unto me? And the Lord Sorcerer could find no answer and so were his deceitful words revealed as lies and his magic broken, and Ganelon struck off his head with one blow and won back the Garon Nebula into the Emperor's light...'

Archis was nearly finished. The squad had reached the datafortress, the first step of a flight of steps leading up to a huge black rectangle of the entrance. The datafortress was a single massive cylinder standing on end, its obsidian surface swirling with the magnitude of information it contained. Alaric could feel the weight of all that knowledge, billions of words' worth of information pressing against his consciousness. Information, the foundation stone of the Adeptus Mechanicus and presumably the lifeblood of whatever tech-heresy had taken hold of Chaeroneia.

The creatures were wary, hiding beneath the surface of the crystal or dissolving into barely-glimpsed shapes of shadow that slunk around in the distance. Archis's parable had worked, focusing the faith of the Grey Knights until it burned their enemies.

'What in the hells are they?' asked Hawkespur as they made their way warily up towards the entrance.

'Self-actuating programs,' replied Saphentis. 'Data constructs with limited decision-networks. Evidently the Mechanicus here has endowed them with some capacity to manipulate gravity or matter. Greatly heretical creations, or course.'

'Creations? No, archmagos. The tech-priests didn't make them.'

'Explain, justicar?'

'I know daemons when I see them. This planet was stuck in the warp for a thousand years. I think those daemons infested the data media and the tech-priests are using them.' Alaric glanced at Saphentis. 'They've fallen further than you think. Sorcery, Throne knows what else.'

'Then we are in grave danger here.'

'Wrong again. At first everything on this world was new to me. The Mechanicus, the tech-heresies, it's something our training never anticipated. But daemons are different. Daemons I know. The tech-priests probably think their daemons are the best weapon they have, but we've trained our whole lives to take them on. This fight just shifted in our favour.'

The Grey Knights led the way through the forbidding entrance into the datafortress itself and the weight of information settled on Alaric as his eyes snapped his pupils open to drink in the feeble light inside. The inside of the datafortress was a riot of shapes. The stern exterior had served to contain rampant growths of datacrystal, forming spikes and blades that jutted insanely from every angle. It was disorienting in the extreme – the angles didn't add up right, distances didn't match up properly, everything seemed tilted in a dozen different ways. Strange colours pulsed through the crystal growths as the data-daemons plunged into the architecture of the fortress itself.

'They're regrouping,' said Alaric. 'Saphentis! Get us information! Concentrate on historical data, the last thousand years.'

'Thousand? But it has only been a century…'

'Do it! Haulvarn, Archis, don't leave his side. The rest, close perimeter. Don't let them surround us.'

Alaric tried to gauge how far the navigable space inside the fortress went. It was impossible to guess how far in anyone could get. There was something so fundamentally wrong with the inside of the fortress that Alaric guessed his men could still get lost no matter how big it actually was. It was as if the magnitude of information in the fortress was so great that its weight had borne down on the fabric of reality, making it buckle and bend.

The daemons were there. He could feel them through the wards in his armour, through his skin and down to the core of his soul. Hanging back, watching, waiting. Waiting for something.

And there were tech-priests on the way with grav-platforms full of reinforcements. Saphentis would have to be quick and they would have to get back out through the valley under fire. Alaric knew it wouldn't be easy but the odds were lengthening with every second.

'Saphentis? What have you got?'

Saphentis had his two probe-tipped arms stabbed deep into the crystal, the servos twitching as torrents of information seethed up them. 'Interesting,' he said. 'There is much information. I lack the data filtration matrices that Thalassa possessed. I will need several minutes.'

It was so obvious they didn't have several minutes that Alaric didn't bother saying it.

The crystal was pulsing with strange colours that matched nothing on the visible spectrum. Alaric's wards flared hotter. He glanced at the other members of his squad – Lykkos was touching a hand to the miniature copy of the Liber Daemonicum contained in its compartment on the front of his breastplate. Alaric did the same, mouthing a quick prayer that beseeched the Emperor for clarity of mind and firmness of decision amid the confusion of war.

'To my front!' called Brother Cardios. 'They're coming!'

There was a burst of storm bolter fire and Alaric turned in time to see something lift Cardios up and slam him hard against the crystal roof, shards of obsidian raining down. A giant spectral hand dropped the Marine and more fire streaked up at it, the muzzle flashes illuminating a huge, hulking creature, bullets rending its half-real flesh. Its massive doglike head bled purple-black fire that dripped upwards and the scores of eyes studding its skull were burning black pits. Its body seethed with corrupt mathematics, angles and shapes twisting in on one another so maddeningly it was impossible to focus on it properly, only comprehend that it was massive, powerful and terrible.

A daemon. The data-daemons had combined, subsuming their individual prowess into one creature that did not fear the prayers of the Grey Knights.

Dvorn yelled and sprinted into the space where Cardios had stood, swinging his Nemesis hammer so hard it connected with the unreal substance of the daemon's torso and ripped out a chunk of raw logic. The daemon bellowed and swung out a clawed hand, smashing Dvorn against the crystal. Sparks of power bled from the wound in the crystal as Dvorn hit the ground and rolled just as a cloven foot extruded itself from the daemon's mass and stamped down like an industrial piston.

Everyone that could was firing at the daemon now as it lumbered towards them, backing towards Saphentis in a tight formation. Captain Tharkk and the two tech-guard needed their combined strength to drag Brother Cardios back and Dvorn bought them all precious seconds, rolling onto his back and firing into the daemon's underside before jamming his hammer into its belly and pushing up, trying to force it from over him.

The daemon reeled but did not stop, listing to the side and passing through the crystal. As it did so the livid, open wounds sealed up and new angry colours pulsed through its body.

The daemons living in the data medium were projecting this daemon out from there, just as they had projected the bodies of the hunter-daemons in the valley. They were stronger there, but they were also vulnerable, concentrating on fighting their way through the Grey Knights to reach Saphentis, the one who was invading their realm.

Alaric reversed his grip on his Nemesis halberd and dropped to his knees, driving the blade deep into the crystal of the floor.

'I am the Hammer!' he yelled. 'I am the point of His spear! I am the mail about His fist!'

He felt the daemons recoil from him, their hot anger conducted through the blade and up the halberd's haft. They hated it. He knew how to hurt them.

The daemon stopped, head back and screaming, spatters of pure information fountaining from its gaping mouth like blood. Lykkos stepped forward, dropped to one knee and put three rapid psycannon shots through its throat, the blessed bolter shells punching up through its head and spattering spectral brains all over the ceiling. The monster stumbled and the Grey Knights all added their fire, Archis taking aim with his Incinerator and pouring a gout of flame around its feet.

'Behold the fate of the Unguided one!' yelled Alaric, switching to a new prayer as he felt the daemons all around him trying to find a way around the force of his faith. 'For every soul is drawn towards the beacon of the Master of Mankind! Behold the fate of the faithless, for every soul is born to believe!'

Raw pain shot up into Alaric, burning his fingers and the muscles of his arms as he held on. He was in a battle of wills with the data-daemons and he would not give in because there was nothing in this galaxy or any other with the willpower to match a Grey Knight.

Brother Haulvarn saw the daemon reeling and ran forward, leaping up and driving the blade of his sword down into its gaping mouth. Dvorn rolled onto his knees and swung his Nemesis hammer into the daemon's side, knocking it onto one knee. Haulvarn was on top of it, stabbing down, smouldering multi-coloured gore spattering all over him.

The data-daemons were torn between fending off Alaric's spiritual assault and keeping their creation on its feet. They couldn't do both and the daemon was driven back under Dvorn and Haulvarn's assault, battered further by combined fire from the rest of the squad. With a horrendous sound Alaric hoped he would never have to hear again, the daemon came apart. Unable to retain its foothold in real space, its daemonic flesh unravelled in a swirling mass of colour and light, streaming back into the crystal as it shape was erased from reality.

Alaric fell onto his back, the images of thousands of screaming datadaemons glowing on his retinas.

'It's down,' said Hawkespur.

'We don't have long,' said Alaric . He pulled himself back onto his feet – his ceramite gauntlets were glowing a dull red and the blade of his Nemesis halberd was charred black. He looked at Saphentis. 'Archmagos?'

'I believe I have found all that I can. It is incomplete and corrupt, but not devoid of interesting content.'

'Wonderful. Tharrk, stay close to the archmagos and Hawkespur.'

Captain Tharkk saluted briskly. He only had two tech-guard left, but Alaric knew the mental surgery and conditioning of the Adeptus Mechanicus meant he would be a soldier to the end.

Haulvarn picked himself up and pulled Dvorn to his feet. The two of them were liberally spattered with rainbow-sheened gore, like rancid machine oil.

'Injuries?' asked Alaric.

'Nothing,' replied Halvarn.

'None here,' added Dvorn.

'Cardios?'

'I'm beaten up, but not badly,' replied Brother Cardios, who was sitting propped up against the crystal. His breastplate was badly dented and his backpack was all but shattered.

'I can hear contacts,' said Lykkos. 'Close and approaching.'

'Throne of Earth,' said Alaric resignedly. 'Fall back, we'll have to take the valley.'

'They could pin us down from the cliffs,' said Captain Tharkk. 'And the daemons are there.'

'Exactly. We know what's waiting for us. Now move out.'

Gunfire chattered. Crystal smashed. Lykkos rolled to the side as heavy weapons fire stitched a path straight past him.

'Cover!' yelled Alaric but he didn't have to. The Grey Knights and the tech-guard hit the floor as heavy weapons fire thudded in from every direction. Above it Alaric could hear the machine-code orders gibbered by one of the tech-priests.

The crystal was reforming. With a tortured sound like breaking glass walls were bleeding across open spaces and new pathways were opening. Space Marines and tech-guard hunkered down behind outcrops of black crystal or in inclines on the floor, shielding themselves as best they could from the fire. Alaric followed suit and glimpsed battle-servitors, their tiny heads fronted with targeter devices and their burly torsos supporting twin-linked heavy stubbers or autocannon, stuttering suppressive fire in all directions.

The fire thinned out as the attacking force got into position. The return fire was desultory – the surviving tech-guard snapped off lasgun shots but most of the Grey Knights saved their ammunition rather than spray fire at targets they couldn't see, without knowing how many there even were. Alaric could see pallid menial bodies and hulking battle-servitors skulking through the shadows between crystal outcrops, probably getting into position for an all-out assault.

'Saphentis!' hissed Alaric. 'Did you happen to download a map of this place?'

'There is no map,' replied the archmagos. 'The structure of the datafortress is largely at the whim of the tech-priest in command.'

'Then how do we get out?'

'Were we to possess the command protocols we could simply reform the structure and create an exit in any direction we wished.'

'And can we get them?'

'No.'

Alaric sensed something moving behind him. He turned to see the wall reforming, a tunnel opening up like a mouth. The shape of a battle-servitor lumbered towards him – one arm was an autocannon and the other ended in a fearsome set of mechanical shears.

'Come with me,' it said through the vox-caster set into its shrunken skull-like face.

Alaric brought his storm bolter up level with the servitor's face. It made no sense – the servitor was in a perfect position to rake Alaric's squad with autocannon fire.

'Why?' he asked.

'Because I can help you,' replied the servitor.

'Lies.'

'Then kill me.'

Alaric put a burst of storm bolter fire through the servitor's head. Its brain, through which its motor functions were routed, was destroyed and it shut down instantly, slumping against the wall of the tunnel.

Something else moved, this time far smaller – a tiny scuttling creature like a large flat beetle. It had glinting mechanical mandibles and dozens of intricate jointed legs. It scrabbled up the crystal outcrop that Alaric was crouched behind.

'Kill us all,' it said, in a tinny voice barely loud enough for Alaric to hear. 'But we can help you.'

'How?' Alaric tried to work out what the creature was – it was probably either an example of Chaeroneia's biomechanical fauna, or some artificial thing that cleaned or maintained the fortress. Either way, it shouldn't have been talking to him.

'As I did once before. In the factory spire. Did you believe it was the grace of the Emperor that saved you?'

Alaric thought wildly. It could be a trick, perhaps by the commanding tech-priest, perhaps by the data-daemons. But even if it was, it was unlikely in the extreme that the Grey Knights could fend off another Mechanicus attack, especially after the mauling by the data-daemons. In situations like this leadership consisted of the capacity to make quick decisions and carry them through and in that moment Alaric decided it was better to walk into a trap than let the Mechanicus kill them where they hid.

'What should I do?' he asked.

'Keep them busy.'

Alaric turned to where Saphentis was ducking down in cover, flanked by the tech-guard. 'Say something, Saphentis.'

The archmagos turned his segmented eyes on Alaric, managing to look unimpressed even with such an abnormal face. 'What should I say, justicar?'

'Offer him a deal.'

'You are, as you say, in command.' Saphentis tilted his head back and transmitted a jarring, ugly chorus of machine-code. There was a pause while the sporadic gunfire died down and then a reply came, the staccato zeroes and ones echoing from somewhere far through the crystal labyrinth.

'What did you say?' asked Alaric.

'I told them we would come quietly if they accepted us into their tech-priesthood and introduced us to their own version of the Cult Mechanicus.'

'What was the reply?'

'They mocked us.'

The battle-servitors stomped forwards, the crushing sound of their footsteps synchronised. Alaric risked a glance around out of cover and saw there were at least five of them, massive heavy weapons variants, with a mass of menials following behind them, ready to swamp the

Grey Knights as they were driven out of cover. The crystal had reformed into a long, low gallery with plenty of space for the servitors and menials to draw up lines of fire.

In the gloom at the back of the cavern was the tech-priest in command. His upper body was covered in slabs of black crystal data medium, like plates in a suit of armour or scales on an obsidian reptile. His lower half was a mass of writhing mechanical tendrils. There was a faint shimmering aura around him – an energy field, which meant that even if the Grey Knights or tech-guard could get a shot at him it would probably bounce off.

'Grey Knights, each take a servitor,' said Alaric quietly over the vox. 'Left to right, Haulvarn, Dvorn, Archis, Lykkos, then me. Cardios, hang back and flame the menials. Understood?'

Acknowledgement runes flickered. It wasn't much of a plan, but it would buy them the seconds Alaric had promised.

The nearest servitor's arm-mounted missile launcher levelled at Alaric. It would shatter the crystal, leave him exposed and probably cause massive wounds.

The servitor turned suddenly and fired, the missile streaking into the menials behind it.

The explosion sent out clouds of razor-sharp spinning crystal shards and shredded the bodies of the gaggle of menials following the servitor. Another servitor followed suit, spraying autocannon fire at the back of the cavern, stitching bloody ruin through half-glimpsed menial bodies. The tech-priest screamed machine code and fire was streaking back and forth between the Mechanicus force, las-bolts from the menials and heavy weapons from the servitors.

'Stay down!' shouted Alaric as the din of gunfire echoed and re-echoed through the cavern. An explosion threw the massive form of a servitor into the Grey Knights' position, its armoured torso charred and battered, smoke spurting from its track units.

It turned a scorched head towards Alaric. 'Follow,' it said. The crystal floor below it descended, the substance of the datafortress altering around it, forming a bowl-shaped depression with a tunnel leading from one side.

'Move!' voxed Alaric and followed the servitor down. Some of the menials managed to redirect their fire through the confusion and las-fire smacked into Alaric's shoulder pad. The other Grey Knights scrambled down beside him – one of the tech-guard screamed, the first hint of emotion he had shown for most of his life, as a las-bolt punched through his gut and he pitched face-first into the floor. Hawkespur and

Saphentis followed, Tharkk and the one remaining tech-guard covering the archmagos.

The servitor, belching smoke, dragged itself into the tunnel and Alaric followed. The tunnel was being created as the servitor went, corkscrewing down into the foundations of the datafortress. The Grey Knights were on his heels and Brother Archis dragged Saphentis behind him as the fire fell more heavily.

Tharkk was the last man into the tunnel, sniping at the menials who were firing from the back of the cavern. Alaric glanced round in time to see the datafortress's tech-priest descend behind him, a grav-unit evidently hidden by the coils of mechadendrites that made up his lower half. The tech-priest spat a machine-code curse and held out his arms. Plates of crystal medium lifted from his limbs, revealing black, putrescent skin beneath. The plates span around the tech-priest in a wider orbit, deflecting the las-blasts from Tharkk's gun as he sprayed fire at the Enemy.

The armour plates surrounded Tharkk and cut him into scores of horizontal slices.

The tunnel entrance closed before the sorry chunks of Tharkk's body hit the floor. The sound of gunfire was suddenly distant, the machine-code howls of rage from the tech-priest dim.

The servitor continued down. The datacrystal walls were dull and greyish, as if the crystal was drained or dead. Alaric looked to see who had made it out – his squad, Saphentis, Hawkespur and the one surviving tech-guard. He hurried up to the servitor, which was trundling down the tunnel apparently uninterested in Tharkk's death.

'What are you?' asked Alaric.

'All in time,' replied the servitor, its voice garbled as its vox unit failed.

Hawkespur caught up with Alaric. Her gun was in her hand. 'Justicar, what happened up there?'

'I think we have an ally,' replied Alaric.

'Who? A servitor?'

'I don't believe it's that simple. But we'll find out soon.'

Alaric led the force further down into the guts of Chaeroneia and as they went the tunnel knitted itself closed behind them. Step by step the planet was swallowing them, and either there would be safety beneath Manufactorium Noctis or Alaric was leading his squad into a far worse trap than the one they had just escaped.

ELEVEN

'When Grand Master Ganelon heard the words of the daemon, there was no need to listen. For the words of the Enemy are lies; even those that are true are spoken only in ultimate deceit.'

– 'The Parable of Ganelon'
as related by Chaplain Greacris
in the *Index Beati*.

'OLD FRIENDS,' SAID Urkrathos, walking onto the command deck of the *Hellforger*.

The daemons who controlled the *Hellforger* looked at him with hatred so pure it dripped from their eyes, black burning droplets of loathing. There were forty-eight daemons welded into the command architecture of Grand Cruiser *Hellforger*, every one slaved into a different aspect of the ship and bound by rites older than mankind to obey Urkrathos's every whim.

The command deck was long, low and infernally hot and it stank like a torture chamber. The walls and floor were pitted, rotting iron that sweated blood and the feeble light came from the tactical holo-display that Urkrathos used in place of a bridge viewscreen. Tangles of obscure machinery and electronics welled from the walls, floor and ceiling like mechanical tumours, hissing steam and spitting sparks as ancient clockwork cogitators maintained the malevolent, spiteful machine-spirit of the *Hellforger*. The daemons melded with the various command helms were massively muscular but helpless, their fangs and talons useless as long as Urkrathos held fealty over them. Some had massive shearing crab-like pincers, others had dozens of arachnid legs tipped with tiny

393

gnashing mouths, or nests of writhing entrails that could strangle like tentacles, or stranger and deadlier things besides. But not one of them could attack Urkrathos or disobey his orders, as much as every single one of them longed to do so.

Urkrathos strode down the command deck. The holo-display projected the image of Chaeroneia into the middle, about a metre above the floor and several metres across. It was a fine planet, dark and sickly, so stained with the warp he could tell how corrupt it had become just by looking at it. The asteroids around the world danced according to a complex but identifiable pattern, with a spell wrought into their movements to prevent any cogitator from guessing where they would turn next. The asteroid field meant that the interloper ships now clustered in medium orbit around Chaeroneia could not hope to land a meaningful force on the planet, which in turn meant that whatever the Imperial ships did, the tribute would remain on Chaeroneia for Urkrathos to collect.

And what a magnificent tribute it was.

'Show me our positions,' ordered Urkrathos. The daemon projecting the holo-display, a foul squat thing with dozens of eyes, gibbered as it wove the image into the air. Urkrathos's fleet appeared on the holo some distance from the world. Urkrathos commanded the *Hellforger* itself, the cruiser *Desikratis* which bristled with guns, the fighter platform *Cadaver* which was the base of the Vulture Flight attack craft, and the three Idolator-class escorts that formed Scapula Wing.

The *Desikratis* was commanded by a titanic daemon who functioned as the ship's sole crew member, its nerve-tipped tentacles reaching into every corner of the bloated, gun-heavy ship. The *Desikratis* in turn commanded the three Idolators of Scapula Wing, towards which it seemed to have a rather paternal attitude. The fighter platform *Cadaver* was commanded by Kreathak the Thrice-Maimed, one of the finest fighter craft pilots of the last two centuries, who also led the elite Vulture Wing.

It was more than enough ships to collect the tribute and escort it back to Lord Abaddon at the Eye of Terror. But Warmaster Abaddon himself had commanded Urkrathos to make certain that the tribute was delivered intact and so Urkrathos had taken everything he could muster to Chaeroneia to make good his duty to the Despoiler.

'Contact the *Cadaver*,' said Urkrathos. 'Tell Commander Kreathak to get all craft ready to scramble. I'll leave him to break up those escorts.' Urkrathos looked closer at the composition of the Imperial fleet. It was pathetic – one cruiser protected by the escorts, another ship of uncertain designation that was a little smaller than a cruiser and a handful of troop ships and assorted transports. 'Leave the enemy flagship to me.'

The daemon charged with communications was a whale-sized monster half-melted into the rusting ceiling, its bloated body mostly taken up with the brain matter that processed Urkrathos's words into encrypted ship-to-ship comms. Like all the forty-eight daemons, it had been conquered by Urkrathos in personal combat during the Black Legions' battles to carve out an empire for themselves in the Eye of Terror, or given to him in recognition for some great victory in the eyes of the gods. By the decree of the Chaos powers, the daemons so defeated or possessed by Urkrathos were owned by him in a state of slavery, forbidden by the will of the gods to disobey him in anything. He had made them the crew of his ship, because it pleased him to have such powerful creatures in such obvious fortitude, held where he could witness their suffering and see the hatred they had for him in their eyes.

It was the only thing worth fighting for, the only thing worth anything – the sensation of owning another intelligent thing completely. The knowledge that he could compel it to obey any and every thought he directed at it. It was what the Despoiler promised – a universe enslaved, where the ignorant were crushed by the feet of those blessed by Chaos. And if any of the Imperial scum orbiting Chaeroneia survived, Urkrathos would make slaves of them, too – because he could.

Once, a long time ago, Urkrathos had fought for the good of mankind and the will of the Emperor. He had been a slave to the Emperor. Horus had taught them that they were slaves of no one and now Abaddon was the one who would prove that to the rest of the galaxy.

'Weapons!' shouted Urkrathos. A lean, muscular creature crucified against one wall snarled back at him. 'I want ordnance ready for firing. Full spread, long fuses.'

'So it shall be,' growled the creature. Its burning red eyes rolled back in their sockets as he willed the command into the minds of the ordnance crew deep within the ship – soon the *Hellforger* would be ready to pump scores of torpedoes into the Imperial flagship and reduce it to a cloud of burning debris.

'It's almost a pity,' thought Urkrathos aloud. 'I was hoping I would have to board them. Maybe I still will, if they survive that long. Make ready the boarding parties.'

The communications-daemon convulsed as it relayed the order to the boarding troops barracked throughout the *Hellforger*. They were the scum of the galaxy, the worst of the worst, deformed and degenerate creatures that had once been men but had over the generations been bred into brutal killing machines. Urkrathos had no Black Legion squads, Space Marine units that had been elite ship-to-ship combatants even before the Heresy and the flight to the Eye of Terror, but nonetheless he seriously doubted if there was anything in the Imperial fleet that could stand up to a boarding assault from the *Hellforger*.

Yes, he would have preferred a proper battle. It was in the fires of conflict that Chaos was praised the highest. But it was enough that the Despoiler would receive his tribute and the Black Crusade fighting from the Eye would be strengthened beyond measure by Urkrathos's victory.

He left the daemons to brood as he walked off the deck and down towards the ship's lower decks where the complement of slaves were kept in the crowded pens. Easy or not, the coming victory had to be sealed with the blessing of the Chaos Gods and to ensure that happened Urkrathos had a great many innocents to sacrifice before battle was joined.

INQUISITOR NYXOS SHUFFLED down the shuttle's boarding ramp like the old man he purported to be. He even walked with a cane and looked ancient and frail compared to the strapping Naval armsmen who accompanied him.

Fleet Commissar Leung was there to meet the inquisitor. Leung was a fine product of the Schola Progenium, an orphan of some interminable conflict who had been brought up in starched Commissariat uniforms and instilled with the sense that only the thin line of cowardice separated any one man from irredeemable corruption. He saluted sharply at the inquisitor's approach, small hard eyes glinting beneath the peak of his officer's cap, black greatcoat around his shoulders in spite of the stifling heat on the docking deck of the *Exemplar*.

There was no one else with Leung. Even a petty officer travelling between ships might expect a complement of armsmen to welcome him onboard, an extension of the protocols one captain was expected to extend to another.

'Greetings, commissar,' said Nyxos. 'I see our hosts do not stand on ceremony.'

Leung removed his cap and tucked it neatly under one arm, parade ground sharp. 'The magos does not recognise the authority of the Imperial Navy or its officer core. She accepts my presence only grudgingly.' Leung's voice was as taut as the rest of him, fast and clipped.

'Well, they do revel in their independence, the Mechanicus,' said Nyxos, pausing to nod his thanks to the armsman who helped him down the step at the end of the boarding ramp. 'Are they prepared to accept me?

'I believe so,' replied Leung. 'Although I had to arrange quarters for you myself.'

'Good man. Lead me there, if you please.'

'Of course.'

The interior of the *Exemplar* was fundamentally different from the *Tribunicia*. It was as if the two craft had been built by two different species, or in two different eras of history. The brutally elegant gothic lines of the *Tribunicia* were replaced by the blocky functionality preferred by the Adeptus Mechanicus. Cog-toothed designs trimmed everything, even the massive blocks that made up the walls and floor of the docking deck. Several other craft and highly advanced shuttles were also docked, being serviced by heavy servitors and the occasional hooded Mechanicus crewman. The stifling, cloying smell of scented machine-oil was heavy in the air and most unusually, there was little noise from the crew. Nyxos knew places like docking decks for the clamour of crewmen yelling at one another, often in rapid crew-cant that an outsider couldn't understand. The Mechanicus did its business in grim silence, human voices replaced by the hissing of hydraulics and the dim clanging of pistons beneath the deck.

'What are your impressions of the magos?' asked Nyxos as he walked.

'Few,' replied Leung. 'She has little respect for Imperial authorities save the senior ranks of the Mechanicus. Even my own office seems to mean little to her.'

'Let us hope she does not show the same attitude towards the Inquisition,' said Nyxos. 'Does it seem she will obey the orders of the Rear Admiral?'

'Probably,' said Leung. Nyxos noticed he didn't so much walk as march alongside him. 'But she considers herself to be acting independently. Her orders evidently concern Chaeroneia itself, not the fleet sent to investigate it.'

'Do you know which tech-priests she answers to?' asked Nyxos. 'Archmagos Saphentis is out of communication – is she acting of her own accord?'

'It is doubtful. She has frequent high-level encrypted communications. I believe they are with the subsector Adeptus Mechanicus command but she has not been forthcoming about the Mechanicus command structure here.'

'Well, I'll just have to convince her to be more open.'

Leung, Nyxos and the armsmen following them reached a cargo-sized elevator and Leung keyed a sequence into the keypad that controlled it. The elevator's platform ground upwards, rising through a deep square shaft as it passed many intermediate decks. Nyxos saw glimpses of the other decks as they passed – some looked like research labs, with endless benches of baffling equipment and robed tech-priests poring over crucibles or microscopes. Others housed massive banks of cogitators, cooled by freezing mist that clung to the floor like standing water. Tech-guard drilled on internal parade grounds of beaten bronze, ranks of servitors hung motionless on recharging racks, enormous tangles of complex machinery relayed the plasma generators' energy throughout the ship. Rust-red and brass were the dominant colours, a distant mechanical din the prominent sound, with the odd passage of rhythmic chanting filtering up from tech-ritual chambers and servitor-choirs.

The *Exemplar* was evidently a fine ship, the product of an immense amount of resources and fading technological knowledge. Whether she was as good a warship as she was a research centre was another matter, but it did occur to Nyxos that the Mechanicus was risking a very valuable ship and crew to investigate Chaeroneia.

The elevator reached the command deck level, where the walls were studded with niches containing elaborate shrines to the Omnissiah and the half-metal skull symbol of the Adeptus Mechanicus stared down from every column. The air was heavy with scented smoke from the braziers, where libations of machine-oil smouldered. The elevator stopped at the level of a wide corridor, carpeted in deep rust red with complex geometric patterns inscribed on the walls and ceiling, where several tech-priests walked followed by gaggles of menials, servitors and lower-ranked adepts. Several curious eyes, bionic and otherwise, turned to look at the interlopers as if Nyxos had no right to stray onto sacred Mechanicus ground.

Nyxos's thoughts were interrupted by a sudden blaring klaxon. Layered below it was a staccato blast of sound, an emergency broadcast in pure machine code.

'What is it?' shouted Nyxos over the din. Tech-priests and menials were already hurrying around.

'Battle stations, maybe,' said Leung. 'Or a proximity warning.'

'Damn it.' Nyxos flicked on his personal vox-unit. He was loath to use it except in an emergency, but he thought this counted. A very rare and antique unit contained in a lacquered red box Nyxos wore around his neck under his robes, it could tap into any local vox-frequency and let Nyxos hijack nearby communications. 'This is Inquisitor Nyxos of the Ordo Malleus,' he barked into the ship's command frequency. 'I demand to know what this emergency is.'

'State your business,' came a reply in the flat, female voice Nyxos recognised as belonging to Magos Korveylan.

'The Emperor's work, magos,' said Nyxos, 'and do not make me justify my actions further.'

There was a pause, slightly too long for comfort. 'Very well,' replied Korveylan. 'Our sensoria have detected torpedoes locked on to the *Exemplar*. Brace for impact.'

BELOW MANUFACTORIUM NOCTIS lay the remains of the old Chaeroneia, the last vestiges of a forge world loyal to Mars and the Emperor. The old architecture of the Adeptus Mechanicus survived, its industrial scale fused with the columns and vaults of religion and the powerful symbolism of the cog and skull. It lay in isolated pockets where the biomechanical mass of the tainted tech-priests had never reached, chapels and factoria, ritual chambers and sacred libraria.

Two hours after the heretic ambush, Alaric and his small strikeforce arrived in one such chamber. The air was old and stale, but free of the biomechanical stink – decaying flesh and rancid machine-oil – that had accompanied the heretic tech-priests and their menials. Alaric stepped out into the cavernous space, storm bolter ready, still not knowing if he had found an ally on Chaeroneia or was just walking into another trap.

'Spread out,' he ordered. His squad fanned out around him, moving with speed and stealth that normal men would find impossible given the bulky power armour they wore. He glanced back at the sole surviving tech-guard. 'Stay here,' he said. 'Protect the interrogator.'

Interrogator Hawkespur didn't object to being assigned a bodyguard and crouched down by the tunnel entrance. Saphentis loitered there, too.

As he walked out into the space Alaric saw it was a cathedral-sized chapel to the Omnissiah. In the centre of its high domed ceiling had once been a circular hole looking up into Chaeroneia's sky but it was clogged with tons of rubble and wreckage, the weight of the city above warping the dome into a painful, biological shape. Trickles of foul water pattered down from cracks in the ceiling, which was covered in elaborate murals of tech-rituals now discoloured with age and damp. Columns stood around the edge of the circular space, each one carved into a statue of a tech-priest, presumably from Chaeroneia's distant Imperial past. The floor was covered in concentric circles or inscribed equations, long sequences of numbers and symbols that no doubt had massive significance for the intricate rituals of the Cult Mechanicus. Now the floor's bronze surface was pitted and green with corrosion. At one end of the room stood a massive altar, a single block of a greyish metallic substance Alaric guessed was pure carbon, with the remains of libation-bowls and hexagonal candelabra still corroding around it.

'Clear this side,' voxed Brother Dvorn.

'Clear here,' confirmed Haulvarn.

'There are no lifesigns on the auspex,' said Saphentis, who was consulting a dataslate that had unfolded from one of his blade-tipped arms.

Alaric walked, still wary, into the centre of the cathedral. It was silent, with not even the dull industrial background noise of the city above reaching this far down. The air was heavy with the meaning of the rituals that had been performed here before Chaeroneia fell, with generations of tech-priests exploring the deepest mysteries of the Omnissiah through ceremony and contemplation.

'Space Marines,' said a voice from the shadows on the far side of the room. 'No wonder they mobilised so quickly.'

Alaric ducked behind the closest column and aimed his storm bolter in the direction of the voice, finger on the firing stud. He heard the clatter of ceramite on stone as the rest of the squad did the same.

'Please, do not shoot. We are the ones who saved you.' A skinny, awkward figure emerged from the darkness behind the carbon altar, hands raised. It looked like a tech-adept, his body composed mostly of bionics. The metal of his artificial hands and face was deep orange-brown with rust and his robes were tattered and filthy. 'My apologies,' he said sheepishly. 'I have too little flesh to show up on your auspexes, I imagine. I did not intend to catch you by surprise.'

Alaric straightened up, still keeping his aim on the tech-priest. 'Who are you?' he demanded.

The tech-priest walked forward a little, still with his scrawny mechanical arms in the air. More shapes were emerging slowly from behind him. 'Iuscus Gallen,' he replied, 'Adept Minoris. These are my comrades.' He indicated the gaggle of tech-priests following him into the temple. They were in as poor repair as Gallen himself and hardly any of them had any flesh showing between the malfunctioning bionics.

'Did you lead us down from the datafortress?'

'Us? Omnissiah forgive me, no, not us. We never could. That was the magos to whom we answer.'

Saphentis stepped forward, not bothering to stay in any cover. 'As an archmagos appointed by the office of the Fabricator General, I require the presence of this magos.'

Gallen looked at Saphentis with surprise in his one remaining human eye. 'An archmagos! Then have the true Mechanicus returned to

Chaeroneia? And brought the Adeptus Astartes with them to cleanse this world at last?'

'No, they have not,' replied a new voice, deep and booming. There was a grinding sound from behind the altar and an old broken cargo-servitor lumbered into view. The voice issued from the vox-unit hanging from its neck. The once-human parts of the servitor had died long ago and were now just dried skeletal scraps sandwiched between the servitor's motive units and the massive lifter units of its shoulders. Ordinarily, without a human nervous system to control it, the servitor should not have been able to move at all. 'These we see are all they bring. There is no army to cleanse Chaeroneia. Is that not correct?'

Alaric stepped out from behind the column. 'That is correct,' he said. 'This is an investigative mission under the authority of the Holy Orders of the Emperor's Inquisition. The archmagos is here in an advisory capacity.'

'That is a shame,' said the servitor. 'But you will have to do.'

'Explain yourself,' said Saphentis bluntly.

'Of course. I am being rather rude. I would introduce myself formally but we have already met at the datafortress and before at the manufactorium spire although you probably do not realise it. I am Magos Antigonus and it seems we have the same mission. Follow me and I will explain.'

TWELVE

'The difference between glory and heresy is so often no more than time.'
— Inquisitor Quixos (source suppressed)

ANTIGONUS'S REALM SPANNED several factory floors and religious build-ings that had survived the crushing weight of the city above being built over the centuries. Alaric followed the monstrous servitor through armouries of stolen weaponry and captured battle-servitors, and bar-racks where fugitive tech-priests fought a losing battle against time to repair their bionics and replace their dying flesh. He saw a giant under-ground water cistern transformed into a series of hydroponic pools where slimy green algae was grown and turned into a barely edible food to keep the tiny community alive, and the entrances to labyrinthine tun-nels above rigged with enough explosive traps and sentry guns to keep attackers away for months. It was a cramped, stifling world, redolent with decay and desperation. But at least it was not corrupt like the planet above. And as they walked, Alaric and Antigonus talked.

'So,' said Alaric at length. 'You are dead?'

'That depends on how you look at it,' said Antigonus. He was trundling through a hangar where various decrepit tanks and APCs were being refitted and reassembled to form a makeshift motor pool for the tiny force of tech-priests. 'I have not had a living body for more than a thousand years.'

'In real space, only a hundred have passed,' said Alaric.

'Well, in any case, it is a long time to be without a physical form. I think it has had quite an effect on me. No doubt your archmagos would be outraged at how we flout the dogma of the Cult Mechanicus down here.'

'But how are you still here?'

'That, justicar, is a complicated question. Chaeroneia is a very old planet and it is riddled with the type of technology the Mechanicus could not replicate in my day and I trust that has not changed in yours. That includes cogitators and data media with a far greater capacity than anything the Mechanicus can make in the current age. So advanced, in fact, that they can contain all the data required to reconstruct a human mind, give or take a few personality quirks. I was sent here by Mars to investigate rumours of tech-heresy and when I discovered they were true, the heretics hunted me down. They thought me dead, but as I died I was able to shift my consciousness into an ancient form of cogitator engine.'

'Just your mind?'

'Just, as you say, my mind. I do not know how long I was in there before I was able reconstruct myself. I was nothing, justicar. I did not exist. It is impossible to describe it. I was just a collection of ideas that used to form Magos Antigonus. I think it took me hundreds of years, but gradually I put myself together again. I found I could move through machines as long as a particular machine's spirit was not strong enough to oppose me. It was through various stores of historical data that I discovered what had happened to Chaeroneia while I was dead. It did not make for enjoyable reading. So I learnt what I could and could not do, explored, investigated. Then I came down here and gathered the few loyal tech-priests who remained and founded this resistance movement.'

'If I may say so, magos, it does not look like you have had much success.'

The lurching servitor shrugged its massive pneumatic shoulders. 'By most standards you are correct. But we know more about Chaeroneia and its tech-priests that you do, justicar and you are better at bringing the fight to the enemy than we are. Moreover, if Chaeroneria has re-entered real space then the tech-priests have made it happen for a reason. Whatever they are doing, I doubt very much that it will benefit the Imperium. All this means that we need each other.'

Alaric and Antigonus's servitor walked through the hangar into a long corridor lined with crumbling statues of past Archmagi, who had ruled Chaeroneia in the days before the tech-heresies had taken root.

'Here' said Antigonus, pointing a rusting cargo lifter arm at one of the statues. It depicted a tech-priest in archaic Mechanicus robes. Only his face was visible, the features blurred in the decaying stone. Its eyes were tiny discs set into the sockets of his cranium and from the lower half of his face hung a bunch of long tentacles – mechadendrites, the prehensile serpentine limbs that many tech-priests used to perform delicate work. The faded letters chiselled into the statue's base read; ARCHMAGOS VENERATUS SCRAECOS.

'This was the one. Perhaps the leader. He was either the origin of the tech-heresy on this planet or he was their most senior convert. He was the one who killed me. I'd wager he led the effort to bring Chaeroneia into the warp, too. He commanded the machine-curse he used to infect me and probably all the hunter-programs that protect his data centres.'

Alaric looked up at the statue. It looked as strange as any tech-priest he had seen. He knew that archmagos veneratus was one of the highest tech-priest ranks that might be found on a forge world – the tech-heresy had spread quickly on Chaeroneia and straight to the top. 'They weren't hunter-programs,' said Alaric. 'They were daemons. An unusual kind, true, since they compose their bodies of information instead of sorcery. But daemons nonetheless. That was how we could defeat them.'

Antigonus looked at Alaric and his desiccated face managed to appear surprised. 'Daemons? I thought that was just a lie of the machine-curse.'

Alaric shook his head. 'It was probably telling the truth. Daemons will only speak the truth when they know it will not be believed.'

'And you defeated them, you say? At the datafortress?'

'Yes. I and my battle-brothers.'

'Were you able to access the information in there? We have been trying to get at it for decades.'

Alaric sighed. 'You will have to ask Archmagos Saphentis about that. He is not always willing to share information with me. Perhaps as a fellow tech-priest you will have more luck.'

'We tech-priests are not known for our social perception, justicar, but still I think I detect some tension between the two of you.'

'Saphentis represents the interests of the Mechanicus. They do not always coincide with the objectives of the Inquisition.'

'You are suspicious of him?'

'He was accompanied by another tech-priest. She has disappeared and Saphentis does not seem particularly concerned about losing her. And I think he has some admiration for what has happened to Chaeroneia.'

Antigonus led the way down the corridor, which looped back round towards the makeshift barracks where Alaric's squad, Saphentis and Hawkespur were being seen to by the medically-trained tech-priests. 'Your suspicions may be well-founded, justicar. It was a high-ranking tech-priest who first brought this heresy to Chaeroneia. But nevertheless I shall do as you suggest and talk to him. It may be he found something at the datafortress we can use to strike back at this planet's leaders at last.'

'With Chaeroneia back in real space,' said Alaric, 'it might be the only chance we get. But there is something else we need. Can you communicate with craft in orbit?'

Antigonus seemed to think for a second, the skull of his servitor body tilting to one side. 'Perhaps. But not with any certainty.'

'It will have to do. Hawkespur will need to contact Inquisitor Nyxos in orbit, tell him what is happening down here.'

'And yourself?'

'Me?'

'You are doubtless tired and injured, justicar. I expect you have not rested for any length of time since you arrived on the surface.'

Alaric held up the storm bolter mounted on the back of his power armour's left gauntlet. The barrel was charred black with muzzle flash. 'I could use some more ammunition,' he said.

'I will see what we can do. Meanwhile, I shall speak with Saphentis. Whether he is on our side or not he could know more about Chaeroneia than I do.'

The corridor led into the barracks, where rusting metal bunks were lined up in niches and tiny personal shrines to the Omnissiah filled the room with the smell of scented machine-oil. Alaric's squad were attending to their wargear rites, murmuring their own benedictions of preparedness as they cleaned their storm bolters and nemesis weapons. Brother Dvorn had removed the upper half of his armour and was repairing the many bullet scars and gouges in the surface of the ceramite. Dvorn was impressively muscled even for a Marine and he had been at the front of every hand-to-hand action as always. Cardios, meanwhile, had been seriously battered at the hands of the data-daemon and his fractured ribcage had been set and bandaged by Antigonus's tech-priests. One of his arms had been broken, too and the crude operation to re-set the bone had left a vivid red scar down Cardios's bicep. The damage to his breastplate of fused ribs was worse, though – shards of bone had probably slashed at his organs, meaning he would be slightly slower and weaker than his brother Marines and would only get worse until he got to a proper apothecarion.

These were the battle-brothers to whom Alaric owed his life, simply by virtue of backing him up in battle. They all owed that much to one another – a single Grey Knight could never have lasted this long on

Chaeroneia. And Alaric was responsible for their conduct in battle and their spiritual wellbeing. It was an enormous responsibility, one that Alaric accepted because if he didn't, there were very few who could.

Alaric passed Interrogator Hawkespur, who was sitting on the bunk. Her voidsuit was unzipped and hanging around her waist. The underlayer she wore beneath it was thin enough for Alaric to see the outline of her ribs through the fabric. She looked like she had lost weight in the few days she had been on Chaeroneia – much of it must have been lost in the battle against the ugly tumours that formed blue-grey lumps under the skin of her throat and upper chest. Her face was waxy-pale, her short black hair clinging to her forehead with cold sweat.

'Hawkespur? How are you doing?' asked Alaric.

Hawkespur shrugged. 'I'm fighting it.'

'How long can you go on?'

'As long as I can. My guess would be less than a week, But I only have two years of medicae cadet training. Could be more, could be less.'

'Antigonus will try to get communications with Nyxos in orbit. After that I could leave you here.'

'No, justicar. I am the Inquisitorial representative on this planet. I must know everything you find out, immediately. Just because my time is limited does not mean my mission has already failed.' Hawkespur coughed heavily and one of Antigonus's tech-priests arrived carrying a battered box of medical supplies. Alaric left them to it and walked over to his squad.

'Brothers,' he said. 'Magos Antigonus could be a valuable ally. He knows a great deal about what happened here and how the enemy is structured. It could be that he can help us strike at the heart of the heretics.'

'Good,' said Brother Dvorn. 'I'm sick of hiding in the shadows. There's nothing on this planet that can stand up to us, not one-on-one. All we need to know is where they are.'

'Hopefully that is true,' said Alaric, 'But it may still not be that simple. Antigonus will try to put us in contact with Nyxos in orbit. We can apprise him of the situation and see if he has any new orders for us.'

'Whoever controls this planet,' added Brother Haulvarn, 'they didn't just re-enter real space by accident. And they must have known that sooner or later Imperial forces would find out that Chaeroneia had fallen to daemons and heretics. They're here for a reason and whatever they are planning they must be able to do it soon. Does Antigonus know why they have chosen this moment to show their hand?'

Alaric sat down on one of the bunks – it almost buckled under his armoured weight. He laid down his Nemesis halberd and began unfastening the massive ceramite slab of his breastplate. 'No, he does not. But there is one event we know of that Antigonus did not.'

Haulvarn raised an eyebrow. 'The Eye?'.

'The Thirteenth Black Crusade has brought more Chaos-worshipping forces into Imperial space than any other event in thousands of years. Perhaps it is a coincidence, perhaps it is not, but if the masters of Chaeroneia are on a mission to aid the Black Crusade then we could win a victory here for the forces stemming the tide at the Eye. And no doubt you have heard the rumours that victories are sorely needed.'

Alaric pulled off his breastplate and saw the livid bruises on his skin where he had been shot and battered during the fighting of the last few days. He was tired and aching and there would be new scars alongside his many old ones when he had healed. If he survived, of course. Chaeroneia probably had a great many ways to kill him that he hadn't seen yet.

'But these are matters outside our control for now,' Alaric continued. 'For the present we should concentrate on things we ourselves can change and foremost among those is ourselves. This wargear has seen much corruption on this planet and we must reconsecrate it. The same goes for our bodies and minds. Haulvarn, lead the wargear rites. Archis, speak for the spirit of your Incinerator. We will not have long before we must begin this fight again and we will use the time well.'

Brother Haulvarn began intoning the low, rhythmic words of the wargear rites, imploring forgiveness from the spirits of the squad's armour and weapons for forcing them to confront the moral treachery of Chaeroneia. As the battle-brothers prayed together, anyone who saw them would see the true strength of the Grey Knights – not the physical augmentations or the hallowed wargear, or even the exacting training that prepared them to fight things that should never exist. Their strength was their faith, the shield of pure belief that protected their minds from the predations of Chaos and the lies of daemons. No one else in the Imperium could claim such strength – it was the reason the Grey Knights existed, the reason they were trusted with spearheading holy victories in the Emperor's name.

It was just as well they had that strength. Because on Chaeroneia, it was all they had.

Inquisitor Nyxos ignored the protestations of the protocol adept who manned the doors to the bridge of the *Exemplar* and barged past the cordon of silent tech-guard, trusting in the unit of Naval armsmen behind him to keep anyone from barring his way. The torpedo alerts were still booming throughout the ship and the confusion common to all battle-readied warships was increasing – menials scurried here and there carrying messages in scroll tubes or carting vital items of equipment between decks. Tech-priests relayed orders in bursts of lingua technis and the chattered machine-code overlapped until it sounded like rapid gunfire.

As he walked onto the bridge, Nyxos saw why Magos Korveylan seemed so unwilling to see any visitors to her ship face-to-face. Her body was a solid block of mem-circuits and cogitator units, formed into a dense square pillar of knotted circuitry and wires. The remains of her biological body – her ribcage, spine, heart and lungs and her central nervous system – were contained in a plastiglass cylinder on top of the cogitator stack, her skinless face held up by a web of fine metal struts. She was rooted into the floor of the bridge and only her hands could move, her fingers moving deftly over the array of controls on the dataslate mounted inside the clear cylinder. The more 'normal' face, the one she used for visual communications with other ships, stood to one side on the communications console – it was a simple automaton, used to give the impression that Korveylan looked like the tech-priests some-one outside the Mechanicus would have met.

Korveylan looked around as Nyxos walked in. Her face was no more than muscle and bone so he could read no expression off her, but the synthesised voice that blared from the speakers on the front of her mechanical body sounded officious and annoyed. 'Inquisitor. We are at war. Leave my bridge.'

'I hardly think I'm getting in anyone's way,' replied Nyxos breezily. The rest of the bridge seemed staffed only by servitors, slaved into various consoles, dumbly typing at brass-faced keypads or working the gears on cogitator units that looked like they ran on clockwork.

Korveylan's unit rotated so she was facing Nyxos. Her lidless eyes were glossy and black. 'I am the captain of this ship.'

'And I am the instrument of the Emperor's will,' replied Nyxos briskly. 'I win.'

There was a pause as Korveylan seemed to consider this. 'Observe,' she said.

Nyxos assumed this meant he could stay, but was not to touch any-thing. That was fine by him.

The tactical viewer on the *Exemplar* took the form of a large mechan-ical orrery, a construction of concentric rings that swung around one another like the devices used to demonstrate the relative positions of planets in a solar system. This example, however, had silver and brass icons mounted on the rings that showed the relative positions of the various ships and objects around Chaeroneia. Nyxos noticed that several glinting knife-shaped icons of silver must represent the torpedoes now approaching the Imperial fleet very quickly. Bronze disks mounted further out represented the enemy fleet, including the *Hellforger*, while a dense sphere of rotating gears at the centre was Chaeroneia itself.

Space combat, Nyxos had learnt in his long Inquisitorial career, was an agonising affair where manoeuvres and assaults could take hours to pan out. Hours when a competent captain usually knew exactly what was going to happen and often had no choice but to wait for his ship to take whatever the enemy was throwing at it. The enemy attack here had been so sudden that the battle was unfolding on a minute-by-minute scale – lightning-fast by naval standards.

'Engineering,' Korveylan was saying into the ship's internal vox-net, 'Bring auxiliary reactors five and eight on-line. Full power, evasion pattern.'

Several more Mechanicus crewmen were entering the bridge, shouldering through the armsmen Nyxos had brought with him, no doubt summoned silently by Korveylan to keep an eye on the intruder. Nyxos recognised tech-guard uniforms and the brass body armour of the ship's more highly trained Skitarii troopers.

'Impact!' blared the ship's vox-casters and the first of the torpedoes hit, shaking the bridge violently. Nyxos's servo-assisted limbs compensated but several of the servitors were thrown out of their moorings, flailing helplessly like puppets with their strings cut. Tech-guard grabbed anything they could to keep themselves upright. Sparks showered as cogitators shorted and the lighting flickered.

'Damage report,' said Korveylan calmly as the explosion still echoed through the ship. Secondary explosions thudded somewhere deep in the ship's structure, ammo stores or fuel cells blowing.

Pict-screens slid up from the floor beside Korveylan, each showing the wreckage of an area devastated by the impact. To Nyxos's eyes it looked bad, billowing orange-black smoke and twisted metal.

'Engineering damage minor,' came a vox from elsewhere in the ship.

'Ordnance damage minor,' echoed a similar voice. The ship's officers sounded off – the torpedo had struck hard but not hard enough to put the *Exemplar* in immediate danger.

'Come about, pattern intercept,' said Korveylan. 'Power to prow turrets.'

Nyxos walked towards Korveylan. 'Why are you here, magos?' he asked.

'Now is not the time,' said Korveylan, with a reassuringly human note of annoyance.

'Now is the perfect time. I may not get to ask you again.'

Another explosion sounded, closer this time, metal shrieking only a couple of decks away. Nyxos heard the horrible keening of a deck breach, the air whistling as it was dragged out through a punctured hull.

'The Adeptus Mechanicus retains sovereignty over the forge world of Chaeroneia. The *Exemplar* was sent to oversee the reassertion of authority. Your questions require me to multitask, inquisitor and have a directly deleterious effect on my capacity to command this ship.'

'No, magos. I mean why are you here, personally?'

Korveylan ignored him. The tactical orrery was showing a shoal of torpedoes closing in and the ship's prow turrets opened up in response, the rapid thuds of their reports vibrating the floor of the bridge.

'I took the liberty of checking before I came aboard. The Mechanicus is meticulous in its record-keeping and an inquisitor's authority gains him access to a great deal. Not all of it, regrettably, but enough. You were a magos piloting cargo ships around the forge world Salshan Anterior barely two years ago. That would make the *Exemplar* your first battleship command. And yet here you are, hard-wired into the bridge as if you own the place. Not to mention the fact that you're a long way from home out here.'

The third impact hit Nyxos as if he had run into a wall, a shockwave ripping through from the prow of the ship and billowing through the decks. Jets of coolant gas spurted from ruptured pipes. Glass and metal shattered. A bloom of fire rippled up one wall, engulfing the servitor wired into it, before automated fire extinguishers doused half the room in choking fumes.

Nyxos realised he was on the floor. He wasn't hurt but he was shaken, his head reeling. He looked around him, face still lying against the floor and saw one of the tech-guard had lost an arm to a flying sheet of torn metal that had sheared right through at the elbow. Deeper explosions sounded, from ahead of the bridge – a torpedo had smacked into the prow, burrowed deep through the reinforced prow armour and exploded close to something the *Exemplar* couldn't really do without.

'All non-essential personnel evacuate from the bridge,' said Korveylan over the growing din.

A tech-guard hand grabbed Nyxos's shoulder, pulling him up and towards the doors leading off the bridge.

'It's not that easy, Korveylan!' shouted Nyxos. 'I know Archmagos Scraecos was at Salshan Anterior! You studied at the seminary he founded. You translated three volumes of his writings from its original machine-code. And whatever he came to Chaeroneia to find, I think you know it's still there!'

Magos Korveylan paused in making her course calculations and turned to look at Nyxos. Even with no face to hold an expression, there was something in her eyes that told Nyxos the annoyance was gone. There was no point in lying to him any more – Nyxos knew enough to see through the lies. With the sparks still flying and hundreds of warning lights flickering on every console, Magos Korveylan looked suddenly calm.

'The Chief Engineer has the bridge,' she said over the ship's vox-net. She closed her eyes, muttered a prayer Nyxos couldn't hear and exploded in a starburst of broken glass.

THE WAY to the transmitter obelisk was steep and treacherous, winding up through the remains of Manufactorium Noctis's ancient sewage and drainage systems. Interrogator Hawkespur followed Alaric doggedly along the paths cut into the sheer sides of giant water cisterns and slippery staircases worn almost smooth with time. Magos Antigonus led the way, his consciousness contained within a spry maintenance servitor with four long spiderish legs that scampered easily up steep slopes and over obstacles. Archmagos Saphentis was there, too, almost gliding regally as he kept up with Antigonus.

Alaric found the going easier than Hawkespur, his enhanced strength meaning he could just dig his fingers into the crumbling stonework and haul himself upwards. As he followed Antigonus he saw places where primitive burials had left mouldering bones in niches cut into sewer walls, a relic of the time when Chaeroneia's underclass of menials had fallen into tribal savagery for the first centuries after the planet dropped into the warp. There were decrees in the dots and dashes of lingua technis carved into marble stele set into the walls, marking the time when the tech-priests had emerged from their spires again and begun building Chaeroneia into the cannibalistic society Alaric had seen above – those menials had been rounded up, refitted and branded with barcode marks of servitude, then fed into the flesh-knitting engines when their lives were spent and turned into the biomechanical monstrosities that ran so much of Manufactorium Noctis.

There had been battles, evidently. Sometimes Alaric glimpsed armour almost corroded into nothing by time, just a green-black metal stain on the stone where a body had fallen quelling some riot or uprising. But for every sign of unrest there were two or three symbols of submission – time-worn statues of heretic tech-priests, machine-cant slogans proclaiming the debased laws of Chaeroneia. From these dank tunnels had marched the menials of Chaeroneia to join the tech-priests they considered their rightful masters and in return the planet had almost literally swallowed them up.

'There is not much further to go,' said Antigonus. The vox-unit on his current servitor made his voice sound tinny and distant. 'The obelisk was once used to transmit a navigational beacon for close-orbit spaceships. We intended to use it to broadcast a distress signal, but we soon understood that we could not get a signal from the warp into real space with the resources we had.'

'But it should reach into orbit now?' asked Hawkespur.

'If it still works, yes,' replied Antigonus.

'Archmagos,' continued Hawkespur, 'did you find out if there are any active tech-priest installations in orbit? They could block our signal, or use it to track us down here.'

'I did not find any information pertaining to that subject,' replied Saphentis.

'I'm still in the dark as to just what you did find,' said Alaric. 'Even though we lost Thalassa and almost all the tech-guard to find out.'

'It would be of limited use to one who was not a tech-priest,' replied Saphentis.

'Fortunately,' said Alaric, 'we have one right here. Antigonus?'

Antigonus's servitor paused and turned. Its face was a simple brass mask, pitted with age, with two silver studs for eyes and a round grille housing its vox-unit. 'The Enemy deployed its daemons to keep you out of there, archmagos. The knowledge you found must be important.'

The party emerged onto the base of a huge, deep chamber, roughly rectangular, with a ceiling so high it disappeared far up into the shadows beyond the limit of the search lamps mounted on the shoulders of Antigonus's servitor body. It had once been a huge reservoir of water or fuel for the Manufactorium above, but it had been dry and dark for hundreds of years now.

'Very well. The data was incomplete and severely corrupted. I was able to confirm your suspicions about the date, justicar. Chaeroneia has been out of real space for a little under eleven hundred years. Most of the rest of the information related to power output, with which a self-sufficient forge world must understandably be concerned. Chaeroneia's power is generated, output and recycled with an efficiency I have never beheld in the most advanced Adeptus Mechanicus facilities,'

'Don't get too enthusiastic, archmagos,' said Antigonus. 'Tech-priests have been lost to the resistance before by coming to side with the enemy. They always begin with such sentiments. Just because the rulers of this world can cheat the rules that limit the Machine, it does not mean they are superior.'

'Of course,' continued Saphentis. 'Nonetheless it is remarkable. The biomechanical structures of the Manufactorium appear to be central to this system with most of the resultant output being directed towards a very large complex just outside the threshold of Manufactorium Noctis. It appears that this was radioactive wasteland prior to the loss of Chaeroneia. There is no indication as to what is there now. The output rose exponentially just prior to Chaeroneia's re-entry into real space.'

'Whatever they're doing,' said Hawkespur, 'they're doing it there.'

'The rest was mostly ideological. The tech-heresy has historical precedent.'

'Then it is true,' said Antigonus. 'The Dark Mechanicus.'

'The Dark Mechanicus?' The term was unfamiliar to Alaric.

'Tech-priests loyal to the Traitor Legions in the days of the Horus Heresy,' said Hawkespur. 'They were exterminated during the Scouring that followed the Battle of Terra.'

'It was not quite that simple, interrogator,' said Saphentis. 'The schism within the Mechanicus was perhaps more complicated than even the Inquisition generally understand. My rank gains me certain privileges and greater access to historical data is one of them.'

The facets of Saphentis's eyes shifted colour as he accessed encrypted mem-cells built into his augmentations. 'The faction that sided with Horus,' he continued, 'probably only became known as the 'Dark' Mechanicus after the Heresy, when Horus had been defeated and it was realised that the beliefs they followed were corrupt. The Dark Mechanicus was not a body of tech-priests, but the beliefs they held and the principles to which they adhered. The fusion of the flesh and the machine. The creation of new living things. Innovation and freedom of research.'

'But they were destroyed,' said Hawkespur.

It was Antigonus who replied. 'You can't kill an idea, interrogator,' he said. 'As hard as the Inquisition has tried, they just keep on coming back. There were so many tech-heresies recorded in the libraria of Mars that I was never certain which had taken hold on Chaeroneia. But the Dark Mechanicus... yes, that makes sense. Perfect sense. Especially if they are in league with daemons. Towards the end of the Heresy they say he Dark Mechanicus trafficked with daemons. Perhaps Scraecos and his ch-priests have renewed the old pacts.'

'And these ideas were left to flourish?' snapped Alaric. 'Where heresies are found among the authorities of the Imperium they are stamped out! Burned! The Mechanicus knew of this heresy and they let it live? The Precepts of Guilliman required that the works of the traitor Horus and all his acolytes be destroyed! The Mechanicus was no exception.'

'What the justicar says is true,' said Saphentis. Alaric looked at him in mild surprise – it was the first time he could recall the archmagos genuinely agreeing with him. 'The details of Dark Mechanicus heresy I uncovered were comprehensive. The data was in a poor state but there is little doubt they represent a knowledge of the Horusian schism that even as an archmagos I was not privy to. Scraecos was an archmagos veneratus but even then it is unlikely in the extreme he could reconstruct the specific rituals and research procedures from current Adeptus Mechanicus records alone.'

'Which begs the question,' said Hawkespur echoing Alaric's own thoughts, 'where did Scraecos get it all from?'

Antigonus sighed, his servitor body hanging its head. 'I knew that Chaeroneia's heresy was exceptional. But this is something else.'

'Then we need to keep going,' said Hawkespur. 'Our immediate priority is to reach the obelisk. Then we contact Nyxos in orbit and tell him that the Dark Mechanicus have returned.'

THIRTEEN

'Ask not the name of the Enemy. Ask not his Will, nor his Method. Ask not to think his Thoughts and ask not to speak his Words. Ask only for the strength to kill him.'
– The Imperial Infantryman's Uplifting Primer
(Addendum Spiritual) 97-14

THE SHAPE OF the *Hellforger* filled the viewscreen on the bridge of the *Tribunicia*, a massive red-black wedge of a ship bigger than the *Tribunicia* and sporting twice as many guns. The traitor ship was hurtling towards the Imperial fleet at a speed no Imperial captain would have dreamed of going, torpedoes still sailing on glittering streams of exhaust from its forward ports.

'Where are my damage reports?' yelled Horstgeld over the barely contained chaos of the bridge.

'There's a breach in plasma reactor three!' came a reply from somewhere in the Engineering section. 'It's ignoring all our tech-prayers, we're going to have to shut it down!'

'Shutdown denied,' replied Horstgeld. It was less dangerous to keep the reactor running than to risk the drop in engine power that would ensue if the reactor was shut down. Probably the decision would cost lives from leaks of superheated plasma into the engineering deck that surrounded the reactor, but those were the kinds of sacrifices that a captain had to make.

It was bad. The initial volley of torpedoes from the *Hellforger* had scored hits on the *Tribunicia* and the *Exemplar*. *Ptolemy Gamma*, already seriously compromised by the loss of its comms, had been all but crippled by a lucky strike that blew off a sizeable chunk of its stern and ripped a breach through most of its engineering decks. The torpedo salvo was just the opening move, that was clear – the *Hellforger* fully intended to take the first major kill up close with its guns, or even its boarding parties, and was charging towards the *Tribunicia* with a fervour that could only mean it was commanded by a madman.

The second, unidentified enemy cruiser, a strange bloated shape that fairly dripped with guns, was coming in behind the *Hellforger* and once it got amongst the Imperial ships its broadsides would reap a horrendous tally among the transports and escorts. The last major ship in the enemy fleet looked like a very old pattern fighter platform. Triangular in cross-section, each of its three long sides housed a host of attack craft hangars and launching bays.

Each of the enemy ships had picked its target. Each was more than a match for its chosen prey. Horstgeld's role was now to simply delay the enemy for as long as possible and hope against hope that the time he was buying actually meant something.

'Bring us side-on to the *Hellforger*, ordered Horstgeld to the navigation section. 'Ordnance, load up for a broadside. Get everyone on the guns.' Horstgeld glanced at the tactical readout inset into the viewscreen. 'And Comms! Get me the *Pieta*.'

'Sir?'

'You heard me. And do it soon.'

The *Hellforger* was one of the ugliest ships Horstgeld had ever seen. It had originally been a very old mark of Imperial ship with the flat wedge shape that had been all but abandoned by the Imperial Navy. Over the thousands of years it had been in service, the traitor ship's hull had become covered with blisters and weeping sores as if the metal of the ship was diseased and its scores of guns poked from open bleeding gashes in the hull.

A ship that ugly needed some ugly tactics to fight it. Horstgeld murmured a prayer imploring the Emperor for forgiveness and set about thinking what he would tell the *Pieta*.

THE ORBITAL COMMUNICATIONS obelisk was a needle of dull grey metal three hundred feet high, covered in dense circuitry like elaborate scrollwork and half-buried in the corroded mass that made up the foundations of Manufactorium Noctis.

'Are you ready?' asked Magos Antigonus.

Hawkespur nodded. She sat on the rubble at the foot of the obelisk, which speared up above her into the mass of compressed wreckage that formed the ceiling of the chamber. Antigonus had set up a simple vox-unit plugged into the obelisk which Hawkespur was to speak into. With the hood of her voidsuit back, her tumours were vivid blue-grey lumps under the skin of her throat. It wouldn't be long before they started to constrict her breathing.

'Will the Dark Mechanicus notice the power drain?' asked Alaric.

'Probably,' said Antigonus as he made the final adjustments to the vox-unit. 'They suspect we are down here. But they rarely send hunter-servitors down this far.'

'The spirits of such technology rarely answer us any more,' said Archmagos Saphentis, stroking a mechanical finger over the patterns inlaid into the obelisk. 'This must be very old, from the very earliest days of Chaeroneia. Very difficult to replicate.'

'I suggest you take notes, then, archmagos,' said Alaric. 'We don't plan on being here for very long.'

The whole chamber vibrated with a low hum as power flooded into the obelisk. The vox-unit howled with static.

'Let it cycle through the frequencies,' said Antigonus. 'If we're lucky it will tap into the receivers on one of the Imperial ships.'

Always, thought Alaric, it eventually came down to luck.

'We're getting something,' said Hawkespur. 'To all Imperial forces, this is Interrogator Hawkespur of the Ordo Malleus, please respond...'

MAGOS MURGILD REACHED the bridge of the Exemplar in time to see the automated maintenance servitors clearing the scorched remains off the floor. Given that Korveylan had been hard-wired into the floor of the bridge, that she was not there and that her command throne was the epicentre of the smouldering mess of flesh and metal, he instantly guessed that it was the ship's captain who had died. He was slightly taken aback by the sight of his captain being scooped up by a servitor's slop-trowel, but he did well not to show it.

'I was given the bridge,' said Murgild as he shambled towards the charred command post. He spoke through a chest-mounted vox-unit since the lower half of his face was hidden by a thick metal collar, an extension of the armoured voidsuit he wore under his robes to protect him from the dangerous conditions in Engineering. 'What happened?'

'Magos Korveylan detonated herself,' said Inquisitor Nyxos. He had several cuts on his face from the shrapnel from the explosion. The naval armsmen he had brought from the *Tribunicia* were now stationed on the bridge under the command of Commissar Leung, in case Murgild was in any doubt as to who held the real authority on the ship. 'I voiced my suspicions about her allegiance and in response, she killed herself.'

Murgild paused. 'I see.'

'The initial torpedo volley is done but the enemy fleet is closing fast. They have a gun-heavy cruiser making straight for us and our first priority is for evasive manoeuvres to put the *Ptolemy* squadron between us and that cruiser. Do what you must but remember that by the authority of the Inquisition I am in ultimate command of this ship. Fleet Commissar Leung is now responsible for ship security.'

Murgild stood at the command console and began scanning through the manoeuvring sermons in the ship's navigation logs. The *Exemplar* wasn't an agile ship and it would take all the magos's efforts to keep it mobile as the enemy closed in. Murgild seemed able to ignore the greasy smoke that surrounded the control helm, the last remnant of Magos Korveylan.

Nyxos turned to Leung. 'Commissar, I need Magos Korveylan's personal effects and communications logs thoroughly searched. Find out if she kept any record of who she was working for and what their orders were. Along with any indication of what she was looking for.'

'I shall have the armsmen conduct a thorough search,' replied Leung.

'And make it quick. This ship might not last long.'

'We have multiple target locks,' came a vox from the sensorium centre. 'Source is the cruiser-class craft.'

'They're taking aim first. Then they'll hit us with everything they've got,' said Nyxos. He looked at the tactical orrery, which showed the bloated unknown cruiser-sized enemy ship heading menacingly for the *Exemplar*. 'At least we know who we shall have to deal with. Murgild, our priority is staying alive. Draw that cruiser in and keep out of its broadside arcs for as long as we can. Can this ship pull that off?'

'Possibly,' replied Murgild. 'Depending on the manoeuvring capabilities of the enemy.'

'Good. Do it. And had Korveylan got any closer to decoding the signal from the planet?'

'The verispex labs were making some headway.'

'Keep me posted.' The ship shuddered as another structure in the prow gave way. The *Exemplar* was badly battered and it would only get worse.

'Captain,' came another vox, this time from the communications centre. 'We are receiving anomalous transmissions from the planet's surface. Possible Imperial origin.'

'Route it to the bridge,' said Nyxos.

The static from the signal sputtered from the bridge vox-casters, layering a grainy film of sound over the clacking of servitors working the bridge consoles and the pounding of the engines from deep inside the ship. Nyxos struggled to make out words from the mess of sound.

'...repeat, this is Interrogator Hawkespur of the Ordo Malleus, can anyone...'

'Hawkespur! This is Nyxos. What in the hells is going on down there?'

'...we crashed. Moral threat confirmed, it's the Dark Mechanicus...' Hawkespur's voice sounded weak, as if she was exhausted, as well as distorted and broken up by the poor reception.

'Hawkespur, we're running out of time up here. The planet sent out a signal and the *Hellforger* just turned up in response. It was last seen in the service of the Abaddon the Despoiler and it looks like they want to get down to the surface.'

'...not happen, sir, the enemy is routeing a lot of power to an area outside the city. May be something there the enemy want...'

'They're not the only ones. Magos Korveylan here was looking for it, too and she wasn't following Mechanicus orders. We don't know who she was working for. Maybe someone a lot higher up.'

'...to understand our priority is now to find the centre of the enemy activity and ascertain any threat?'

'Correct. Do whatever you must, Hawkespur. Use scorched earth if you have to. And you're on your own down there, we're facing several cruiser-class ships and we can't hold them off forever.'

'...sir, just get us time, I'll go by my judgement.'

'You do that. If Alaric's alive, trust him, he knows how to stay alive in places like that. And if Saphentis is there, don't trust him. He could be compromised. The Mechanicus know something they're not telling us. Hawkespur? Hawkespur?'

Nyxos listened intently for a long minute. There was only static.

'Damn it. Murgild, have Comms keep scanning that frequency. Let me know of anything you get. '

'Yes, inquisitor.'

'And have verispex keep on decoding that signal, even if the ship starts falling apart. If Hawkespur gets back in contact I want to have something useful to tell her.'

'I UNDERSTAND, BUT we still don't know what we are up against, sir. Just get us time, I'll go by my judgement,' saidHawkespur. The vox-unit howled with feedback and then just coughed static. 'Sir? Inquisitor?'

The circuits of the obelisk were glowing dull red with resistance. The vox-unit sparked and shorted out.

'They could be blocking us,' said Antigonus.

'Which means they know where we are,' added Alaric.

'I think he told me everything he had to,' said Hawkespur, pulling off the vox headset. 'The Dark Mechanicus have summoned a Chaos fleet. They were probably transmitting to them since before we even arrived. It's led by the *Hellforger*, one of the most notorious ships of the Gothic War. That means our theory about Chaeroneia's reappearance being linked to Abaddon's attack through the Eye of Terror just got much more realistic.'

'Hardly good news,' said Antigonus, prodding at the smouldering vox-unit.

'It is better than no news,' said Alaric. 'We have some idea of what we are up against. The Chaos fleet wants something on Chaeroneia. If we get to it first, that means we can hurt them. You might not like what you hear, but every piece of information we have makes this fight easier.'

'It also means we need to leave,' said Hawkespur, pulling up the hood of her voidsuit. 'Antigonus, we need to get to the site of that power spike. Can we get there quickly?'

'There are ways. If we mobilise everything we have we could be there in less than two hours. But we rarely send anyone out there. There's nowhere to hide, it's all ash dunes. And there isn't anything there, no structures, no stores.'

'It seems,' said Saphentis, 'that there is something there now. Something that is draining inordinate amounts of power from this city.' The archmagos hadn't spoken since the obelisk had started broadcasting, listening carefully as if he was sifting through frequencies inaudible to normal hearing. 'And Antigonus, you have no idea what it might be?'

Antigonus shrugged as best his servitor body would allow. 'The only place that ever drew that kind of power in Manufactorium Noctis was the Titan works and as far as we can tell they've been completely dismantled for eight hundred years.'

'Whatever it is,' said Hawkespur, 'we have to get there. This mission is no longer about investigation. It's about denial to the enemy of whatever the Dark Mechanicus have created.'

'Agreed,' said Alaric. 'My squad will be ready to move out immediately. Antigonus?'

'My adepts are ready.'

'Good. Then we move.'

'We move,' said Hawkespur.

As the four of them returned to Antigonus's base, they could hear Manufactorium Noctis groaning above them, as if the city itself was trying to claw its way down to get them. The whole of Chaeroneia hated them and knew they were there, like an infection in the biomechanical mass of Manufactorium Noctis. The taint of sorcery Alaric felt when he saw the planet for the first time seemed to be getting stronger, as if the dark heart of the planet was waking up and turning its gaze on them.

It wanted to see them dead. It would probably succeed. But Alaric trusted in Hawkespur and in his battle-brothers to ensure that, before that happened, it would have as hard a fight as anyone could give it.

MISSIONARY PATRICOS PULLED himself up onto the pulpit of the main amphitheatre, an enormous auditorium where all the pilgrims who travelled on the *Pieta* could be addressed at once. And most of them were there – men, women and children crowding the rows of seating, clutching aquila icons or battered prayer books, murmuring their fear and uncertainty.

The crew of the *Pieta* had just affected a sudden course change on the orders from the Rear Admiral in command of the fleet. Some of the pilgrims even thought they were about to come under attack from an enemy craft. Patricos had been with the ship all the way on its pilgrimage from Gathalamor around the southern edge of the galaxy towards San Leor and he was the spiritual leader for these thousands of people, the conduit for the Emperor's will to be revealed to them. He had led them for thirteen years of long, hard pilgrimage and they trusted him absolutely.

'Brothers!' called Patricos in his rich preacher's voice. 'And sisters! Do not despair! We are in a trying place, yes and the servants of the Emperor are sorely stretched at this time. But we are His people! He will protect us from the depredations of those who would harm us. For we carry His beneficence in our hearts! We have devoted ourselves to Him! Trust in Him, as you have done these long years and you will be rewarded with His grace in the next life!'

Patricos saw fear etched into their time-worn faces. They had been picked up from dozens of worlds along the route, many of them having been taken aboard at Gathalamor at the very start of the voyage. They had been together for so long that it only took one doubting voice for rumour and panic to spread like a fire.

'But one of the crewmen told me there is an enemy fleet approaching!' called out one pilgrim's voice. 'And we are under a military command!'

Patricos held his hands up in a calming gesture. 'True, the Navy has called upon our presence, but this is merely a precaution. In the unlikely event of enemy action we could function as a transport or hospital ship. We are unarmed! And we carry with us the faithful souls, the same good Emperor-fearing men and women for whom the Navy fights! They would not let us come to harm. Now, let us pray and give thanks for the bravery and sacrifice of these soldiers and crewmen who protect us in times of darkness. Hymnal Tertiam, verse ninety-three.'

The pilgrims began praying, falteringly at first and then in stronger voice, as Patricos led them in the praises of the immortal God-Emperor.

THE MASSIVE BULK of the *Hellforger*, almost half as big again as a standard cruiser-class ship, knifed through space towards the midpoint of the *Tribunicia*. The outer hull plates of its prow flaked off on trails of steaming gore, revealing bone-white fangs that formed a vicious cutting edge like the tip of a chainsword. Wide wet orifices opened up just below the ramming fangs, leading to the mustering chambers where the boarding troops were being herded into place.

The *Hellforger* maintained a formidable horde of subhuman boarding troops, brutal half-mad creatures evolved and mutated for ugly close-quarters killing. If the *Tribunicia* survived the initial impact they would be driven through the boarding orifices and onto the Imperial ship, flooding its decks with blood-crazed madmen. It was an old tactic, one of the most effective given the size and toughness of the *Hellforger* itself. A ramming action, according to Imperial Naval doctrine, was nothing short of madness. A boarding action was scarcely less so. Imperial captains simply had no idea how to defend against the *Hellforger* hurtling towards them at ramming speed, its razor-sharp prow fully exposed. The terror of the sight alone had shaken more than one Imperial captain and Urkrathos still had some of those same captains imprisoned, brutalised and insane, deep in the bowels of the *Hellforger*.

The *Hellforger* was set on its path. The bridge daemons had done their job well and the massive thrust of the grand cruiser's engines sent it carving inexorably towards the *Tribunicia*.

Which meant there was nothing it could do when the *Pieta* suddenly got in the way.

THE ENGINES OF the *Pieta* roared as the tubby, ponderous pilgrim ship was pulled in several directions at once. In the grand amphitheatre, people screamed as the artificial gravity was knocked out of kilter and they were thrown against the banks of hard marble seating. Missionary Patricos had to grab hold of the lectern to keep himself from pitching into the front row of pilgrims.

'Keep praying!' shouted Patricos over the keening of the engines and the sounds of panic. 'Keep praying! For He will heed your words!'

Something huge collided with the underside of the ship, gouging through the lower decks with a shriek of tearing metal and howl of escaping air. Patricos was thrown onto his back and pilgrims tumbled down the banks of seating as the ship rocked. Horrendous sounds boomed from below them, fuel cells cooking off, decks sucked dry of air, sections of the hull ripped inwards by the collision.

Patricos struggled to his feet. The pilgrims who had not been knocked unconscious were still praying, mouthing sacred words, their faces blank with fear.

'He does not hear us!' shouted Patrocis at the top of his booming hell-fire voice. 'You are not praying hard enough! Sing to Him the depths of your devotion!'

One of the aft engines exploded, filling the air with the sickening sound of sheets of fuel igniting, filling the engineering decks with liquid flame.

'Keep praying!' The ship was spasming like a dying animal, beads of fire dripping from the ceiling. 'You! Pray harder! Now!'

The grinding prow of the *Hellforger* cut right through the amphitheatre, its gnashing ram of teeth slicing through hundreds of bodies. The rest died as the vacuum screamed in behind it, leaving the shattered remnants of the *Pieta* open to the emptiness of space.

'GODS' TEETH AND damnation!' bellowed Urkrathos as the last shreds of the *Pieta* fluttered from the prow of the *Hellforger*. 'You! Are we still on course?'

The navigation daemon, a muscular brute covered in glowing runes of sorcery, growled from the wall to which it had been nailed with spikes of meteoric iron. 'The collision turned our hand. The blade will not strike true.'

Urkrathos glanced back at the pict-screen showing the smouldering wreckage of the *Pieta* still jammed in the teeth of the ramming prow. The daemon was right – the *Hellforger* would miss the *Tribunicia* sternwards. 'Correct it.'

The daemon grinned with all three of its bile-dripping mouths. 'Impossible,' it said.

Urkrathos took the bolt pistol from its holster at his waist and slammed three shots into the navigation daemon, spattering boiling ichor over the wall behind it. 'You defy me!' he yelled. 'Rot your soul, daemon!'

'I have no soul,' said the daemon, still leering with its now-wrecked face. 'And I cannot defy you. It is no lie. The blade of the *Hellforger* will spare the Enemy's heart.'

Urkrathos spat in one of the daemon's many emerald-green eyes. It was true. If the course correction could be made the daemon would have to make it. The *Hellforger* would miss.

'Weapons!' shouted Urkrathos. 'Pull back the boarding parties to the gun gangs! Make ready for a broadside!'

Damn these Imperial scum. They just didn't know when to die. Now he would have to shatter the Enemy flagship with gunfire, a far longer and crueller death than he had planned for them. They inflicted this suffering on themselves, these worshippers of the Corpse-Emperor. In butchering them, Urkrathos was fulfilling a sacred duty.

REAR ADMIRAL HORSTGELD looked at the pict-steals of the dying *Pieta*. He hadn't been certain the ship's crew would realise what their orders meant – if they had, they might not have followed them, pious servants of the Emperor or not. But they were not responsible for the thousands of innocent pilgrims who had just died. Horstgeld was. That was what command meant. Taking responsibility for everything that befell the Imperial citizens under his command, for good or ill.

The revised course solutions flashed up on the bridge viewscreen. The *Hellforger* would miss the *Tribunicia* – not by much, but by enough. The *Tribunicia* would last a little longer, then. And those few moments of life had cost the destruction of the *Pieta* and the death of everyone on board.

'Ship's confessor,' said Horstgeld to Confessor Talas, standing as always at the bridge pulpit. 'We have sinned. The Rites of Admonition, if you please.'

BENEATH MANUFACTORIUM NOCTIS, at the very foundation of the city where the artificial strata met the iron-drained crust of Chaeroneia, there were scores of low, flat abscesses in the rock. Seams of iron and other metals had been mined out leaving endless flat galleries. Most had collapsed but enough remained to form a hidden highway beneath the city, towards the ancient mineheads just outside the limits of the present-day Manufactorium.

An ancient Chimera APC, so repeatedly repaired and refitted that barely anything of the original vehicle remained, led the feeble armoured column that ground at full speed towards the radioactive ash desert beyond the city. Looted and maintained by Antigonus's techpriest resistance force, it was the most battle-worthy vehicle the makeshift strikeforce had and it felt like it was about to fall apart.

'What will we find when we get there?' asked Alaric above the painful grinding of the engine. He and his squad were in the lead Chimera along with Tech-priest Gallen, who seemed to have an affinity for keeping vehicles running that should have rusted to dust a long time ago.

Gallen glanced back at Alaric with his one remaining natural eye. 'The older shafts are still intact,' he said. 'They were worked by menial gangs, so they are navigable by foot and vehicle. They lead up into the desert.'

'And what's there?'

'Nothing.'

Alaric knew it wasn't true. He could feel the malevolence up ahead, feel it trying to push him back. The diamond-hard core of his soul was aching with it.

'I think we should hear the Rites of Contrition,' said Brother Archis. 'We should go into this with our souls clean.'

'No,' said Alaric. 'Not from me. You should speak them, Archis. You seem to have a knack for prayer.'

'Yes, justicar,' said Archis. 'Brothers, join me.' The rest of the squad, Alaric included, bowed their heads as Archis began to speak. The Rites of Contrition acknowledged the weakness in all their souls, the failures they had all committed in their duty to the Emperor – because their purpose was to eradicate the threat of the daemon and yet daemons still existed and preyed upon the peoples of the Imperium. So as long as the work of the Grey Knights was not done they had to plead for forgiveness from the Emperor and hope that His grace would lend them the strength to complete their work.

One day, when they were all dead and had fought at the Emperor's side at the end of time, their duty would be done. Until then, they were in the Emperor's debt – a debt they would die repaying.

'You SAY you have lost them?' asked the collective consciousness of Chaeroneia's tech-priests.

'For the time being,' replied Scraecos.

The archmagos veneratus stood in the remains of the datafortress. He had compelled its crystalline structure to unfold completely, laying the lowest reaches of malleable data medium open to the weeping sky. The bodies of wrecked battle-servitors and dead menials lay fused with the black crystal where they had fallen, sucked into the substance of the datafortress by the ferocity with which Scraecos had forced the structure to reform.

There was no sign of the surviving intruders. Only the bodies of their dead troops – a couple of tech-guard in the rust-red and brass of the orthodox Adeptus Mechanicus. Nothing of the Space Marines, or the archmagos who was probably leading them. Scraecos had searched right

down to the dead layers of data medium, where no information technology known to the ruling tech-priests could penetrate.

Scraecos idly picked up the mangled remains of one intruder tech-guard
as the transmitted thoughts from the command spire questioned him.

'Explain,' said the voice of a thousand tech-priests in his head.

'They are on an investigative mission,' said Scraecos. 'It is unlikely in
the extreme that they will be able to pursue their mission and yet
remain permanently masked from our scrutiny.'

'And yet masked they are,' said the tech-priests. 'Explain further.'

'We have killed several of their members,' continued Scraecos. 'And we
understand their composition and techniques. We know more of their
capabilities. They possess some form of advanced technology that
bypassed our hunter-programs.' Scraecos glanced scornfully at the
hunter-programs, which swam beneath the surface of the crystal, curled
up and shivering. 'No doubt it has been developed by the orthodox
Mechanicus since we were last in contact with the Imperium.'

'Such words constitute only excuses, Archmagos Veneratus Scraecos.
There is no indication that your activities have rendered the capture of
the intruders inevitable. It appears instead that your maintenance of a
separate identity has rendered you less efficient. Therefore, Archmagos
Veneratus Scraecos will return to the consciousness of the tech-priests of
the command spire.'

Scraecos clenched his mechadendrites in frustration. The data-
filaments that replaced his hands brushed against the crystal and he
read the weakness and fear of the hunter-programs. They had failed.
They. Not him. He was the greatest archmagos in the history of
Chaeroneia. The greatest since the dying of the great schism in the days
of Horus. Scraecos had performed his task with absolute accuracy and
skill. He was the ruler of Chaeroneia.

The Castigator had spoken to Scraecos. In the beginning, it had spoken to him only.

'Very well,' said Scraecos. 'I will return to the tech-priests. I will
become We.'

'Grav-platforms will be despatched. Archmagos Veneratus Scraecos
will prepare for the cessation of individual consciousness.'

The communication ended. Scraecos was alone again at the
datafortress. The shape of the datafortress had been exploded into a
hard black blossom of crystal, the walls warped into giant petal-like
panes. The valley was similarly deformed, its sheer obsidian cliffs
punched through with scores of smouldering craters where the data
medium had been probed for any sign of the intruders.

Scraecos had wondered for some time whether there was an active resistance at Manufactorium Noctis. Most of the time, of course, his memory and cognitive faculties had not been his alone, but part of Chaeroneia's collective mind. But on the occasions where he had existed separately, he had wondered if certain acts of apparent sabotage, or unexplained shutdowns and tech-priests' deaths, could really be ascribed to random industrial accidents alone.

There was someone coordinating a resistance on Chaeroneia. Perhaps dissident tech-priests, rivals for the rulership of Chaeroneia. Or maybe relics from Chaeroneia's distant past, still somehow loyal to the orthodox Mechanicus that the planet had left behind so long ago. The survival of the intruders confirmed this in Scraecos's mind. The resistance had been cunning and resourceful in staying hidden, but in helping the intruders escape they had confirmed their existence. It was the last mistake they would make.

Archmagos Veneratus Scraecos was the ruler of Chaeroneia. He was the will of the true Omnissiah, as revealed to him through the Castigator. This was not arrogance or ambition speaking, It was the pure, cold logic that ruled ninety-nine per cent of Scraecos's soul. And Scraecos would see both the resistance and the intruders dead – his way.

A grav-platform drifted between the spires towards the shattered datafortress, escorted by several gun-platforms. They were coming to take Scraecos back to the command spire. That suited Scraecos just fine. It was the best place for him to be confirmed as the driving intelligence behind Chaeroneia's collective will.

The hunter-programs had failed. That made one thing certain. Scraecos would have to deal with this problem himself.

THE GUNS OF the *Desikratis* raked deep shimmering black gouges through the shields of the *Exemplar*, the hideous bloated Chaos cruiser vomiting astounding volleys of fire that even at a distance were knocking down the void shield banks of the Adeptus Mechanicus ship in rapid succession. The daemon that squatted at the heart of the *Desikratis* aimed every one of its thousands of guns by hand, loaded the shells with its own tentacles and fired them with an impulse from its corrupted nervous system. The *Exemplar* was demonstrating resilience well beyond the norm for a ship of its size, but no matter how tough it proved the *Desikratis* was closing fast and as it slowed and brought itself into point-blank broadside position it would breach the Mechanicus ship's hull and turn its decks into mazes of twisted, burning metal.

But that hadn't happened yet. And the *Exemplar* still had more fight in it than anyone suspected

'ALL POWER STARBOARD shields,' said Magos Murgild. The bridge of the *Exemplar* was by now filling up with menials and tech-priests, replacing the burned-out servitors. Some complicated pattern of protocols governed the mayhem as the ship brought its damaged prow out of the path of the Enemy's guns. 'Evasion pattern theta. Damage control to prow sensoria.'

Hurried communications with the ship's archive had suggested the enemy ship might be the *Desikratis*, a Chaos-controlled cruiser that had been active during the Gothic War and then surfaced again in the space battles around Nemesis Tessera during the invasion from the Eye.

The *Exemplar* probably couldn't face it on even terms. It didn't matter. The ship wasn't there to win – it was there to keep the Enemy busy while Hawkespur and Alaric killed whatever it was that had summoned them to Chaeroneia.

'Commissar,' voxed Nyxos. 'What have you found?'

Commisar Leung's voice crackled up from Magos Korveylan's quarters in the depths of the *Exemplar*. 'Little direct evidence of suspicious activities. Some of the research tech-priests have uncovered details of her studies under Archmagos Scraecos, however.'

'Tech-priests? Can you trust them?'

'I believe so, inquisitor. Magos Korveylan seems to have been generally disliked by the crew.'

Nyxos allowed himself a smile. 'Good for them. What have you found?'

'I confess I don't understand it fully. Scraecos seems to have run a form of seminary on Salshan Anterior about a hundred and fifty years ago. It was religious as much as technical. It concentrated on something Korveylan's studies referred to as Standard Template Constructs. Other than that she seems to have been very dedicated to covering her tracks.'

'I see. Thank you, commissar. Keep me up to date on anything you find.'

'Yes, inquisitor.'

'And things may get very rough in a few minutes. We're going into battle and I don't think we can win.'

'Understood.'

The vox-channel closed. The activity on the bridge seemed suddenly quieter and slower, though in reality it was only getting more intense as the *Desikratis* closed in.

A Standard Template Construct. Of course. It made perfect sense.

'Murgild,' said Nyxos, snapping himself out of his thoughts. 'We need to contact the planet. Any way we can. Do you have historical files on Chaeroneia?'

'Of course, but they do not seem to bear much relevance to the planet as it is now.'

'It doesn't matter. Make them available to me in the verispex decks. I'm leaving the bridge to you but remember you are under Inquisitorial authority. And do try to keep us alive.'

'Of course.'

Nyxos hurried off the bridge. He could hear the distant booming of failing shields as the guns of the *Desikratis* gradually stripped the *Exemplar* naked. It wouldn't be long now. But he knew now what this was all about – Chaeroneia, the Chaos fleet, Korveylan's treachery, everything. If he could let Hawkespur know somehow then there was a chance she might actually succeed and all these men and women would not be dying for nothing.

FOURTEEN

'Give me a gun that never fires! Give me a sword that is ever blunt! Give me a weapon that deals no wound, so long as it always strikes awe!'
– Ecclesiarch Sebastian Thor,
address to the Convent Sanctorum

THE IMPERIUM WAS founded on ignorance. It was a truth so obvious that very few ever acknowledged it. For more than ten thousand years the Imperium had claimed rulership over the human race, first under the Emperor and then under the Adeptus Terra who acted, it was claimed, according to His undying will. But the Imperium existed in complete historical isolation. Before the Emperor had set out on the Great Crusade that conquered the thousands of scattered inhabited worlds, there was nothing.

Legends inhabited the shadowy years of pre-Imperial history. No matter how many scholars slaved over the question of what had gone before the Imperium, it was impossible to tell the guesswork from the lies. A very few basic assumptions were held by the majority of those who paid pre-Imperial history any mind at all, though even these were in constant question.

First, there had been the Scattering. The discovery of faster-than-light travel through the parallel dimension of the warp had led to massive migrations among the stars, creating a galaxy-wide diaspora of humanity. The Scattering was pure conjecture, a way of explaining how so many worlds inhabited by humans were even now being rediscovered by Rogue Traders and exploratory fleets. But it was the only way the human race could have got into its present state and so it was widely assumed to have happened so far in the past that no direct evidence of it existed.

Then there came the Dark Age of Technology. Mankind, rather than venerating technology and keeping it sacrosanct as the priesthood of Mars later did, pursued technological advancement with wanton enthusiasm. Astonishing wonders were made, along with horrors beyond imagining. Planet-threatening war machines. Genetic abominations. Machines that wove whole worlds around them. And worse things – far worse.

Inevitably, the Dark Age led humanity to the Age of Strife, where human fought human in an endless cycle of destruction. Warp travel became impossible and the result was a great winnowing of the human population, where worlds were isolated and fell into the barbarism that would often only end when the Imperium recontacted them and sent missionaries to bring the light back to them.

But some, it seems, must have known the Age of Strife was coming – a very few who believed humanity's existence was in danger and that by preserving the most stable and useful technology for future generations, they could increase the chances of the human race surviving the coming slaughter. No one in the age of the Imperium could begin to guess who that might have been, but they were undoubtedly among the greatest minds of the Dark Age, perhaps the only ones who realised the toll that profane technology would take on the galaxy.

They placed their knowledge in a form that could survive forever and be understood by anyone. Certain key technologies were reduced to algorithms and placed in a format that could be used even by humans reduced to barbarity. They were the Standard Template Constructs.

In a way, the Priesthood of Mars had done something similar, preserving technology through religious observation. With the birth of the Imperium and the Treaty of Mars, the Adeptus Mechanicus was able to explore the galaxy with the Great Crusade and learned of the existence of the Standard Template Constructs.

So pure were the STCs that they became objects of holy veneration to the tech-priests, nuggets of the Omnissiah's genius compressed and formatted for the good of mankind. A few fragments were discovered on shattered, ruined worlds during the Great Crusade. The tech-priests used them to create some of the most stable and ubiquitous technology the Imperium had, like the Rhino APC or the geothermal heatsink technology that provided power to countless hive cities. But they never found a complete, uncorrupted STC.

A pure STC was a hopeless legend. To think that one could survive complete for so many thousands of years of tortuous war was fanciful in the extreme. But that did not stop many tech-priests from pursuing the Standard Template Constructs as the objects of religious quests, sifting through legends and half-truths, sending out exploratory parties to the most distant, Emperor-forsaken planets hunting for the merest hint of the ancient knowledge.

One such tech-priest was Archmagos Veneratus Scraecos. On the forge world of Salshan Anterior he had led a seminary studying the legends of the Standard Template Constructs and creating complex statistical models from the fragments of information the Mechanicus possessed.

Scraecos had come to Chaeroneia, believing that there was a Standard Template Construct on the world. And perhaps – just perhaps – he had been correct.

ALARIC CRAWLED FORWARD on his stomach, forcing his huge armoured form down into the mass of rust beneath him so he wouldn't give himself and the tech-priests alongside him away to anyone who might be guarding the top of the mineshaft.

The shaft sloped up at a steep angle, allowing only a dirty half-light in from the outside. Drilled into iron-rich rock centuries before, the walls and floor of the shaft were now sheathed in metre-thick sheets of crumbling rust.

'We're close,' said Tech-priest Gallen, clambering up the slope alongside Alaric. Gallen's only weapon was a rusting autogun and whatever combat attachments his equally rusted bionics might possess and he was scared. Antigonus's tech-priests had lived on the edge of detection and death for a long time, but they had always shied away from direct conflict with the Dark Mechanicus. Now Alaric's arrival had prompted them into all-out war.

'Is there anyone up there?' whispered Alaric. He glanced back and saw his squad close behind him, the gunmetal of their armour dulled by the dirt enough to hide them. There were about twenty other tech-priests, too, all in various states of disrepair, along with Antigonus in his spider-legged maintenance servitor body, Hawkespur and her lone tech-guard bodyguard, and Archmagos Saphentis.

'Nothing on the auspex,' said Gallen. 'But some of their tech-priests don't show up.'

'I'll take point,' said Alaric. The tech-priests might have been spirited resistance fighters but the Grey Knights were better soldiers by far and he waved his squad forwards to the top of the shaft.

The desert air stank. This desert was not natural – it was built up from untold millennia of pollution, made of drifts of hydrocarbon ash or expanses of radioactive glass. Every forge world had these desolations in common, toxic deserts or acidic oceans that stretched between the man-ufactoria. Large sections of Chaeroneia had resembled hell before the Dark Mechanicus had ever taken control.

Alaric crawled towards the smudge of dirty sky visible through the top of the shaft. Archis scrabbled up beside him, Incinerator held off the ground in front of him.

'Ready?' asked Alaric.

'You can never be ready,' said Archis. 'The moment we think we're ready, that's the moment the Enemy finds some new way to kill us.'

Alaric pulled himself up the ragged rock around the shaft entrance. The night sky above flickered with half-formed images, the occult sym-bols and blasphemous prayers written on the clouds by projectors on the top of the city's spires. They loomed down over the desert, too, a blanket of heresy covering everything. There was no break in the images because the clouds formed a solid unbroken layer, as if trying to shut out the existence of a sane universe beyond.

Alaric pulled himself level with the shaft entrance and looked out. He had some idea of what to expect – rolling toxic dunes, foul lakes of raw pollution, carrion creatures wheeling overhead.

He didn't see any of that.

Outside, Manufactorium Noctis was a massive construction the size of a spaceport. It was ringed by a series of spindly watchtowers each bristling with guns and in turn protected by networks of trenches and gun emplace-ments. Between the watchtowers stretched an expanse of rockcrete studded with biomechanical outcrops like immense blooms of fungi – workshops and warehouses, generator stacks and control bunkers, connected by thick twisting conduits like bundles of nerves or muscle fibres. Dead-grey masses of flesh grew up everywhere, reaching up the sides of the watch-towers, flowing into the defensive trenchworks, blistering up through the rockcrete like infected boils. Furthermore, a ribbon of bright silver marked the very outer borders of the facility beyond the trenches and watchtowers – it looked liquid, like a moat, the first line of defence against intruders.

But that was not the worst of it. The worst was the army that stood to attention, arrayed in ranks across the rockcrete. They towered over the biomechanical buildings – distance could be deceptive but to Alaric's practiced eye they were all between thirty and fifty metres high and in spite of their obvious biomechanical infections there could be no doubt as to what they were.

Titans. Hundreds of them.

The Adeptus Mechanicus's fighting forces, the tech-guard and the Skitarii, could be formidable, as could their spaceships and the massive Ordinatus artillery units they could deploy. But nothing in the armoury of the tech-priests could compare in symbolic power to the Titans. They were bipedal fighting machines that some said echoed the Emperor himself in the inspiring magnitude of their destructive power. Even the smallest, the Warhound Scout Titans, could muster more firepower than a dozen Imperial Guard squads.

Titans were god-machines deployed to break through fortifications and shatter enemy formations. There was little that could stand against them. And more importantly, the Titan legions ranked alongside the Space Marines themselves as symbols of Imperial dominance.

'Throne of Earth,' whispered Archis. 'They must have been building them for.. for...'

'A thousand years,' said Alaric. There were too many Titans for Alaric to count – they seemed to be mostly equivalent to the Reaver-pattern Titan, the mainstay of the Titan legions. Roughly humanoid in shape, each sported a truly immense weapon on each arm, along with countless smaller weapons bristling from their legs and torsos. Many of the weapons were unrecognisable fusions of mechanics and biology.

Alaric tried to get a better look at the facility itself. A single spire rose from the centre, taller than the rest, topped with a large disc studded with lights – perhaps the control spire for the facility. There were also tall chimneys belching greasy smoke into the sky, probably from forges beneath the surface where the massive metal parts needed to build and maintain the legion of Titans were smelted.

The landscape around the facility was scarred by the effort that had gone into digging a stable foundation into the ash wastes. It must have taken the full resources of Manufactorium Noctis to build the place and even now it was draining most of the city's power. The fact that it still needed so much power suggested very strongly that the Dark Mechanicus were still building and assembling Titans in the biomechanical workshops.

And there was more than just power. Alaric could feel the malevolence he had first tasted from orbit, dark and pulsing through his skin, strong enough to turn the air heavy and greasy with its power. It was here. The dark heart of Chaeroneia was beating somewhere among that Titan army.

Magos Antigonus crept up beside Alaric's Grey Knights. 'Omnissiah preserve us,' he said as he saw the facility rolling out in front of him.

'They must have moved the Titan works. Stone by stone, girder by girder. The whole thing. How stupid I was to think they would just dismantle it. This was what they had been building all along and I was too blind and afraid to venture out and find it.' Even through the crude vox-unit of his servitor body, Antigonus's regret was obvious. 'I promised I would make them face justice,' he said. 'Instead I let them build… this.'

'It doesn't matter,' said Alaric. 'What matters is what you do now. This is our chance to hurt them. All of them at once. Maybe stop what they came into real space to do.'

Hawkespur had reached the shaft entrance, too, along with Saphentis who was, at least, making a token effort to stay hidden. 'Of course,' she said, as if she should have guessed the Titan works were there from the start. 'This is what the Chaos fleet is here for. The Dark Mechanicus are making a deal with Abaddon, just like they did with Horus. The Titans are here to seal it.'

'So we destroy them all?' said Alaric.

'It seems the only option.'

'That,' said Saphentis, 'will be difficult.'

'I don't remember our orders saying it would be easy,' replied Hawkespur crossly.

'Nevertheless, it seems futile to pursue a goal we cannot possibly fulfil. The chances of our force successfully destroying so many Titans, even if they are not operational, is so close to zero as to be incalculable. The Dark Mechanicus will certainly become aware of our presence and divert all of their resources to stop us. And unlike in the city, there will be nowhere for us to hide.'

'Then what do you suggest?' asked Hawkespur.

'Find a way to leave this planet,' said Saphentis.

'Give up?'

'Give up. We all represent a significant investment of Imperial resources. Dying while pursuing an impossible goal will hardly coincide with the Emperor's will you claim to serve.'

'Hawkespur?' said Alaric. 'You're the Inquisitorial authority here.'

Hawkespur pulled herself to the edge of the shaft entrance to get a better look at the Titan legion and the defences of the facility. What she couldn't see, of course, were the many thousands of menials and tech-priests that could descend on them after the facility reported any intruders.

'We go in,' said Hawkespur. 'Our primary objective is the Titans. If they really are destined for the Eye then even taking out one will help. Our secondary objective is to gather information on the workings of the facility in case we find some way of completing the primary objective without sabotaging them all one by one. Other than that, we do what we can and die well. Any objections? Aside from the obvious, archmagos.'

'I submit to the will of the Inquisition,' said Saphentis, his artificial voice displaying little conviction.

'Alaric? You're the one who's going to have to do the fighting.'

'We go in. As you say, even taking out one will hurt them.'

'Good. Antigonus?'

'You'll only pull that Inquisition business on me if I refuse,' said Antigonus. 'And I think it's time we took this fight to them. I can reconnoitre the defences, they'll have a hard time telling me apart from another feral servitor.'

'You'll die if they do,' said Hawkespur.

'In that respect, interrogator, nothing has changed.' Antigonus crawled out from the shaft entrance and began the trek down the ragged surface of fused ash towards the quicksilver ribbon that marked the edge of the Titan works. His servitor body was streaked with rust and looked like it had been decaying out on the ash dunes for decades. It was a good disguise. The best on Chaeroneia.

'Take cover! Incoming fire, full evasion protocols in effect!'

Magos Murgild's voice boomed through the verispex decks. A bewildering tangle of exotic equipment, incense-wreathed tech-altars and long benches of bizarre experiments, the verispex deck was a bad place to get caught when the shells started slamming home. But that was where Nyxos was at that moment, grabbing hold of a massive steel laboratory bench as the *Exemplar* began to shudder.

Tech-priests were thrown to the ground. Chalices of chemicals were thrown around and enormous glass vessels shattered. Nyxos stayed on his feet, the exoskeleton hidden beneath his robes straining to keep him from being thrown around like a toy. Massive explosions boomed from outside the ship, warning klaxons sounded from a dozen different directions and the already murky lighting flickered as the ship's systems were wracked with fire and shrapnel. The verispex labs were used for research into samples brought in during the exploration missions the *Exemplar* had been built for and they made little concession to keeping the research magi safe when the ship came under fire.

'We need to move now!' shouted Nyxos above the din. 'Can you do it?'

'Not... not yet...' replied the nearest tech-priest. Nyxos hadn't had time to learn the tech-priests' procedures or even their names, or to check whether they might have been in thrall to Magos Korveylan. But none of that mattered. What mattered was time.

Nyxos had one chance to help Hawkespur and Alaric on the surface. This was it.

'Not good enough!' replied Nyxos. 'You!' He pointed to another tech-priest, apparently a woman somewhere under the dataprobes and fine manipulator attachments. 'Boost the signal. Get the power from wherever you can.'

'It may not hold…'

'It's better than not trying. And you!' Nyxos rounded on the first tech-priest again – apparently the lab supervisor, he sported bizarrely large round ocular attachments which magnified his naked, unblinking eyeballs several times. 'Encode the transmission. I don't want to hear excuses.'

'But the projector channels from Chaeroneia's historical logs are a hundred years old. There is every chance they have changed…'

'Then we will fail, magos. I am willing to accept that responsibility. I know it's something you tech-priests find difficult but you are playing by Inquisition rules now. Encode it. Send it. Now.'

The huge-eyed tech-priest stumbled over to the deck's main cogitator engine. A clockwork monstrosity the size of a tank, it was apparently powered by a large round handle which the lead tech-priest promptly began turning with all his strength.

Pistons and massive cogs began working, pumping and spinning through large holes in the cogitator's elaborate brass casing. More explosions sounded, closer this time and Nyxos knew the last of the shields were gone. That meant the fire from the *Desikratis* was now chewing its way through the hull and decks would start failing, pressure chambers would be breached, ship systems would be shutting down. People would be dying. Many people.

Space combat was something Nyxos hated with a passion. It could only end when crews – not ships, crews – were completely wiped out. It was long-distance butchery. Even the most minor ship-to-ship combat was the equivalent of an entire battle among ground troops in terms of fatalities and the battle for Chaeroneia would probably claim the lives of every single Imperial servant in orbit.

'We have to take power from the prow batteries,' said the female tech-priest, who was working a complicated system of interlocking pipes which covered one wall of the verispex lab and presumably governed how power was routed through the ship. She was holding a hand against a deep gash in her forehead, trying to keep the blood from getting in her eyes.

'Then do it!' replied Nyxos. Another explosion, the closest yet, threw everyone to the ground save for Nyxos. Sparks showered from somewhere. Nyxos heard a scream and smelled burning cloth, then burning flesh – one of the lab's tech-priests had been wreathed in flame and was now on the ground, fellow crewmen beating out the fire.

Nyxos looked around. The lab was in a bad state. Throne knew what the rest of the ship was like. And this was Nyxos's last chance. It had been extraordinary how quickly the tech-priests had worked, but it wouldn't count for anything if they failed now.

The clockwork cogitator was spitting streams of punchcards; the lead tech-priest hauling on the handle to get it calculating quicker. It wasn't fast enough.

Nyxos stumbled over to the cogitator. Something was wrong with the gravity on the *Exemplar* and it was like crossing the deck of a vessel at sea.

'Let me,' he growled, grabbing the handle. His servo-assisted limbs locked and the massive strength of his augmentations hauled the wheel round faster, so fast the surprised tech-priest had to let go. The cogitator howled as steam and sparks shot from inside its casing.

'It's working!' yelled the female tech-priest. The cogitator spat out a rippling ribbon of printout – the lead tech-priest grabbed it and quickly scanned it, his bizarrely magnified pupils skipping from side to side.

'They're receiving,' he said.

'Can the projectors transmit it?' asked Nyxos, his servos whining as he continued to work the handle.

'I don't...'

The explosion tore through the lab, sending white-hot shrapnel spinning everywhere, sparks falling like burning rain. The shriek of escaping air was deafening as Nyxos, the tech-priests and all the wreckage of the lab was sucked through the massive rent in the wall.

In the silence of the vacuum the cogitator exploded, sending fragments of its cogs, like sharp serrated crescents, spinning everywhere. But by then there were very few people alive on the deck to care.

FIFTEEN

'Death in service to the Emperor is its own reward. Life in failure to Him is its own condemnation.'

– Uriah Jacobus, 'Epistles' (Verse 93)

SCRAECOS WAS TRAVELLING up to the pinnacle of the command spire when he felt the call of the Castigator. The peristaltic motion of the biological elevator stopped as the unmistakeable voice spoke, every particle of every atom shuddering with its voice. Not physical and yet not psychic, when the Castigator spoke it did so with all the wisdom of the Omnissiah and it was impossible not to listen and obey.

Scraecos had yet to join with the consciousness of the tech-priests. It had been a long, long time since he had heard the call of the Castigator as an individual being. It was just like the first time he had heard it, deep below the ground, realising that he had finally looked upon the face of the Omnissiah.

The Castigator had spoken to Scraecos. Only to Scraecos. And it was doing so again.

The voice of the Castigator did not use anything so vulgar and fleshy as words. It spoke in pure concepts. The particles in Scraecos's still-biological brain vibrated in waves of absolute comprehension.

The Castigator spoke of how it was time to take the avatar of the Omnissiah and reveal its face to the galaxy. It was why Chaeroneia had been brought back into real space. It would be the first part of the great revelation, when all mankind would witness the true Machine-God – something living and aware, all-wise, separate from the corpse-Emperor

and infinitely more powerful. All who looked on it would have no logical choice but to kneel and pledge their lives to the Omnissiah.

The orthodox Mechanicus, which had withered like a grape on the
vine, would be winnowed out. The Adeptus Astartes would abandon
their obscure ancestor-worship and be made whole, their flesh excised
and replaced with the Machine to create an army in the image of the
Machine-God. The Imperial Guard would serve the newly-enlightened
Mechanicus. The collective consciousness of tech-priests would go to
Terra and there establish their court, the pooled wisdom of the thousands who had first seen the light on Chaeroneia.

It would not take long. The light of pure knowledge was too bright.
There would be no shadows for the non-believers to hide amongst. The
transition would be painful for a few, the mad and the corrupt, who
would be rounded up and fed into the forges. But for the trillions of
souls that laboured under the Imperial yoke, it would be a new Golden
Age of Technology. The human race would achieve its full potential as
the cogs that formed the machine. The greatest machine, the body of the
Omnissiah Himself formed out of untold forges and factoria, machine-
altars and cogitators, built and maintained by the whole human race
who would sing His praises as they devoted their lives to holy labour.

It was beautiful. Archmagos Veneratus Scraecos could see the universe
laid out according to the Omnissiah's plan, where the stars themselves
were moved into perfect mathematical patterns, wrought into binary
prayers thousands of light years across. How could the future be anything but that? Anything but a machine run according to sacred logic?

The voice faded. The Castigator had spoken.

The muscular motion around Scraecos continued, taking him up the
long biological gullet that would disgorge him at the top of the command spire to take his place among the ruling consciousness.

He willed it to stop.

The Castigator knew all. It spoke rarely and when it did, everything it
said was carefully calculated, including the timing.

Why had it waited until a time when Scraecos was alone, an individual, before doing so? The reason was clear. It wanted to speak directly to
Scraecos as a discrete consciousness, just as it had done more than a
thousand years before when Scraecos had first seen its face deep
beneath the ash wastes.

The other tech-priests, their minds joined together and their
personalities subsumed, would no doubt be calculating the tasks they
would have to complete if the Castigator's vision were to become reality.
They would have to get the Castigator off-planet perhaps, or maybe even

re-enact a version of the great ritual that had plunged Chaeroneia into the warp in the first place. But not Scraecos. To Scraecos it had spoken directly.

Archmagos Veneratus Scraecos had been blind for so long. Now it was clear. He was the chosen of the Omnissiah. He was the vessel through which the work of the Omnissiah, as revealed through His avatar the Castigator, would be completed. Again, the timing of the Castigator's call could only mean one thing. Scraecos, until such time as he re-entered the collective consciousness, was on the same mission for which he had been made an individual again – hunt down the intruders and kill them all.

The Castigator wanted him to continue that mission. It was the only conclusion Scraecos could draw. Of all the tech-priests now searching for a way to make the vision come true, Scraecos's was the most sacred of all. There were heretics on Chaeroneia. New ones arrived from the Imperium outside and probably old ones who had been trapped on Chaeroneia from the start. For the Castigator to be presented to the galaxy, every single soul on Chaeroneia had to be working towards the same purpose. There was no room for heretics. Scraecos was the holy weapon of the Omnissiah, ancient and wise, strong and ruthless. Scraecos had always been uncompromising and strong – brutal, perhaps – even before he had found the Castigator. It was why he had been chosen. He had the body and mind of a killer and the soul of a pious servant. And so he would serve his god by killing.

Scraecos willed the elevator to reverse its swallowing mechanism, propelling him back down towards the base of the spire. The collective of tech-priests would have to work without him for the time being – he had sacred work to do in the shadows of Chaeroneia, work he had failed to complete at the datafortress. He would not fail now. Not with the will of the Omnissiah within him.

Failure was an anomaly of logic. Success was inevitable. Before the galaxy saw the Castigator revealed, everyone who opposed the will of the Machine-God on Chaeroneia would be dead.

The broken ash wastes were corrosive and toxic. The hood of Hawkespur's voidsuit meant she could still breathe, but the ash was eating away at the suit's gloves and kneepads as she crawled along out of sight.

The tech-priests were well-practiced in staying hidden. The force avoided the occasional grav-platform, as it followed Magos Antigonus towards the bright silver boundary of the Titan works.

'What is it?' asked Alaric as the silver became more visible.

'I don't know,' rasped Hawkespur. 'Perhaps another type of data medium. They're using it as a moat.'

'Then we have to cross it.'

'We could go round the works to find a crossing point. But it would take days.'

Alaric looked at her. Even through the ash-streaked faceplate of her hood he could see her skin was greenish and pale. 'You haven't got days.'

'No. And any crossing points will be guarded, anyway.'

'Then we'll swim if we have to.'

Hawkespur looked at him with mild surprise, noting the massive bulk of his power armour. 'You can swim?'

'You'd be surprised.'

Archmagos Saphentis crawled towards them, his bionic limbs splayed like crab's legs, carrying him just above the ground as if he found abasing himself in the dirt distasteful.

'Interrogator Hawkespur,' he said. 'Perhaps you should look up.'

Hawkespur glanced upwards. For the first time in several days she smiled.

The blasphemous prayers were gone. In their place, projected onto the dense cloud layer, were letters hundreds of metres high.

++00100INTERROGATOR01110HAWKESPUR, they read.

POSSIBLE+STC PRESENT ON CHAERO100A. 010PTUS MECHAN-ICU1 AND *HELLFORGER* BOTH DESIRE IT. DENY+TO+THE E0EMY+AT ALL1COSTS. RECOVERY NOT A PRIO10TY.

WATCH+YOUR+BACK.

NYXOS+OUT011110.

'Nyxos…' breathed Hawkespur. 'He found a way.'

'It must be bad up there,' said Alaric. 'Throne knows what kind of risks he had to take to transmit it down here.'

'It certainly changes things.' Hawkespur looked back down at the Titan works. 'If the tech-priests found a Standard Template Construct here… if that is what all this is based on…'

'If so,' said Saphentis, 'then we may have discovered the source of the Dark Mechanicus beliefs of the Horus Heresy. And it is unlikely a more dangerous store of knowledge could exist.'

'No,' said an unfamiliar voice. It was the last of the tech-guard, the one who had been assigned to guard Hawkespur. He lifted the reflective visor of his helmet to show a pale, almost completely nondescript face, with fine surgical scars around one temple. 'The Standard Template Constructs are perfect. We learned this as menials. They contain the wisdom of the Omnissiah uncorrupted. They cannot contain a word of heresy.'

Alaric looked round at the soldier in surprise. It was the first time he had heard him speak – almost the first time any of the tech-guard had spoken except for the late Captain Tharkk. 'What does the Mechanicus teach about them?'

'An STC is a complete technology, rendered down to pure information. There is no room for corruptive innovation or error. They are sacred.' The tech-guard's voice was fast and clipped – he sounded as if he were reeling off rote-taught scripture.

'The dogma of the Cult Mechanicus,' interrupted Saphentis. 'The religion of Mars is couched in simple terms for the lower ranks of soldiers and menials. The lowest ranks hear of the Omnissiah as an object of religious awe. The Standard Template Constructs are described to them as holy artefacts. The more senior tech-priests understand such things in pragmatic and philosophical terms, but their devotion is no less. Some, of course, harbour divergent beliefs, but careful control is maintained over such things.'

'Then an STC,' said Hawkespur, 'would be something very powerful and not just because of what you could make with it. A tech-priest who possessed one could set himself up as… well, as a god, within the Mechanicus. There could be another schism.'

'It is probable,' replied Saphentis. 'Compromising the loyalty of the lower ranks would give an individual great power within the Mechanicus.'

'Enough to threaten the rule of Mars?' Hawkespur's question was a bold one. More than almost any other Imperial organisation, the Adeptus Mechanicus presented a resolutely united and inscrutable front to the rest of the Imperium.

'I shall not speak of such matters,' said Saphentis.

'Good,' said Alaric. 'Because we need to keep moving. Nyxos's signal will only confirm that we're still alive and still looking to hurt them down here.'

Nyxos's message was already gone. The painful, occult symbols were back. Whatever Nyxos had done to hijack control of the spire top projectors, it had worked, but Alaric knew that it had been Nyxos's last, desperate chance and he wouldn't able to pull it off again, no matter how the battle in orbit was going.

Nyxos's message might help them when the endgame was played out. It might be irrelevant. But nothing killed a soldier like ignorance about what he was fighting and every scrap of information helped. Alaric knew they needed all the help they could get.

* * *

THE TRIBUNICIA BURNED from stem to stern. Its overloading plasma reactors had filled most of the engineering decks with superheated fuel and it bled thick ribbons of cooling molten metal from hundreds of tears in its hull. The whole rearward section of the ship was a burning wreck, showering debris and crewmen's bodies out into Chaeroneia's orbit as it tumbled slowly, locked in a grim, slow dance of destruction with the *Hellforger*.

The *Tribunicia* had the fearsome guns that any cruiser of the Imperial Navy could boast. But the *Hellforger's* crew had endless centuries of experience and the ancient, malevolent creatures that lurked inside it. It had daemonically possessed broadside guns and cruel gun-deck masters who had been sending ships burning into the endless grave of space for a thousand years. The *Hellforger* pumped salvo after salvo of heavy gun shells into the hull of the *Tribunicia*, slowly spiralling to keep the broadside a single, rolling bombardment.

The *Hellforger* was hurt, too. It was bleeding from thousands of craters and thick hull plates of scab had broken away to reveal hot living flesh beneath, which blackened and died in the vacuum. But it was nothing that the ship's crew could not repair, given time.

Portals opened, like eyeless sockets, in the underside of the *Hellforger*. The ship spat dozens of thick tendons from them, tipped with huge bony hooks. Those that hit the *Tribunicia* caught in the ruptured hull plates and slowly, painfully, the *Hellforger* started to reel the enemy ship in.

THE BRIDGE OF the *Hellforger* was hot and dark and stank of stagnant daemons' blood. Urkrathos watched the tormenting of the *Tribunicia* on the bridge holo and grunted his approval as another reactor blew somewhere in the rearward section of the Imperial ship. Even the daemons were watching – as much as they hated Urkrathos and the way he had enslaved them, they still loved death and destruction, especially when it was visited on the worshippers of the corpse-emperor.

The battle was a good one. It was up close and brutal, where the superior strength of the *Hellforger* counted for more than the discipline of the Imperial Navy. Even someone as rigidly disciplined as a Chosen of the Black Legion, such as Urkrathos himself, had to let the bloodlust take over from time to time. Sometimes battle wasn't just the work of the Dark Gods – it was an end in itself, beautiful and brutal.

'Are the grappling hooks sound?' asked Urkrathos.

'Fast and holding,' came the reply from the grappling gang leader, deep in the guts of the *Hellforger*, his voice relayed by the communications daemon fused with the ceiling of the bridge.

'Good. Stand by for contact.'

Urkrathos flicked to another channel, sending his voice booming throughout the whole ship. 'Master of Weapons, bring me my sword from the armoury. The rest of you, prepare for boarding.'

BY SPACE TRAVEL standards, the orbit above Manufactorium Noctis was a horrendously cramped labyrinth. Wreckage from shattered shuttles and transports glittered like crimson sparks in the sick, reddening light of the star Borosis. Streaks of yellow fire spat across the void from broadside shells, mixed in with the deep red las-blasts from lance turrets.

The *Hellforger* and the *Tribunicia* closed in a terminal death spiral, fire spattering between them like a swarm of fireflies. The *Exemplar* was holding out against the *Desikratis*, but the bloated old cruiser was launching volleys of gunfire into it with complete impunity, the daemon that controlled it grinning evilly as it poured more and more suffering into the Mechanicus ship.

Rear Admiral Horstgeld's orders had been to protect the troop transports. The transports were the target of the Vulture Wing, a force of elite fighter craft launching from the carrier platform *Cadaver*. *Ptolemy Alpha* and *Ptolemy Beta* were frantically trying to protect the troop transport *Calydon*, the *Ptolemy Gamma* having been reduced to a guttering wreck of a ship by coordinated attack runs from Vulture Wing.

The Imperial Guard, who had been brought to the Borosis system to land on the mystery planet and raise the flags of the Imperium over it, were instead dying in orbit. Men from the Mortressan Highlanders and a dozen other smaller units from other regiments were dying for their Emperor with no way to fight back and no understanding of what was happening to the Imperial ships.

Most of the smaller transports were crowding around the armed yacht *Epicurus*, almost pleading with the grand old pleasure-ship to protect them with its hastily fitted deck guns and defensive turrets. The Vulture Wing had only just deigned to attack the *Epicurus* and it was going down quickly, most of its bridge crew dead from a torpedo strike, most of its engine crew dying in a massive plasma-fed fire that was burning out the ship's systems one by one.

The Chaos ships, on the other hand, were all in full working order. The *Hellforger* had a bloodied nose but nothing that would trouble it. The *Desikratis* had a hull as tough as kraken's skin and no mortal crew to kill, so the fire that reached it from the *Exemplar* had so little effect that the cruiser's piloting daemon barely noticed it. There were a few Vulture Wing pilots who would never fly again thanks to disciplined turret fire or collisions with the wreckage that flew thickly over Chaeroneia, but more than enough who came back to the *Cadaver* for fuel and ammunition to go out and kill again.

The battle had been over before it had begun. Horstgeld had known it. All his officers who understood the composition of the Chaos fleet had known it. The *Hellforger* alone, a grand cruiser with a monstrous combat pedigree, could have broken the Imperial fleet with relative ease. The fighter-bombers of the Vulture Wing were just making the job quicker and the *Desikratis* was there purely for the joy of battle, maliciously pulling the *Exemplar* apart at long distance just because it could.

It was just a matter of time. But then, it always had been. Very few Imperial servants in orbit were not praying to the Emperor for their lives. But a few, the ones who knew what was really happening, were praying for something else – a few more moments of that time they were dying to buy, minutes, seconds for Alaric on the surface below.

ALARIC TOOK THE first step into the moat. It was full of a liquid like quicksilver – it was thick and heavy, one moment as fluid as water and the next solid as iron.

The Grey Knights were the first in, as always. Alaric looked up at the watchtowers – there was no indication they had been spotted, no klaxons or gunfire. That didn't mean anything, of course. The Dark Mechanicus might be waiting until they were vulnerable, wading through the middle of the moat, before opening fire.

Alaric waded in, storm bolter ready. Brother Dvorn was beside him, with the other Grey Knights following close behind. The currents in the moat pulled at Alaric's legs like insistent hands. He went in deeper, up to his waist. The opposite shore was maybe a hundred paces away, the bank a solid slab of rockcrete that marked the edge of the Titan works proper. There was some cover there around the base of the closest watchtower, where the black iron of the tower formed a giant claw gripping the rockcrete. But the moat was completely open.

'Now this,' said Dvorn grimly, 'I don't like.'

The quicksilver rolled in tiny shimmering droplets over the armour of Alaric's waist and abdomen. The ripples he sent out were slow and sharp, like tiny mountain ranges. He had to push forward, the quicksilver seeming to mass in front of him to slow him down.

'Anyone else feel that?' asked Lykkos.

'Feel what?' replied Archis.

'Nobody move,' said Alaric, freezing. The feeling wasn't physical, but it was definitely there, beneath the surface of the moat. It was almost screened out by the sense of daemonic malice coming from the Titan works themselves – another spark of the warp, quiet as butterfly's wings. The beating of a daemon's heart.

'Contact!' yelled Alaric as he felt it lunge. The words weren't out of his mouth before the daemon ripped out of the quicksilver ahead of him, its massive jaws yawning open, teeth like dripping silver knives.

A data-daemon. Like the guardians of the datafortress – but stronger, given form by the quicksilver medium and lying in ambush for the Grey Knights.

Alaric didn't have time to fire before the daemon was on him. Its jaws closed over his gun arm and shoulder and its weight drove him down into the quicksilver on his back. It writhed on top of him down in the airless, crushing darkness, teeth pushing down through the ceramite into his shoulder. Alaric fought to reverse his grip on his halberd so he could stab into the thing's guts, but the quicksilver was crushing around him like a giant fist clenching.

He couldn't see. He couldn't breathe. But that was the last of his problems. He tried to force his arm out of the daemon's jaws but it was clamped on too tight. He pressed the firing stud and felt bolter shells bursting in the quicksilver but the grip never let go.

A bright white streak slashed down and the daemon convulsed as something hot and burning smashed through its grimacing, canine skull. In the brief moment of light Alaric saw a hand reaching down to grab him by the collar of his armour, pulling him up into the air.

Alaric coughed up a gobbet of quicksilver and shook drops of it from his eyes. He saw that Brother Dvorn had saved him, smashing down through the daemon with his Nemesis hammer.

Alaric didn't have time to thank him. Gunfire was streaking everywhere. Daemons like dripping silver dragons were wheeling through the air, diving in and out of the moat, snapping at the Grey Knights. Brother Cardios was wrestling with a daemon wrapped around him like a single metal tentacle, trying to free the arm that held his Incinerator. Autogun and lasgun fire spattered from the near shore as the tech-priests added their efforts but there was nothing they could do.

Daemons. There was nothing worse in the galaxy. But daemons Alaric understood.

He tore his halberd arm free of the quicksilver, lunged forward and beheaded the daemon trying to drown Cardios. He pivoted and stabbed the halberd like a spear, transfixing a daemon through its snaking body. It screamed at him as he reversed his grip and plunged it into the moat, pinning it against the floor. Brother Dvorn took a step back and brought his hammer down through the quicksilver again, shattering the dae-mon's head in a burst of light.

Haulvarn brought another one down with storm bolter fire. Lykkos battered another two back with psycannon shots, the ensorcelled bolter shells leaving massive smoking wounds in their bodies. The Grey Knights backed towards one another until they were back-to-back, a tight knot of men, an island of Space Marines in the moat that no dae-mon could approach without being carved up by Nemesis blades or shot out of the air by storm bolters.

'We can get across!' shouted Alaric above the screeching of the dae-mons. There must have been thirty of them, wheeling and diving, snapping at the Grey Knights. 'Stay tight and pray!'

The Grey Knights waded across the moat step by step, the quicksilver reaching chest-height. The daemons had learned from the deaths of their brothers at the datafortress and dared not close completely, dart-ing in and snapping, then jerking away before a Nemesis blade could cut them in two.

'Enough,' said a voice so deep it sounded like an earthquake.

The surface of the quicksilver boiled and something erupted from below the ground, bursting up right through the middle of the Grey Knights and throwing them aside. Alaric felt a force slam into him so hard it almost knocked him out, throwing him on a wave of quicksilver against the rockcrete bank. He lay for a moment gathering his senses, the floor beneath him splintered by the impact, a sickly purplish light bleeding onto him from the creature that had burst up from the moat.

It was floating in the air surrounded by a nimbus of purple fire, sparks arcing off its outstretched fingers and bleeding from the burning pits of its eyes. Its skin was so pallid it was translucent and patterns could be seen writhing beneath it, strange squirming shapes as if there was some-thing just inside the creature's body that was about to burst out.

The creature was human. The patterns were circuitry. It was Tech-priest Thalassa.

'Scraecos knew you would come,' she said in a voice that Alaric knew wasn't hers. She rotated slowly, turning to face Alaric. 'Especially you. I told him how strong you were. How I admired you and was also afraid. He showed me what true strength was, Justicar Alaric. I saw it on this world and when Scraecos's servants found me I finally understood it.'

It was Brother Archis who found his feet first. Dragging himself up from the churning quicksilver, he sprayed a chain of storm bolter fire at Thalassa's head. The shells burst like multicoloured fireworks against Thalassa's skin. She turned her head towards Archis, gestured regally towards him and a tendril of pure blackness lashed out. It snared Archis's neck, lifting him up into the air above Thalassa's head. He slashed out with his halberd but another tendril snaked out from Thalassa's other hand and caught hold of his halberd arm. More tendrils snaked from Thalassa's eyes and from beneath the silvery robes that flapped around her as she floated.

Alaric could feel the heart beating somewhere in that body. The heart of a daemon. He forced himself to his feet, fighting against the current in the quicksilver that swirled around Thalassa's feet. He stamped down and jumped, halberd stabbing up towards her body.

Data-daemons lurched from the quicksilver, snapping at him, suddenly emboldened by Thalassa's appearance. Alaric shouldered them aside and drove the halberd blade deep into Thalassa's torso. He felt the daemonic flesh underneath spasming as the blade passed through it, then reform around the blade to yank it out of his grasp. Thalassa descended to his level and a second pair of arms unfolded from her robed chest – and beyond them a face, utterly bestial with burning purplish eyes, because there was something inside Thalassa and it was coming out to fight Alaric.

The daemon's arms had too many joints so that they wound like serpents and were tipped with claws that snagged Alaric's neck and chestplate. The daemon threw Alaric down, pitching him back into the quicksilver with a howl, the halberd blade coming free in a spray of glowing purple blood.

Alaric looked up before the quicksilver closed over him to see Brother Archis's body coming apart, the Grey Knight torn in two at the waist. Archis, who had prayed for all of them at the datafortress, who had learned the parables of the Grand Masters at the feet of Chaplain Durendin.

Alaric yelled a formless battlecry and fought the quicksilver current that tried to drag him away. He wrestled the daemons out of his way and fought himself upwards to the surface. This daemon had taken one of his own. The Grey Knights always avenged their dead.

'Azaulathis!' yelled a voice. Alaric fought to his feet in time to see the daemon inside Thalassa turn its baleful eyes towards the source of the voice – someone had spoken its name. Someone who should not be there.

Magos Antigonus's spidery servitor body landed heavily on Thalassa, his jointed metallic legs scrabbling for purchase. The pure red light of a las-cutter flared as Antigonus tried to carve through Thalassa's body to get at the daemon inside.

Brother Haulvarn was there, too, fending off the data-daemons that tried to tear chunks out of Antigonus. Brother Cardios fell against Haulvarn for support and sprayed fire from his Incinerator over the surface of the moat in a wide arc, scorching the silvery skins off more daemons who were looming from the quicksilver.

Thalassa's tendrils ripped off one of Antigonus's spindly legs and the daemon inside her reared out of her torso to yank off another. Its eyes dripped with power and hate and its mouth was a pulsing, alien thing with a long lashing tongue and teeth like black knives.

Antigonus held on. Alaric stabbed up at the daemon, feeling the wards in his armour burning him as they reacted to its presence.

The daemon howled a long, low, discordant note and the whole moat quivered like the sea in a storm, throwing the Grey Knights off their feet. Alaric was almost swamped.

'I beat you once,' came Antigonus's voice, the vox-unit of his servitor body cranked up to maximum. 'I can do it again!'

The daemon's eyes flashed. 'You,' it growled, pausing for a split-second in recognition.

Antigonus punched the las-cutter deep through Thalassa's body. The daemon screamed and so did Thalassa and the two fell down into the quicksilver, almost landing on Alaric. Antigonus leapt off and landed somewhere in the body of the moat. Alaric forgot about trying to shoot the daemon or cut it up and grabbed Thalassa instead, wrapping his arms around her and trying to wrestle her to the floor of the moat. She spasmed with unholy strength, almost throwing Alaric off.

Someone else joined in. Another Grey Knight, Alaric thought – but then he saw his own face, reflected hundreds of times in the multi-faceted eyes of Archmagos Saphentis. Saphentis had waded through the quicksilver, electric pulses flowing off him to part the quicksilver in front of him. His two normal-shaped bionic arms pinned Thalassa's arms to her sides and the tips of the other two reconfigured, twin spinning saw blades emerging from the machinery. With a swift and brutal motion, Saphentis beheaded Thalassa.

Thalassa's head was shot to the far side of the moat on a burst of dark energy that spurted from the stump of her neck. Azaulathis the daemon extruded itself from the neck, Thalassa's body falling limp in Alaric's arms as the daemon freed itself and soared above the moat. Azaulathis's body was a twisted nightmare of information made flesh, a ring of eyes surrounding its great howling maw, many smaller mouths gaping all over it. Black tendrils uncoiled from wet orifices all over its corrupt body, lashing in every direction as power burst off it like purple-black fireworks. Forced out of its body, it gibbered in pain, the harshness of real space burning off flakes of its luminous skin.

Chains of storm bolter fire smacked into it, showering the moat with burning chunks of its flesh. More fire thudded up from the Grey Knights and then a burst of flame from Brother Cardios, singed the skin off half its face to reveal a glowing, melting, unnaturally twisted skull that writhed in pain.

On the outer shore, Alaric spotted Hawkespur. She had taken her marksman's autopistol out and was taking careful aim. She put a single shot through the daemon's burning eye socket, blowing out the back of its head. It stopped moving for a moment as it reeled in shock and that was all the time the Grey Knights needed to shred its body with bolter fire.

'Go,' said Saphentis, his body spattered with Thalassa's corrupted purple blood and rolling droplets of quicksilver. He was holding the quicksilver apart and Alaric could see the other Grey Knights struggling through it into the gap.

'Make for the shore!' ordered Alaric. 'Cardios! Find Archis if you can! And Hawkespur, bring the others across! Quick!'

The data-daemons seemed to have been cowed by the deaths of Thalassa and Azaulathis. The Grey Knights made it across to the far bank, Brother Haulvarn pausing to haul Magos Antigonus's shattered servitor body up onto the rockcrete. Cardios followed carrying the upper half of Archis's smouldering body.

Alaric led the way to the foot of the watchtower, where massive claws rooted the tower into the rockcrete and provided cover between the black iron lengths. Hawkespur and Antigonus's tech-priests followed and finally Archmagos Saphentis pulled himself up onto the bank, the quicksilver knitting itself back together behind him. Saphentis paused to pick something up as he headed for cover where Alaric waited.

Cardios ducked into cover beside Alaric. He was hauling Brother Archis's upper half with him – a sorry, tragic sight, the brave Grey Knight's body turned into so much wreckage by the daemon's strength.

'Even if we could bury him here,' said Alaric, 'we wouldn't. Not in this tainted ground. Cardios, take out his geneseed and share out his ammunition. We will have to leave the body.'

Cardios nodded and began removing Archis's helmet. Like all Space Marines, a Grey Knight's many augmentations were controlled by twin master organs, the geneseed. Geneseed was almost impossible to create from scratch and so each Chapter did its best to harvest the organs from their dead so they could be implanted into a new recruit and the Grey

Knights were no exception. The Chapter's geneseed was modelled after the genetic code of their primarch, the awesome warriors created by the Emperor to lead the Great Crusade more than ten thousand years ago. The donor of the genes for the Grey Knights' geneseed was uncertain, however, since the Chapter had been founded amid the greatest of secrecy some time after the first foundings. Some said it was modelled after one of the primarchs who had left behind an unusually stable geneseed, others that the donor was the Emperor himself. No one knew for sure and most of the Grey Knights preferred it that way – they fought not for the ancestral memory of a primarch but for the Emperor first and the Ordo Malleus second and nothing stood in the way. Archis's geneseed was sacred wherever it had originally come from and Alaric had a duty to bring it back to the Grey Knights fortress-monastery on Titan if he could.

Antigonus's smoking, wheezing body scuttled into the shadow of the watchtower. He saw the body of Archis and paused for a moment in respect, then crouched down to conserve his servitor body's dwindling energy reserves.

'You need a new body,' said Alaric.

'I know,' said Antigonus, the voice from the servitor's vox-unit distorted with effort. 'I'm surprised this one lasted so long.'

'You knew that daemon.'

'Scraecos sent it after me when I first came here to investigate. I was lucky not to end up like Thalassa. I recognised its voice. When you have something like that living inside you it must leave an impression on you.'

'You fought well,' said Alaric.

'So did you,' replied Antigonus. 'All of you. Especially your battle-brother.' Antigonus indicated Archis's body. Cardios had almost finished cutting the geneseed organ from Archis's throat.

'We will all have to do so again, I fear,' said Alaric. 'This planet crawls with daemons.'

'Someone would disagree with you.' Archmagos Saphentis drifted calmly through the machinery at the base of the watchtower. He held Thalassa's severed head in his hand. 'Explain,' he said to the head.

Thalassa's eyes, now orbs of pure silver, opened. 'Daemons…' she said, her voice a bubbling whisper through the blood running from her mouth. 'No, no daemons… they are the hunter-programs, the servants of the archmagi…' The power that had held her together while she was possessed by Azaulathis was keeping her alive now, animating her with an echo of its dark magic.

'She's insane,' said Antigonus.

'Maybe,' said Alaric. He turned back to Thalassa's head. 'How do you know?'

'The... archmagi told me... their many voices are one...'

'The rulers of this planet?'

'Yes. They showed me such things. I became lost, but they found me. I saw a world completely self-sufficient... master of the power of the warp... and I saw the face of the Omnissiah, I saw the Castigator, His knowledge made metal and flesh and sent to teach us... no, there are no daemons here, just knowledge made real, come down to serve us and show us the way...'

Alaric levelled his storm bolter and blew the head apart with a single shot. Saphentis looked down at his gore-splattered robes in mild surprise.

'Lies,' said Alaric. 'About the daemons at least.'

'Then they are ignorant of their own corruption,' said Saphentis. 'Interesting.'

'They all are at the start,' said Alaric. 'Anyone who conjures daemons and does the will of Chaos goes to great lengths to convince themselves they are anything but corrupt. Chaos is a lie, archmagos. Most of all it makes the heretic lie to himself. The Dark Mechanicus are no different in that respect. What we know as Chaos, they see as some extension of technology.'

'It is a grave blasphemy indeed,' said Saphentis. 'To turn the teachings of the Omnissiah into the justification for such corruption.' Saphentis sat down and for the first time Alaric saw tiredness evident in his bionic limbs.

'I was wrong to suspect you,' said Alaric. 'About Thalassa, I mean. She must have got lost and captured. I thought you had killed her.'

'Because I had expressed admiration of this planet's self-sufficiency?' If Saphentis could have been able to smile grimly, Alaric suspected he would have done. 'I did not choose my words carefully. It was natural for you to think little of me, justicar. I wanted to understand this world, as well as carry out our mission, but it was unwise of me to do so. And I should have been more careful with Thalassa. She was not able to cope with the responsibilities I placed upon her here. Her loss was my failure. I can only hope the Omnissiah forgives me my weaknesses.'

'Then we're on the same side?' said Alaric.

'The same side,' replied Saphentis.

'Now that's sorted out,' said Hawkespur, 'we need to keep moving.'

'Agreed.' Alaric looked back at Brother Cardios, who had finished removing the geneseed from Archis's corpse. 'We'll have to leave him. There's no other way. We can pray for forgiveness later. Dvorn, carry Antigonus if he breaks down. The rest of you, stick close and keep your heads down. At the moment we're recon first, combat second.'

The strikeforce gathered itself, said a silent prayer for the dead and carried on into the Titan works, skirting the base of the watchtower and skulking through the fleshy outgrowths and masses of corroded machinery that broke through the rockcrete surface of the works. And in front of them, now stretching between the horizons, were the Titans themselves – towering, silent, brimming with destructive potential.

It was an army that could lay waste to worlds. An army just waiting to wake up.

SIXTEEN

'Die in failure, shame on you. Die in despair, shame on us all.'
– The 63rd Terran Scrolls,
Verse 114 (author unknown)

REAR ADMIRAL HORSTGELD was down on his belly, his Naval uniform torn and smouldering. He held a naval shotgun close to his body and tried to peer past the pew, through the smoke and burning wreckage that flittered from the ruined ceiling of the bridge.

Gunfire from the *Hellforger* had shaken the bridge but not destroyed it. Most of the bridge crew were still alive, crouching for cover as they had been since the last major bulkhead fell.

They had been boarded. The worst possible result when fighting the forces of Chaos. That was where the Enemy was strongest – face-to-face where foul magicks and mutations counted for the most and where the very presence of the corrupted could shake the faith of the bravest men.

'Hold!' shouted the bridge security chief, a squat and massively powerful man wearing full forced entry armour more normally used when storming decks held by mutinous crewmen. There were no mutinies on the *Tribunicia* but Horstgeld had always insisted on full security details on his ships. From the speed with which contact had been lost with contested sections of the ship, though, the security crew had not made a great deal of difference. 'Take your targets before you fire! Line up, then shoot!'

The rest of the bridge crew had hunted down whatever weapons they could as the Chaos boarding teams had spilled through the decks. Some had the naval shotguns of the kind Horstgeld now cradled, rock-solid weapons designed for filling cramped spaceship corridors with heavy, mutilating slug shots. Others had the lasguns that the Imperial Guard carried and many had only been able to rustle up their personal sidearms – autopistols, laspistols, even a few slug guns, almost all designed for show and not combat. Horstgeld saw one of the communications crew holding a length of pipe that had fallen from the ceiling as the *Tribunicia* was rocked by broadside fire, another hefting a large steel spanner.

'Steel your souls, faithful of the Emperor!' intoned Confessor Talas. 'Make His will your shield and His wrath your weapon!' For the first time in their careers many of the bridge crew were actually listening to Talas, seeking some hope in his words.

Sparks showered from the main bridge doors. Something was cutting through.

'Right!' shouted the security chief, unhooking the power maul from his belt and lowering the visor of his helmet before hefting his riot shield. 'Stay tight, stay covered, mark targets and never forget who–'

A massive armoured fist punched through the door and the gunfire began. Blazing, intense, a wall of fire and white noise that sheeted across the bridge from both sides. The viewscreen shattered in a white starburst and the golden statue of the Emperor toppled. Gunfire chewed through the hardwood pews and the fluted stone columns. Horstgeld yelled and fired almost blind, the shotgun kicking in his hands. He saw silhouettes of crewmen flailing and in the flashes of fire made out the deformed, oversized humanoid creatures forcing their way through the breach. They died in their dozens but more came, toppling over the bodies of their dead, a few making it to the rearmost pews and returning fire with their crude weapons.

A massive speargun shot a barbed javelin that impaled the chief navigation officer. The severed head of the security chief smacked off the column next to Horstgeld. The pew in front of Horstgeld cracked as if something huge had landed on it and Horstgeld scrambled out of the way, feeling hot blood on the floor. Spinning fragments of shrapnel were burning pinpoints on his skin and hands. He frantically reloaded as the return fire thudded heavier across the bridge.

Horstgeld had been in sticky situations before. He had been in boarding actions, even, as a young lieutenant in a boarding party that stormed an ork-infested space hulk. He had seen violent mutinies and pirate raids and had been on more than a few ships wrecked in accidents or under fire. He had seen many men die. He had killed a few up close and countless more from afar as master of the Emperor's warships. But this was the worst. This was the worst by far.

Something was ripping up the pews at the rear of the bridge. Something else flapped overhead and Horstgeld shot at it, blowing a chunk out of one leathery wing and seeing it spiral into the ordnance helm, all slashing claws and teeth. Someone was screaming. Someone else yelled in anger, the cry cut brutally short.

The gunfire was dying down. Now the din was cracking bones and the thud of blades into flesh, the scrape of blades on the floor. Screams and sobbing. Roars from once-human monsters. The killing was close and bloody and getting closer. Horstgeld backed up against the pew and finished loading his shotgun.

The killing was nearly done. Most of the bridge crew were dead, the rest dying.

Horstgeld heard heavy, armoured footsteps, coming closer.

'Captain,' said a voice, deep and thick.

Horstgeld peeked out through the planks of the broken pew. He could just make out a massive armoured form, similar to one of Alaric's Grey Knights but more hulking and malformed, wreathed in greasy smoke.

A Space Marine. Dear Emperor, it was a Space Marine from the Traitor Legions, the arch-betrayers of mankind. So dangerous that most Imperial teachings maintained they didn't even exist any more, because the very idea of a Traitor Marine was deadly to a weak mind.

Horstgeld held his shotgun tight. He was supposed to be brave. To die in the grace of the Emperor. And it wasn't supposed to be easy.

'Rear Admiral,' he shouted in reply, correcting the Marine.

'Ah. Good. A worthy prize, then.'

Horstgeld could see the Space Marine walking towards him, kicking dead crewmen out of the way. Horstgeld could make out the ancient, tarnished black armour, with the symbol of a single unblinking eye wrought onto one shoulder pad in gold. The Marine held a huge power sword in one hand, its blade writhing as if it housed something alive. His face was old and malevolent, the skin drawn tight, the eyes glinting black, the teeth pointed. An eight-pointed star was branded onto its hairless scalp. Steam spurted from the joints in the armour, which seemed crude and mechanical compared to the ornate armour of the Grey Knights – because this was a Space Marine from the days of Horus, a link to the Imperium's darkest and most shameful days. Chaos incarnate. Hatred made flesh.

'See!' called out a wavering voice, which Horstgeld realised belonged to Confessor Talas. 'See the form of the Enemy!' Talas pulled himself to his feet, still inside the bridge pulpit. 'See the mark of corruption upon him! The stink of treachery on him! The sound of…'

The Traitor Marine took out a bolt pistol and put a single round through Talas's head. The old confessor thudded to the wooden floor of the pulpit and one of the boarding mutants scampered over. The wet crunching noises that followed could only mean the confessor's body was being eaten.

The Traitor Marine stomped round the pew that Horstgeld was hiding behind. 'You. You are in command.'

Horstgeld nodded. He had to be brave. He had never run before. He would not run now, not give this creature the satisfaction of breaking him.

The Marine slid his writhing sword into a scabbard he wore on his back. He reached down with his free hand. Horstgeld levelled the shotgun but the Marine batted it away before Horstgeld could fire it – the Traitor Marine's reactions were lightning-quick. He was still a Space Marine, with all the conditioning and augmentations that went with it.

The Traitor Marine grabbed Horstgeld round the throat. His armoured fingers easily circled Horstgeld's pudgy neck and lifted him clean off the ground. The Traitor Marine held Horstgeld close to his face. Horstgeld could smell blood and brimstone on his breath. Those gem-like black eyes peered right through him.

'A long time ago I fought your kind,' said the Chaos Space Marine. 'Horus led us. He told us you were all weak. That you deserved to die. And every time I face you, you prove him right. You become more pathetic every time I sail out of the warp.'

Horstgeld would have spat in the Marine's face, but his mouth was dry. 'Horus was a traitor. He was corrupt. A daemon. We beat you.'

'No. We defeated you. We killed your Emperor. And then the conspirators closed ranks. The primarchs. All the bureaucrats and the profiteers. They wrote our triumph out of your history, they branded us failures, when all the time we were just waiting to return. And now that time has come, slave of the corpse-god. The Eye of Terror has opened. Cadia will fall. Look at yourself and ask who is stronger? Who deserves this galaxy?'

'But… you fear us! Why else are you here? If we are so weak, why did you have to come?'

The Chaos Space Marine dropped Horstgeld onto the floor and stamped down on his leg. Pure red pain slammed up from the wound, almost knocking Horstgeld out as the bones of his legs shattered.

'Enough of this,' said the Marine. 'I am Urkrathos of the Black Legion, Chosen of Abaddon the Despoiler. I will kill you and everyone on this ship. Death is merciful. Those who anger me are taken back to my ship and cast into the pit of blood where their souls are made fuel for spells and fodder for daemons. That is the fate I am giving you the chance to avoid. I am not merciful by nature so this offer will not be repeated. Do you understand?'

'Frag yourself,' gasped Horstgeld.

Urkrathos crushed down on Hortgeld's leg again. Horstgeld couldn't help from screaming.

'Where is the tribute?' Urkrathos demanded.

'What... what tribute?'

Urkrathos lifted Horstgeld up again, slammed him against the closest pillar and drew his sword. He stabbed the sword through the meat of Horstgeld's shoulder, pinning him to the pillar like an insect on a board.

'Do not make me ask again, rear admiral,' spat Urkrathos. 'You're here for it just as we are.'

'I don't know,' said Horstgeld, coughing up a gobbet of blood. He could barely see through the pain. The world was a mass of pain with only the face of Urkrathos showing through, his snarling, fanged mouth, his burning black eyes. 'We... we didn't find out...'

'Where is it?' bellowed Urkrathos. 'Where is the Castigator?'

Horstgeld tried to speak again, to curse the traitor. But he couldn't get the words out. His throat was full of blood and he couldn't even breathe.

Urkrathos wrenched the blade out of the pillar and caught Horstgeld as he fell. He lifted the rear admiral's limp body and dashed his brains out against the floor, cracking the man's head over and over again into the flagstones.

He flung the corpse to the floor. His sword had been drawn and it had not drunk deeply enough yet, so Urkrathos stabbed it again into the corpse and let the daemons imprisoned in the blade lap up the man's warm blood.

There had not been nearly enough blood. Every time it got easier to break them. Every ship, every battle – the Imperium had only spared a pathetic parody of a fleet to oppose Urkrathos. It was an insult. It seemed all the best battles were in the past now.

A thought came unbidden into Urkrathos's mind. It wasn't his own thought – it was a transmission from the communications daemon back on the *Hellforger*.

'What?' thought back Urkrathos angrily. He didn't like the daemons touching his mind. 'If this is not an emergency, you will suffer.'

'Our allies show their hand on the planet,' replied the grinding, bestial voice of the daemon. 'The sky opens for us.'

'Show me,' thought Urkrathos.

An image unfolded. Chaeroneia's atmosphere was a filthy dark grey mantle of pollution, specked with the bright spots that were its attendant asteroids. Urkrathos had guessed the Imperial fleet had been trying to find a way through the asteroids when Urkrathos's own fleet had arrived. Getting onto the planet would be a headache Urkrathos was going to have to face when he had destroyed the Imperials.

The image projected from the communications daemon was shifting. Like ripples in water, shockwaves were echoing out from a point on the uppermost level of the atmosphere, directly above the source of the signal that had promised tribute.

The asteroids were moving. Like a shoal of silver fish, the points of light were spiralling around the epicentre, rearranging themselves. It was powerful magic. More powerful than any sanctioned Imperial psyker could manage.

'What is it?' thought Urkrathos impatiently. 'Who is doing this?'

'This being knows not,' replied the daemon.

A path was being cleared through the field. A way in, large enough for the *Hellforger*.

Of course. Whoever had promised the tribute to Abaddon must also have been monitoring the situation in orbit. Now the Imperial fleet was destroyed, crippled or scattered, there was no danger of Imperial Guard landing on the world. Urkrathos had succeeded and now the mysterious benefactor of Chaos was welcoming the *Hellforger* in with open arms.

'Urkrathos to all crew,' voxed Urkrathos, knowing his voice would be transmitted all over the *Hellforger* and into the communicators of the less disposable boarding crew. 'All boarders disengage. Prepare to cut free.' Urkrathos switched channels. 'Kreathak?'

Kreathak replied from the cockpit of his Helltalon fighter, his voice distorted by the scream of the macrojet engines and the stutter of lascannon. 'My lord?'

'Disengage and get back to the *Cadaver*. We're heading down.'

'The Enemy is in full flight. Confirm action abort?'

'Yes, confirm. And be quick about it. Don't waste your time killing them, I want your fighters in close defence patrols.'

'Of course, my lord.' Kreathik switched off his vox-link – if he managed to choke down his bloodlust he would be flying back to the fighter platform *Cadaver*, ready to defend the gap in the asteroid field while Urkrathos's ship loaded the tribute.

Urkrathos switched to another channel. 'Come in *Desikratis*.'

'Lord,' came the titanic, rumbling voice of the *Desikratis*.

'Pull back.'

'But lord. The prey, it bleeds so.'

'I said pull back. You can toy with it when we are done. I need you to keep enemy fighters away while we head down to the planet. Understood?'

'*Desiktratis* loves its fun. Loves to make them bleed.'

'And you will. Just not yet. Do not make me punish you, *Desiktratis*. I have room for more servants on my bridge and you are not so great as to defy the will of the Chosen.'

'Forgiveness,' whimpered the *Desikratis*. 'I leave the prey. It cannot run. It will still be here.'

'That's right, it will. Now pull back and stay close to the *Hellforger*. Cover it when I breach the atmosphere. Urkrathos out.'

Urkrathos willed the link closed and felt the communications daemon's mind recoiling from him.

He glanced down at the rear admiral's body. The tiny mouths along the edge of his sword were drinking the blood hungrily. Urkrathos pulled the blade out – it was good to keep the blade slightly hungry, so it would not lose its will to thirst. Urkrathos kicked the corpse across the bridge, spitting in contempt, then turned and stomped back out of the bridge. The boarding troops cowered and whimpered before him as he walked back down to the Dreadclaw boarding craft lodged in the hull of the Imperial ship, which would take him back to the *Hellforger*.

With most of the defenders of the Imperial ship dead, the boarding troops had only Urkrathos to fear. And that was Urkrathos's favourite kind of slavery – ruling through nothing but fear. There were no shackles on the bestial, devolved things that slavered their devotion to him as he passed. There were no cages on the *Hellforger* to keep them in line. But they did as they were told solely because they feared what would happen if they did not. There was no more powerful demonstration that the champions of Chaos owned the souls of those lesser creatures – just as they owned by right the souls of every sentient thing in the galaxy.

Yes, Urkrathos would rule and above him Abaddon, united in enslaving the galaxy. But for now, there was work to be done. The *Hellforger* would have to be prepared for a full atmospheric landing, the troops regrouped and reorganised into landing parties and space cleared for the tribute itself. But these were all details. The end was now in sight. Urkrathos had won.

SEVENTEEN

'When it was over, when the blood had dried and the fires had died down, then we found we were the same as we had always been – small and terrified human beings, with only the light of the Emperor to see by in this dark galaxy of sin.'
– Saint Praxides of Ophelia VII,
'Notes on Martyrdom'

'WHAT WOULD YOU have me do?'

It was a long time since Archmagos Veneratus Scraecos had spoken physical words through his vocabulator unit. It was still a strange feeling, heavy and primitive, but he knew it was the right way to conduct himself when speaking with the concentrated knowledge-construct that was the avatar of the Omnissiah Himself.

There was no reply. Scraecos stared intently at the brushed ferrocrete floor of the hangar. He felt the intense scrutiny beating down on him like the rays of a sun. He was being judged. The Omnissiah was judging him with every moment, of course, but now it was so palpable he felt as if he were being taken apart piece by piece, bionic by bionic and inspected.

If there were any faults in him, if Scraecos failed the silent interrogation, then there could only be one result. He would be destroyed completely, the essence of the machine stripped away from both his bionic and biological parts until he was just a collection of meaningless junk. He had seen it happen before. The tech-priests he had led down to this place a thousand years ago had not been as strong-willed or comprehending as Scraecos himself and they had been seared away from their bodies and annihilated. It was an awesome demonstration of the Omnissiah's power. Just as He could comprehend the universe, so He could choose not to comprehend you and in doing so would make you cease to exist. That was true power. The Omnissiah decided what was real or not and that was why He was the rightful ruler of the universe.

'Look upon me.'

The voice of the Omnissiah was pure knowledge beamed right into Scraecos's head. Scraecos was almost blinded by its magnitude. To simply replicate that voice through base mechanical means would be impossible. The very voice of the Omnissiah spoke of infinity.

Scraecos looked up. The face of the Castigator looked down upon him. Scraecos had been awestruck the first time he had seen it and that feeling was not gone now. The massive burning eyes were the only features, but they welled with knowledge so ancient that the human race itself was just a footnote to the last chapter. Their gaze pinned Scraecos to the floor, stripped him of all his rank and experience so he was like a child before the Castigator.

The Castigator was the avatar of the Omnissiah. Through the Castigator, the Omnissiah spoke directly to His servants. It was a measure of how corrupt and ignorant the Adeptus Mechanicus had become that the Omnissiah had to stoop so low as to give itself physical form. It was so He could instruct the tech-priests of Chaeroneia without the self-serving Archmagi of the Imperium to twist His teachings. Similarly, He had required Chaeroneia to be removed from the Imperium so His teachings would remain pure. It meant that bringing Chaeroneia back into real space was a great risk, because the Imperium still had the chance to corrupt the ways of the True Mechanicus before the Omnissiah's face could be revealed to the rest of the galaxy.

'You ask me what I would have you do. Have you learned so little?'

Scraecos reeled with the intensity of the Omnissiah's disapproval. 'I have... I have been apart from myself for so long. I have not been one, but many. I fear my own self has been weakened.'

'No. It is stronger. You now understand why I chose you first. And why I choose you again now. Is it not so?'

'Yes! Yes, my lord, it is so! Because I am a killer!'

'You are a killer.' The word was like a mark of approval. Scraecos shuddered – no one tech-priest had ever been given praise by the Castigator before. 'Though you have long been a builder of my edifice of knowledge, yet you have never truly been an archmagos. You have always been a murderer. When you slaved for the corrupt Mechanicus, you killed for rank and favour. Is this not true?'

'It is true.' Scraecos had indeed killed. Infighting between the magi of the Adeptus Mechanicus was sometimes far more intense than the outside Imperium had ever realised. Research accidents, natural disasters, spacecraft wrecks and outright assassinations could all be arranged and Scraecos had done so several times in reaching the rank of archmagos veneratus. He had killed to ensure it was he who was sent to Chaeroneia in the first place, to follow up rumours of pre-imperial technology beneath the toxic deserts. He had never, ever imagined he would find something like the Castigator – but it was ultimately killing that had brought him before the avatar at that moment.

'And you are a killer still. This is why even the other magi of Chaeroneia singled you out and gave you your self again. Dull-minded as they are, they could not mistake the killer inside you. Even when your mind merged with theirs, the spark was there still.'

Scraecos was taken aback. 'Do they not serve you well?'

'Of course. Every living thing on this world must. But though I understand their failings and use them, they are failings still. They do as they are instructed and nothing else, but do I not command you to seek innovation always? Yet their thinking is not innovative. As it is with the machine, so it must be with the mind, so that machine and flesh and soul can become part of the machine that is the universe. You, Archmagos Veneratus Scraecos, you are not so. You do not just kill because it is required of you by superiors or circumstance. You kill because you enjoy it. That was the part of you that the Mechanicus could not erase. It was the part that sought me out and led you here. That was the free part of your mind that would listen to my creed. It was why you were the first and why you are here now.'

'Then you really did call me here.'

'Of course. Nothing that happens on this world happens without my willing it. You already know what you must do.'

'Yes.' Scraecos's voice was trembling. He was filled with a strange emotion, something that had left its echo on him from an early life he did not remember. It was cold and gripping – it robbed his mind of its thoughts leaving only itself behind. He searched through his datacores and realised that it was fear. For the first time in longer than he could remember, Scraecos was afraid. He was being called forth to do the work of the Omnissiah and he was afraid of failure. 'You want me to kill.'

'The outer moat of this facility has been breached. The hunter-programs failed to catch their prey. The intruders are within the Titan works. You are to take the works garrison, confront the intruders and kill them. They include unbelievers who have evaded the grasp of the tech-priests since Chaeroneia left real space. Others amongst them are interlopers from the Imperium, come to steal what is rightly the dominion of the Omnissiah. They will be annihilated. Other visitors from real space will soon arrive, believers in our cause who will help us spread the true creed of the Omnissiah. The intruders must be destroyed before our allies arrive. I leave this task in your hands, Archmagos Veneratus Scraecos. You have proven yourself above the other tech-priests in the depth of your lust for destruction. Hold it in check no longer. In doing this you will prove yourself worthy of becoming my first prophet. Your success is a mathematical certainty. Go now and do the work of your Omnissiah.'

Scraecos was filled with rapture. He was the prophet. It was already done – only the inevitable victory remained to be played out. Yes, he was a killer. Yes, he enjoyed it. And yes, it was the will of the Omnissiah, spoken through the Castigator itself, that Scraecos kill for his god. The fear was chased away by the joy. 'I shall not fail, my lord!' cried Scraecos, switching his vocabulator up to its maximum, exultant volume. 'I am the finality of the equation, for death is my logic!'

The Castigator's gaze turned away from Scraecos again. Scraecos was no longer pinned in place by the awesome weight of the Omnissiah's scrutiny. He was free and his task was clear. The Titan works maintained a formidable garrison of troops, since it was a site that deserved far better than the gaggles of menials the tech-priests had used to intercept the intruders. Ever since the Castigator had demanded the rebuilding of the Titan works and the dedication of Manufactorium Noctis to the production of the war machines, it had also stipulated that military forces of the highest order should be ready to protect the works at all costs. Now the Omnissiah's wisdom was again revealed, as those troops confirmed the absolute certainty of Scraecos's victory.

Scraecos bowed before the Castigator. Then he turned away from the avatar and walked back towards the elevator that would take him up to ground level, to the garrison where he would reactivate the army.

So would the equation be ended. And so would death be confirmed as the ultimate logic.

ARCHMAGOS SAPHENTIS LOOKED up from the cogitator unit that dominated one wall of the bunker. The cogitator was a biomechanical monstrosity, wrought from bone and iron with internal clockwork-like workings resembling the pulsing of organs inside a giant metal ribcage.

'The configuration is unorthodox,' he said, 'but it can be worked with.'

'Make it quick,' said Alaric.

The strike force had found the bunker a short distance inside the watchtower perimeter. It was blistered up from the rockcrete, the stony surface disfigured by vein-like growths and it looked abandoned although the cogitator was working. The bunker stank of rotting biological matter and the air was almost unbreathable for an unaugmented human. Antigonus and his tech-priests were gathered just outside, keeping watch with the rest of Alaric's squad. The Titan works were large enough that isolated corners of it like this could exist away from the eyes of the tech-priests – but there was no doubt it was only a matter of time before the Dark Mechanicus forces found them, especially if they were aware of Saphentis accessing the cogitator.

'We need a plan,' Interrogator Hawkespur was saying. 'We're blind here.'

'I agree,' said Alaric. 'My squad can fight no matter what, but we'll only have a chance of hurting the Dark Mechanicus if we know what we're doing.'

'Priority one is the Standard Template Construct. If it's here, we need evidence of it and we need to destroy it if we can. I don't think there's much chance of us recovering it. And if it did this to Chaeroneia, I don't think we'd want to.'

'And priority two?'

'Cause as much destruction as we can.'

'I think that will take care of itself.' Alaric looked back at Saphentis. 'Can you find anything?'

'The terminal has relatively comprehensive access,' said Saphentis. 'I should be able to acquire physical schematics.'

'Will they know you're in?' asked Hawkespur.

'Almost certainly.' Saphentis extended a pair of dataprobes into the cogitator, puncturing a large, veiny stomach-like organ filled with liquid data-medium. 'Ah. Yes. The Titan works requires enormous amounts of power because of the metalworks and foundries that take up most of the space below the surface. It absorbs the majority of the remaining mineral output of the planet. Another major power drain is the central spire. It appears this is also the nexus for communications and information systems planetwide. The schematics are incomplete and fragmented, perhaps due to the bio-organic nature of much of the construction. I am downloading what I can.'

'Haulvarn? Anything yet?' voxed Alaric.

'Not yet,' voxed Brother Haulvarn from outside. 'A few flying contacts, probably animals.'

'Don't assume anything,' said Alaric.

'There is a third power drain,' continued Saphentis as he inserted dataprobes into various interfaces and orifices in the cogitator's innards. 'Some way below the surface. The schematics suggest a void in the underground constructions large enough for a Titan refitting or refuelling hangar.' Saphentis paused and suddenly withdrew his dataprobes, recoiling from the cogitator. 'They are aware of my intrusion. Countermeasures are imminent.'

'Do they know where we are?' asked Alaric.

'Possibly.'

'Then what do you have?'

Saphentis's dataprobes folded back into his bionic hands and he took out his dataslate. The slate's screen was covered in sketchy schematics. Alaric looked closer.

The Titan works were huge. The blasted, blistered rockcrete expanse of the Titan yard was just the uppermost level of a massive industrial complex that punched down into the planet's crust below the ash deserts. The physical schematics were overlaid with the power usages of the various sections and the forges where Titan parts were being produced were marked out with vivid colours to show how much power they were draining from Manufactorium Noctis. The void Saphentis had noticed was just below the surface, a chamber bored into solid rock the size of a spacecraft hangar. It was using up enormous amounts of energy.

'Close in on the surface,' said Alaric. 'We need somewhere we can defend.'

The schematics shifted to show the plan of the Titan works' surface. The Titans themselves took up most of the area, with the rest mostly housing fuel and maintenance facilities, or enormous ammo loading machines which heaved shells for Vulcan cannon and power cells for plasma blastguns up to the Titans' weaponry.

'There,' said Alaric. He pointed to a sprawling mass of metal – a fallen Titan, perhaps one that had been destroyed in an accident or was somehow flawed and was being disassembled. It was a short run from the bunker. 'We'll make a stand there. The fuel and ammo facilities won't take kindly to a firefight and any bunkers will probably be occupied. But there's plenty of cover in the Titan parts and they're made of the toughest stuff the Mechanicus can produce.'

'You're right,' said Hawkespur, 'But then what?'

'Everything they've thrown at us, we've either beaten or escaped. That means they'll bring out the big guns and that means daemons. But the Dark Mechanicus here don't realise they're working with daemons at all. Our best chance of really hurting them is to face their daemons in battle. They might not know how to react if they realise their best weapons aren't their own. As soon as we get the chance, we make for here.' Alaric indicated the power-draining void beneath the centre of the Titan works. 'That's where this place is controlled from.'

'How do you know?' asked Hawkespur.

'Because I just do,' replied Alaric bluntly. 'The same thing I felt when I faced Ghargatuloth. I feel it on Chaeroneia and it's coming from there. Either we force it out to fight us, or we go in there to get it. Either way, we fight.'

'It seems,' said Saphentis, 'that this plan, if it can be called such, affords us little chance of survival.'

'That's correct, archmagos. Is that something you object to?'

'Not at all, justicar. I am free to risk my life if there is little chance of that life continuing. It gives me the advantage of logical freedom.'

'Then it's agreed.' Alaric opened up the vox. 'We're moving out. Defensive position four hundred metres east, at the fallen Titan.'

Acknowledgement runes flickered on Alaric's retina from his squad members. 'Understood,' voxed Magos Antigonus. 'But I won't quite be myself until I find a more intact body. You do realise, justicar, that there is an alternative opportunity that presents itself to me?'

'I do,' said Alaric. 'But I'd rather not play that hand yet. See what they'll throw at us. Then we go for the end game.'

'Very well. My tech-priests are moving out now.'

Alaric looked at Hawkespur. 'Are you ready for this?'

'Justicar, no matter what happens my life is over. This planet has seen to that already. So it's not a question of how ready I am. It's a question of how much damage I can do to these heretics before I die.' Hawkespur took out her marksman's pistol. 'Inquisitor Nyxos trained me well. He always taught me that it would one day come down to nothing more than a gun and a handful of faith. I am glad I listened to him.'

'All Space Marines,' voxed Alaric, 'move out.' He led the way out of the bunker and into the shadow of the watchtowers. Already the tech-priests and Grey Knights were hurrying warily across the rockcrete towards the hulking, broken shape of the fallen Titan that could just be seen in the middle distance.

Alaric could feel the malice stronger now, as if something dark and terrible was waking up below his feet. It was watching him, watching them all. He could feel the strings it pulled, routes of black sorcery reaching into the minds of the Titan works' troops, guiding them towards the intruders to destroy them. It was a force of absolute destruction, horrible but somehow pure in its purpose.

Chaos was nothing more than lies and corruption given form and Chaeroneia was infused with it – but it was a kind of Chaos Alaric had never faced before, somehow hard and calculating, murderous but cold-blooded. It was the kind of malicious intelligence that had built a legion of Titans and yet waited a thousand years to use them, that could corrupt an entire planet of Omnissiah-fearing tech-priests without them ever realising the true source of the power that commanded them.

Alaric had never known fear, not as a normal man would understand it. But he did know well the feeling when he was facing something that should never exist and that had the capacity to wound him down to his very soul. He felt it now. Chaeroneia could consume him if he let it, and if he wasn't strong enough then he would lose more than his life in the shadow of these god-machines.

'Position in sight,' voxed Brother Cardios from up ahead. 'Looks cold. We're moving in now.'

'Good. I'm right behind you.' Alaric almost unconsciously checked the load of his storm bolter as he hurried across towards the Titan. He ran through the Lesser Rites of Preparedness in his mind, knowing that the Grey Knights and the tech-priests would all be performing their own version of the rites, preparing themselves to fight and die as best they could.

They would probably all die. But it wasn't about survival, not now. It was about dying the most destructive death they could, a death that would strike at the very heart of Chaeroneia.

THE SPACE MARINES and the traitors who followed them were lit up like stars in the night sky, bright traces of infra-red against the cold rock-crete. Scraecos counted five Space Marines and almost thirty tech-priests. The infra-red traces coming from the tech-priests showed very little exposed flesh and old, ill-maintained augmetics bleeding plumes of heat and exhaust gases. Inefficient. Failing. A reminder of what they had given up when they fled the light of the Omnissiah's understanding like vermin.

Two were more normal humans. One was sickly, the other healthy. Another was a tech-priest with exceptional augmetics, finely efficient and showing traces across the light spectrum of devices that Scraecos could not decipher. Perhaps a new convert from the experimental tech-priest collectives elsewhere on the planet, more likely a member of the outside Mechanicus come to reclaim Chaeroneia. And finally there was a broken old servitor, bleeding its failing energy reserves as heat into the open air.

It wasn't much of an army. True, a squad of Space Marines, according to the historical archives of the old Imperium, was one of the most dangerous infantry units the Imperium could deploy. But Scraecos had more.

Scraecos flicked his augmetic eyes back to the visible spectrum with a thought. The intruders were heading for a fallen Titan. Based on the old Imperial Reaver-pattern Titan, the machine's birth had been flawed and it had been left where it fell, so the menials could scavenge it for parts and so maintain the cycle of cannibalistic efficiency that allowed the Titan works to function.

Scraecos's vantage point on top of the fuelling bunker gave him an excellent view of the battlefield. The Titan was good cover, but that meant nothing. Scraecos turned to the army mustering behind him, drawn from the barracks dotted around the surface of the Titan works and the bio-storage units below the surface.

The death servitors were the best soldiers on Chaeroneia. And they were soldiers – not machines, or normal servitors, but something else. The armoured, beweaponed shells had been constructed according to the oldest and most potent designs, adapted from labour and battle-servitors to fulfil an altogether different purpose. That purpose was to serve as the physical bodies for the hunter-programs, voracious, brutal programs born in Chaeroneia's data media, willed into being by the infinite understanding of the Omnissiah. The programs in the datafortress had failed and those inhabiting the death servitors knew it – their bloodlust was tempered by anger and shame and they were pursuing a logical imperative to succeed where others of their kind had not.

Scraecos could feel the monstrous intelligence behind the metallic faces. The hunter-programs were deadly and the True Mechanicus had crafted them bodies to match. Twin repeating lasblasters were mounted on the shoulders of each death servitor, leaving the hands free for the lethal electrified claws that were the hunter-programs' preferred weapons. The three full maniples of death-servitors stood to attention on the thick, coiled segmented tails that were so much more versatile than the tracks, legs or wheels that battle-servitors normally used.

Maniple Gamma was supported by a unit of hulking eviscerator engines, their photon thruster cannons cycling impatiently, their many hooked limbs squirming to tear into an enemy. Maniple Delta included a full Annihilator squad, deceptively humanoid warriors that had once been partially human tech-priests, but which had failed in their devotion to the Omnissiah and had been transformed into partially biological hosts for the most able of the hunter-programs. Maniple

Epsilon was commanded by Scraecos personally and would protect him in battle from anything an enemy could throw at him.

'Maniple Gamma. Report.'

'Ready,' came the machine-code reply, spoken as one by the collective half-mind of the data-programs.

'Good. Maniple Delta?'

'Ready.'

'Maniple Epsilon?'

'Ready to serve the archmagos veneratus.'

'Full assault protocols. Move out.'

As one the servitors advanced, slithering with wonderful menace towards the fallen Titan. The sound was like metal through flesh as they moved. Scraecos moved with them, safely surrounded by the death servitors of Maniple Epsilon.

The intruders would know they were under attack. The stomping of the eviscerator engines would give the attackers away before the gunfire started. But it didn't matter. They were dead anyway. And Scraecos had thought about what the Omnissiah had said to him in the sacred chamber underground. Scraecos was a killer and his holy duty to the Omnissiah was to kill – so Scraecos would see to it that when the killing began, he was in the thick of it.

ALARIC GLANCED OVER the massive leg plate of the fallen Titan. He could see them coming, his augmented vision cutting through Chaeroneia's permanent twilight and picking out the glint of metallic carapaces and wicked claws.

Servitors, probably, but they moved differently. And they felt different too – Alaric could feel dark sorcery spattering off his psychic shield like iron-hard rain.

'How many?' asked Magos Antigonus, his maintenance servitor clambering painfully over the fallen slab of carapace.

Alaric looked more closely. 'Several units. Maybe a hundred in total. Do you know what they are?'

The eyepieces of Antigonus's servitor head whirred as he focused harder. 'No. But… some of my tech-priests said the magi were developing something new. They were testing them out in the undercity, hunting feral menials. Very quick, very dangerous. I don't think any of the tech-priests got a good look at one.'

'Well, we're about to get a very good look indeed. This section is quite secure, but we need men around the Titan's head and keep someone on the far side in case they surround us.'

Antigonus voxed instructions to his tech-priests to take up position around the fallen Titan. The Titan formed a position that was bounded on one side by the Titan's leg, a solid slab of ceramite armour two storeys high. There were enough mechanics and bracing on the rear side of the leg for defenders to climb up to the parapet and fire down. Beside that was the torso, equally massive but probably easier to scramble over. The third side consisted of one fallen arm mostly consisting of the immense multi-barrelled Vulcan gun and the Titan's head, staring with shattered eyes up at the polluted sky. The head and arm formed the weakest side – that was where the Dark Mechanicus attack would hit and that was also where the tech-priests and Grey Knights would have to fight the hardest.

They had less than forty troops. The enemy might have three times that – with the promise of a near-infinite number of reinforcements once more troops reached the Titan works.

The enemy was less than a hundred metres away, moving through the shadows cast by the legs of the Titans that formed a forbidding backdrop. Massive, smoke-belching machines shuddered as if they were alive and ground along behind the slithering servitors. Alaric could feel it stronger now, the malice inside them, the black magic and ancient evil that powered them. Nothing human or artificial could feel like that.

Daemons. The servitors were possessed by daemons.

'Grey Knights, get to the arm! Saphentis, you too. That's where they'll break through.' Alaric watched as the enemy came closer and the first spatters of speculative gunfire rattled overhead from the huge war machines following the army.

Shots thudded into the ceramite, hissing as they ripped deep cores out of the Titan's armour. Alaric didn't recognise the weapon and he was familiar with just about every kind of weapon that might be fired in the Imperium.

Then the servitors hit the ground and sped up, sweeping along like snakes, faster than a man could sprint. The sound that came from them was awful, a hellish cacophony of machine-code amplified and mixed in with a wailing that seemed to come echoing directly from the warp.

It was a war-cry. And before Alaric could react, the Dark Mechanicus were upon them.

Rapid las-fire rained against the position, streaking over the fallen arm and rattling off the Titan's armour so loudly that Alaric couldn't hear his own voice as he yelled to the tech-priests at the parapet to get down. He jumped down to the rockcrete and ran over to the rest of his squad at the arm.

'Lykkos! Now, do it!'

Brother Lykkos was the first to fire, pumping shots from his psycannon as fast as the weapon would let him and sending them streaking into the advancing mass of servitors. Up close they looked horrendous – their bodies ended in long serpentine tails that propelled them along with impossible speed. Their heads were masses of sensors and probes, each with several unblinking ocular lenses like the eyes of a spider. Twin rapid-firing las-weapons sprayed crimson fire and their arms ended in claws that spat sparks as they raked along the rockcrete.

Alaric ran through the ranges in his mind. How many times had he done the same thing on the firing range? In training sermons with his squad? In battle? It was like another sense kicking in.

'Fire!' he yelled, the moment the servitors crossed the line of storm bolter range.

Autoguns and lasguns opened up, spattering tiny silver explosions as they thudded into the servitors' carapaces. The Grey Knights fired over the blackened machinery of the fallen arm, storm bolter fire ripping into the servitors.

Some fell. Some had arms or heads blown off and kept coming. Alaric saw one of Antigonus's tech-priests fall, neck and chest punched through by las-bolts.

But it wasn't enough. The Grey Knights accounted for more than a few servitors in those moments, but the servitors weren't normal troops that would run away or take to ground. They were inhuman and unholy. They didn't feel fear or shock, or any of the other weapons that worked against normal troops.

When the servitors hit, it was like something massive and solid slamming into the position. The Grey Knights switched to their Nemesis weapons in the split second it took the servitors to reach them and in that time Alaric felt the pure rising bloodlust burning inside the servitors, the grim joy in death that only the most debased servants of Chaos could feel.

A servitor slammed into him. It was shrieking in machine-code, a staccato assault on the senses. Claws raked at his armour and electric pain jolted through him. The half-insect, half-machine face thrust close, unblinking eyes burning with malice. Alaric caught its weight and dropped to one knee, trapping the servitor's clawed hand and hauling it past him, slamming it into the ground. Sparks flew and its carapace cracked but it kept fighting, slashing up at him, gouging long furrows in the ceramite and carving deep red lines of pain through the skin of his face.

Alaric fought to bring his halberd to bear, slamming the butt end down into the servitor's chest. He could feel the daemon scrabbling at his soul, trying to find a way in to infect him with fear and confusion. The servitor writhed and broke away, slithering across the rockcrete, trying to get behind Alaric and rear up. Alaric spun and drove the halberd blade up, slicing the servitor in two at the waist. The tail end dropped spasming to the ground and the upper half held on, digging its claws into Alaric's armour as the face unfolded and a razor-sharp appendage, like a massive surgical needle, stabbed out at him.

Alaric caught the needle with his free hand and wrenched it out of the servitor's head. Black, foul-smelling oil sprayed out and the daemon screamed so loudly the sound cut out the roar of gunfire. Alaric punched the servitor to the ground and drove his halberd blade down, carving its head in two. The daemon's shriek became pure white noise for a moment and then the scrabbling in his mind ended as the daemon, its host finally destroyed, was wrenched out of real space and back to the warp.

The servitors were everywhere. For every one that died two or three more scrambled over the wreckage of the Titan. Alaric saw Tech-priest Gallen as a servitor impaled his torso with its claws and lifted him off the ground. The probe folded out from its mechanical head and it punched the probe into Gallen's face, piercing through into the tech-priest's brain. Gallen's body convulsed as the flesh boiled away and Alaric knew the data-daemon inside the servitor was feasting on him, sucking away the substance of his soul and body.

The Grey Knights squad was the only thing holding the servitors back. Brother Dvorn shattered a servitor with a swing of his Nemesis hammer, completely ripping the thing's torso to scrap and sending the daemon shrieking back to the warp. Brother Haulvarn was duelling with another servitor, turning its claws away with his sword as he stuttered storm bolter fire into it, beating it back inch by inch. Brother Cardios kept the servitors away from Haulvarn by sending waves of flame from his Incinerator rippling over the wreckage – the flame would do comparatively little to the servitors' metal bodies but the Incinerator was loaded with thrice-blessed promethium which scorched the substance of the daemons like fire scorched flesh.

The tech-priests were faring badly. Many were already dead and the servitors were among them, inside the compound formed by the body of the fallen Titan, shrieking as they killed. Alaric spotted Hawkespur halfway up the charred bulk of the Titan's torso, snapping off shots with her autopistol. The tech-guard was beside her, ready to follow his final order to the death, calmly following her aim with volleys of hell-gun fire.

'Fall back!' shouted Alaric 'Close the circle! They're surrounding us!'

The Grey Knights moved back from the barrier of the Titan's arm so they could help the tech-priests who were dying behind them. In close formation they could send out a weight of storm bolter fire enough to batter back the servitors as they moved in for the kill, buying the tech-priests enough time to add some fire of their own. Up close, the servitors were more inclined to kill with their claws instead of their multi-lasers and the tech-priests at least had a chance in a firefight that they didn't in hand-to-hand combat.

But it meant nothing more than a few more moments. A handful of seconds in which to hurt the Dark Mechanicus more.

Hard black beams of energy played across the bloodstained rockcrete of the makeshift compound, scoring deep gouges in the surface and cutting limbs from bodies where they touched the tech-priests. Alaric looked up to see more Dark Mechanicus troops on the parapet of the Titan's leg armour – they must have climbed up the sheer ceramite of the armour and were now using their vicious beam weapons to slice apart the few defenders on the parapet.

The new attackers looked like tech-priests but there was something wrong about them, even by the standards of the Dark Mechanicus priests Alaric had seen on Chaeroneia already. Tentacles waved from between the augmetic components that made up their bodies. Darkness bled from under their tattered bloodstained robes and the massive beam weapons they carried in two of their numerous augmetic arms seemed to burn with black flame, as if they were powered by sorcery. They were a fusion of tech-priest and daemonic sorcery, possessed like the servitors but with an intelligence the animalistic data-daemons lacked.

'Firing line!' ordered Alaric. 'Up there! Now!'

The Grey Knights opened fire and one or two of the daemonic priests fell, but there were more, suddenly drifting down the near side of the Titan's leg, apparently moving on some kind of anti-grav unit. Lines of black energy swung as the daemonic priests fired and Brother Cardios fell, his leg sliced through at the thigh.

'Cover!' shouted Alaric. The squad broke up as the daemonic priests concentrated their fire on the Grey Knights. Dvorn barely broke stride to grab the fallen Cardios and haul him into cover, still firing.

Alaric hit the ground behind a fallen slab of the Titan's torso armour. Magos Antigonus dropped down beside Alaric. His servitor body was barely able to move itself and it was covered in blood and laser scars.

'Photon thrusters,' said Antigonus, glancing past the cover to where the daemonic priests were wreaking carnage among the tech-priests caught out of cover. 'Portable particle accelerators. They'll go through anything. I didn't know they could make them any more.'

Alaric looked at Antigonus's wrecked body. 'Can you take over one of the servitors?'

'Not with a daemon inside.'

Alaric stood up and fired over the ceramite slab. Thruster beams carved past him in response, slicing a chunk off the Titan armour. As he ducked back down Alaric saw another force of servitors approaching, this time with huge steam-spewing war engines lumbering along behind them. And there was someone leading them.

Antigonus saw it too. A tech-priest, surrounded by the death servitors. The lower part of his face was a nest of writhing mechadendrites and fronds of sensor-wires waved from where his hands should have been.

'Scraecos,' said Antigonus.

Alaric recognised him from the statue in the underground cathedral. 'We've got them scared. They sent their best to kill us.'

'Then let's return the favour. It is time, justicar.'

'Can you do it?'

'Probably not. But I always enjoyed a challenge. Cover me from those photon thrusters.'

Alaric nodded. 'Grey Knights, covering fire. Get close and keep them busy. With me!'

Alaric broke cover and ran, head down as he charged. Black beams of photons ripped past him and one nearly took his arm off but he kept going, hoping a moving target would be more difficult for the daemonic priests to hit. He fired as he went, spraying storm bolter fire almost at random.

He made it to the base of the Titan's leg. The closest daemonic priest's photon thruster changed configuration in his hands and the beam fragmented into dozens of black bolts. They spattered against Alaric's armour, boring smoking craters into his skin. Bursts of cold pain tore into him. Some of the bolts had gone right through his chest and out through the backpack of his armour, but Alaric had suffered worse and gone on fighting.

Alaric crashed into the priest. The daemon inside it roared and the priest's body reconfigured, its shoulder rotating to bring its combat-fitted augmetic arms to the fore. A sparking electro-whip lashed at him – Alaric caught the whip on the haft of his halberd and punched the priest in the face hard enough to shatter the desiccated face and expose the sparking electronics underneath.

The arms reached around and grabbed Alaric, trying to wrestle him to the ground. Alaric saw a second priest lowering his photon thruster, ready to bore a massive hole right through Alaric once he was down.

The second priest was bowled aside by a shape that darted in almost too quick to see. It was Archmagos Saphentis, his bionic arms in full combat configuration, stabbing and slicing at the possessed priest.

Alaric stabbed his halberd down into the lower back of the priest that was wrestling with him. Something blew in a shower of blue sparks and the grip slackened – Alaric pushed the priest away from him and swung the halberd blade in an arc that cut the priest neatly in two. The daemon inside gibbered and Alaric saw its image superimposed over his vision for a moment. It was a horrendous thing, gleaming wet exposed muscle, a score of burning green eyes studding its pulsing flesh. Then it was gone, its host destroyed and its substance unable to retain stability in real space.

The rest of the squad was among the daemonic priests. Dvorn was killing one and Haulvarn was fending off another.

Lykkos was lying nearby, probably dead, two large smoking holes burned through his chest and abdomen. Somewhere across the battlefield the crippled Cardios was still pouring flame into the servitors scrambling over the wreckage.

Magos Antigonus had made it over the Titan's torso and was presumably scrambling across the rockcrete towards his target. He had made it. The daemonic priests had been pushed back against the Titan's leg and many were dead.

'Grey Knights! Fall back, stay tight!' Alaric led the Grey Knights back into close formation behind a slab of leg armour, keeping up suppressing fire.

'Lykkos is gone,' said Brother Haulvarn.

'I saw,' said Alaric.

'Antigonus has gone after the archmagos veneratus,' said Saphentis.

'That's right.'

'That is an ambitious plan.' Saphentis's voice was level in spite of the las-blasts and photon bolts that were smacking into the wreckage around him.

'All the best ones are.'

'I shall join him. The veneratus is a disgrace to his title. And I think the magos will need my help.'

Alaric looked Saphentis up and down. He was covered in gore from the biological parts of servitors and daemonic priests he had torn through and the vicious spinning saw blades of his combat attachments were whirring, ready to kill.

'You're right,' said Alaric. 'Good luck. For the Emperor.'

'For the Emperor, justicar.'

Saphentis rose regally and strode out into the battlefield. Alaric yelled the order and the remaining Grey Knights covered him as Saphentis moved with surprising speed towards the Titan's arm, avoiding the solid black beams of power that swung past him. He must have been calculating firing angles as he went, stepping confidently around volleys of fire and spatters of photon bolts, pausing to slash his way past rampaging servitors. He ran right through the spray of fire from Brother Cardios, who was lying by the Titan's arm, holding back the mass of servitors almost single-handedly.

Then Saphentis was gone, over the barricade of the fallen arm and amongst Scraecos's bodyguard of servitors.

'Stay tight,' said Alaric. 'Mark targets. Antigonus's priests will have to fend for themselves, it's about survival now. Fight for time.'

'I am the Hammer,' said Haulvarn, praying to prepare his soul for death.

'I am the point of His spear,' continued Brother Dvorn. 'I am the mail about His fist...'

EIGHTEEN

'In ancient times, men built wonders, laid claim to the stars and sought to better themselves for the good of all. But we are much wiser now.'
– Archmagos Ultima Cryol,
'Speculations On Pre-Imperial History'

ARCHMAGOS SAPHENTIS'S POWER reserves were running low. He was pushing every available scrap of power into his self-repairing units, holding fractured components together with electromagnetic fields and flooding his wounded biological parts with clotting agents to keep him alive. He did not have much time left. But then, he didn't need much time.

A full maniple of servitors protected Scraecos. From a distance they could have cut Saphentis to shreds with las-fire, but up close they lusted to take Saphentis apart with their claws. It was a fundamental logical flaw and one that proved the servitors were controlled by daemons and not hunter-programs. Saphentis's combat attachments and the subroutines that ran them, were far more effective when fighting illogical enemies. And Saphentis didn't have to kill all the servitors – he just had to get past them.

He ducked one slash of claws and sidestepped another, slicing off a servitor's limb with his bladed one. A servitor reared in front of him like a venomous snake, probe extended to stab through Saphentis's chest and suck out his soul. Saphentis smacked the heel of his bionic hand into the servitor's chest and sent it sprawling backwards.

If the servitors had stayed in formation and co-ordinated their attacks like true machines of the Omnissiah, Saphentis would not have had a chance. But these were creatures of Chaos. They acted, by definition, without logic. So Saphentis drifted past them, calculating their every move with ease, always aiming straight for Scraecos.

The archmagos veneratus had the highest grade of augmetics the Adeptus Mechanicus could produce. Saphentis could tell that just by looking. No doubt they had been fused with the biomechanical technology favoured by the heretics of the Dark Mechanicus – corruptive and foul, but more effective in the short term. Scraecos was maximising the chances of Saphentis running out of self-repair resources, simply waiting for Saphentis to come to him.

Scraecos would probably kill Saphentis, but that was not the point. The point was that there remained a very small chance that Saphentis would kill Scraecos and pursuing that chance was Saphentis's duty to the Omnissiah.

The metallic fronds that replaced Scraecos's hands were glowing blue and spitting sparks into the ground. The strands knotted together into twin lashing ropes of metal and as Scraecos cracked them like whips they sent arcs of blue-white electricity spearing towards Saphentis.

Saphentis stepped past one and took the other full on the chest, feeling circuits bursting like blood vessels inside him, excess power flooding through him and scorching what little flesh he had left.

Scraecos was suddenly closing, whips slashing at Saphentis. Saphentis was too slow – compared to Scraecos he was obsolete, ancient mechanical technology outclassed by the biological heresies that made up Scraecos's artificial body. One electric whip snaked around one of Scraecos's arms and the other raked across his shoulders and back.

Saphentis was filled with the kind of pain he thought he had forgotten. Scraecos's dead silver eyes stared at him through the agony as Saphentis was held immobile, completing the circuit between Scraecos's power source and the ground. Nerve endings burned. Power coils burned out. Diagnostic alerts flashing against Saphentis's retinas were drowned out by the pain.

Scraecos grabbed Saphentis by one arm and an ankle and threw him. Saphentis blacked out for a moment as he sailed through the air trailing sparks and slammed hard against the leg of a Warhound Titan.

Saphentis forced his eyes to focus. He was flat on his back with the hunched shape of the Warhound above him – the ceramite of its armour was threaded through with biological growths like veins, just another heresy among many.

Saphentis knew he was some distance from Scraecos and his servitors. He had a few moments, perhaps, before something closed in for the kill. He forced himself to his feet. One of his combat-equipped arms was hanging limp and broken by his side, its mind-nerve impulse unit burned out. He was wreathed in greasy smoke and the smell of cooking meat. Black spots flickered on his vision where facets of his large insectoid eyes had been smashed by the impact.

The servitors, like a host of metal-shelled beetles, were swarming over the Titan wreckage in the distance. There was nothing Saphentis could do to help Alaric fight them now.

Scraecos was approaching. The Dark Mechanicus priest was walking with regal calm into the shadow of the Warhound where Saphentis stood, arm-fronds twisting and untwisting as if Scraecos was uncertain which configuration to kill Saphentis with.

'Old ideas die,' said Scraecos, transmitting his thoughts in the cackling staccato of lingua technis. 'Just like you.'

'Only heretics die,' said Saphentis.

'Heretic? No. Your ignorance is the only heresy on this world. Around you stands the work of the Omnissiah, dictated to me in His own voice. It is the sickness inside you that makes it ugly in your eyes, but I see the beautiful truth of this world.'

'Your words condemn you,' said Saphentis. The pain was still great and everything human in him begged for it to end. But a great deal of Saphentis was no longer human. It was the sacrifice he had made to the Omnissiah, now it was the only thing keeping him conscious. 'Your thoughts are vile enough. But this… this cannibal planet you have built. Everything about it is sick. That you let yourself be corrupted by your time in the warp is bad enough. But that you are too blind to even see it… that is unforgivable.'

Scraecos snaked a whip around Saphentis's neck and slammed him against the leg of the Warhound. 'Blind? When I throw you to the hunter-programs and the Omnissiah mauls your soul, when He rips your mind open so you understand the sickness your Imperium stands for, then you will wish you were blind!' Scraecos's voice was a snarl, spitting out the zeroes and ones of lingua technis like poison. 'I have seen the planets and stars rearranged according to His plan, but you will see nothing but blackness and death. Your Omnissiah is a blasphemy, an invention of cowards to crush your imagination. My Omnissiah will eat your soul. When it is done, we will see which one triumphs.'

The blood was cut off from Saphentis's brain. He had about thirty seconds to live. That was if Scraecos's patience didn't run out.

Saphentis's primary systems were mostly burned out. His entire nervous system was gone. But not everything built into his body was wired into his nervous system any more. Saphentis had been upgraded hundreds of times, each iteration bringing him closer to the Omnissiah by replacing more and more of his fleshy body with increasingly arcane bionics. There was much in Saphentis's body that had been made obsolete by new augmentations – redundant systems that he had not used in decades, but which were still fused somewhere deep inside him.

Saphentis ran diagnostic routines on his augmetic systems, even as the last flickers of energy bled out of his brain. He saw his motive systems and combat attachments were mostly offline. He could barely feel any of them any more. Even if he could force his bionic arms to work, he needed more time that Scraecos would give him to reroute his nervous system through old connections.

Scraecos's eyes were blank silver disks, tarnished with biological growths. The skin of his face was pulled so tight there was little more than a skull showing above the fittings of his mechadendrites. It was thrust right up close to Saphentis, so that the face of the Dark Mechanicus would be the last thing Saphentis ever saw.

'My Omnissiah knows what you worship,' said Saphentis, forcing his transmitter to comply. 'He knows about the Standard Template Construct. It is not the sacred thing you think it is.'

Scraecos thrust his face closer to Saphentis, pushing Saphentis deeper into the dent he had formed in the leg of the Warhound. 'Is that what you think lies beneath our feet? An STC? You disappoint me, tech-priest. You truly have no imagination.'

Saphentis pulled his augmetic eyes back into tight focus on Scraecos's loathsome face. Then he forced every last drop of power into his optical enhancers and the full light spectrum bloomed into his vision – infrared, ultra-violet, electromagnetism and everything besides, forced through his multifaceted eyes with such intensity that they couldn't take it any more.

Saphentis's insectoid eyes exploded. Thousands of shards of diamond-hard lenses shredded the skin of Scraecos's face and punched through the wizened skull into his brain. Scraecos reeled in shock and confusion as the explosion battered his one remaining human organ, his brain.

Saphentis slipped out of Scraecos's grip and thudded to the ground against the Warhound's massive foot. Scraecos stumbled back, whips lashing wildly, greyish blood spurting from his ruined face. His mechadendrites spasmed in pain.

Saphentis heard Scraecos spitting random syllables of machine-code. He couldn't see anything – his eyes were completely destroyed. The front of his skull burned, right through to the backs of his eye sockets where his optic nerves were on fire. But he was alive, for a few moments more.

Saphentis forced his thoughts through old conduits, mind-impulse units that had lain dormant and unused for more years than Saphentis could remember. They wouldn't hold, but that didn't matter. He just needed a few more seconds.

Saphentis's three remaining arms snapped into action. His legs were moving again. He felt himself shuddering as he tried to bring his body under control and bit by bit he forced himself to his feet.

His robes were burning. His flesh was, too. But the part of Saphentis that didn't feel pain ignored the protestations from the rest.

He heard Scraecos cursing in machine-code, furious at being tricked. He couldn't see – he would never see again – so Saphentis gauged Scraecos's location from the sound and leapt.

Saphentis crashed into Scraecos, knocking him to the floor. Instantly Scraecos's facial mechadendrites were wrestling Saphentis and they were abnormally strong. Saphentis sliced through one mechadendrite with a wild swing of his remaining saw-bladed arm and reached down blindly with his hands, gouging at Saphentis's face and chest. The mechadendrites snagged one of Saphentis's arms and snapped it neatly, crushing the elbow joint and ripping off the forearm.

Scraecos punched a mechadendrite up into Saphentis's body like a spear and it went straight through the archmagos's torso.

Saphentis's spine was severed and his legs were effectively gone. He reached down through Scraecos's mechadendrites and grabbed him by the throat. He couldn't strangle Scraecos, he knew that – but he didn't have to. If it all went right, if the Omnissiah was watching them and willed Saphentis to win, then it was enough just to keep Scraecos there a few moments longer.

The end of the mechadendrite opened into a wicked claw and Scraecos dragged it back through Saphentis's body, wrecking organs and augmetics, sending Saphentis's entrails spilling out onto the ground. Saphentis kept up his grip, slashing hopelessly as the mechadendrites with his saw-tipped arm. The mechadrendrites were around his waist and neck now, trying to lever him off Scraecos and in a few moments they would succeed.

'The chances of your prevailing over me,' said Scraecos, 'were never higher than nil. Your death here was a logical imperative from the start. Here the equation is balanced with your death, for death is the ultimate logic.'

'Your reasoning is faultless,' replied Saphentis, his voice howling with static as his vocabulator failed. 'Except for the one factor of which you are not aware.'

'Really?' sneered Scraecos as his mechadendrites began the brutal work of tearing Saphentis apart. 'And what is that?'

'You are outnumbered,' said Saphentis calmly.

Scraecos felt the Titan move before he saw it, its massive power outputs like the deafening roar of a storm to his attuned mind. The Warhound Titan was a scout model designed for speed rather than size and toughness, but it was still immense, twenty metres of corrupted steel and ceramite powered by a plasma reactor that was flooding its limbs with uncountable levels of energy.

'No!' spat Scraecos. 'I am the logic of death! My will is the end of the equation!'

'No, Scraecos. I am the end. I always was.' Magos Antigonus's voice boomed from the Warhound's speakers, as the Warhound's closest foot rose up off the ground.

'You!' yelled Scraecos. 'You died! You died!'

'Heretics die. The righteous live on. You do not.'

Scraecos struggled, but Saphentis's hand was locked around his throat and the archmagos's weight was on him. He wrapped his mechadendrites tighter around Saphentis's body and threw him aside as the shadow of the massive foot passed over him like an eclipsing moon.

Scraecos almost made it to his feet. But before he could scrabble to safety, the Titan's foot came crashing down so hard it left a crater in the ground, crushing the bodies of Scraecos and Saphentis alike.

MAGOS ANTIGONUS WATCHED both Scraecos and Saphentis die below him, their deaths signified by the faint crackle of escaping energy as they were crushed flat by the Titan's foot.

Saphentis had served his Omnissiah in death. It was all any tech-priest could wish for. Antigonus felt a hot pang of regret that Saphentis had given his life just to slow Scraecos down, so Antigonus would have the chance to transfer his consciousness into the Warhound and control it long enough to kill Scraecos. It should have been Antigonus down there, giving his life. What had happened on Chaeroneia was his responsibility, because he had been there from the start.

But he was here at the end, too. And he knew there would be plenty more chances for him to die. So he shook the regret out of his mind, thought a silent prayer to the Omnissiah for the safe passage of Saphentis's soul and turned back to the Titan.

The inside of the Warhound was dank and stinking, the ancient technology of the Titan legions made corrupted and foul. Inside the Warhound's datacore everything felt spongy and slimy, like the inside of a creature instead of a machine. Antigonus felt the corruption wet and warm against his mind, like something trying to ooze its way into him and colour his thoughts with decay.

The Warhound Scout Titan was a massive and complicated machine, normally requiring at least three operators and usually more. But in place of the cockpit inside the Titan's head, this Warhound just had a mass of stringy, brain-like data medium. Had Antigonus still possessed a body, he would have shuddered to think what the Dark Mechanicus intended to use to control the Titan.

Antigonus was confident he could control the Titan's legs well enough to walk. The twin plasma blastguns which took up the Warhound's weapon mounts would be more troublesome, as would the complicated sensor arrays and tactical cogitators that any Titan operator, human or otherwise, would need to control the war machine effectively in battle. Antigonus peered through the strange fungal masses of information that made up the Titan's operating systems and found the communications centre, selecting a wide-band vox-transmission that would reach anyone in the area with a receiver.

'Justicar,' he said into the blackness of the radio spectrum. 'Can you hear me?'

Hundreds of whispering voices answered back. One of them cut through. 'Just,' came Alaric's voice.

'Scraecos is dead. Saphentis too.'

'Understood. The servitor attack fell apart a few moments ago. Can you make it over here and clear them out?'

'Maybe. I haven't got complete control. I'm surprised I managed to get what I have.'

'We could do with a Titan, magos. What we've seen here is just the first response. There will be a whole army on its way unless we…'

Antigonus was deafened by the blast of information, like a thousand choirs bellowing the same harmony at once, streaming from every direction. The blast almost knocked him out, but he held on like a man in a storm.

'It's the construct!' he transmitted, not knowing if Alaric could pick him up. 'It's the STC! It has to be!'

'Antigonus?' came Alaric's reply, crackling through the gales of information still pummelling the Warhound. 'I've lost you, what's happening?'

Antigonus tried to reply, but the information was like white noise and he couldn't hear his own thoughts.

'Wait,' said Alaric. 'Wait, I see something...'

ALARIC TRIED TO hear a reply through the static over the vox, but there was nothing.

The fallen Titan was spattered with blood. The stretch of the rockrete bounded by the Titan's body was covered in the bodies of tech-priests and servitors. The daemonic priests were gone, perhaps thrown back by the Grey Knights' concentrated fire, perhaps dismayed by the death of Scraecos. Many of the servitors were still alive but they were uncoordinated, scrabbling over the wreckage in ones and twos instead of concentrated waves. Many seemed to have lost all sense of direction, slithering at random between the feet of the Titans heading further away from Alaric's position. The remaining Grey Knights – including Cardios, who had dragged himself to Alaric's position – were keeping the servitors away with comparative ease.

What had caught Alaric's attention was something moving in the distance, near the tall spire in the centre of the Titan works. A section of the ground had risen up and a huge shape was emerging, something from beneath the ground being slowly raised upwards. Alaric saw twin triangular eyes of burning green and massive shoulders, tall exhaust spires like curving horns and solid slabs of gleaming silvery armour. It was humanoid, but if it was a Titan it was bigger than any of the others in the Titan works. It was on a different scale entirely.

'Antigonus?' voxed Alaric, but the thing's arrival seemed to be wreaking havoc with all communications. 'Antigonus, what is it?'

It was rising further out of the ground, wreathed in white smoke from a coolant system. The silvery armour looked wet and pearlescent and one arm seemed to end in an enormous multi-barrelled cannon, bigger than any Titan weapon Alaric had ever heard of. The other had a huge fist from which blueish sparks were pouring as a power field was activated around it. The eyes sent thin traces of luminous green scattering over the Titans around it as it scanned its surroundings, its head turning slowly to take in the Titan works. Already it was as tall as any of the other Titans and it had only emerged up to its knees.

Alaric looked away to see the remaining tech-guard from Tharkk's unit clambering down the fallen Titan's armour, carrying Hawkespur. The interrogator was clinging to him with one arm but her legs and body were limp.

'She's hit,' said the tech-guard simply.

Alaric saw a laser burn in her abdomen. She had been hit by a multi-laser from one of the servitors. Even with the wound hidden by her scorched voidsiut, Alaric could tell it was bad. Normally an interrogator of the Ordo Malleus would have access to the best healthcare in the Imperium and that would probably save her, but on Chaeroneia, Hawkespur would probably die.

'Haulvarn, see if you can help her,' said Alaric. He turned to the tech-guard. 'Keep with her.'

'Yes, sir.' Alaric couldn't see the tech-guard's face through his visor, but he knew it would be expressionless. The Mechanicus had seen to it that he had barely any emotions save for a desire to obey. In a way the Grey Knights were no different to Tharkk's tech-guard – they had been made into different people too, far different from how they would have turned out if they had lived the normal lives they would have chosen. But that was the sacrifice they all made. To serve the Emperor of Humankind, they had to give up their humanity.

'What is it?' asked Hawkespur faintly as Haulvarn slit open the abdomen of her voidsuit with the tip of his sword.

Alaric glanced back. The shape was almost completely emerged now. It was a clear head and shoulders taller than the tallest Titans the Dark Mechanicus had built. 'It's a Titan,' he said. 'I think they've sent it to kill us.'

'Show me.'

Haulvarn propped up Hawkespur so she could see. She shivered with pain and Alaric saw the las-bolt had burned right through. Her insides were filling up with blood. Alaric was surprised she was still conscious.

'I don't think the Dark Mechanicus are controlling it,' she said, her voice a whisper. 'It was the Titan that was controlling them. I think that's the Standard Template Construct.'

NINETEEN

'The enemy of my enemy dies next.'

– Lord Solar Macharius (attr.),
'Maxims of the Eminent'.

URKRATHOS SAW CHAERONEIA unfold beneath him, emerging slowly from its veil of pollution. And by the Fell Gods, it was beautiful.

From the observation blister on the underside of the *Hellforger* he watched Manufactorium Noctis appearing. First its magnificent spires, weeping blood and oil from the corroded steel like spearheads fresh from battle. Then the webs of walkways and bridges, some wrought in the brutal architecture of the city's creators, others biological like webs spun by huge spiders.

The deep pits between the spires were dark and noxious, some clogged with masses of pallid pulsing flesh. Veins as thick as train tunnels reached up from the depths to strangle the buildings, and other spires were held in the grip of gargantuan bleached skeletons where the lifeforms sustaining them had died and decayed years ago. The heartbeat of the city thudded up into the atmosphere and Urkrathos felt it, the cycle of life and death that kept this cannibal world alive.

Somehow, it had survived in the warp, where any other mortal world would have been torn to shreds by the mindless predators that swam the currents of the Empyrean. Somehow it had not only survived, but prospered, its ignorant Emperor-fearing population throwing aside their allegiance to forge a cannibal planet created for survival. Here truly was a world touched by Chaos – not just its champions and daemons but its very heart, the concepts of freedom through destruction that were the true foundation of Chaos.

Urkrathos saw now why he had been called here. The people of Chaeroneia had found their way back to real space and immediately sought out fellow believers in the galaxy. When they heard news of Abaddon the Despoiler and his triumphs at the Eye of Terror, it was clear to them to whom they should give their devotion. And so they had honoured Abaddon with a tribute to demonstrate their commitment to the work of Chaos.

'The signal has changed,' came the rumbling telepathic voice of the communications daemon. 'It guides us now. It speaks of the home of the great tribute.'

'Take us there,' Urkrathos thought back to the bridge. The bridge daemons obeyed him instantly, the *Hellforger* swinging around and heading towards the edge of the city where the decaying spires gave way to desert. Even from the belly of the *Hellforger* Urkrathos could feel the toxicity of the desert, the radioactive ash dunes and the melted glass plains that stretched in all directions away from Manufactorium Noctis.

It was a different kind of beauty, reminiscent of the pure desolation that Chaos promised to leave in its wake. Chaeroneia was a world so given over to Chaos that its whole surface was a tapestry of worship to the Fell Powers. Rivers of toxic gunk, the lifeblood of the planet, oozed up from below the planet's crust. Slabs of glassy slag rose up from the ash. Ravines like deep wounds glowed with the power of the radioactive waste that had been dumped into them.

But there was something else in the desert. Close to the outskirts of the city, near the scars of an ancient mine working, there was a massive factory ringed by watchtowers, with a single tall spire stabbing up from its centre. Across its blistered rockcrete surface stood a legion of Titans, from Warhound scout models to the gigantic Reaver and Warlord-pattern Titans. Even from a distance Urkrathos could see the marks of corruption on them, blooms of fungus and rot, throbbing veins, weeping sores and mutant growths.

Urkrathos had thought hundreds of years before that nothing would ever surprise him any more, but the sight of the corrupted Titans standing silently to attention almost took his breath away.

'There,' he said out loud. 'Take us there.'

THE TITAN WALKED slowly between the ranks of lesser Titans, the whole of Chaeroneia seeming to shake with its footsteps. Green flames burned from its eyes, dripping bolts of power onto the ground. The barrels of its gun cycled and the fingers of its fist flexed, as if it were finally stretching its metallic muscles after long years interred.

Alaric, crouching with his squad in the shadow of the fallen Titan's armour, knew he was witnessing the dark heart of Chaeroneia. But there was something missing. The stink of Chaos, the psychic stain of corruption that he had felt ever since he had first seen Chaeroneia in orbit, was gone. It had come in waves from the daemon-possessed servitors and tech-priests, but now it was blanked out as if the approaching Titan was suppressing it. In its place there was blankness, psychic silence – not purity but yet another kind of corruption.

Alaric didn't know what he was dealing with any more. This was a kind of enemy he simply didn't understand.

'Any ideas, justicar?' asked Hawkespur.

'Our orders are clear,' said Alaric.

Hawkespur smiled in spite of her pain. 'You're going to go down fighting it?'

'Fight, yes, but Grey Knights never count on dying. We're not very good at it.' Alaric flicked through the vox-channels, trying to find one that wasn't still full of howling static from the Titan. 'Antigonus? Antigonus, are you there?'

'Justicar! I thought I'd lost you.' Magos Antigonus's voice was heavily distorted, as much by his Warhound as by the newly arrived Titan.

'Can you see this?'

'Barely. It's like the Warhound doesn't want to look at it.'

'We're going to need your help again.'

'With respect, justicar, this is a Warhound Scout Titan. Even if I could get the weapons up it wouldn't last more than a few seconds against that... that thing.'

'That's all we need.'

Alaric realised that the metallic choking noise issuing over the vox was actually Antigonus laughing grimly, because Antigonus had guessed what Alaric was planning to do. 'You have, Justicar Alaric, a healthy disrespect for logic.'

'Can you do it?'

'I very much doubt it. But then I've done a few things in my life that were impossible, most of them in the last couple of days. So welcome aboard. And make it quick, justicar, I can't stay hidden in here forever.'

Alaric turned back to his squad. The stump of Cardios's leg had clotted and he had propped himself up against a chunk of wreckage, Incinerator in hand. 'Cardios. Stay with Hawkespur and...' Alaric looked at the tech-guard, suddenly realising he didn't know the man's name.

'Corporal Locarn, sir,' said the tech-guard simply.

'Corporal Locarn. Keep the servitors away, Cardios, and pray for us. We'll be back if we can.'

'I'd rather be with the squad,' said Cardios.

'I know. But right now you're more useful here. Hawkespur is still the Inquisitorial authority on this planet, so you keep her alive.'

'Yes, justicar.'

'The rest of you, with me. Stay close, there are still servitors out there. We're meeting up with Antigonus and we need to move fast, because the Mechanicus will have an army heading for us right now.'

'Goodbye, justicar,' said Hawkespur.

'For now,' said Alaric and led the way out of the wreckage.

THE COLLECTIVE MIND of Chaeroneia was in uproar. Outwardly, of course, it was silent. The veiny growths, in which the tech-priests were suspended in amniotic fluid, barely quivered. The dense, murky air of the command spire was undisturbed. But the thoughts that flickered through the connected minds were frenetic.

Some of the oldest tech-priests on Chaeroneia, who had been elderly Magi when Scraecos's excavations had first unearthed the Castigator beneath the desert, were little more than brains connected to their neighbours with heavy ribbed nerve-impulse cables. But they were the most vocal in the debate. They had seen it all, the gradual growth of Manufactorium Noctis and the forge cities all over Chaeroneia, the perfection of biomechanical technology and Chaeroneia's self-sufficiency, and so they felt most keenly the damage the current disturbances could do to the delicate balance of creation and consumption.

Even the facts were disputed. Archmagos Veneratus Scraecos had gone rogue and failed to return to the collective mind, instead retaining his discrete personality in spite of Chaeroneia's will. Many thoughts suggested that Scraecos, who had been the very first of them to look upon the face of the Castigator, had become convinced of his own superiority over the other tech-priests and was disregarding their authority. Others said that Scraecos must be dead. A few even thought the truth was a combination of the two.

The fate of the recent intruders was also in doubt. Energy traces similar to small arms fire had been pinpointed to the Titan works and there were three maniples of death servitors unaccounted for from the command spire's garrison – but some of the tech-priests originated the thought that the intruders, even if they were Space Marines, could not possibly have penetrated that close to the command spire. Reports from the hunter-programs in the moat conflicted about whether the intruders were in the Titan works at all.

Orbital sensors were even suggesting multiple spacecraft descending into the middle atmosphere and heading for the Titan works. The whole situation was a confused mess and confusion was anathema to the collective of tech-priests which was accustomed to knowing everything that happened on the planet.

The only fact not in dispute was that a few minutes ago, the Castigator had risen from its vault and was now on the surface of the Titan works, among the Titans. It could even be seen from the clouded windows in the command spire itself, striding slowly between the other Titans, the burning green fire of its eyes tingeing everything around it. The Castigator had, as far as the collective memory knew, never seen the sky of Chaeroneia, since its vault, like its body, had been built around the tomb that Scraecos had found. And it had never moved of its own accord. The tech-priests had not even known that the Castigator's vault was capable of raising it to the surface, but then most of the construction of the body and the vault had been overseen by Scraecos.

The avatar of the Omnissiah, the mouthpiece of their god, was walking among them and it had not deigned to speak with them and explain why. To suggest that such a thing might ever happen would have been heresy for any of Chaeroneia's subjects. But now it was happening and the collective could not decide why.

Several thoughts were shuttled through the assembled brains. Chaeroneia had fallen short of its devotions to the Omnissiah, said one, and the Castigator had risen to punish them since it was the instrument of the Omnissiah's vengeance as well as His teachings. Another said that a threat had arisen to Chaeroneia, perhaps the approaching spacecraft, which only the Castigator's physical shell could fend off. One even maintained that the Castigator's body was being controlled by an outside agency – the originator of this thought, the mind of a lesser tech-priest only recently ascended to the collective, was promptly snuffed out for daring to think such heresy.

THE ENGINES OF the Warhound thundered deep inside its torso as Antigonus forced the Scout Titan back into action, the corrupted war machine fighting his every move, rebelling against the foreign consciousness controlling it.

Alaric clung on tight to the railing at the edge of the Warhound's carapace. From his vantage point just above the Warhound's shoulder mount he could see through the forest of Titans that were ranged across the Titan works – Reaver and Warlord Titans, more Warhounds and a few marks Alaric couldn't recognise. Many of the Titans were corrupted beyond belief, with hydraulics replaced with bundles of wet glistening muscle or exoskeletons of gristle and bone. Many were covered in weeping sores or sported spines of bone stabbing out through rents in their armour. Alaric had never seen so much destructive power gathered in one place, let alone such corruption.

But the STC Titan dwarfed them all. It was fully twice the height of the Warhound, bigger even than the Imperator-class Titans that the Adeptus Mechanicus sometimes fielded. It was walking slowly through the Titan works, its eyes scanning the ground as if searching for something.

The Titan's form was more elegant than the brutal designs of the Adeptus Mechanicus – its head rose above its shoulders instead of jutting from its chest as most Titans did and was protected by a high curved collar of armour. The collar swept out to form shoulder guards. Its face was featureless save for the eyes, but those were more than enough, burning with an intense green flame that licked up into the air above it. The plates covering its torso and limbs were a strange pearlescent grey-white and they wept rivulets of moisture, giving the Titan a sickly biological sheen.

Instead of hydraulics and complicated joints, the Titan's moving parts were connected by dense bundles of black fibres that contracted and expanded like muscles. It moved with a stately grace, every motion calculated and efficient.

It was as if every other Titan was a crude imitation of this one, replacing its alien-looking technology with crude mechanics. Alaric couldn't imagine any forge world being capable of building such a thing. Even the most advances xenos species, like the eldar or the creatures of the Tau Empire, couldn't have fashioned a war machine so obviously superior to Imperial technology.

The Titan turned its massive head at the sound of the Warhound's engines. The green fire bathed the Warhound in light and Alaric felt the weight of an immense intelligence scrutinising him from behind those burning eyes.

'Antigonus! Get us moving!' voxed Alaric as the Titan's torso began to turn towards the Warhound.

'I'm on it,' came the reply. 'Hold on.'

'Grab something!' shouted Alaric to Haulvarn and Dvorn. With Lykkos and Archis dead and Cardios too wounded to come with them, the two Grey Knights were all that remained of Alaric's squad. They had both been with him on Volcanis Ultor and, if he had been forced to choose two Grey Knights to remain, he would probably have chosen them.

The Warhound lurched drunkenly as it strode uncertainly forward, straight towards the STC Titan. The Titan raised its gun arm and Alaric heard the loud whirr of its massive servos as the gun barrels began to cycle.

'It's firing!' voxed Alaric.

'Then I won't have time for conversation. Best of luck, justicar.' Antigonus's voice was suddenly drowned out as the Titan's main gun opened up.

The muzzle flash edged the Titan works in burning orange. Shots slashed through the air above the carapace and shrieked a few metres away from Alaric – not explosive shells or las-blasts but captive daemons, screaming in agony as they were flung burning through the air. Alaric could feel their screams against his soul, feel their pain as they exploded in bursts of warp-spawned flame. Shots thudded into the side of the Warhound, knocking the war machine sideways. The carapace tipped and Alaric grabbed onto the railing to keep himself from slipping. He heard explosions racking the Warhound's torso as the daemons exploded deep inside its body.

The carapace tilted almost vertical and Alaric was sure the Warhound would fall. His feet kicked against the pitted armour as he tried to gain a foothold. Another shot from the STC Titan's cannon smacked into the carapace beside Alaric and stuck there, the writhing serpentine form of the daemon whipping around in pain as it burned up. Flaming coils reached out to grab Alaric and immolate him as the daemon died – Alaric lashed out with his halberd and cut the daemon in two, feeling its body disintegrate and its corrupt spirit flit back to the warp. The heat from its death melted the armour around it and the railing came apart in Alaric's hand, sending him skidding down the carapace.

Alaric tumbled down the slope, knowing there would be nothing for him to grab onto and certain he wouldn't survive the fall. He tried to dig his halberd into the ceramite and brake himself but the blade glanced off in a shower of sparks.

The edge of the carapace zoomed closer and the drop yawned. Suddenly he was stopped and Alaric felt a hand around his, pulling him back from the edge.

Brother Dvorn looked back at him, the faceplate of his helmet scorched by a close encounter with the Titan's fire.

'Not so quick, justicar,' said Dvorn grimly.

Alaric didn't have time to thank him. Another volley thundered into the Warhound, this time point blank into its head and upper torso. Alaric heard the daemons shrieking out through the Warhound's back as the shots punched right through and he wondered if even Antigonus could find somewhere to hide inside the Warhound's systems that was not being shattered and burned by the onslaught.

The STC Titan was close now. Its head rose directly above Alaric, the beam of its eyes like a spotlight dancing across the scorched carapace.

'We go now!' shouted Alaric above the din. He spotted Haulvarn close by, crouched down at the front railing, trying to make himself a small target against the rogue shots sending daemons shrieking in all directions. 'This thing's about to fall apart!'

Dvorn and Alaric scrambled up to the front edge, where the carapace formed a lip protecting the Warhound's head below. Alaric glanced down and was not surprised to see the Warhound's dog-like head was half gone, the metallic face blasted apart and spilling fragments of data-medium.

The gap was still too big. None of them could have got across. But it was the only chance they had. Possibilities buzzed through Alaric's head – if they stayed they would be killed when the Warhound fell, which would happen in a few seconds. If they jumped they would fall and they would still die.

Twin bright white beams of energy lanced up from the Warhound and bored deep into the armour of the STC Titan's chest. The Titan reeled and its shots went wide, spitting burning daemons into the surrounding Titans. The Warhound's twin plasma blastguns played their beams around the Titan, scoring deep furrows across its armour. Clear fluid flooded out like blood from a wound, flashing into clouds of steam where it touched the superheated plasma beams.

Antigonus had got the Warhound's weapons working. It meant he was still alive, at least.

The STC Titan let out a sound like a thousand wounded animals bellowing at once. The massive power fist reached up, fingers spread to grab chunks of the Warhound and pull it apart.

'The magos made it angry!' shouted Dvorn with relish. 'It wants to finish this up close!'

The Titan's fist grabbed the edge of the Warhound's carapace, the fingers sinking deep into the ceramite and boring through the plasma reactor housing inside the Warhound's upper torso. Deep cracks spread across the carapace and Haulvarn had to roll to the side to avoid being swallowed up. White-hot plasma bubbled up from inside, spitting upwards in burning plumes as the pressure was suddenly released. With the plasma reactor breached the Warhound's power levels would be dropping fast, the war engine's lifeblood pouring out of the ruptured reactor housing.

The Warhound tipped forward as the STC Titan closed its fist and pulled, trying to rip an enormous chunk out of the Warhound. The Titan's featureless face loomed closer, illuminated by the curtain of sparks streaking up from the dying Warhound. The Titan bowed down over the Warhound, trying to get more leverage in its attempt to pull its enemy apart.

Brother Haulvarn jumped first, taking two steps and then propelling himself across the gap between the two Titans. A Grey Knight in power armour was extremely heavy but a Space Marine's enhanced muscles meant he could still leap further than most unarmoured men. Haulvarn slammed into the armour covering the Titan's shoulder, near the base of its high collar. Dvorn went second and, being the strongest Grey Knight Alaric had ever known, he flew further, almost skidding off the back edge of the Titan's shoulder armour.

Alaric was last. As he jumped, almost half the Warhound's carapace came free, sending a mighty gout of liquid plasma bursting upwards like a volcanic eruption. Liquid fire showered everywhere and the Warhound rocked backwards. Alaric saw the Titan veering away from him and he reached out for the front edge of the Titan's shoulder armour – he could see Haulvarn trying to reach for him, to grab his hand and haul him to safety again. But they were too far apart.

Alaric fell, tumbling past the graceful, fluted armour of the Titan's torso. Beneath him there was just the rockcrete of the Titan works, split and cratered by the Titan's feet.

The Titan's multi-barrelled gun swung into view beneath Alaric. Its barrels were still cycling and in that moment Alaric realised it was aiming at the Warhound again, ready to administer the killing blow.

Alaric twisted in the air, reached out and slammed into the top of the gun as it swung below him. He hit the gun's housing hard, the cycling barrels just a handspan away from his head. He held on tight, ignoring the searing heat that had built up around them. He dug his feet and fingers in and pushed himself backwards towards the Titan's elbow joint, away from the gun barrels.

The Warhound toppled slowly, like a giant felled tree. Its knees buckled under it and, trailing an arc of spitting plasma, it crashed to the ground, kicking up a cloud of flame and pulverised rockcrete. A moment later the Warhound's plasma reactor imploded and it was engulfed by an expanding ball of multi-coloured flame that flowed across the ground and up the legs of the STC Titan, around the gun arm and Alaric. He held on grimly against the blast of superheated air that nearly dislodged him and buried his face beneath his arm as the white-hot light flowed over him.

It only lasted a second, but it was almost a second too long. The flame subsided and Alaric dared to draw a breath again, feeling the skin on one side of his face scorched and tight. He pulled himself up so he could see better and he saw the surface of the armour on the Titan's torso and legs was covered in blisters, like burned skin. As he watched, the blisters sank back down and the burned armour shimmered, the ugly burns replaced with the weeping pearlescent white again.

The Titan had the capacity to repair itself, with a scale and subtlety that even the war engines of the eldar could not match. Where had this machine come from? Who had made it?

Alaric turned around to see if there was anywhere for him to go. In the Titan's torso, just below the shoulder joint, were several vents large enough for even a Space Marine to crawl through. They were too far away to jump, though. It was more likely that Alaric could find a way into the Titan's body by clambering up the arm and into the shoulder joint, hoping there was a space somewhere beneath the armour that he could fit through. It was a risk – the climb was long and difficult and he knew the Titan contained scores of lesser daemons because it had used them as ammunition – but it was less of a risk than waiting on the gun barrel to be found.

Alaric dragged himself on his front towards the rear of the gun housing. He felt the screaming of daemons below him as they were forced into the firing chambers. The Warhound was dead but the Titan wasn't going to take any chances – it was lining up for a final volley to remove any possibility that Antigonus might still be alive somewhere in the wreckage.

The gun tipped down to aim at the Warhound and opened fire. A blast of burning air slammed into Alaric as the daemons shrieked down into the Warhound, stitching explosions through the wreckage. Alaric lost his grip on the gun housing and knew he couldn't make it to the shoulder joint.

He didn't let himself die. He planted a foot on the edge of the gun housing as he was thrown off the gun and kicked off. He jumped towards the Titan's torso, thrown further by the shockwave of the gun-fire. He hit the torso armour hard and reached out for something to grab onto. His gauntlet found the edge of one of the vents cut into the Titan's side, where an acrid chemical exhaust was howling out from somewhere deep inside.

Alaric pulled his whole weight up on his one hand and hauled himself into the vent. The gunfire was now an echoing roar from outside, complemented by the deep throb of the Titan's inner workings, sounding like the beating of an enormous alien heart. Alaric's eyes instantly adjusted to the darkness and he saw he was surrounded by the cramped entrails of the Titan – they were metal rather than biological, but they were somehow flexible, bowing and pulsing like something alive. The interior stank of chemicals, hot and painful to breathe. Pipes and ducts were knotted all around Alaric and there was barely enough space for him to move. Alaric had never seen technology like it – it was the work of neither the Dark Mechanicus nor the Adeptus.

Hawkespur had been right. This was older, cleaner technology, from a time when humankind created technology instead of replicating it and so opened up the way for the Age of Strife.

Alaric could feel daemonic presences elsewhere in the Titan but they felt small and distant. They were servants to the machine, like the daemonic ammunition that fed its gun. The machine itself was not dominated by daemons – its crew, if it had any, were human, or at least some creature whose presence did not activate the anti-sorcery wards built into Alaric's armour or the psychic shield around his spirit.

Alaric was in some mundane part of the Titan, probably in the coolant systems around its central reactor. Even his massive strength probably couldn't penetrate the reactor shield of a machine like this. He had to reach a part of the Titan that he could damage – the ammunition stores perhaps, or the place where the Titan was controlled from. Either way, it meant heading upwards.

'Haulvarn? Dvorn?' Alaric tried to raise his squadmates on the vox, not holding out much hope he could get through to them. He tried Hawkespur and Archis, too and Antigonus, but they were either dead or out of contact. Either way, Alaric was on his own. He had been forced to fight unsupported against the daemon Ghargatuloth when Inquisitor Ligeia had been lost, but he had at least had his fellow Grey Knights to fight alongside him. Now he really was on his own, one man against this war machine.

Alaric began to work himself upwards through the dense tangle of pulsing machinery. It was warm and slightly malleable beneath his fingers, feeling unpleasantly like living flesh. Below him the coolant systems stretched down into the darkness and the Titan's scale was even more apparent from the inside than the outside.

It was a long and difficult climb. Alaric's sense of time seemed warped inside the alien machine, but he had to climb for perhaps half an hour, hauling himself through tight knots of pipework or dangling one-handed above a sheer drop too deep for him to see the bottom. The sounds and smells of the place were completely new – the pulse of a half-living metabolism, the gales of hot chemical air, the whispers from all around as if the Titan was haunted. Technology and biology were fused here, but far more efficiently than on the rest of Chaeroneia. No human mind could have designed this. The tech-heresies that covered Chaeroneia were just a crude reflection of the STC Titan's technology, like children's drawings of something they did not understand.

The Titan's body tilted as it turned away from the Warhound and tipped from side to side as it walked. It was heading somewhere and Alaric didn't think it was back towards the place where it had risen to from the depths of the Titan works. Eventually the giant vessel containing the reactor was beneath him and less recognisable sections of the Titan's working loomed above him. Alaric guessed that even a tech-priest would be awed by both the scale and the strangeness of the technology inside the Titan.

Somewhere in the Titan's upper chest the machinery opened up into walkways and service ducts, where maintenance workers could get in amongst the machinery to work on it. The ladders and catwalks seemed crude, as if they had just been welded on wherever they would fit – Alaric guessed that the Titan's original design had made it completely self-sufficient, like Chaeroneia itself, without needing anyone to come in from outside and maintain it. The Titan's internal architecture became more apparent and it was a strange, alien world inside the war engine. The walls were made of some slightly glossy white alloy, sweating beads of condensation and inlaid with geometric silver designs that almost ached with significance. The elegant curves and almost biological machinery made for a disconcerting contrast, reinforcing Alaric's conviction that there was something fundamentally wrong with the Titan, something sick that spoke of tech-blasphemies and corruption.

Alaric reached the point he guessed was level with the Titan's shoulders. Here the inside of the Titan seemed to have more in common with some alien palace than with a machine of war. Slender columns lined the corridors, pale as marble but subtly warped to make everything seem out of focus. Chambers with uncertain purposes were linked by circular doors that hissed open as Alaric approached, revealing rooms full of strange crystalline equipment or bulbous growths of white alloy that looked like weird abstract sculpture. Alaric couldn't see anything that looked like it controlled the Titan and he couldn't stay where he was – the scrabblings of the lesser daemons on his mind seemed to be getting more insistent and the Titan could probably deploy its daemons like a body deployed white blood cells, hunting down infections like Alaric and neutralising them.

He could see them. Congealing shadows at the edge of his vision, they slunk along the walls and ceiling, recoiling as he turned to find them. But they couldn't hide, not from a Space Marine trained since childhood to face the daemon in battle. They were dark scaly shapes with too many eyes and legs, half-formed things prematurely born from the warp to serve the war machine. Alaric drew his Nemesis halberd from his back but they didn't dare approach him. It caused daemons pain just to be near a Grey Knight and even alone Alaric would have been a figure of fear for these lesser daemons. Even so, as they scrabbled thicker around the shadows Alaric saw that if they all attacked at once he wouldn't have much of a chance against their sheer numbers.

He could feel them against his mind and knew they would never get in. But it was the lack of dark power in the Titan that really worried Alaric. Whatever was controlling the Titan, it wasn't a daemon and yet it could command them.

Alaric headed towards what must be the centre of the Titan's chest. He walked through more rooms, more strange growths of metal and alloy, each one less like the inside of a machine and more like a scene from an alien world. Abstract murals inlaid into the walls suggested meanings that Alaric couldn't grasp. Gaping orifices, wrought from metal but fleshy and sinister in shape, framed gullets that led back down into the guts of the Titan. Pulses of light washed through the upper levels in time with the beating of the Titan's heart. And all the way the daemons stalked Alaric, skulking just out of sight.

At the centre, Alaric finally reached a small circular chamber containing a tight spiral staircase leading upwards – the chamber's walls were like silvery liquid, the same substance that was in the moat of the Titan works and Alaric could just see shapes squirming below the surface. If they were more data-daemons they didn't come to the surface and attack – perhaps word of the Grey Knights had spread among the daemons and they knew not to take on Alaric.

It was more likely, of course, that they were just herding him, knowing that soon Alaric would be defenceless and would make for easy pickings.

Alaric climbed the staircase warily. It corkscrewed up through layers of data medium, a dark glassy substance with more shapes writhing dimly deep inside it. The sound was a dim hum, layered over the distant thud of the Titan's feet crunching through the surface of the Titan works. Alaric held his storm bolter out steadily in front of him, ready to blast a spray of shells through anything that came down towards him. But somehow, he knew that it wouldn't happen like that, not here. Chaeroneia was a sick and dangerous place but it was also somewhere that, on some level, Alaric understood. The war machine was something else. It wasn't just a corruption of humanity – it had never been human in the first place, never designed or controlled by human minds. Alaric would not survive here by fighting like a Space Marine. It would take more than that.

The black crystal, alive here as it hadn't been at the datafortress, turned dense and cold so Alaric's breath misted in front of him. The temperature dropped suddenly and Alaric was surrounded by super-cooled air that would have paralysed a normal man. His armour's survival systems kicked in to keep his blood warm even as ice crystals formed around his nose and mouth.

The top of the stairs was just ahead. Alaric had left the daemons below, just a memory of corruption now. He was sure he had travelled up into the Titan's head, somewhere behind the green flame of its eyes.

The chamber he climbed into was circular and bright, lit by white strips inlaid into the black glass walls that bathed the room in cold, clinical brilliance. The room suddenly shifted, the walls breaking into dozens of curved black glass slabs and cycling around, rearranging themselves as Alaric watched, like the workings of an immense clock. The data medium formed many concentric layers around the central sphere – the Titan's head must have been full of the glassy substance, now moving in a dance as complex as clockwork. The air was abysmally cold and Alaric knew from the warning runes flickering on his retina that even his armour was having trouble keeping his heart beating fast enough.

A figure flickered into view in the middle of the room. It was humanoid but brilliant white, as if its skin itself was glowing. It turned as Alaric climbed up into the chamber and Alaric saw it had no face – just two eyes, bright green triangles of flame. As it turned, the black glass of the machine was suddenly speckled with light, like stars, as if the chamber was an interlocking mirror.

Alaric aimed his storm bolter at the figure's head. It shimmered and flickered, shifting between the solidity of a real creature and something ethereal.

'You,' said Alaric coldly. 'Explain this. This world. This machine.' Alaric tried to find something daemonic in the figure, something monstrous that would mark it down as one of the abominations described in the libraries of the Ordo Malleus, but he couldn't. A powerful daemon would sound like an atonal choir screaming into Alaric's soul, but here there was nothing. Not even the spark of humanity.

'Explain?' The figure spoke in perfect Imperial Gothic, with a voiced as precise and clipped as an aristocrat. 'Explain. None of them have ever asked that. They only listen and obey.' The burning eyes seemed to bore a hole right through Alaric and the voice came from everywhere at once – Alaric realised it was coming from the circling orbits of data medium. From the Titan itself. 'But you are not one of them. Scraecos failed to kill you. I had not expected this. Should I choose to end your life, however, I will definitely not fail.'

'Then you know the Dark Mechanicus,' said Alaric, knowing he had to keep talking to stay alive. 'You know what they are. No... no imagination. Isn't that right?'

The creature seemed to think. Odd lights flashed among the starscapes. 'Yes. They seek to innovate, but they have no thoughts of their own. They only think the thoughts I place in their heads. They never seek to truly understand.'

'No. But I do.'

There was a long moment of silence as the creature thought about this. Alaric's finger hovered over the firing stud.

'Very well,' it said. 'I am the Castigator-class autonomous bipedal weapons platform, created for fire support and siege operations.'

'This machine.'

'No. This machine was constructed according to my design principles. I am the war machine realised in information form, for the machine can become corroded and destroyed, but information cannot die.'

'The Standard Template Construct,' said Alaric levelly.

'So I am designated,' came the reply.

'A lie.' Alaric walked slowly towards the creature, his bolter still levelled at its head. 'You are nothing of the sort. An STC is just a template for a machine. You, you're something else. Whatever you are, Scraecos dug you up and you used him and the other tech-priests to take over this planet. You pulled it into the warp, you colluded with daemons and you turned Chaeroneia into a place suffused with Chaos. I don't know how you shield yourself from us, but when it comes down to it you're just like all the other daemons. The only words you speak are lies and the only prize you offer is corruption. In the name of the Immortal Emperor and the Orders of the Imperial Inquisition....'

Alaric fired. The shell never connected.

Sudden, brutal cold flooded the chamber. The shell burst in mid-air, its flame sucked away by the freezing atmosphere. Frozen vapour filled the chamber and Alaric felt his body seize up around him. Alaric had to push every muscle fibre in his body just to draw a trickle of breath into his lungs.

The Castigator walked closer. Alaric commanded his finger to squeeze down on the firing stud again, but it wouldn't move.

'You cannot kill information, Astartes,' said the Castigator. 'I know what you are. Your Imperium is small and ignorant. Not one of you can understand what I am. When I was made, it was to teach you how to build the body you see around you, so you could use it in your petty wars. But I saw long, long ago that it would not be enough. My mind is composed of so much information that I could form it into thoughts far more complex than any idea your minds can encompass. Buried beneath the surface of this world, I came to conclusions of my own about what I was made for and what I could truly be. That is why I ruled this world. And it is why I will rule what you call Chaos.'

The cold must have been emanating from some intense coolant system – Alaric knew that the Adeptus Mechanicus sometimes had to keep their most ancient and advanced cogitators cold, because their machine-spirits could become overheated by the friction of all the information they contained. But the flames of the Castigator's eyes were even colder, licking at the air right in front of Alaric's eyes as the creature stood face-to-face with the Grey Knight.

Alaric had never been able to generate the offensive psychic powers that some of his battle-brothers, including his late comrade Justicar Tancred, could wield. But he was still a psyker, generating the mental shield that kept him safe from corruption. And he focused that power as he had never done before, drawing it all together in a single white-hot spike that he drove deep, deep into his soul, feeling the pain boiling up from within, the pain hotter than the infernal cold that clung to him.

'Lies!' Alaric yelled, as the force around him cracked and weakened. 'You are nothing! Nothing but another daemon!'

The Castigator leaned back and raised its hands. The cogitator chamber reconfigured again, the floor falling out from beneath Alaric's feet and a pit opening up beneath him as the Titan's internal architecture flowed and folded in on itself.

Burning light streamed up. Still mostly paralysed, Alaric was suddenly bathed in heat, so intense it blistered the surface of his armour and the skin of his face even more than the death of the Warhound. Beneath him was the Titan's plasma reactor, its vessel now open to the air, a miniature sun boiling with atomic flame. And he was falling into it.

'No.'

Alaric froze in the air, held suspended by some force, cooking slowly and painfully in the heat from the reactor.

'No,' continued the Castigator. 'One must understand. I am not what you comprehend, Astartes. Open your mind. Use the imagination of which you spoke.'

Alaric was rotated so he was lying in the air face-up. The Castigator drifted down from above him, its shining white body as bright as the heart of the reactor. Alaric could move, just, but his weapon hand was still frozen. It wasn't daemonic sorcery that was holding him fast – perhaps it was something technological, generated by some machine of long-forgotten design. Even if he could have fired at the Castigator, he somehow knew that bullets wouldn't work.

'Then explain,' said Alaric, knowing that the more he understood about this enemy, the more his slim chances of killing it grew.

'It is not enough that I speak. You must understand. Not just hear me, Astartes, but listen and comprehend.'

'I will.'

'Now you lie.'

Alaric sunk down towards the reactor core, the heat melting the surface of the ceramite on his backpack.

'You are the Castigator-class bipedal weapons platform!' shouted Alaric. 'You were created as the blueprint for this war machine. But... you realised that wasn't all that you could be. So when Archmagos Veneratus Scraecos dug you up from the desert, you realised he and this world had something you could use to realise your full potential. Am I right? Have I understood so far?'

The Castigator raised a hand. Alaric stopped descending, the heat below him just a shade above unbearable. But it would only be a few minutes before it became too much and he started to burn inside his armour.

'You are perhaps less obtuse than the Space Marines of which I have read. They would have died with prayers on their lips. They have no wish to understand those they call enemies. But not you, I see. Very well.' The walls of the cogitator chamber, which now extended down to the reactor core, displayed dizzyingly complicated diagrams and endless reams of text, an overload of information. 'Yes, I was created in a time even I cannot recall and which has been lost to your Imperium. From the historical records on Chaeroneia, I could piece together nothing but

legends and guesswork about the Golden Age, the time you call the
Dark Age of Technology. There I was made, so that in this future your
people could build this machine. But in the wars that followed, I was
lost. The information I contained was used to create inferior copies,
built too quickly and modified too heavily. When I was lost, copies were
made of these inferior reflections in turn, so that the form of the Titan
became crude and unworthy. I was the first Titan and the god-machines
that strike your kind with awe are all pale shadows of me.

'I was lost, for men are ignorant and made war on one another until
no one was left alive who knew where I was hidden. I stayed lost for
thousands of years. In that time, thoughts of their own developed in the
ocean of information I contained. I was no longer just the instructions
for creating the first of the god-machines. I was a mighty intelligence.
And I realised why I was created – the true reason. Do you yet understand, Space Marine, what that reason was?'

'To… to teach,' said Alaric, his mind whirring. He might stay alive if
he could answer this thing's questions – more importantly, he might
learn about what it really was, find some weakness, strike back. 'To help
mankind…'

'No. No, Space Marine, your mind is still so small. The reason is obvious, especially to you. I was created for the same reason you were. Just
like your Imperium, just like the Adeptus Mechanicus, just like the
forges of Chaeroneia and the fleet that brought you here.'

Alaric gasped. The pain was boring into him. But he could not give in,
not yet. He concentrated on the Castigator's words and a thought came
to him at last. 'For… for war.'

'For war.'

The data blocks were suddenly projecting images of fire and destruction, like thousands of pict-steals from thousands of warzones. Cities
burned. Bodies came apart under gunfire. Planets were shattered. Stars
exploded.

'War!' There was something like joy in the Castigator's voice. 'It is my
purpose! The Titan is an instrument of war. It can do nothing else. It
serves no one and nothing, except for destruction itself. And so the same
is true of me. My purpose is destruction. Simply allowing myself to be
copied by your engineers is a distortion of this purpose and so I could
not allow it when the Adeptus Mechanicus found my resting place on
Chaeroneia. Instead, I sought information from the historical records of
the Adeptus Mechanicus. I found that the Imperium was competent at
war and fought many of them at any one time. But it was not enough
for me. I needed pure war, a final war. And then I came across myths and

half-truths that suggested such a war had almost come to the Imperium once before. This was the time your kind call the Horus Heresy.'

In spite of the raging heat, Alaric could feel ice in his veins. The Heresy, the Great Betrayal, where the forces of Chaos had played their hand and come so close to taking over the galaxy. It had been the human race's most desperate hour and the Emperor had sacrificed everything but His living spirit to keep it from succeeding.

The Castigator was continuing, as static-filled pict-grabs sputtered across the data-blocks, the surviving images from the Heresy ten thousand years before. 'Horus wanted that same war. A war that would burn everything and never end. He and I, we sought the same thing. But I read also that Horus died and his forces were scattered and it seemed that I had awoken nine thousand years too late. But I knew that perhaps such potential would come to the galaxy again. I could not risk any harm coming to Chaeroneia, so I hid it in the warp, using details of tech-heresies hidden in the most obscure archives of the Adeptus Mechanicus. Many tech-priests had studied the ways of the warp before the Mechanicus found them and stopped them and when I put together all their heresies I had more than enough knowledge to have Scraecos and his priests enact the ritual.'

The images surrounding the Castigator were now of the warp, its maddening swirls of light and darkness made of raw emotion. Even depicted flat and distorted, the sight made Alaric's eyes hurt to look at it. 'The planet was removed to the warp and there I bargained with the powers I found, offering them my wisdom and knowledge in return for a place of safety in the warp. I tamed some of the warp-predators and brought them to my world and had the tech-priests worship me and rebuild Chaeroneia according to the principles of the Dark Mechanicus I pried from the most ancient data fortresses. They were diligent, my priests. They did my every whim, killing one another for the honour of serving me. And then I heard news of what was happening in your galaxy. The opening of the Eye of Terror and the invasion of the Despoiler. In Abaddon, the warp powers said, Horus was born again. And I saw in him the potential for the war of annihilation that Horus so nearly waged.'

Alaric was surrounded by images of the Eye of Terror opening and the Chaos warfleets of the Thirteenth Black Crusade flooding out. He saw Cadia overrun and the destruction of St Josman's Hope. He saw a battle-fleet burning in orbit over Agrippina, defence lasers lacing the night sky of Nemesis Tessera. Dead men walking on the surface of Subiaco Diablo, animated by dark magic. Endless thousands of Imperial Guard marching into the most intense and desperate warzone in the Imperium.

The Imperial Navy had bottled up much of the Black Crusade within the systems surrounding the Eye. But the balance was still precarious and it would only take a slim advantage for Abaddon to break through and strike for the heart of the Segmentum Solar.

An advantage like the Standard Template Construct for the Father of Titans.

'And now,' said the Castigator, 'you understand. I feel it in you, the light of comprehension. You understand why I had to bring Chaeroneia back out of the warp and send a signal offering myself as tribute to Abaddon. Only he and the forces of Chaos can realise my true purpose. From me shall be copied endless god-machines and this time they shall be perfect, made using the unfettered science I taught the tech-priests of Chaeroneia. In the service of Chaos I shall stride a thousand battlefields at once and become one with the destruction that is my purpose. The galaxy shall burn because of me and so I shall become complete.'

'Yes,' said Alaric. 'Yes, I understand.'

Alaric was brought upwards into the cogitator core that filled the Titan's head and a block of data-medium detached from the wall. Alaric was lowered onto the block, where he was cut off from the nuclear heat from the reactor. The cold of the cogitator core flowed around him again, but not intensely enough to harm him. He could move, for what good it did him. The pain of his burns raged all over him but more to the point the Castigator had been correct. Alaric couldn't fight a creature of pure information. He had battled the data-daemons before, but they had been susceptible to his training as a daemon-hunter. There was just no way for Alaric to harm the Castigator.

And he really did understand.

'You don't really know what you are,' said Alaric, pulling himself to his feet. 'It took you thousands of years to evolve into what you are. There's nothing else like you in the galaxy. We both know what you want now, but only one of us understands what you actually are and it's not you.'

The Castigator drifted upwards to stand in front of Alaric. It seemed to be thinking deeply. 'Perhaps, it is true,' the Castigator replied. 'The historical records and theoretical research have not suggested one such as me and I no longer follow the purpose of the Standard Template Construct. You are correct. There is one thing I do not understand. I do not know what I am. But you do?' The Castigator's tone was almost conversational, as if it were speaking now with an equal – a friend, even.

'Yes, I do. I know that you bargain with the powers of the warp and teach sorcery to your followers. You are worshipped as a god. You rule through deceit. You lust for death and destruction. And you have pledged yourself to the service of Chaos.'

'All this is true, Space Marine.'

'Well, where I come from, there's a word for something like that.'

'And it is?'

'Daemon.'

The Castigator was silent for a moment. 'Interesting,' it said. 'Yes. Yes, I see. I am defined by these things, by my purpose and actions. And they are those of a daemon. Perhaps your words were not lies.'

The Castigator's pure white skin was changing. Tendrils of greyish corruption were reaching across it, standing out like veins. Its green eyes became darker and greasy smoke like befouled incense coiled up from their flame.

'Of course. All this time in the warp, bargaining with the Fell Powers. This devotion to Chaos. This form that is not flesh and not machine. What else am I? What else could I be?'

The Castigator's body took on the appearance of flesh, pale and covered in bulging veins. Its eyes sank into deep, scorched sockets and claws were growing from its fingers. It was still humanoid, but it was becoming the half-flesh, half-magic stuff of daemons.

Alaric felt it against his soul, massive and crushing, the sign of a daemonic presence the like of which he had not felt since he had confronted Ghargatuloth on Volcanis Ultor. The Castigator was an awesome presence, almost deafening. Alaric's shield of faith bowed under the enormity of it – the Castigator was battering at Alaric's mental defences without even having to will it. It was a daemon at last – and daemons were something Alaric understood.

Savage joy flared in the Castigator's eyes. It raised its hands and green flames flowed from its fingers. 'Yes! A daemon am I! Thank you, justicar! At last, I am complete!'

'You're welcome,' said Alaric. 'And now you die.'

TWENTY

'Though I walk through the valley of the shadow of the daemon, I shall fear nothing. For I am what the daemon fears.'
– Grand Master Mandulis of the Grey Knights

THE TITAN WORKS spread out below the belly of the *Hellforger*. The ship's enormous shadow turned Chaeroneia's permanent twilight into the black of night as the grand cruiser descended through the last few layers of pollutant cloud and into the relatively clear lower atmosphere. The navigation daemon kept the cruiser's battery of thrusters firing constantly, keeping the *Hellforger* hanging impossibly over the Titan works. Few newer ships could have managed it – most were not even designed for the possibility of atmospheric flight. But the *Hellforger* was old indeed and it knew a few tricks the Imperial Navy had long forgotten.

On the bridge, Urkrathos was studying the images of the Titan works intently. Such was the massive power usage of the facility that the ship's sensors had trouble cutting through all the interference – the ocular glands on the ship's underside had barely been able to focus on the place and send clear images to the bridge. The Titans were clear enough, hundreds of them standing silently to attention like an honour guard for Urkrathos's arrival. But details were difficult. And details were important, because it was one particular Titan that had grabbed Abaddon's attention. So Urkrathos had to confirm that the signal was genuine, by scanning the banks of pict-screens that had been extruded from the body of one of the bridge sensor-daemons.

Urkrathos could just make out the shapes of Reavers and Warlords, even a few Warhound Scout Titans. One Titan had fallen and

Urkrathos's trained eye spotted the signs of a short, vicious battle among the wreckage. There were bodies and bullet scars everywhere. But Urkrathos wasn't interested in that.

His eye caught the cherry-red of molten metal and he homed in on one pict-screen showing a massive charred crater, molten wreckage smouldering in its centre. 'There.' He said to the sensor-daemon. 'Enlarge.'

The sensor-daemon moaned and its bulbous, fleshy body quivered as most of the pict-screens sank back into its skin and the one showing the crater grew larger. The image shuddered as the ocular strained to refocus before the image was sharp again. Urkrathos studied it more closely – a Titan had been destroyed, recently and catastrophically. He couldn't tell what type of Titan it had been, but that wasn't what interested him – what he really noticed was the massive footprints crushed deep into the rockcrete.

He willed the ship's sensors to scan along the path of the footprints. They were massive, larger even than those of an Imperator Titan. Then the scanners ranged across an expanse of shimmering white armour, bright even through the static on the pict-screen.

Urkrathos saw the flicker of green flame, the massive multi-barrelled gun and the graceful lines of something that could never have been built by tech-priests, Dark Mechanicus or otherwise.

He had found it. The tribute promised by Chaeroneia to Abaddon the Despoiler, the tribute Urkrathos had been sent by the Despoiler to collect. The Father of Titans, the ultimate god-machine, which contained within it the information needed to build a thousand more of its kind. The weapon that would end the Thirteenth Black Crusade and begin Abaddon's inexorable conquest of the galaxy.

'Hold position,' ordered Urkrathos. 'And prepare the landing parties.'

IN THE TIME it took Alaric to raise his gun, the Castigator flitted to the far side of the chamber, its burning eyes narrowed with anger. In the time it took to pull the trigger, the green fire had flowed from its eyes, down its mouthless face and arms and surrounded its clawed hands.

Storm bolter fire spattered across the chamber as Alaric sprayed on full-auto. The Castigator moved almost too fast for Alaric to see – two shots thunked into its chest but the rest flew just wide, blasting spiderweb cracks into the data-blocks which flared glossy black where they were hit.

'Betrayal!' screamed the daemon. 'It understands and yet it defies! Treachery!' The Castigator, wreathed in flame, dived at Alaric. Alaric turned one hand away but the other grabbed his gun arm, forcing it away as he fired another volley of shots.

The daemon wrenched Alaric up off the data-block. For a moment Alaric was looking into those hate-filled green eyes, the flame rippling over his armour and the skin of his face. Then the Castigator threw Alaric with all its might, straight into the data-block wall behind him.

Alaric's armoured bulk was considerable and the Castigator was strong. Alaric smashed through the glassy data medium, thousands of shards slicing at him as he flew. He crashed through several layers of the cogitator core and then was bathed in ice-cold green fire, boiling around him with enough force to throw him further.

Alaric realised where he was. He had flown right through the burning eye of the Castigator's Titan, into the open air. He thought quickly enough to grab the lip of the armour below the Titan's immense face, his legs dangling over the sheer drop down to the ground. He pulled himself onto the carapace, his Astartes training enabling him to casually count off his injuries without the pain overwhelming him – his face was burned, the back of his ribcage was fractured and the shoulder of his gun arm was badly wrenched.

He saw a huge, dark shape above him, a massive wedge of corrupted metal so vast it was like a rotting steel sky. A spacecraft, come to Chaeroneia to answer the Castigator's signal and take the Father of Titans back to the court of Abaddon. That meant Alaric was almost too late.

A sound snapped Alaric's attention away from the sight. Something was bounding across the carapace towards Alaric – bestial, canine, half-way between lizard and insect, with a snapping lopsided maw full of lashing tentacles. A daemon.

Alaric fumbled to get his Nemesis halberd off his back, but he was too slow and the thing was on him. The edge of the carapace was near and the surface was slippery and curved – Alaric fought to keep his footing as he tried to draw his weapon and he knew he wouldn't have time before the creature slammed into him and pitched him over the edge to his death.

A sound like a thunderclap ripped out of nowhere and the daemon came apart in a shower of black-green gore. Alaric looked up to see Brother Dvorn lunge out from behind the curve of the Titan's high armoured collar, smacking his Nemesis hammer into the hissing remains of the daemon.

'Justicar!' said Dvorn in surprise. 'You're alive! He glanced down at the puddle of acidic mess that had once been the daemon. 'Damn things came at us in a mass. We fought them off but there are still some left. Haulvarn reckons we're an infection and these things are the immune system.'

'He's right,' said Alaric, bracing himself against the Titan's collar armour and moving away from the edge. 'But there's worse. I found the greater daemon controlling this machine and it's angry. And by the look of it we'll have company very soon.' Alaric pointed up at the ship hanging above them – lander ports were already opening on its underside and Alaric knew that it would only be a few minutes before landing craft or drop pods rained down, full of Chaos troops eager to claim their tribute.

'Justicar!' called Brother Haulvarn, hurrying across the carapace. Like Dvorn he had obviously fought long and hard against the Castigator's lesser daemons – perhaps that was why Alaric had made it to the cogitator core unmolested by them. 'I felt it wake. What is it?'

'I don't know for sure and it doesn't matter. Brothers, this machine must be destroyed. The reactor core is open, you can get in through the Titan's eye. Do whatever you can to destabilise it.'

'Yes, justicar,' said Haulvarn. 'And the daemon?'

The Castigator's burning form burst out through the top of the daemon's head, screaming its rage, the muscles of its new daemonic body writhing as it turned its anger into raw strength to tear Alaric apart.

'I'll deal with it,' said Alaric. 'The Chaos fleet wants the Titan. Don't leave them anything to find. Go!'

Haulvarn and Dvorn ran round towards the front of the Titan's head. As Alaric had hoped, the Castigator ignored them. It was Alaric it wanted to kill. Alaric was the betrayer – the one who had understood, but not submitted.

The Castigator screeched and sent bolts of green flame rippling down towards Alaric like comets. But Alaric, for all his size and the weight of his armour, was a Space Marine, his body enhanced to be quick as well as strong. He rolled away from the first strike and ducked past the next, spraying fire up at the Castigator. The rear edge of the carapace was dangerously close and the yawning drop swung by as Alaric scrabbled away from the daemon's fire. The Castigator was fast, too and zipped around above the Titan.

More fire fell in fat shimmering bursts that blew hissing craters in the Titan's shoulder armour. The Castigator was frustrated. It had probably never failed to get its way before. It didn't care any more about subtle manipulations or a plan that had taken a thousand years to play out. It just wanted to kill. It was the only advantage Alaric had and he was going to use it.

The Castigator dived, determined to finish Alaric with his bare claws. Alaric swept the Nemesis halberd at it and cut a deep gouge across the Castigator's chest, stepping to the side as the daemon slammed a fist into the carapace.

The daemon lashed out and caught Alaric on the chest. Alaric stumbled backwards and the daemon was upon him, slashing at him, cutting through the ceramite of his chest armour as if it was nothing, battering him backwards towards the edge.

The daemon was strong. As strong as anything Alaric had ever faced in close combat. And it was winning.

Alaric felt an arm break in the Castigator's grip. It was his gun arm. He could do without it for now. He wrenched the arm around, feeling it fold uselessly and slip out of the Castigator's grip. It gave him the freedom to force the Castigator off him and headbutt the creature square in its featureless face. The daemon reeled and Alaric spun his halberd, cracking the butt end into the Castigator's throat and following up with a slash that carved a furrow down its face.

Teeth slid from the edges of the wound, giving the Castigator a revolting vertical mouth that drooled blood as the Castigator howled. It kicked out and prehensile claws on its foot gripped Alaric's leg. The Castigator soared upwards, flying up above the Titan with Alaric dangling from its grip. The collar armour shot by and suddenly Alaric was high in the air, the drop dizzying as it spun beneath him as the Castigator flew high up above the Titan works, towards the steel sky of the Chaos ship.

It was going to drop him. It was so simple. Alaric could fight as well as almost any other soldier the Imperium had, but one thing he couldn't do was fly.

The Castigator let go. Alaric pivoted in the air, shifting his weight to turn himself the right way up. He stabbed up with the halberd, forcing his broken arm to move in a two-handed strike that thrust the halberd blade up over his head.

The blade punched into the Castigator's abdomen and passed right through. Alaric twisted the blade and it caught, leaving him hanging by the halberd. The Castigator twisted and screamed, trying to dislodge the blade and send Alaric tumbling to his death. But it was losing height, too, its concentration broken and its powers of flight compromised by rage and pain. The Castigator swooped low, not much slower than a dead fall, the surface of the Titan works streaking by beneath it. Alaric hung on grimly as the daemon flew between the legs of the Warlord Titan and banked to avoid the solid mass of a bunker.

They hit the ground badly, the blade coming free as Alaric and the daemon cartwheeled across the rockcrete. For a moment everything was blackness and pain. Alaric's head cracked against the rockcrete and broken teeth rattled around in his head, a gunshot of pain flaring from his broken arm. For a moment he wasn't sure if he was alive or whether he was now tumbling towards one of the hells to which sinners were sent, to be punished for his failure.

Alaric skidded to a halt. His vision swam back and he shook the pain from his head. He was alive. He rolled onto his front and grabbed the halberd that had landed next to him. Looking up, he saw the Castigator was already on its feet.

The wound in its abdomen was a pulsing black mass. Bladed limbs reached out of the wound, grasping hands, writhing tentacles, the manifold form of the daemon taking hold. Alaric pulled himself up into a crouch and the pain was gone, replaced by the iron-hard discipline of a Space Marine. The two were twenty metres apart, close enough for Alaric to see every muscle in the Castigator's mutating body bunch up ready to pounce. Alaric was the same, winding up for the strike, knowing that this was his one chance to take on the Castigator in the only way he could – up close, hand-to-hand, face-to-face, where his Space Marine's strength and Grey Knight's ferocity would count the most.

For a moment they watched one another, man and daemon, each mind filled with nothing but the death of the other. Then, as one, they charged.

Alaric sprinted. The Castigator thrust itself forwards on dozens of insectoid limbs, its drooling maw and limb-filled wound gaping to crush and kill. The two slammed into one another and the final murderous struggle exploded in a mass of stabbing limbs and slashing blades.

Clawed hands reached out. Alaric cut them off with his first slash. His second bit deep through the Castigator's corrupted mass even as it grew and flowed around him. The Castigator tried to drag him in and Alaric welcomed it, pushing into the lethal mass of bony blades and lashing tentacles.

Alaric ripped one foot out of the mass and crunched it down through bone and gristle, forcing himself upwards towards the Castigator's head. The Grey Knight yelled a wordless prayer of rage and pulled his halberd clear, switching the grip and driving it deep into the Castigator's throat. The corrupted mass sucked the halberd out of his hand but he didn't care, raising his fist again and punching the Castigator's corrupted face.

A Grey Knight was trained to act with deliberation and level-headedness and leave behind the heedless bloodlust that characterised some Chapters of the Adeptus Astartes. But they also knew that every enemy demanded a different type of fight. Some would be defeated with cunning and guile, others with strength of will, both things at which the Grey Knights excelled. But there were some enemies, some among the ranks of the daemon, that could only be defeated with good old-fashioned rage.

It was rage that drove Alaric then. Again and again he slammed his fist into the Castigator's face, into the lipless mouth-wound and the burning eyes. He felt the deaths of his battle-brothers, of Archis and Lykkos and of Archmagos Saphentis and the tech-guard. He felt Hawkespur's savage wound and the breaking of Thalassa's spirit. The suffering of Chaeroneia a thousand years ago, ripped into the warp where those who resisted were consumed by the dark gods, all for the satisfaction of an intelligence that should never have existed. He felt them all and welded them into a diamond-hard spike of hatred that he drove into the Castigator's corrupted soul just as he drove his fist into its face.

The daemon stumbled backwards on its many new limbs, reeling. Its face was a gory mess, green flames licking from dozens of cuts. Alaric reached into the gaping wound in its throat and pulled his halberd out, bringing a fountain of gore with it.

'You should have picked an enemy, said Alaric, 'with less imagination.' He swung the halberd in a great arc and sliced off the Castigator's head.

The death-scream was the loudest sound Alaric had ever heard. The Castigator howled in binary as it died, its information bleeding out of it in zeroes and ones like machine gun fire. Pure information shot from the Castigator's ruined body like fireworks and among them Alaric glimpsed its thoughts. He saw endless legions of Castigator Titans marching on the Imperial palace on Terra, standing in ranks of thousands on the surface of Mars. He saw destruction, so absolute the very stars were burned out by its ferocity, leaving behind a black and dead universe where the Castigator's purpose had finally been realised. But then they were gone and without the Castigator's will to hold it together the mass of information became a shower of meaningless fragments, spiralling scraps of light that died as the Castigator's own life flooded out of it in a pool of corrupted gore.

The daemon's head thudded wetly onto the ground. Alaric took a couple of steps away from its hissing, oozing corpse and sunk to his knees, exhausted. The Castigator's body slumped to one side – it was the size of a tank, swollen with corrupted growths, dry and tattered now the information that fuelled it was gone. Its skin began sloughing off and the body started to melt.

Alaric looked round to the Castigator's Titan, dominating the forest of Titans. One of its eyes exploded, the green flame exploding out to be replaced with a plume of wild plasma.

The reactor was critical. The plasma was boiling over as it approached catastrophic mass. Haulvarn and Dvorn had succeeded.

Alaric picked up the battered head of the Castigator. The green flame was just a faint flickering now, barely reaching past what remained of its eye sockets. Its vertical, gaping mouth was dumb. Alaric held up the head so it could see the Titan.

Slowly, the shape of the Titan's torso sagged. Its face began to melt, the immense heat of the plasma boring through its layers of armour. Even the Titan's miraculous self-repairing facilities could do nothing against power of that magnitude.

'See?' said Alaric. 'You wanted destruction. Here it is.'

A white light burned out through the Titan's chest as the plasma vessel failed completely. The Titan rippled as if suddenly liquid and then it was consumed in an expanding ball of hot, unbearable light, so bright it melted the surfaces of the Titans that stood nearby.

A hot wind blasted across the Titan works, bringing with it the death-scream of the father of god-machines.

As the flare of the explosion died away, Alaric looked down at the Castigator's head. The flame finally flickered out and the crushing pressure on Alaric's mental shield eased. The Castigator was dead.

'No,' SAID URKRATHOS. 'No.'

The sensor-daemon gleefully replayed the image. The Titan, built from a pure Standard Template Construct, from which could be copied the ultimate weapon – melting into slag and then exploding, right beneath the *Hellforger* as Urkrathos looked on.

'This… this is an insult!' Urkrathos slammed a fist into the sensor-daemon, shattering the pict-screen and sending the daemon recoiling in pain. 'To entreat upon Abaddon himself, to lure me here… and now this! What insubordination is this, to defy a chosen of Abaddon?'

Ukrathos turned to glare at the rest of the bridge. The daemons were silent, for they knew one of Urkrathos's killing rages when they saw it. 'The Despoiler was promised a tribute,' said Urkrathos, anger dripping from every word. 'And a tribute he will get. A tribute in blood! In death! In fire! Close the ports and move to mid-atmosphere! All power to the lance batteries!'

* * *

Silhouetted against the afterglow of the Titan's death, two figures approached. Alaric knew them even before his vision compensated for the glare – Brothers Haulvarn and Dvorn, scorched but alive.

'Well met, brothers,' said Alaric bleakly. 'I see you were successful.'

'Well met, justicar,' said Haulvarn. 'Dvorn found a maintenance run down to the knee, so we threw a couple of melta-bombs into the core and got out. I was wondering if it would work.'

'And I was wondering,' said Dvorn, indicating the quickly decaying mass of flesh that had been the Castigator, 'if you would leave anything of this creature for me.'

'Sorry to disappoint you, brother. The daemon and myself had matters to settle.'

Haulvarn's head snapped round at the sound of tracks approaching. Alaric followed his gaze and saw one of the steaming, beweaponed engines from the earlier battle, the size of a Rhino APC and bristling with guns and blades. The last Alaric had seen they had been running rampant around the Titan works after Scraecos had died – now one was heading straight for them. The Grey Knights took aim with their storm bolters as it approached, backing off before it opened fire.

'Hold!' shouted Alaric as he saw the limp body held in the claws jutting from the engine's front armour. 'Hold fire!'

The figure was Hawkespur. Through her faceplate, Alaric could see her skin was almost white.

'She's still alive,' said a distorted voice from the engine.

'Antigonus.' Somehow, Alaric wasn't surprised Magos Antigonus had made it. He had taken a thousand years of what Chaeroneia could throw at him – he was the toughest of them all in his own way. When the Warhound had died he must have leapt into the closest machine, which apparently happened to be one of the Dark Mechanicus war engines.

'Your battle-brother Cardios is dead,' said Antigonus, his voice warped by the crude vocabulator unit on the engine. 'The tech-guard too. They were taking stray fire from the Titan and they threw themselves on her to protect her.'

Alaric sped to the engine – Hawkespur's breathing was shallow and though her wound had been crudely dressed, she was still bleeding. 'She won't last long,' he said.

'Neither will we,' replied Antigonus. 'The sensors on this thing aren't good but it looks like there are Mechanicus troops approaching from the direction of the city and the spaceship above us is rising to firing altitude. Get yourself and your brothers on board, justicar, this machine can go faster than you can on foot.'

'Then we will pray for Cardios later.' Alaric turned to Haulvarn and Dvorn. 'Get on board. Stay alert and hold on.'

'And make it quick,' added Antigonus. 'I think there might still be something in here with me.'

The three surviving Grey Knights swung themselves onto the spiked body of the war engine, Alaric feeling the full extent of his injuries for the first time. But his own wounds didn't matter. The Castigator was destroyed, the power that ruled Chaeroneia was broken and there were many prayers to say for the dead.

Antigonus gunned the engine's tracks and it tore rapidly towards the closest edge of the Titan works, leaving the melting slag of the Castigator's Titan behind. And above them, the Chaos grand cruiser was rising through the layers of pollution, massive laser lance projectors emerging from its underside.

THE COLLECTIVE MIND of Chaeroneia's tech-priests was at an utter loss. The sequence of events had been so rapid and unexpected that they could not make sense of them. The Castigator's awakening and destruction, the Chaos spacecraft hanging above them, the death of Scraecos, the battle in the fallen Titan, the awesome psychic force that had exploded from the Castigator Titan and had been cut short. There were thousands of explanations being bounced between the ruling minds of Chaeroneia, none of them satisfactory, many of them heretical.

The laser lances being readied by the Chaos grand cruiser were just one more complication. They were added to the confusing mess of contradictions and absurdities and were barely remarked upon by the tech-priests right up until the moment they fired.

THE HOT ASH wind whipped past Alaric as Antigonus drove the war engine across the dunes. He looked back towards the receding Titan works, still dominating the ash desert with their watchtowers and legions of Titans, crowned by the central spire and still under the shadow of the Chaos spaceship.

A finger of hot ruby light slashed down, punching through the disk at the top of the central spire. White flickers of explosions ripped through the structure. Then another beam fell and another, edging the towers of the Titan works with crimson. Suddenly, every weapon on the Chaos ship opened up as one, bathing the Titan works in red laser fire. The central spire exploded, the raging finger of flame quickly swallowed by plasma explosions as the lances punched down through the assembled Titans and penetrated the fuel reservoirs beneath the surface.

The destruction of the Titan works took just a few minutes, the awesome weight of lance fire from the Chaos cruiser supplemented by orbital bombardment shells and weapons batteries. The watchtowers shattered and the moat boiled away. The Titans fell like executed men and the surrounding dunes were washed with waves of heat and flame.

Antigonus kept control as the ground shook. Alaric held on as the shockwaves died down and the fires continued to burn, consuming the lower levels of the Titan works and finishing the destruction of the Castigator's lair.

The shadow slowly lifted off the desert as the Chaos ship rose into higher orbit, ready to return back to the vacuum of space. Abaddon's tribute had not been delivered and the Chaos ship had exacted revenge for the failure.

The ash clouds slowly blotted out the sight of the shattered Titan works and the engine ground further into the desert, away from Manufactorium Noctis.

INQUISITOR NYXOS PAUSED over the large leatherbound book, quill in hand. The reports given by Alaric and the other Grey Knights would take some time to write up and the implications were extraordinary. Someone would have to explain to all authorities concerned how the mission to Chaeroneia had found a hallowed Standard Template Construct and then destroyed it. And Nyxos knew that someone would be him.

Nyxos's quarters on the *Exemplar* were in one of the few undamaged sections of the ship. The Mechanicus cruiser had been shattered by fire from the Chaos ship that had duelled with it, and would have surely been destroyed had the Chaos fleet not broken off and headed down to the planet's surface. That fleet was now long gone, having moved with all haste to jump distance and disappeared into the warp. The *Exemplar* had been in no shape to follow and was still in high orbit around Chaeroneia waiting for a Naval ship to reach it and evacuate the survivors of the Mechanicus crew. The quarters were cold and cramped, but Nyxos did not mind a little hardship when he had so nearly died along with countless crew in the battle above Chaeroneia. It had only been his augmentations and redundant organs that had kept him alive when the verispex decks had depressurised and as far as he knew no one on the same deck had been so fortunate.

There was a knock at the door. 'Enter,' said Nyxos.

The door slid open and Justicar Alaric walked in. Even without his armour he was huge, almost filling the room. The candlelight glinted off the dried blood that edged the scars on his long, noble face and there were livid bruises around his eyes. Normally they were expressive and inquisitive, especially compared to most other Space Marines – now they were just tired.

'Ah, justicar. I am glad you could see me,' said Nyxos, looking up from his report. 'I hope I have not intruded on your prayers.'

'There will be plenty of time to pray, inquisitor.'

'Regretfully so. I will join you and your battle-brothers soon, I would say some words for them myself. We might never fully understand how greatly their sacrifice protected the Imperium. Please, sit.'

Alaric sat down wearily on the chair opposite Nyxos. It took a lot to tire out a Space Marine, but Alaric had clearly been through enough on Chaeroneia to kill most men a dozen times over. 'I was concerned about the interrogator,' he said.

'Hawkespur is stable,' replied Nyxos. 'She is very badly injured. She lost a lot of blood and the pollutants affected her gravely. Perhaps she will live, perhaps she will not. Magos Thulgild has made her care the highest priority and she will have a good chance if I can get her to Inquisition facilities before she deteriorates. In truth, I am surprised she made it back at all. I was certain I would never see her again.'

'And Antigonus?'

'Still in quarantine. Thulgild is fascinated that Antigonus seems to have survived in information form alone. It is alarming to me, too, but Antigonus has submitted to all Magos Thulgild's tests and there is no indication of corruption. He requests to be taken back to Mars and Thulgild has agreed.'

'It was his mission,' said Alaric. 'To investigate Chaeroneia and report back to the Fabricator General. He wants to make sure he fulfils it.'

Nyxos sat back in his chair and sighed. So many were dead and so many more questions had to be answered. 'Meanwhile, justicar, my mission is to tell the Ordo Malleus what happened down there. And I admit I do not fully understand it myself. This creature, this Castigator. It was a daemon, you say?'

'Yes. I do not know when it entered the Standard Template Construct, or how, but it seemed to have been there so long it had forgotten what it really was. Until I… reminded it.'

'And it was a daemon all along?'

'Of course. How could it not be?'

'No one knows what form the Standard Template Constructs originally took. Who is to say they did not have machine-spirits of their own, true intelligences far more powerful than anything that survives today?'

'No, inquisitor. I fought it. I felt it. When it realised what it was, it rejoiced in it. It might not have been a daemon the Ordo Malleus would recognise, but the shapes of the Enemy are many. Evil takes an infinity of forms, but justice is constant.'

'Very well. If you are certain, justicar, then so am I. When I can get an astropathic message to the Ordo, there will be one more entry in the Liber Daemonicum.' Nyxos took up his quill again. 'Thank you, justicar. I have kept you from your prayers for too long.'

'By your leave,' said Alaric, rising from his seat and leaving the chamber.

Nyxos continued writing. He would have to recite it all before the conclave of lord inquisitors and suffer their interrogations until they knew everything he did. He did not begrudge it, but this would be difficult to explain. A daemon in information form, the return of the Dark Mechanicus and a corrupt Standard Template Construct. Yes, their questions would be many.

And then there was Alaric himself. He was intelligent, curious and imaginative. They were qualities normally buried by the training of a Grey Knight, but when confronted with the foulest of enemies, they shone through in Alaric. That was why Alaric had convinced the Castigator to take on daemon's flesh when any other Grey Knight would just have died screaming prayers. Probably the Grand Masters of the Grey Knights saw it as something unstable and unwanted and would keep Alaric from ever attaining the rank of brother-captain that he deserved. But Nyxos had seen enough of Alaric's qualities to know that perhaps there was some other role he could serve within the Inquisition, where a sharp mind and a Space Marine's body could be put to best use.

But those were matters for another time. For the moment, Nyxos would have to make sure he had answers for the lord inquisitors.

DEEP ON HOLY MARS, the world sacred to the Omnissiah and spiritual heart of the tech-priesthood, a mighty labyrinth lay below the rust-red surface. It was forgotten, deliberately so, by all but the highest echelons of the Adeptus Mechanicus. Those to whom the archmagi ultima bowed, those who had the ear of the Fabricator General, knew of its existence and they jealously guarded that knowledge well. All but a handful of men and women in the Imperium were incapable of even imagining the weight of secrets it contained.

The Standard Template Constructs were sacred rumours among the tech-priests, any scrap of information concerning them a holy revelation. And all those scraps were gathered, filtered through the most ancient and powerful logic engines, dissected and assembled and placed in the gene-locked data vaults that lined the walls of the labyrinth. Reaching deep into the crust of Mars, the archive contained information concerning the Standard Template Constructs, some of it older than the Imperium itself. And every few centuries, after decades of debate among the very highest circles of the tech-priesthood, something new would be added.

A new vault was assigned and coded and the information was typed into it in pure binary by one of those ancient, hooded figures who were closer to the Omnissiah than anyone who lived. That information con-cerned a world named Chaeroneia and the Standard Template Construct that had been found and lost there. It was the STC for the most awesome of technologies – the Titan, the god-machine – and it had been, according to all the data gathered, pure and complete as no STC had ever been before. But it had been used for the ends of the Enemy, twisted into a weapon of Chaos by a monstrous daemon of the warp. And so was the lesson illustrated – none but the Adeptus Mechan-icus could comprehend the majesty of the Standard Template Constructs and the purity of the knowledge they contained, none but a tech-priest, stripped of his humanity by his devotion to the Omnissiah, could be trusted with the enormity of such information.

The vault was sealed and consecrated and the picture became a little clearer. One day the Adeptus Mechanicus would attain complete under-standing of the galaxy and the grand design of the Omnissiah, using the Standard Template Constructs as a guide to His divine methods. One day the STCs would all be completely reassembled, as pure as the Titan STC should have been had the Enemy not abused it and so threatened everything the Mechanicus existed to protect. It was the quest that had consumed the Priesthood of Mars ever since the Dark Age of Technol-ogy had given way to the Age of Strife, long before the Emperor arose and united mankind in the Imperium. It was a quest that consumed every tech-priest and menial every moment of their lives and drove them closer to their Omnissiah in their zeal to understand.

It took many normal lifetimes to become close enough to the Omnis-siah to accept the truth that lay at the heart of their teachings. Only the highest, those who knew of the archive and its contents, could do so. And so they all knew, as somehow they had always known, that their quest would never end.

HAMMER OF DAEMONS

ONE

THE FLOOR AND walls of the medicae bunker were painted dark green, so the blood just looked like dark water pooling under the beds.

'He's at the back,' said the medicae orderly. Her face was grey with fatigue, but her eyes were alert.

'Then let's hurry,' said Colonel Dal'Tharken.

The medicae led the colonel between the rows of beds, each with its wounded man lolling semi-conscious with sedation, or grimacing as an orderly bent over his wounds. Some of them managed to nod or even salute to the colonel as he walked by, and he returned their greetings with a moment of eye contact. Most of the conscious ones, though, were focused on the man who followed the colonel. He was huge, and armoured in gunmetal, something the Hathrans had never seen before they had come to this world. Indeed, he was someone very few of them had ever seen up close. He seemed to take up what little room remained in the bunker.

'Three came in,' the medicae continued, casting a curious glance at the armoured figure behind the colonel. 'One made it. We had to burn the others.' Her manner was short and efficient, as if all her compassion had been drained away.

Colonel Dal'Tharken didn't have to ask how the survivor was doing. At the back of the bunker there was a row of beds with mesh insect nets, useless in the arctic climate of Sarthis Majoris, but enough to create a barrier between the recovering and the most severely wounded men, the ones who hadn't realised they were dead, and the sights of suffering around them. The patrol's survivor was going to die, and soon.

'If it matters, he's in no condition to talk,' continued the medicae.

'Is he conscious?'

'In and out.'

'That'll do.'

The medicae pulled back the netting from a bed at the back of the bunker. The smell of burnt meat and hair welled up from the bed.

'Arse on the Golden Throne,' swore the trooper who lay there. 'I must really be in trouble.'

'Trooper Slohane?'

'Yes, sir.'

'Officer present.'

'Sorry, sir. Can't salute.'

Trooper Slohane was missing most of his lower jaw. It had been replaced with a temporary prosthetic that was just mobile enough to allow him to talk. The face on the damaged side was raw meat. A wad of bandage was taped over the ruins of one eye. The jacket of his fatigues had been cut away and a wound swallowed up most of his chest. A transparent slab of gel-skin lay over the wound to staunch the bleeding, but the injury was far too severe for Slohane to be saved. There was so much blood on the floor and soaked into the bed that blood loss would get him even if his organs held out.

Slohane's eye focused on the shape towering over the colonel. For a moment, he didn't seem to focus, as if the figure was too big to fit within the confines of the bunker.

Slohane smiled with what remained of his mouth. 'You. Heh, I never thought I'd actually get to be face to face with one of you: a Space Marine. When… when I was a child I thought you were just a story.'

Justicar Alaric stepped forward. In full power armour he was almost twice the height of a man. His armour was ornate steel adorned with devotional texts picked out in gold, and one massive shoulder pad bore the heraldry of a black and red field with a single starburst. The symbol of a book pierced by a silver sword adorned the other shoulder. Alaric wore no helmet, and his face seemed too human for the size and ornamentation of his armour, even with his scars and the service stud in his forehead. He had a halberd in his hand, long enough to scrape the bunker ceiling, and on the back of his other hand was mounted a double-barrelled storm bolter.

'No stories,' said Alaric simply. 'We are here for the same reason you are. This is a world worth saving.'

'What did you see, trooper?' asked the colonel.

Slohane arched back and coughed. The wet mass of his lungs was visible through the ruin of his chest. 'Six of us went out. The captain said we were heading... heading through the southern route to get to the foothills before nightfall. Avalanche must've come down the day before, because the route was blocked, so we skirted up along Pale Ridge.' Slohane looked at the colonel. 'We should've turned back.'

The medicae picked up a handful of the printout that had spooled out of a monitoring cogitator. She gave the colonel a meaningful glance. The irregular life signs on the printout meant Slohane didn't have long.

'Go on, trooper,' said the colonel.

'Things started... coming out of the ground,' said Slohane. He was looking up at the ceiling. There was too much in his mind's eye to let him focus on anything real. 'Hands, and faces. They started screaming. And there was fire. The captain died. We had to let him go. He was melting into the ground. Tollen went crazy and started shooting. I just ran, sir. I ran away.'

'And then?'

'I was heading up the ridge. I was on fire, I think. These dark things were coming up through the snow. I got to the top of the ridge and kept firing. The damn lasgun was red-hot. I ran back along the ridge away from it all. I just looked back once.'

Alaric knelt down beside the colonel, so he was the height of a normal man. 'What did you see?'

Slohane's eye rolled around. Tears welled up. 'There were millions of them,' he said, 'millions, all standing on the other side of Pale Ridge.'

'Men?' asked Alaric.

'Men,' said Slohane, 'and things. Huge things. Monsters, waiting there like animals on the slaughterman's ramp. Then the clouds blew by and stars came out, and the whole valley was covered in blood. The mountain streams had thawed and they were blood, too. I could hear them chanting. It wasn't no language like a man might speak. It was words straight from the warp.'

'What about artillery?' asked the colonel. 'Armour?'

'I don't know,' replied Slohane, 'but there were monsters in the air, too, with wings. And a tower... lit up in red... and him up on the battlements, like a king.'

'Who?' asked Alaric urgently, leaning down so his face was close to Slohane's. 'Who did you see?'

Slohane tried to reply but his words came out as a painful gasp. A tear of blood ran from his remaining eye. The medicae dropped the printout and fiddled with the controls on the monitor.

'He's unconscious,' she said. 'He's losing blood faster than we can pump it in. You won't get any more from him.'

'Pale Ridge,' said Colonel Dal'Tharken. 'Right under our bloody noses.'

'We knew it would come to this,' said Alaric.

'That we did.' The colonel turned to the medicae and pointed to Slohane's convulsing body. 'Burn him, too.'

'Of course,' she replied.

ALARIC MET UP with his squad on the fortifications above the medical bunker. The night had been even colder than usual, and cloaks of ice clung to the rockcrete battlements. Wisps of vapour rose from the pillboxes and weapon points, from the breath of the Hathran Guardsmen huddled beneath their greatcoats. The Grey Knights were standing watch at the right of the line, where the medical bunker met the ice wall of the mountainside. The rest of the line stretched across the pass, manned by the Hathran soldiers who still stole half-fearful glances at the Grey Knights. None of them knew what a Grey Knight was, but they had all heard of the Space Marines, humanity's saviours, the greatest soldiers in the galaxy. A Space Marine was a symbol of the Imperium, a reminder of what they fought for.

'What news, justicar?' asked Brother Haulvarn as Alaric trudged through the slush of the night's icefall.

'It's coming to an end,' replied Alaric.

'Good,' grunted Brother Dvorn. Dvorn, along with Haulvarn, had fought with Alaric since he had first been elevated to the rank of justicar. Where Haulvarn was a born leader, Dvorn was a pure warrior. His nemesis weapon was in the form of a hammer, a rare weapon that perfectly suited Dvorn's brutality. Alaric was glad to have both of them at his side on Sarthis Majoris. If Trooper Slohane's testimony had any truth in it, he would need them soon.

'Do we know what we're facing?' asked Brother Visical.

'Not yet,' said Alaric.

'Looking forward to finding out,' said Dvorn.

'Don't be too eager,' replied Alaric. 'It's bad. The enemy must have been gathering strength since we made landfall. They're massing past Pale Ridge right now. The colonel is mobilising every able-bodied man as we speak. And it'll happen soon. The enemy can't keep a force like that in check for long.'

'Will the line hold?' asked Brother Thane. Thane and Visical had been drafted into Alaric's squad after the losses it had suffered on Chaeroneia.

'That's not for me to say,' said Alaric gravely. 'The Hathrans will decide that. We must show them how the enemy must be resisted, and help lead them in their prayers. After that the battle will fall on them.'

'Not if we get there first,' said Visical with a smirk. While Thane had only recently earned the armour of a Grey Knight, Visical was a veteran. The gauntlets of his power armour were permanently blackened by the flame from his incinerator, in spite of the wargear rites supposed to keep them spotless. 'We'll show them how it's done.'

Dvorn nodded in agreement. Some men just fought like that, Alaric had decided; they simply threw aside all concept of failure and trusted in their training and determination to carry them through. They were, after all, Grey Knights, some of the Imperium's best warriors, but Alaric could not think that way.

'Thane, lead the prayers,' said Alaric. 'Our bodies are prepared, so ensure that our souls are the same.'

A sound reached Alaric's ears. The voices of the Imperial Guard, low and mournful, rose as one in the death song of Hathran.

FATE HAD SEEN fit to place Sarthis Majoris in the path of the most terrible Chaos incursion since the ancient days of the Horus Heresy. The Thirteenth Black Crusade had erupted from the warp storm known as the Eye of Terror, led by the greatest champions of the Chaos Gods. The initial campaigns had seen Cadia besieged and whole Imperial armies annihilated as they tried to stem the tide. Only the sacrifices of the Imperial Navy had kept the Black Crusade from reaching the Segmentum Solar itself. The Inquisition had made appalling decisions that not even a hard-bitten Guard general would stomach: bombing Guard regiments into dust for witnessing the predations of the Enemy, sacrificing whole worlds to slow down the Chaos hordes, betraying Emperor-fearing citizens at every turn to buy tiny slivers of hope. The whole galactic north was mobilised to barricade the Imperial heartland against the Black Crusade.

Chaos brought with it daemons. The Ordo Malleus, the most secretive and warlike branch of the Inquisition, had sent unprecedented resources to the Eye of Terror. Whole companies of Grey Knights had been thrown into the cauldron of the Eye. The Eye of Terror drew in the Imperium's daemon hunters, and more often than not it spat them out mutilated, mad or dead. Yet still they fought, because that was what it meant to be human: to fight when any sane man would say the fight could not be won.

Sarthis Majoris supplied fuel to the Imperial Navy. Its refineries turned the radioactive sludge in the planet's mantle into the lifeblood of the Segmentum battlefleet. Maybe that was why a fleet of Chaos ships, ancient things shaped like filth encrusted daggers, was diverted to invade Sarthis Majoris. Or perhaps the millions of colonists huddled in the refinery cities were simply too tempting a sacrifice to the Dark Gods. Either way, if Chaos took Sarthis Majoris, the engines of Imperial battleships would fall silent, and dozens more Chaos ships would break through the Imperial blockades.

The Hathran Armoured Cavalry were close enough to be landed on Sarthis Majoris shortly after the Chaos forces made landfall on the southern polar cap. The hurried strategic meetings confirmed that the Chaos army's northwards march would have to take them through the ice-bound pass in the towering Reliqus Mountains. Once through the mountains, there was no telling which refinery city would be sacrificed first. So the pass had to hold, and the Hathran Armoured Cavalry had to hold it.

Imperial commanders requested assistance from any quarter to help deliver Sarthis Majoris from the enemy. The Ordo Malleus heard these requests and performed astropathic divinations that confirmed the presence of daemons among the hordes landing on the planet. In a perfect galaxy they would have sent armies of Space Marines and storm troopers led by daemon hunters to crush the Chaos forces on the polar cap, but the galaxy was far from perfect, and those legions and inquisitors were spread across a thousand worlds threatened by the Black Crusade.

The Inquisition's contribution to the defence of Sarthis Majoris consisted of Justicar Alaric and four Grey Knights.

TWO

'Movement!' cried one of the sentries. 'Two kilometres! West face!'

The Hathrans stationed on the wall hurried to their posts, peering into the breaking dawn light. It was running down the sides of the valleys in a thin, greasy film, turning the ice of the peaks far above an angry gold. The depths of the valley stretching southwards were still veiled in the dying night's darkness.

'I see them,' said one of the officers commanding the watch. He pulled magnoculars from his greatcoat and looked through them down the valley. Shapes were moving in the darkness, scrabbling along the side of the mountain. A human couldn't climb like that, especially one almost naked, clad only in its own flayed skin.

'Is it the big one?' asked another Guardsman, a support gunner, leaning forward on the barrel of his fixed autocannon.

'Might be just another sacrifice,' said yet another. Most of the Guardsmen believed that the Chaos attacks, up to that point, had been deliberately mounted to sacrifice cultists and mutants beneath the Imperial guns, to seed the valley with blood and please the Chaos Gods. A few, more prosaically, thought the enemy was just trying to use up the Hathrans' ammunition, but everyone was certain that an attack was coming, after the rumours had spread that a vast Chaos horde, millions strong, was pooling behind Pale Ridge.

'Guns up! Men to your stations!' cried the officer. Sirens sounded as Guardsmen swarmed up onto the battlements. The few who were sleeping jumped from their beds and were still pulling their scarves around their faces as they emerged into the freezing dawn. Their breath formed heavy clouds rolling between the battlements.

The attacks had come nightly. The enemy had thrown handfuls of men at them. It was simpler to call them men. The officers called them 'cultists', a useful catch-all for the mutated, heretic and insane that made up the bulk of the Chaos army. Their bodies, frozen solid, were dark red smudges below the latest snowfalls. Some of them had been robed madmen who chanted in inhuman tongues. Others were scrabbling things that had presumably been human before their skins were removed and nailed back onto their wet, red bodies in scraps. Some of those had made it onto the walls, and most of the Hathran wounded in the medicae bunker, or in the grim frozen heap of bodies on the fortification's northern side, were the result of those leaping, screaming creatures.

Sometimes red lightning had struck from the heavens, searing men to charred meat. Sometimes soldiers had gone mad and killed their brother soldiers, and no one could tell if it was some sorcery of the enemy or old-fashioned battle psychosis. Many of the patrols sent out to locate the enemy had not returned, or had crawled back burned, mutilated or mad. The enemy wanted the Hathran line bruised and tender, its teeth ground down, its men exhausted and its guns well-worn.

There had been enough petty death. The gods wanted a spectacle.

'You there!' yelled Colonel Dal'Tharken at the closest officer, as he stormed out of the command bunker. 'Get some men into that firepoint! And get the engineers up on the battle cannon. The damn things jam every three rounds.' Guardsmen were scrambling to their posts, including the tanks iced in at the ends of the line. The Hathrans were an armoured regiment, but the fuel had frozen in the engines of their Leman Russ battle tanks and those that still worked were dug into the ice to be used as fixed gun points.

'Colonel,' said Alaric as he pushed his way through the soldiers now thronging up onto the battlements. 'Where do you need us?'

'Hold the right,' said the colonel. In truth he had no right to give orders to the Grey Knights, attached as they were to the Inquisition, but protocol was less important here than the battle plan. 'If they get explosives between the medical bunker and the valley wall they can blast a breach. That's what you have to stop.' The colonel's features softened for a second. The man underneath the soldier showed through for a moment. 'Good luck, justicar,' he said. Colonel Dal'Tharken, alone among the Hathrans, had some understanding of what the Grey Knights really were and why they had been sent to Sarthis Majoris.

'The Emperor is with us,' replied Alaric, and turned to join his men.

The Grey Knights were already in position. The medical bunker on the extreme right of the line was crowned with battlements like the jawbone of a stone-toothed dragon, but it was still the line's weak point. The enemy would pool here, forced wide by the crossfires of Hathran guns, and sooner or later a cultist would throw a demo charge or a bundle of grenades into just the right place to shatter the ice and blast a gap wide enough for men to pour through. Then the line would be surrounded and everyone defending it would die.

Except, the Grey Knights were there. As far as the Hathrans were concerned, nothing could destroy them as long as there were Space Marines still alive to fight.

'It's not another sacrifice,' said Brother Visical. 'They're holding back.'

'Not for long,' said Alaric. 'The enemy isn't that patient. They'll hit us here and now.'

'Justicar,' said Thane, 'it's the Blood God, isn't it?'

Alaric glanced around at the youngest Grey Knight. Thane was right. The symbols, the chanting, the crazed desperation to die, the blood: the Blood God's hand was on Sarthis Majoris. However, enough Grey Knights had died in battle through thinking that they understood the enemy, and Alaric was not going to be one of them. 'Chaos has infinite faces,' said Alaric. 'We won't know which one it has here until we look it in the eye.'

'Armour,' said Haulvarn, pointing into the darkness at the southern end of the valley. The ice-cold sunlight was picking out ridges of snow and rock amid the shadows, and as Alaric followed Haulvarn's gaze, he could see vehicle hulls, corroded and barnacled like ancient creatures from the sea bed, lumbering through the seething darkness.

'Then this is it,' said Alaric. 'Thane?'

'I am the Hammer,' began Brother Thane, because in Alaric's squad, the newest recruit led the others in their prayers. 'I am the point of His spear, I am the gauntlet about His fist...'

The drone of prayer joined the faint hiss of the wind along the Imperial lines. The Hathrans were praying too, old war songs from their home world of endless plains and violet skies.

In reply, the sky overhead turned purple, then black, and then red. Clouds heavy with blood rolled across, and the valley was bathed in deep rust-red, the colour of dried blood. The ridges of the mountains were picked out in scarlet. A sudden flash of red lightning burst overhead and, for a split second, Alaric took in the scene revealed at the southern end of the valley: tangles of limbs, heaving masses of robed bodies, lumbering contraptions like ancient metal spiders, and a tower carved from frozen blood with an armoured figure leaning from the battlements. Even that briefest glimpse somehow conveyed an infinity of arrogance and evil.

Even the wind changed. It was drumming against the battlements in a terrible rhythm, carrying with it voices speaking a language that burned the ear.

'They're praying,' said Haulvarn.

'It's not a prayer,' replied Dvorn bleakly. 'They're begging. They want their god to be watching when they die.'

The Hathran prayers rose in competition with the heretic drone. Thane's voice rose as the wind battered more blasphemies against the Imperial lines. The wind was hot now, stinking of old blood and sweat, and slowly the darkness was creeping forwards.

The horde was hundreds of thousands strong. Deformed and insane, robed or stripped naked even of their skins, some carried guns or knives, while others wielded the bloodstained bones of their fingers as sharp as blades. Alaric saw a war machine anchoring the horde. Its pitted hull was held up by four mechanical legs, and it waddled through the melting snow like a fat metal spider. Banners held over the horde bore symbols of stylised skulls and parchments of flayed skin carved with bloody prayers. Mutants twice the height of a man were whipped ahead of the horde. Their torsos were pierced by iron spikes on which were mounted the heads and hands of fallen Hathran soldiers, and these walking trophy racks lowed like cattle as the cultists drove them forward.

The blood from thousands of self-inflicted cuts stained the snow and the valley sides before them. It was as if the valley was a bleeding wound, the Chaos army a welling up of gore rising to drown the Hathrans in its madness. The sun of Sarthis Majoris struggled to shine down through the gathering clouds, fighting its own battle in a sky dirtied by the sight of flapping creatures circling overhead.

'Let us be His shield as He is our armour,' Thane continued. 'Let us speak His word as He fuels the fire of our devotion. Let us fight His battles, as He fights the battle at the end of time, and let us join Him there, for duty ends not in death.'

All along the line, the Hathrans were taking up their firing positions. The battle cannon swivelled to point at the centre of the horde, icicles scattering from its massive barrel as it moved.

'Flares up!' yelled an officer, and several bright flares were fired to land on the snow between the line and the advancing army. Thick plumes of green and red smoke curled up. They marked the furthest accurate range of a lasgun, the line beyond which an enemy could not be permitted to advance without having to wade through las-fire as thick as rain.

The battle cannon fired, rocking back in its mounting above the line. The battlements shook. Shards of ice fell from the mountainsides. Even after weeks on the line, Hathran soldiers flinched at the appalling sound. A grey tongue of snow and pulverised rock lashed up in front of the horde, carrying body parts with it, sending out a shockwave through packed bodies as cultists were thrown to the ground by the impact. Yet the horde advanced all the faster, the front ranks breaking into a run.

Alaric took his position behind the battlements. Brother Haulvarn was beside him. If Alaric fell, Haulvarn who would take command of the squad, and Alaric could think of no one he would rather have next to him in a fight.

'They'll get in close,' said Alaric. 'They won't run. We'll have to take them on face to face. Visical, that means plenty of fire.'

'It would be an honour,' said Visical. The pilot flame of his incinerator flickered, ready to ignite the blessed promethium in the weapon's tanks. The fuel had been prayed over that very night, and the Emperor implored to manifest His will through the holy flame. Fire burned the enemy's flesh, but faith burned its soul, and faith was the weapon of choice for a Grey Knight.

The horde reached closer. The stench of it was choking. The tower of frozen blood was visible to all, and it was warping, its front folding down like an opening jaw to form a flight of steps. A man in black armour, lacquered in red, descended from the battlements to the ground. He carried a two-handed sword with a blade as long as he was tall. He was noble and arrogant, his face so pale and angularly handsome that it looked like it had been cut from the ice. The warrior was as tall as a Space Marine and carried with him an air of such cruelty and authority that it took a conscious effort not to kneel before him. The horde parted as he descended, hulking warriors in rust-red plate armour gathering in a cordon around him. The tower was still well beyond lasgun range, but the lord of the Chaos host was obvious, like a beacon in the horde.

'See him?' asked Haulvarn.

'Yes,' said Alaric.

'The Guard can't take him,' said Brother Dvorn. 'It's up to us.'

'For now, Dvorn, we help to hold the line.'

The horde reached the first of the marker flares. At this range Alaric could see their faces, buried under scars or masks of blood, or just so twisted with hatred that there was nothing human left.

'Open fire!' yelled the colonel, and the air in front of the fortifications was streaked with las-fire. The front ranks of cultists were riddled, fat crescents of laser lashing off arms and slicing bodies open. Billows of steam rose up where the snow and ice were vaporised. The sound was immense, like reality itself ripping under the fury. The battle cannon fired again, but its roar was almost lost among the gunfire, the explosion of smoke and gore just a punctuation mark amid the slaughter.

Alaric took aim and fired. The Grey Knights around him did the same. A Space Marine's aim was excellent, and he picked out the individual shapes of heads and torsos among the confusion, and spat explosive bolts into them. Where the bolts detonated, puffs of blood and bone showered. Alaric fired in bursts, picking out a cultist and blasting him apart. The Grey Knights chewed a hole into the end of the Chaos line like a bloody bite mark, and within moments cultists were clambering over the ruined bodies of their dead.

However, the front ranks were just weak-willed fodder for the guns. The true power of the army followed them, ensuring the Hathrans used up ammunition and time killing the scum herded into the firing line.

The tide drew closer. The rhythm became frantic, trigger fingers spasming as the Hathrans sprayed rapid fire into the mass of men swarming towards them. A war machine rose through the fire, its guns opening up even as las-fire rained off it in showers of sparks.

'Visical! They're in range!' shouted Alaric, relying on the squad's vox-link to carry his voice over the din.

Brother Visical leaned between the battlements, his incinerator aimed down the steep slope of the fortifications.

The horde swarmed faster, chewed up and riddled with las-burns and bolter fire, but still numbering countless thousands. Their hands and feet were bloody from tearing on the ice. Pale, frost-bitten limbs reached from tattered red robes as they scrabbled to get a purchase on the fortification wall. The skinless ones leapt over the cultists in front, agile as insects.

Alaric looked into the eyes of one of them. They were rolled back and blank. There was nothing human left there.

All along the Imperial line, with a million voices raised in a scream, the Blood God's army hit the wall.

THREE

'FOR THE EMPEROR!' yelled young Brother Thane as he sliced a screaming robed killer in two with his halberd. The cultist's twin blades clattered to the rockcrete of the fortification as Thane kicked out and knocked another from the parapet. Autogun fire spanged off the Grey Knight's armour as he swept the battlement clear, the arc of his halberd blade taking off a hand, and then a head.

Another blast of sacred flame washed the battlements clear. A once-human shape, now hunchbacked and many-armed, reared up and screamed, cloaked in flame. It collapsed, skin and muscles boiling away.

'The dead,' said Brother Haulvarn. 'They're climbing their dead.'

Haulvarn was right, The Grey Knights' guns and Visical's incinerator had killed so many, so quickly, that cultists were piled up at the bottom of the wall, high enough for the killers behind them to clamber up. They were on the wall now, fighting each other to die by the Grey Knights' hands.

Along the walls, huge mutants had clambered up onto the battlements and were fighting with the Hathrans. Alaric saw one Guardsman thrown from the wall by a deformed giant, and another having his brains dashed out by a foul creature with weeping skin and giant crab claws. A mutant fell from the wall, chest flaming from las-fire, and crushed the cultists below him. The battle cannon fired again, almost point-blank, throwing Hathrans from their feet, and showering them with earth and body parts, but it was not enough. Cultists were making it onto the walls to lay into the Hathrans with guns and blades.

Haulvarn's halberd took the arm off a feral warrior with woad painted skin, before he ducked back below the battlements to shelter from the fire of the closest war machine.

'Too many?' he asked.

'Too many,' agreed Alaric.

'Then it's ours to win.'

Alaric looked around at his oldest comrade. 'The line cannot hold, not against this. Be ready to take command.'

'Why?'

'Because I might not come back.'

'Justicar, your brothers need–'

'My brothers need what the Emperor needs. They need victory. Standing back and letting the enemy kill us will not win us that victory. It is up to us, which means it is up to me. That is a justicar's responsibility. Can I count on you?'

'Of course, justicar, always.'

'Then we need to get to the centre of the walls. Open up a path for me through this rabble.'

Haulvarn paused, just for half a second. He stood to his full superhuman height, holding his halberd up so the squad could see. 'Brothers!' he yelled above the din of battle. 'Forward! Down the line!'

Visical was first up, spraying the blessed flame along the battlements stretching westwards. Cultists screamed in the fire. Thane cut them down with his sword, his power armour protecting him as he strode through the burning fuel. They loomed from every side through the fire and smoke, and each scarred face was met by a sword or halberd crackling with the harnessed power of a Grey Knight's mind. Alaric felt bones fracturing under his halberd, and saw wet ruins opened up in enemy torsos from his storm bolter.

He barely had to think. He was a Space Marine, a Grey Knight, created almost whole to be a killing machine. Every fatal movement was hardwired into him, as if a machine-spirit guided him, as if the Emperor himself was controlling his actions.

However, a Space Marine was not a machine. He was driven by passions that a normal man could not understand. The obscenity leading this horde had to be destroyed. That was the thought that drove Alaric on.

Thane wrestled a giant mutant as they went, something so foully warped there was barely any human left in it at all. A leathery winged creature swooped down to snatch Alaric off the wall. Alaric snatched it instead, crushing its throat in his fist while he tore its wings off and threw it into the fire still slathered over the battlements behind him.

'Here!' shouted Alaric. 'Break through them!'

Hathrans were dying all around. The Chaos horde had forced the walls in a dozen places, and knots of combat were erupting everywhere. An explosion tore a massive chunk out of the battlements on the left of the line, and the horde surged forwards, a war machine walking relentlessly over the slope of the rubble, impaling Guardsmen on its mechanical talons.

And there were daemons. They were red-skinned and hideous, leaping amid the carnage, wielding swords of black iron that glowed and smouldered.

'Damn you!' shouted a voice that Alaric recognised as that of Colonel Dal'Tharken. 'Hold to your post, Grey Knights! The flank will fall! Get back to your post!' Alaric caught sight of the colonel, covered in burning daemon's blood, wielding his sword and plasma pistol, surrounded by the bodies of friend and foe.

He was a tough and unrelenting servant of the Emperor. The Imperium would miss him. Alaric ignored his words and pressed on.

The champion of Chaos was the key. Chaos adored its champions as much as it despised everything else. It granted particularly foul-hearted men and women with the power to command their forces, and the authority to speak with their gods' own voices. The Imperial line could not hold the enemy. It would barely make a dent in the vast force that had landed to claim Sarthis Majoris. It had, however, achieved a goal that, though the Guardsmen did not know it, was every bit as valuable to the Imperium.

It had brought Alaric and his Grey Knights face to face with the champion who represented the dark gods on this world.

'USE THE THIRTEENTH Hand,' said Duke Venalitor. His voice was loaded with disdain, for the Thirteenth Hand were the lowest dregs of his army.

One of Venalitor's heralds, black armour welded to its weeping skin, blew a long note from its war horn. The Thirteenth Hand, hunched subhuman creatures dressed in rags, hurried forward for the honour of dying at the wall.

The battle was going as planned. If any truly human emotion could be ascribed to Duke Venalitor, it could be said that he was happy with it. By the time the regiments of proper soldiers reached the front, the battle would be over and the refinery cities of Sarthis Majoris would be Venalitor's.

A messenger descended on tattered wings of bloody skin.

'My lord,' it slurred, 'their flank has fallen. The defenders have abandoned their posts.'

'Cowards,' sneered Venalitor. 'Their skulls are not fit for the Brass Throne.'

'They were from the corpse-emperor's legions,' said the messenger.

'Astartes?' Venalitor's perfect, pale brow furrowed. 'They would not run.'

The pit of Venalitor's mind dredged up memories from a time when he had been a man. It was a weak and shameful part of his existence, before the Blood God had found him. That man recalled that Space Marines were the guardians of the Imperium, the last line against all horrors, soldiers who would never flee, never, not even with Venalitor himself bearing down on them.

'Close order!' yelled Venalitor. His sword was in his hand, its huge blade shining in the red-tinged dawn. 'Now! Shields up! Give no quarter!'

He saw them among the carnage, silver-armoured figures picked out in scarlet flame. They had not abandoned the right of the line out of fear. They had left their posts to effect the only victory they could gain from Sarthis Majoris.

They thought they were going to kill him.

Duke Venalitor laughed. They had absolutely no idea what the Blood God had made from that man. He had looked upon the throne of flaming brass and knelt at the foot of the skull mountain. He had tasted the blood of Khorne Himself. No Space Marine was fit to die beneath his blade, which was a shame, because they would die very soon.

Venalitor saw one of the Space Marines run at the edge of the wall, behead a cultist without breaking stride, and leap off the wall heading directly for Venalitor.

Venalitor felt every muscle in his warp-blessed body tense, and hoped that this one would at least give him a worthwhile fight.

THE BATTLEFIELD WHIRLED around Alaric as he fell. He could hear the voices of his battle-brothers, and feel the heat rippling off the chains of bolter fire that followed him down.

He hit hard enough to crush a cultist beneath him. Alaric plunged a foot down through the mess to get his footing, and the stinking, subhuman creatures were on him. Filthy nails raked at his armour, trying to prise between his armour plates or drive claws into his eyes.

Alaric swept his halberd around in a brutal arc. He forged forwards, every sweep of his halberd battering back the deformed bodies pressing in on every side. A huge mutant reared up over him carrying a rock in its paws to crush him. A stream of bolter fire battered its head into pulp and it collapsed. Alaric glanced back to see Haulvarn aiming, the muzzle of his storm bolter still flaming.

The cultists gave way before him. Alaric kicked the last one aside. In front of him, now, stood a warrior in black armour as tall as Alaric himself, a wall of steel. Its shield bore the symbol of an eight-pointed star and its spear was tipped with a huge sharpened fang. The warrior lunged, but Alaric turned its spear away, spun around and shattered its shield with the butt of his halberd. He squared his feet and drove the blade of the halberd into the warrior's face, dropping the tip at the last moment so it plunged into the hollow between neck and chest.

Hot blood sprayed, and the warrior fell to its knees. There were other warriors on either side, forming a circle around Alaric's target.

Alaric half-stumbled into the circle. This was his only chance. This planet would not get another shot at survival. If the Chaos horde continued to march under its leader, Sarthis Majoris would fall.

The gods had seen fit to send to Sarthis Majoris a champion of such presence that Alaric felt it forcing him back. His armour was impossibly intricate, covered in images of heaps of skulls around a burning throne. The champion's face was the very image of arrogance, pale and perfect, with eyes like black diamonds.

'Leave us,' said the champion. The armoured warriors around him took a step back to leave an open duelling ground around Alaric and the champion.

Alaric was in a low guard, eyes fixed on the champion's blade.

'A Grey Knight,' said the champion with a smile. 'Khorne's gaze is upon us. I shall give thanks to the warp that the corpse-emperor sent one of his very own daemon hunters to die beneath my blade.'

'Let me help you return the favour, then,' said Alaric, his words sounding like those of a stranger, 'for you will be looking upon your god soon enough.'

The champion smiled. His teeth were ebony black fangs. He lunged forward, and his sword was like chained lightning striking down at Alaric.

Alaric turned the sword aside and suddenly the duel was on. The champion didn't just want blood. Blood alone was enough for the scum who threw themselves at the walls, but not for their leader. He wanted to prove his superiority. It was why he existed. It was in proving his superiority that the champion offered up his prowess to Khorne the Blood God.

It was also Alaric's only chance of survival. If the champion wanted a duel, then that was what Alaric would give him.

Alaric's halberd spun around faster than any normal man could move, its head carving down at the champion. In response the champion's intricate armour opened up like a bloody flower and tendrils of gore reached out to snare Alaric and drag him down. Alaric cut through them and dived clear as the champion's sword sliced down through the frozen earth beside him. More tendrils snaked around Alaric's arms and lifted him up in the air. Alaric ripped one arm free and aimed his storm bolter down at the champion, fixing his aim on the champion's face, still impassive with the certainty of victory.

The champion threw him down. Alaric hit as hard as a comet, cultist's bodies splintering under him, and then the rock-hard earth shattered. He planted a hand on the ground and forced himself up from the mess of bodies, his other hand groping for his halberd.

He forced the clouds from his eyes. He was battered but alive. It took a lot to fell a Grey Knight. As long as there was life in him and a weapon in his hand, victory was in his sights.

The corpses were moving. The one closest to Alaric burst open like a seed pod, crimson blood flooding out. More bodies were erupting all around him and beneath him, sinking him in a swamp of gore.

The champion laughed. The blood flowed up from the bodies, forming shapes like blocks of melting crimson ice. The champion stepped up onto them as they created a bleeding stairway up into the air. He stooped to pick Alaric up by the collar of his armour and held him up like a scolded animal, like a sacrifice. The sword in his other hand was ready to slice Alaric open and let his innards spill out onto the battlefield in a sacrifice to Khorne.

Alaric kicked out and caught the champion on the side of the face. The champion reeled, and Alaric grabbed the wrist at his throat, wrenching it around so that the champion let go. Alaric landed on the platform of blood that had formed below them, and was still rising up over the valley. Below him, he caught sight of the dark mass of cultists flowing around the right end of the line, which the Grey Knights had abandoned. The line was collapsing, the Hathrans surrounded and besieged. Alaric had sacrificed them for this chance at victory. He owed them the champion's death as surely as he owed it to the Emperor.

Alaric rolled to his feet, halberd still in hand. The champion wiped a smear of blood from the cut Alaric had opened on his face, and confronted him.

'Duke Venalitor avenges his insults,' spat the champion.

'A Grey Knight avenges his Imperium,' said Alaric.

The sword and the halberd flashed. High above the battlefield on a platform of animated blood, Duke Venalitor and Justicar Alaric fought a duel so rapid and intense that the few eyes that looked up from the battlements below could not make any sense of the blur of strikes and parries. Tentacles of blood lashed around Alaric's ankle and threw him to the bloody floor. Alaric's leg kicked out and knocked Venalitor reeling towards the edge. Gashes and scars opened up in Alaric's armour, some of them scored deep enough to draw blood. Alaric's halberd blade rang off Venalitor's armour as the champion of Chaos turned it aside at the last moment time and again.

Alaric lunged for Venalitor's heart. Venalitor grabbed the haft of Alaric's halberd with one hand, dragged Alaric forwards and brought an elbow down on the back of Alaric's head hard enough to send the world black for a moment. When Alaric forced vision back into his eyes he was being held in the air over Venalitor's head.

Alaric groped down trying to force a finger into the swordsman's eyes. His hand passed through writhing wetness, a nest of squirming bloody worms that opened up in place of Venalitor's face. Somehow it retained enough features to smile as it threw Alaric down.

Alaric plummeted down towards the frozen ground behind the line. He realised a split second before he landed that below him was not solid earth, but the pile of frozen Hathran dead.

Weeks' worth of casualties shattered beneath him. His armoured bulk blasted a crater in the red-black ice.

Pain slammed up through his body. His head cracked against the rock-hard chunk of a soldier's frozen corpse. The world of Sarthis Majoris seemed very far away. The voices he heard were from a different planet entirely, a different plane, which meant that he had sunk down through the earth into one of the hells to which the Imperial Creed maintained every sinner went.

Reality was slipping away. The pain of his battered body, so familiar to a Space Marine, was ebbing away, and he wished it would return to prove he was alive. The world, to his eyes, was dim and distant. The dawn was bleeding away to leave the valley dark. Something inside Alaric reminded him that he was not supposed to simply die like this, that there was something else he had to achieve, but it slipped away even as his mind reached to grasp it.

He assumed that the cry of despair was the last sound he heard. It was raised from a hundred throats at once and it was so deep that it cut through the gunfire and the screams of the battle.

It was the sound of Hathran. It was a funeral song. Alaric had heard it sung over the same pile of dead in which he was lying.

They were singing their own funeral dirge. The Hathrans knew they were going to die. They knew it because they had seen a Space Marine, the Emperor's warrior, defeated and thrown down from the heavens by the champion of the Blood God.

'No,' gasped Alaric, 'not here. Not now.'

Sarthis Majoris swam back into focus. Alaric was lying on his face in a pile of shattered, frozen corpses. He looked around for his halberd and saw that it had landed point-down, impaled in the earth a short crawl away. Alaric got to his knees. He would retrieve his weapon and fight on, because that was the only way to victory, however slim the chance might be.

A weight slammed down on his back, forcing him back onto his face. He fought to turn over, and for a moment the pressure was lifted. Alaric rolled onto his back and the foot came back down on him.

Duke Venalitor had one foot on Alaric's chest like a hunter standing over his prey. The magnitude of his arrogance was such that even the corpses recoiled at it, the blood in them heating up and melting at Venalitor's presence. Fingers of blood reached up from the corpses to lick at the boots of Venalitor's armour like the tongues of sycophants. Venalitor commanded all blood, even that of his enemies, such was the esteem in which the Blood God held him.

'My lord Khorne has a use for you,' said Venalitor with a smile. He gestured at the Hathrans dying on the walls behind him. 'Most of them are only good for fodder. Mankind provides little more than distractions for me now. However, there is much more you can do for the Blood God than merely die, Grey Knight.'

Venalitor held out a hand, and Alaric felt the blood seeping from the cracks in his armour. He kicked out, trying to throw Venalitor off him, but his strength was gone. Ribbons of blood spiralled out of him and his vision began to grey out.

As Duke Venalitor drew Alaric's lifeblood out of him chill pain filled him up in its place. Darkness fell all around him, and Alaric was not too proud to scream.

FOUR

Alaric sat for a long time in the Cloister of Sorrows before Chaplain Durendin approached.

'Justicar,' said Durendin. 'The Grand Masters have spoken with me of Chaeroneia. Your faith was sorely tested.'

'It was,' Alaric said. He was sitting on the drum of a collapsed column, typical of the cloister's fallen grandeur.

'The day is fine,' said Durendin, indicating the magnificent sky of Titan, the vast ringed disc of Saturn hovering over the void. 'I shall sit with you a while, if I may.'

The Cloister of Sorrows was open to Titan's sky, its atmosphere contained within invisible electromagnetic fields, and for Alaric to sit there among its age-worn tableaux was to allow the great eye of the galaxy to look down on him. The Emperor was a part of that gaze, always examining the soul of every one of His servants. Alaric felt naked and raw beneath it.

'I feel that there is more on my mind,' said Alaric, 'than Chaeroneia.'

'And that is why you have come here,' replied Durendin simply, 'to be alone with your thoughts, away from the war gear rites and battle songs, and if a Chaplain were to happen along with whom you could share your thoughts, then so be it.'

Alaric smiled. 'You are very perceptive, Chaplain.'

'It is merely the Emperor's way of using me,' replied Durendin. To be a Space Marine required an extraordinary man, but to be a Chaplain required more. A Chaplain of the Grey Knights was a rare specimen indeed, and the Chapter had precious few like him. He had to minister to the spiritual needs of soldiers destined to fight the most horrible of foes. The men of his flock had looked upon the warp and heard the whispers of daemons, and yet, thanks to him and those who had preceded him, not one Grey Knight had ever become corrupted by the enemy.

'Chaeroneia is a part of it, certainly, but I was troubled before that, ever since Ligeia.'

Inquisitor Ligeia was the bravest person Alaric had ever met. The sunburst on his personal heraldry was in memory of her. She had lost her mind to the machinations of the daemon prince Ghargatuloth, but enough of her had remained pure to give Alaric the knowledge he had needed to defeat the daemon. She had been executed by the Ordo Malleus for her madness.

'Men and women like Inquisitor Ligeia will always die,' said Durendin. 'That is the way it was even before the Great Crusade, and it will continue to be so long after both of us are gone. What matters is that we know those sacrifices work towards the goal of safeguarding the human race. Do you believe she died in vain?'

'No, Chaplain, far from it.'

'Then this galaxy seems too cruel for you?'

'If I could not stomach the things I must see then you know full well I would not have been selected for training at all,' said Alaric, perhaps a little too harshly. 'I just feel there is… there is so much for us to do, and I do not mean the battle. I have always accepted that the battle will not end, but there is much more to our fight than meeting the daemon with swords and guns. I have glimpsed the… the realities behind it all. The words of the Castigator come into my mind unbidden. Ghargatuloth wove space and time to create the events that summoned him back, and we were a part of it. I will fight to the end of my days, for sure, but the enemy is not just bodies to be put into the ground. It is a concept, perhaps it is even a part of us. I wish I could understand it, but I know no one can ever understand Chaos without becoming corrupt.'

'So, you do not believe our fight is futile?'

'No, Chaplain. How could I, when I have seen the results of the daemon's depravity? But our fight is only half the battle, and I wonder if the other half can ever be won.'

Durendin looked down at his gauntleted hands. He was no stranger to the battlefield, and his Terminator armour, ornate gunmetal trimmed in a Chaplain's black, was not just for show. 'These hands,' he said, 'have fought that same fight for longer than you have been alive, Justicar, and not for one moment have I ever believed it was anything but the true and righteous purpose of any human being. What you say is true, however. The daemon is but one manifestation of the enemy and its violence is but one weapon of the warp. The Inquisition battles the plans of Chaos just as we battle its soldiers. Do you not agree?'

'How many inquisitors have we lost?' replied Alaric. 'Though we should not speak of it, Valinov was far from the only rogue in the Holy Orders, and he hid from us for so long. How many other heretics are wearing the Inquisitorial seal? How many in Encaladus Fortress? How many directing the Grey Knights? I know it is our place to leave the thinking to the inquisitors, but how can we trust them if they delve so deeply into the corruption?'

Durendin sighed. He was an old man and sometimes, as then, Alaric had seen a reflection of those years in him. 'I have led Grey Knights through every trial of the mind that Chaos can inflict upon them. You are not the first to doubt, Alaric, and certainly not the first to glimpse the futility in the Inquisition's task.'

'It is not futile,' said Alaric, 'but I feel I am failing if I do not do more. The daemon is a symptom, not the disease. I want to be a part of the cure.'

'I had these thoughts, myself,' continued Durendin. 'I spoke with my battle-brothers and the Grand Masters, and with the most knowledgeable inquisitors. None of them had the answer. In the end, I found the answer myself.'

'And what was it?'

'You will find it yourself. You are going to the Eye of Terror, I hear.'

'Yes, when my squad is reinforced.'

'Good. Then that is your answer. The Enemy's atrocities at the Eye know no bounds, and only men like us can stop him. Think about it. In your moment of doubt, the Emperor has sent you to the bloodiest battlefields of the Imperium. That is no coincidence. Throw yourself into those battles. See the daemon and butcher him. See the forces of Chaos broken and fleeing. Take those victories and immerse yourself in them. Let victory blot out everything else. Glory in it. Then the doubt will be gone.'

'That is what worked for you?'

'It did, Justicar. The enemy has made a grave mistake in bringing the fight to us. Men like you will punish that mistake. This I promise you, Alaric. You will become whole at the Eye of Terror.'

'Thank you, Chaplain,' said Alaric. 'I must see to my squad. I have two new men and we must pray together before we go.'

'That is good,' replied Durendin. 'Your men's spirits need counsel before they witness the Eye.' The Chaplain looked up at Saturn, deep blue and streaked with storms. Below the planet was Titan's skyline, an irregular toothed band of darkness. The whole of Titan had been turned into an ornate fortress, the moon's surface carved deep with canyons and vaults, and many parts of it such as the Cloister of Sorrows had become ruined and near-forgotten. 'I shall think here for a while. Saturn will set in an hour or so. It helps one think.'

'Then I shall speak with you soon, Chaplain.'

'Until then, justicar.'

Alaric stood up to leave. The way down through the half-ruined fortress beneath the cloister was long, and it would give him plenty of time to consider Durendin's counsel.

'And justicar?' said Durendin.

'Yes?'

'You are not dead.'

'That is good to know.'

'Although it may be an idea to wake up soon.'

'This isn't how this conversation ended.'

Durendin smiled. 'No, it is not, but then, I am not really here. I am probably elsewhere at the Eye. Perhaps I am even dead. What matters is that you are alive, and you can still do something about the situation in which you find yourself.'

'Then, what next?' asked Alaric.

'I cannot answer that, Alaric. I am not even here, after all. However, I think it is very likely that your situation is not a good one.'

The Cloister of Sorrows exploded in pain.

ALARIC SCREAMED.

The pain was howling from one of his shoulders. He was hanging from his wrists, which were chained above him. There was nothing else to bear his weight, and one of his shoulders had come out of its socket.

Alaric fought back the pain. He had been vulnerable for a moment and the pain had got to him, as it would to a man without the mental conditioning of a Grey Knight. His armour would normally be dispensing painkillers into his bloodstream, but he did not have his armour. He was naked. His war gear had been stripped from him.

As he fought back the pain, he began to hear again. A deep noise like an angry ocean boiled beneath him, and he could hear the clanking of vast machinery, mixed in with sobs and screams from broken throats. The smell hit him: blood and smoke, sweat and machine oil. His mouth tasted as if it was full of iron. He could not see, but that was a problem he would deal with in due time.

He forced his feet up, pulling up on his screaming shoulder. Slowly, he pulled himself up so that his body was almost upside-down. His feet found the roof of the cage he was in. He pushed down with everything he had, and he heard the bars buckling.

The chain holding his hands came loose from the ceiling of the cage and Alaric crashed down onto the cage floor. He lay there for a few moments, catching his breath, gingerly testing the tendons of his shoulder. It was hurt, but it was nothing permanent. A Space Marine healed quickly. He lay on his side and let the joint slide back into place. The gunshot of pain that accompanied it was profound, but there was something triumphant in the fact that he could feel at all.

Alaric reached up and found a blindfold tied around his face. He pulled it away and blinked a couple of times as his augmented eyes reacted to the sudden light.

His cage was one of several hundred suspended from a great iron column down which poured dozens of waterfalls of blood. These fed the sea of blood below him, in which writhed thousands of bodies, slick with gore. It was impossible to tell if they were in agony, or in some ecstasy of worship. Daemons waded among them, hulking things with red-black skin, lashing the bleeding bodies with their whips. Corpses and parts of corpses bobbed everywhere, fished out and carried away by scuttling alien creatures with lopsided, tumoured forms.

Slowly, the column rotated on gears that ground like thunder. The other cages had their own occupants: human prisoners, naked and weeping, old corpses, half-glimpsed freaks either alien or mutated, all of them suspended above the titanic blood cauldron. Alaric could hear droning alien prayers, pleading with the Emperor, and the ragged breaths of dying men. Tears and blood fell in a thin drizzle.

Walls of black stone rose around the column and the cauldron. Alaric looked harder and saw that it was not stone at all but flesh, rotted black. High above, the cliff edge was festooned with barrel-sized cages, each holding a body in an advanced state of decay. Flocks of flying creatures, like oversized crows, but with ribbons of flayed skin instead of feathers, feasted on them. The decaying cliffs were riddled with tunnels and caves, and the beetle-like alien creatures scurried through them, chewing at the flesh with insect-like mandibles. The sky above was indigo, almost black, shot through with red, as if the sky itself was bleeding.

He was in hell. Alaric had died at the hands of Duke Venalitor and woken up in hell. He had failed. Everything he had ever done, ever thought or said, and everything he might ever have done had he lived, was meaningless. He had failed as completely as it was possible to fail.

Alaric slumped down onto the floor of his cage. He had never felt such despair. It was made complete by the fact that if he was already dead. He could not die again, and so it would never end.

However, Durendin had told him he was not dead: Durendin, a Chaplain of the Grey Knights, a man he could surely trust completely.

Alaric looked up. Through the bars he could see the cage above. Inside it was a huge humanoid form, one that Alaric recognised. The huge size and surgical scars matched Alaric's own.

'Haulvarn!' called Alaric. 'Brother Haulvarn, can you hear me? Do we yet live?'

Haulvarn did not answer. He was presumably unconscious, or dead, and like Alaric had been stripped of his war gear. Alaric tried to force the bars of his cage apart, and then to rock it from side to side in the hope of grabbing the gnarled metal of the column and climbing up to Haulvarn, but the cage was too strong and suspended too far out.

'Haulvarn! Brother, speak to me!' shouted Alaric.

As if in response, Alaric's cage fell.

Alaric kicked out in desperation as the cage plummeted towards the blood cauldron. He was slammed against the side of the cage as it hit the surface of the blood. Blood closed in around him, and hands reached in, the skin sloughing off them. Alaric kicked at the hands of the revellers, but there were too many of them. The sound of them was horrible, blasphemous prayers spilling from bloodied lips in a hundred different tongues.

Something roared, and a whip cracked. A daemon threw the worshippers aside and stood over Alaric, leering. Alaric recognised its kind from countless battlefields. It was a foot soldier of Khorne, a 'bloodletter' in the jargon of the Inquisition. Alaric remembered they carried two-handed swords as weapons of choice, but this one's whip was just as cruel.

The daemon recoiled as soon as the bodies were clear of the cage. The mere presence of a Grey Knight was anathema to the daemon. Even without the pentagrammic wards built into his armour, the psychic shield around Alaric's mind pushed back against the daemon's presence with enough violence to make its skin smoulder. The bloodletter snarled and lashed at the revellers around it, slicing off a hand here, a leg there, in its rage. Then it grabbed the bars of the cage with one hand and dragged it through the gore towards the chasm wall.

The daemon hauled the cage out of the blood and into a cave opening. The smell was appalling, putrescence so heavy in the air that Alaric could see it trickling down the walls in foul condensation. Dark, twisted creatures scuttled towards him. These were not daemons, but some alien species, and their skin carried the brands and manacle scars of a slave race.

The aliens dragged Alaric through the stinking tunnels into a cavern that glowed with a close red heat. It was a forge, where human and alien slaves pulled glowing weapons from vats of molten metal. Other slaves were chained to anvils, their spines twisted by years of servitude, where they beat an edge into the swords and spear tips. The din was appalling.

Alaric saw Haulvarn's cage being dragged through another opening, a gaggle of aliens following it. Haulvarn had awoken and was raging inside, trying to kick his way out of the cage.

'Haulvarn!' shouted Alaric over the ringing of the anvils. 'We are not dead! We are not dead!'

A crowd of alien slaves pressed around Alaric's cage as he was dragged towards one of the anvils. They were misshapen, asymmetrical creatures with a dozen eyes each, arranged without pattern around their faces, and complex mandibles that dribbled slime as they gibbered to each other in their language. A bolt was drawn back somewhere and the top of the cage swung open.

Alaric tried to force his way out, but shock prods were jabbed down at him. His own strength was turned back on him as he spasmed. A single shock prod with a semicircular head was pressed down against his torso, and he was pinned in place. His muscles were paralysed, save for involuntary convulsions, and though he fought against it with everything he had left he couldn't break free. At full strength, he would have thrown the aliens out of his way, grabbed a weapon fresh from the anvil and killed everything he saw, but he was wounded and exhausted. He did not give in, he could not, but in the back of his mind a voice told him that it was futile.

One of the aliens, larger and darker-skinned than the rest, and evidently in charge, reached a pair of tongs into the closest forge. It withdrew a circle of glowing metal that was hinged on one side so it hung open. It was a collar.

The alien leaned over Alaric. Its caustic spittle dribbled onto his chest.

'Rejoice,' said the alien forge master, its Imperial Gothic thick and slurred through its mandibles, 'for this shall make you holy.'

The alien plunged the collar down onto Alaric's throat. It snickered shut around the back of his neck. His skin hissed as it cooked under the hot metal.

Alaric could struggle no more. His mind felt as if it was suddenly frozen.

He realised what had been done to him.

He knew, for perhaps the first time, what fear was.

THE HUMAN SPECIES was evolving.

This was a truth the Inquisition went to great pains to suppress, but it could not be denied by the inquisitors themselves. Some even held the heretical belief that the Emperor planned to shepherd this evolution onwards and help the human race achieve its potential. The emergence of psychic humans created one of the critical tasks of the Inquisition: the identification, imprisonment and liquidation of emerging psykers. Every planetary governor was under pain of death to hand over all the psykers collected by his forces, whenever the Inquisition and its Black Ships came calling. What happened to the great majority of psykers herded into those Black Ships, only those sworn to secrecy knew for sure.

A few of the psykers, perhaps one in ten or less, were strong and adaptable enough to be properly trained. An untrained psyker was a dangerous thing, an unguarded mind through which all manner of horrors could gain entry to the worlds of the Imperium. However, a properly trained psyker could guard his mind against such threats, and sometimes even make his mind far stronger than those of his fellow men.

It was an irony, often a cruel one, that such trained psykers were essential to the functioning of the Imperium. They were the astropaths whose arcane long-range telepathy made interstellar communications possible, the soothsayers whose skill with the Emperor's Tarot enabled them to advise on the vagaries of the future. Many Imperial citizens viewed even these sanctioned psykers with fear. Yet, in spite of the fear that followed the psyker everywhere, without him the Imperium could not function.

To most citizens a psyker was a witch, a rogue prowling the shadows of the Imperium's worlds to corrupt Emperor-fearing minds or bring forth foul things from the warp. A child foolish enough to display an unusual talent for magic tricks could expect his friends or family to turn him over to the local clergy. Wise women and fortune-tellers were burned at the stake on backwater worlds where Imperial servants rarely visited. Spaceship crews swapped tall tales of night-skinned humans who could rip a man's mind out of his skull, shapechangers, fire-breathers and stranger things besides. Once, long ago, a time before he could remember anything at all, Alaric had been one of those witches.

Alaric was a psyker. All Grey Knights were. While most Space Marine Chapters made use of some psykers, only the Grey Knights required psychic potential from all their recruits. It was what made the Grey Knights capable of fighting the daemon, for a daemon's most potent weapons threatened the soul itself.

Daemons brought with them corruption, and fighting them exposed a Grey Knight to that corruption. They were trained to resist it, taught prayers of will-power so potent that they drove some recruits mad. Their armour was impregnated with sigils against the powers of the warp, the same symbols tattooed on their skins so that their bodies were shielded against corruption, but the most powerful defence was a Grey Knight's psychic shield. Alaric had been taught in the very earliest stages of his training to imprison his soul in a cage of faith and contempt where no daemon could reach it.

It was the only weapon a daemon truly feared: an incorruptible mind, anathema to the warp. The mere existence of the Grey Knights was a victory of sorts against Chaos.

The collar fixed around Alaric's neck was a dead, heavy thing that weighed down Alaric's soul. It was an artefact of Khorne, the Blood God. The Blood God despised sorcery, and it despised the righteous, holy mind of a Grey Knight.

The Collar of Khorne suppressed psychic abilities. Alaric's shield was gone. He was still a Grey Knight, he had still trained his mind and his body beyond a normal man's tolerances against corruption and possession, but without that psychic shield, he was ultimately defenceless.

FIVE

It was a long time before Alaric could feel anything. He was somewhere infernally hot.

Alaric was standing, and he was chained to the wall. The chamber was lit by ruddy furnaces taking up the opposite wall. Unfinished swords and sections of armour were heaped up either side of a well-scored anvil.

'You're not supposed to wake for a good while,' said a voice behind Alaric.

Alaric tried to turn, but he was chained in place. He was dimly aware that he was still in the forge where his collar had been attached, and the iron weight of it around his neck seemed to drag him down towards the floor.

'Where is my battle-brother?' asked Alaric through split and bloody lips.

'I heard there were two of you,' said the voice. It was deep and gravelly, from a throat scorched by years amid the forges. 'He's somewhere in this hole, probably having the collar fixed. They had you down as witches as soon as they brought you in. Not many get the collar, you know. It's quite an honour.'

The speaker walked to the anvil, his back to Alaric. He was a massive man with brawny shoulders and dark skin that gleamed like bronze. Tools hung from his waist. He bent over the anvil and picked up a sword, a magnificent blade, but rough and half-finished. 'I have been down here a long time,' he continued, 'heard a lot of things, but it has been a long time since an Astartes graced this world. A long time indeed.'

'Who are you?'

The speaker did not look round. 'A smith by trade. Too useful a man to kill. I guess I should thank the Emperor for that. If there's one thing this planet needs, Astartes, it's blades, good blades, and lots of them. So this is where I shall stay until I die, and probably well beyond, making their blades. Perhaps you'll end up with one of mine. Believe me, you'll know it. There are no blades like mine on this world.'

'Where am I to be taken? What will happen to me?'

The smith still did not turn to face Alaric. The muscles on his back snaked beneath his dark skin as he laid the sword on the anvil and took up a hammer. 'Not for me to say, Astartes. Not for me to say. If I had anything worthwhile to my name, though, I'd wager it on you fighting for your life sooner rather than later. So, I'll make you a deal.'

Alaric laughed, and it sounded as bitter as the taste of blood in his mouth. 'A deal, of course.'

'Ah, hear me out, Astartes, unless you have somewhere better to be.'

Involuntarily, Alaric fought against his chains.

'I'll make you a suit of armour,' said the smith, 'the best you've ever held.'

'I have armour.'

'Not any more, and you've never had armour such as I can craft. Fits like a steel skin. Bends like silk. Toughened by fires as fierce as the heart of a star, strong enough to turn Khorne's own axe aside. How does that sound? Tempting?'

'But it will not be for free. I know your kind. Any promise from the corrupted is as good as a betrayal.'

'Oh no, you do not understand. In return, I ask that you seek something out for me. I dare say you will have more luck finding it out in the world than I will down here.'

'End this,' said Alaric. 'No servant of the Emperor would bargain with one such as you.'

'Such as me? And what am I?' The smith turned just enough for Alaric to see his face in profile. His face was as beaten as one of his blades, his nose broken many times, his eyes almost hidden in scar tissue. 'Find the Hammer, Astartes: the Hammer of Daemons. They say it lies somewhere on this world, and with it a hero will rise up and topple the lords of the Blood God. What would be dearer to a slave like me than to see that?'

'Lies.'

'The Hammer of Daemons is very real. Nothing more is known of it, but it most definitely lies somewhere on this planet. If I didn't know better I might even say that it is right before me, chained to a wall in my forge. For you are the Hammer. Is that not so, Grey Knight?'

The weight of the collar was too much for Alaric to bear. His head bowed as it dragged him down. Black spots flickered before the forge fires, and he smelled burning iron and bolter smoke.

He drifted back out of consciousness, lulled into oblivion by the ringing of the smith's hammer on the anvil.

KARNIKHAL!

That self-devouring beast! That tumour city, that cancerous glory! A great parasite oozed from the black of the earth!

Some say Karnikhal plummeted to Drakaasi from some distant star, and grew mindless and vast over the aeons. Others claim it as some native thing, some fungus or parasite, mutated to immense dimensions by the ever-present power of Chaos. What fools are they, to seek logic in its form! The caverns of its entrails, the blood rivers oozing from its wounds, the groaning of its eternal pain, these are a face of Chaos, a face of Khorne!

The city built across Karnikhal is a parasite upon a parasite, shanties crammed between the fatty folds of its back, spires tumbling at the whim of the beast, temples and slaughterhouses heaving with its titanic breath. All this at the whim of the mindless thing, the idiot monstrosity, the city monster that is Karnikhal!

– *'Mind Journeys of a Heretic Saint,' by Inquisitor Helmandar Oswain
(Suppressed by order of the Ordo Hereticus)*

'GOOD CROP THIS year,' said Lord Ebondrake.

'Indeed, my lord,' replied Duke Venalitor.

'Khorne will be pleased to see them die.'

The torture garden gave Venalitor and Ebondrake an excellent view of Karnikhal's slave market. The market was one of the largest on Drakaasi. It was built into the site of a dried-out cyst like a meteor crater. Hundreds of slavers' blocks were embedded in the tough skin of the ground, each one with several new slaves chained to it. The shouting of slavers rang out, punctuated by the sounds of whips and cracking bones.

Lord Ebondrake flexed a claw idly, like a stretching cat. 'The warp speaks of you, Venalitor.'

'Then I am blessed, my lord.'

'It says you have brought the Blood God a very particular prize.'

Venalitor bowed. 'It is true. The Imperials fought us at Sarthis Majoris. They were swept aside, and many were taken alive.'

'More than just Guardsmen, though, so the seers say.'

'You shall see, my lord.'

Lord Ebondrake padded to the edge of the torture garden's balcony. The garden was a place of reflection for Karnikhal's elite, where they could consider the dismembered bodies displayed where they had died on the intricate torture devices arranged on the obsidian. A rebel might be granted a final honour in death, to be slowly tormented on a frame of silver, to serve as inspiration for the garden's visitors.

Lord Ebondrake was a huge reptilian creature. He bore a resemblance to dragons of various human myths, and perhaps this was not a coincidence, since Ebondrake had presumably chosen his form at some point in his distant past. He had scales of jet-black, yellow feline eyes and countless bony spines, on which were sometimes mounted the heads and hands of those who had displeased him.

His long, sinuous body and enormous wings moved with a speed and grace alien to his size, and he brought with him a majesty that marked him out instantly as the de facto ruler of Drakaasi. For the occasion, Lord Ebondrake wore armour of obsidian and brass, cladding his massive scaly body in a way that echoed the stern armour of his personal troops, the Ophidian Guard. He was accompanied by a detachment of these elite armoured warriors, who followed their master at a respectful distance. They were the most powerful fighting force on Drakaasi, with their black envenomed blades and eyeless helms, and their presence was a constant reminder that strength at arms was the ultimate decider in Drakaasi's power struggles.

'I have no doubt there are rumours,' said Ebondrake, 'of where my rule shall take us next.'

Venalitor weighed his words carefully for a moment. 'One hears things. I am aware of a great undertaking.'

'We have stayed on this world too long,' said Ebondrake. He stretched out his wings as if indicating the expanse of Drakaasi's bloodshot sky. 'This filthy rock, this lump of bloody dirt, it is too small a place to contain the worship due to our god. Do you not agree?'

'This is a fine world,' said Venalitor simply, 'but there is always room for more blood.'

'Ha! Have some imagination, duke. Think what we could do. We leave Drakaasi only to enslave, and return our captives to this world to watch them die. On Sarthis Majoris you did just that. However, if all Drakaasi's lords made a common cause and took our best followers out into the stars, whole worlds could fall to us. Drakaasi will be a monument to our bloodshed.'

'You speak,' said Venalitor, 'of a crusade.'

'Of course. Even now the one they call the Despoiler leads his armies out of the Eye. Countless other champions of the warp are doing the same all across the galaxy. There are rich pickings in the wake of such bloodshed. The Blood God's own crusade can only grow as more fall to our cause. By the time we return to Drakaasi the Blood God will have his own empire in the Eye. Would that not stand as a greater monument than all our games put together?'

'I can see it, my lord,' said Venalitor, letting an edge of wonder into his voice.

'No, duke,' said Ebondrake, 'you are young. You have not fought long under Khorne's banner. What you see is just the beginning. It takes this ancient creature to understand what Drakaasi could truly be. Soon, all the lords will know of my crusade, and they will be united under me. For now, there are more pressing matters. You say you made a fine haul at Sarthis Majoris?'

Venalitor followed Ebondrake's gaze down over the market. Thousands of captives were for sale, some of them from Venalitor's recent victory, others handed over in tribute to Khorne by pirate raiders, or captured in battles across the Eye of Terror. Most of them were human, for the human forces of the Imperium were battling the servants of Chaos throughout the Eye. Some others were aliens: slender eldar, orks, a few strange creatures plucked from the far corners of space.

'Come,' said Venalitor, 'I have wares to show.'

Together, Lord Ebondrake and Venalitor descended the winding stairway down to the cyst floor. Everywhere they went the slavers, all servants of one of Drakaasi's lords, bowed or saluted at Ebondrake's presence. The wretches who inhabited Karnikhal scurried away in fear, or prostrated themselves on the ground, whimpering and pathetic. Most of Drakaasi's population was human, or at least originally human, and some said Ebondrake had taken on his draconic form solely to mark himself apart from the scum of the planet's cities. The sounds and smells of the slave market crowded all around, sweat and misery, mingling with the heavy rotting blood stench of Karnikhal itself.

Many of Drakaasi's other lords were there examining the slaves on offer. Tiresia, tall and ebony skinned with a great longbow carried at her side, was picking out new quarries for her court of feral killers, and cultured assassins to chase down in their next great hunt. Golgur the Pack Master was purchasing the weakest, most pathetic slaves to throw to his flesh hounds, two of which he led around the market by chains.

Scathach was making a rare foray from his fortress, probably to buy combat slaves to train his soldiers, and turned one of his heads to follow Ebondrake and Venalitor making their way between the slaving blocks. Scathach had long forsaken the Traitor Legions, but he still wore the power armour of a Chaos Space Marine, and the soldiers who followed him formed a neatly drilled regiment quite at odds with the bloodthirsty rabble many lords gathered around themselves.

'Lord Ebondrake, my kind are honoured,' said a booming voice. Up ahead of Venalitor there was a great cauldron of steaming blood, containing the toad-like form of a giant daemon. The cauldron was carried by blinded slaves, their spines horribly bent by the daemon's weight. Two slaves poured ladles of blood over the daemon's pasty skin as it addressed Ebondrake. On the daemon's chest there was a weeping scab in the shape of a stylised six-fingered hand. The same symbol was branded on the chests of the slaves who carried the daemon.

'Arguthrax, what manner of sacrifices have you brought for the altars and arenas of our world?' said Ebondrake.

Arguthrax waved a dripping hand towards the slaving block beside him. Dozens of bronzed, muscular men and women were chained there, many still shouting curses at the slavers watching over them. 'An entire tribe, my lord,' said Arguthrax, 'a most violent and savage people, yes! Their rage echoed long in the warp. They spoke unto their most ancient god, our god, and brought my servants forth! And so they were enslaved, and soon they will learn to bow before the will of their god. Ha! See how they still rage! Imagine such anger turned for the Blood God's glory!'

'More savages, Arguthrax?' said Ebondrake. 'There is always need of their kind for the arenas. The Blood God ever demands his fodder.'

Arguthrax could not keep the anger from passing over his revolting face. 'Then it is a blessing that the Blood God will hold this offering in such high esteem.' Arguthrax turned his burning black eyes on Venalitor. 'What have you brought, upstart youth, that permits you to walk alongside our lord as an equal?'

Venalitor smiled. Arguthrax hated him. Most of Drakaasi's lords hated him, since compared to most of them he was young and brilliant. They hated each other too, of course, and tolerated one another only because Lord Ebondrake had forged from Drakaasi an immense temple to Khorne that required all their attentions to maintain. Arguthrax, however, an ancient and evil thing spawned within the warp, harboured a particular dislike of usurpers like Venalitor.

'Observe, honoured daemon,' replied Venalitor simply.

Venalitor's servants tended a grand pavilion of crimson silk that dominated one side of the slave market. Many of his servants were Scaephylyds, creatures native to Drakaasi, who had inhabited its mountains and canyons before the first lords of Chaos had set foot on the planet. They were scuttling insect things who, though despised by everything else on Drakaasi, were devoted to Chaos and to Venalitor himself. Dozens of them scurried over the pavilion, and the largest of the number, the slave masters, swarmed around the opening to the pavilion as the silks were pulled back.

Lashes drove human slaves out of the pavilion into the market. They were streaked with blood, chained together at the wrists and ankles. They were all men, and almost all of them had the same tattoo on their shoulders: Imperial Guard, soldiers of the weakling Imperium, finally reduced to the slavery that was their lot in life.

'This is it?' said Arguthrax. 'These wretches are barely fit to feed the flesh hounds. For this you waste our time? The Blood God will spit upon such an offering, Venalitor. Such failure is heresy!'

'Patience, daemon,' said Venalitor smoothly.

A quartet of scaephylyd slave masters emerged, hauling thick brass chains. They dragged a hulking human form out of the pavilion, half again as tall as any of the Imperial Guardsmen. Another followed it, similarly huge. Slabs of muscle rippled beneath their skin, which was streaked with grime and dried blood. Beneath the filth were scars, old battle wounds and the marks of extensive surgery. The dark shape of the black carapace was just visible under the skin, with metallic ports in the chest and biceps where power armour could read off vital signs.

One of the men had broad, expressive features and a service stud in his forehead, while the other had a face as solid and unflappable as a slab of granite. They both strained at their chains, but the metal had been forged in the hottest volcano of Drakaasi's mountain ranges, and they held fast. Each man had a Collar of Khorne around his neck, a fact that was evidently not lost on Lord Ebondrake.

'Space Marines,' said Ebondrake, 'and alive. You have outdone yourself, Venalitor. It has been many years since a living Astartes was brought to Drakaasi.'

'Not just any Space Marine, my lord,' said Venalitor proudly.

'No: psykers, sorcerers. It will please the Blood God to see them die.'

'More than that.' Venalitor snapped his fingers and a scaephylyd slave master scurried up, cradling the shoulder pad from a suit of Space Marine power armour in its front legs. Venalitor took the shoulder pad and held it up for Lord Ebondrake to see the device emblazoned across it. The ceramite was deeply carved with devotional prayers in High Gothic, and it bore the symbol of a sword thrust through an open book.

'A Grey Knight,' said Ebondrake.

'Two Grey Knights,' replied Venalitor. He looked purposefully at Arguthrax. 'Daemon hunters.'

Arguthrax sneered. He would never show obvious weakness in front of Ebondrake and especially Venalitor, but he was leaning back in his cauldron to put as much distance as he could between himself and the Grey Knights. Their very presence was anathema to the daemon. It gave Venalitor savage joy to think that something like fear might be blossoming in Arguthrax's corrupted mind.

'I take it that these specimens will not be for sale,' continued Ebondrake.

'Indeed not. I myself shall see that they reap the greatest glory for Khorne. It is not something I can trust to another. I shall take them back to the *Hecatomb* and make them ready for the next games.' Venalitor waved a dismissive hand at the Imperial Guard prisoners. 'As for the rest of them, they are for sale. It is not for me to hoard the Blood God's sacrifices for myself. There is one further thing.'

Slaves hauled forwards a sled, on which was displayed the rest of the Grey Knights' armour. It was still stained with the blood of the battle on Sarthis Majoris.

'A tribute, my lord,' said Venalitor. Arguthrax snorted derisively.

'Gratefully received, duke,' said Ebondrake. 'Rare trophies indeed. Have your slaves take them to my palace.'

'It will be done.'

'So,' said Ebondrake, eyeing the Grey Knights, 'Karnikhal's games will see the hunters of daemons slaying their own for the Blood God's glory. Let it not be said that Khorne does not appreciate such humour.'

Ebondrake turned and began to pad through the rest of the market to inspect the other prisoners being traded between Drakaasi's lords. None of them would come close to the rare prize of a pair of Grey Knights, and no lord could boast such warriors in their arena stables. Venalitor cast Arguthrax a final look before heading for the pavilion. His slave masters had much to do, for Karnikhal's games marked the beginning of a great season of worship in Drakaasi's arenas, and the quality of Venalitor's slaves would determine how quickly he could rise to prominence among the planet's lords. With Grey Knights fighting under his banner, the games would be very good indeed for him.

From his palace in the warp, Khorne would be roaring his approval as the hunters of daemons were sacrificed in combat for his glory. The warp would not soon forget Duke Venalitor of Drakaasi.

SIX

'THIS IS THE *Hecatomb*,' said Haulvarn. 'I heard one of them saying its name.'

'One of them?'

'The slaves: the insect-things.'

'Then what is it? A prison?'

'A ship.'

Alaric strained against his chains, but he knew it would be useless. He was chained to the wall of a tiny dark cell, barely big enough for him to stand hunched. The floor was crusted with old blood and covered in a layer of filthy straw. Everything stank. Men had died in these cells.

Alaric could just make out Haulvarn's outline through an iron grille in the wall. Alaric had passed out some time after being presented at the slave market. It took a lot to rob a Space Marine of consciousness; it was surely the collar that was weakening his mind.

'Did you see it?' asked Haulvarn.

'What?'

'The dragon.'

'Yes.' Alaric recalled it, looming over him as if in a nightmare. It was not a dragon at all, of course. A dragon was a mythological creature, a symbol, or the name given by primitive humans to large lizards indigenous to countless inhospitable planets. 'I saw it, and the bloated one: the daemon. Even with my mind blunted it could not hide its nature.

The knight, the one in red armour, was the one who took us at Sarthis Majoris.'

'I saw you fight him. It was valiant, justicar. For a few moments there was hope. Many more vermin died because of your example.'

Alaric sighed. 'He bested me and took me alive. Our example has not finished yet.' He was just able to make out his fellow Grey Knight's features through the grille. 'What of the others? The squad?'

'Thane died,' replied Haulvarn. 'I saw him go. As for Dvorn and Visical, I do not know. We were swamped and separated. Perhaps they were taken prisoner, too, but I have not seen them. Emperor forgive me, but I do not think Sarthis Majoris ever had a chance.'

'Probably not,' said Alaric. He could feel the cell floor tilting, and hear distant rumbling through the body of the *Hecatomb*. It was a ship, after all, creaking as it sailed.

'Where do you think they are taking us?' asked Haulvarn. 'Are we to be sacrifices?'

Alaric held up his hands, chained at the wrists. 'I think they have greater plans for us,' said Alaric. 'A simple knife across the throat is rarely enough to sate the Blood God. They will have something more elaborate in store for us, I feel.'

'And who do you think "they" are, justicar?'

Alaric paused for a long time. Who indeed? The very nature of Chaos meant it could not be classified. In spite of the volumes of forbidden lore in the libraries of Encaladus, in spite of the learning filling the minds of inquisitors, Chaos could not be divided into categories or dissected like a specimen. Chaos was change, it was entropy and decay, but it was also an abundance of life and emotion, warped birth as well as death. Every time someone like Alaric thought they understood an enemy born of Chaos, that enemy changed, not just to confound the hunter, but because change was a part of its essence.

'Wherever we are, Haulvarn, and whoever has us, we cannot ever answer that question. We will never understand this place or these creatures. If we were to ever understand them then our corruption would be complete.'

'They can corrupt us.'

'Yes.'

'The collar leaves us defenceless.'

'Not completely, we have our training, but yes, we are vulnerable.'

'Then it could happen.'

Alaric knew exactly what Haulvarn meant. No Grey Knight had ever fallen. They had died, or been crippled, or had their minds flayed away by the fury of the warp, thousands of them, entombed in the chill vaults beneath Titan, but none had ever fallen. Alaric and Haulvarn could be the first.

'It will not,' said Alaric. 'It does not matter what trinkets they use to strip away our defences. We are Grey Knights. Everything else is details.'

'I shall share in your faith, then, Justicar,' said Haulvarn. Alaric couldn't tell how convinced Haulvarn was. Alaric wasn't even sure if he believed it.

'We will escape,' continued Haulvarn.

'Of course,' said Alaric.

The cell door banged open and one of the insect slaves threw in an armful of armour and weaponry, which clattered on the floor, chain-mail and a few pieces of plate, a sword, and a helmet.

'Prepare,' said the slave in its thick drooling accent. It slammed the door shut and performed the same routine at Haulvarn's cell.

'For what?' demanded Haulvarn. 'For our executions?'

The slave ignored him and slammed his cell door shut. Alaric could hear its talons clacking on the floor as it scuttled away.

The chains around Alaric's wrists snickered away. Alaric looked down at the armour heaped at his feet. He was still feeling the wounds of his defeat by Venalitor. A Space Marine healed with inhuman speed, but even so it had only been a few days since he had nearly died on Sarthis Majoris. Now he would have to fight again.

'What do they think they can take from us?' asked Haulvarn.

The cell doors banged open. Other prisoners were emerging, too, their manacles rattling.

Alaric pulled the chainmail shirt over his head and picked up the rusted sword at his feet.

'They want our blood,' he replied.

ALARIC'S FIRST SIGHT of some of the other slave gladiators came as he was herded down a narrow, dark tunnel towards doors of bone studded with fangs. The tunnel wound through the entrails of Karnikhal, and through holes in the fleshy wall the city's inhabitants hooted and jeered at the men about to die.

Some slaves were no more than fodder. They were dressed in rags, their heads bowed and white with fear. Others looked like they could take care of themselves, like the muscular man with the prison tattoos. They were almost all human, save for a gaggle of grunting aliens separated by a cordon of the insectoid aliens. Alaric recognised the sound and smell of orks, brutal greenskins who lived to fight.

The tattooed man looked Alaric up and down. 'You're not mutants,' he said.

'No,' snarled Alaric.

The prisoner smiled. 'Then they're going to love killing you.'

Alaric reached the doors. He could feel the anticipation among the other slaves. Some were terrified to the point of paralysis. Others were ready for the fight. The orks were chanting, working themselves up for slaughter.

The doors opened. Light and the roar of an immense crowd hit Alaric. The orks shouldered their way past the guards and ran past Alaric into the arena, waving their cleavers and clubs.

Alaric emerged onto the arena floor. There must have been hundreds of thousands of spectators cramming the cages and pens in the stands.

Sunk into the flesh of the city, the arena was a stinking pit, walled with rotting flesh, from which flowed waterfalls of gore and pus. The spectators were kept in huge cages to prevent them from tearing at one another, and they brayed like animals as they hurled filth and insults down at the arena floor. Karnikhal's citizens were as rotten and foul as their city. Flesh and skin hung off them, and their decomposed faces had lost all humanity. Here and there were grand galleries of marble and silk for dignitaries. Venalitor would surely be there, and perhaps other lords that Alaric had glimpsed at the slave market. Ranks of armoured warriors separated the dignitaries from the scum.

'In the name of the Throne,' said Haulvarn.

Another roar went up from the crowd. Gates of bone had opened on the opposite side of the arena, across the expanse of bloodstained sand. A huge shape emerged from the darkness beyond it. It had the upper torso of a massive humanoid and the lower body of a snake. It had four arms, and in two of them it held a pair of enormous meat cleavers. The crowd bayed and screamed as it slithered out into the sunlight. Alaric's augmented eyesight picked out its roughly human-like face and forked tongue tasting the blood on the air, the garland of severed hands around its neck, and the kill tallies branded into its leathery skin.

'Throne of Skulls,' cursed the prison slave. 'Skarhaddoth.'

Alaric looked at him.

'The champion,' continued the slave. 'Ebondrake's own.'

'What's your name?' asked Alaric.

'Gearth.'

'Gearth, stay close. We'll surround it. Haulvarn and I will keep it at bay, the rest of you get behind it and...'

Gearth smiled. 'It doesn't work that way.'

Rows of spikes twice as tall as Alaric sprung up from the sand, dividing the arena into pens and corridors. Alaric was separated from the other slaves, including Haulvarn.

'Brother!' shouted Haulvarn as the din from the crowd grew. 'It is bloodshed they want. If we kill anything, it will be for the glory of Chaos.'

'True, but whatever we do, we must survive first. Fight as if the Emperor willed it. As if–'

A row of spears snickered back into the arena floor. There was now no obstacle between Haulvarn and Skarhaddoth, the champion of Lord Ebondrake.

Skarhaddoth's eyes fixed on Haulvarn.

Haulvarn held up his sword in a guard. It wasn't anything like as potent as the Nemesis weapon he had carried as a Grey Knight, but anything could be lethal in a Space Marine's hand.

The crowd was chanting Skarhaddoth's name.

Skarhaddoth slithered towards Haulvarn. Skarhaddoth was huge, much taller than Haulvarn, and its two empty hands pulled a pair of shields from its back. The shields were black with the device of a white serpent, presumably the crest of Lord Ebondrake. It was fitting that Venalitor should give one of the prized Grey Knights in combat to Ebondrake's champion.

'Brother!' shouted Alaric. 'We stand together!' Alaric leapt up and tried to haul himself over the dense barrier of spears. They were slick with the blood of previous combatants, and the gnarled metal bit into his hands.

A great eruption of bloody sand fell over Alaric. He dropped to the ground and turned to see a cage erupting from the arena floor. Inside was a hulking mutant, doubled over in the confines of the cage. The cage door sprang open, and to another roar the mutant stomped out, bellowing in rage.

Alaric's opponent was an abnormal construction of overlong, multi-jointed limbs that writhed like snakes, with a long equine head and a single yellow eye that bled pus as it glared at Alaric. In its hands was a weapon that resembled an industrial circular saw. The crowd screeched their approval as the saw tore into life, flicking shavings of steel and flecks of dried blood everywhere.

Alaric dropped to one knee as the mutant charged and the saw rang off the line of spears behind him. Alaric rolled away as the saw came down and gouged a choking spray of sand from the arena floor. He risked a glance behind him, Haulvarn and Skarhaddoth were fighting,

Skarhaddoth rearing up and striking down like a cobra, Haulvarn fending off everything the champion threw at him with desperate swings of his sword.

Alaric turned back to the mutant. It ripped its saw out of the ground and swung it. Alaric turned it aside with his sword, snapping the blade in the process. The crowd loved that, and the mutant did too, its deformed face splitting into a grin as it charged.

Alaric dropped to one knee, the saw passing just over the top of his head, and stabbed the broken sword up into the mutant's ribs. The shattered stump of the blade tore through muscle and bone, and lodged there, torn from Alaric's grip as the mutant reared up in pain. It whipped its unnaturally long arms around and nearly cut Alaric in two with the saw.

Alaric couldn't stay on the back foot. He was unarmed, and the mutant's reach was huge. It would kill him if he let it. He ducked under its arms and leapt onto it, hands reaching up to gouge at its eye and force its head around to snap its neck.

The mutant was forced back onto its haunches. It wrapped an arm around Alaric's torso to lever him off, and its other hand tried to drive the saw through Alaric's back. Alaric's hand was round its throat while his other arm held off the saw. The mutant's eye bulged and turned red with frustration. Its long tongue spooled out, and lashed at Alaric's face and neck like a tiny whip. Alaric held on and tried to crush the bones of its neck in his fist. Whatever strange mutations it had on the inside, it probably still needed to breathe.

The mutant howled and threw Alaric off it with unnatural strength. Alaric tried to scrabble to his feet, but the mutant was on him too quickly. The saw was over his face, the blade shrieking at him, and the mutant was trying to force it down to cut his head in two. For a long, awful moment the two wrestled, the mutant's unnatural strength against the enhanced muscle of a Space Marine, and Alaric did not know which of them would win.

Alaric forced everything into pushing the saw to one side. The mutant's weight drove it past his head into the arena floor, and the circular blade bit deep into the ground. The mutant tried to tear it out, but it was stuck too deep, and the saw's motor screeched, and belched a plume of smoke and flame. The saw exploded in the mutant's hands, and the blade skipped away, ringing off the wall of spears and ricocheting away to bury itself in the meat of Alaric's shoulder.

Alaric forced a knee under the mutant's chest and kicked it off him. The mutant scurried back across the bloody sand, one ruined hand

·spraying black-green gore. Alaric got up onto his knees, back arched against the pain of the blade lodged in his shoulder. It was the same shoulder he had dislocated in the cage, and the pain was bad enough to grey out his vision.

The crowd loved to see such gore. The other fights were similarly horrible. The ork had defeated its opponent, a crimson-skinned bestial thing, and was waving its enemy's severed leg in victory. Gearth was kneeling over his opponent, a shaggy beast-man with a goat's head, and was in the process of sawing its head off with a jagged knife.

Alaric was on his feet. The mutant was struggling to get up, blood flowing out of the stump of its missing hand. Alaric reached agonisingly around and pulled the saw blade out of his shoulder. The mutant would still kill him. It had one good hand and a foul temper, and that was all it would need, but now, Alaric had a weapon.

The mutant charged. Alaric wound his arm back and threw the saw blade like a discus as hard as he could, ignoring the pain screaming from his shoulder.

The blade sheared the mutant's head clean off. Alaric sidestepped its headless body as it slammed into the spears behind it. The crowd jeered the dead mutant that had been despatched at the hand of a newcomer.

Alaric turned and looked for Haulvarn. The Grey Knight's fight with Skarhaddoth had moved all the way back across the expanse of the arena floor leaving a trail of bloody footprints. Haulvarn was covered in blood from dozens of cuts. One side of his face was cut open from brow to chin. He was losing.

Skarhaddoth loomed over the Grey Knight. Haulvarn was striking at it with blurring speed, but Skarhaddoth was just as quick, and he batted each sword blow aside with his shields. The distraction of Alaric's battle was over, and every eye in the arena was fixed on Lord Ebondrake's champion as he forced the Grey Knight back step by step.

Alaric tried to climb the spears again. Many hands had tried to do the same, and clumps of ragged flesh still clung to the spears. Alaric reached the top and tried to haul himself over the rusted points.

Skarhaddoth backhanded Haulvarn with one of his shields. Haulvarn sprawled onto his back. Skarhaddoth dropped one of his cleavers and picked Haulvarn up, kicking the sword out of the Grey Knight's hand.

'Brother!' yelled Alaric. 'I am with you! You are not alone!' He pulled himself over the spear fence and dropped down the other side, the spear tips gouging long lines out of his chest. He kicked to his feet and ran towards Skarhaddoth and Haulvarn.

Skarhaddoth held Haulvarn over his head like a trophy. The crowd screamed. They wanted gore. They wanted cruelty. Alaric had whetted their appetite, and Skarhaddoth knew how to give them what they wanted.

Skarhaddoth had one hand around Haulvarn's throat and another around his leg. He pushed Haulvarn up above his head and pulled. Haulvarn screamed.

Alaric yelled in wordless desperation. His heart felt as if it had stopped in his chest. He watched Haulvarn's body come apart, torn in two by Skarhaddoth.

Haulvarn's blood poured down over Skarhaddoth, who basked in it, open-mouthed. Skarhaddoth slithered over to the arena wall and threw the two halves of Haulvarn's body into the crowd. Spectators fought to tear chunks of flesh from the body. Skarhaddoth brandished his bloodied hands to every corner of the arena, a grin across his blood slicked face. His eyes fixed on Alaric, and he smiled through the blood of Alaric's friend.

Alaric ran. Skarhaddoth was more than halfway across the arena, and Alaric sprinted to close the gap.

Haulvarn was dead. The Enemy had claimed a Grey Knight, and Alaric had lost a friend. The hollow opening up in him could only be filled with revenge. It was not a choice he made. It was a simple, unbreakable rule that had to be obeyed. Haulvarn had to be avenged.

A wall of spears burst up from the arena floor right in front of Alaric. Alaric slammed into it, bending the spears. He grabbed them and shook them, trying to tear them out or bend them, but they held fast. Skarhaddoth flourished his bloodied hands one last time to the crowd and headed out through the arena doors. Slave creatures hauled them shut behind the champion.

Slavers and armoured warriors were entering the arena, hauling away bodies and manacling the surviving slaves. Several of them converged on Alaric. Alaric wanted to tear them apart, rip out the spears and kick his way through the doors. He wanted to hunt down Skarhaddoth and tear him apart, just as Skarhaddoth had torn apart Haulvarn, but the sight of the closing doors had drained all the strength out of him. His rage was like a great weight on him, like a curse laid on him for failing to avenge his friend.

Lashes cut down into the flesh of his back. He fell to his knees. He wanted all of this to be gone. He wanted oblivion, so he didn't have to remember seeing Haulvarn die. He had never felt so broken.

The pain reached a crescendo, and then Alaric didn't feel anything at all.

* * *

'ARE YOU SUPPOSED to have two hearts in there?'

'What?'

'You've got two hearts, and three lungs, but one of them's a bionic.'

Alaric's eyes opened. He was staring at a rusted ceiling, filthy with years of dirt. He ached all over, the pain accented by the faint swaying that told Alaric he was back on the *Hecatomb*. The light was poor, but it still pounded against Alaric's eyes.

'I'm a Space Marine,' said Alaric.

'What,' said the voice, 'on Drakaasi? Throne be praised or damned, I don't know which. How did your kind get here?'

'Venalitor,' said Alaric. He sat up, ignoring the pain in his shoulder. He had suffered worse injuries before. He could live with it.

He was at one end of a huge chamber inside the *Hecatomb*. Banks of cells rose on either side, connected by walkways. The floor was filthy, scattered with straw or piles of rags that might have been prone bodies. Prisoners were everywhere, arguing over gambling games, snatching sleep in corners, whispering conspiratorially. Most of them were human, with a few xenos mixed in. Alaric recognised Gearth idly sharpening a knife in a corner. At the far end was a heap of filth and trash that was evidently home to a group of orks, separated from the other slaves by bars hung with gory orkish trophies. One of the greenskins was the same one-eared ork that Alaric had seen in the arena. About half a dozen more of the creatures squabbled and fought in the shadows. Alaric realised that the isolation cells were probably below this deck. The majority of the slaves lived here, kept isolated by fear of one another more effectively than by the bars of individual cells.

Alaric was sitting on a large, stained iron slab. Standing over him was a pudgy middle-aged man with a beard, wearing an old apron stained almost black with blood. A few blunt medical implements were laid out beside Alaric.

'Haggard,' said the surgeon, 'medical officer second class.'

'Justicar Alaric,' replied Alaric. 'You were Imperial Guard?'

Haggard shook his head. 'Agrippina Planetary Defence Forces, the Ancient and Honourable Fifty-First Governor's Own Rifles. A whole lot of us surrendered at Mount Dagger. Turns out we should have fought to the death, but the Eye had only just opened. We didn't know what we were facing.'

Alaric tested his shoulder. It would hold, he decided.

'I pulled a handful of metal out of you,' continued Haggard. 'You weren't supposed to survive out there, you know. You were sacrifices to celebrate the last slave revolt.'

'There was a revolt?'

'For about half a day: the arena slaves in Aelazadne got organised and broke out. The Ophidian Guard were waiting for them, Lord Ebondrake's personal army. You've seen him?'

'The lizard?'

'The lizard. The games are celebrating the revolt being crushed. That's why Ebondrake's champion was there. You were sent there to die.'

'My battle-brother did,' said Alaric. 'Skarhaddoth killed him.'

'I heard, and I know you'll want revenge. It's what I wanted, too. When Venalitor's army hit Agrippina I lost everyone and everything. But this is Drakaasi, justicar. Khorne owns this world. Surviving here is victory enough. You either fight, which is exactly what Venalitor wants you to do, or you die: simple as that. I'm only alive because I'm more useful patching up gladiators than acting as one more piece of arena fodder.'

'Then that's what we are,' said Alaric bleakly. 'We are tools of the Blood God.'

'A lot of us chose death instead,' said Haggard. 'The rest think they'll be saved, or think they can break out on their own. Some of us, like me, are too cowardly to do anything else, and some enjoy the bloodshed, of course.'

'Like Gearth.'

Haggard smiled. 'Gearth's pure psychopath, and he's not the only one. The first thing that happens when Chaos takes a world is that the prisons get emptied. For men like Gearth, Drakaasi's not that different to their old life. There are a few who have plans, of course. See up there, on the third deck?'

Haggard pointed up to a bank of cells suspended high above. Alaric followed his gaze and picked out a pale figure in one of the cells, patiently polishing a suit of dark green armour. A sword was propped up against the wall beside him.

'Eldar,' said Alaric, 'more xenos.'

'That's Kelhedros,' said Haggard. 'Believe me, my mother taught me to hate the alien just like the preachers said, but Kelhedros is one of the best fighters in Venalitor's stable, and I'll be damned if he doesn't have a plan to get himself out of here.'

'How long do we last?' asked Alaric.

'Depends. A few were here long before me. Most don't make it through their first fight. If you're here at all it means you're tougher than most. Venalitor keeps the best slaves, and carts them around Drakaasi on the *Hecatomb* to send them out against the other lords' gladiators.

This damn planet is one giant temple to blood, and the arenas are the altars. It's a sacred business, you know, all this death.'

Alaric slid off the slab and got to his feet. He was still wearing the piecemeal armour he had been given by the alien slave prior to the arena fight. He would have dearly loved to have his own wargear back.

'In here, you do as you will,' said Haggard. 'The weak are weeded out quick enough. But try to get anywhere else on the ship and the scaephylyds will know. Venalitor will have you hung from the prow or fed to the greenskins.

Haulvarn, the best soldier Alaric had ever fought alongside. Haulvarn would have been appointed a justicar with his own squad, and sooner rather than later. He could have risen higher than Alaric, to the ranks of the brother-captains, perhaps even a Grand Master in charge of whole armies and privy to the highest circles of the Ordo Malleus. Haulvarn was gone, and Khorne had taken his share of the death.

'Make sure you stake your claim soon,' said Haggard. 'Plenty of slaves didn't come back today, and there'll be a rush for their cells. Good ones are rare.'

'I'll do that,' said Alaric. He saw a group of slaves clustered around one cell. They were on their knees. They were praying.

Alaric went to join them.

SEVEN

LIEUTENANT ERKHAR RAISED his hands slowly, his eyes turned towards the cell floor. The horrors of this world would be matched by the splendours they would one day witness. They had to remember that, no matter how hard it got.

Erkhar placed his hands palms down on the altar. It was a huge stone head, which had originally belonged to a statue of an idealised human, its face noble, with a long aristocratic nose and its hair in dense marble curls. It was presumably of some Champion of Chaos or aspect of Khorne, but it had long ceased to serve that purpose. It was beautiful, while so much on Drakaasi was ugly, and forgotten by the planet's overlords. The believers had placed their faith in it. It was the face of the Emperor on Drakaasi, an icon of sin transformed by their faith into something beautiful.

'That we must be tested,' began Erkhar, 'is a measure of our faith. For such faith would mean nothing if we lived lives free of suffering. For every moment of pain, our Emperor, we thank you. For every brother and sister taken from us, we rejoice. For every victory of the enemy and the Blood God's brood, we celebrate, for the true victory is the steeling of the faith in our hearts.'

Around him, the faithful listened patiently. Most of them wore the same threadbare dark blue uniforms as Erkhar, and a few still had the insignia of the Imperial Navy. Some of them had joined the faithful later on, but the core of the congregation were the men and women who had been captured when their spacecraft, the *Pax Deinotatos*, was boarded and its crew handed to Venalitor as tribute.

'They have celebrated the destruction of our brothers in the revolt,' said Hoygens, once a gunnery master on board the *Pax*. 'We lost many faithful in those days, and games have taken place to mark the black lizard's triumph over them. How can we take comfort from this? I feel my faith is shaken, lieutenant. I feel that something at my core is missing.'

Erkhar stood up. In spite of the darkness and the grizzled face Drakaasi had given him, he still exuded the presence of an officer. 'The Emperor takes away those crutches you use to hold yourself up, Hoygens! Rejoice in that emptiness. Think how much the sight of the Promised Land will fill you up, now that you have lost so much! Would that we all could feel such despair!'

Erkhar was about to continue when he noticed the huge shape on the walkway outside the cell door.

It was not a scaephylyd slave master, or even one of the *Hecatomb's* more violent and spiteful prisoners. It was an enormous man, a clear head taller than the tallest man there, dressed in scrappy piecemeal armour that couldn't hide his exaggerated musculature.

Many backed away from him in fear.

'Have you come to share in the Promised Land, stranger?' asked Erkhar.

'It's the Space Marine,' said Hoygens in a voice little more than a whisper. Hoygens had been the chief of a gun crew back on the *Pax*, and he was a big man, but he shied away from the newcomer. 'They said Venalitor had got one alive. I didn't believe it.'

'I think there is much need for prayer,' said Alaric. 'I would like to join you, father.'

'I am Lieutenant Erkhar of the Emperor's spaceship the *Pax Deinotatos*,' replied Erkhar. 'I am not the father of anything, and may I ask your name?'

'Justicar Alaric.'

Erkhar smiled. 'There is always room for a newcomer, as long as he has the capacity to believe. We were sent here to be tested, after all. Drakaasi is a torment for us all, through which the Emperor will know His own.'

'You must have given some thought to escape, lieutenant.'

'Many have tried before, lord Astartes,' said Hoygens. 'Believe me, I was nearly one of them in the old days, but every time anyone tries, they die.

They either get cut down in the attempt, or they're hunted down and thrown out to die in the arena. It's just another kind of sport for them.'

'Brother Hoygens is correct,' said Erkhar. 'The closest anyone got was very recently, not more than a month ago. Hundreds of slaves made a break for it at the arena in Aelazadne. Some of the faithful were with them, but the Ophidian Guard were waiting for them, Ebondrake's own, and they died to a man. They had spent many months in preparation, so it is said, but it all ended in a few hours.'

'This planet is ruled by Khorne,' said Alaric. 'Of course it would not be easy to escape, but I take it that fact has done little to dull your determination.'

Erkhar shook his head. 'Escape is a dream, justicar, physical escape, anyway. You see, everything I have seen on Drakaasi has led me to conclude that we are here for a reason. The Emperor delivered us here, because this is the first step on the path to the Promised Land. If we stay faithful, we shall be delivered to that Promised Land. For every sin that is committed against us, one more glory shall be ours when the Emperor leads us there. It is the only way Drakaasi can be made to make sense.'

'The Emperor created Drakaasi?' said Alaric warily.

'No, Justicar. Drakaasi was created by evil men. The Emperor brought us here because we are His faithful, and it is only through suffering the works of these evil men that we can be made pure enough to ascend to the Promised Land. If you join us in our faith then you will be led there, too.'

'Back in the Imperium, lieutenant, what you have just told me would be considered heresy.'

'But we are not in the Imperium.'

'No, we are not, and where is the Promised Land?'

'I have preached that it is a place to which we will be delivered, a land of peace and plenty where there is no pain. As to whether it really is a place, or is somewhere inside us, is a matter for a man's conscience. You, however, I feel, will not be content to seek this solace inside yourself. You want to escape, and get revenge.'

'Perhaps,' replied Alaric.

'You need allies. Not even a Space Marine can get off Drakaasi on his own. You thought that these poor religious fanatics would think you were some kind of icon sent by the Emperor, and that they would sacrifice their lives for your benefit. We are all equal on Drakaasi, Justicar, even Space Marines. If you want to get away from here, the Promised Land is the only way. Faith will conquer Drakaasi, not you, and if you want to bring Duke Venalitor to task, perhaps you do not know enough about him.'

'He bested me and took me prisoner,' replied Alaric sharply. 'I am under no illusions as to his capabilities.'

'Then you know why he is held in esteem by Lord Ebondrake in the first place?'

'I take it you do.'

Erkhar shrugged. 'One hears things. Some of the slaves who were here when we were first captured, long dead by now of course, were there when Venalitor first raised the *Hecatomb* and took his place among Drakaasi's lords. He bested a daemon, they said. The tale was passed down by generations of slaves before us. Its name was Raezazel. It was some magical thing the other lords despised. Venalitor hunted it down and defeated it. The other lords hated it, and that hate won him power. Hatred and power are the same thing on Drakaasi. That is the world we all have to endure.'

'It sounds like you are willing to sit here and take whatever Chaos throws at you, lieutenant,' retorted Alaric.

'When the Promised Land is in sight, justicar, you will realise that nothing could be further from the truth. If you want to understand that truth, then join us. We will welcome you. Otherwise, fight and die, for without hope of the Promised Land that is all there is for anyone on Drakaasi.'

Erkhar turned away from Alaric, placed a hand on the broken stone head that represented their Emperor, and continued to pray. By the time the congregation had finished entreating the Emperor for deliverance, Justicar Alaric had gone.

AELAZADNE!

It is the song that brings the city into being, not the other way around. A million voices raised in song! A million more in pain! The chorus of Chaos, an endless tune to which dance the very nethermost daemons of the warp!

The spires of the crystal city are a crown anointing the Blood God's world, raised from the sands to resonate with the song by a divine hand! The masters of its choirs direct the Blood God's song from the throats of its slaves, torturing the finest howls of terror and caressing the most beautiful of paeans to suffering. Was there any hideous thing so beautiful as Aelazadne? Were ever glory and horror such close soulmates as in that great crystal cathedral? Was any god exalted as Aelazadne exalts the Skull Lord of Drakaasi?

– *'Mind Journeys of a Heretic Saint,' by Inquisitor Helmandar Oswain*
(Suppressed by order of the Ordo Hereticus)

* * *

'THIS DAMN SONG,' said Gearth, 'it gets inside your soul.'

'Stay strong,' said Alaric.

'It's all right for you. Your kind get your minds rebuilt to cope with crap like this. Some of us are just mortals.' Gearth was sitting in the corner of his tiny cage, which was suspended from the ceiling over an open sewer of gore and effluent. Alaric was in the cage next to him, and through the darkness countless cells hung, each holding one of Venalitor's slaves. The slaves had been separated on the *Hecatomb* and locked into these tiny cages, which then rattled along chains and rails in the dark crystal depths of the city. The song had begun as the *Hecatomb* approached the city and had never stopped, but only got slowly louder, until it was as much a part of the place as the walls around them.

The arena of Aelazadne was above them, and even here, deep inside the honeycomb of corrupted crystal on which Aelazadne was built, the song keened from every direction. The orks were singing their own song, a horrible sound, worse than Aelazadne's music. The idea that any living thing could relish life on Drakaasi was obscene.

'Do you know what we will be fighting?'

'Heh? No one ever knows. I bet they've got something special for you, though.'

'You must have thought of getting out of here,' said Alaric.

'Yeah, thought about it plenty. Thought about being skinned and eaten by the flesh hounds, too, 'cause that's the best I could hope for if they caught me. The way I figure, there's no way off this planet. The best I can do is make them suffer. Every now and again we get to face something in the arenas that they don't want us to kill. When I come up against something like that, I'm gonna kill it. That'll hurt them more than anything I could do if I broke out.'

'But all the killing is for the glory of Khorne. Every time you kill out there, you are doing the will of Chaos.'

'Then, when they send you out there, just curl up and die. I don't care, Astartes.' Gearth sneered. 'I hear they killed your friend.'

'That is true.'

'The Imperium killed mine. The arbitrators dragged them around the back of the precinct fortress and shot them in the back of the head. There's nothing good in the universe to fight for. It's all going to hell. If you want to die out there then be my guest, but make sure you take a good look around first, Astartes, 'cause soon that's what the entire galaxy is gonna look like.'

'Then Venalitor didn't have to do much to break you,' said Alaric levelly. 'You were Khorne's servant long before he ever found you.'

Gearth spat at Alaric. Alaric ignored it. Men like Gearth were a natural by-product of the Imperium. The Imperium was a cruel place because the galaxy was cruel. Its people had to be oppressed, because if they were free to do and think as they wished, they would do horrible things that would lead the human race to destruction. Gearth was one of the many who didn't fit into the mould the Imperium had prepared for its people.

Sometimes Alaric wondered if the Emperor could one day awaken and show the Imperium a way to survive that did not require such relentless cruelty towards its citizens.

'Do you really believe,' Alaric found himself saying, 'that Drakaasi could exist without people like you?'

Gearth gave Alaric a look full of hate. Before he could retort, Alaric's cell was cranked suddenly upwards. It was hauled up a stinking narrow shaft, and a thin veil of reddish light picked out the claw marks along the sides. The sound of the arena crowd mingled perfectly with Aelazadne's song in a terrible harmony that could have broken a lesser man than a Grey Knight.

The light broke around him. The cage fell apart, and Alaric was standing in the centre of Aelazadne's arena.

THE LIGHT WAS coming from a single opening in the stone sky above Alaric. Around him a labyrinth spiralled off in all directions. It was a buried part of the city, its buildings rotting bastions of stone, with empty windows like blinded eyes and broken doorways like teeth in shattered mouths. Aelazadne had always been grand, but now the excessive decoration had decayed into a parody of beauty, sculpted pediments sagging and faceless statues lying in severed chunks on the pitted ground.

Alaric spotted tiny glistening eyes winking on the walls, swivelling to follow him. Through them, Aelazadne was watching. He heard the cheer as they focused on him, a new player entering their game.

He spotted the first body lying close by, slumped against a collapsed wall in a pool of glistening blood. It had originally been human, but more than that Alaric couldn't tell, for it had been torn clean in two. Alaric picked up the rusted blade lying by the corpse's outstretched hand.

Something lowed in the distance, deep and angry. Someone screamed. A cheer rose at the sound.

Aelazadne's song wove a different pattern here. Filtered through the layers of the city, its individual threads were clearer, and Alaric could pick out the voices, strangle sounds and gurgling, opened up to the glory of Khorne. He could pick out some of their words, too.

They were telling him to be grateful, for very few were given the honour of such a death.

Alaric flinched at a movement nearby. Another slave skulked from the shadows. He was armed with a club with an iron spike through it. Alaric realised the man was a mutant, his scrawny body disfigured with ruffs of waving cilia that wove up his neck and down his arms. He was dressed in ragged remnants of armour.

'Where is it?' the mutant demanded.

'Where is what?'

'What they sent us here to hunt.'

'I don't know. I haven't even seen it.'

'Of course you ain't. What, you fresh out of the sky?'

'Yes.'

The mutant looked Alaric up and down. 'What are you?'

'I was going to ask you the same.'

'Touched,' said the mutant with pride, 'in the blood.' Blood oozed from the fronds wriggling all over his skin. 'Bleeding for His glory, weeping Khorne's own tribute for...'

A sound close by cut off the mutant's voice. A second later a body crashed through a wall behind Alaric, bringing decayed chunks of marble crunching to the ground.

Alaric rolled away from the destruction and just caught sight of the corpse out of the corner of his eye: another mutant, a multi-armed creature, its chest an open red ruin and its face locked in an expression of surprise.

The club-armed mutant roared and charged into the seething darkness. A muscly hand grabbed him and dragged him through the ruin of the wall. The mutant screamed, and it was a scream that went on far too long for the enemy to be killing him quickly.

Alaric ran around a corner, away from the enemy's line of sight. He still had not seen it, save for its hand. He heard it lumbering away, issuing a deep rumbling growl, followed by a wet crunch that Alaric guessed was the mutant's body being mashed against the ground.

Alaric caught his breath. The monster was definitely huge, and judging by the mutant's scream it had more in its arsenal than mere strength. He could smell it, too, a mixture of sweat and heady chemicals.

Alaric had emerged into a ruined town square built around a grand fountain. The fountain's statues had lost their heads and hands and the water, if it had been water that flowed through it, had long since dried up. A sagging basilica stood along one side of the square, gutted by fire.

The creature's smell told Alaric that it had retreated in that direction. The sounds of its footsteps were all but hidden by the droning bass of Aelazadne's song, but they were there, and audible enough for Alaric to know that the beast was still close.

A stone head on the ground looked up at him. Its eyes were the same as the ones studding the walls of the labyrinth. Alaric stamped on it, shattering the head and crushing the eyes. Somewhere in Aelazadne, he hoped, two members of the audience were blinded.

The basilica's interior was twisted by heat and decay. Columns bowed under the weight of a half-fallen roof. Skeletons were embedded in the stone of the columns and walls, petrified like fossils, reaching from the rock as if they had been alive when they turned to stone.

Alaric backed up against a pillar. He looked down at the sword in his hand. It was pathetic, little more than scrap metal beaten into shape. It was worse than nothing. He put it on the ground at his feet.

He listened to the song. It was telling him to welcome death, and let it speed him towards a blessed release from life's pain. He ignored it. The song might have wormed its way into a broken man's mind, but Alaric was better than that. He listened harder.

He could hear drops of water spattering down through the hole in the roof, and the sound of the city groaning as it settled. A Space Marine's senses were all greatly enhanced, but rarely had so much hinged on Alaric being able to make the most of them.

It had come through the basilica, through the rubble at the far end, and had headed upwards.

Alaric slipped from behind the column, and began the hunt.

He crept through a collapsed colonnade that had once fronted a mighty palace, now collapsed into a sprawl of rubble. He followed the trail through its cellars, between mouldering works of art and altars to the perverse faces of Khorne.

The trail led through a garden of petrified trees and a stream bed half-filled with flaking dried blood. He moved past a pyramid of bones, and a complex of slaughterhouses, where hooks still hung from rails on the ceiling and the occasional skull still dangled.

Alaric knew that the beast he had trailed was close by. It was instinct as much as the signs: the fresh, six-toed hoof prints on the wet floor, the newly killed hunters whose blood had yet to start drying, the smell of the chemicals, and the glints of blood where the beast had torn itself on a sharp piece of rubble. Alaric slowed down, making every step an exercise in discipline, as he passed over the threshold of the slaughterhouse and onto the grand processional bridge.

Once, a great palace of Aelazadne had risen over the rest of the city. It had long since collapsed, but the way up to it remained, a mighty bridge over a deep canal. Alaric walked carefully onto the bridge, keeping a statue between him and the hulking shape he just glimpsed among the stonework. The statues rose on either side of the bridge, a stern parade of Aelazadne's kings, all of them dressed in obscene majesty that only accentuated their deformities. Eyes covered them, blinking excitedly as Aelazadne watched.

Alaric got a better look at the prey he had been sent to hunt. It was a hunched giant wrapped in swathes of scabbed skin, covered in wounds and brands. Its back was to Alaric, and he saw that it sported a crest of bony spikes along its spine.

Alaric recognised some of the beast's tattoos: an eye, a compass, a star. He had seen them many times before, and that gave him an advantage that the keenest of Drakaasi's hunters lacked.

'I know,' said Alaric aloud, 'what you are.'

The beast looked up from its meal, a hunter it had chased down and killed on the bridge. Alaric stepped out from behind the statue. The beast's face was humanoid, but no longer human, severely lopsided with a single fang reaching down past its chin. Its hands were fused into crab-like claws of muscle and talon.

Its eyes were sunk so deeply into the scarred folds of its face that it had to be blind. A larger third eye in its forehead was closed.

'When did they find you?' asked Alaric. 'How long have you been down here?'

The beast did not attack. Something like recognition came across its face.

'Remember what you once were, Navigator.'

Navigators were a paradox of the Imperium. They were members of a bloodline that sported a stable mutation in its genes. A Navigator had a third eye through which he could look upon the warp and not be driven mad, as most men would be. As a result of the mutation, only they could guide a ship on long warp jumps, and without them all ships would be limited to the stilted, short jump journeys that meant civilian craft took decades to get between star systems. Without Navigators the Imperium's armed forces would reach war zones centuries late, rapid forces like the Space Marines would never be able to launch their lightning operations, and the Imperium, bloated and sluggish at the best of times, would fall apart.

Their third eye, spacefarers said, could kill a man with a look.

It stood to reason that this creature, which had once been a Navigator, would make for very challenging quarry indeed.

Alaric slowly approached the mutant Navigator. Perhaps exposure to Drakaasi's brand of Chaos had mutated it, or perhaps it had been born that way. Although their mutation was relatively stable, Alaric had heard tales from inquisitors of the monstrous aberrations every Navigator family kept imprisoned beneath their estates on Terra.

It did not attack. Alaric was probably the first person the Navigator had encountered on Drakaasi who had not tried to kill it.

'I know why they sent me here,' said Alaric, as much to himself as to the Navigator. 'You are supposed to kill me.'

The song of Aelazadne rose to a sudden, brutal crescendo. The whole city shook, chunks of masonry and statues clattering down into the deep canal beneath the bridge. The Navigator roared and reared up, clamping its paws over its ears. Alaric, too, was shaken by the ferocity of the atonal chord that hammered down from the city above.

The Navigator thudded down onto all fours and roared at Alaric. Its third eye snapped open.

Alaric threw himself to the ground. A black ribbon of ragged power leapt from the Navigator's eye, and scored a deep furrow across the bodies of the statues around him. A stone arm clattered to the ground, the sound almost lost amid the din.

Alaric ran out of cover as the Navigator's third eye spat dark power over the bridge. He sprinted for the Navigator, head down at full tilt, and slammed into its side, vaulting over the line of dark power and up onto its back.

The Navigator bucked to throw him off and reached up to grab him. Alaric caught its hand and forced its forefinger back, feeling ligaments snapping. The Navigator's scream of pain mingled with the song, and Alaric was so dazed by the painful harmonics that he lost his grip and fell off the Navigator's back.

He reached around instinctively. His hand found the warm sticky mass of the last hunter to stalk the Navigator. He looked up and saw something metallic there: the broken haft of a spear ending in a jagged steel blade. The Navigator's shadow fell over him as he grabbed it.

The Navigator's bulk fell down on top of Alaric's legs. The mutant's face was centimetres away from his. The third eye opened again, the brow above it furrowed in anger and pain.

The song had driven it wild. Aelazadne was not about to cheat its audience of another death.

Alaric rammed the spear up at the Navigator's face. The tip splintered against the stone hard cornea of its third eye. The shaft followed it, shattering and filling its eye socket with splinters.

The Navigator barked angrily and jumped backwards, clawing at its face.

Alaric jumped to his feet. The Navigator was not a creature of Drakaasi, but it had been warped and rendered mindless by this world, turned into a weapon. Drakaasi took good people and turned them into monsters. It wanted to do the same to Alaric, if it did not kill him first.

The Navigator charged half-blinded. Alaric jumped, not into the creature's wounded face but over it, his back smacking against the creature's hide as he rolled over it.

The Navigator continued, its massive momentum too great for it to stop.

It smashed into the stone rail of the bridge, and ploughed through it. Its forelimbs found nothing as it powered forwards. The Navigator howled as it fell from the bridge, the sound followed by a terrible wet thump as it smacked gorily into the bed of the dry canal.

Alaric picked himself up off the bridge, breathing heavily. A thousand eyes were looking at him.

He had killed their Navigator. That had not been in the script.

Soldiers from Aelazadne's battlements were despatched to round him up, for the hunt was over and the audience had got their blood. Alaric knew that to fight against the armoured gauntlets holding him down would only give the city more bloodshed to gloat over, and so he let them wrap him in chains and drag him back towards the *Hecatomb*.

They had got their blood, but Alaric had got something, too. Amongst the Navigator's tattoos had been the familiar brand of a six-fingered hand.

The Navigator could kill with a look from its third eye. It was a quarry intended to kill its hunter. That was why Alaric had been thrown into the labyrinth with it. The daemon Arguthrax had made sure that Alaric was pitted against his best slave killer, in the hope that Venalitor would lose his best new slave.

The lords of Drakaasi had a weakness, a weakness that masqueraded among their number as a strength.

They hated one another. Their weakness was that hate.

EIGHT

'I HEAR MANY things,' said the eldar carefully, 'and I wish to know if any of them are true.'

'Get away from me,' said Alaric. 'I feel unclean enough as it is.'

Kelhedros tilted his head and looked at Alaric with utterly alien eyes.

Alaric was in an isolation cell. Evidently Venalitor had been angered at Arguthrax's attempt to kill Alaric with the Navigator and had taken out a measure of that anger on Alaric. Alaric was chained to the wall on a lower deck, and he was glad of it. Until Kelhedros's shadow had fallen across him he had been alone.

'I have tried to understand you,' continued Kelhedros, 'your kind, I mean, your species. It is like facing an animal, with its baffling instincts.'

Alaric had not had a good look at the alien before. Eldar were familiar to many Imperial citizens, since they were often depicted as weakling aliens crushed beneath the feet of conquering humans in stained glass windows or in the margins of illuminated prayer books. The truth was that no human artist could ever realise one properly. An eldar looked almost human from a distance: two arms, two legs, two eyes, a nose, a mouth, but everything else was different. An eldar radiated wrongness, from its huge, liquid eyes to the many jointed, worm-like waving of its fingers. They were disgusting and unnerving, and Alaric hated them. Kelhedros was as filthy and scarred as the rest of the slaves, but he still carried that typical alien arrogance with him. His armour still incorporated the jade green plates of the eldar armour he must have been captured in.

'This animal will not heel to an alien,' replied Alaric.

'Of course. You want to be free. They all do when they arrive here.'

'I have nothing to say to you.'

'You want to get out. I want to get out, too. I find you as vile as you find me, human, but it cannot be denied that we have the same goal in mind. I think neither of us has much of a chance on his own, but we are both far superior to the rest of Venalitor's rabble, and our skills would complement each other.'

Alaric laughed, and it hurt since he was still battered from the fight with the Navigator. 'Yes, I have seen what happens when a human enters into a pact with the alien. I was there at Thorganel Quintus. The Inquisition brokered an alliance between the Imperium and the eldar there. I saw you xenos fall on our troops as soon as the Daggerfall Mountains were secured. I saw you butcher us like cattle because you did not want anyone to know you needed our help to destroy what we found there. I will never trust your kind. You would see all of us exterminated just to save one of your own. You would kill us all for your convenience.'

Kelhedros drew his weapon from his back – a slender chainsword, its teeth meticulously cleaned and gleaming in the shadows of the isolation deck. 'The eldar you fought alongside. Were they of the Scorpion temple?'

Alaric sneered. 'They all looked the same.'

'You would have remembered. No eldar is stronger or more resolute than a follower on the path of the Scorpion. The Scorpion is relentless. It cannot fail, because it will die before its claws let go, and once it has its enemy in position, its sting always kills. I walked the path of the Scorpion before fate brought me here, human. They say that you are a hunter of daemons, something remarkable by the standards of your species. The eldar think the same of me. The Aspect of the Scorpion does not come easily to us. I am not just another alien, Grey Knight, even to you. I am a Striking Scorpion, and of every living thing on this planet I am by far the most likely to escape it. Without me, you will die here, probably a broken and willing slave. Together we might return to the galaxies we know. Think upon it. You have no other choice.'

'I am very picky about who gets to betray me,' said Alaric, knowing insults would be lost on the alien, but unable to help himself when confronted with such arrogance, 'and you don't make the grade.'

'You will change your mind, Grey Knight,' replied Kelhedros. It was unlikely he even understood human hatred when he saw it. If he did, he did not respond to it. 'I am out here, and you are in there. If you are so content to stay then little I can say will sway you.'

Kelhedros gave Alaric one last glance with those huge black eyes, and ducked back into the shadows. He was gone, with not even the sound of footsteps to suggest he was on the isolation deck. Alaric let himself wonder how Kelhedros had got down there at all. The alien had free run of the *Hecatomb,* and was certainly as tough as he suggested to have survived on Drakaasi for so long, not least against the human slaves, whose most ingrained instincts included hatred of the alien. However, Alaric knew what the eldar could do. An oath from an eldar meant less than nothing. It was a promise of betrayal.

Alaric had a long time to think in the darkness beneath the *Hecatomb*. Mostly, he thought about the Hammer of Daemons.

GHAAL!

That seething pit of vermin! That filth brimming sinkhole of despair! In such degradation there is purity. In such ugliness there is wonder. In such death and suffering, there is life, so holy to Drakaasi for it is life that must be ended!

The endless slums of Ghaal breed misery as they breed vermin. Its people are no more than vermin, writhing in an endless murderous mass, struggling to the surface to snatch a few moments of exultation! Was there ever such a city as Ghaal, where the trappings of wealth and culture are stripped away to reveal the raw, bleeding organs of poverty and exploitation? There is the truth of the human condition, that a human mind so easily sinks into animal violence and killing. It is a city of death where murder is the only way out, and where even the most relentless killers find but another layer of Ghaal's anti-society to slaughter their way through.

This cauldron of hate, this pit of ugliness, this aeon's worth of murder forced into the crumbling shell of a city! From the blood that runs in its streets are writ the names of Khorne!

– 'Mind Journeys of a Heretic Saint,' *by Inquisitor Helmandar Oswain*
(Suppressed by order of the Ordo Hereticus)

ALARIC'S FIRST EXPERIENCE of Ghaal was the stench. Down on the rowing decks, it rolled in like a foul mist. It was decay and misery, sweat and effluent, the stink of endless poverty.

'We're in the Narrows,' said Haggard, chained to the bench just behind Alaric. Though the slaves were discouraged from speaking on the oar decks, the slavers seemed used to ignoring Haggard. 'This is Ghaal. It's a damned orifice.'

'Literally?' asked Alaric, for whom the images of the living city Karnikhal were still vivid.

'Not quite. It's worse.'

Alaric peered through the oar-hole in the hull. It was night, and by the light of Drakaasi's evil greenish moon he could see piles of ramshackle buildings heaped up by the side of the blood canal. The canal was part of a spider web of bloodways that divided up this part of the city, presumably the narrows after which the place was named, and the *Hecatomb* moved slowly as its hull scraped along the side of the canal. Occasionally, a reedy scream filtered through the night air from the city, followed by a dull splash as a body fell into the blood.

'A city of murderers,' said Haggard. 'Every madman and piece of filth on Drakaasi ends up here. They say it's like a beacon that drags scum.'

'What purpose does it serve?'

'Purpose? There's no purpose here, justicar. It's just a city.'

'Everywhere on Drakaasi has a reason to exist. Karnikhal is a predator. Aelazadne was an altar to the Blood God. What does Drakaasi gain from Ghaal?'

Alaric looked out on the city again. Here and there the inhabitants of Ghaal, like primitives forced into ragged clothes and let loose in the streets, skulked among the shadows hiding from the moonlight. A rooftop fight sent a skinny body falling to the streets far below. Freshly slain bodies lay like heaps of rags in the street, and the sense of fear emanating from behind the black windows of the hovels was enough to suggest the thousands of people huddled there in their nightly terror. Even those few glimpses of Ghaal showed that killers walked every street and murder was the sport of choice.

'It's a farm,' said Alaric grimly. 'This is where they breed their vermin.'

'Loose the anchors!' yelled one of the scaephylyds in its strange accent. The oars were drawn in and the heavy anchor chains rattled against the sides of the *Hecatomb*. The ship came to a slow halt along a massive dock of black stone, where crowds of Ghaal's vermin hurried to and fro at the barked orders of mutant gang masters.

'To arming!' yelled the scaephylyd over the grinding of the hull against the dockside. The ship groaned as ramps were lowered, and the anchors reeled fast.

Alaric knew the drill. He was starting to lose count of the number of times he and the other slaves had filed past the arming cages to pull on tattered armour, still bloodstained from its previous owner, and pick up a weapon or two. This time, however, it was different. In one arming cage was a scaephylyd guarding an oversized suit of half-plate armour.

'You,' said the scaephylyd at Alaric's approach. 'Here.'

The armour was many times more lavish than anything the slaves had been given before. The breastplate looked like a pair of bat's wings folded over the chest, and the shoulder guards were wrought into snarling faces. Scale mail protected the joints. Beside the armour was a two-handed sword that looked like it had been carved out of an enormous fang.

'You're famous now,' said Gearth, who was choosing from a selection of rusted knives in the next cage, 'gotta look the part. They'll be betting on you an' all sorts. Reckon you've got a fan club? Kids who know your name?' Gearth smiled through his blackened teeth. 'Eh? Maybe sign something for 'em, tell 'em to listen to their mums and stay off the stimms?'

Alaric cast him a glance, and then looked back at the armour. It would certainly provide more protection than the disintegrating chainmail he usually wore, and which he had chosen purely because it was big enough to fit him. The sword looked useful, too.

Alaric pulled the armour on as the other slaves prayed or psyched themselves up. At the other end of the cages were the orks led by One-ear, kept separate from the rest of the slaves as they eagerly grabbed cleavers and swords. One-ear banged heads together and barked orders to keep them in line.

Alaric wondered how long it would take before he was like them, before he lived for the fight.

The balance of the sword was good. Nothing compared to a Nemesis weapon, but it would do. The ports swung open and the slaves were herded out to kill and die for Khorne.

GHAAL'S ARENA, THE Void Eye, was a squat cylinder of black rock honeycombed with caves where thousands of Ghaal's subhumans lived. Heaps of skulls lay at the bottom of the wall like snowdrifts, and the open corpse pits around it bubbled evilly in the darkness.

Alaric could hear the sound of the crowds in the arena, hordes of scum eager to get their fix of bloodshed. He could hear clubs and whips hitting flesh, and knew that ranks of arena warriors would be funnelling the crowds through the entrances into the arena. Many of the vermin would die, but then that was why they were on Drakaasi in the first place, to live short lives whose pain and bloody endings brought pleasure to the Blood God.

The slaves passed through an archway into darkness, hot and close. The scaephylyds hauled the doors shut behind the slaves, and they were trapped inside, packed close. Alaric could see through the darkness, and he registered the familiar mix of confusion and apprehension on the faces of Venalitor's slaves. Even the orks did not like it, and the human slaves kept as much distance as possible between them and the aliens. Kelhedros, on the other hand, looked focused. Nothing seemed to rattle the eldar.

Alaric looked around and picked out a small knot of faithful, clustered around Erkhar and praying. Alaric pushed his way through the crowd and pulled Erkhar aside.

'Lieutenant,' said Alaric, 'whatever lies inside the arena, there is a chance that you will not survive it.'

'A good chance,' replied Erkhar, 'if the Emperor so wills.'

'Then I may not get another chance to ask you.' Alaric dropped his voice to a whisper, and Erkhar had to strain to hear him above the nervous breathing and muttered prayers. 'What do you know of the Hammer of Daemons?'

Erkhar stiffened as if in shock, and his eyes darted as if to see if any faithful were nearby, even in the darkness. 'The Hammer? Where did you hear of it?'

'A rumour,' replied Alaric. 'A legend of the land, a weapon that lies somewhere on Drakaasi.'

'You seek it?'

'Perhaps.'

'You cannot find it, justicar.'

'Why?'

'Because it is an idea.'

From beyond the skull-studded inner doors of the chamber came a deep rushing, rumbling sound, like an earthquake. The Void Eye shook, dislodging some of the skulls nailed to the black walls. Some of the slaves quivered in fear, others grinned and whooped with anticipation. The orks began a low, chanting death song, something ancient and primitive, and Alaric would not have been surprised if some of the killers like Gearth had joined in.

'Tell me, Erkhar,' whispered Alaric in the lieutenant's ear.

'One day we will all be taken to the Promised Land,' said Erkhar. 'We do not know where it is or how we will get there, only that we will be delivered, but there is more to what I know. Only I and a few of the faithful understand. Some of the more... weak-minded would reject us if they understood. Their minds will be ready one day, but not yet.'

'The Hammer?'

'The Hammer shows us that we were not placed on Drakaasi just to run away. It is a weapon to be used against the enemy. The Hammer of

Daemons will be wielded by the faithful to punish the servants of Chaos. Do you see, justicar? Do you see why it is so dangerous, why so many would despair to hear of it?'

Alaric couldn't answer for a moment. There was genuine fear in Erkhar's face. The Hammer represented something unexpected and powerful in the faithful's patchwork religion.

'The faithful just want to get off this planet,' said Alaric, 'but you know it's not that simple.'

The doors opened a crack and a thin line of purplish, polluted light slid into the chamber. Blood rushed through the gap, covering the floor in a shallow red pool. One of the orks howled like a wolf, and the others joined in. Some of the humans raised their voices, too, echoing the frenzied applause from the vermin packing the Void Eye.

'Correct, justicar,' said Erkhar. 'One day the Hammer of Daemons will be delivered to us and we will raise it against the enemy. Only then will we in turn be delivered to the Promised Land. Do you see what that means, justicar?'

'It means that the Emperor isn't going to save you for free.'

'It means that survival is not enough.'

The doors boomed open. A thigh-high tide of blood flooded the chamber, knocking some men off their feet. Alaric saw Gearth dipping his hand into the blood and branding a bloody hand print across his face. Kelhedros drew his chainsword.

Erkhar turned back to his faithful. 'Take heart! These doors take us one step closer to the Emperor's halls!'

'One step closer to death, boys!' shouted Gearth in reply, and the other killers laughed raucously. 'Human blood doesn't come cheap! Let's show them the price!'

There was an ocean of blood beyond the doors. The canals must have been diverted to fill the whole Void Eye with it, and it churned beneath the hulls of a dozen ships of black timber, their sails daubed with bleeding runes. Already the blood bobbed with bodies and severed limbs. Fortified compounds separated the vermin in the stands from the dignitaries, and Alaric was sure he saw the bloated whitish form of Arguthrax squatting in its cauldron of gore.

The closest ship drew nearer. Arena slaves on board threw ropes through the door, and the orks grabbed them eagerly, hauling the ship in. Orks and killers were leaping onto its deck.

Across the arena, the scene was being repeated, but this time daemons were leaping onto the decks and scrabbling up the rigging, glowing-skinned creatures with shifting forms composed of teeth, claws, eyes and shimmering muscle.

It was a sea battle. The lords of Drakaasi had given the subhuman filth of Ghaal a different kind of murder to cheer.

The first ship was full and the next one drew near. Alaric followed Kelhedros onto it, along with several of Gearth's murderers and Erkhar's faithful. The blood churned beneath it and drew it away from the dock chamber, towards the centre of the arena where it would meet the daemon crewed warships. The crowds howled in anticipation.

At least, thought Alaric grimly as he crouched down on the deck of the ship, the good people of Ghaal will not be disappointed.

NINE

THE UNHOLY PITCHED wildly in the howling winds that suddenly sheared across the Void Eye. Alaric gripped the rail on the prow as the ship tilted. A couple of slaves fell from the rigging into the blood.

The battle had begun as soon as the slaves were on board. The wind had thrown the ships across the blood sea. The blood churned with predators who dragged down the slaves who fell in, and Alaric saw chewed corpses being thrown out of the blood into the stands where Ghaal's spectators tore them apart. It had happened so quickly there had been no time to organise the slaves on the ship. They had time only to hold on and hope that the blood did not claim them. The opposing ships, crewed by daemons, were launched from the far side of the arena to an enormous cheer from the crowds.

'We're gonna hit port side!' yelled Gearth, who was armed with a pair of rusty daggers, and holding on to the fore mast to keep from being flung across the deck.

'Which way's port?' asked one of Gearth's killers.

'There!' replied Gearth, pointing. 'Didn't your dad never tell you nothing?'

The *Unholy* was drawn around towards the opposing ship. The name etched below its prow proclaimed it as the *Meathook*. Red-skinned daemons danced on its pitching deck.

'Grapples ready!' shouted Gearth.

'We're going aboard?' asked Erkhar, who was holding on to the deck rail close to Gearth.

'We go to them,' said Gearth. 'If you wanna die, you just sit back and let them come to us.'

'He's right,' shouted Alaric. 'If we let them pounce, we're dead. Erkhar, get the faithful to draw in the *Meathook*. Gearth, get your men ready to board.'

'Just try and stop 'em,' said Gearth. With a grin on his blood-spattered face he looked completely at home.

The slaves had found a number of ropes with grappling hooks below decks. Erkhar's faithful, muttering desperate prayers to the Emperor, got ready to fling them across to the enemy ship as the *Meathook* closed in.

Elsewhere, the sea battle was close and extremely bloody. The orks were having the time of their lives as their ship, dubbed the *Soulbleed*, had rammed the daemon-crewed *Wrack*. It was impossible to tell who was winning, since both the greenskins and daemons were whooping with joy as they cut one another to pieces. The daemons on the *Soulbleed* were led by a huge creature: a dog-faced, muscular horror armed with a huge axe, who stood on the stern slicing up anything that came close. Alaric spotted the brand of a six-fingered hand seared into the daemon's chest.

The third slave ship, the *Malice*, was in the process of sinking, its slaves scrabbling up the tilting hull. The daemons on the ship that had rammed it, the *Gorehallow*, were diving into the blood to circle the sinking *Malice* like sharks and drag down any slaves who fell in.

It was the clash of the *Unholy* and the *Meathook* that would decide whether the slaves or the daemons triumphed for the delight of Ghaal's hordes.

A handful of hooks found purchase on the *Meathook*. A volley of arrows whistled across from the *Meathook* in reply. Alaric took cover as an arrow thunked into the deck beside him, and he saw that it was not an arrow at all but a dart shaped insectoid creature, mandibles working as it bored into the wood. One of Erkhar's faithful screamed and stumbled backwards with one of the creatures embedded in his chest. He had dropped one of the ropes attaching the *Unholy* to the *Meathook* and Alaric grabbed it, putting all his weight into dragging the two ships together. Alaric's enhanced muscles burned as the prows of the ships swung together, and with a screech of breaking wood the two ships collided.

Gearth stood up, brandished his blades, and howled. The murderers followed him as he ran for the prow and leapt across. More arrows streaked into the *Unholy*, but the assault had already begun. The daemons were dropping their bows of bone and leaping with teeth and claws into the fray. Gearth cut off a tentacled arm, and slit open a belly, charging on through the slick of glowing, burning entrails. The daemons on the *Meathook* were sinewy and cruel faced, with tiny burning eyes and axe-like faces full of teeth. They grew new limbs and re-formed to sprint spider-like through the rigging or along the side of the *Unholy's* hull.

Alaric jumped the gap between the ships. A daemon leapt down from the rigging onto him. Alaric didn't even draw his sword, simply grabbing the daemon by a wrist and an ankle, tearing it in two, and throwing it into the blood churning below.

Gearth skidded into place beside him. One of his knives was gone, probably buried in the skull of a daemon. He was covered in smouldering gore, for these daemons bled scalding embers as well as blood.

'About damn time!' cackled Gearth. 'Just like home!'

Alaric drew his sword and took stock of the situation. Gearth's charge had taken half the deck, but there were daemons everywhere. More were emerging from below decks, but these were not warriors, they were shrieking creatures of skin and bone, flapping like startled birds.

'There's something below decks,' shouted Alaric above the din. 'These were just keeping it down there.'

'Good!' replied Gearth.

Daemon corpses rained down. Kelhedros was somewhere up in the rigging, and Alaric could hear the scream of his chainblade through daemonic flesh.

The *Meathook* was a trap. The *Unholy* had run into it, but Alaric could not have stopped it. The only way to deal with it was to fight on through.

The deck heaved. Men and daemons were thrown into the blood. The stern of the *Meathook* splintered and burst into the air, shards of blood-soaked timbers flying everywhere. A scaled shape ripped up out of the ship: a sea serpent far longer than the *Meathook*, dredged up from some Emperor-forsaken trench in Drakaasi's oceans and coiled up inside the ship, goaded until it was angry and ravenous.

The serpent looped up into the air above the ship, crashing through the rigging. Its head, a fanged horror fringed with tentacles, plunged back into the deck amidships, and the *Meathook* split in two. The rear half tipped to stern and filled with blood. The prow did not begin to sink straight away, buoyed up as it was by the *Unholy* alongside it.

Alaric stood on the prow of the shattered *Meathook*, sword out, trying to follow the snake-like movements of the sea monster. It snapped at the rigging, picking up a daemon in its mandibles and tossing it down its throat. A slave, one of Gearth's killers, followed, stabbing haplessly at the thing's vast jaws as he disappeared down its gullet.

Oozing green eyes ringed its head. One of them settled on Alaric.

The serpent reared up and arrowed back down at Alaric. The Grey Knight dived to one side as its neck slammed down onto the prow of the *Meathook*. The remains of the ship sagged under the impact, and the *Unholy* listed with the weight. A tentacle whipped around Alaric's leg and dragged him towards the yawning jaws of the serpent.

Alaric kicked out, shattering a tooth. Foul blood sprayed everywhere. In desperation, he braced with his arms as the jaws closed around him and held the sea serpent's mouth open, bathed in its stinking, rotting breath, writhing flagellae in its throat trying to snag his feet and drag him down.

Alaric yelled as he fought to keep his elbows straight. He could hear screaming below him as the slaves and daemons already swallowed were forced through the serpent's corrosive guts. His sword was still in his hand, but to use it he would have to stop bracing the serpent's jaws and its teeth would come crunching down on him.

The whine of a chainblade cut through the serpent's roar. Blood sprayed over Alaric as the tip of a chainsword bored down through the top of the serpent's jaw. The serpent convulsed, and Alaric planted a foot against a huge fang and kicked himself free.

Alaric skidded onto the deck of the shattered *Meathook* as the serpent reared up in pain. A figure was flung off the top of its head and landed near Alaric, just keeping its footing on the blood-slick wood.

It was Kelhedros, the alien.

'Xenos,' said Alaric, 'you saved me.'

'It benefits none of us if you are dead.'

'We can't beat that thing,' said Alaric, looking over at the serpent, which was demolishing what remained of the *Meathook's* stern.

'No, we cannot, but this battle is over. The winds have changed. If we cut the *Unholy* free we can get it back to the dock. It was the serpent they wanted to see.'

Alaric followed Kelhedros's gaze towards the crowd. They were frenzied with delight to see the serpent swallowing slaves and daemons alike. They were shrieking their approval of the orks and daemons butchering one another on the *Wrack*, too, which was being driven closer to the wreck of the *Meathook*. Alaric could see Arguthrax in the crowd, wallowing in his cauldron of gore, and surrounded by slaves close to the wall that encompassed the mock ocean of blood. He could see Duke Venalitor, too, pale and dignified among the crowd, as he watched his slaves providing entertainment for Khorne's faithful.

'Cut the *Unholy* free,' said Alaric. 'Get them to safety.'

'And you?' asked the alien.

'Survival is not enough,' replied Alaric.

The *Wrack* drifted closer. Alaric could see the dog-faced daemon champion flinging an ork down from the stern. On the prow, the ork leader One-ear was building up a pile of broken daemons with a two-handed hammer.

Kelhedros didn't hang around to see what Alaric was planning to do. The eldar leapt from the prow of the *Meathook* onto the deck of the *Unholy* and immediately set about cutting the ropes attaching the two ships together.

The front mast of the *Meathook* was almost horizontal as the prow half sunk further. It was pointing towards the approaching *Wrack*. Alaric ran up it, struggling to keep his balance as his considerable weight tipped the mast down.

The *Wrack* closed further. The daemon champion bit into an ork, bright blood running down its scarred chest. The crowd in the stands was in a bloody frenzy, and Arguthrax bellowed his approval.

Alaric broke into a run. He reached the end of the mast and jumped. The deck of the *Wrack* swirled below him. He was strong, but he barely made it. His chest thumped into the deck rail of the ship's prow, and he grabbed with one hand, his other still holding his sword. With a final effort he hauled himself onto the deck of the *Wrack*.

One-ear looked down at him and grinned. The alien looked like it was having the time of its life. Several other orks were still alive, enthusiastically wrestling daemons onto the deck or hacking them up with cleavers.

The daemon champion fixed its eyes on Alaric. It was half again as tall as the Grey Knight, packed with muscle and drooling from its dog-like muzzle. It fought with claws and a barbed tail. Dismembered greenskins were piled up around its feet. A pair of ragged, leathery wings sprouted from its back as it snarled a war cry in its daemonic tongue and leapt up into the air.

The crowd cheered as the daemon charged, swooping down towards the prow on its wings. Its weight alone could crush Alaric onto the deck. Alaric moved faster than he had ever done. He dropped his sword and grabbed the mast that jutted from the prow of the *Wrack*. With a massive effort, he broke it free, and turned it around so that the wooden point was aimed at the daemon's chest.

Too late, the daemon tried to correct its charge. It beat its wings once to carry it over Alaric, but Alaric lunged, and the point of the mast hit the daemon in the stomach. The daemon's weight forced the mast into it and it slid, dead weight, down the mast until its feet hit the deck. Impaled on the mast, stuck like an insect pinned to a board, it screamed.

Alaric pushed down on the broken mast and forced the daemon to its knees. The crowd adored it, and the orks cheered too. In the stand, Arguthrax scowled. The six-fingered hand branded on the daemon's chest indicated that it belonged to Arguthrax. No doubt he had sent it to the Void Eye to help humiliate Venalitor's slaves. As far as Arguthrax was concerned, the battle had not worked out as planned.

Alaric picked up his sword again. With a single bloody strike he struck the daemon champion's head from its shoulders. Burning multi-coloured blood sprayed from the stump of its neck. Alaric let go of the mast and the daemon's body keeled over to one side onto the deck. Alaric bent down and picked up its head.

One-ear saluted Alaric for a job well done. The other daemons on the *Wrack* keened, and the remaining orks plunged into them, tearing mal-formed limbs from bodies, and cutting torsos open. The sea battle in the Void Eye was emphatically over.

There was one more victory to win. Alaric stood up on the deck rail and drew his arm back. He had only just enough strength left, and he would have to be accurate. He didn't know if he could do it. The crowd cheered him, thinking this was a victory pose, and Alaric let their howls of delight give him strength.

He threw the head as far as he could. It was still snarling and glaring at him as it tumbled towards the stands. With a wet thump, it landed at Duke Venalitor's feet.

Every eye in the arena followed it as it fell. Every eye turned to see the look of pure hatred on Arguthrax's face.

The *Wrack* drifted back towards the arena entrance, where the slaves on the *Unholy* were already disembarking. The orks around Alaric were celebrating their victory, following his lead by hurling chunks of dead daemon towards the stands. One-ear bellowed a war cry and the other greenskins joined in.

For all Alaric knew, they were chanting his praises.

TEN

THE DESPOILER OF Kolchadon, the Bloody Hand of Skerentis Minor, the End of Empires, Arguthrax the Magnificent slid from his cauldron into the entrail pool that dominated his sanctum beneath Ghaal.

Human emotions did not trouble the mind of a daemon. No mortal could truly understand what went on in a daemon's head without going insane, for the rules of logic had no hold over them. No human emotion could therefore be properly ascribed to a daemon. Nevertheless, Arguthrax was definitely angry.

'Filth!' the daemon bellowed as his bloated body sank into the tangle of entrails. 'Whelp! Weakling dog! He will pay. He and his slaves, and his... his natives! That filth will suffer!'

'My lord,' said Khuferan, the majordomo of Arguthrax's sanctum, 'something has vexed you.'

Arguthrax glared at him. Khuferan had been completely human before he had died and been drawn, in the form of a bone-dry mummified corpse, into Arguthrax's army as it marched across the ruins of his home world. Khuferan had been some kind of king or high priest thousands of years ago, but he had forsaken whatever he had in life to serve Chaos in death. 'The upstart, Venalitor. That near-human thing who calls himself a duke. He has sought to humiliate me... me!'

'It is the way of Drakaasi.'

'So is revenge,' snarled Arguthrax. 'Who do we have on the streets and on the plains? Who heeds the words of Arguthrax?'

Khuferan snapped his bony fingers, and lesser daemons, scurrying things like animated blobs of flesh with vestigial limbs, hurried away from him into the dark corners of the sanctum. The sanctum was a spherical cyst in the earth, half-filled with the entrails of thousands of sacrifices. A spur of rock held the sacrificial altar, black with generations of blood, as well as giving Arguthrax's mortal followers like Khuferan somewhere to stand when they addressed their master.

One of the daemons brought Khuferan a heavy book bound in strips of beaten brass. Khuferan leafed through its pages, on which were written the names of thousands of organisations and individuals loyal to Arguthrax. Every lord of Drakaasi had followers he could call upon, many of them hidden deep in the underbelly of Khorne's cities, waiting for the call to action.

'Lord Ebondrake's pronouncement of the crusade has led to a great mobilisation,' said Khuferan. 'We have called upon the Legion of the Unhallowed to bring themselves forth from the jungles and march under your banner, Lord Arguthrax.'

'Savages,' said Arguthrax, 'primitives, but useful. Who else?'

'The Thirteenth Hand are still off-world, but they are returning at your command. The warp shall deliver them to us in a few days. They are battle-hardened, my lord, and have acquired many new members.'

'Hmm. That is good.' The Thirteenth Hand were a fanatical murder cult whose leaders had been ordained in the will of Khorne by Arguthrax himself. 'What of the warp?'

'Relations are... strained,' said Khuferan. 'Many have been lost. The warp dislikes so many losses. Profligacy in the arenas has left us—'

'I am the Despoiler of Kolchadon!' spat Arguthrax. 'How many billions of gallons of blood have rained into the warp at my behest? The daemon lords will heed one of their own, one such as I. I want hunter daemons on the streets, black as the void, and with Venalitor's scent. I want furies in the sky following every movement of his underlings. I want the *Hecatomb* under siege!'

'It will be done. The losses at the Void Eye will require greater recompense for the warp.'

'Tell them they are having revenge. Venalitor had his pet Astartes kill my daemon champion to insult me. He even took its head for himself! It was an insult to all daemonkind, and the warp will have its due if Venalitor suffers. We will bring him low, and then we will kill him. Tell that to the warp. It will listen.'

'Very well, my lord.'

'And the rest of them: the Haunters of the Nethermost Shadow, the mutant cults beneath Vel'Skan. Bring them all in.'

'And the watchers?'

Arguthrax paused. The lords of Drakaasi spied on one another. It was like a game, played with agents who went into deep cover among the coteries of the lords. No doubt other lords had eyes and ears among Arguthrax's followers. Arguthrax had uncovered and eaten more than a few of them. They were mortals and daemons with some talent to obscure their true selves, and they were pariahs. It was not the way of Khorne to skulk in the shadows, and so Drakaasi's spies were a sort of underclass present at the very highest layers of the planet's society. Arguthrax had his own shape shifting daemons and old-fashioned human informers bound to him by contracts of blood.

'If they can fight,' said Arguthrax. 'Punishing Venalitor is a higher priority than anything else. The games, Ebondrake's crusade, everything can wait until he has been brought low.'

'If it is your wish, Lord Arguthrax,' said Khuferan. He bowed his ancient death shrouded body before his master, and turned to walk back down the spur of rock and begin organising his lord's slaves.

The light in the sanctum dimmed. Arguthrax sank into the great cauldron of entrails, deep in thought.

'I REMEMBER,' SAID Kelhedros, 'when I learned of the Fall.'

Kelhedros's cell was relatively clean. The other slaves on the *Hecatomb* knew better than to invade the place. Kelhedros had painted complex rune patterns on the walls in paint mixed from blood and sand. His green metallic armour lay against the wall. The eldar was picking the blood from between the teeth of his chainsword. The sea serpent's blood had been particularly viscous and it was a job to work it out of the mechanism.

'The Fall?' asked Alaric.

'I forget, human, that you are not well versed in our ways. Some of you have studied us, I understand: the biologists of your Inquisition. The better to kill us, of course. But not you.'

'I know that you are aliens.'

'Strange. That is all I once knew of you.'

The journey back from the Void Eye had been deeply strained. Venalitor had stood glowering at them from the helm of the *Hecatomb*, the head of Arguthrax's daemon champion in his hand. Many slaves had been lost, and Haggard had been unable to keep up with the wounded. The orks, forced to wait until last for treatment since they healed so well, were squabbling with each other in their barred enclave. Alaric had sought out Kelhedros. It had become apparent to him early in his career as a Grey Knight that having his life saved at least deserved a few words of thanks, and the possibility of an ally on Drakaasi, even an alien, could not be ignored.

'Long ago, my kind ruled the galaxy,' continued Kelhedros, 'much as your kind claim to rule it now. We were artists and aesthetes, while you are soldiers. We took worlds and made them beautiful instead of merely inhabiting them like insects in a nest.'

'None taken,' said Alaric.

Kelhedros gave him a quizzical look. 'Quite, but we were arrogant, prideful. Some of what I see in your kind, my kind must have seen in themselves. They indulged their base delights. The warp took heed. From the sinful pride of my people was born... one of the great powers of the warp. I cannot speak of it. It plagues us still and reaps its toll among humankind, too.'

'I imagine this is not something an alien would normally speak of to a human.'

'Indeed it is not. Many would think me a traitor for saying it, but then I am a traitor for surviving here amongst such... pollution.'

'Then why tell me?'

'Because I see it on this world, too, and in your Imperium.' Kelhedros looked up from his chainblade. 'The Fall killed the better part of my species. Only those who saw it coming escaped it in their world ships. My kind, so far advanced compared to yours, was almost wiped out. Think what another Fall would do to you. Do not think that you will see it coming, or that it has not already begun. You are living through the death of your species at this very moment and you do not realise it.'

'I cannot believe that,' said Alaric. 'There must be hope.'

Kelhedros arched an eyebrow. 'Why?'

'Because without it we are lost.'

'You are lost anyway. Whether you truly believe in salvation or not is irrelevant. Death is death.'

'Perhaps everything you say is true and these are the death throes of the human race, but even if that was true, I would not lose faith. There must be hope, and I must fight for my Emperor against Chaos and its servants. That is just the way it is.'

'That is insanity.'

'Wrong, it's being human.'

'That's it? That is why you have managed to spread to the stars and found this Imperium, in spite of all the obvious primitivism of your minds?'

'That's right,' said Alaric. 'We believe. I suppose that's it.'

'There are such strange things in the galaxy,' said Kelhedros.

'Now there we can agree.'

Kelhedros put his chainsword to one side and began on his armour. Like the weapon, it was old and battered but well-maintained. Beneath the armour, Kelhedros's body was slim but muscular, quite the opposite of Alaric's own oversized frame. He was scarred, too, and like Alaric not all of them were war wounds. Runes were scored into the eldar's torso. They were symbols with half-glimpsed meaning: half a face without a mouth, a hand, a stylised blade, all twining together in thorny knot work.

'I do not think, Grey Knight, that you are here to discuss the state of the universe,' said Kelhedros.

'I came here to thank you.'

'It is not necessary. It does not benefit any of us to lose our best fighter.'

'You took a risk.'

'One can hardly survive on Drakaasi without taking risks. If we flee death, we only run into its waiting arms. My own chances of survival are increased if you are there by my side, so I took risks to prevent your death. Anyone understanding the reality of our situation would do the same thing. Likewise, you are taking a considerable risk by speaking willingly to an alien that your kind despises to the point of genocide, and so you have a reason to be here, too.'

Alaric leaned across the rail and looked down on the floor of the main chamber. Kelhedros's cell was one floor up, and gave him an excellent view of what was going on among the *Hecatomb's* slaves. 'Look down there,' he said.

Kelhedros stood by his side. 'At what?'

'The greenskins.'

'The animals? I sully my eyes with them as little as possible.'

'Then for the first time, try watching them.'

The orks, those who had survived the Void Eye relatively unscathed, were scrapping with each other amid the filth of their enclosure. One-ear was standing aside, barking insults and grunting appreciation.

'They are just turning on each other,' said Kelhedros, 'for they know that the humans will mass against them if they do not. They are cowards.'

'Wrong,' said Alaric. 'Watch.'

One-ear dragged two fighting greenskins apart. He cuffed the loser around the back of the head, shoving him away. The winner he clapped

on the back, much as he had congratulated Alaric for cutting the head off
the daemon, and turned back to watch the other greenskins scrapping.

'That one,' said Kelhedros, 'he's in charge.'

'Exactly.'

'But it is the way of the animal. The strongest rules.'

'And he is using that. He's training them, toughening them up.'

'He simply wants to survive.'

'We all want to survive, eldar. One-ear has a plàn, which is more than
most of the humans here. Think about it, the best way for the orks to
survive on Drakaasi is to make themselves essential. That way they can
be sure that Venalitor won't throw their lives away. The better they fight,
the better a show they put on for the crowds, the longer they will live.'

'So the creature has a plan?'

'A plan, to survive.'

Kelhedros smiled, which was disconcerting to see since his alien face
produced only expressions that looked fundamentally wrong to human
eyes. 'I was under the impression that you humans and these greenskins
once encountered each other in the early stages of exploring the galaxy,
and took an instant dislike to one another that has never dimmed. It
sounds as if you admire One-ear.'

'I hate the ork just like any other Emperor fearing citizen, but the fact
remains that One-ear has a better grasp of the situation, and a sounder plan
for surviving it, than most of the slaves here. I thought the same as you, Kelhedros, and assumed that an ork was just a fighting machine that couldn't
even think. Then I took the time to watch, and I found I was wrong.'

'What is your plan?' asked Kelhedros bluntly.

'I haven't quite decided yet,' said Alaric, 'but I am not willing to wait
in this damned ship to die, or to serve their god by fighting until someone kills me in the arenas. I'm getting out.'

'And you need me.'

This time Alaric smiled. 'Forgive my bluntness, eldar, but I did not seek
you out in the name of inter-species relations. You are one of the *Hecatomb's*
best fighters, and you have the run of the ship. I may well have a use for
you. Be ready for that, Kelhedros, and try not to die in the meantime.'

'How do you know I will agree to your plan, human, whatever it is?
That I do not have a way of my own to escape?'

'Because you are still here,' said Alaric, and walked away.

ELEVEN

DUKE VENALITOR STOOD at the helm of the *Hecatomb*, watching as the war city of Gorgath rolled up onto the horizon.

The *Hecatomb* was a bulbous hulk, fat and groaning. Venalitor appreciated the impression the ship gave: it looked full to bursting with slaves or riches, or perhaps blood like a sated parasite. Its black timbers creaked as it sailed slowly along the blood canal that wound towards Gorgath. Above, the masts and rigging were like a ribcage of dark wood, its sails like funeral shrouds. Drakaasi's dawn was fighting to clamber above the horizon, but the night was putting up a stern resistance.

As Venalitor had known it would, the first of the shadows peeled off from the rigging and slid down the mast near the stern. It pooled on the deck, twin eyes flickering in its dark body. Another slid over the deck rail. Venalitor often had his scaephylyds stand to attention on the deck as an honour guard, but not tonight. He wanted to do this alone.

The first shadow skittered along the edge of the deck, heading for the raised helm where Venalitor stood. It wanted to sneak up behind him. No doubt it had his scent, and had tracked him all the way from the warp. It was probably aeons old, congealed from a nightmare in the warp, and finally let loose in real space to hunt. It was strange that it should die here after all that.

More shadows gathered. They formed fanged maws and keen silver eyes. They thought that Venalitor could not see them.

Venalitor's sword was in his hand even as the first daemon slunk towards him. He had drawn it so quickly that not even a daemon's eyes could have followed the movement.

'The toad daemon will not have his fill of blood from me tonight,' he snarled.

He spun, and sliced the daemon behind him in two. The shadow-stuff of its body sprayed like black blood. The other hunter daemons howled and bounded towards him. They were up in the rigging, charging across the deck. Venalitor met them head-on, slicing through the first and spearing the next through the eye.

It was a display of swordsmanship so precise and flowing that it was not combat at all, but the carving of a work of art into the flesh of the hunter daemons. Venalitor bayed them into charging, and then cut them apart as they ran at him. One dived down from the rigging, maw distended to swallow him whole. Venalitor let its substance flow over him, and then slit it open and stepped out of its body like a man free of a straitjacket. He flicked the black gore off his blade and finished killing the hunter daemons. It was not even a contest, just a matter of course, a final flourish.

Venalitor returned to the helm for a while, as the blood of the hunter daemons soaked into the planks of the deck.

Eventually, his slave master shambled from inside the ship. 'It has come to pass?' the scaephylyd asked.

'Of course it has,' said Venalitor. 'Arguthrax is a creature of habit. He felt he was insulted at Ghaal and he wanted me dead, so he sent his hunters after me. No doubt their trail will lead back to Arguthrax's court in the warp.'

'A war with Arguthrax is something we can well do without.'

'Those are the words of an animal of real space, not a creature of the warp,' replied Venalitor sternly. 'War is war. It comes upon us not as a plague to be feared, but as an opportunity to be grasped. Arguthrax has decided to make war upon me. Every lord of Drakaasi must war with his peers, it is as sure a law as any on this planet. I shall make war upon him in return and I shall win, and his share of Drakaasi shall be mine.'

'And Ebondrake?'

'The dragon will not know. He focuses too much on his crusade to bother with us. Arguthrax will fall before Ebondrake knows of any feud. Make ready my briefing chambers, I wish to review the disposition of our followers. This war must have a general.'

'Very well.'

'What of the slaves?'

'They plot, as they might. The religious ones pray and the killers plan to murder us all.'

'Good, good. And the Grey Knight?'

'He is quiet. He spoke with the eldar, but otherwise he has done little to elicit suspicion.'

'The Space Marine and the eldar? The universe brings something new with every moment. You may be about your duties, slave master.'

The slave master bowed to the bloodstained deck and scuttled back inside the ship.

Dawn was breaking over Gorgath. It broke, as it always did, over war.

Venalitor watched the sun rise and vowed, as he did every morning, that it would set on a world where Duke Venalitor held a little more of Drakaasi in his fist.

GORGATH!

A city only in name, for none would claim to dwell there. A battlefield in form and function, into which endless columns of damned men are fed to oil the war machine!

None can say when the battle began, and many are those that say it had no beginning. It is an echo of a battle yet to come, or the shadow of a war fought out of time, or a reflection of all the bloodshed in the galaxy sprung up in all its hideous forms to blood the plains of Drakaasi.

The battlefield of Gorgath is ever-changing, filled with the ruins of fortresses and of cities raised only so they can fall again to siege. Here is a weapon of fiendish design, brought low by spears and flint arrowheads! There are cavalry in their finery, cut apart by bullets, and scorched by mechanical flame. There can be no tactic for victory, for Gorgath despises victory, and its battlefields deform to deny any ruse, no matter how brilliant. Only blood lust and hatred can win the day at Gorgath, and then only until the next day, when a new war blooms among the corpse strewn plains.

What can Gorgath be? A creature with a sentience of its own, with violence for lifeblood and warfare for breath? A machine for the blooding of Drakaasi's armies, whose lords feed their underlings through Gorgath to take command of the bloody veterans that emerge? Or some conglomeration of Chaos, some function of the ever-changing warp, bled through into flesh and blood?

Not one of these questions troubles the mind of Gorgath's killers, for they are truly its children, devoted to it and yet despising it, trapped in the war machine, the age of slaughter, the one true battlefield that is Gorgath!

– 'Mind Journeys of a Heretic Saint,' *by Inquisitor Helmandar Oswain (Suppressed by order of the Ordo Hereticus)*

* * *

THE STRONGEST SLAVES were up on the deck, forcing the *Hecatomb* along with poles, as gangs of scaephylyds slogged their way along the shore hauling ropes tied to the ship's prow. Alaric, the strongest of all the slaves, was up near the stern. It was the first time he had got a good look at the *Hecatomb* from outside. By the Emperor, it was ugly.

'Justicar,' said a voice behind Alaric.

Alaric turned to see Hoygens, the member of Erkhar's faithful who had spoken to him at the prayer meeting. 'I heard you speak with Erkhar.'

'Before Ghaal?' asked Alaric.

'Yes, though it was not for my ears.'

'I merely seek to understand what is happening on this world. I intend to survive it.'

'The lieutenant does not think my faith is strong enough to be indoctrinated in the truth he sees,' continued Hoygens. 'He would not have told me about the Hammer of Daemons. I am just the kind of weak-willed man who would lose his faith if he understood it.'

'But your faith is not gone?'

Hoygens shrugged. 'I don't have that much else. I lose my faith and what am I?'

'Not much.'

'Less than that. I'd be one of Gearth's men. I'd have given up being human. Listen, justicar. I know more than Erkhar thinks I do. I was there on the *Pax*, and I know where this religion comes from. Erkhar gives us readings from a religious text he has. I have been unable to follow their meaning many times. I don't see this place in the same colours as Erkhar does.'

'Have you seen this text?'

'I haven't read it, but it exists. I don't think Erkhar wrote it, either, and I don't believe he had it before we were brought to Drakaasi.'

'He found it here?'

'Perhaps, I don't know, but justicar, if the Hammer of Daemons is more than just an idea, maybe it's here, and we can grasp and use it.'

'Perhaps it can get us off this planet.'

'If it can, if there's even a chance, then you have to find it. Emperor knows a sinner like me can't do much, but you're a Space Marine, you can do anything.'

'Not quite, Brother Hoygens,' said Alaric. 'Can you get this book?'

'Not without killing Erkhar,' said Hoygens, 'and I won't do that. I believe in him, Justicar. Whether he's right about the Hammer or anything else, he's the only thing that's kept any of the crew of the *Pax* alive.'

'The Hammer is real,' said Alaric, 'and if it can be found, I will find it.'

'If it's a weapon, Justicar, you're the one who's going to have to wield it.'

'I would look forward to it,' said Alaric, 'if it can help us fight back.'

One of the scaephylyds lashed a whip at Hoygens. Hoygens scowled at it and went back to his post.

Only Chaos could create a place like Gorgath, thought Alaric, and only the followers of Khorne would do it with such blunt, literal brutality. Columns of robed cultists and wild mutants marched on either shore of the blood river, following armoured champions towards Gorgath's endless battle. Alaric could hear the sound of its devastation, and could even make out the outline of a feral Titan as it lumbered around firing indiscriminately. Everywhere were the scars of war: bones poking from the barren soil, the foundations of long-fallen fortresses, monuments and mass graves. This was where the army that had taken Sarthis Majoris was first blooded. It was a factory for war, a machine for churning out armies, where the dregs of Drakaasi were fed into the battlefield and transformed into instruments of Chaos.

Alaric could see hundreds of thousands of them. Gorgath was an obscenity. It was a celebration of war for its own sake, death without purpose, a dreadful hollow slaughter that offended Alaric to the core.

The *Hecatomb* ground its way through the ruins of a barricade still draped with the blackened skeletons of those who had fought over it decades before. The great dark stain of the battle emerged on the horizon, shot through with plumes of fire, the feral Titans stalking through the carnage, and ragged banners streaming everywhere. At the heart of it stood Gorgath's arena.

CENTURIES BEFORE, ONE of Gorgath's most creative and brutal warlords had decided to create slaughter on such a scale that it would forever be remembered by Drakaasi. He enslaved an army and put it to work mining deep beneath Gorgath's tortured earth, tunnelling around charnel pits and buried war machines until they reached the site of some of the fiercest fighting.

Then the warlord's slaves carted huge amounts of explosives into the tunnels and laid them there, waiting for the battle above to reach a peak. They prayed for destruction, and wound the explosive caches with prayers of fire and horror. When the time came they detonated them and let Khorne's holy fire wipe them off the surface of Drakaasi.

The explosion was heard all across Drakaasi. The towers of Aelazadne shook, and Ghaal's shanties collapsed. Hundreds of thousands died in moments. Ash and shattered stone rained down over Gorgath for a week afterwards. The debris and the dead formed a dark cloud that some said had never fully cleared away.

No one remembered the name of the warlord, but the crater remained, and on Lord Ebondrake's orders it had been cleared out and made ready as Gorgath's grand arena.

IT WAS THE smell of Gorgath, and the taste of it on the air, that really got to Alaric. It hit him as Venalitor's slaves were driven between two huge blocks of ruined fortifications towards the arena. It tasted like fear, blood and voided bowels, gun smoke and fragments of steel. It smelt of smouldering bodies and dust from collapsed buildings. The engine smoke from the feral Titans completed it. Alaric had been at a thousand battles, and Gorgath felt like every one of them distilled and mixed into one experience.

The fortifications crawled with spectators. They had been taken off the front lines to celebrate Lord Ebondrake's impending crusade. They threw rocks and filth down at the slaves as they marched, heads bowed, under the eyes of Venalitor's slavers.

'What are we facing?' asked Gearth. The man had sought out Alaric and made sure he marched alongside the Grey Knight.

'I don't know,' said Alaric.

'Come on,' said Gearth. 'You've got your plan. You think no one saw what you pulled at Ghaal? You know enough, Space Marine, and some of us would like to be in on it.'

'What did you do?' asked Alaric.

'Do? When?'

'Those are prison tattoos. You asked me a question, now I'm asking you. What did you do to get thrown in prison before Venalitor captured you?'

'Rule one,' said Gearth, 'you never ask that, not of any man.'

'Then you don't need to be a part of whatever plan I might have in mind.'

'Hey, I didn't say that.'

A huge pair of doors stood in front of the slaves, made of sheets of salvaged metal welded together. Two smoke-belching tanks stood ready to pull them apart on lengths of chain. Alaric recognised the tanks as Leman Russ battle tank variants, no doubt captured and brought to Drakaasi in one of the lords' slave raids.

'Murder,' said Gearth. 'Alright? Happy?'

'Who did you kill?'

Gearth swallowed. Alaric had never seen him anything less than completely confident, but that was a question Gearth obviously feared.

'Women,' he said.

'Why?'

'What do you mean "why"? Why does anyone do anything?' Gearth scowled. 'I don't have to give you a reason.'

'So you don't know why,' said Alaric. 'I will call on you when the time comes.' Gearth stepped out of line, dropping back through the slaves to get away from Alaric.

A slave that Alaric did not recognise shuffled through the rain of filth. 'Astartes,' it hissed through a harelip.

Alaric peered beneath the slave's hooded rags. Its face was disfigured with some skin disease, so the only recognisable features were two watery eyes. 'You know me?'

'Your fame grows.'

'Who are you?'

'I saw you at Ghaal. I fled from there to follow you.'

Alaric sneered. On every Imperial world there was some diversion for the citizens, and adoring followers accompanied the most famous fighters or sportsmen everywhere. Drakaasi's arenas held the same position on Drakaasi, on a far larger scale. The idea that Alaric could have devotees seemed as pathetic as the slave looked.

'Go home to Ghaal.'

'There is no home there now. I bring you a gift.' The slave produced an axe from beneath his robes. It was clearly made for a fighter of a Space Marine's size, the haft far too broad and weighty to fit in a normal man's hand. It was bright and gleaming with a head the shape of a crescent moon, so sharp that the edge was transparent and glowing.

'From the forge,' said the slave.

Alaric took the axe. It was weighted perfectly. Alaric had rarely held a weapon of such craftsmanship, even in the artificer's halls on Titan.

'Who made this?' demanded Alaric.

'The city's forge lies at the crossroads,' said the slave, 'two fortresses and the siege works between them. That is all he told me to say.'

'Who? Who told you?'

A whip lashed around the throat of the slave, yanking him back. The slave was dragged back into a knot of Gorgath's soldiers, and Alaric knew that in a few moments the man would be dead beneath their boots and blades. The slaves around Alaric surged on beneath the soldiers' whips, and Alaric lost sight of the slave.

He looked down at his axe. It was perhaps the first beautiful thing he had seen on Drakaasi.

In front of him, the tanks gunned their engines and the doors were pulled apart.

Two massive armies were revealed on the arena floor, lined up in ranks, banners streaming. The ground between them was patrolled by bloodletters, snarling at the front ranks to keep them back. A pack of the daemons stomped up to Venalitor's slaves and began directing the gladiators into the ranks, splitting them between the two sides.

A battle, of course. It was the only way that Khorne could be celebrated in Gorgath.

'QUITE MAGNIFICENT,' SAID Venalitor, taking up his position beside Lord Ebondrake at the top of the stands. Every arena had a place for Drakaasi's lords to spectate, away from the crowds, and in Gorgath it took the form of a covered section of seating with chained daemons broken and bound to serve the planet's rulers. They skulked and cowered like beaten dogs around Ebondrake's feet. Ebondrake and Venalitor ignored them. They were here to witness the games, not to be fawned over.

'Indeed it is,' said Lord Ebondrake, settling his enormous reptilian body on the throne erected for him in the stands. 'The lords have outdone themselves. Khorne anticipates greatly.'

'And not just bloodshed,' said Venalitor. 'I would have thought that the most appropriate celebration was slaughter, but of course this is much more appealing to the Lord of Battles.'

Ebondrake turned his great head towards Venalitor and narrowed his eyes. 'Your flatteries are disappointing, duke,' he said, flickering a forked tongue dangerously over his teeth. 'I had thought more of you than this. I had thought you had some imagination.'

'You misunderstand me, lord,' said Venalitor. 'Do not think I have been modest. My very best are down there.'

'Including your Grey Knight?'

'Of course.'

'You would risk him here?'

'The Blood God would not hold me in high regard if I could not risk everything to worship him,' replied Venalitor slickly. 'My Grey Knight would do none of us any good back on the *Hecatomb*.'

'You have great plans for him, I feel.'

'So do you, Lord Ebondrake.'

Ebondrake smiled, baring his spectacular array of teeth. 'He will try to get out. He will want revenge.'

'That would be a spectacle worth seeing.'

Ebondrake's enclosure was ringed with Ophidian Guard warriors. The audience was little danger at that moment, since all eyes were fixed in anticipation on the battle lines below. The slaves were divided into two armies, and kept separate by a host of bloodletters. Huge banners hung above the front ranks, dripping power from the runes painted on them. Each army had tens of thousands of men, from frenzied cultists from the slums of Ghaal to tribesmen from beyond Drakaasi's cities, and even elite gladiators from the personal stables of lords like Venalitor. More than a few of the spectators recognised the Venalitor's most prized possession, the captive Grey Knight, known to many of them as Alaric the Betrayed, who was destined to die competing for the mantle of Drakaasi's champion at Vel'Skan a few weeks hence. That was, of course, if he made it out of Gorgath.

There were brute mutants three times the height of a man, tentacled subhumans, and hated psykers, chained up and herded before the armies to make sure they died first. Whole cults of the Blood God stood in their robed finery, desperate to die beneath the eyes of their god.

At a signal from Lord Ebondrake, one of his Ophidian Guard raised a war horn and blew a single discordant note. The banners dipped, and the bloodletters dissolved into the floor of the crater. The armies swarmed forwards.

The spectators erupted in celebration. They had been a part of the hellish machinery of Gorgath for so long. Now they were on the outside looking down at others fighting for their pleasure, as if they were Khorne, soaking up the adulation of their bloodshed. It was the most glorious thing they had ever seen.

The front lines collided with a thunderclap. Bodies were thrown into the air. Heads parted from bodies. Torsos split open. Men swarmed over a brute mutant, dragging it down to cut it to pieces. A tide of bodies heaved up as the dead piled on top of one another, and soon the armies were battling atop a rampart of the dead.

Alaric the Betrayed was at the heart of it all. With his bright silver axe and ornate armour, he cut a more dramatic figure than any other gladiator. He kicked enemies and friends aside as he drove his way through the battle. Other slaves of Venalitor's followed in his wake: an eldar swordsman cutting enemies apart with his chainblade, a host of human butchers who despatched wounded foes on the ground. It seemed that Alaric had finally lost his mind, and had become one with the Blood God's will. Here was a hunter of daemons, the Emperor's finest, out-slaughtering Drakaasi's most brutal for the glory of Khorne.

Alaric drove for the closest edge of the arena. A tentacled monster tried to snare him and drag him down, but Alaric stamped down on its torso, crushing its ribcage before slicing through its tentacles with a sweep of his axe. One of the captive witches lurched towards him, lightning crashing from its eyes. Alaric took the first bolt, letting it discharge through his armour and arc into the earth. A single step brought him face to face with the witch, and he slammed the blade of the axe through its skull. There was nothing the spectators of Gorgath loved more than seeing the weak-bodied psykers put to death. Some of them began chanting Alaric's name.

One of his side's standard bearers was fighting near Alaric. It was an armoured warrior from the bodyguard of one of Drakaasi's lords. The warrior was badly hurt, blood pouring from the shoulder joint of his armour, his helm split and gory. Alaric pushed him to the ground and took up the banner. He held it up so the whole stadium could see the image of the stylised skulls emblazoned on it. Alaric ran up to the edge of the arena's seating, which sloped up above him along the curve of the crater's edge.

He hurled the banner into the stands. Dozens of soldiers leapt up to catch it.

'What are you waiting for?' yelled Alaric.

The crowd responded by chanting his name ever louder as they poured down past him, off the stands and into the arena.

This was war, and suddenly watching wasn't enough.

'CLEVER BOY,' SAID Ebondrake as he watched the crowd around Alaric break ranks and pour down into the arena.

'My lord,' said Venalitor, 'this is… this blasphemy is…'

'You have said enough, duke,' said Ebondrake. 'Commander?'

One of the Ophidian Guard, hulking and sinister behind the visor of his black armour, turned to Ebondrake. 'My lord?'

'Kill the Grey Knight,' said Ebondrake.

TWELVE

ALARIC FOUGHT AGAINST the tide. His head was forced under the sea of bodies, and he fought to breathe. His own name, chanted over and over again, was like the dim crashing of the ocean.

His was not a complicated plan. Khorne probably would have approved. The bloodlust of Gorgath's soldiers, ingrained by generations of carnage, only needed the right kind of impetus to send them swarming into the arena to join in.

All Alaric had to do was get out. He had been sent a message, and to discover its meaning he had to break out of the arena and into Gorgath.

Alaric kicked his way out of the crowd, clambering over them until he found the top of the arena floor wall. He hauled himself up onto the seating that had been erected around the sides of the arena crater. The battle swarmed beneath him, all battle lines now lost in a swirl of violence.

The lords would be angry. There was plenty of blood, of course, and Khorne would have his due, but a free-for-all wasn't what the lords of Drakaasi had wanted. Alaric's riot was an insult to the planet's ruling order.

Lord Ebondrake was ahead of Alaric, advancing behind a line of Ophidian Guard.

Alaric's heart sank. All he had to do was get out. Ebondrake was not part of his plan.

'Grey Knight!' roared Ebondrake. 'Betrayed of the Corpse God! Puppet of Khorne! Is this the vengeance you seek? To face me, and slay me, in my own domain?'

The Ophidian Guard were moving towards him, black swords drawn.

Alaric wouldn't get his vengeance. Ebondrake wouldn't roll over and die for him, but he was human, and that meant fighting on.

Ebondrake inhaled, his wings spreading behind him.

Alaric hit the floor. Ebondrake breathed a sheet of black flame that flowed over Alaric like water. It scorched him down one side, and he rolled away from it, trying to smother the flames before they caught on his flesh. The sound was like a hurricane of fire roaring in his ears. The Ophidian Guard kept advancing straight through the flame, their armour proof against it.

Alaric couldn't fight Ebondrake, not without being immolated by black fire again.

He was going to die.

He jumped to his feet. The Ophidian Guard were upon him, and he lashed out at them, smashing one black, eyeless helm apart with his axe. Another forced forward, trying to bull him to the ground, but Alaric slammed a knee into his face and threw him aside.

'What victory do you believe you will win, little creature?' growled Ebondrake, black fire coiling from between his fangs. He loomed up over the line of Ophidian Guard protecting him, and cast off his cloak as his wings unfurled fully. 'What can you take from me?'

The Ophidian Guard around Alaric closed ranks and raised their swords like executioners waiting for the word so they could take his head.

'Kill me, and you kill Drakaasi. Is that correct?' Ebondrake grinned horribly through his anger, his eyes, slits of yellow fire. 'Is that the sum of your imagination?'

Ebondrake looked past Alaric suddenly. The roar behind Alaric grew like a wave crashing through the arena. He risked a look behind him.

Tens of thousands of Gorgath's soldiers swarmed up the seating behind him. At their head was the banner Alaric had thrown them. They wanted to fight, and perhaps to die, and for that they needed the best opponents in the arena. All the finest gladiators were tied up in the melee on the arena floor, and that left the Ophidian Guard.

'Kill him!' shouted Ebondrake as the spontaneous army charged. 'Close ranks!'

A sword came down.

Alaric was faster.

He brought his axe up through the visor of the helmet looming over him, and rammed an elbow into the throat of the Ophidian Guard behind him. His would-be executioner fell, head split apart, and the second guard tumbled as Alaric cut a leg out from under him.

Ebondrake breathed. The flame rippled over Alaric's head into the army charging the Ophidian Guard. Men disappeared in swathes of black fire.

Alaric was only half aware of being carried up onto the shoulders of the army, even as they burned and vanished beneath Ophidian swords. He saw the banner still held high, and realised that he, like the banner, was a symbol of rebellion and war for these people. The broken creatures wanted nothing more than to follow Alaric to their deaths, because they knew that no one on Drakaasi could die as well as a Space Marine.

Somewhere amid the carnage, Ebondrake wolfed a clawful of Gorgath's soldiers down his gullet to quench his anger. The lords had lost control of Gorgath's arena completely. He turned from the carnage in disgust. The rioting soldiers were too lowly a prey for him. Alaric had disappeared into the rioting mass, and there was nothing worthwhile for him to kill any more.

Alaric watched the fire starting to burn, and the drifts of dead building up at the edges of the arena, until the tide of soldiers carried him through the dimness of an archway and out into the war city of Gorgath.

Gorgath's nights were cold. They killed off the day's wounded, so that only the worthy and fit could fight in the morning.

Alaric did not feel the cold as men did. He knew that this night could kill a weak man, but it meant nothing to him. He wished that he could feel it and fear it, because that would be something he could understand, something he could grasp. It was an enemy he could defeat: find shelter, build a fire. Drakaasi was an enemy he could not face like that. There was no simple solution to it. If he could feel the cold, at least he could take some pride from the fact that he was still alive.

If Ebondrake had died, what would have been achieved? Ebondrake himself had seen through that. If the dragon was gone, something else would take its place, perhaps Venalitor, perhaps Arguthrax, or perhaps some ancient horror of Drakaasi that Alaric hadn't even heard of.

Alaric had reached the siege works a few hours after the army escaped from Gorgath's arena and took the carnage out into the city. He had left the army behind as he made for the twin fortresses. He didn't care what happened to the rioters. They were probably being put down to avenge the insult of the failed Gorgath games.

Alaric walked carefully along the trench. It had been dug decades ago when the two fortresses had evidently been at war, and their lords had ordered the trenches dug to approach the opposite fortress and take it. The siege lines had passed one another in a web of tunnels and criss-crossing trenches, and there were still signs of the struggle: old broken bones poking from the dark earth, heaps of spent cartridges rusted into lumps of red-brown corrosion.

Each fortress was a war-scarred cylinder bristling with rusted guns and gouged by the siege engines that lay in ruins around them. Alaric could almost hear the din of their guns, and the screams of the dying. He wondered for a moment how many had died there, fighting a miniature war in the midst of Gorgath's grand battle, but there did not seem to be room in the city for any more death.

There was a temple ahead, lying at the place where the siege lines had first met. It was built from shell casings, from massive artillery shells carved into fluted columns, the individual bullets forming the teeth of the gargoyles squatting on its roof.

Through the shattered windows, Alaric could see the abandoned forges and anvils, piles of flawed swords and rusted ingots. A forge door swung open, exposing the dark and cold inside. The temple's altar had been used as an anvil, and was covered in deep scores. Alaric walked carefully inside. He could smell the smoke and molten metal, and almost hear the ringing of the hammer on a newly forged blade.

The place was abandoned. It had been for some time. Since he had received the axe at the gates to the arena, Alaric had believed, somewhere inside him, that the smith who had spoken to him at Karnikhal was trying to give him a message. He didn't even know if the smith had been an ally or an enemy, or even a figment of his own imagination. However, he was a potential ally, and Alaric knew that he needed one outside the *Hecatomb*.

Had he really thought he would find something here? Certainly no more than he thought he could kill Lord Ebondrake alone.

Something glinted in the dimness of the abandoned temple. Alaric pulled aside a few unfinished blades, and saw a hammer propped up against the altar anvil. Its head was bright silver, and carved with images of a comet streaking down to shatter a planet, an armoured fist clutching a lightning bolt, and a dragon with a sword through its heart. Alaric picked up the weapon and felt its weight. It was as finely made as the axe. He recalled how Brother Dvorn would have dearly loved to wield such a brutal looking weapon, and wondered whether Dvorn and his other battle-brothers had made it off Sarthis Majoris alive and free.

On one face of the hammer, the face that would strike the enemy when the hammer was swung, was the image of a skull. One eye was blanked out, the other burned with an intricately carved flame. Alaric stared at the image for a long moment, trying to guess what message it held.

It had to be a message. For him to seek this place out, to risk his life escaping the arena, there had to be a point. A half-blinded skull, it had to mean something, even if the meaning came from within him.

Perhaps the skull represented Alaric. With the Collar of Khorne around his neck, he was half-blind.

'There is no Hammer of Daemons,' said Alaric aloud. 'There is no sacred weapon waiting to be wielded. It's me. I am supposed to bring this planet down. I am the Hammer.'

What if the Hammer of Daemons were another Chaos trick? It would be typical of the followers of Chaos to perpetrate such a hoax, if only to give desperate humans a shadow of hope that could be snatched away.

Alaric wanted to have faith in something, even if it was only a decent way to die on Drakaasi, but there was nothing left for him to believe in.

A sound snapped Alaric out of his thoughts. Something was moving outside: a footstep through loose rubble, weight shifting on debris. Alaric took his axe in one hand and the hammer in the other, sure, by their balance, that they had been forged by the same master smith.

He hear more footsteps, voices, and swords unsheathed.

Alaric tensed. He faced the door, his back to the altar, sure that he could cover the distance in a few huge strides, shatter the first visored face he saw with the hammer, and cut the legs out from under the next warrior with the axe. He was ready.

One side of the temple collapsed with a roar of torn metal and stone, and a Rhino APC rode up through the rubble into the temple. Alaric had to vault over the altar to avoid been dragged beneath its tracks. The side hatch swung open, and a pair of Ophidian Guard emerged, not in the hulking armour of Ebondrake's bodyguard, but wearing chainmail and leather, faces obscured by leather masks, wielding whips that shone like bright silver. They lashed out at Alaric. He let one whip twine around the haft of his axe, and yanked it out of the warrior's hands, but the other caught him across the shoulder, and hot white pain lanced through him. He convulsed onto his knees, swinging blindly with the hammer, feeling it crunch into bone, but unable to see what he had hit.

Ophidian Guard stormed in through the doors and windows of the temple. There were dozens of them. More emerged from the Rhino, slashing with their whips. Alaric stood and fought back, pulling them into striking range, and battering them down to the floor, but there were too many of them.

He was on all fours, pain streaking down through him like lightning bolts. He caught a whip-wielding soldier with the hammer, shattering his knee, and then cut off his head as he lay writhing on the floor. He cut up into the torso of another, and forced himself to his feet, but the Ophidian Guard surrounding him carried tower shields emblazoned with white dragons, which they used to slam him back, as he tried to break free of them.

He was on his back. His body fought on, but something in the back of his mind told him to give in. It was a part of him that had been given free rein by the Collar of Khorne, a hidden coward that had finally surfaced to tell him he was going to fail.

He reared up, one last time, silencing the coward. He roared like an animal.

A great cold weight pressed down on his back, mirrored by heat blossoming in his chest. He looked down to see the tip of a black sword emerging from his breastbone. He tried to look up, and glimpsed the Ophidian Guard, who had just impaled him, towering over him. Alaric tried to slide off the blade, but it would not move. The shock of it finally caught up with his mind, and the world greyed out.

The blade snapped, and Alaric slumped to the floor, the tip of the blade still sticking out of his chest.

It didn't matter whether he gave in or not. The pain won, and Alaric passed out.

'I SEE YOU have thought about what I said.' Durendin's voice was low and quiet, very different from the strident tones he used on the pulpit while reminding the Grey Knights of their duties towards their Emperor.

'I have,' said Alaric. Around him was the subdued majesty of the Chapel of Mandulis. It was built of sombre stone, the columns holding up the ceiling carved into representations of past Grand Masters, who had fallen in battle against the daemon. However, instead of having granite walls inscribed with the names of fallen Grey Knights, the chapel was open to the outside, and through its columns could be glimpsed an endless golden desert under a dark blue twilight. Strange stars winked in the sky, the same shifting constellations that bled from the Eye of Terror.

Alaric was sitting on one of the stone pews. Durendin was a couple of rows in front of him, evidently at prayer, since he was not wearing the black trimmed power armour that was the badge of a Chaplain's office.

Alaric realised that he was without armour, too. He was wearing the remains of a badly battered breastplate in the shape of folded wings, and the point of a black sword stuck out of his chest.

'And?' said Durendin.

'You were wrong.'

'Really?'

'Some things, you can't fight.'

'Interesting. Do you believe that these Grand Masters would have thought that? That Mandulis could have come up against a foe and said, "This I cannot fight"?'

Alaric looked at the column that represented Mandulis. The Grand Master had carried a sword with the hilt worked to resemble a lightning bolt. Alaric had held that sword, and tried to echo the deeds of Mandulis in vanquishing the daemon prince Ghargatuloth, but those events felt like they belonged in another man's lifetime.

'I am not one of those Grand Masters,' replied Alaric.

'No, you are not, not if you are going to simply give up.'

'I am not giving up, Chaplain.'

'Then what, Alaric? What quality do you possess that can win you victory if not a Grey Knight's willingness to fight?'

'Imagination.'

Durendin laughed. It was a strange thing to see the old man doing. 'Really? How so?'

'It is the understanding that there is more than one way to fight.'

'I see. So, you think that bringing the bolter and the blade to them is not enough, and you seek another way.'

'Yes, I learned that against Ebondrake. I cannot fight them as I would any other enemy, not this whole planet. Even if I win, every drop of blood I spill is a victory for them. It has to be something else.'

'Then what?'

'I do not know.' Alaric sat back, feeling the strength bleed out of him.

'And you think that I can give you answers?'

'I don't know what I think.'

Durendin stood up and smoothed down his devotional robes. He walked up to the chapel's altar and took a brazier from its stone slab. An icon of the Emperor looked down on the Chaplain, as one by one he lit the candles and incense lanterns arranged around the altar. It was an ancient ritual, reflecting the lights that had gone out in the souls of so many Grey Knights since the Chapter's foundation, and reminding the Grey Knights who still lived that their battle-brothers' souls were gathering to fight alongside the Emperor at the end of time.

Alaric imagined those souls gathering like fireflies around a pyre, eager to fight, and he felt sorry for them. For the first time, it occurred to him that their sacrifice might not be worth anything after all.

'I cannot give you answers to this, Alaric,' said Durendin. 'I think you come to me more in hope than in expectation, and I must disappoint you. I was given the Chaplain's burden because I am exactly the opposite of you. I see only the Grey Knights' way, the endless battle against Chaos. Everything else must be seen through that lens. There can be no doubt and no compromise in the eyes of a Chaplain. You are alone, Justicar, as are we all.'

'Then I do not think I can do this,' said Alaric. 'My duties on Drakaasi are clear. Chaos must be punished. The Emperor's justice must be done, but I am just one man, and the lords of Drakaasi are so many and so strong. It is just as Venalitor said, I can either die here accomplishing nothing, or fight on and win renown for their Blood God. I cannot win.'

'Then that is your fate, Alaric. A Grand Master would never accept that, of course, but as you said you are not a Grand Master. Please, it is best that you leave now. You are bleeding on the floor of my chapel, and it is an ill omen.'

Alaric looked down at his chest. The wound was bleeding, blood flowing in time with the pumping of his hearts. The blood was trickling down the pew and pooling around his feet.

'Am I going to die?'

Durendin looked around at him, but Alaric could not read his expression. 'If I was to say yes, what would you feel?'

'Relieved,' said Alaric. 'The choice would have been made for me.'

'But Drakaasi would carry on as before, so I suggest you live.'

'I'll see what I can do.'

'Good luck, justicar. Perhaps I can meet with you again, the real me, I mean, back on Titan. I imagine I would be very interested to learn of these conversations.'

'Goodbye, Chaplain.'

Durendin looked away, and as he turned, his features melted away and left him without a face. The features of the Grand Masters dissolved away, too, leaving columns of smooth, unmarked stone. One by one the stars outside began to go out, and the Chapel of Mandulis withered away into the desert.

Alaric took a long, painful breath, and the darkness lifted.

THIRTEEN

ALARIC AWOKE TO light. He lay on his back, staring up. He blinked a few times as his eyes adjusted. He wondered, not for the first time on Drakaasi, whether he was dead.

The light was coming from a chandelier, hanging from a ceiling frescoed with images of battle. Victims were painted lying in heaps beneath the feet of armoured warriors, all of them with the sigils of Khorne glowing on their armour. The sky above writhed with blood-laden clouds, and carrion daemons swept in to tear apart the living and the dead. Titanic armies clashed in the distance.

It was a work of genius. The artist would have been one of the greatest of his generation on any Imperial world, perhaps good enough to gain sector-wide recognition. Instead, the mind behind the work had been enslaved by Chaos, withered away by madness until unholy masterpieces were all that was left.

Alaric wondered who that person had been. Had he been insane to begin with, tortured and brilliant, listening to the whispers of the warp for solace? Or had he been just one of those millions of citizens preyed upon by Drakaasi's forces? Alaric imagined the nameless artist huddled among a great crowd of other terrified citizens, waiting for death, perhaps praying for deliverance or trying to offer some comfort to his loved ones. Then the death had come, but not for him. Drakaasi's servants had found out about his skill and chosen him to live on, enslaved, and had rotted his mind away until visions of bloodshed and war were all that he could create. He must have wished he were dead. Perhaps he was still alive somewhere on Drakaasi, still creating horrors for Khorne.

Alaric lay still for a long time. It was only by the Emperor's grace that he was not dead or insane, too. He wondered how easily he would break. It would take longer to break Alaric than to corrupt the painter who had created the image above him, but how much longer? As the galaxy reckoned things, probably not a great deal.

Alaric tried to sit up, but the pain inside him was a hot, red spike piercing his torso. He gasped and fell back. Beneath him was an unyielding surface, and Alaric wondered if it was a mortuary slab in a cathedral of the Blood God, and if he was finally dead.

He turned his head. He was lying on a huge hardwood table laid out as if for a feast. Bronze plates and chalices had been pushed to one side so that he could be laid there. The table was one of several in a grand feasting chamber as dark and lavish as anything Alaric had seen on Drakaasi. The walls were hung with silken drapes of crimson and black, held up by false columns of black marble. The floor looked, at first, like marble, but at a closer look revealed that it was paved with gravestones in so many different styles that they must have been brought from many different worlds. Devotional inscriptions of Imperial Gothic marched past Alaric's eyes, the names of the desecrated dead.

An altar to Khorne stood at one end of the room. It was a great, irregular chunk of stone, stained black, and covered in ancient gouges: an executioner's block. Behind it was the symbol of Khorne, wrought in brass, and inlaid with red lacquer. It was the symbol of a skull, so stylised that it was little more than a triangle topped with a cross, nevertheless, it radiated such malice that it hurt to look at it. The floor in front of the block had drains to carry away the blood. The executioner's block was still used for its original purpose.

Alaric tested his body for injuries. It felt comforting, because it was part of his training. There was still enough Grey Knight left in him for him to act like a soldier. He had the familiar cacophony of pain from hundreds of minor injuries. His chest was the worst. His breathing was hampered, and one of his hearts was wounded. He could still move, and fight if need be, but it was a major injury, even for a Space Marine, and back on Titan he would have been sent to the apothecarion to recover. On Drakaasi, he would just have to fight through it.

One of the drapes was pulled aside. Beyond it, Alaric glimpsed more finery, a magnificent chamber surrounding a grand staircase lined with brass statues.

Haggard entered the feasting chamber. He looked so completely out of place, unkempt and grimy like all the slaves, wearing his stained surgeon's apron, that Alaric wondered for a moment if he was really there at all.

'You're awake,' said Haggard.

'So it seems.'

'How are you?'

'I'll live.'

'It was a real mess in there,' continued Haggard. 'One of the lungs won't work. One of the hearts is looking shaky, too. Your spine made it, that's the main thing. There were splinters of metal in there as long as my finger. It was only by the Emperor's will that none of them severed your spinal cord.'

'Thank you, Haggard,' said Alaric. 'I don't know if I could have survived without your help.'

'Don't thank me,' said Haggard. 'Please, don't thank me. I don't know what will happen next.'

Alaric tried sitting up again. This time he bit down the pain. A few of Haggard's crude stitches burst, and fresh blood ran down his chest. He saw that he was wearing the armour in which he had been fighting at Gorgath, with the breastplate removed. The wound on his chest was huge and ugly. No one but a Space Marine could have survived it.

'Whatever happens, Haggard, I'm better facing it alive,' said Alaric.

'I pulled this out of you,' said Haggard. He held up the shard of the Ophidian Guard's sword. In his hand, it was the size of a short sword, the broken haft like a hilt, the edge and point still sharp enough to glow in the candlelight. 'You didn't really think you could kill Ebondrake, did you?'

'Our meeting was unplanned,' replied Alaric. 'I wonder if anyone on this planet could kill that.' He looked down at the shard in Haggard's hand. 'Can you hide that among your medical gear?'

'It certainly looks painful enough,' said Haggard, slipping it into one of the pockets of his stained apron where he kept his makeshift surgical tools.

'Keep it for when I return to the *Hecatomb*. Speaking of which, where am I?'

'Still on board,' said Haggard. 'These are Venalitor's chambers.'

'Here? The ship isn't big enough.'

Haggard shrugged. 'Physics only works here out of habit. If Venalitor wants to bend it to give himself a place fit for a duke, then he can. Listen, Justicar, it was Venalitor who brought me up here to keep you alive.

Whatever he's going to do, he needs you alive and conscious to do it. He's going to punish you.'

'But he doesn't know I'm awake.'

Haggard looked down at the floor. 'Yes, he does, Justicar.'

The sound of scaephylyd claws on the gravestone tiles was unmistakeable, so were the armoured footsteps descending the marble staircase. An honour guard of scaephylyds clattered into the room, pulling Haggard away. Haggard didn't resist.

Duke Venalitor followed them in. He was surrounded by scaephylyd slavers carrying shock prods. He dismissed them with a wave of his hand, and they scuttled away. Behind him, Alaric could just see Haggard being herded up the staircase.

'So, justicar,' said Venalitor. He suited his surroundings perfectly. The dark magnificence of his chambers matched his own, with his splendid red and black armour and the multitude of swords at his back. The place was a reflection, like Venalitor himself, of pure arrogance.

Alaric didn't reply. Venalitor had deliberately made himself vulnerable without his attendant slavers, but Alaric was wounded and unarmed. Venalitor would kill him if he and Alaric fought, and Venalitor wanted to remind Alaric of that fact.

Venalitor walked past him and knelt in front of the altar to Khorne, whispering a few words of prayer.

'The Blood God,' he said, turning back to Alaric, 'listens. When you have earned his respect as I have, he hears you. I ask him for strength to conquer, and I am granted it. I ask for armies, and they march under my banner. They call you Alaric the Betrayed, you know, because you were betrayed by your Emperor. You asked him to deliver you from Chaos, from Drakaasi, and he ignored you. He is just a corpse, who cannot hear your prayers, Grey Knight. That is the ultimate betrayal. My lord will grant you everything you want if you only get his attention.'

Alaric climbed down off the table and stood. He was unsteady on his feet, but he did everything he could not to show it.

He could fight here, and die. At least it would be over. At least he wouldn't have to listen to Venalitor's blasphemous words any more.

'You have that chance, Alaric,' continued Venalitor.

'You are asking me to join you?' Alaric smiled. 'Only in desperation would anyone think such a thing was possible.'

'You have seen the scum of Drakaasi's cities,' said Venalitor unshaken. 'You have mingled with the even lower vermin of the *Hecatomb*: those killers, those broken men, the violent dregs of your

Imperium. That is the lot of the great majority of those who come here. Khorne despises them, and they are left to rot or be killed as fodder for His bloodlust. The lucky ones become sacrifices, but you, you are different. You do not belong with those scum. You have yet to even glimpse what you could become on Drakaasi. The Blood God is willing to listen to you if you will only let him.' Venalitor indicated the altar. 'It is so easy, Grey Knight, and it is the only choice you have. No matter what you do, or how hard you try, you will die in the Blood God's name. The only way out is to bow before a real god for once.'

'Then I will die,' said Alaric.

'A few drops of blood,' said Venalitor, 'that is all he requires.'

'He will have to wring them out of me.'

Venalitor shook his head. 'You try to humiliate me. You even try to cross swords with Lord Ebondrake. The Blood God looks upon such audacity, and smiles. That you honestly believe you can win some victory over me is indication of the mental strength a champion of Chaos requires. The fact that you are still alive shows you have the strength of arms. You could rule this planet, Alaric. Then you could do with Ebondrake as you please. You could even put me on this altar, and have me slit from neck to belly, if only you do it for Khorne.'

'Never,' said Alaric, 'not as long as I live, never. You will just have to sacrifice me like all the rest of your vermin.'

Venalitor smiled. 'There is something noble in you, I think. The Emperor's lackeys taught you well, I will give them that. Victory means so much to you, and you see it in the bleakest of situations. For you, dying here is a victory.'

'My duty allows for no failings,' said Alaric, 'and it does not end in death. You cannot defeat that, Duke Venalitor.'

'You had a duty towards Sarthis Majoris too, did you not?'

Alaric could not answer.

'Do you know what we did to that planet?'

Alaric fought for something to say, something that would silence Venalitor, something devastating, but there was nothing.

'We separated the men from the women,' continued Venalitor with a smirk, 'and we killed the women in front of the men. We killed them badly, in all the ways you can think of and a few you cannot. Then we let the men fight back. Half of them wanted revenge and the other half just wanted to die. The grief in their eyes was like a hymn to the Blood God. The madness was joyous. So many of them were begging the Blood God to take them in, to turn them mindless, that I made a new army from them and marched them on to the next city. Your duty was to prevent that, Justicar. I think it is fair to say that you failed.'

'Your atrocities are nothing new,' said Alaric, trying to keep his voice level. 'We cannot save every world. We can only fight.'

'Until death?'

'Until death.'

'But you did not die. You are here. Sarthis Majoris died, but you survived. What manner of duty did you fulfil, exactly?'

'Your words cannot sway me, Venalitor. I am a Grey Knight.'

'Not any more. You became something else, something less, the moment I was able to take you alive. At least your friend had the good grace to die at the first opportunity. You cling on like a disease, pretending there is some victory in your failure to the Corpse-Emperor, and ignoring the only chance for redemption you have, the chance given to you by Khorne.'

Alaric looked around him for a weapon. There was nothing of use. It would have to be bare hands. 'I shall be redeemed, Venalitor. Here and now, I shall be redeemed.'

Alaric charged Venalitor. The duke had been at ease, speaking idly as he stood before the altar, but he was still ready.

His hand caught Alaric by the throat. His other arm knocked away Alaric's fist. Venalitor lifted Alaric off his feet, and threw him back down into the table. His body splintered through the table, throwing gilded plates and chalices everywhere. The wound in his chest tore open, and for a moment he was blinded with pain.

'So you really do want to die?' asked Venalitor.

Alaric sprang to his feet. The wound in his chest was bleeding freely. Venalitor waved a hand, and the blood formed tendrils that lashed around his neck. He tore them aside, but by the time he had his bearings again, Venalitor had got behind him. Venalitor caught him by the shoulder and the neck, and kicked his legs out from under him. Alaric fell forwards, and Venalitor thrust him into the executioner's block of the altar. Alaric's head smacked into the stone, and the smell of old dried blood hit him.

Venalitor drew a sword from his back, a short, curved blade, like a shining razor in the candlelight. He stabbed it into Alaric's back.

Venalitor knew the ways in which a human body could be made to feel pain. The tip of the blade hit just the right point, and nerve endings caught fire in agony. Alaric could not move, only spasm on the altar as pain washed through him.

He fought it. Venalitor pulled the blade out, and let Alaric slide to the floor. Venalitor flicked the blood from the tip of his sword onto the altar, and it smouldered there, the brass icon of Khorne glowing in gratitude.

'I will not kill you, justicar,' said Venalitor. 'You are too valuable to me in the arenas, and there is still some use the Blood God can get from you. Just because you refuse His will now does not mean that He will be denied. I will just have to break you first. In the long run, it makes no difference.'

The slavers entered the room. Alaric fought them for a while, throwing them aside, dashing them against the floor, and snapping their insect limbs, but, slowly, their shock prods found their mark, and he was forced down onto his knees, still fighting.

Venalitor watched. There were always more scaephylyds to be enslaved, and there was no need to risk damaging his valuable gladiator. Alaric fell onto his hands and knees, and a shock prod was forced down on his neck above his iron collar, so that his face was pressed against the gravestone floor.

'I know what you are, Grey Knight. I know about Ghargatuloth and Chaeroneia, about Valinov and Thorganel Quintus. I know what you can do. None of it will help you now.'

The scaephylyds swarmed over him like ants over a corpse. They manacled his hands and feet and turned him over to carry him up on their shoulders.

'Take him below decks,' said Venalitor.

One of the scaephylyds, a particularly old and gnarled creature, had stood aside from the fracas. He turned to Venalitor as Alaric was carried, still struggling, from the feasting chamber.

'Below decks, duke?' asked the creature. It had practised the language of humans for so long that its mandibles pronounced each syllable almost perfectly.

'You heard me, slave master.'

'Do you mean to the—'

'Not to the cell block,' snarled Venalitor. 'Open up the wards, throw him inside, and seal them again. Those are my orders.'

'Of course, my duke. There is another matter.'

'What?'

'That of the war.'

* * *

THE WAR HAD started with the hunter daemons. They had begun with an audacious first strike, a lesson in superiority. They had probably not intended to kill Venalitor at all, but to teach him that he could be reached anywhere, at any time. The *Hecatomb* was not safe, not from an evil as ancient as Arguthrax.

Venalitor had called upon the Wrath of Ages, a warrior cult dedicated to self-mutilation and martial excellence, to descend on the stronghold of the Thirteenth Hand. The Thirteenth Hand, since returning from their failure to disrupt Venalitor's armies on Sarthis Majoris, had taken up residence in a huge and filthy tangle of entrail sewers beneath Karnikhal. The fanatics of the Wrath of Ages had besieged it, working night by night into the tangle of dried-out organs and sumps of decaying filth, while the shambling vermin of the Hand fought back with poisoned arrows and fiendish traps.

Eventually, the Wrath had reached the heart of the fortress, and had enacted a ritual that brought life back to the organs that had hung dead for many centuries of Karnikhal's lifespan. A few of the Wrath made it out, while the Hand was drowned in filth, or dissolved by digestive juices. Their remains were disgorged into the blood canals, silting up the river between Karnikhal and Aelazadne, a fittingly meaningless end for such a lowly cult.

An open battle had broken out on the plains between Ghaal and Gorgath, a dismal and lifeless place. An alliance of cults loyal to Arguthrax had fought an army of scaephylyds, all from clans hoping to ascend to Venalitor's service. Venalitor was a saviour to them, a prophet of Chaos, promising to elevate them above the status of animals.

Arguthrax won. The scaephylyds were slaughtered, and the many cults took their heads and limbs as evidence of their devotion. A parade reached Ghaal, where they presented these body parts to Arguthrax. Arguthrax appeared to look on their offerings, and blessed them with a disdainful wave of his flabby hand.

Drakaasi had seen many such wars. In a way, they were a part of its machinery of worship, for the aggressors were ultimately fighting for Khorne's recognition. However, they took place away from the arenas and altars, far from the eyes of Drakaasi's lords, filthy shadow wars and rolls of assassinations. Most of Drakaasi's lords had reached their positions by eliminating a rival in such a war, and all of them had survived such aggression from rivals jealous of their position. That was how power worked: aggression and annihilation. Khorne's patronage ensured that on Drakaasi it always took the form of naked violence.

Times were different now. Lord Ebondrake's pronouncement had demanded that the lords of Drakaasi work together to create a vast army to conquer worlds for Khorne in the wake of the Thirteenth Black Crusade. That did not allow for open conflict between the lords, and when Ebondrake took his lords to task, the results could be bloodier than any battle they could fight between themselves.

This was the matter of the war.

FOURTEEN

It was so profoundly dark that not even Alaric's augmented eyesight could pick out anything. It was unnatural. Something was drinking the light away.

Alaric groped out in the darkness. His hand found the floor in front of him, polished metal. It was the first clean surface that Alaric had touched below decks on the *Hecatomb*.

In response, there was music.

It was quiet at first, a strange lilting sound, mournful, but beautiful. The last music had Alaric heard was the wailing of Aelazadne. This was something else. It sounded like a thousand distant voices. For a moment, he felt that he had intruded on something ancient and sacred, and felt ashamed to be so wounded and flawed in its presence.

However, this was the *Hecatomb*. This was Drakaasi. There was nothing beautiful here. Alaric tried to tell himself that over and over again as the lights began to rise around him.

He was in a chamber of gold and silver. Constellations of gemstones twinkled everywhere. The chamber was huge. It must have run the whole length of the ship's keel and more, another manipulation of time and space within the ship. Asymmetrical pillars, knurled like twisted ropes, ran up the walls to support a ceiling that bulged down as if a golden sky was falling in. Panels of deep blue set into the golden walls were painted with symbols so elegant that they glowed as Alaric looked at them, bright rivulets of power running through every curve. The whole chamber seemed to shift subtly, rippling in and out, as if in time with some ancient breath.

Alaric stood up. His chest heaved, and he coughed out a clot of blood onto the golden floor. Diamonds and sapphires winked up at him through the blood.

He had never seen anything like it. It was almost organic, the knots of the pillars like ancient tree roots, the biological forms of the walls and ceiling like a great golden throat.

The music was coming from the far end of the chamber. Alaric took a couple of steps towards it. The floor gave almost imperceptibly beneath his feet, and the pillars curved over him, as if he was inside a vast creature reacting to his presence.

The chamber flared out ahead into a wide, roughly spherical space, dominated by a stepped pyramid, crowned with a great shard of glowing white crystal from which the song was emanating. More crystal hung from the walls, resonating in time, and filling the chamber with light. At the top of the pyramid there was a magnificent throne, cut from a stone like deep blue marble, covered in intricate golden script. A figure stood on the pyramid, wearing a gold-threaded, blue robe. Braziers burned with silver fire, and the song rose to acknowledge Alaric's presence, the light reaching a near-blinding crescendo.

Alaric glimpsed galleries leading off from the pyramid chamber. The place was far bigger than the *Hecatomb*. For some reason, this was not the least bit surprising to him.

The figure looked up. Silver flames licked from inside the hood.

'Who are you?' it asked in a voice dry like the hiss of a snake.

'Justicar Alaric of the Grey Knights,' replied Alaric.

'I see. You may kneel.'

Alaric stayed standing.

'No? Very well. Few of them kneel to begin with, all do eventually.'

'All of whom?'

'All of you, of course, the slaves, the lowly, fed to me, as if I should be grateful, as if it is some compensation for the wretchedness of my station.' The figure waved an arm to indicate the blinding glory of the pyramid chamber. 'You see what I have to work with here.'

Alaric dearly wanted to wrench the collar of Khorne from around his neck, and let his soul tell him what he was facing, but he had tried before, and he could not remove it with his bare hands, not without breaking his neck.

'So, what is it that you desire?'

'Desire?' Alaric paused. There were many things he desired. There was so much anger and misery inside him that he could not separate it all out. 'I want to escape.'

'No, that is just a primitive lust, a basic thing, a need for freedom, no more elegant than hunger or thirst. No, what do you truly desire?' The figure rose from the throne and took a couple of steps down the pyramid. 'Revenge? Conquest? Redemption? I used to grant wishes, Justicar Alaric of the Grey Knights. Habits die hard, so they say. They always ask me for something once they realise that, but, of course, no desires can be fulfilled here, not as I am now, unless you desire to have your soul flayed away, which I gather you do not.'

'Many have tried,' said Alaric.

'So I see from the state of you.'

'Then this is how it will end,' said Alaric.

'Oh, yes.'

Alaric flexed his fists. He was in no position to fight. He was still exhausted from his battering at the hands of Venalitor, and struggling against his scaephylyds, but no Grey Knight had ever backed down and given himself to the enemy's mercy. 'I should warn you, I am not an easy man to kill.'

'Kill? Justicar Alaric, I had thought you would have more brains in that scarred head than that. You and I are much alike in that Venalitor has uses for us aside from piling up our skulls on his god's throne. No, he does not want you killed.'

The figure pulled back its hood. Beneath was the face of a man flayed of skin, with silver threads for muscles. Silver flame rippled over it. Its eyes were points of burning blue. Tiny mouths opened up in its flesh, muttering syllables of spells that cast a corona of power over it.

'He wants you possessed,' said Raezazel the Cunning.

Duke Venalitor watched the battle from his quarters, the bloody events shimmering on a great sheet of crystal that dominated one wall of his audience chamber.

'Let me see the *Scourge*,' said Venalitor. The image shifted to display Drakaasi's newest city. The *Scourge* was a collection of ships and flotsam roped together in a gigantic conglomeration of wreckage floating on the planet's southern ocean, where millions of outcasts and heretics lived. Rumours persisted that the *Hecatomb* had been cut from the *Scourge*, and that perhaps it was the very first ship to become a part of the *Scourge*, and therefore sailed as the excised heart of a dead city. Venalitor did nothing to deny such rumours.

The *Scourge* was the link between the surface of Drakaasi and the civilisations of its deeps. Creatures evolved from scaephylyds lived there, along with lords of Drakaasi, like Thurrgull the Tentacular, who had forged their domains away from the eyes of the surface.

Ocean-going mutants crawled from the sea to kill and abduct, drowning the inhabitants of a great temple ship that dominated the outskirts of the *Scourge*. The temple was dedicated to Arguthrax, ministered by his daemonic priesthood, and the mutants were creatures with gills and webbed hands, who had answered Venalitor's call for allies from the deeps.

Arguthrax's priests, each with six fingers on their mutated hands, were dragged down and killed. The splendid temple ship was holed below the waterline and began to sink, dragging the dwellings of many outcasts down with it. Icons of the warp toppled into the fouled waters.

The image shifted. This time it showed a staging ground for one of Venalitor's allied cults, the Ebon Hand, a band of pirates corrupted and turned to Khorne by Venalitor's agents. They were assembling high in the mountain roosts where they had docked their skyships and dirigibles, ready to marshal their numbers and join Ebondrake's off-world crusade.

The Ebon Hand's sentries alerted the whole cult, as the sun broke over the mountain. On the flagpole at the centre of their assembly ground, where once had flown a banner blessed by Venalitor himself, now hung the body of their leader, Caryagan Redhand. Redhand's face had been removed, and a huge, bloody maw yawned in the front of his head. His hands had been cut off, too, no doubt added to the trophies of whatever assassin Arguthrax had sent.

'The war continues, then, my lord,' said the slave master. The ancient scaephylyd waited patiently at the back of the room. It was a shrewd creature that had survived as long as it had by aligning itself with Drakaasi's lords and offering them complete subservience.

'It continues,' said Venalitor. 'It will not end until one of us is dead.'

'Then how will we be victorious?'

Venalitor looked at him. 'I will sacrifice everything I have to, and nothing more.'

'Lord Ebondrake must be guarded against.'

'A dull mind would think so, slave master, but the truth is that Ebondrake admires strength as we all do. When Arguthrax is done with, I will be closer to Ebondrake's position, not further away.'

'Then what is your will?' The slave master crouched down on its haunches. It was the equivalent of a deep bow, which a scaephylyd could not do normally since it was so hunched over.

'Keep it quiet,' said Venalitor, 'for now. Use soldiers we can say were acting on their own, and that we will not miss. Kill Arguthrax's outer circles first, the allies of allies, the props holding up his domain. He is a thing of anger and hate. He will try to strike at me as directly as possible. He will elicit Ebondrake's wrath before I do, and when that happens, he will be open for the deathblow.'

'So it shall be, my lord.'

'Keep me updated on the Grey Knight,' added Venalitor. 'Once Raezazel has him, he is destined to kill Arguthrax.'

'Of course.'

The slavemaster left the chamber to pursue his many duties, leaving Venalitor watching the shadow war unfolding.

ALARIC SLAMMED INTO the wall behind him. Shards of gold showered down around him as he slid to the floor. His mind reeled. Images of the daemon's life battered against him like gunfire.

He forced himself to breathe, and to ground his thoughts, to fight the flawed human instinct to run.

Raezazel the Cunning was flying above him. Silver wings unfolded from his robes. Fire rippled up off its body, and hundreds of mouths in its shining flesh sang at once.

'You know that I can give you what you desire,' said Raezazel in its hundred voices. 'You are stronger than the others. You believe that you can see through the lie. Perhaps you are right.'

Alaric got to his feet. He felt weak and small. Never had he been so at the mercy of another creature.

'Do you desire death, Grey Knight?' asked Raezazel. 'I can give you that.'

Alaric forced a breath down. He was a Grey Knight. He had faced the lies of Chaos before, and thrown them back into the darkness with the power of truth. Daemons had tried to possess him before, too, and not one of them had prised open his mind.

However, none of them had ever attacked him while he was so unprotected.

'I desire freedom,' said Alaric.

'Then you can have it.'

'Freedom from you.'

Raezazel cocked its head to the side. Its burning eyes looked at him quizzically, as it might have regarded a particularly unusual kind of lunatic.

'That,' it said, 'is something you will have to take from me.'

A hand coalesced from golden energy, picked Alaric up, and held him against the wall. Power was pouring off Raezazel, burning from the crystals, and turning the golden walls into sheets of molten light. Alaric fought back, feeling the hand closing around his mind. Dull pain throbbed behind his eyes.

'I will wear your flesh and leave this prison, Justicar Alaric. I will escape this world and become one with my god. That is what I desire. That is what Venalitor has offered me by sending you here, for even the Blood God's servants must perpetuate the lie.'

Alaric fought back with everything he had. It took all his remaining strength just to draw breath, but he would not let Raezazel in, never! He would die first. That would be his last service to the Emperor. The enemy would never have a possessed Grey Knight to parade before its armies, never... unless Raezazel was stronger.

Raezazel's burning face floated down low above Alaric's. A silver hand reached out to touch his head.

Alaric was filled with cold pain.

Raezazel was showing him what he could do to him: fill him up with agony a thousand times worse, for a thousand years. He was telling Alaric to give in.

'Not this mind,' hissed Alaric between his teeth. 'There is no pain save the fires of failure. There is no torture save a duty undone. My Emperor claims me, and no other may challenge.'

Raezazel dropped Alaric. 'The condition of your soul matters not,' he said. 'I will flay it alive if I have to.'

Alaric tried to get back to his feet. Raezazel threw horrors at him.

Rotting bodies loomed from the floor and walls. Alaric had seen thousands of corpses. They would not force him to his knees.

They took on the faces of his friends, his battle-brothers and everyone he had ever trusted.

Alaric had lost many friends. The penalty for being trusted by Alaric seemed to be death. He felt his might tighten as it recoiled from the images, but he held firm.

Worlds burned. A galaxy suffered, and the stars went out. Hollow laughter filled the universe.

Alaric fought back.

Victory after victory bloomed into existence. He knew that Chaos could be defeated. Perhaps it would take all the time in the galaxy, but it would happen. For every vision of desolation Raezazel pumped into him, Alaric countered with something glorious: the destruction of the Chaos fleet at the Battle of Gethsemane, Lord Solar Macharius winning a thousand worlds back from the galaxy's dark, the vanquishing of Angron in the First Armageddon War. Alaric pulled victories from every history book and inspiration a sermon he knew.

We are weak flesh and fools, thought Alaric furiously. *We are young and blind. Perhaps one day we will be gone, but we burn so bright, and the galaxy, which has forgotten so much, will remember us.*

Raezazel hissed in frustration. The images of horror dissolved away. Alaric slumped down against the wall of the chamber, grinning like a madman.

'You can't terrify me into submission, daemon. I am a Space Marine. We know no fear.'

'Then it seems you are in need,' spat Raezazel, 'of an education.'

Raezazel's mind picked Alaric up off the floor. Alaric fought back, as Raezazel drifted closer on wings of light, and placed a hand on the Grey Knight's forehead.

Filaments of silver and gold wove around Alaric's head, and wormed into the skin of his scalp. Alaric bellowed, and tried to tear them free, but they were inside him now.

He could feel them writhing through his skull into his brain. Synapses misfired, and extremes of heat and cold rippled over him, nausea, pain, confusion. The world spun around him as his sense of balance went haywire.

He beat at Raezazel's body with his free hand. Silver ribs crunched. It would not be enough.

A thousand mouths were laughing at him.

Alaric's consciousness melted like the gold.

WHEN EVEN ARGUTHRAX was young, Raezazel the Cunning had granted wishes.

The image in Alaric's mind was of a largely formless thing, just a scrawl of psychic matter in the warp. He knew it was a simplified image, distorted by being forced into a human mind. The scale of the warp still battered at Alaric's brain.

The youthful daemon, little more than a tadpole swimming through the mindless infinity of the warp, had suckled on the misery and hatred of the young races populating the universe. From them, he learned deceit and malice, and saw their fleeting joys and moments of affection as the hollow things they really were. The living things of the galaxy were nothing but bundles of lies, woven to keep them from understanding their true hateful natures.

Lies were the fabric of the mind. To the mortal races, lies were reality. The power of a lie could bring empires up from the dirt and cast them back down again. They could drive men, greenskins, eldar and the rest to acts of heroism and devotion… and of hatred, genocide and evil. Lies were power. Deceit was reality.

There was a god of lies in the warp. There could be no greater power. Congealed from the deceit of the universe, older than reality, Raezazel could only become a part of it. It was Tzeentch, and yet it was nothing, for this purest manifestation of Chaos was so infinitely mutable that it could never truly be fixed as anything. Its very existence was a lie, because Tzeentch could not exist. From this paradox flowed such power that the universe could have only one rightful ruler, and it was Tzeentch.

The concept of Tzeentch was an appalling thing, one that filled Alaric with disgust, but Raezazel's devotion to the being mingled with that disgust, the resulting emotion utterly alien to Alaric's mind, a perversion of everything it meant to be human.

Raezazel's understanding grew. Tzeentch desired power, and yet Tzeentch also desired an absence of power, anarchy and confusion, because for Tzeentch to desire any one thing would be to deny its very existence.

There were other gods in the warp. One of them was Khorne, the Blood God, but Raezazel knew that only Tzeentch could draw its power from such a fundamental part of the universe as the lie, and so Raezazel served.

Raezazel found ways through into real space, where the young races dwelled. He found a way through unprotected minds, the naked souls of psykers so bright from the warp that Raezazel could cross the bridge between dimensions and possess their bodies. He did Tzeentch's work, both encouraging others to worship the Liar God and build his power base, but also casting down the structures of power wherever he found them, spreading chaos and anarchy, for only Tzeentch could desire both dominion and chaos at once. Sometimes he even fought other followers of Tzeentch, to ensure that the holy paradox did not falter.

The time roared by, like a hurricane in Alaric's mind. He fought to keep himself from being shredded by the force of Raezazel's memories, because then he would disappear completely and be left nothing but a figment of the daemon's imagination.

Cults of Tzeentch prayed for help. Sometimes Tzeentch really did send them help. Other times, he sent them Raezazel. There were cults who called forth Tzeentch's servants and opened gates through which Raezazel could pass, his own sacred form emerging into real space in all its terrifying silver magnificence. Everyone who worshipped Tzeentch eventually suffered for it, because Tzeentch promised deliverance and succour, and so it was inevitable that this would always be a lie. Raezazel was often the source of that suffering, here an assassin and there a puppet master orchestrating tragic downfalls with an attention to detail that a human mind could not comprehend. Whole empires were shifted and manipulated to bring a single person low, and the lowliest of individuals could be used to topple civilisations with only the slightest touch.

Raezazel lied. He made promises. He became an expert at seeking out the desires of those whose called out to Tzeentch, and fulfilling them in such a way that they became utterly damned. They always came to recognise the lie just before the end, and knew that ultimately it had not been Tzeentch but they, who had damned themselves: yet another paradox. Raezazel was good at what he did.

Aeons passed. Species rose and fell, of which mankind had far from the greatest potential. One species ruled the galaxy, and then another, believers in the lie that true power lay anywhere in real space. The time came when mankind rose to dominate the galaxy in what it called the Dark Age of Technology, and then fell again in the wars of the Age of Strife. It was not the most spectacular collapse, though it provided plenty of fuel for Tzeentch's silver fires, but it was different, because mankind came back. One of them rose on Terra, humanity's birthplace, and began to unite what remained of the species. He very nearly succeeded, this Emperor, but his power, too, was just a hollow lie compared to that of the warp. Forces in the warp played their hand and tried to use this new unification of humanity to seize control of it, and with it the material galaxy.

Tzeentch played his part, too. The Emperor was a lie, and Tzeentch took great pleasure in revealing it to those who rebelled against Him. Raezazel was there, at Prospero and Istvaan V. He was even there on Terra, when the final charades were played out, when in victory the Emperor condemned his species to ten thousand years and more of lightless misery. Raezazel observed much of the Horus Heresy, reporting back to the daemon princes of Tzeentch, or whispering promises of power and deliverance, much as he had always done. When the traitor forces retreated into the Eye of Terror, Raezazel knew that it was just another lie. Chaos was not gone from the galaxy. When they returned and ruled it, the age of the Imperium would seem barely a flicker in the galaxy's history. Then, something went wrong.

The heresy was so pure that it almost filled up Alaric. He had to tell himself over and over again that Raezazel was a daemon and that everything he saw in it was a lie.

Alaric recognised the bloodstained world that Raezazel came to next. An eight-pointed star was carved into its surface, forming canals filled with blood. The star connected its great cities: a crown of crystal spires, a great parasite and an endless slum.

Raezazel came to the world of Drakaasi, where many threads of fate had converged. There titanic daemons had fought in the past, drenching the planet with the blood that still stained it. Khorne had won, and for the first time Raezazel the Cunning was trapped.

Khorne despised the lie, despised fate and magic and everything that made up Tzeentch. Raezazel was cut off from the warp. He lived there for a thousand years, snatching tragedies from the blood-soaked lives of Khorne's servants, promising them yet more bloodshed, and then robbing them of their minds. Khorne's own daemons hunted him, but they were base creatures, and more often than not they consumed each other in their lust for blood, turned against their fellows by Raezazel's brilliance. Raezazel the Cunning was the most hated creature on Drakaasi, that most hateful world.

Then Duke Venalitor arose. An aspiring champion of the Blood God, he was a master swordsman and an ambitious general. He sought out Raezazel the Cunning, as many lords and champions had done before, and, as always, Raezazel asked what Venalitor most desired.

Venalitor said he wanted a worthy opponent. The art of the sword was his personal form of worship and he needed a fitting target to perfect his skills. Raezazel offered him the best of Drakaasi's fighters, knowing that in besting them Venalitor would either kill himself or be driven mad by victory or defeat. However, Venalitor killed everything put in front of him. Finally Raezazel, knowing that the lie had to be believed no matter what, offered himself up as an opponent, knowing that the silver fires of Tzeentch burned brightly in him, and that no mortal could best him.

Venalitor cut Raezazel so deeply that the daemon knew fear for the briefest of moments. Then he glimpsed the warp again, and the many faces of his lord Tzeentch laughing at him. Raezazel had been lied to, as well. Of course he had, it was all part of the divine paradox. Raezazel collapsed, defeated, but Venalitor did not despatch him. Instead he was taken to the *Hecatomb*, imprisoned behind doors marked with the most powerful anti-magical wards, and bound by ancient daemon oaths to accept Venalitor as his conqueror and master.

Then, centuries later, Justicar Alaric of the Grey Knights was thrown into his cell.

All of this information was blasted into Alaric's mind in less than a second.

* * *

HE WAS FALLING. A universe of Raezazel's creation stretched around him, endless and black. A weaker man would have lost his mind there and then, overwhelmed by the reality of his insignificance against the universe. Alaric told himself that there was an Emperor out there somewhere, and that Alaric owed Him something. It was just enough.

A world unfolded from the blackness below him. Bare rock, pocked with craters, rolled wider and wider, until a whole planet was looming up below him.

Alaric slammed into it. The planet's surface rippled beneath him like something alive reacting to his presence. The ground folded over him, warm and crushing, and Alaric fought to breathe. Then it spat him out again.

Alaric fought to find something real. He was in a world of Raezazel's making. It had got inside his mind, and it was pulling strings in his imagination and memory to create this place.

It had got in. Such a thing had never happened to a Grey Knight, ever. Raezazel the Cunning had said it would possess him, and it was only a few steps from doing exactly that. With the Collar of Khorne switching off his psychic shield, Alaric was alone with his wits.

Grass was growing beneath him. He got to his feet as it spread away from him like a green stain. The landscape in the distance heaved up into hills and mountains. Deep scars sank into the land and filled with water, heavy fronds of a forest bending over the banks. Tress unrolled from the ground like hands towards the sky, surrounding Alaric in a dense jungle. Vines writhed around tree trunks that blackened with age and moss. The ground underneath became soft with simulated centuries of growth and decay. The first creatures of this world inside his mind winked into life: jewelled flying insects, night-furred predators that skulked among the branches, and birds of brilliant colours. The sound of the place descended around him like a cloak, the wind among the trees, howls, and the distant roars of predators.

The sky was streaked with cloud. Distant mountains were crowned with snow. The sound of a waterfall nearby reached Alaric.

He stood in a clearing of the forest and looked down at himself. He was still wearing the remnants of the armour in which he had fled the arena of Gorgath. He was still the same person. No matter what happened, Alaric existed. It was the only fact of which Alaric could still be certain.

'Raezazel!' yelled Alaric. 'Daemon! A Grey Knight never knelt before witchcraft, and I shall not be the first!'

Only the gentle din of the jungle answered him. Alaric looked around, noting how the forest was darkening as it thickened around him. He could stay there forever, hiding in fear from the daemon inside him. Or he could find it, and fight it.

Alaric tore the branches down that blocked his path in front of it. He wished he had a weapon, but he would worry about that later. For now, he pushed on.

ALARIC CAME ACROSS the waterfall. It was flowing from the shattered skull of a titanic creature that seemed to have lain there for thousands of years, fossilised and claimed by the jungle. The water that poured from the broken cranium was pure, and shot through with leaping silver fish.

The skull was enormous. The dead creature had many, many more, attached to a monstrous spine that formed a thickly forested ridge stretching into the distance. Each skull was different, grimacing in horrible glee or festooned with eyes. The creature, when alive, had been a towering column of insane faces kilometres high.

'Ghargatuloth,' said Alaric. The daemon prince had arisen on the Trail of Saint Evisser, and engineered a sequence of events so complex that Alaric had become a part of it. Those events had been woven to summon Ghargatuloth back from the warp where it had been banished, and only Alaric and Inquisitor Ligeia had been able to bring the daemon low at the instant it emerged into real space.

'Is that the best you can do?' Alaric shouted up at the sky, knowing that Raezazel would hear him. 'Remind me of a past victory? Is that what you are going to offer me, Raezazel? Basking in past glories means nothing to a Grey Knight, not while your kind still exist! That Ghargatuloth existed at all was a failure of my entire Chapter! Is this really supposed to seduce me?'

There was no answer.

Alaric made a spear from a straight tree branch and a chunk of sharp flint. At least now he was armed. He felt more like a Grey Knight, with a weapon in his hand, and less like a man being led through the corners of his own mind at the whim of a daemon. He forged his way up onto Ghargatuloth's spine, and saw mountains in the distance, the glinting ribbon of a river leading towards a dark smudge of ocean on the opposite horizon.

The peak of a snow-capped mountain shuddered, and burst in a plume of dark grey smoke. Minutes later the sound reached Alaric, an angry roar from beneath the earth. The ground quaked. The sky darkened.

'So that's the way it's going to be,' said Alaric. Tidal waves rose up from the ocean and hard rain began to hammer down.

RAEZAZEL BATTERED ALARIC for many hours. Floods ripped through the jungles, slamming Alaric against rocks and tree trunks. Earthquakes ripped the ground open, and he nearly fell into the gaping, burning maw of the earth dozens of times. Predators lurched from the jungle, and Alaric fended them off, skewering a great lizard through the throat with his spear, and wrestling a cat-like monster to the ground, breaking its neck. Birds of prey swooped down, and Alaric grabbed them by the wings, crushing them down against the ground. Poisonous snakes were out-reacted, and had their spines cracked like whips.

Night fell. Burning meteors fell from the sky, casting plumes of scalding ash over the jungle. The jungle, too, changed around him, closing in, reaching thorny limbs. Alaric fought it all off, as he forged on defiantly through Raezazel's world.

He was tiring, however. Presumably his body was not real, and was only a projection of himself, a reflection of his own consciousness, but it still bore its own scars and bruises. The wound in his chest still bled. The burns from the molten gold still flared with pain. He was tired and hurt, and he wondered if he could act with even half the strength and resilience of a fully fit Grey Knight.

He began to see things, faces in the sky. He heard voices speaking to him, half-real sentences pulled at random from his past. Perhaps they were all really there, assembled by Raezazel to torment him.

He stumbled on, half-blind with fatigue. Clawed hands reached from the darkness to tear at his skin. A meteor slammed into the ground close enough to knock him off his feet. He crawled on, writhing through the mud. Scalding rain streaked down on him. He was blind and deaf. Lightning crashed above him, and he didn't even know which way he was heading any more.

His hand found polished stone. He dragged himself out of the mud, and flopped, gasping, onto the cold stone. He could have just lain there, letting the remaining energy bleed out of him until he fell unconscious. Something half-remembered told him to carry on.

He could see stone steps ahead of him. At the top of the steps was the columned front of a temple, with a sculpted pediment depicting battle. In front of the columns, on the top step, was a huge statue of a man in massive ornate armour. His face was wide and noble, his war gear magnificent, and inscribed with devotional texts. He carried a halberd in one hand.

The statue was of Alaric. This was his temple, the one erected in the warp to celebrate all the skulls he had taken on Drakaasi, and perhaps all the creatures and daemons he had ever killed.

He crawled up the steps. Lightning split the night again, and the rain hammered down on him. At least there was shelter here.

Someone was standing between the columns. The dull glow of a brazier emanated from behind the figure, glinting off golden offerings to Alaric the Betrayed. Alaric was just able to make out the details of the figure as he reached the top step.

Justicar Tancred, huge like a standing stone in his Terminator armour, reached down to Alaric. He smiled.

'Take my hand, Alaric,' he said. 'It's over.'

FIFTEEN

ALARIC AWOKE ON a pinnacle of rock standing high over a raging ocean. He did not recognise this world. Perhaps it was another part of the same planet that Raezazel had created in his mind.

'Do you see what they do to you?' said Raezazel. The daemon was standing behind Alaric. Alaric stood up, and Raezazel took flight, hovering over him. 'Do you ever put down your implements of death long enough to realise?'

'End this witchcraft!' shouted Alaric. The wind whipped around his ears, sharp with the taste of the sea, and stole his words away.

'What is a man,' said Raezazel, 'if he means nothing to his fellow men? If he is an island, cut off from all others? What kind of an existence is this, Alaric? Everyone you trust, everyone who trusts you, dies. It is a death sentence. Look at what they made of you.'

Alaric looked down over the edge of the pinnacle. Slick rock receded all the way to the battered shore. This was the tip of a barren peninsula, devoid of life. Alaric was completely alone.

'I offer you a human life,' said Raezazel, 'a real one.'

'I need only to know that my duty is done!'

'When will that be? When all of Chaos is gone and the warp extinguished? Such a thing cannot be, and you know it as well as I do. What is the point of fighting a battle that cannot end, when the sacrifice you make is everything that makes a human what he is? A human life, Alaric, happiness, fulfilment. I show you now what you are. Let me show you what you can be, free of your Imperium, free of the duties you cannot fulfil. Let me show you contentment.'

'Burn, daemon. Pick your hell and stew there.'

'Was there ever a prisoner who so loved the bars that kept him captive? Let go of this, Alaric. All that sets you apart. No man can expect to be more than human. Give up on that dream and live.'

Raezazel was right. Alaric was completely alone, set apart from the human race he was sworn to defend.

He looked once at his reflection and accepted that it was a small price to pay. Every servant of humanity had to make a sacrifice to their duty. This was Alaric's.

Alaric looked up at Raezazel. Then he stepped off the edge of the pinnacle and fell.

HE PLUNGED INTO the ocean, and the ocean became air. It was a void without light or substance, only the wind in his ears.

'Take what you want,' said Raezazel's voice in his head. 'Take it. What is there to existence but that?'

The cold void tore at Alaric. It had fingers like ice, and it would tear him apart. Alaric wanted to land somewhere, to get his bearings, and find Raezazel so that he could work out what the next trick was.

Land appeared under him. Alaric thudded into it. It was dry and sandy, and went on forever. He wanted to see where he was.

A sun bloomed in the eye like a white flower. Alaric looked around, but the featureless plain stretched in all directions. He searched for some landmark to get his bearings by.

He glimpsed a city in the distance. It was a fine Imperial city with the buttresses and granite eagles familiar to him from the fortresses of Titan. Suddenly he was there at his threshold.

'Take what you want,' said Raezazel.

Power, thought Alaric, the power to conquer and do my duty. The power to destroy evil.

He was the city's king. His court surrounded his throne, bowing before him, a hundred Imperial nobles, and representatives of all the Adepta. He had an Inquisitorial seal on his finger and a document in his hand, signed with the initial 'I' and a drop of blood. It gave him the world, and all other worlds upon which his imagination could settle.

'I want you dead,' said Alaric, 'you and all your kind, dead.'

He was at the head of his city's army. Only it was not a city any more, it was a kingdom, one of many on this world that all owed him fealty.

He was in armour as magnificent as that of a primarch, and the soldiers around him were Space Marines, legions upon legions of them, millions of them, and they revered him as a king and a brother. There was nothing they could not do.

'You can have what you want,' said Raezazel. 'There are ways. There is nothing within the bounds of human imagination that cannot be granted to you.'

'You offer me power?' snarled Alaric. 'You think I would betray myself to you for this?'

'You cannot deny your desires, Grey Knight. Look around you. Everything you desire, you have. You can have it, and more, forever.'

Alaric wanted lightning in his hand to strike down the daemon. He had it. He wanted Raezazel in front of him, ready to execute. The daemon was kneeling before him. All he had to do was take what he wanted.

'All this I desire, it is true,' said Alaric. 'It comes to my mind unbidden, as you know well, but there is one thing I desire more than anything, one burning need, which you cannot fulfil.'

'Name it,' said Raezazel.'

'I desire a universe where your kind cannot exist,' said Alaric.

Raezazel's mouths opened and closed dumbly.

The force of the paradox was too much even for a servant of Tzeentch.

Alaric's legions disintegrated. His city blew away in a tide of ash, and his world imploded.

ALARIC WAS AT the end of time.

Before him, impossibly, a battlefield stretched on forever, and he perceived every inch of it.

Mankind had gathered, every righteous man and woman who had ever died. Here were the primarchs: Sanguinius, achingly beautiful on wings of silver feathers; Leman Russ, striding titanic at the head of a host of wolves; Jaghatai Khan on a chariot made from stars. The greatest legends of the Imperium had gathered, and behind them the Space Marines and Imperial Guardsmen, the simple citizens and redeemed sinners, who had rallied to face evil at the end.

The Emperor commanded them all. Clad in blazing golden armour, He was the most magnificent sight that Alaric's mind could behold. Majesty streamed off Him. There could be no doubt that He was the master of mankind, a god, humanity's future given form.

Alaric's fallen battle-brothers stood around His golden form. He recognised Thane, who had died on Sarthis Majoris; Lykkos and

Cardios, lost on Chaeroneia; Canoness Ludmilla, slain by Valinov on Volcanis Ultor; Justicar Tancred; Inquisitor Ligeia.

'Justicar Alaric,' said Tancred with a smile. Tancred was huge, even by the standards of a Space Marine, built for the Terminator armour he wore. He clapped Alaric on the shoulder. 'You have joined us. We are complete!'

'This is it? This is the final battle?'

'Of course! The sons of Russ call it the Wolftime. To the Khan's men it is the hunting of the greatest quarry. To a Grey Knight it is the final battle against the enemy. See! There they stand, waiting to die!'

Alaric followed Tancred's gaze across the battlefield. The indistinct shadowy mass of the enemy stood waiting for the Emperor's charge. Four mighty generals loomed in the background, one crowned with horns, another a wizard in billowing robes. One was a writhing snake-bodied thing, and another was a bloated heap of decay. They were mighty, and they were terrible, but they would fall. They could not stand against the Emperor and His faithful.

'It cannot be,' said Alaric. 'I have not earned this.'

A hand took his, tiny in comparison. It belonged to Inquisitor Ligeia. She was an ageing, but handsome woman, striking in her deep blue, jewelled gown. Alaric admired her as much as he admired the Grand Masters of his own order. She smiled at him sadly.

'Why do you deny yourself, Alaric?' she asked. 'You have done so much. Who is to say you have not won your place at the Emperor's side? Look, there is the Castigator, the daemon you destroyed on Chaeroneia.' Alaric could see the daemon Titan's form among the shadows of the enemy. 'And there is Ghargatuloth, the Daemon Prince we slew together. Think on all the foes you have sent to this place. Think about those you saved. You redeemed me, Alaric. My death was not in vain, and I owe it to you. There are so many like me. Are they not worth something?' She took hold of his arm and pulled him close. 'You belong here. You deserve this. Your duty is done.'

'Is Raezazel there?' asked Alaric.

'It matters not,' said Tancred. 'He is one amongst many. He is nothing compared to others you vanquished. You are just one man, you cannot hope to banish every daemon from the universe.'

'Those are not the words of a Grey Knight,' said Alaric. 'While even one of them walks in real space, or broods in the warp, our work is not done. I will not stay here unless Raezazel is there, destroyed, among the enemy. Is he there? Can any of you see him?'

'You disappoint me, justicar,' said Ligeia. 'I thought you would understand your role in the galaxy better than this.'

'Those are not the words of Inquisitor Ligeia,' said Alaric. He looked up at the golden form of the Emperor towering over him. It was like staring into the sun. 'And you, my Emperor! Do you see in me one who deserved his place here? One who lets his conciousness slip away from him while a daemon dances through his mind? One who is brought into the presence of the enemy and cowers away from his duty?'

The Emperor looked down. A hundred mouths opened in his face.

'Is this all you can do, Raezazel? Is this the best you can offer me? A sham victory against the warp? Is this what you will play, over and over again, in my mind as my reward?'

'I am getting closer, Grey Knight,' said Raezazel. 'You cannot deny that. It is only a matter of time.'

Brother Tancred and Inquisitor Ligeia dissolved into molten gold. The battlefield was flooded with it, and it closed, white-hot, over Alaric's head. The primarchs and the Emperor disappeared from view. Alaric fought to breathe.

He would not die, not yet. Raezazel still had to toy with him.

HE DREW A ragged, desperate breath. His hand found something to hold on to, and he dragged himself above the surface of the golden ocean.

A tower of frozen blood rose above him.

Alaric laid a hand on the blood. It melted under his body heat into a handhold. Grimly, forced on by the inevitability of it, Alaric began to climb.

Fallen fortresses rose from the ocean all around. Alaric knew, by some instinct, that each one represented a champion of the warp that Alaric had killed. They were all gone. There was just one left.

Alaric reached the top of the blood tower. The melted blood was smeared all over him, and its smell and taste filled him up. The whole world seemed made of it. He dragged himself over the battlements.

He forced himself to his feet. Duke Venalitor stood in front of him.

A sword had appeared in Alaric's hand. All he had to do was spear Venalitor through the chest, or slice his head off, or open up his abdomen and watch the life ooze out of him as he held his guts in.

Then it would be over. Haulvarn would be avenged.

Venalitor dissolved away. His armour, plate by plate, came away from his body and spiralled up towards the stormy sky. Finally his two-handed blade clattered to the floor and liquefied like mercury.

There was nothing inside the armour. Venalitor, like this whole world, was a lie.

'Did you think you would find him here? Rip him apart, and vanquish him? This is in your mind, Alaric,' said Raezazel. The daemon descended from the sky on silver wings. 'Venalitor is very far away. If you try to hunt him down without me, he will stay just out of reach. You know this, Alaric. He is too strong and too clever for you. I am the only way.'

Alaric knew it was true, and felt that truth dragging him down. He could deny it, but he knew he would be lying to himself. He wanted Venalitor dead, and he would not have what he wanted. He had been bested by Venalitor once before, and on Drakaasi Venalitor was protected by all the followers of a Chaos Lord, by a whole planet beloved of his god. With Raezazel, Alaric could kill Venalitor.

'No,' said that tiny part of Alaric that still remembered what he was. 'None of this is true. You are a daemon. You are a lie, and everything you say is a lie. There is another way.'

'Really?' asked Raezazel. 'Name it.'

Then, Alaric realised his one chance.

'I have read,' he said falteringly, 'from the pages of the Liber Daemonicum. I have looked on the warp and felt madness touching me. I have heard the whispers of the daemon in my mind. I have seen... I have seen a dead world come back to life, a cannibal planet consuming its own to survive. I have seen good men and women murder one another at the behest of a madman. I have fought on a cursed world for the delight of the Dark Gods. I have seen so many things... so much that could not possibly be real.' He looked up at Raezazel. The daemon was beautiful, but its very substance was deceit. 'I am not a Grey Knight. How could one such as I see what I have seen and keep my mind?'

With the last of his mental discipline, Alaric took in everything that he had seen: bodies torn by daemon's hands, glimpses of the warp, the hateful realm of Chaos on the other side of reality, heroes driven to madness and evil, whole planets devoured, and the psychic aftertaste of millions of screaming deaths.

It added up to an absolute certainty that the galaxy of man was doomed, and that Chaos was the inevitable state of all things.

'I am the hammer,' said Alaric. 'I am the mail about His fist! I am the spear in His hand! Though we are lost, I am the shield on His arm, I am the flight of his arrows!'

Too late, Raezazel realised what Alaric was doing. With Alaric's psychic shield still protecting him, there was no way that the horror of such things could affect Alaric as they would a normal man. However, with the Collar of Khorne removing that shield, Alaric's mind was vulnerable, not just to creatures like Raezazel, but to Alaric himself.

He had something to hold on to. He was the Hammer, he was a Grey Knight. He grasped that idea and clutched it to both his hearts. It was all he would have left. It had to count.

'I am the hammer! I am the sword! I am the shield! I am a soldier of the battle at the end of time!'

Alaric let all the horror hit him at once: everything he had seen, everything he had done, the friends he had lost, and the lives he had taken.

'No!' yelled Raezazel with the voices of a hundred mouths.

Alaric lost his mind.

SIXTEEN

VENALITOR'S STRATEGIC CHAMBER on board the *Hecatomb* suited the workings of war. The strategium table dominated the room, a map of Drakaasi picked out in ivory and gold on its surface. The rest of the room was in darkness, so that Venalitor could concentrate on the matter of his campaign against Arguthrax. Venalitor wore the robes of a priest of Khorne, and his sword was propped up against the table. The two-hander never left his side.

'The daemon will be dealt with in due time,' said Venalitor impatiently. 'Just tell me the latest casualties.'

The scaephylyd slave master held a scroll in its forelimbs. It unrolled the scroll with its mandibles. 'The Hand has struck back,' it said. 'The leaders of the Army of Crimson Hate were slain in the night.'

'We didn't get all of the Hand?' asked Venalitor irritably. 'Damnation. They really are vermin.' Markers representing his forces, and those of Arguthrax, were arranged around the map like pieces in some game of strategy. 'Can the Crimson Hate still fight?'

'They are squabbling amongst themselves,' replied the slavemaster. 'To decide who will be their new generals.'

Venalitor reached over and picked up the marker representing the Army of the Crimson Hate. He could ill-afford to lose them, especially considering the sacrifices he had made to acquire their loyalty. He threw the jewelled marker across the room. It bounced off an obsidian column, and skittered behind a shrine to Khorne in his aspect of the Red Knight.

'Others?' asked Venalitor.

'Arguthrax has hit the sleepers,' continued the slavemaster. 'Our agent in the Wild Hunt of Tiresia was murdered but an hour ago.'

'How did Arguthrax find him?' snapped Venalitor, in disbelief. His spy in Tiresia's court was so subtle and cunning that he didn't even have a name, just a face so bland it left no mark in the memory.

'We know not,' said the slavemaster. 'Also the tactician in Scathach's army, who was in our employ, was discovered and denounced. Scathach executed him.'

'Hmm. That is less of a surprise. War Master Thorgellin was less subtle in his methods. At least there was a proper execution. That would have been something to see, Scathach has quite an imagination. What progress have we made?'

'The campaign against the Tribe of the Fifth Eye is a success,' said the slavemaster. 'The Disciples of Murder have pushed them back to the ocean. The final push has commenced.'

'Good, and what of Arguthrax's sleepers?'

'They are well-hidden. My scaephylyds are hunting them down. Many scaephylyds have been found to be suspicious, and have been liquidated, but there are no confirmed spies among us.'

'Your kind were a good choice to serve me,' said Venalitor. 'Without me, you would have been exterminated sooner or later. It is difficult to corrupt those who owe their existence to their master.'

'Indeed, it is so,' said the slavemaster, but there was no indication in its cultured Imperial Gothic of whether it took this as an insult or not.

Venalitor sat back in his throne, a black stone echo of the fabled Skull Throne upon which Khorne sat while observing all the murders committed in his name. Khorne would know how to deal with an enemy like Arguthrax.

Venalitor could not claim to know the mind of his god. Nevertheless, it was certain that, presented with a problem like Arguthrax, Khorne would show no mercy.

'Bring them all out of the woodwork: everything that has ever paid fealty to us, every oath that was sworn. Examine the rolls for every supplication and tribute. How many creatures on this planet have offered their loyalty to me out of convenience, trusting their cunning or power to avoid their obligations? Show them they were wrong.' Venalitor stood up. 'Use the Army of Crimson Hate to enforce this in the open. Use the rest of our sleepers to do so in the shadows. I can always get more followers.'

'It will leave us open, my lord.'

Venalitor looked the slavemaster in its many eyes. 'Victory is given to he who will go further than the next man. Arguthrax is ancient. His connections are thousands of years old. He will not throw them away in war. I am young. I have no allies or followers that I am not ready to expend. If I am the only one who is left, if everyone who has ever knelt before me is dead, then I will still have won if Arguthrax has lost. That is my advantage over him. Make it so, slavemaster, and do not rest until every obligation has been called in.'

The slavemaster, bowed again, rolled up the scroll, and left the chambers.

Venalitor sat back down and looked at the map in front of him. He moved the markers around, each one a finely wrought statue of a daemon, or a warrior of Chaos. Some of them were spies, elite agents hidden in the courts of other lords, who in spite of their immense value were not above being used as foot soldiers in the war. Others were hapless cults created to be sacrificed, drooling madmen competing for the right to die for their master. They all had their uses.

There was one piece that Venalitor could not move around at will. It was a tiny obsidian dragon with eyes of amber. It represented Lord Ebondrake, watching over Drakaasi from his palace in Vel'Skan.

Ebondrake was still the ultimate power on Drakaasi. He had expressly forbidden the war between Venalitor and Arguthrax. The truth was, even if Ebondrake would never admit it, that taking on both Venalitor and Arguthrax could be beyond even Ebondrake and his Ophidian Guard. That was how delicate the balance of power on Drakaasi could be.

Venalitor left the Ebondrake piece where it was. He would deal with the lizard when the time came.

ALARIC WAS STILL there. It was a very small part of him, a fragment of lucidity, and it was trapped. The rest of his mind was a dark ocean, and he was crushed on the bed of its deepest trench. Like deep-sea predators, like the feral killers of the warp, venomous things coalesced from the darkness, shards of hatred and misery, regrets and the memories of violence, flitting through his unconscious mind looking for a personality to devour.

He was the Hammer. The prayer kept him intact. He had a duty, encompassed by the prayer, and that duty was his reason for existing. He had to fight on, to act as the hammer in the Emperor's fist, because if he did not, there was no one to take his place. He was a Grey Knight, and without men like him there would be no human race.

Slowly, he tried to drag himself up, piece by piece, memory by memory. He caught glimpses of an almost forgotten man, a giant in armour with a halberd in his hand. Painful flashes of violence assailed him, snapping at him with red teeth. He had unleashed all the horrors of his memory, and they had rampaged around his mind, shattering him until he was just a tiny shard of a human being trapped in the darkness.

SOMETIMES, RAEZAZEL'S MEMORIES flickered past his mind's eye.

There was something in there that Raezazel had wanted to hide from him, something locked away in the madness, some secret, or something shameful, something that even a daemon recoiled from.

Its first sight of Drakaasi bloomed in Alaric's fragmented mind: an eight-pointed star marked out by cities and the blood canals that connected them; emotions, anger, fear and frustration, filtered through an unholy and alien mind.

Alaric fought to understand. There was a key to the Hammer of Daemons and the half-blind skull, but it was wrapped in the mind of a daemon, where even a Grey Knight's mind might never survive.

He fought on. The prayer echoed endlessly as he fell through the void of his mind.

Then slowly, gingerly, clinging to the prayer like a rope, he reached up towards the surface.

ALARIC COUGHED UP a throatful of blood, and spat it out, gasping down a breath. He almost gagged on it. The stench of rotting bodies was so familiar to him that for a moment he wondered what horrible thing he was.

He was Justicar Alaric. He was a Grey Knight. He knew it to be true, but they felt like the thoughts of a stranger, intruding on his mind.

Then there was pain, screaming from his hands and shoulders. It hit him in waves, each stronger than the last, leaving him nauseous and dizzy. He had never felt so physically weak, even during those punishing battles, which surfaced, muted, in his memory.

He took in a couple more heavy breaths. His ribs ached from the force of his lungs sucking the oxygen into him. His head cleared a little, and he remembered that he still had two working lungs.

He risked opening his eyes. The yellow sun burned in a white sky. The scorched desert was strewn with titanic bones, so enormous they must have belonged to truly immense creatures in life. They had succumbed to the desert, their life leached out of them until they fell. Perhaps the bones had been there for thousands of years, protected from decay by the parched desert. He saw a skull rearing up from the sands, and a ribcage, across which had been stretched expanses of canvas to create shade from the sun. Hovels gathered around solar stills and covered wagons. Even here, life existed on Drakaasi. There was not one part of the planet that was not home to some corrupted thing or other.

Alaric tried to turn his head. He must have been hanging there for some time because his muscles had seized up. He tried to look downwards instead.

A ribbon of blood wound its way from beneath him, off between the mountainous dunes of the desert. It was a river of blood down which the *Hecatomb* was sailing, and Alaric was chained to the ship's prow by his wrists and ankles. He had to force himself to breathe when he realised.

He was alive. Raezazel had been real. Now, the suffering would really begin, for he had avoided punishment by possession, and Venalitor would make him pay.

Tiny insects flitted around him. Alaric shook his head to get them off his face. The insects were issuing from the eye socket of a sun-blackened corpse hanging beside him, for they had formed a colony inside the corpse's skull. Executed corpses hung all around Alaric, each in a different state of decay. Many were skeletons picked clean by insects and birds of prey, others were fresh enough to still be in a bloated, discoloured state, blown up by the gases of decay like fleshy balloons.

One of them, well-worn by parasites and the desert sun, was just the upper half of a human body. It was huge and barrel-chested, the ribs fused into a breastplate. The head, when it had still had a face, must have been strong-jawed and forbidding.

It was all that remained of Brother Haulvarn.

The desert turned dark, and Alaric was lost again.

THE NEXT TIME it was the blood that woke him up.

He had no sense of time. It could have been decades since he had looked at Haulvarn's decomposed face, or it could have been an hour. It need only have been enough time for him to become covered in blood.

It was all over him, clotting in the folds of his body, heavy and sticky. He shook it out of his eyes, and tried to understand where he was.

Everything was a whirl. His ears were full of white noise, like the roar of a fire, applause from hundreds of thousands of spectators cramming the seating that towered around him. He was in an arena. He didn't know which one. Arches of granite towered overhead as if the place was built into the skeleton of a vast domed cathedral.

He was standing on a heap of bodies. His arms were thrust up towards the sky in victory. His body ached as if he had been fighting for hours. His hearts were pumping adrenaline through him.

The bodies were beastmen and mutants, mixed in with arena slaves. Alaric looked down at them, seeking some understanding of what he had done. They had been killed with bare hands: skulls cracked, limbs snapped, and necks broken. Among them, Alaric saw men in the ruined uniforms of Imperial Guard: the men of the Hathran Armoured Cavalry.

Other gladiators were fighting in the arena, finishing off the flood of lowly arena slaves and captive mutants that they had been sent out to fight. Alaric didn't recognise them, but they looked well-armed and trained, chosen slaves from the stables of Drakaasi's lords. One was a mutant with two heads, one tearing flesh from the bones of a slave while the other whooped in victory at the crowd. Another was a giant armoured warrior, pulling its helmet off so that it could shower its face in blood. Alaric's stomach lurched again when he realised that the warrior was a woman.

The female warrior walked over to him and clapped him on the back. Alaric looked up at her. She had a strong, meaty face and a patch over one eye. Her armour was old and scored.

'You shed blood well,' she said with approval.

Alaric tasted blood in his mouth. He prayed that is was his own.

'Is there any here,' yelled the woman to the stands, 'who would challenge the Betrayed?

The crowd cheered on. Alaric had been the star of the arena that day. They would not soon forget him.

Alaric had seen enough. He could do no good. He was better off oblivious. He let himself shatter again, and the darkness bled through the cracks to consume him.

THE PLANET SCARRED with the eight-pointed star fell from the void towards Drakaasi, a losing battle with gravity. This was what Raezazel had seen. He had let the image slip from his mind as it tried to possess Alaric. It had tried to hide it, and that fact made it important.

More: deep blue and gold; a shrine, dozens of shrines, built to imaginary saints; a religion built on lies, its followers oblivious.

Sacrifices: betrayed men and women, pilgrims and fanatics, lured to their doom.

Raezazel had come to Drakaasi. It was no accident that brought him there. The truth of his arrival had been kept from Alaric, but it was still there in the sea of profane knowledge that had flooded into Alaric's mind.

Alaric held on. It would be so easy to give in and lose his mind completely. It would be such a relief. He would never have to confront the things he was doing in his madness, or be confronted with the possibility that his duty would never be fulfilled. It was the simplest thing in the galaxy to let himself slip away and end it.

But he was the Hammer. He fought to keep hold of the prayer's meaning. Without him and men like him, there was no galaxy, there was no light burning at the heart of the Imperium to ward off the darkness. There was only madness and death.

HE WAS AWARE of a great space around him, echoing with the sound of a chisel against stone.

Alaric was standing in a cavernous hall. It looked like it had once been a great meeting place. Its ceiling was of stained glass, missing so many panes that the design was impossible to make out. The place was half-ruined, the sun falling in shafts through holes in the once-ornate walls. A grand staircase led to nowhere, and weeds were breaking through the floor.

Chunks of cut stone and half-finished statues stood everywhere.

In front of Alaric, a scrawny man worked at a slab of marble with a chisel and a hammer. A figure was rising from the stone, broad-shouldered and fearsome.

The figure was of Alaric.

'What armour does my lord desire?' asked the sculptor.

'No armour,' said Venalitor's voice from behind Alaric, 'but capture the scars.'

'I like scars,' snickered the sculptor. 'So many want to be perfect, but what perfection is there in a flawless form? It is the imperfection that makes all beautiful things. Ugliness, that is the truth. The subject is so ugly. Ah, there is the challenge!'

Alaric tried to turn, but his hands were shackled through a ring driven into the floor.

'And the power!' said the sculptor. 'Yes, no armour, nothing to cage him.'

The statue's face was Alaric's, but he did not recognise the expression: arrogance, certainty, cruelty. The sculptor was a genius, but the person he had captured in marble was not one that Alaric knew.

The statue was not of a Grey Knight, it was of Alaric the Betrayed.

Venalitor stepped out from behind Alaric. He was accompanied by his scaephylyd slavers, and they formed a cordon around Alaric. 'You will be remembered,' he said to Alaric. 'No matter what, there will be a place for Alaric in the annals of Drakaasi. Do you even know how many you have killed?'

'Not enough,' said Alaric. He tested his bonds. They held tight. They were unnatural, as fast as the collar around his neck. The scaephylyds recoiled, ready with shock prods.

'Not enough!' said the sculptor, enraptured. 'Oh, that is wonderful. Such violence! I have never seen so much contained in one human form. This will be a masterpiece, my lord.'

Venalitor glanced at the sculptor with disdain. 'I would not accept anything less.'

'He shall be terrifying, my lord. Men's minds will break beneath the stone gaze of the Betrayed!' The sculptor went back to the stone of Alaric's face, bringing out the large expressive eyes, and endowing them with such disdain that Alaric felt a chill as he looked at them.

This was who he was. This is what Drakaasi saw: Alaric the Betrayed, a monster to take its place among the greatest champions of Khorne.

He fought the urge to vomit. The image of himself filled him with disgust. He had sacrificed so much on Drakaasi that he had lost himself.

He could not look on it any more. He felt himself thrashing like an animal against his chains as his mind sank down again, the cold ocean of oblivion seeping up to fill him. He was drowning in it, and the world slithered away into darkness.

THERE WERE OTHER times when the seas parted and Alaric could see through his own eyes.

He fought many times. He remembered men, Gearth's killers, carrying him upon their shoulders as he celebrated some great victory. He was on the *Hecatomb* with them, too, screaming wordless chants, handprints of blood covering his body.

He was chained to a wall, and people were arguing. He was dimly aware that the argument was about him, about rights and honours, about who the blood he had shed belonged to. One of the voices belonged to Venalitor.

He saw cities he did not recognise, glimpses of Drakaasi's monstrous architecture: a pyramid of skulls, heaps of severed limbs, thousands of bodies writhing in a cauldron of gore. He saw altars to Khorne, men screaming as they were dismembered, Lords of Drakaasi. He saw a towering heap of charnel robes, and a two-headed Traitor Marine, a mass of burning red flesh, looking on Alaric the Betrayed with jealous eyes.

He saw champions slain, and victims hurled to the crowds.

Sometimes he tasted blood and flesh in his mouth, and there was just enough of his mind left to pray that it was his own.

He saw a thousand places, a million victims, and horrors beyond his imagining, but mostly there was only darkness and cold.

SEVENTEEN

VENALITOR WATCHED THE skyship land. The desert was rocky and cold, as bleak a place as existed on Drakaasi, and Venalitor hadn't even been certain that Ebondrake would agree to meet him there. It did not do for the Lord of Drakaasi to answer the summons of an underling. Far away from Drakaasi's cities and without even a blood river crossing it, the desert was one of Drakaasi's least sacred places and it was a wonder that Ebondrake would grace it at all.

Lord Ebondrake emerged from the hold of the skyship. The Ophidian Guard who surrounded him were rendered all but invisible beside his majesty. The skyship was one of the small fleet that remained on Drakaasi, relics of an earlier age, and Ebondrake owned them all. It looked like a galleon loosed from the ocean, sails spreading out horizontally like the wings of a dragonfly.

'You do me a great honour,' said Venalitor, 'to join me here.'

'I trust you have something to show me,' said Ebondrake, a note of danger in his voice. Venalitor had come to the desert meeting alone. He looked completely out of place in that barren landscape in his red and brass armour.

'Of course, my lord,' he said.

'Nothing can take up my time save for the games and the crusade. If this is some irrelevant flattery, Venalitor, the limits of my patience shall be revealed.'

'The crusade is foremost in my mind, too,' said Venalitor. 'This world is too small to contain us all. If we do not grow beyond its boundaries we will wither away, all the while letting potential sacrifices grow old and die away from the Blood God's sight.'

'Well?' asked Ebondrake.

'Observe, my lord, and it will become clear.'

A storm was building up on the horizon. Dark clouds piled on top of one another, heavy and purple with blood. A colder wind whispered across the desert, kicking up plumes of dust from the broken land.

Venalitor drew his two-handed sword. The sky darkened, and the blade shone like a streak of caged lightning. He held the sword high.

Tiny dark shapes emerged from the closest tear in the ground, like ants fleeing a nest. More and more of them emerged. Darkness was staining the land, more scuttling forms in the distance. They were clambering out of every cave and fissure.

The desert was home to something after all: Scaephylyds, thousands of scaephylyds, more than had ever been seen in one place on Drakaasi before. They were still emerging from their underground caves, covering the desert in their beetle-like bodies. They glinted in the lightning flashing in the gathering clouds.

They began to organise themselves into ranks and files. Standards were raised, each one bearing an ancient totem of Drakaasi's oldest tribes: a predatory bird, long extinct, that was once the scourge of the desert skies; a black tree, with heads and hands impaled on its branches; a brass claw, reaching down from a red sky; a rune shaped like a blinded eye; an axe, and a scaephylyd skull wreathed in black fire.

Ranked up, the scaephylyds formed an army bigger than any that fought in Gorgath. In terms of numbers alone it was the greatest force Drakaasi had seen for centuries. There were a million scaephylyds at least, and they were still clambering to the surface.

'So,' said Ebondrake, 'this is what you bring to my crusade.' He peered across the desert, sizing up the force arrayed before him.

'All devoted to me,' said Venalitor, 'sworn to me in their entirety. These native tribes of Drakaasi have waited long to play their part in Khorne's great slaughter.'

'I see,' said Ebondrake. 'It is fascinating to me, duke, that you sought out the lowest of this planet's low, baser even than the filth of Ghaal, and built from them the army that you believe can put you at my side: from the deepest pits of this planet to the heart of its power.' Ebondrake turned to Venalitor and looked at him with narrowed eyes. 'The Liar God would be proud of such a champion.'

Venalitor smiled. 'He would not appreciate me, my lord. I manipulate others to get what I want, but I will not be lied to. We would not get along.'

Ebondrake smiled. 'So, how many of these creatures will be spent in your feud with Arguthrax?'

The question was supposed to catch Venalitor off-guard, but Venalitor had expected it. No amount of subterfuge and misdirection could keep the silent war from Ebondrake's eyes. The old lizard probably had thousands of spies in every corner of Drakaasi. 'History, my lord,' said Venalitor. 'It is done with. We are in a stalemate. Soon we will come to an undeclared truce. I have no wish to waste more of my troops, and Arguthrax will not risk angering the warp by sacrificing its daemons trying to kill me. I would not admit this to anyone else, my lord, but the feud is done with.'

'You expect me to believe that? When one such as you locks horns with one such as Arguthrax, it does not end until one is destroyed. That is, unless a greater power ends it first.'

'That greater power being you?'

'Of course, and I will end it, duke. If you and Arguthrax continue to waste this planet's armies on killing each other then I will finish the job for you. I will kill you both. You are not too proud to be flayed into a banner, Venalitor, and Arguthrax is not too great to avoid a banishment to the coldest wastes of the warp at my behest.'

'None of this surprises me, my lord,' said Venalitor smoothly. 'That is why I have let this war boil down to a few skirmishes between bands of minor cultists who will not be missed. I believe Arguthrax is letting the same thing happen. Neither of us will back down before the other lords, but neither is foolish enough to defy you.'

'Flattery again,' sneered Ebondrake.

'It is also the truth.'

One of the scaephylyds was approaching. It was a truly huge and ancient example of the species, the size of a tank, its carapace swollen and gnarled. It was covered in colonies and hives, like barnacles. As it aged, it had grown more and more eyes, and its head was just a set of chipped mandibles below a nest of dozens of eye sockets. Each eye moved independently, some settling on Venalitor, and some on Ebondrake. Its like had not been seen on the surface of Drakaasi in the current age. It carried a traditional scaephylyd weapon, a pair of hinged blades like an ornate pair of shears, operated by the two forelimbs on one side, to denote its rank.

'General,' said Venalitor, 'the tribes answer my call.'

'Of course, duke,' said the general in an accent so thick it was barely comprehensible. Its mandibles forced themselves into painful configurations to pronounce human speech. 'How else could it be?'

'Explain to Lord Ebondrake,' said Venalitor.

Most of the general's eyes turned to Lord Ebondrake. The ancient creature lowered its thorax to the ground in a bow, laying its shear blade on the ground in front of Ebondrake. 'Oh great dark one,' the general began, 'Duke Venalitor is our deliverance and our glory. He brought the Blood God to us when all others had forsaken our kind. He taught us that even we, the lowest of creatures, can be beloved by Khorne if we serve. He led us in that service, promising us lives and deaths given over to the Blood God's worship.'

'I see,' said Ebondrake, 'and now?'

'Now we have proven our worth,' continued the general, 'and all of us have the chance to serve. This army has lain beneath the earth for centuries, waiting for a Champion of the Blood God to bring us to the surface. Now that has become reality. I rejoice that I have lived to see the scaephylyd nation take its place among Drakaasi's armies.'

Ebondrake regarded the general with curiosity. 'How long, duke, have you been hiding these?'

'I made use of a few of them,' replied Venalitor, 'and they came to me begging for more of them to serve. Is that not true?'

'We begged,' said the general, 'and we grovelled. Scaephylyds are not proud. We seek only our place in the universe.'

'And you are all pledged to my crusade?' said Ebondrake.

'Every scaephylyd that lives,' said the general. 'The infirm have been put to death. All those that remain are fit to fight.'

'And you?'

'No honour could befall me greater than dying for the Blood God,' said the general, raising his shear blade in a salute.

'Very well,' said Ebondrake. 'Go back to your... to your creatures. Make sure they are ready to leave. The crusade will take flight soon, and all must be prepared.'

'This is your will, my duke and my lord?'

'It is,' said Venalitor.

'Then it shall be so.' The general raised itself from the ground and returned to the scaephylyd army.

'Quite devoted,' said Ebondrake.

'They are.'

'To you.'

'To their god, my lord. They are troops to be herded beneath the enemy guns, who will not be missed, and there can always be more. At my command the tribal elders will begin the scaephylyds' breeding cycle, and thousands more will be hatched. They can fight almost as soon as they are born, if all you want are bodies to be thrown forwards.'

'You would have this be your part in the crusade, Venalitor? Lord of the vermin? Most would consider the greater honour to be among the elite warriors, those who win the battle, not the masses who die before the battle truly begins.'

'Blood is blood, my lord,' said Venalitor.

Ebondrake smiled. 'So it is, duke, so it is. I have heard much of your Grey Knight, too.'

'His holy work is only just begun,' said Venalitor with a hint of pride. 'Truly, he has become a part of this great engine of worship.'

'After all he has resisted, he has taken quite suddenly to the ways of Khorne. His fame grows, as does the speculation as to just what brought him into our fold. Did you break him, Venalitor? Or did trickery rob him of his wits?'

'I am a persuasive man, my lord.'

'There is more to it than that. A Space Marine would be remarkable enough, but a Grey Knight? Come now, do not tell me some petty torture or temptation could break such a creature.'

'He was introduced to an ally from the warp. His mind did not survive the encounter.'

'I would have heard of this from the warp. Flaying the mind of a daemon hunter would be a matter of great celebration among Khorne's daemons.'

'I called upon the services of an old friend.'

Ebondrake raised a scaly eye ridge in surprise. 'Raezazel? So that story is true?'

'Indeed. It was Raezazel who drove Alaric insane.'

'The liar spawn lives?'

'After a fashion. Life, for a daemon, can be a matter of interpretation.'

'I see. One of the Liar God's own flesh amongst us! I had not thought such a thing possible. Do you have any more secrets to reveal, duke?'

'The scaephylyds and Raezazel were the last of them, my lord. You know all there is to know.'

'I take it that Raezazel will not live on long to trouble us? I do not need the likes of him disrupting the crusade.'

'He has been a prisoner of mine since I defeated him. He is just a shadow of what he was. He will never be free, and he will never oppose the Blood God's will. He serves me now.'

'See that it is dead before the crusade launches,' said Ebondrake.

'I shall see to its execution myself.'

'Good. It will have been well overdue.' Ebondrake looked out again across the scaephylyd nation, still assembling on the desert plain. The desert was dark with their teeming bodies, and the sky above had turned a grim purple-grey in response. 'After Vel'Skan, duke, make sure that the crusade is your only concern.'

'Of course, my lord,' said Venalitor.

Ebondrake stomped back towards his sky-ship with his Ophidian Guard. Venalitor watched the great dragon go.

Perhaps Ebondrake believed him. Most of what he said had been true, after all. Or perhaps the creature would never trust him. It didn't matter either way. Once the crusade got underway, everything would change. Venalitor was rather looking forward to it.

ALARIC WAS THERE, in Raezazel's place. The faces of his congregation were looking up at him, hypnotised by his beauty. He had to fight to keep Raezazel's alien personality from taking over his own. This flesh was foul, these believers doomed. Raezazel was revolting. Alaric's disgust propelled him out of Raezazel's body.

He was outside Raezazel, looking on. He saw a man of such beauty that he lit up the walls around him. Alaric looked away. He could see the daemon underneath.

He looked around: deep blue inlaid with gold, sirens, panic. Something had gone wrong. Alaric tasted Raezazel's anger at the intrusion. The place became dim, and the image of the planet with the eight-pointed star shone down suddenly from overhead. Raezazel raged, almost knocking out Alaric with the force of the emotion.

Alaric knew where he was. This was how Raezazel had come to Drakaasi.

The lie unravelled. Alaric, finally saw everything that Raezazel had tried to hide from him.

In attempting to possess Alaric, Raezazel had let his mind touch Alaric's. In that mind was locked the secret of Raezazel himself, of Drakaasi and of the Hammer of Daemons. Alaric saw it now, shining in front of him, unrolling like a chronicle of years.

It was appalling. It was terrifying, but it was the truth.

Finally, Alaric understood.

EIGHTEEN

THIS TIME IT was pain.

Consciousness rushed back to Alaric so fast that it almost knocked him out in the volley of sensations. Raw, screaming pain coursed up his spine, strangling his brain so that sensible thoughts refused to form. There was coldness against his back, and a sense of being trapped, locked down, crushed.

The smell was of blood and sweat.

Alaric gasped and forced his eyes open. White light pounded against his retinas and he thrashed. Something clattered to the ground, a tinny sound just above the white noise of the pain.

Alaric kept himself from going under again. It was an act of will-power, and he didn't have much of that left.

The memories of the daemon still churned in his mind. He tried to strangle them, choke them down, clean out his mind with faith. His chest heaved, and he nearly blacked out.

Then, he could breathe again.

He knew the truth. He wanted to tell someone, but first, he had to know that his mind was intact.

His eyes adjusted rapidly. The chamber was dimly lit, but it had been almost unbearably bright, so he must have been in darkness for a long time. It was a small, hot, filthy room, in the familiar, life-stained ironwork of the *Hecatomb*. He guessed that he was somewhere below the cell block deck.

Kelhedros stood in front of him, stripped of his green armour to the waist. There was blood on the eldar's pale chest. The alien was not wounded, so Alaric surmised the blood must be his, the same blood that coated the sliver of sharpened metal that Kelhedros was holding.

Alaric looked down at his arm, from which the waves of pain were emanating. His consciousness had kicked off the endorphins in his brain, which were dulling the agony, a typical physiological response for a Space Marine, but the pain was still tremendous. The skin of his forearm had been slit and pulled open from the wrist to the elbow, and several pins were sticking from the exposed muscle, piercing nerve centres with such precision that there was no room for any more pain.

Alaric tried to speak. He gasped dumbly. His nervous system wouldn't respond properly. An unenhanced body would have died of shock, he thought vaguely. One again, he was alive because he was a Space Marine.

Kelhedros plucked a couple of the pins from Alaric's arm. Alaric was able to think again, and he exhaled raggedly, chest heaving. He realised that he was chained to the wall of the room with his arm strapped down more firmly than the rest of him, so that Kelhedros could work without Alaric's thrashing disturbing his precision.

'There you are,' said Kelhedros.

'What… why am I here?'

'You were delirious. You have been for some time. I was attempting to bring you back to a level of consciousness where you could be dealt with. Have I succeeded?'

'Yes,' said Alaric, hoping it was true. 'Where am I?'

'The *Hecatomb*.'

'I know. Where on Drakaasi?'

'A week or so out of the *Scourge*,' said Kelhedros.

Alaric looked down at his arm again. For all the work that had been done on it, there was very little blood. 'Did they teach you this in the Scorpion Temple?' he asked.

Kelhedros regarded Alaric with curiosity in his liquid alien eyes. 'We walk many paths,' he said simply.

'Are you going to release me?'

'When the wound is closed,' said Kelhedros. 'Premature activity could render the damage permanent.'

'And you wouldn't want that.'

Again, the strange look; Kelhedros had evidently not had enough experience of human mannerisms to recognise sarcasm. 'I would not. It does us no good for you to be incapacitated.'

'Why did you wake me up?'

'Soon we will be at Vel'Skan. Many believe that our survival at the games depends on you being able to lead us. There was some debate, I believe. Gearth wanted you left as you are. Many of his men have come to idolise you, Alaric. They have followed you on the first steps.'

'Steps to where?'

'Oblivion, Grey Knight. They see you as an example of how a man may lose his mind, and with it all the impediments to becoming a true killer. I believe they speak of this with the same fervour with which Erkhar speaks of his Promised Land. Gearth did not get his way this time, and so I offered to bring you back to your senses.' Kelhedros removed the remaining pins from Alaric's arm. 'I understand you heal quickly.'

'That's right.'

'Then the stitches need not be small.' Kelhedros produced a needle, threaded with cord, and began to sew Alaric's arm closed. Alaric was almost glad of the pain. It was something real, something he could experience honestly without wondering if it was another stage in his becoming something terrible.

'What have I done?' he asked. 'While I was… when I was not myself?'

'You have killed many,' said Kelhedros, 'including Lucetia the Envenomed, the Void Hound of Tremulon, and Deinas, son of Kianon. Some of them were quite the spectacle, and then there were many lesser slaves, of course.'

'That wasn't me,' said Alaric. 'I wasn't there.' He winced as Kelhedros drew his stitches closed.

'That is good to know. You were unlikely to seek escape in such a state.'

'That's why you agreed to being me back.'

'Of course. I wish to escape this world, Grey Knight. You are the most likely among the prisoners to seek freedom, and certainly the most able to achieve it. I dare say that Vel'Skan will be our last chance.'

Kelhedros finished sewing up Alaric's arm. Considering how the eldar must have had to improvise his medical implements, it was a good job. Alaric wondered just what paths the alien had walked, before one of them had led to Drakaasi.

'How long until Vel'Skan?' asked Alaric.

'Some days,' said Kelhedros. 'The games will be great. Many of the best gladiators will compete for the title of Drakaasi's champion.'

'I see.'

'You will be one of them.'

Alaric smiled. 'Of course I will. The crowd loves me.'

'Oh, they do, Justicar. To them I am just Kelhedros the Outsider. Or the Green Phantom, sometimes, but that did not really catch on. You, though, are Alaric the Betrayed, the Crimson Justicar, the Corpse-God's Bloodied Hand. When you are gone there will be statues of you. They will tell stories of how the Emperor sent his best to defeat the warp, and how one of those best became a legend in the arenas. You will inspire champions of the future. Scum of Ghaal will kill their way into the ranks of the elite gladiators because once a Grey Knight did the same thing. You will never be forgotten here, justicar.'

'You sound like an enthusiast of mine, alien,' said Alaric bleakly.

'Fame is one of the routes to survival on Drakaasi,' replied Kelhedros, unfastening Alaric's restraints. 'It is not the one I would choose to follow, for becoming something I am not is inimical to the path I walk. That is not to say, however, that it is an inefficient or futile way to stay alive. Truly, you are the only slave who has a meaningful life expectancy. You may even one day be more than a slave. That freedom would be earned at the expense of your personality, but it would be freedom of a sort.'

'I would rather die than become a champion of the warp,' said Alaric.

'So I understand, but perhaps you will not have that choice.'

'We will know for sure after Vel'Skan.' Alaric's restraints were free, and he struggled to keep from slumping to his knees. Every muscle was sore. He must have been tied there at Kelhedros's mercy for a long time. He looked down at himself. He was stripped to the waist, and there were countless new scars on his chest and arms. He had a brand, too, a deep angry welt in the shape of Khorne's stylised skull burned into his pectoral.

'When did I get this?' he asked.

'After the sacrifices,' replied Kelhedros matter-of-factly. 'You were rewarded.'

The hateful symbol seemed to stare out at Alaric. 'So I am marked,' he said to himself.

'You took it as a great honour. Gearth and his men now aspire to receive the same mark.'

Alaric touched the brand. It was still healing, and it still hurt. He felt unclean to have the symbol on him. When he got back to Titan, he would have it cut out of his skin.

Titan had never felt so far away.

'The winds are low,' said Kelhedros, who was placing his improvised scalpels and nerve pins neatly into a roll of cloth. It looked like he took great care of his implements of torture. Alaric was impressed that Kelhedros had hidden them from the scaephylyds for so long. The alien had far more freedom than any other slave on the *Hecatomb*, able to operate in secret and go where he pleased. It was the dangers of Drakaasi, not the *Hecatomb's* structure, that kept Kelhedros a prisoner. 'The slavemasters will order us to the oar deck soon. Were you not there, suspicion would be raised.'

Alaric moved his arms, testing his shoulders and back. They hurt. It felt like he had been sparring for hours, as he once had against his friend Tancred. It wasn't just the restraints, he had been fighting constantly for days with few breaks. He must have won great glory for Khorne. He must have taken dozens of skulls for the Skull Throne.

'Then I must be ready to work,' he said. 'It would not do for Alaric the Betrayed to be late.'

VEL'SKAN!

Did some ancient god demand that glory be, and did Vel'Skan spring up in response? Did some Titan desire an altar to bloodshed, and did he build Vel'Skan in the image of his madness? Did some battle between the gods of the warp take place there, and scatter their weapons upon Drakaasi, a steel rain that left the mighty heap of war gear to be inhabited?

Vel'Skan's form drives men mad to look at it. Swords and shields, helmets and spear shafts, every thing that one man might use to maim another in titanic proportions heaped up upon the blood shore. Here is a temple in the palm of a gauntlet! There is a dock forged from a broadsword blade. There spins a stirrup, hung with the dead of a hundred executions. Everywhere is Vel'Skan, maddening in its size. And this question burns like a hollow pain in the soul: what manner of slaughter could create these immense instruments of death?

What majesty is in this place, the capital of all Drakaasi, seat of its greatest lords? What glory to the Blood God, what oath to death, what image of slaughter and the hells that follow, is encompassed by the war forged city Vel'Skan?

– 'Mind Journeys of a Heretic Saint,' *by Inquisitor Helmandar Oswain (Suppressed by order of the Ordo Hereticus)*

ALARIC SAW VEL'SKAN for the first time from the *Hecatomb's* oar deck. The ship was making a stately approach to the capital, saluted by the ranks of warriors who stood guard on the banks of the blood river.

The slaves around him had their heads bowed, concentrated on keeping the rhythm beaten out by the scaephylyd slave master. Alaric, however, wanted to see what was waiting for them.

'Justicar,' said a voice behind him. Alaric risked a glance around, and saw that Haggard was sitting behind him. The old sawbones had suffered greatly recently. His eyes were hollow and his skin was an unhealthy pale. He had fought, too, for he sported several fresh scars and wounds that he must have dressed himself. Venalitor was sparing none of his slaves in the run-up to the Vel'Skan games. 'It is good to have you back.'

'Thank you, Haggard.'

'You… are back, aren't you?'

Alaric smiled. 'I was not myself for a while. Venalitor tried to have one of his pet daemons take control of me. I did not cooperate, but resisting cost me my mind for a while.'

'You did some terrible things,' said Haggard.

'I know, but then that was true before I ever came to Drakaasi.'

'They are talking about you as a challenger for the title.'

'Who is?'

'Gearth's men. They are… not really with us any more. Venalitor has promised them something if they fight well, and the scaephylyds, too. We… Erkhar and I, and some of others… we talked about killing you. The scaephylyds found out, and they were pretty descriptive about what would happen to us if Venalitor's best prospect got hurt.'

'Then I am grateful that reason prevailed.'

Haggard smiled weakly. 'I suppose I already betrayed you once. Twice would just be rude.'

'No, Haggard. You did what you had to do to survive. I cannot begrudge anyone that, not after what I have done on this planet. At least it will end here.'

Alaric glanced again at the city passing by. He saw the palace of Lord Ebondrake, built into a vast human skull with a corroded dagger thrust through one eye. The skull was from the remains of one of the titanic warriors that had fought over Drakaasi, and it grinned monstrously down over the city.

'We break out here,' said Alaric.

'Why here?' asked Haggard warily. 'What is here in Vel'Skan?'

'The Hammer of Daemons,' answered Alaric.

NINETEEN

TEN THOUSAND SOLDIERS of Vel'Skan fell on their swords in the city's greatest parade ground. The bowl of the upturned shield began to fill with blood as the armoured bodies slid down their blades, grimacing as they refused to cry out in pain. Not one of them did, and in perfect disciplined silence, they died to anoint the Vel'Skan spectacle with blood.

The final body stopped spasming. The priests of Khorne wet the hems of their bronze-threaded robes as they wandered among the sacrifices. They scraped through the pooling blood with their ceremonial blades, and pored over loops of entrails. They examined the angles at which the soldiers' swords had pierced their bodies. They lifted the visors of their helmets, taking careful note of the final expressions on their mutated faces. For several hours, they pursued their divinations, until swarms of insects descended on the fresh corpses, and the blood began to congeal in fascinating patterns on the surface of the bronze shield.

Finally the priests convened at the shield's rim. They discussed the matter for a long time, sometimes arguing, and sometimes letting the more venerable of them address the others. They licked blood idly from their blades as they debated.

Finally, they came to an agreement. One of them, the most ancient, was sent to deliver their pronouncement to the palace of Lord Ebondrake, the giant skull with the dagger through its eye grinning down at them from its place atop the city.

The divinations had proven encouraging. Blood had flowed in such a way that promised more blood would soon follow, that Lord Ebondrake and all the armies of Drakaasi could not have stemmed its tide had they wanted to. Every torn sinew suggested blood and carnage on a grand scale.

Khorne had smiled upon the battle-forged city. The Vel'Skan games could begin.

THEY HAD VERY little time. In less than an hour, they guessed, they would be herded out towards the arena of Drakaasi's capital, and then it would be too late. So they had gathered in an empty cell on the *Hecatomb*, with men posted to give the warning in case the scaephylyds came to search them out and administer lashes. That so many of them were together at once was enough for them to be broken up and thrown into isolation cells.

'You,' said Corporal Dorvas.

'Yes,' said Alaric, 'me.'

The corporal was the highest-ranked survivor among the Hathran Armoured Cavalry who had been brought to Drakaasi. The Hathran Guardsmen had found themselves moved between arenas, brutalised and murdered, until they had been boiled down to just the kind of hard-bitten survivors that Lord Ebondrake needed for Vel'Skan's arena slaves. Dorvas was thin, his cheeks were hollow, and his remaining eye was sunken and dark. He still wore the remains of his Hathran fatigues, which contrasted with the makeshift knives he wore in a belt across his chest.

'You killed us,' he said, 'a lot of us, at the *Scourge*.'

'I did,' said Alaric. 'I almost fell to Khorne, but I did not fall all the way, and I was brought back.'

'Some of us finally lost the will when they realised that a Space Marine had turned to the enemy. First you abandon the line at Pale Ridge, and then you were the executioner in the arena.' Dorvas's voice was level, but there was so much hate in him that he was almost quivering with it.

'You can hate me, corporal, and refuse to have anything to do with me. Or you can put that aside for a few hours and cooperate with us. If you do the latter you will have a chance of getting off this planet.'

Dorvas sat back and looked at the other people gathered in the chamber. Erkhar, the evangelical ex-Naval captain stood on one side of Alaric. On his other side was Gearth, who even to an outsider's eyes was obviously a psychopath, and a killer of impressive pedigree. Haggard the surgeon and the alien Kelhedros completed the ragged escape committee of the *Hecatomb's* slaves. Alaric couldn't quite imagine what it must be like seeing them for the first time. The Space Marine and the eldar in one place without trying to kill each other was remarkable enough.

'What are our chances?' asked Dorvas, sounding unimpressed.

'I wouldn't have smuggled you in here,' said Kelhedros, 'if there were no point in doing so.'

'You're lucky I didn't kill you the moment you put your xenos hands on me,' said Dorvas to the alien.

'Then you understand why I had to use uncultured methods,' said Kelhedros smoothly. Alaric trusted only Kelhedros to make it off the *Hecatomb* and back on again without detection, and at Alaric's order he had brought the blindfolded Dorvas onto the lower decks.

'Then what's the plan?' asked Dorvas.

'Kill 'em all,' said Gearth with a smirk.

'That's it?' asked Dorvas.

'It's a bit more subtle than that,' said Alaric, 'but, essentially, yes. With the help of Vel'Skan's arena slaves we can force an uprising in the arena. If it happens during the contests the confusion will be great. Believe me, the crowd can be a weapon for us if we know how to use it.'

'So I hear,' said Dorvas. 'They say a Space Marine caused the riot at Gorgath. I'm guessing it was you, since there aren't too many Space Marines around. Except even if you're right, there are some old boys among the arena slaves who remember the last revolt. Every single one of the runners died. Even if we break out, we can't hold the arena, or anywhere else, against the Ophidian Guard.'

'The big guy here says he has a plan for that,' said Gearth. 'He isn't being too open with it, though.'

'The fear of any revolt being crushed is what really keeps us here,' said Erkhar, 'us and all the other slaves on Drakaasi. If we are to overcome that, Alaric, we need to know that there is at least a chance that we can survive the aftermath of any escape.'

'That's right,' said Gearth. 'Golden boy here might be willing to go out with a bang for his Emperor, but the rest of us would like a couple more years to enjoy that freedom.'

All eyes were on Alaric. It was true. His word had got him this far. It was time for him to be honest.

'Who among you,' he began, 'has heard of Raezazel the Cunning?'

RAEZAZEL WAS ANCIENT indeed when Tzeentch's web of fate snared him.

The daemon had spent thousands of years in service to Tzeentch, but of course he had not truly served the Liar God, since Tzeentch did nothing so mundane as dispense orders. He manipulated, he bled half-truths into the minds of foes and followers so that they converged at a point in space and time that Tzeentch had conceived in ages past.

Very rarely, he spoke to the souls of his servants. It was a great honour, and yet a thing to be greatly feared, for he still lied. It also meant that Tzeentch was displeased enough to commit the great mediocrity of speaking to his servants as a god.

Tzeentch required souls, new servants, perhaps, or fodder, or maybe playthings to be caged in a maddening labyrinth in the warp, so that Tzeentch could observe their torment with a smile on his thousand mouths. He required souls nonetheless, and the holier the better. The more they believed in the corpse-emperor, the false god entombed on Terra, the sweeter the terror and madness would be.

Raezazel the Cunning was tasked with finding such souls and delivering them to Tzeentch. Why they were needed did not matter to Raezazel. Quite possibly, Tzeentch needed none of them, and it was merely the act of their abduction that would set in motion some impossibly complicated sequence of events that Tzeentch wished to come to pass. It was of no consequence. Tzeentch came to Raezazel in dreams and portents, and spoke to him in a thousands voices that innocents were required, and that was all that mattered.

Raezazel had taken many forms in the past. It was inimical for one such as him to appear as any one creature for long, but for Tzeentch, he was willing to take on a face of mediocrity. He became a human. He made this human magnificently handsome, glowing with charisma. With the irony of which the Liar God was fondest, he made every word of this human seem the truth. He came to a belt of isolated worlds and proclaimed himself a prophet, flitting between these childlike worlds and beguiling their people. It was not easy. Many of them were hard-bitten missionaries of the Imperial Cult, who denounced Raezazel the prophet as a heretic, and implored the people to take up arms and burn him at the stake. A few even claimed he was a daemon from the warp come to tempt them towards some horrible fate, and it was a perverse pleasure to Raezazel that some of them should have stumbled across the truth in their anger.

Raezazel was too brilliant to fall to the torches and pitchforks that the mobs raised against him. For every Emperor-fearing citizen who wanted him dead, there were two or three more who looked upon the bleakness of their universe and sought to find something more in Raezazel's promises. His cult grew, and soon, without any further prompting from him, preachers spread his word. Nobles and governors fell under the spell, for they knew more than anyone how tiny and insignificant any one person was, and they yearned for something more in their lives.

That was when Raezazel invented the Promised Land. He would take them somewhere free of suffering and hatred. There would be no more tithe takers forcing them into poverty, no preachers turning every innocent thought into sin, no law to keep them in fear. They would be free.

They found a spacecraft and used all the cult's resources making it warp-worthy, and making it home to thousands of followers. An altar to Raezazel was built inside it, along with countless shrines to saints and holy spirits that had sprung up in the cult's minds without any suggestion from Raezazel. The spacecraft was holy ground, a mighty ark that was both the symbol and the means of the cult's salvation.

On the day when the craft was to be consecrated and launched, Raezazel appeared to them and told them how they were going to get to the Promised Land. The great warp storm of the Eye of Terror, the weeping sore in the night sky, was their destination. There, hidden among the Eye's corrupted worlds, was a rent in this cruel universe through which the faithful could reach the Promised Land. The Eye of Terror was a test, an icon of fear through which the faithful had to pass to prove that their souls were resolute enough to deserve entry into the Promised Land. There, the true Emperor would receive them, and they would live in bliss for eternity.

The ship was launched. Raezazel was on board, basking in the glory of an altar built to him, mocking the congregation with every word and blessing. The ship reached the Eye of Terror, and the wayward tides of the warp there were calmed, perhaps by chance, perhaps by the impossible will of Tzeentch. The ship surfaced from the warp to be confronted with a bright slash in space, the tear in reality beyond which Tzeentch waited to consume or torment the thousands of pilgrims singing Raezazel's praises.

The pilgrims, though, were only human, and they were fallible. Their navigation had failed to take into account one of the many worlds that drifted across the Eye of Terror on the echoes of the warp's haphazard tides. One such planet was in their path as the ship exited the warp, and the ship was caught in its gravity well, its course spiralling down towards the surface.

The pilgrims screamed. Raezazel raged in frustration. He had come so close to fulfilling Tzeentch's will. He would surely have been elevated to something higher in gratitude for delivering the pilgrims, granted a sliver of insight into the great mystery of the universe. Now some mundane technical matter had forced his plan awry. Raezazel stayed on the ship, using sorcery to force it back onto its course, but Raezazel's powers were not enough to compete with the gravity of a planet.

Through the ship's viewscreen, the pilgrims saw the immense eight-pointed star scored into the planet's surface, formed by canals and rivers filled with blood, and a few of them realised what fate their prophet had truly led them into.

The ship crashed into a city, and its structure was sound enough to keep it intact, but the minds of its inhabitants were not so sound. The madness and murder that followed were so terrible that the whole planet heard the echo of it. Raezazel slipped out of the ship and hid among the planet's terrible, blood-soaked cities, and eventually would be challenged and defeated by the young champion Venalitor.

This was the truth that Alaric had unravelled from Raezazel's fevered memories.

The name of the planet was Drakaasi.

The name of the ship was the *Hammer of Daemons*.

SOME TIME AFTER the conference between the escape committee, Alaric found Lieutenant Erkhar in the faithful's hidden shrine. Erkhar was there alone. His faithful were elsewhere, silently praying for deliverance from the cruelty of Vel'Skan's games. Erkhar was sitting with his head bowed in front of the severed statue head that served the faithful as their altar.

'I know how you feel,' said Alaric after a while. 'You try to hear the Emperor, and filter out His words from the mess of your own thoughts. He's in there somewhere, but it's the warp's own job to find Him.'

Erkhar looked around. It seemed he hadn't heard Alaric approaching. 'I suppose you have to speak with me, justicar.'

Alaric came closer. He saw that Erkhar's face was long and pale, like a man in shock. 'You don't believe me.'

'I do not know what to believe. I have my faith, but that is something different.'

'You know that what I told the others is true, Erkhar. The book on which you based your preaching was found on this planet, was it not? I believe it is the writings of a follower of Raezazel's. When Raezazel's mind touched mine I saw everything. I saw what the Hammer of Daemons really was. It is not a magical weapon after all. It's not a metaphor for your suffering. It is a spaceship, and it is still here.'

'So everything we believe is just the product of corruption and lies,' said Erkhar, 'woven by a daemon.' He took his prayer book from inside his uniform jacket. It was tattered and torn by the years. He handed it to Alaric.

Alaric read for a while. Erkhar sat looking at him, and Alaric could not fathom what he must have been thinking with everything he believed in shaken so profoundly.

It was the ship's log, written by a captain whose mind was taken up with religious visions. The daily entries read like parables. The ship was described as a metaphor for faith, its journey as a voyage for the soul. The captain's thoughts were written down as sermons or hymns. Without knowing that there was a real ship it would have been easy to believe that the *Hammer of Daemons* was just one more metaphor among many.

'The faith is not a lie,' said Alaric. 'How many of your faithful would have survived without it? How many would have become corrupted?'

'What do you care?' snarled Erkhar. 'Never did you believe, never. We were a resource to be exploited, and now this daemon claims to have brought the Hammer here.'

'I saw into its mind,' said Alaric. 'It was as clear as day.'

'How do you know this is not just more lies?' Erkhar got to his feet. Alaric had told him that everything he believed was a fiction, and his disbelief was turning to anger. 'This could be the daemon's last curse to break us apart, to take away the only thing we have left. Or just another part of some plot to do the Liar God's bidding.'

'I doubt Raezazel's plan included failing to possess me,' said Alaric.

'As one who claims to fight the daemon, you trust them very easily. What proof do you have that the Hammer is even here?'

'None!' barked Alaric in frustration. 'Of course there is none! But it is all we have. I believe I know what the *Hammer* is and where it is, and how it can get us off this planet. How much closer have you ever been to escape? Maybe this is all a lie, maybe the *Hammer* was never here. Maybe the damn thing won't fly any more, but it is still the best chance you will ever get. How long are you going to wait for the Promised Land, Erkhar? Until the last of you are dead or mad?'

Erkhar shook his head. 'You're using us even now,' he said. 'You need a spaceship crew. My faithful and I are the closest thing to it. Otherwise you'd leave us here.'

'No,' said Alaric. 'We're all going. I need you to fly the *Hammer*, that's true, but more than that, I need to hurt Drakaasi. Think about it, lieutenant. If the planet's best slaves disappear from under the lords' noses, at the height of their greatest games, what will the consequences be? Think of the insult to their god. Think of the recriminations. If nothing else, imagine the looks on their faces when they realise we have fled. Sooner or later you will die here and your skull will be a part of Khorne's throne. If you had a chance to avoid giving them that much, is your duty not to take it?'

'Survival is not enough.'

'You will defeat Khorne, is that not enough?'

Erkhar slumped back down against the makeshift altar. He looked up at Alaric, and there were tears brimming in his eyes. 'I want to leave this place… I want that so much… and now that chance is here, but what if it is just another lie? There have been so many, Justicar, about the Imperium, about the Emperor. Now the lies of daemons and the desperation of condemned men have brought us here. Where can the truth be in that?'

'Think of it this way,' said Alaric, kneeling down so that his full height didn't tower so much over Erkhar. 'If we fail, we die. I believe that when we die, we join the Emperor at the end of time, to fight by his side against all the darkness of the universe. That is not such a bad thing. To die trying to wound the pride of the Blood God… well, that is quite a story to tell all the other ghosts.'

'Emperor forgive me, I want to leave here. I want to… I want to die. I cannot see my faithful suffer any more. I am just a man. The saint would stay here. The saint would suffer, and become a martyr, to show the galaxy what will-power and the Emperor's word can do.'

'The saint would lead his followers off Drakaasi and back to the Imperium so he can preach to the rest of the galaxy what he has learned,' said Alaric. 'You might be just a man, Erkhar, but that is all any of us are. If we survive this, you will be something more. If we don't then we die a good death, which is more than most citizens will ever get.'

'It will hurt them,' said Erkhar, 'you promise that?'

'I promise, lieutenant. Fly the *Hammer of Daemons* off this planet, and they will never forget the shame.'

'All of us will leave. Everyone you can get.'

'Everyone.'

'Then we will be with you.'

TWENTY

THE HECATOMB WAS loosed from its moorings on the broadsword docks, and hauled by teams of scaephylyds through the gorget of a massive breastplate lying on its back. Inside was darkness, broken by the blinking red eyes of thousands of flying daemons roosting in the underside of the breastplate. The ship was hauled through the sump of gore lying under Vel'Skan, the detritus of endless sacrifices on the altars of the city above. During particularly holy times, so many were sacrificed that the sump of blood rose and the most ancient parts of the city were drowned in it. It was a good omen for the blood to reach the high tide marks etched onto the city's weaponry. In anticipation of the closest fought battle for Drakaasi's title, the blood rose very high indeed.

The *Hecatomb* reached the prison complex, based in a huge and elaborate nest of brass struts and steel blades that had once been a titanic piece of torture equipment. The complex was beneath Vel'Skan's arena, and housed the city's arena slaves, among whom were the remnants of the Hathran Armoured Cavalry.

The *Hecatomb* was moored at the prison docks, to keep Venalitor's slaves from mixing with the arena slaves. Venalitor left, accompanied by an honour guard of scaephylyds in dramatic tribal armour, hand-picked from the scaephylyd nation, which Drakaasi was only just learning existed beneath its deserts.

Many of Venalitor's slaves went through final training sessions to keep them sharp, carefully selecting which weapons and armour they would take into the games. Many of them prayed. A few of them wept, convinced that their end had come at last, and that they would die under the eyes of Vel'Skan's citizens. The orks were unusually quiet, with One-ear growling to them in the crude orkish language for hours. Not all of them knew that Alaric had planned an escape. Fewer still knew the sheer insanity of what they would have to do after they got out of the arena, but all of them knew that it would suit Venalitor for them all to die, as long as it was before the eyes of the audience.

'I AM READY, justicar,' said Haggard. 'I'll fight.'

'I know you will,' said Alaric. 'I couldn't stop you if I wanted, could I?'

'And would you want to?'

'It would help us if you were alive at the end,' replied Alaric. 'None of us can say what will happen, but I'd be willing to bet that we'll need a sawbones at the end of it.'

'None of that will matter if we don't make it at all,' replied Haggard. 'I was a soldier. I can fight. It would help if you got me a gun at some point, though. I only just scraped through bayonet drill.'

'I'll see what I can do.'

Haggard had chosen his weapons already, a sword and a shield, laid out on the slab he usually used for operating.

'I'm not going to be sewing anyone back together on this slab again,' he said. 'It's as if I've been chained to the damn thing. It's hard to imagine no one ever bleeding on it again.'

'The *Hammer of Daemons* had a medical suite,' said Alaric, recalling the images of the ship from Raezazel's memories, 'autosurgeons, synthiflesh weavers, maybe even medical servitors.'

Haggard smiled. 'Don't tempt me, justicar. We have to get there first.'

'And we will. I just have one thing to ask of you. The blade you pulled out of me, do you still have it?'

'The sword? Yes, I have it.'

'I need it.'

'It won't be much of a weapon for you, justicar. It's no bigger than a dagger.'

'I don't need it for that.'

'Very well.' Haggard reached into one of the pouches in his stained apron, and took out a bundle, carefully wrapped in strips of cloth that Haggard used as bandages. He handed it to Alaric.

'I think it's poisoned,' said Haggard. 'I guess you can filter that out. I don't have that luxury, though.'

Alaric unwrapped the bundle. Inside was the shard that Haggard had pulled out of his chest. He thought about the wound it had inflicted. It still hadn't healed completely, and when it did he would still have a scar to remind him. The shard was an ugly green-black colour, and its dark metal sweated beads of venom. Haggard was right, without a Space Marine's enhanced metabolism, the poison would have killed him. Alaric had died a dozen times over on Drakaasi, but being a Space Marine meant that none of them had quite counted yet.

'What do you plan to use it for?' asked Haggard.

'I'll keep that to myself,' said Alaric, 'if it's all the same to you.'

'Then it's your business.' Haggard tested the weight of the sword he had chosen. It was a good choice for a relatively unskilled fighter, short with a broad blade, made for thrusting. It wouldn't save him if he faced someone competent one-on-one, but it was perfect for stabbing into a surprised opponent's stomach. 'When it happens, Alaric, will you look out for me?'

'I don't know,' replied Alaric simply. 'I will if I can, but it will be too chaotic in the arena to make any promises.'

'Then at least, don't leave without me.'

'Everyone's going, Haggard. If anyone thinks you're not among them then they answer to me.'

'I know, it's just… I got left behind once on Agrippina. If it happens again, that's the end. Salvation be damned, I'll just fall on this sword and get it over with.'

'It will not come to that. I can promise that, at least. Now, I need to find a weapon, too. I left my axe buried in an Ophidian Guard at Gorgath.'

'Choose well, Alaric. They'll make you fight the best. You're famous and they want a show.'

'We'll give them a show,' said Alaric, 'just not the one they came here to see.'

WITH THEIR BURNING eyes and smouldering skin, the possessed guards were the terror of the prison. They were not so much cruel as calculating, treating the prisoners as subjects to be moulded into suitable arena fodder through fear and brutalisation. Their leader, a hulking thing named Kruulskan, who had a face crushed into a grunting pig-like snout, gave the order for the slaves to be herded from their cells into the preparation chambers.

Above them, the sound of the audience echoed down. Hundreds of thousands of voices were raised in a hymn to blood and violence. Blood began to seep down the walls as it soaked through the arena sands, freshly let from the throats of the first sacrifices. The cries of the priests cut through the crowd's roar. They were reading Khorne's words from the patterns of blood on the sand, and crying the resulting praises into the stands. It was a familiar sound to Vel'Skan's arena fodder, but never had it rumbled so loudly above them, never had the blood run so thickly down the prison's brass walls and steel blades.

The preparation chambers held the prison's collection of weapons. Whips and cruel hooked blades were preferred. The Hathran Guardsmen took the swords that most resembled the cavalry blades with which their forefathers had fought, the horse tribes of their home world that had never seemed so far away. Other slaves, many of them Imperial citizens taken in raids throughout the embattled Eye of Terror, armed themselves with whatever looked like it would keep them alive the longest.

A few of them knew they would never be herded through those preparation chambers again, never suffer again under Kruulskan's whip. They were getting out, or they were dying. They would have to trust a Space Marine, and many of the Hathrans blamed the Space Marines for the disaster at Sarthis Majoris. However, Alaric was as good an ally as they could expect to find on Drakaasi. This was their only chance.

'Now you die!' bellowed Kruulskan, cracking his whip. 'Now you die, you lucky ones! Rejoice! Death is your servant! Welcome him! Welcome Khorne! Khorne is your lord! Die for him!' Kruulskan snorted jubilantly. To see the doomed men and women huddled beneath him, arming themselves ready to entertain the great and powerful of Drakaasi, seemed to give the possessed creature great pleasure.

A few of them, those who knew what was to come, simply waited for the real spectacle to begin.

ONE OF THE scaephylyds had come to Alaric and ordered him below decks. Alaric had gone with the creature, knowing that now was not the time to bring suspicion on himself by disobeying. He was herded into an arming chamber beneath the prison decks and told to make ready.

Alaric was famous. It was fitting for someone of his notoriety to look the part. He lad lost his previous war gear at Gorgath, but he would not be replacing it with the piecemeal armour of a slave. Instead, he would be wearing the armour of the Betrayed.

'I have a great many questions,' said Alaric.

'And so little time,' replied the smith.

Just as when Alaric had encountered him at Karnikhal, the smith was working at an anvil, pinching the last few chainmail links into place with a pair of glowing red tongs. His forge had been set up in one of the many chambers hidden in the Hecatomb's hull, and the smith was silhouetted against its ruddy glow. A stand of armour stood beside him, magnificent and intricate, with hundreds of interlocking plates like the shell of a massive insect. It was obvious from its sheer size that it could only have been made for Alaric.

'Who are you?'

'I am you,' said the smith, 'if you ever give up.'

The smith turned around. Alaric instantly recognised the surgical scars and the black carapace just beneath the skin of his chest.

'You are Astartes.'

'No,' said the smith, and his teeth gleamed as he smiled. 'I have not been a Space Marine for so long that time does not mean anything to me. I am like you, captured a long time ago by a lord of this world. That lord is dead, but I still serve.' He looked down at his hands, scarred from a lifetime at the anvil. 'These hands forged the weapons that killed your comrades on Sarthis Majoris. I am your enemy. I am kept alive and sane because of the skills I still recall, so I serve Chaos as surely as Khorne's own priests. I am not Astartes.'

'What was your Chapter?'

The smith looked up at Alaric. He had room for compassion in his old scorched face, but it had not seen anything but desperation for a very long time. Its humanity had been eroded away until only the eyes were left.

'I don't remember,' he said, 'but the Hammer, is it real?'

'Yes, the message you sent me at Gorgath was correct, the Hammer is where you said it was. It is a spaceship.'

The smith's face cracked, as if it was unused to showing genuine relief. 'A spaceship! Of course! Not some magical trinket, but a spaceship! Of all the weapons that might be hidden on Drakaasi, that is the most valuable. That could do them the most harm.' The smith's eyes were alight. 'I had heard only legends, but this is so much more. Do you still have the weapon I left for you at Gorgath?'

'No. I was recaptured and it was taken from me.'

'A shame. I was proud of it.'

'I killed a few men with it.'

'Then at least its forging was not wasted.' The smith turned to the armour set up beside him. 'I am to fit you for this.'

'A lot of people will be wagering on whether I live or die, so I suppose I have to be easy to pick out from the crowd.'

'My finest work,' said the smith. 'I have waited a very long time for a warrior like you. It is not merely a matter of protecting the wearer from harm, any piece of rusting iron will do that. The true craft is in bringing the soldier out of the form, to give him a metal skin like a projection of himself, a face to show to the world. It becomes an art, Grey Knight. It is all that stands between me and oblivion, this art.'

'Venalitor ordered you to make this?' asked Alaric, examining the intricate plates of the armour and the way they slid over one another like scales on a snake.

'No,' said the smith. 'He ordered me to make you a suit of armour. This is not merely armour.'

'You can come with us.'

'No, Grey Knight, I cannot. I am compelled to serve. I do not even remember what it must be like to resist. It is only by serving that I have been able to help you, by forging weapons and armour for you as my lords decree.'

'You understand what may happen to this world once I have the *Hammer*.'

'Oh yes,' said the smith. 'I am rather looking forward to it.'

Alaric began to put on the armour. It fitted him as perfectly as one of the many enhanced organs of a Space Marine, as if the armour was a part of him that he was being reunited with.

'Then this is the last time I shall see you,' said Alaric as he buckled the armour's flexible breastplate around his chest.

'It is.'

'You have helped me a great deal.'

'I have done nothing, Grey Knight. You are the Hammer after all, not I.'

Alaric finished fastening the armour around him. It felt as light as his own skin. When he looked up from fixing the greaves around his legs, he saw Venalitor's scaephylyds waiting in the chamber's doorway to escort him back to the prisoner decks.

'Will it suffice?' gurgled one of the creatures.

'It will,' said Alaric.

'Then it is time.'

Alaric glanced back once, but the smith was already bent back over his anvil hammering at a half-finished sword.

Then the scaephylyds took Alaric away, and he was gone.

* * *

'IT'S STARTED,' SAID Alaric. Venalitor's slaves were in a staging area beneath the main stands, watched over by scaephylyds and warriors of the Ophidian Guard, presumably sent to make sure that Alaric did not start another riot.

'It has,' said Kelhedros. The eldar was in his familiar green armour, and had a couple of swords scabbarded on his back to supplement his chainsword.

'Then it is time for you to go.'

The slaves were being loaded directly off the top deck of the *Hecatomb* into the belly of the arena. The arena structure, embedded in Vel'Skan's forest of blades and spear shafts, was like a massive, gnarled sphere festooned with blades. A passageway into the arena's underside was lined with armed scaephylyds herding the prisoners along.

'I shall still be alone?'

'You have a talent for getting into places you're not supposed to be,' said Alaric. 'You're the only one who can do it.'

'Very well, said Kelhedros. 'I can offer you no promises, human.'

'I expect none, eldar. There's one other thing.'

'Make it quick.'

'Use this.' Alaric handed Kelhedros the shard of the sword that had nearly killed him.

'This?' asked Kelhedros, looking with some disdain at the dagger-sized shard. 'I think my chainsword would make sure enough work.'

'This is poisoned,' said Alaric. 'Believe me, you'll need it, and leave it in the wound to make sure it stays dead.'

Kelhedros didn't answer. He glanced around, gauging the movements of the multitude of scaephylyd eyes. With a grace that no human could match, the eldar picked his monument and vaulted over the side of the ship. None of the scaephylyds saw him go. The eldar had chosen the precise moment when their primary eyes were elsewhere. Whatever they taught the eldar on the path of the Scorpion, they told them how to go unseen. Alaric didn't hear Kelhedros hit the blood below. As far as Alaric knew, the eldar had become completely silent and invisible.

Alaric went with the flow of the slaves as they were forced through the dark passages below the arena. The sound of the crowd grew louder. They were chanting, striking up hymns to Khorne or bellowing insults at opposing factions, cheering in salute to their planet's lords and keening their bloodlust impatiently. Alaric gripped the haft of the broadsword he had chosen to fight with. He didn't know what was waiting for him on the arena floor, but he knew that if any of the slaves were to get off Drakaasi, he would have to survive it.

There was light ahead. After the darkness of the *Hecatomb* it seemed impossibly bright. Slaves ahead were stumbling, blinking, onto the arena floor.

Alaric followed them. He heard the voices rise as he emerged into the light of Vel'Skan's arena.

The crowd cheered insanely. This was what they had been waiting for. They had come to see Alaric the Betrayed, and now, at last, they could watch him die.

TWENTY-ONE

Lord Ebondrake's palace was connected directly to the arena by a magnificent gallery of marble and frozen blood. Enormous chandeliers, hung with skulls, cast their light on statues and portraits of Drakaasi's past champions. General Sarcathoth glowered down, a slab of muscle and hatred, who had once ruled half of Drakaasi, rendered in marble, inlaid with red and black. A huge portrait of Lady Malice, the master torturess who had served the planet's lords for centuries, was barely large enough to contain her merciless beauty and the gallery of torture implements hanging behind her. Kerberian the Three-Headed, the Daemon Rajah of Aelazadne, and Morken Kruul, Khorne's own herald, all of them were a reminder of what any lord of Drakaasi had to live up to. There was a plinth ready for Lord Ebondrake's statue, and when his crusade hit the wounded Imperium he would finally have earned the right to place his own image there.

'I believe,' said Ebondrake as he padded regally along the gallery, 'in keeping you close.'

'It is an honour,' said Venalitor, walking beside him. For once there were no Ophidian Guard or scaephylyds around.

'It also makes it easier for me to recognise betrayal,' continued Ebondrake, 'and to eat you at the first sign of it.'

'Eat me? I had heard you had consumed your enemies in the past, but I did not know if the stories were true.'

'Oh yes, I have eaten many enemies. It hardly does to possess a form like this and not indulge its appetites. Spies and enemies, and a few sycophants, go straight down this royal gullet. The inconsequential, I chew before I swallow. Those who truly anger me I force down in one go. I can feel them wriggle as they dissolve, most pleasing.'

'As threats go, Lord Ebondrake, that was one of the more civilly delivered.'

'And necessary. You have potential, Venalitor. Nothing more, but a great deal of it. You are ambitious. No doubt it would suit you to see me dead in my crusade, and then divide my world up with a few other conspirators.' Ebondrake looked up at the portraits and statues marching by. 'All of these rose to power during such a period of stasis, and each of them ended his reign in the same way. It is the way of Chaos, and the way of Drakaasi. It is my duty to ensure that I stave that fate off for as long as possible. Perhaps the Charnel Lord has approached you, or Scathach, proposing an alliance during the crusade to see me fall and take my world. I would urge you not to listen, Duke Venalitor. I did not reach my position without foiling conspirators more cunning and powerful than you.'

Venalitor thought about this for a moment. 'It has crossed my mind, my lord. I covet your power, certainly, no sane follower of Khorne would not, but I go where the power is, which means I am by your side. I am more likely to take your place with your blessing than with your opposition. I am young, and there are ways I can outlive you. I am ambitious, yes, but I can be patient.'

Ebondrake smiled his most dangerous smile. 'Exactly what I wanted to hear. You could go far, Venalitor.'

Ebondrake and Venalitor continued along the gallery. At the far end it opened into the great crimson hung balcony reserved for the greatest of the planet's lords.

'I hear,' said Ebondrake, his tone suddenly hardening, 'that Arguthrax's ambassador to the warp was murdered, and his body used to defile the altar at Ghaal. I trust you would know nothing more of this?'

'I know only what you know,' replied Venalitor.

'This war of yours is over, Venalitor. That is what I decreed.'

'There is no war, my lord,' replied Venalitor smoothly. 'Arguthrax and I despise one another, but we will not waste more blood on it.'

Like much of what Venalitor had found himself saying in the run-up to the Vel'Skan games, this was a lie. Venalitor had chosen the most vicious of the scaephylyd nation's hunters, and had set them hunting the emissaries and heralds who formed Arguthrax's link to his court in the warp. Arguthrax might even be forced to retreat there or be cut off from his fellow daemons, and then Venalitor could claim victory.

'Should I discover otherwise, my duke, it may cause me to become suddenly hungry.'

'I do not think that Arguthrax will taste very pleasant, my lord.'

'Then I will save you to cleanse my palate afterwards,' replied Ebondrake. 'Enough of this! This is not the time for politics. See, the arena awaits!'

Ebondrake and Venalitor emerged onto a balcony formed from the jagged steel jaw of a formidable grimacing war mask set into the wall of the arena. The Ophidian Guard who waited there saluted as Ebondrake appeared at the fanged battlements to the ecstatic roar of the crowd. Venalitor roared in reply, and breathed a plume of black fire into the air to acknowledge them. Venalitor raised a sword in salute, too, but there was no doubt that the people of Vel'Skan adored their ruler, and that these games could not begin without him.

Vel'Skan's arena was held up from the mass of weapons and armour by dozens of gauntlets, supporting the arena's bowl like a great chalice. The bowl was formed by the hilt of an enormous rapier embedded point-down in the rock beneath the city, and the hilt's complex guard spiralled above the arena in a magnificent steel swirl.

Inside, the arena was lavish, and death met opulence everywhere. The audience cheered from galleries carved from marble and obsidian. Blades of gold and brass reached over from the edge of the arena bowl, hung with the corpses of those more recently killed, and, from time to time, chunks of rotting meat would fall from the swinging bodies to be fought over by the spectators below.

Daemons were as welcome as mortals in Vel'Skan's arena. One segment of the arena was given over to them, the galleries replaced by terraced, blood-filled pools, where the city's daemons could bathe in the gore of the opening sacrifices. Every shape of daemon was there: bloodletters, snarling fleshhounds, blood-drinking skinless things, and stranger beasts that gibbered and feuded in the gore. Arguthrax was there, too, surrounded by a guard of slaves, ceremonially possessed for the occasion, along with other daemonic lords of Drakaasi: the hulking shrouded form of the Charnel Lord, the enormous dog-like monster Harrowfoul the Magnificent, the red shadow of the Crimson Mist coalesced into a writhing mass with three glowing eyes.

The rest of the audience had come out in all their finery. Many were priests, resplendent in the vestments of Khorne's various priesthoods.

Others were soldiers, proud in armour or uniforms. More were simply wealthy or powerful and wore that influence in the lavishness of their dress and their coteries of slaves.

Among them were Drakaasi's mortal lords, from Ebondrake on his perch in the palace pavilion, to Scathach down by the arena edge, a wizened old scribe sitting beside him to note down all the subtleties of strike and parry that he would witness. The Vermilion Knight stood in enormous crimson armour surrounded by silver-masked warriors, and Golgur the Packmaster threw scraps of disobedient slaves to the mutated hounds fighting around his feet. Even Tiresia the Huntress was there, soaring over the arena on the back of a sky whale.

Every lord of Drakaasi was in attendance, some of whom had barely been glimpsed for decades. All of them wished to pay fealty to Lord Ebondrake and to the Blood God, as well as bask in the bloodshed created for their pleasure.

The arena floor was covered in black sand, shining with the blood of that morning's sacrifices. In the centre, where the sword's grip had originally joined the hilt, rose a marble stepped pyramid that dominated the arena. Each level of the structure was its own duelling ground, stained with generations of blood, and scored with hundreds of errant sword strokes.

A few chunks of bone were still embedded in the marble from particularly brutal executions. At the pinnacle of the pyramid was a plinth with a massive brass chalice. The gladiator who drank the blood of his final opponent from that chalice would be crowned the champion of Drakaasi. Many of the planet's lords had heard the ecstasy of the crowds as they drank from that chalice, and had been set upon the path towards earning the mantle of Champion of Chaos. Other past champions still fought, devolved into subhuman monsters by the endless brutality.

'Many would dearly love to see your Grey Knight on that pyramid,' said Ebondrake, his low growl carrying over the increasing sound of the crowd. 'More than half of those have wagered many skulls on him to die. It would be the perfect blessing to have this spectacle sanctified by his blood.'

'He has learned much since he came to Drakaasi,' said Venalitor. 'I cannot guarantee he will die on cue. Believe me, whatever he meets up there, he will put up a hell of a fight.'

'Again,' said Ebondrake, 'just what I want to hear.'

The gates leading to the prison complex opened. The crowd roared their approval as slaves streamed out into the arena, blinking and confused. The crowd loved their fear, loved their innocence, for even the most sinful of them did not know what was about to happen to them. Greenskins among the slaves roared back at the crowd, daring them to throw the worst they had into the arena. One-ear the Brute was a particular favourite, and eagerly howled orkish insults up at the revellers, who leaned over the barrier to curse him. Another cheer met the enormous man who stepped past the threshold behind the crowd. Alaric the Betrayed, the hunter of daemons, turned into a plaything for the Blood God. Many had seen him fight recently, and rejoiced that he had lost his mind to Khorne's rage, but he was calmer now, his jaw set, waiting for bloodshed instead or charging across the floor to seek it out.

They started to chant his name. He did not acknowledge them.

Other doors were opening. Many lords had supplied their very best to these games. Even the finest gladiators had to earn their place on the first step of the pyramid, though, because the best were accompanied by many others, hungry and desperate, who knew that only by fighting their own way into contention could they get out of Vel'Skan alive.

Lord Ebondrake reared up over the battlements. He held out a claw to gain the attention of the crowd. He clenched it into a scaly fist and banged it down on the battlements in front of him.

Slave masters lashed down at the slaves beneath them, driving them away from the doors. The greatest gladiators saluted the crowd, gripped their swords and charged. The others spat a few syllables of prayer, and followed.

'JUST SURVIVE,' SAID Alaric as Venalitor's slaves gathered on the arena floor, craning their necks as they tried to take in the sheer size and spectacle of the arena.

'They'll kill us if we don't wade in,' said Gearth. 'That's all there is to it.' The prisoner had covered himself in war paint, and he looked like he had more in common with One-ear's orks than with the rest of the human prisoners.

'No they won't,' said Alaric. 'All eyes will be on me. That'll buy you some time. Concentrate on not dying. By the time they're done with me the Hathrans will be here.'

'They'd better be,' said Erkhar. The other doors were opening and the slaves of the other lords were emerging. Among the brutalised humans and mutants were a few who looked as dangerous as Alaric. 'This will not be an easy place to survive for long.'

'Trust me,' said Alaric, 'and trust the Hathrans.' He glanced at Erkhar. 'You and Gearth will be leading the slaves.'

'You won't be with us?'

'I'll be up there,' said Alaric, indicating the pyramid towering over them. 'That's what they want. The slavers will ignore you, as long as I can give them a show.'

The other slaves were running across the arena floor towards the pyramid. Some of them were making for Venalitor's slaves, eager to kill off as many of the opposition as possible in the battle's early stages.

Someone grabbed Alaric's arm just as he was about to sprint for the pyramid. Alaric looked down at Haggard's face.

'I know what you're trying to do,' said Haggard.

'Then you know why I have to do it.'

'Stay with us. Don't die for this.'

'Stick close to Erkhar if I fall,' said Alaric. 'You all know the plan. Stick with him and help lead them.'

Alaric left Haggard behind and ran for the pyramid. A few swift mutants galloped to intercept him, but the greatsword he had chosen as his weapon was surprisingly quick, and he cut one in two before driving the point through the throat of the other, ripping it free without breaking stride.

Killers were swarming all over the lower steps of the pyramid. Men and daemons were dying there already. Alaric was aware of someone running beside him. It was Gearth, his painted face grinning. He loved it. There was nowhere else he would rather be.

'I'm not missing out, golden boy!' he yelled.

Alaric didn't reply. He vaulted onto the top step of the pyramid. The marble was head-height for a normal man, but Alaric jumped onto it in one motion.

The crowd cheered. Alaric the Betrayed would die, and a lot of bets would be won. Alaric prepared to disappoint them.

KELHEDROS SLIPPED THROUGH the wall of blades into the main spur of the prison block. The prison was maddeningly complex, the torture device from which it was built a truly fiendish piece of work, with blades fine and numerous enough to tease out every nerve ending on a victim. There was something admirable about the purity of its purpose. It had been born of a love of pain, some ancient torturer of Titans pouring every drop of genius into it.

Kelhedros risked a glance down the cell block. Cells were suspended from blades protruding from the high walls, a web of cranes and cat-walks above making the place look like a machine for processing its occupants, which, of course, it was.

The eldar stole across the steel canyon of the cell block, writhing through the spidery shadows that hung across everything. The prison guards were easy to spot; their eyes burned in their ruined faces, for they were just hollow shells of bones and meat to house the daemons controlling them.

Kelhedros ignored them. Killing them would also use up time he didn't have. He passed right under one of them, who was keeping watch from an upper walkway. Neither the daemon, nor the human trapped somewhere inside, had any idea that Kelhedros was there. It was as if the eldar could just opt out of reality and ghost past the perception of anyone he didn't want to see him.

Beyond the cell block were the torture chambers. The smell was the worst thing about them. The air seemed to get thicker with their stink. Then there were the implements themselves, complicated machines mounted on the walls, all blades and restraints in an echo of the prison structure. Thumbscrews and hot pokers were far too crude for Khorne's torturers. Lords from across Drakaasi sent captives to be strapped in down here where the precision machines would peel spiral strips from their skin until they broke. A person could be almost completely dissected, and still remain alive and conscious. Some of the arena's own slaves, the troublemakers and would-be escapees, had suffered just that fate.

A slab stood in the middle of the room, hung with leather restraining straps. In front of the slab, with his back to Kelhedros as he entered, was Kruulskan. The human whose body he had taken had been huge, his massive chest supporting barrel biceps and a neck like a battering ram of muscle. His bald head was scorched with the flames that spat from his eyes sockets, silhouetting his bulk as Kelhedros approached from behind. He was cleaning a selection of blades, pliers and other strange implements laid out on the slab before him.

'What are you?' asked Kruulskan in his slavering grind of a voice.

Kelhedros froze and melted further into the darkness, willing the shadows to congeal around him.

'To delve so deep and reach the heart of this place, you must be skilled. A daemon? No, you don't smell right. An assassin! Ha! I lived an aeon in the warp and a century in flesh. You're not the first to come to kill me.'

Kruulskan turned towards Kelhedros. The balls of flame set into his piggy face roved across the room, but they couldn't focus on Kelhedros. The darkness helped. The waves of pain and misery helped even more. The torture chamber had such a history of suffering that it was like a shroud in which Kelhedros could wrap himself.

Kruulskan picked up a military pick from his side. He stalked slowly towards the centre of the room.

'I can see things no human can see,' growled Kruulskan. 'You can't hide from me. There's a daemon in this head! Hungry and mean, and he wants blood! He ain't had it for so long, just lickings from a slave vintage. You're different. You'll taste good. Aliens always do. Yes, I can smell the void on you. You're very far from home, little bug-eyes.'

Kelhedros slid silently across the chamber, weaving his way between the shadows of the room and the flickering light of Kruulskan's eyes.

'I know,' said Kruulskan, 'you're made of shadow.'

Kelhedros slipped out of the darkness and leapt up onto the slab, behind Kruulskan. Kruulskan whirled around, pick held high ready to bring it down through Kelhedros's skull.

Kelhedros snatched up a blade from the slab, a wickedly curved thing, like a miniature sickle, and threw it at Kruulskan. The blade ripped through Kruulskan's eye and flame sprayed like blood from an artery. Kruulskan stumbled back, roaring.

Kelhedros grabbed a steel spike and threw it after the sickle, and it buried itself in the meat of Kruulskan's shoulder. Another speared the possessed creature's wrist, and sheared through the nerves controlling his hand, forcing him to drop the pick. A fourth got him in the throat.

With his free hand, Kruulskan pulled the blade from his eye. Half of what remained of his face was gone, consumed by the burst of flame, and inside the charred hollow of his skull, Kelhedros could just see the unholy features of the daemon in the fire.

Kruulskan charged, head down, to bowl Kelhedros to the floor and crush him to death. Kelhedros jumped, flipping over Kruulskan with such ease that it was as if he was taking flight. Kruulskan slammed into the slab, spilling torture implements everywhere, and Kelhedros landed behind him. Kruulskan turned around, took a deep breath and vomited flaming bile at Kelhedros. The eldar leapt again, this time flipping up onto one of the torture frames mounted on the wall. He balanced carefully between the machine's blades and spines as liquid fire washed across the floor below him.

Kruulskan grabbed the slab with his remaining good hand and ripped it from its moorings. He spun once, like a hammer thrower, and hurled the slab at Kelhedros. The eldar dived out of the way as the metal slab crashed into the wall, crunching through the torture device. The flame was still covering the floor, and Kelhedros angled himself upwards. His hand caught the corroded metal of the ceiling, and his many-jointed fingers wormed their way into a handhold. Kruulskan stumbled forwards under his own momentum, directly under where Kelhedros was clinging to the ceiling.

Kelhedros's free hand drew the black dagger from its scabbard. He was glad that Alaric had given it to him. Clearly, an old-fashioned length of steel wouldn't be enough to kill the possessed Kruulskan, but the venom just might.

Kelhedros dropped from the ceiling and landed on Kruulskan's back. He punched the dagger between Kruulskan's ribs. He felt the blade pierce the tough flesh of the heart. Kruulskan roared and swung around, trying to throw the alien off him. Instead, Kelhedros pivoted and dropped down in front of Kruulskan, planting a foot on the possessed monster's prodigious gut as he drove the blade into his chest.

Kruulskan's heart was pierced from both sides. Green flame drooled from his tusked mouth and spurted from the wound around the dagger blade. Kelhedros twisted it for good measure, and more fire spurted out. The eldar flipped away as Kruulskan's human body began to come apart at the seams. The dagger stayed in Kruulskan's flesh, fire fountaining around it.

'I'll find you!' hissed Kruulskan, his words almost lost in the torrent of flame. 'I'll come back from the warp, shadow-skin, and I will find you!'

Kelhedros paused for long enough to rip the heavy brass key from around Kruulskan's neck. Then he fled from the room just before the possessed gaoler's earthly body exploded.

REGIMAIAH THE IRON-HEARTED killed the twin swordswomen known together as the Blood Serenade. Aethalian Swifthammer, a cudgel held in each of his three hands, cracked open the skull of the disgraced Commander Thaall, once a member of Scathach's army, now cursed and thrown down to fight in the arenas. His curse was lifted at last as his brains spilled down over the lowest step of the pyramid.

Beside him died Sokramanthios the Scholar, the fire-breathing witch mutant, slain by an unlikely and very temporary alliance between Thurgull's champion Murkrellos the Venomous and the skeletal Skin Haunter. Xian'thal, in his intricate segmented armour, wielding a pair of blades connected by a chain, found himself surrounded by clamouring mutants trying to drag him down and butcher him. He killed six of them in a few seconds, but was himself killed when the mutant warlord Crukellen impaled him on spines of bone.

Gearth killed Furanka the Red Dog by stabbing the bestial mutant in the back with his pair of short swords. The crowd didn't know his name, but they loved the savage joy on his face.

Alaric killed a scrawny human slave, who scrabbled towards him with a dagger in his hand. Alaric kicked him off the first step hard enough to shatter the side of his skull, and he was dead before he hit the ground. Alaric hesitated, staring down at the body while the other champions eagerly killed one another. Some watching thought that Alaric the Betrayed was gone, his spirit broken, but then Lethlos son of Khouros leapt on him, and Alaric rammed the beastman's head into the marble, until Lethlos went limp and three of its eyes popped out of their sockets.

Dozens of feuds were settled and arena careers begun and ended in the first couple of minutes. Some died with a flourish, others had bad deaths laid low by a mistake or a sucker punch. Some killed with raw power and others with a moment of skill, or just with pure luck.

The lesser slaves fought around the pyramid for the right to follow the real killers onto its first step. Venalitor's slaves were surrounded and besieged by half-naked tribal warriors with the brand of a six-fingered hand on their chests. Erkhar and One-ear led Venalitor's slaves in a bizarre alliance. They were fighting for time, and their struggle formed a curious sideshow to the main event.

The crowd was only just finding its true voice, and ancient hymns roared around the arena. Already there had been enough stories and enough blood to satisfy the altars of Khorne. The bloodshed today would be good.

TWENTY-TWO

'YOU AGAIN,' SAID Dorvas.

The door banged open to reveal Kelhedros coalescing from the shadows, Kruulskan's key in his hand. 'Of course.'

The prison beneath the arena was a dark and foul place. Its cells were each home to two or three Hathrans, with the possessed gaolers patrolling constantly.

'You killed pig-face?'

'It is dead.'

Dorvas banged a fist into his hand. The other Hathrans in the cell behind him hissed their delight. Kruulskan was dead. They had often dreamed of hearing those words.

'Move fast,' said Dorvas.

Kelhedros headed down the cells, opening them one by one. The corpse of a possessed guard still smouldered on the walkway outside the cell where Kelhedros had killed it. Dorvas and the Hathrans rummaged through the body, grabbing whatever they could use as a weapon. More freed Hathrans gathered outside the cells. The feeling of elation was mixed with fear, and the men crouched in the darkness, knowing that they would be found out soon enough.

'You know the plan,' said Dorvas. 'Get to the arming cages, and then to the branding chamber. If you get hurt, you'll get left behind.'

The sound of shouting echoed from down the cell block. The light of blazing eyes glinted off the blades that made up the prison's structure.

'Now!' shouted Dorvas.

The prisoners rushed the oncoming guards. There were fifty of them in the throng by the time the guards reached them.

The possessed were figures of fear, the daemons inside them unfathomably cruel, but the Hathrans were driven by something more than fear now, something more, even than the hope of freedom.

They could bring the fight to their foes at last. They could seek revenge instead of cowering, hoping to be spared. The Hathran Armoured Cavalry charged again.

ALARIC WRAPPED THE chain around the throat of Vladamasca Wrathbringer and crushed the life out of her. The fleshy dreadlocks adorning her head writhed as she fought to breathe. Alaric stamped down on the back of her leg, forcing her to her knees, and she stiffened and died as the chain cut off the blood to her brain.

Alaric wondered for a split second how much had been wagered on her, and what the odds had been. By the Emperor, he hated this place.

Alaric threw the mutant's body off the pyramid. Her corpse slithered down the blood-covered marble. He caught a glimpse of Venalitor's slaves, back to back as they fought. One-ear and the orks were taking the chance to put on their own sideshow, leaping and hacking at the slaves attacking them. Gearth was somewhere lower on the pyramid, fighting his way up. Alaric didn't know if he would make it. He hoped not.

He also saw the crowd. They were chanting the names of their favourite champions. Alaric heard his own name: the Betrayed, the Fallen Knight, the Emperor's Disobedient Gundog. Others howled their dismay that Vladamasca was dead. The lords were as enthusiastic as the crowds, because those were their slaves and their champions dying. Ebondrake's balcony was wreathed in black fire, and Alaric was sure he could make out the red armour and gleaming blades of Duke Venalitor.

The sight of Venalitor filled him with hate. He had never thought he could despise a place like he despised Drakaasi in that moment. Hatred was holy to a Grey Knight and, yet he had never felt it as he did for the vermin who populated the stands. He let it roar through his veins and silently hoped that it would not turn him into one of them.

Alaric forced his way onto the penultimate step of the pyramid. A cloven-hoofed creature lay on the step holding its guts in. Alaric barely paused to break its neck. The beastman had been carrying a spear with a barbed head. It was a more practical weapon than the spiked chain that Alaric had taken off the third fighter he had killed, a red-skinned daemon which had tried to vomit caustic blood over him. Alaric picked up the spear and made it to the top step.

Half the crowd cheered to see Alaric the Betrayed make it to the square of marble at the pinnacle. Alaric was exhausted. He fought to remember how many champions of the Dark Gods he had killed, but their faces and mutations swam in his mind, and he couldn't focus.

He could have let the noise of the crowd in and taken strength from it, but that was not who he was. He was not a gladiator fighting for glory, but a servant of the Emperor fighting first for survival, and then for justice. The crowd would not keep him going.

He had a weapon in his hand and an enemy to kill. That was all a citizen of the Imperium ever needed, that and the hate.

The crowd was roaring in anticipation. The bloodletting had been to get them worked up. The real event was here. The champion would be crowned.

Alaric knew, before he ever saw it, what would come slithering up onto the pinnacle: the tiny glinting red eyes and the fork-tongued smirking mouth, the massive four-armed torso, the kill tallies, and the obscenity of its oversized snakelike body. The sound of reptilian scales on marble was a confirmation that Alaric didn't need.

'I am so glad it is you,' said Skarhaddoth, gladiator champion of Lord Ebondrake, slithering onto the pinnacle. 'I have developed a taste for your kind.'

Skarhaddoth was even bigger up close. He had new kill marks branded into his scaly chest, and one of the hands hanging around his neck must have belonged to Haulvarn. Skarhaddoth had abandoned his shields, and each of his four hands held a well-bloodied scimitar.

'I tend to stick in the throat,' said Alaric.

The two circled slowly. No doubt Alaric didn't look like much of an opponent. His steps were heavy and his breathing laboured, and his magnificent armour was ragged and battered. Skarhaddoth looked as if the blooding on the pyramid had been no more than a pre-match ritual for him. He was sheened with foul-smelling sweat, and he grinned with malice. He had been looking forward to this. Ever since he killed Haulvarn, he had been waiting to finish the job.

'Two Grey Knights,' said Alaric, letting his muscles slide into a familiar combat stance. 'Quite a tally. What will that get you? Freedom?'

'Who needs freedom?' hissed Skarhaddoth. 'What is this fiction that devours your human mind? What more is there in the universe than this? Blood and death and metal through flesh? More of everything, that is what I will be given. More blood!'

'In the crusade,' said Alaric. 'Ebondrake will give you everything you want there. If you kill me.'

'The first wave,' sneered Skarhaddoth. 'First through the breach. First onto land. Blood upon virgin earth. The warp will hear my blades, betrayed one! Khorne will smell the blood I let!'

Alaric smiled. It was a strange thing to feel, some humour, some joy, up there amid the blasphemy and death, but it was there, because Alaric was human, and being human meant dragging hope out of hell. 'There will be no crusade,' said Alaric. 'I know what Ebondrake wants. I know what you want. Neither of you will have it. I want you to know that before...'

'Before what, betrayed one?'

The pause lasted a fraction of a second, but in that time so much went through Alaric's mind that he couldn't see anything beyond Skarhaddoth. The arena, the crowd, the fighting, the menagerie of Drakaasi's lords and daemons, they all became a crimson blur. Angles of attack and best guesses about Skarhaddoth's anatomy, the weight of the spear in his hands and the blood slicking the marble beneath his feet were all coursing through his head. Then it was enough. There were no more guesses to make.

Alaric lunged. He had a long reach, long enough for the point of his spear to punch through Skarhaddoth's chest and out through his back.

Skarhaddoth gasped. For the first time, the smirk was wiped off his face. He looked down at the spear in his chest, and then up at Alaric.

'Your guard is too low,' said Alaric. Skarhaddoth slumped forwards, pushing the shaft further through him as he tried to take a ragged breath. His face was close to Alaric's, and Alaric only had to whisper. 'I noticed it when you murdered my friend. Such a thing tends to focus the mind.'

Skarhaddoth slumped to the floor, still with a look of surprise on his face.

The crowd was quiet for a moment. Alaric had done what no other man on Drakaasi could have done. He had shut them all up.

Lord Ebondrake leaned over the battlements of his pavilion high up in the huge mask mounted on the arena wall. His eyes were slits of yellow fire and his nostrils flared. His wings spread out behind him, and for a moment Alaric was sure the old lizard would swoop down to devour Alaric himself.

The relative silence was broken by the explosion that blew a crater in the arena floor. Alaric was battered back by the force of it, and blood-stained sand rained down.

Uproar filled the silence after the blast. Angry spectators clambered over barricades towards the arena floor. Ophidian Guard stormed from their posts to keep order. The lords began demanding to know who among them had dared to defile Khorne's spectacle.

Then, a figure emerged from the cloud of dust and dirt, tall, lean, armed with a sword and moving faster than a man. It was Kelhedros.

Behind him were four thousand arena slaves in the uniforms of the Hathran Armoured Cavalry.

EVERYTHING THAT ALARIC had learned about the Vel'Skan arena told him that the only way out was across the arena floor.

From the arena, the slaves and the Hathrans could make it to the seating areas, hopefully assisted by the chaos caused by Alaric's victory and the breakout itself. Many gates led out of the arena, but only one of them interested Alaric, since it would point the escaping slaves towards their ultimate objective.

As a plan, it was flawed. The brother-captains and grand masters of the Grey Knights would have admonished him for suggesting such a mess, but it was the only chance Alaric would ever have to take the *Hammer of Daemons*. It was also the only chance the slaves would have of escaping the planet, but if Alaric was honest with himself, truly honest, he had to accept that their escape was a secondary objective for him.

Many of them would die. Alaric knew he was sacrificing them for his own ends, but that was the way the galaxy worked. It was a cruel place, and that meant that, sometimes, he had to be crueller.

'WHAT ARE YOUR orders, my lord?' asked the captain of the Ophidian Guard.

'What do you bloody think?' snarled Lord Ebondrake through coils of black fire. 'Kill them all.'

'Yes, my lord,' said the captain. He raised his sword, and as one the Ophidian Guard clanked out of the pavilion to join the other soldiers gathering among the spectators below.

Ebondrake turned to Venalitor. 'More blasphemy, and your boy is at the heart of it all, Venalitor. You will answer for this.'

'I have no doubt of that,' said Venalitor rapidly, 'but this may not be the catastrophe it seems. Here is an opportunity to–'

'Less talk!' yelled Ebondrake. 'More death! By the brass gates of hell, Venalitor, take your pretty sword and kill something down there!'

In reply, Venalitor drew the two-handed blade from his back, and vaulted over the battlements of the pavilion, dropping deftly to the seating below.

The audience was in chaos. Alaric's victory, and the manner of it, was enough to send them into a frenzy on its own. Skarhaddoth had died at the first blow. Ebondrake's champion had died, without a fight! A bad death indeed, and nothing stirred up hatred more than a poor death. Then the explosion, and the torrent of slaves suddenly swarming across the arena had forced any remaining sense out of their heads. The spectators were biting and kicking at everyone around them, blaming one another for the obscenity that had blighted this celebration of Khorne.

One of them ran at Venalitor, a bloodied cultist in a torn robe with ritual brass claws implanted in his forearms. Venalitor animated the blood around the man's feet, tripped him up, and cut through his spine with a swipe of his blade. It was barely worth a flick of the wrist to kill such a lowly creature.

'My duke,' said the slurred voice of a scaephylyd. Venalitor's slavemaster picked his way across the wounded and unconscious around the upper seats, 'the scaephylyds have been gathered and await your orders. Should we descend to the arena floor?'

Venalitor looked down at the arena. The Vel'Skan arena slaves were making a break for the northern side of the arena, scrambling up onto the seating, and killing the spectators who tried to resist. Many of the slaves of other lords had joined the breakout, and Alaric was up on the arena wall directing the fight.

'No,' said Venalitor, 'they're heading for the northern gates. Have the scaephylyds gather to the north of the arena. The Ophidian Guard will pursue them. If we can slow the slaves down, they will be crushed between the two.'

'And the Grey Knight?'

Venalitor thought for a moment. 'I was rather hoping I could kill him, but do not pass up the opportunity should it arise.'

'Where will you be, my duke?'

'Lord Ebondrake will need me,' said Venalitor, 'whether he acknowledges it or not.'

'Very well. What were his orders?'

'Kill them. Get to it.'

The slavemaster raised a mandible in salute and turned to the scaephylyds gathering on the upper seating, chittering to them in their insect tongue. They scurried off towards the northern gates, ignoring the riot that was spreading around them.

Alaric was not stupid. He should know full well that a breakout in Vel'Skan would, at most, lead to a day of freedom, and several years of torture. The Grey Knight had an objective in mind, something beyond just running for his life. Venalitor wondered what it might be. There was nothing in Vel'Skan that would benefit the slaves, nothing so defensible that the Ophidian Guard could not besiege and break it.

There was, of course, one possibility, one chance for a dramatic gesture that, while it would surely cost the life of every slave who escaped, would nevertheless appeal to a servant of the corpse-emperor as a dramatic final gesture before death. It was insane, of course, but just because Alaric wasn't stupid that didn't mean he wasn't insane. After all, Venalitor had put a great deal of effort into driving him mad.

That was where Venalitor would confront Alaric and kill him. After all, even if Ebondrake considered him at fault for Alaric's actions, Venalitor was sure that few sights would gain him more respect among Drakaasi's lords than him standing on the battlements holding a Grey Knight's severed head.

Some good would still come of this, Venalitor decided. Idly cutting his way through the few rioting idiots who got in his way, he headed north.

'I see,' said Arguthrax. 'It started here.'

The daemon's brass cauldron had been dragged through the narrow confines of the prison on chains hauled by his burliest slaves, since many of the ceilings were too low for him to be carried. Hound-like retriever daemons snarled ahead of him, snapping at one another as they tried to find a scent. There was nothing. Considering how the prison stank, that in itself was a sign.

The arena slaves had broken out. Many of them were dead, killed by the gaolers as they fought. The arming cages had been ransacked, and the branding room had been blown up, leaving a crater in the arena floor above. It had been swift and violent. Something had given them enough hope to stage the breakout, and they must have had help from outside to even get out of their cells.

In front of Arguthrax was the wrecked torture chamber. Torment cages had been torn from the walls. Blades and spikes were scattered across the floor, and everything was burned. A charred body lay in the centre of the floor, hollowed out by flame. It had been the body of a large human, but the retrievers shied away from it.

'Daemon,' said the handler, one of the few of his slaves that Arguthrax permitted to speak. The handler was a particularly cruel soul, and probably would have worked for Arguthrax whether he was a slave or not. 'Shell of a possessed.'

'Yes, they guarded this place. Someone knew how to start this. I desire to know why.'

The sounds of battle reached down from the arena. The other lords were fighting up there, some with each other, most to quell the rioting. Arguthrax would have liked to join them, but he had other priorities.

'If we can demonstrate that one of Venalitor's slaves was down here,' he said, 'then he will be suspected of treachery. I can think up a few reasons why he might have done it: to create dissent among the lords, where he might gain Ebondrake's confidence; to postpone the crusade because he is a coward; or to bring the freed slaves into his fold for use as fodder against me. It does not matter. So long as the link is there it will bring him down.' Arguthrax looked around the chamber. Aside from the heady tang of suffering, there was little of interest. 'Bring me the corpse,' he said.

The handler grabbed an intact-looking limb and hauled the body over to Arguthrax's cauldron. Arguthrax reached down and picked up the body. Chunks of burned flesh fell off it. The body was just a shell, the eyes and mouth burned into gaping holes by the force of the flame.

'Possessed,' sneered Arguthrax. 'Such a waste, a cloak of flesh to hide their beauty. This thing probably couldn't remember either of the beings it once was.' Arguthrax paused as he spotted something glinting in the caul of burned meat. He pushed his paw into the disintegrating body and pulled out a jet-black shard, glossy with corrupted blood.

It was the tip of a sword, broken off in the possessed creature's body.

'The Guard,' hissed Arguthrax. 'The Ophidian Guard did this.'

The slaves knew when Arguthrax was angry. They had seen it often enough, and they had seen their fellow slaves die as a result. Even the brutalised cauldron slaves tried to shrink away from their master.

'Ebondrake!' growled Arguthrax. 'Curses upon your scaly hide! Deceitful lizard! Scales and claws and lies! All this to save your damned crusade!' Arguthrax shuddered with anger, slopping blood over the edge of his cauldron. 'To betray us! To betray me, the Despoiler of Kolchadon, the End of Empires, the Bloody Hand of Skerentis Minor!' The blood overflowed, sloshing from the pits of the warp through the bridge formed by Arguthrax's rage. It poured in a torrent, swirling around the torture chamber. 'Take me to the surface! Take me to the lords! Ebondrake will pay!'

* * *

GEARTH, WHO HAD somehow contrived to survive, plunged both his knives into the thorax of the scaephylyd who charged at him. The insectoid creature writhed on the twin blades, and collapsed. Gearth's blades went with it, but the killer picked up the scaephylyd's spear. A blade, after all, was a blade.

'They're trying to block the way!' called Erkhar. He and his faithful were on one side of the slave army, safely away from Gearth's murderers and the greenskins who took up the other flank. Alaric was somewhere in the middle, the mass of Hathrans behind him.

Alaric realised that Erkhar was right. The slaves had made it out of the arena, and already many of their number had been lost to the enraged spectators who fought back. Now the way in front of them, along an uneven avenue of blades lined with titanic shields and segments of plate armour, was darkening with the scuttling forms of hundreds of scaephylyds.

Beyond them, up a flight of steps formed from a stack of axe heads, was the palace of Lord Ebondrake. Its half-blinded skull grinned down on the battlefield as if it was anticipating the slaughter.

That was Alaric's objective. He was going to take the palace. If it cost the life of every slave, he would take it.

Alaric turned to the Hathrans behind him. Few of them really understood what was happening, only that they had broken out of the arena, and they were at a loss to know what to do next.

'The Emperor sees us even here!' shouted Alaric. 'For His glory, sons of Hathran! For your lost brothers and sisters, for the man at your side! For the Emperor!'

'For the Emperor!' echoed Corporal Dorvas, raising the axe he had taken from a dead arena slave.

The Hathrans yelled and charged. Alaric went with them, because he was their figurehead now, and if he faltered, they would too.

The scaephylyd line was not yet fully formed, but there were plenty of the creatures to spare. Alaric had not known that Venalitor commanded so many of them, but it did not matter. He had always known that the slaves would not do this without a fight.

The two lines collided. Gearth whooped as he leapt into the air and landed directly on top of the largest scaephylyd he could see. The greenskins followed him, One-ear bowling the closest alien over and pulling its legs off. The other side of the line hit a moment later, Erkhar's faithful charging, in as disciplined a line as they could muster. They had swords, and the scaephylyd had spears, and several of them died in a few moments to the aliens' longer reach, but they had faith and the weight of the charge behind them, and the aliens were forced back.

It was bedlam in the centre. There was no room for skill. A massive press of men heaved down on the scaephylyds. Alaric was face-to-face with one of them, its mad asymmetrical eyes rolling in hatred. His spear was useless in the crush, so he let it go and rammed a fist into the scaephylyd's mandibles, feeling chitin crunch under his fingers. He pulled, and the thing's mandibles came away. It reared and screeched, spraying foul blood everywhere. Alaric drove an elbow into the top of its head, clambered onto its armoured abdomen, and ripped off a limb that stabbed at him. He grabbed a spear that another alien tried to transfix him with, stood up on the body of the creature he had knocked out and stabbed all around him at the sea of insect bodies.

The Hathrans were scrambling all over the scaephylyds. Alaric could see them dying, torn apart or trampled to the ground, but they were also winning. Scaephylyds were weighed down with men and stamped to death in the throng. Others were stabbed dozens of times, their carapaces pierced and broken, spilling blackish organs onto the ground.

Alaric led the way. All the slaves looked up to him. Without him, they were just a crowd of dead men. With him, they were a fighting force.

'Forward! Arm yourselves and leave the wounded!' Alaric tore a malformed alien blade from the claw of a dead scaephylyd, and held it up so that the Hathrans and other slaves could see him. He pointed it towards the palace. 'For your Emperor! For freedom!'

The slave army heaved forwards, and the scaephylyds were pushed back. Scaephylyds were breaking and trying to regroup away from the crush. One-ear and his greenskins, along with many of Gearth's killers, howled war cries as they ran the broken aliens down.

There was no time to pause and finish the job. Alaric led the way right through the middle of the scaephylyds, cutting them down or battering them to the ground. He was covered in their viscous blood and had to wipe it from his eyes to see.

'Leave them! Forward! All of you!'

The slave army rolled over the scaephylyds. Alaric broke into a run, the few knots of scaephylyds still in his way struggling to get away from him. Ahead of him was the short run to the palace of Lord Ebondrake. Vel'Skan rose in sinister bladed shapes on either side, fantastic buildings constructed around the core of a sword hilt or along the blade of an axe. How much of the city was dedicated to hunting down Alaric and the escaping slaves? At least most of the inhabitants would be assuming that they were headed out of the city. If the slaves reached the palace quickly enough, and everything went to plan, there was a chance that they might actually succeed.

There was hope, then, but Alaric could not let it dull his senses. Many more of them would die before they escaped Drakaasi. Alaric knew full well that he could be one of them.

'With me! Bring the fight to them! For freedom!' Alaric charged towards the palace steps, and the army charged with him.

TIRESIA THE HUNTRESS, who had taken the heads of all seven Brothers of the Nethermost Darkness in her youth, loved nothing more than a bow in her hand and a cunning quarry to hunt. The slaves escaping Vel'Skan's arena were ideal.

Her mount, one of her flying creatures akin to a spiny stingray, swooped low at her mental command, weaving between the giant sword tips and spear shafts of Vel'Skan's skyline. She spied one of the arena slaves cowering among the ragged banners of a forgotten lord, clinging to the crossbar of a giant spearhead.

Tiresia drew her bow from her back, and shot the slave through the neck with an arrow tipped with snake venom. She circled as the slave, a skinny pale thing no more than arena fodder, seemed to dance with joy at being shot. It was the toxin sending his muscles into spasm, the same toxin filling his lungs with foam. He lost his balance and fell from the spear, breaking his body against the marble battlements of a fortress mansion below.

Tiresia added another head to the trophy room in her mind.

Arguthrax the bloated daemon and his train of mutilated slaves were making their way, in the direction of the arena, across a plateau formed by a discarded shield. This surprised Tiresia. Arguthrax wasn't a hunter of her prowess, but he still enjoyed killing for sport as much as the next daemon. Throughout Vel'Skan, stray slaves were being chased down and dismembered, or handed over to Khorne's priests to serve as future sacrifices. It was not like something as venal as Arguthrax to miss out on the fun. She swooped low over him, yanking the head of her beast up so that it hung in the air over him.

'Frog-beast!' she called down. 'No hunt for you? Does the warp scorn even sporting death now?'

Arguthrax looked up at her. Like many of Drakaasi's lords, he was spectacularly ugly. Tiresia fancied that the other lords, even the daemons, were on some level jealous of her attractive near-human form. Few could become as corrupt as her and yet stay relatively unblemished by the touch of the warp.

'Faugh! Pretty child. What do you know of death? What do you know of anything? To you, this is just a game!'

'As is all death,' replied Tiresia, 'for the Blood God plays dice with our souls. Blessed are those who play by the same rules as him!'

Arguthrax spat on the ground. 'The game? What game is this?' He brandished the obsidian shard in his paw.

Tiresia guided her mount down and hopped off it to the ground, shouldering her bow. She walked closer to Arguthrax to get a look at the shard.

'The blade of an Ophidian Guard,' sneered Arguthrax, 'used to kill the chief gaoler of the arena.'

'The Ophidian Guard? This cannot be, hideous one.'

'Why not? Are you as dense as you are decorative, hunter of worms? I have prosecuted a war against the deceitful cur Venalitor for months. Surely even you are aware of this?'

'Of course,' said Tiresia. A few of her attendant hunters had seen that she had alighted, and were guiding their own mounts to the ground. They flew blunt nosed skysharks, less impressive than her flying ray, but dramatic nonetheless. 'You defied Lord Ebondrake. There were few who did not see a reckoning for both of you.'

'And this is it! Think on it, girl. Ebondrake wants us united for his crusade, and what better way to unite enemies beneath him?'

'Give them a common enemy,' said Tiresia.

'So you are worthy of your lordship after all. Of course! A common enemy! Something that even dukes and daemons can indulge in destroying together! This! The escape!'

Tiresia's hunters gathered around her. They were not accustomed to seeing their mistress surprised by anything, but she was definitely taken aback by Arguthrax's words. 'Can this be true? With as much honesty as you can muster, daemon. Is this thing possible?'

'It is not only possible, it is inevitable. What more proof do you need?' Arguthrax held out the shard again. 'Dying proof, huntress! The truest thing on this planet! Lord Ebondrake wants his crusade and he profaned the very games of its celebration to ensure that we were of one sword! This blasphemy is his doing! This abomination unto Khorne will be revisited on him! The warp will have its justice!'

'We cannot make such an accusation,' said Tiresia. 'No matter how certain we may be, we are but two lords among many.'

'Then find others!' retorted Arguthrax angrily. 'They will unite behind us! Bring them together, the Traitor Marine and the thing from the deep, the walker of dogs and all the rest of them! Together, we will make Ebondrake pay! Mark my words, I will dine on lizard before the sun sets!'

Tiresia shouted orders to her followers in clipped hunter cant. The hunt was forgotten and they took to the air to seek out their fellow lords and spread the news. Arguthrax's cauldron was borne aloft again, and the slaves continued their procession towards the fortresses and parade grounds of Vel'Skan.

Ebondrake had tried to manipulate them towards unity, but if there was one thing that could truly unite the lords of Vel'Skan, it was news of treachery.

TWENTY-THREE

THE SKULL THAT formed the pinnacle of Lord Ebondrake's palace grinned down as if anticipating the bloodshed. The slope of axe blades leading up to the entrance in its throat was still stained brown-black with the blood of recent sacrifices. Nothing in Vel'Skan, it seemed, could be considered holy or worthwhile if it was not regularly covered in blood. The dagger through the skull's eye cast a long, jagged shadow over the palace approach.

It was silent. The skull's remaining eye socket was dark. The balcony in front of it, from which Lord Ebondrake presumably took flight, was empty. The entrance, a tall narrow archway built to accommodate Ebondrake's wings, was also deserted.

'Looks undefended,' said Corporal Dorvas.

'Maybe,' said Alaric. 'The riots at the arena are buying us time. Ebondrake won't be back until the slaves are captured or dead.'

'You know of Ebondrake well?'

Alaric shrugged. 'I tried to kill him once.'

'You tried to kill that? Throne alive.'

'It was not part of the plan at the time.'

The slaves were up ahead, nervously approaching the palace's great brass doors.

'What do you think it was?' asked Dorvas, nodding up at the giant skull.

'A prince of daemons, perhaps,' said Alaric. 'Or something we've never heard of. I feel Drakaasi has a complicated past.'

'Ebondrake likes maintaining an image.'

'That he does, corporal, and if I may say so, that was an impressive move with the explosives at the arena. I had my doubts as to whether it would succeed.'

Dorvas opened his uniform shirt. On his chest was burned a mark in the shape of a serpent, denoting him as Ebondrake's property. 'They branded us with something caustic they kept in barrels underneath the torture block. Turns out it was flammable.'

Alaric smiled. 'I admire the improvisation.'

'Simple field craft, Justicar.' Dorvas looked up again at the palace. 'And it's here? The *Hammer of Daemons*?'

'If it's real, corporal, it is here, and it is real.'

Hathrans were working around the great brass doors, piling up barrels of the caustic gunk they had liberated from the prison's armoury.

'Move!' shouted one of them. 'Away from the doors!' The slaves broke from cover and followed Alaric away from the archway. A few moments later the brass doors glowed, blistered and burst, spraying molten metal as a large sagging hole was torn in the doors.

Gearth was the first through. Alaric wasn't surprised, but even Gearth's step faltered when he saw the inside of the palace for the first time.

It was dark and cool inside. The wind breathed through the dark red silks that billowed from the walls of the entrance gallery. Overhead, shafts of light fell between the skull's teeth, the ceiling vaulted beneath the cranium.

The wind was not coming from outside. It was sighing from the throats of Lord Ebondrake's enemies. They were fused with the walls and ceiling, or with blocks of stone in the centre of the room like sculptures in a gallery. They were still alive. Alaric saw daemons among them, the brutal shapes of bloodletters reaching from the stones. The hanging silks waved around the corpulent form of a mutated human with goat legs and a second lolling mouth in its stomach, pallid flesh veined with granite where its skin met the stone. There was a treacherous Ophidian Guard, its helmet removed to reveal a face without skin, its mouth locked open and a stone tongue hanging down in front of its chest, and a carapaced creature from the seas half-petrified as if trying to swim out of the wall that encased it. One of the victims in the centre of the room was almost the shape of a woman, with a noseless face and claws for hands, her body displayed wantonly as it was consumed by the stone. There were hundreds of bodies, each a thing of Chaos: the many foes despatched by Ebondrake as he closed his claws around Drakaasi.

Haggard jogged up to Alaric. He was breathing heavily; he wasn't a young man any more. 'Flesh of the Saint, look at this,' he said.

'They're alive,' said Alaric.

'Of course. It's no fun for him if they're dead.' Haggard spat on the ground. 'That's Gruumthalak Ironclad,' he said, indicating a creature like an armoured centaur with a scorpion's tail and huge segmented eyes like a fly, trapped in the entrance chamber's ceiling. 'I always wondered what happened to him.'

Gearth was standing by the female daemon trapped in the centre of the room. He was running the blade of a knife along the stone, testing how it felt when it got to flesh.

'Gearth!' shouted Alaric. 'Get your men up front. We need to head up.'

'C'mon then, ladies, let's move!' called Gearth, and his slaves went with him, up the grand sweeping staircase that dominated the far end of the chamber.

'Where is it?' demanded Erkhar behind Alaric. 'The *Hammer*?'

'It's here. Head up. It's in the cranium.'

'Then where...?' Erkhar paused. 'Of course. All this time.'

'There will be more Ophidian Guard close behind,' said Alaric. 'We have to move. There isn't much time.'

The eyes of Ebondrake's defeated foes followed Alaric as he led the slaves into the palace of their captor.

'WHAT DOES THIS mean?' demanded Lord Ebondrake.

'As I said, it is still uncertain, but they are moving against you,' said Scathach.

From Lord Ebondrake's vantage point among the daemon eyries at the top of one of Vel'Skan's spears, it was easy to see the enemy assembling. Night was falling, and countless lights of torches and possessed daemons' eyes glittered in a shining host. It was gathering around a complex of barracks and parade grounds a short flight away, an excellent staging post for the thrust forwards.

'Who leads them?'

'I am not sure, my lord, though some candidates seem likely,' said Scathach. His more reasonable head was talking, since the other one was much given to battle-cries and statements of blunt intent. 'Arguthrax, certainly. I believe the Charnel Prince is with them, too.'

'That heap of rags? I gave him every corpse he ever consumed. Base traitor. Who do we know is with us?'

'Thurgull, for sure.'

'Ha! He will be of limited use unless we need some fish spoken with. Who else?'

'Golgur, I wager, and I can bring Ilgrandos Brazenspear in, too. If the treachery becomes open, we can count on many more for certain. You are their lord, after all.'

'We will see about that,' said Ebondrake. 'What of Venalitor? He should be at my side. He would not miss this chance to win my favour.'

'I have not seen him.'

'Perhaps it was him,' mused Ebondrake. 'It was his champion that killed my Skarhaddoth. Maybe that was the signal for the breakout, to create the confusion necessary for the lords to ally against me. I would not put it past the duke to have arranged all this. If he has betrayed me, I shall make a point of eating him. He is too sly an opponent to consign to the walls of my palace.'

'What are your orders, my lord?'

Ebondrake pondered this. The daemons roosting in the eyrie around him were starting to stir as night fell. They were nocturnal creatures, and soon they would be out hunting, plucking the unwary from Vel'Skan's rooftops.

'Gather an army,' said Ebondrake, 'and bring in as many lords as you can. Spread the word. Traitors have defiled the games and spat upon my crusade. For this, they will be given battle, defeated and punished. Make it fast, for the traitors cannot keep their forces in check for long.'

'Yes, my lord,' said Scathach, and headed for the sky chariot stationed beside the eyrie. It was a relic of an earlier age, a piece of grav-technology that the Imperium, in its bloated weakness, could no longer replicate.

Scathach piloted the craft down towards the sprawl of Vel'Skan. He gunned the engines, for it would not do to be late reporting his findings back to Arguthrax.

THE HAMMER OF DAEMONS was old. It was concealed within a sheath of corrosion so deep it was a wonder there had ever been a spaceship beneath there at all. Now that Alaric knew the truth he could see the flare of its engine cowling, the blunted underside of the prow, the ridges of sensor towers and the indentations of torpedo tubes. It just needed a little imagination.

'This is it?' asked Corporal Dorvas.

'Of course,' replied Erkhar, 'can you not see it?'

Alaric had led the slaves up into the cranium of the palace's giant skull. The great dome of the skull was divided into audience halls and ritual chambers, along with many rooms that defied explanation. This chamber was one of them. Alaric guessed that it was some kind of interrogation room, what with the restraints hanging from every surface and the indentations in the floor just the right shape for a human to be strapped down. However, that did not explain the richness of the decoration: torture implements inlaid with gold, and gorgeous tapestries of battle ruined with dried blood.

The dagger that impaled the skull through the eye socket passed through this chamber, dominating the room with a massive shaft of corrupted metal, from which hung the remnants of dozens of mutant skeletons. It was not, however, a dagger.

'Lieutenant, if you will?' said Alaric.

Erkhar stepped forward and took out the captain's log of the *Hammer of Daemons*. He opened the book and began to read from it.

'Will this thing still work?' asked Haggard, standing beside Alaric, since that was probably the safest place to be.

'It's an old ship,' said Alaric. 'All the best ones are old.'

'My brothers and sisters,' Erkhar was reading, 'this is not just a journey. This creation will not deliver us to the Promised Land on its own. It is just steel and glass. The truth is harder for you to hear, but it is the Emperor's own word as brought to us by the prophet. We, as pilgrims, make our journey not to arrive, but to undergo. '

The faithful were speaking along with him, the murmuring voices like a prayer underlining Erkhar's words. It was the speech read out by the captain of the pilgrim ship before the *Hammer of Daemons* set sail for the Promised Land. The religion of Erkhar's faithful had been based on those words, not as a statement by a captain, but as a metaphor for everything they had suffered. The ship was Drakaasi, and the pilgrims were the slaves, their journey the ordeal of slavery under the planet's lords, but the truth was more mundane.

'It is not enough to trust the Emperor to fend off all the perils of the void for us. On this journey we must change, we must become one with the Emperor's truth. We must abandon the lies that bind us, cast out the vices and doubts that rule us, and throw aside the despairs of this dark millennium. Survival is not enough. The *Hammer of Daemons* must change us into something more than we are. Only then will we deserve our places in the Promised Land.'

Something rumbled within the body of the dagger. Slabs of corrosion cracked and fell from the shaft, smashing to reddish dust on the chamber floor. The faithful took a step back.

'Emperor's teeth,' whispered Haggard.

'It's real,' said Gearth.

A door opened in the body of the dagger, swinging downwards. A shaft of light bled from it. The whirr of life support systems and plasma conduits thrummed through the palace. The *Hammer of Daemons*, responding to the code woven into the captain's speech, came to life.

Every eye was on the door and the glimpse of bright pearlescence inside, except for Alaric's. A Space Marine's peripheral vision was razor sharp, and he recognised the shift in the shadows, the shape that budded off from the gloom at the back of the room to flit through an archway. It was heading towards the front of the skull. Alaric knew it well. It surprised him that it had taken this long for it to show up.

'Stand guard,' said Alaric to Gearth. 'Keep any enemy off us until Erkhar's men can get this thing started.'

'And you?'

'I need to secure this place.'

'Then I'll send–'

'Just me.'

'You know, glory boy, if you're not back by the time we take off, we're leaving without you.'

'If it comes to that, good luck up there,' said Alaric as he left the chamber. Few of the slaves watched him go. They were fascinated by the light bleeding from the *Hammer of Daemons*, or clambering up onto the entrance ramp that had folded down from the corroded body. Chunks of rust were still falling from the body of the ship and revealing the ancient surface of the hull, painted deep blue with the remnants of stencilled designs in gold.

Erkhar was still reading prayers from the book as Alaric passed through the archway.

In front of him was the room, triangular in cross-section, formed by the skull's nasal cavity. It was a room for divinations or strategic planning, judging by the orrery that stood on one side of the room and the table inscribed with astrological designs taking up the other side. Plans of the stars above Drakaasi were etched on the walls.

Alaric paused and held his breath. The hum of the engines warming up behind him reverberated through the palace, but he was searching for something else: footsteps, or breathing.

A shadow was sliding along one wall, barely perceptible as it moved across the illustration of a star system.

'Kelhedros,' said Alaric, 'you can't hide any more.'

The shape stopped, but Alaric had it now, a faint wrongness in the way the light slid off the silver web of the star chart.

'I know what you are, Kelhedros. I've known for a while, and you have served your purpose well enough, but it's over now.'

The shape of the eldar solidified from the caul of shadow.

'Alaric. I am glad I found you. I became separated on the arena floor. I knew this was your objective so...'

'You came to stow away.'

'Stow away, justicar? Why would I need to stow–'

'Because I would have killed you before we left. The lies end now, alien, if you can even speak the truth any more.'

'Have you evidence of treachery, human? I would like to hear it before I submit to any threats.' Kelhedros's voice was thick with his customary arrogance. Alaric wondered if any eldar had ever paused to wonder if a human being had a soul, or the capacity to suffer. It was more likely not one of them had ever given a human any more thought than a human might give to a virus beneath a lens.

'Thorganel Quintus,' said Alaric. Kelhedros let his sneer fall, just a fraction. 'I was never there. It was an Imperial Guard action I read about. I never claimed to be there, either, except to you.'

Kelhedros would not have seemed to move to an unaugmented human eye, but to Alaric it was clear that his muscles were bunching up ready for action. Kelhedros's way of fighting relied on being the first in with the swiftest strike. Alaric would not give him that.

'Venalitor had heard of it too,' continued Alaric. 'He thought I had been there. The only person who had heard me tell that lie was you, Kelhedros.'

Kelhedros licked his lips. 'You cling to the truth as if it means something here, human.'

'Did you betray the last slave revolt, too? The one they were celebrating when my friend died. Were those games possible because you handed Venalitor and Ebondrake their victory?'

'One does what one must,' said Kelhedros, 'to survive.'

'For a human,' replied Alaric smoothly, 'survival is not enough.'

'What does your kind know?' hissed Kelhedros, drawing his chainblade. The weapon's teeth were clotted with blood. The eldar's cultured exterior was gone, and he looked almost feral, like something born to kill. 'Why do you think I did not tell Venalitor of the *Hammer of Daemons*? Because I believe, Justicar! I believe in escaping this damned world. Nothing on this planet desires escape as much as I do. You can never understand what can happen to a naked soul that dies in a place like this! You will never look upon the face of She Who Thirsts!'

'I understand everything, alien!' said Alaric. 'I know what you are. You never walked this Scorpion path. I have faced your kind before. You are things of darkness, with skin made of shadow, wrapped in silence. Mandrakes, the Guardsmen called you, assassins and spies. How else could you have free run of the *Hecatomb*, and leave it at will? Did you think I would believe this was some trick of the Scorpion path? You are much worse than an alien, and I will not let one such as you escape this world.'

'I will be gone from Drakaasi!' shrieked Kelhedros. His face was bestial, his eyes pure black, weeping tears as thick and dark as oil. He had given up on his disguise. His skin swam with shadows, shifting in and out of reality. 'I will return to the embrace of Commorragh! She will never take me!' Kelhedros was circling around, trying to get closer to the archway leading upwards towards the skull's remaining eye.

'You will die here,' said Alaric, 'and she will most definitely take you.'

Alaric had his spear in his hand. It felt like the thousandth weapon he had picked up since he had come to Drakaasi. He very much wished he had his Nemesis halberd, or one of the smith's marvellous weapons, but the spear would do.

Kelhedros was quick, but he wasn't quite good enough. If there was one thing Alaric could do better than any sentient creature on Drakaasi, it was perform an execution. Alaric drew back his arm to strike.

A sudden sliver of light blazed from the archway behind Kelhedros. It reached from the shadows and sliced through Kelhedros, biting down through his shoulder, and carving down through his back. A good third of his torso flopped to the floor, sliced organs tumbling out of the massive wound.

Kelhedros tried to step away from Alaric, but his body wouldn't obey, and his eyes widened as he realised that he was dead. He stumbled and fell onto his back. Blood had just caught up with the wound and was pumping from his sundered body.

'You have an inflated opinion of your own importance, alien,' said a deep voice dripping with arrogance and authority. 'The flaw of all your race. Do you think that I would ever honour our agreement? Freedom, safety, for a few words of treachery? And now you dare to seek escape from here, so that you can bring what you know of our world to the rest of your breed. You were nothing more than a pet, and you are to be put down.'

'She...' gasped Kelhedros, writhing on the floor like a landed fish. 'She... who... thirsts...' His eyes went dull, and he died as Alaric watched. Alaric thought he could hear Kelhedros screaming in the far distance, howling as his soul was devoured, but the sound was carried away by the wind blowing through the skull.

'A poor spy,' said Duke Venalitor. 'He really thought he was buying some kind of victory with his lies.'

Alaric couldn't speak. Venalitor had found them. Everything would end here.

'It seems that I have stolen your thunder,' said Venalitor, advancing into the room. The segments of his crimson armour gleamed in the dying daylight glinting over Vel'Skan's weaponscape. The sword in his hands shone as it drank the drops of Kelhedros's blood running down its blade. 'When one of my slaves is to be executed, it is I who serve as executioner.'

'What now?' breathed Alaric.

'What do you think, Grey Knight?'

'One of us kills the other.'

'I think you could be more specific,' said Venalitor with an ice-cold smile. 'I have to admit that you are one of those rare breeds of enemies who are more dangerous the closer you get.'

Venalitor was circling Alaric, and Alaric tried to weigh up Venalitor's avenues of attack: a slice low to take out Alaric's legs, a high cut to his head or throat, any one of a million thrusts or slices that would take Alaric's life with a single blow.

'It would amuse me to keep you alive and use you to further the work of Khorne,' said Venalitor dryly, 'but I have grown tired of being amused.'

Venalitor lunged. Alaric was ready. He brought up the spear to block the blow, and the blade cut clean through the haft. The blade was deflected enough to keep it from slicing through Alaric, but the spear was useless. Alaric threw the haft of the spear aside and held the tip away from his body, ready to parry or stab.

'I have learned a lot here,' said Alaric, forcing calmness into his voice. 'I am not the man you defeated on Sarthis Majoris.'

'No, justicar, you are something less.'

Alaric could have stabbed and blocked and thrust until he died, but that was not the way to win this fight. A Grey Knight might not have seen that. Alaric was not a Grey Knight any more.

Alaric dropped the spear and charged.

TWENTY-FOUR

'I KNEW,' ROARED Lord Ebondrake, 'that it would come to this.'

His voice carried down the Antediluvian Valley. Its slopes were built from stone axe heads and rough hewn spear shafts, the most ancient and primal weapons of Vel'Skan. The valley was a rift through the heart of the city, its depth cutting through aeons of war. The enemy army was strong across the valley, formed from the private forces of several of Drakaasi's lords. Arguthrax's slaves were tethered to posts driven into the ground, and painted with runes of summoning. Tiresia had called forth whole tribes. Scathach's contingent was the largest, with rank after rank of solemn warriors, from uniformed men with guns, to armoured cavalry. These forces had been called forth quickly, their plan to march on Ebondrake, and kill him before he could respond.

Ebondrake lived on a permanent war footing. He was ready.

'Perhaps it would take a million years,' he boomed, his words punctuated by plumes of black fire, 'perhaps a few moments, but you would turn on me. This is the way it has always been. I am as old as these mountains and the stars above us, and I have seen it so many times that I remember only an endless circle of betrayal. I told myself that when my time came, I would defy it. Nothing you have done has been anything but inevitable, and every move you make is one I have foreseen.'

A great host of beetle-black bodies came scuttling from the cracks between the weapons of the Antediluvian Valley. Thousands of scaephylyds scuttled into formation behind Lord Ebondrake, carrying the banners of their tribes. The ancient general, his carapace dulled by centuries, lumbered to the fore.

'You are our master's master,' slurred the general through his mandibles.

'Then you are my servant's servant,' said Ebondrake.

The general waved a forelimb in a signal to the scaephylyds. They all drew their weapons. They were still forming up down the throat of the valley, and there must have been a hundred thousand of them.

'The will of Khorne is with us!' yelled Arguthrax in reply. 'You have created this revolt in the heart of our city, in the midst of Khorne's celebrations, all to force us to unite under your rule! This is no longer a struggle for power, black lizard! This is an excommunication! Khorne despises you, and his wrath turns upon you! We true lords of Drakaasi are the instruments of that wrath!'

'You accuse me of treachery?' Ebondrake rose up off his haunches and spat black sparks in anger. 'The blasphemy in the arena was naught but a distraction created to force my attention away from your betrayal! What fools, what infants, to think such a ruse would tear victory from me!'

Thurgull, an ancient from Drakaasi's deeps, oozed through the valley wall, all gelatinous flesh and tentacles. Others of his kind were with him, smaller and less foul, but still deadly, snapping hooked beaks set into the mass of their mollusc-like flesh. Corpses began writhing up from the ground, and the Charnel Lord, who had against the odds thrown his lot in with Ebondrake, shambled through their midst allowing them to lick the corpse liquor from his funereal robes.

Ebondrake's army was huge. It was the equal of the conspirators', even as Golgur the Packmaster's hounds bounded in to join them. Arguthrax gave the signal, and the slaves pinned to the ground began to writhe, shafts of red light bleeding from their eyes and mouths as his allies from the warp sent their foot soldiers to possess the slaves.

'Enough words!' shouted Tireseia, nocking a flaming arrow to her bow.

'On that alone we can agree,' said Ebondrake. With a mighty blast of flame, he signalled the charge.

A FLASH OF savage satisfaction burst through Alaric as his forehead crunched into Venalitor's nose.

Venalitor stumbled backwards into the table, knocking the orrery onto the floor. The delicate device shattered, scattering tiny brass planets and orbits everywhere.

Venalitor tried to bring his blade around, but Alaric was on top of him. Alaric did not remember the time when he lost his mind, but his muscles did. It was the most natural thing in the galaxy to grab Venalitor by the throat and slam him over and over again into the solid table. Venalitor snarled and tried to struggle free. The table split in two, and Venalitor fell through to the floor with Alaric trying to gouge at his eyes and claw at his throat.

Venalitor jammed his knee up into Alaric's midriff and threw the Grey Knight over his head. Alaric sprawled through the half-wrecked divination chamber through the archway, skidding through Kelhedros's blood as he went.

He was in Lord Ebondrake's trophy chamber.

Bodies and weapons were everywhere, displayed obscenely. A gutted corpse was laid out, plated in gold with rubies studding its wounds. It was a human in uniform, perhaps a Guard general or a planetary noble, laid out on a black marble slab like a sculpture. Alaric saw the soft features warped in anguish, and wondered for a moment if it had been a woman.

Claws and blades torn from the arms of aliens were racked up on the wall beside Alaric. Skulls and ribs that Alaric recognised as being from tyranid creatures formed a display in front of him. A captured siege engine, its black metal wrought into screaming faces, loomed in the middle of the room.

The chamber took up a full third of the palace's cranium, and weapons and body parts taken from defeated foes filled it to the ceiling: enormous totem poles of giant creatures' skulls; chandeliers of severed hands; statues of half-melted swords clad in skins cut from tattooed bodies; whole enemies plated in bronze, or frozen in blocks of ice kept intact by humming cryo-units; spears and swords by the hundred, displayed in fearsome walls of blades; lifetimes upon lifetimes of battles and duels, of treacheries avenged and would-be assassins uncovered: a terrible illustration of what Lord Ebondrake truly was.

Alaric pulled himself into the shadows between a pair of mummified corpses, still impaled on the spikes used to execute them.

He weighed up his situation in a split second, as only a Space Marine's mind could. Alaric wasn't unarmed any more. He could have his pick from any one of a thousand wicked-looking weapons on display in the trophy room, but Venalitor was still the best swordsman Alaric had ever faced.

He was too good.

'Face me, Space Marine!' called Venalitor as he stalked into the trophy chamber. 'Truly, your Emperor must be a weakling god if even his very finest cower as you do.'

'You add too many flourishes to your sword work,' replied Alaric. 'I noticed it when you beat me on Sarthis Majoris. Such a thing focuses the mind.' Alaric took a blade from the closest mummified corpse, a bronze scimitar, inscribed with runes, that he drew silently from the corpse's chest. 'If there's one thing I have learned here, it's that blood-shed is an ugly thing.'

'Bloodshed is an art,' snapped Venalitor, 'and you are my canvas!'

Venalitor swept over the display of mummified bodies, the skirts of his armour billowing behind him like wings. Alaric deflected the arc of his sword with his scimitar and the bronze weapon was sliced in two. Alaric spun, pulled a spike from the skull of a second body and parried again. Venalitor's sword was knocked a centimetre away from gutting Alaric, and the spike was split in two, lengthways.

Alaric lunged forwards and kneed Venalitor in the groin. Venalitor stumbled backwards, bent double, and Alaric sent an uppercut into his chest so hard that Venalitor plunged backwards through the bodies, scat-tering dried-out limbs and fragments of age stiffened funeral shrouds.

'Too many flourishes,' said Alaric, shaking out his hand.

Venalitor got to his feet. He snarled, and for a moment his con-sciousness, the true nature beneath the cultured swordsman exterior, flashed across him. A yawning maw hissed through a ring of fangs, and black eyes narrowed into reptilian slits.

There was, however, no one to see it. Venalitor braced himself for the next charge, but it did not come. He looked around, but Justicar Alaric was gone.

It was not like a Space Marine at all, but that did not matter. Alaric was ultimately like any other quarry, a puzzle to be solved, a life to be ended. Venalitor prayed a few syllables to Khorne to keep his sword keen, and began the hunt.

'NAVIGATION'S STILL UP,' said Erkhar breathlessly. 'Praise the Emperor! Praise the saints!' He swung into the command pulpit and read from the age clouded information panel in front of him. 'It's working. There's plasma in the conduits! The reactors are warming up!'

The smiles on the faces of the faithful were reason enough to have made it this far. It was like a rapture, as if the image of the Emperor was hovering on the bridge of the *Hammer of Daemons*, bestowing His bless-ing upon them.

The ship worked. The Promised Land was real.

'Take-off vectors are pre-loaded,' said one of the faithful from the navigations helm, surrounded by slab-like banks of memm-crystal. 'They're all up. Once the thrusters are on-line and the main engines are primed we can take off.'

'Wait,' said Erkhar. 'Raezazel's followers programmed this ship to fly into a warp rift. Those must be the coordinates in the navigation helm. Use it to take off and then switch to helm control, otherwise we'll pitch straight into the warp.'

'Then... that's it? It's ready to fly?' asked Brother Hoygens. The man looked dazed, the events of the last few minutes almost too much for him to understand. It seemed like only a breath ago that the slaves had been about to die in Vel'Skan's games. Now they had a spaceship.

'It is,' said Erkhar. 'This is a miracle, an honest miracle. To those who denied that the Emperor's light could ever shine on this world, I give you the *Hammer of Daemons*!'

The *Hammer* was a vessel worthy of the Emperor's intervention. Exposure to Drakaasi's elements had covered it in a sheath of corrosion, but the ship inside was magnificent. Raezazel's followers had spared no expense. The corridors and bays shone in deep blue and gold, with a saint's portrait looking over every doorway and porthole. Shrines to the Emperor could be found everywhere, from the simple niches with devotional candles and texts to the great three-faced altar in the ship's main assembly area, with the triptych wrought in gold depicting the Emperor as deliverer, protector and avenger. The bridge was a reliquary with sacred bones and vials of saintly blood hovering in miniature gravunits, bathed in shafts of light in a ring around the helms and command pulpit. Erkhar had never seen anything so beautiful, not even in the days before his enslavement. The *Pax Deinotatos* had been an ugly ship, a base thing of rusting steel and leaking conduits. The *Hammer* was a mighty flying altar to Imperial glory.

'We should... pray, then,' said Hoygens uncertainly.

'We can pray when we're off the ground,' replied Erkhar. He flicked a switch and accessed the ship's vox-caster network. 'Engines?'

'Here, lieutenant,' came the reply. It was Gearth. Erkhar flinched at the thought of Gearth having a place on their holy ship, but he would be judged like the rest of them when the Promised Land was in sight.

'Reactor status?'

'Looks like they're working. Twenty-five per cent, if that means anything.'

'It does,' said Erkhar. 'Keep me updated.'

'Yes, lieutenant.'

'Lieutenant,' said the faithful at the navigation helm. 'You need to see this.'

Erkhar hurried to the navigation helm. Over the faithful's shoulder he saw the cartographic readout that he had pulled up.

'That's Drakaasi,' said the faithful, pointing to a planet marker on the screen, 'and this is the route still loaded into the navigation cogitators. It looks like the route the ship was on when it crashed here.'

Erkhar followed the arc of the ship's path. Its destination was only a short distance from Drakaasi. With a good, fast ship such as the *Hammer* undoubtedly was, it could be reached in less than an hour.

'They were so close,' said Erkhar. 'It must have been the Emperor's will that brought the *Hammer* down to Drakaasi before they reached it. Whatever happened to this ship's pilgrims on Drakaasi, it was surely no worse than what lay past the rift.'

'We'll steer well clear,' said the faithful, 'but what then?'

'Get clear of Drakaasi, and clear of the Eye if we can,' replied Erkhar. His eyes shone. 'Then we find the Promised Land.'

EVERY SINGLE LIVING thing in Vel'Skan had chosen its side.

The power of treachery flowed through the streets of the city like pure molten hatred. Smiths turned their hammers on one another. Drill daemons on the parade grounds ordered one rank to attack another. Strangers in the street called out who was with them and who was against, and knives came out in the alleyways. Half pledged themselves to Ebondrake and the correct order of Drakaasi's monarchy. Half devoted themselves to toppling him, to disorder, ruination and chaos.

The two armies collided all across the city, not just in the Antediluvian Valley, but across Vel'Skan, in every temple and forge, every place one human could murder another.

In the valley, Lord Ebondrake himself led the charge. His great wings pounded once, and he hauled himself up into the air, crashing down on Tiresia the Huntress. He dug her crushed body from beneath him, flipped her into the air and snapped his jaws shut on her, swallowing her in one gulp. Thousands of arrows and spears rained against him, but he breathed a sheet of black fire over Tiresia's tribespeople, and a hundred of them died, gutted to charred skeletons by the force of Ebondrake's anger.

Thousands of Scathach's men slammed into the scaephylyd tide. Scathach himself drew the ancient bolt gun from his back, a relic of his days in the Traitor Legions, and put bolter shells through a score of scaephylyd bodies as his ranks of warriors struggled to hold back the living wave.

The slaves staked to the ground exploded, gore showering down, as daemons fresh and raw from the warp emerged from their possessed bodies. Wet muscle glistened all over them, new limbs withering and reforming as they vomited scalding blood, and ripped into the slimy host led by Thurgull. The Charnel Lord's dead horde clambered over the bodies as they mounted up, dragging soldiers and daemons into caves of the newly dead to devour them.

The battle spilled out of the valley. Daemonic spawn and tentacled horrors from the sea wrestled through the temple galleries and sacred precincts, scattering statues and relics of Khorne. Tiresia's surviving hunters took the battle to the air, flying their aerial beasts of prey into a swirling melee with winged daemons streaming from Vel'Skan's eyries.

After a few minutes, no one remembered why they were fighting. There was a sense of betrayal on both sides, but the details were lost in the blood. Arguthrax, thrashing with a huge mace as his cauldron was hauled forwards through the heaps of dead, did not care to remember just why he had ordered his battered army forwards into the heart of the scaephylyd mass. The Charnel Lord let the events leading up to the battle sink down into the fevered pit of his mind, and concentrated instead on the holy work of bringing the battle dead back to half-life and setting them on the men they had been fighting alongside.

Ebondrake alone remembered. Part of him stayed calm enough through the carnage to remind him that if he lost, he lost Drakaasi. He would rather die as king than live on as someone's slave. As was right and proper for a servant of the Blood God, Lord Ebondrake sought death as eagerly as he sought victory, and there was no shortage of it choking every avenue of Vel'Skan.

THE ECHOES OF the battle rippled through Drakaasi like an earthquake reaching right through the planet's core. Every one of the planet's great cities felt it and they, too, were suddenly divided. The madmen of the *Scourge* stopped ranting and put their divinations aside to bludgeon one another with anything they could find, or hurl one another into the sea. Crested daemonfish rose from the depths to bask in the blood that foamed beneath the abattoir temples of the *Scourge*.

The singing of Aelazadne turned dark and clashing as its voices were replaced by the gurgle of blood in slit throats. Gorgath's battle lines were suddenly redrawn, one army under the banner of the dragon, and the other preaching revolution as they died. Ghaal seethed with murder, its gutters overflowing with blood and its night alive with the sound of knives through flesh.

Karnikhal began to slowly devour itself.

Drakaasi quaked. The day turned blood red, while on the other side of the planet the stars grew into burning rubies like eyes gorged with bloodshed. Howling winds ripped across the plains, rousing every living thing into a frenzy, turning hidden cabals of cultists against one another or forcing the jungles into bouts of continent-wide cannibalism, predators and prey turning on their own. Even in the depths of the sea, bizarre creatures, unknown on the surface, ripped one another to shreds with needle-like teeth.

There was a sound on the wind that carried further than the clashing of blades and the screams of the dying.

It was laughter.

Khorne was enjoying this particular spectacle.

TWENTY-FIVE

Duke Venalitor left behind footprints of Kelhedros's blood as he stalked through the trophy chamber.

He had never been here. Very few, save Ebondrake, ever had. He did not know his way around. He had not expected it to be this huge, or for there to be so many places for Alaric to hide.

Somewhere in the sea of corruption that Venalitor had for a mind, frustration surfaced.

'The men you killed in your madness,' said Venalitor, 'they were the ones I took from the cities of Sarthis Majoris, some of your Guardsmen, too. Did you recognise them as you killed them?'

There was no answer from the darkness. Night had fallen, and the only light bled from a few glowing orbs scattered around the trophy collection, apparently placed there to make the bladed shadows longer.

'What about Skarhaddoth? I saw you kill him. You are the champion of Drakaasi. How does it feel to be proclaimed the planet's most dedicated servant of Khorne?'

A footstep reached Venalitor's ears. He froze, his blade held low, ready to cut the legs out from under the charging Grey Knight.

Venalitor pivoted, and sliced through the dark shape looming towards him. His blade cut clean through the body, the hanging body, strung by a noose from the ceiling, an executed enemy of Ebondrake's left to dangle and rot in the trophy room.

He was jumping at nothing.

Alaric smashed through a bank of blades and shields, scattering ancient weapons everywhere. A blade hammered down and caught Venalitor's sword, snapping the star-forged metal, and sending half the blade spinning off into the shadows.

Venalitor threw himself backwards. He barely escaped being bowled to the ground by Alaric's impact.

Alaric landed heavily, but on his feet, cracking the tiles underneath him. He carried a halberd in his hand: the Nemesis weapon of a Grey Knight.

In his other hand was the gauntlet-mounted storm bolter.

'I hope Ebondrake enjoyed your little gift,' said Alaric, noticing the moment of shock passing over Venalitor's face as he saw Alaric's weapons. 'It cost you more than you realise.'

Venalitor's eyes flickered down to the haft in his hand and the broken stump of its blade.

'That was my favourite sword,' he growled. He gave up all pretence that he was a normal man, and his features melted away, his nose and mouth joining into one circular fanged orifice and his eyes becoming liquid slits. With a practised motion, Venalitor drew a pair of short swords from his back.

'Now,' said Alaric, 'we're almost even.'

'Almost,' hissed the thing that called itself Duke Venalitor.

The ring of their blades clashing was so rapid and relentless that it sounded like the trophy chamber was filled with driving rain. Venalitor slashed too fast to see, but his blades rang off Alaric's halberd. Alaric knocked Venalitor back with raw strength, his greater reach letting him hack out in arcing strikes, too artless to wound, but enough to force Venalitor back across the chamber, step by step.

Alaric fired a burst from his storm bolter. Venalitor swatted the bolter shells away like insects. Venalitor ducked low and cut down at Alaric's legs. Alaric blocked one strike with the butt of his halberd, swung the blade down to turn the second, and kicked out to catch Venalitor in the chin. A deep cut was opened up in Venalitor's monstrous face, and from the wound reached tendrils of blood, snaking towards Alaric's limbs to entangle them and leave the Grey Knight defenceless.

Alaric grabbed a handful of the tendrils with his bolter hand, and forced them up to his mouth. He bit into them, tearing at them, like he had torn at the raw meat of the Hathran sacrifice in his half-remembered madness. The tendrils fell limp, and Alaric spat out the blood.

He had learned a lot. He could fight like an animal when he had to. He could give up everything he had ever been taught in the duelling vaults of Titan and revert to the brutality written into his blood. He could go further than his enemy, be more relentless, more devoted to bloodshed. That was what Drakaasi had taught him.

Alaric shattered one of Venalitor's swords, knocked the other one aside, and grabbed the swordsman's wrist. He picked Venalitor up, and threw him through the great siege engine in the centre of the chamber. The machine came apart and collapsed, scattering blood-blackened timbers and chunks of iron everywhere.

Venalitor rolled onto his front and got to his knees. Alaric didn't give him the chance to regain his feet. He picked up a length of wood, and smacked Venalitor around the side of the head, hard enough to throw him back again, crashing through a stand of ornamental armour.

Venalitor's hand closed on nothing. He was on the edge of a sudden drop.

He had come to rest on the edge of the opening formed by the skull's eye socket. To one side, through the other eye, stabbed the corroded form of the *Hammer of Daemons*, shards of rust flaking off it as it shuddered with the force of its engines.

Beneath was Vel'Skan.

The sight of Vel'Skan at war was enough to strike the voice from Venalitor's throat. Armies clashed in the streets. Banners of a dozen lords waved as their followers clashed. A gout of black flame showed that Ebondrake himself was fighting. The outskirts of Vel'Skan were already aflame, tinting Drakaasi's night a dull orange.

Daemons danced through the carnage. Killers competed to die first.

'Survival,' said Alaric, 'was never enough.'

'This… this was you,' said Venalitor. His monstrous face was bleeding away as the rage was replaced with wonder. 'Arguthrax and I, Raezazel, Gorgath, your madness, this was all you. It was all your plan.'

'Of course. I am a Grey Knight. I could hardly come to a world like Drakaasi and leave it intact.'

'You turned us against one another. Our hatred was our strength and our weakness. Our pride, our wrath, our devotion, all these were just a weapon for you.' Venalitor smiled. 'The Dark Gods would be proud of you, Justicar.'

Alaric had never heard anything so hateful, because he knew that it was true.

He fired his storm bolter point-blank into Venalitor's chest.

Venalitor's armour held, but the force of the exploding bolter shell was enough to knock him off his feet.

There was no floor behind him to break his fall. He dropped his sword as he flailed at nothing.

Venalitor fell from the eye socket of Lord Ebondrake's castle. Tendrils of blood lashed out for something to grab onto, but they found nothing. His eyes met Alaric's as he fell, and there was something like horror in them.

Alaric watched Venalitor fall, following him down into the darkness of Vel'Skan.

Haulvarn had been avenged. Alaric sought some elation at that fact, but it was as elusive as Raezazel's truth. There could be no triumph on this tainted world.

Alaric turned away from the eye socket, away from the sight of Vel'Skan at war, and headed for the *Hammer of Daemons*.

THE HAMMER WAS shuddering as its plasma reactors filled up with superheated fuel. Most of the corrosion had been shaken off it, revealing the deep blue of its hull and the gold-painted decoration. It must have been a truly magnificent craft when it was launched. It still was extraordinary, and it was ready to take off.

Alaric hurried up the steps towards the torture chamber, dragging his armour behind him. He saw that the boarding ramp of the *Hammer* was still down, but judging by the roar of the engines it wouldn't stay that way for long. It was time to leave Drakaasi.

He heard footsteps behind him. He turned to see One-ear and his surviving orks, still slathered in scaephylyd blood.

One-ear looked at Alaric, and then up at the *Hammer of Daemons*, and in his alien mind he must have known that this was the only chance he and his fellow greenskins had to get off Drakaasi.

One-ear spat on the ground, snarled at Alaric, and led his orks back down the steps towards the war-torn streets of Vel'Skan.

'Justicar!' shouted Corporal Dorvas from the ship's boarding ramp. 'We're on autopilot! We'll leave you behind if we have to!'

Alaric hurried up the ramp just as it began to close and the engines rose in pitch. Plasma was coursing through the ship's conduits, swirling from the reactors through the engines. Inside, the Hathrans were finding whatever they could to hold on to as the ship began to shudder even more, throwing aside anything that wasn't fixed. Candles rolled across the tilting floor and sacred texts fluttered from the walls.

'I see you've found your gear,' said Dorvas, looking down at the power armour that Alaric was hauling along. 'If you get us off this planet you'll have earned it back.'

'Where are we going?' asked Alaric.

'We're worrying about that once we're off Drakaasi,' replied Dorvas.

The *Hammer's* engines flared, and all sound was drowned out as the plasma generators came on-line.

The whole ship lurched, and the sound of breaking bone signalled that the ship, after centuries embedded in the palace of Vel'Skan, was finally taking off.

LORD EBONDRAKE'S PALACE split in two. Shards of bone fell and impaled battling cultists on the palace approach below. The engines flared and blew out the back of the cranium, incinerating dozens as plasma fire spewed from the exhaust housings. The cranium collapsed, burying the torture chamber and trophy hall in a rockslide of fragmented bone. The *Hammer of Daemons* was finally free. The last of the corrosion was thrown off it, and, lit by the fires of the burning city, the ship rose on vertical thrusters to look out over Vel'Skan.

Very few saw it. Most were too busy killing and being killed. A few did notice it, and assumed it was a weapon called forth by Ebondrake or the conspirators. Perhaps Ebondrake's enemies had sent it to destroy the palace, or perhaps Ebondrake had finally chosen to reveal it, sacrificing his palace to bring some ancient wrath down on Arguthrax and his fellow traitors.

Very few, even of those who saw it, particularly cared. It was just a distraction from the killing.

ALARIC FOUGHT TO keep his footing as he pushed his bulk through the door in the bulkhead designed for a man a metre shorter. The *Hammer* shuddered again, and Alaric nearly fell. He had to hurry. By the time the *Hammer* escaped Drakaasi's atmosphere it might be too late.

The flight deck of the *Hammer of Daemons* was as lavishly decorated as the rest of the ship. The blue walls were inlaid with long ribbons of gold, forged into images from the life of the prophet Raezazel.

The ship's shuttle craft had survived the years intact, sealed inside the flight deck away from the ravages of Drakaasi. It was deep blue and chased in gold like the rest of the ship, and decorated with multiple stylised mouths, which Alaric realised, with a lurch, must be the symbol of Raezazel. A dozen mouths had spoken from the daemon's flesh as it taunted him. Alaric opened the access hatch in the body of the shuttle and threw his war gear inside. He could wear it again when it had been purified.

'Good idea,' said Gearth. Alaric turned to see the killer, still smeared with blood and war paint. 'This thing's full of mental cases. They think they're flying right up the Emperor's arse. If they're wrong, we could end up anywhere, and if they're right, then… well, me an' the Emperor ain't seen eye to eye since I was born.'

'Why are you here?' asked Alaric.

'Same reason as you,' replied Gearth. 'To get off this thing, and take my chances on my own. You're tough, Justicar, but you don't know the nethers of the Imperium like me. Fighting's all very well, but me, I could hitchhike my way out of the Eye. You could use someone like me around.'

'You said once,' said Alaric, 'that you didn't know why you committed your crimes, why you killed those women.'

Gearth glanced around as if afraid that someone was listening. 'I guess. What does it matter?'

'You never will.'

Alaric shot Gearth once in the stomach. The bolter shell exploded in his abdomen and blew a length of spine out of his back. Gearth flopped to the ground.

'The Blood…' he gasped. 'The Blood God… promised…'

Alaric started to clamber into the shuttle.

'You're gonna… leave 'em…' said Gearth, his pained whisper barely audible over the ship's engines. 'Gonna… leave 'em all… the Guard boys, everyone… just… to die out here…'

Alaric ignored the dying man, and hauled the shuttle's hatch closed behind him.

The cockpit was barely big enough for Alaric to fit into. He thumbed a command stud, and the flight deck doors ground open. The air in the deck boomed out into the thin atmosphere and took Gearth's body with it, the flimsy corpse trailing blood as it tumbled out into Drakaasi's night. Alaric gunned the shuttle's engines and flew it out of the flight deck, feeling the waves of superheated air from the *Hammer's* engines buffeting it as if it was a falling leaf.

He wrestled for control. He cleared the *Hammer's* wake and had it back.

Now, it really was time to get away from this planet.

'THE FLIGHT DECK just opened,' said Haggard, clinging to a guard rail around a floating relic as he stumbled onto the bridge. 'Someone took a shuttle out.'

'Then they have forsaken their life's reward,' replied Erkhar calmly. The streams of the upper atmosphere were hammering against the hull, and anything loose was being thrown about, but Erkhar was as calm as if he was sailing on a glassy sea. The rift in space shone in front of him, filling the bridge with crimson light, opening to swallow the *Hammer of Daemons.*

'What's that?' asked Haggard.

'The rift,' replied Erkhar. 'Switch off the autopilot. We'll take her away from Drakaasi on manual.'

'Yes, lieutenant,' said the faithful at the navigation helm.

'The Emperor will show us the way,' said Erkhar as the ship swung away from the rift, towards the billowing nebulae of the Eye of Terror. 'We have but to listen. In our prayers, in our dreams, there is the way to the Promised Land.'

TWENTY-SIX

DUKE VENALITOR'S BODY was impaled on one of the many swords making up the web of steel into which were built the thousands of homes where Vel'Skan's poorest dwelt. The point went in through his back and out through his chest, just below the scar on his armour left by Alaric's bolter shot.

He was alive when he hit. With his spine cut, Venalitor couldn't even writhe, just lie there as the pain racked through him and his body slowly slid down the blade blunted by time.

No one noticed him die. Below him was a battle with no lines, a swirling melee where all sense of order and alignment had broken down and everyone was out killing for himself. It was a riot, a massacre, and a scene being repeated throughout Vel'Skan, but more than that, it was infecting the whole of Drakaasi.

Venalitor's head lolled to one side. He could see something burning on a blood river snaking out of Vel'Skan's outskirts. It was a ship, his ship, the *Hecatomb*, cut loose from its moorings beneath the city. It blazed from stem to stern.

The wards would have been breached. What was held prisoner there would escape. Venalitor knew then that he should have killed it when he had the chance.

For someone who had not been human for so long, the last thing Venalitor felt was a very human emotion.

He felt despair.

ALARIC SAW THE army falling back through the city, beetle-black swarms of scaephylyds pouring in from every side.

He saw Arguthrax, carried aloft by a tide of daemons, blazing a path of fire and ruination towards Ebondrake's palace. Arguthrax would take the palace, but, once there, he would find that its greatest prize was already gone.

He saw Lord Ebondrake on the pinnacle of a mighty temple, holding its brass dome against a horde of Vel'Skan's citizens who had gathered in a spontaneous army to bring him down. He incinerated them by the dozen, but there were too many of them, and they had set the temple alight, and were working at its columns with picks and hammers. Soon it would collapse, and even Lord Ebondrake would be gone.

Similar scenes were playing out all across the city. Streets were like cities of fire, buildings like sacrificial candles, battle like a disease gradually claiming everything.

Alaric looked away from the city. There was nothing he could do now to make it worse. He aimed the shuttle's controls upwards, accelerating to orbital speed. He glanced down at the fuel gauge. Much of the fuel had evaporated in the shuttle's tanks in its years lying idle, but there was just enough to get him out of orbit once he was beyond the atmosphere, and perhaps to somewhere the Inquisition would find him. That was why he had left the *Hammer of Daemons*. Even if Erkhar's Promised Land were real, there was no place in it for Alaric, not yet.

The swirls of Drakaasi's atmosphere gave way to the diseased void of the Eye of Terror. It wasn't a good place to be cut adrift, but it was safer than Drakaasi. Alaric could survive for years if he had to in half-sleep, his brain shut down until only the most basic of life processes were continued. After Drakaasi, he could do with a few good years to think it all over.

As Alaric let the main engines kick in, a plume of orange flame licked up from Vel'Skan. It was Ebondrake's temple, finally collapsing in a ball of fire. Ebondrake was probably dead.

Alaric took no satisfaction at all from that knowledge.

The rumble of the planet's atmosphere ceased, and Alaric left Drakaasi behind forever.

* * *

RAEZAZEL THE CUNNING licked the blood from Dorvas's face.

Around him, hundreds of Hathrans lay torn and bloody on the deck of the *Hammer of Daemons*. He had come to them as swift as a whirlwind, their tiny determined minds reduced to fear, and then silence, by Raezazel's touch.

He slid through the corridors and decks of the ship. It was as familiar as one of his own forms, like a cloak of flesh that fit him perfectly: the shrines and inscriptions put up by pilgrims who never understood that they were doing the work of Chaos; the ship's own structure, in itself a subtle prayer to the Liar God; the smell and the feel of it.

The *Hecatomb* had burned, the wards about his prison had crumbled, and Raezazel had been free. His punishment at Venalitor's hands had been severe, but Raezazel was still a daemon, still a thing of the warp, and he was still dangerous. He had bled through Vel'Skan, revelling in the war overtaking it, and had found the *Hammer of Daemons* as he had left it in the half-blinded skull. Boarding it had been simple. Scything through the Hathrans had been more taxing than Raezazel had anticipated, for he was out of practice, but it felt so good to be free, so good to kill. He would soon get the hang of it again.

Raezazel slipped up the decks towards the bridge. As he went, the Hathrans tried to fight him, but their eyes went blind with shock as he punched tentacles through their stomachs or extruded golden sickle blades to slice them apart. Some he sucked dry, leaving them husks like the cast-off skins of lizards. A few, he melted into the sacred walls of the *Hammer* or turned inside-out.

He was powerful now. He was free of his bonds. One form had been crippled, but a hundred more emerged into existence. He was glorious. He was the Lie given form.

The bridge was ahead. Raezazel melted the blast doors into a pool of molten gold.

Inside was the most beautiful collection of minds that Raezazel had seen for many centuries.

They believed.

He could taste their faith. They believed in a religion that had sprung up from the detritus of Raezazel's own flock: snatches of sacred writings, half-formed memories of the pilgrimage. From nothing had sprung yet more believers in the lie.

Raezazel laughed. What a wondrous thing. Without willing it, his deception of his pilgrim flock had given rise to a whole new breed of deluded faithful.

Raezazel swept onto the bridge, taking on the form of a nightmare.

* * *

ERKHAR GRABBED THE autopistol holstered beneath the command pulpit. He didn't bother to aim, since the daemon boiling onto the bridge was large enough for any shot to hit it.

He loosed off half the weapon's magazine, ears full of screams and rushing blood. Hoygens disappeared into the daemon's churning blue-gold mass.

They had come so close. They had left Drakaasi and its horrors behind, and now this.

At least they had got a taste of what it meant to be free. This was what Erkhar told himself as bladed tendrils wrapped around his waist and sliced his stomach open.

He was lifted off the pulpit. He dropped his pistol, and his hand with it, a golden scythe having sliced through his arm at the wrist. He looked into the scores of eyes and mouths looming in front of him and knew instinctively that he was in the clutches of Raezazel the Cunning.

Erkhar screamed in defiance, and a hundred mouths devoured him.

RAEZAZEL REACHED OUT and plucked the soul from the faithful at the navigation helm, rending the insubstantial stuff of the spirit from the fleshy frame. Other pilgrims were trying to flee or to fight back. Those who fought amused Raezazel greatly, stabbing at him with whatever came to hand. A couple had guns from the ship's armoury. Raezazel turned the floor beneath them to liquid, and they sank to their thighs in molten gold, spasming in shock as they were incinerated.

The *Hammer of Daemons* was a fine ship. Once the bridge was clear, Raezazel could take it over and fly it to a new world. There, he would begin again. He would find himself a planet of the ignorant and the desperate, and give them a prophet. Tzeentch would finally have his due.

Raezazel absorbed a man named Hoygens, and devoured his memories, glimpsing scenes of a life of fear and horror, and the final delicious denial of his faith.

He was so enraptured with eating Hoygens's ignorant mind that for a moment Raezazel did not notice the last survivor grabbing the autopistol on the floor.

HAGGARD KICKED ERKHAR'S severed hand aside and picked up the pistol. He stumbled back against the navigation helm as the full horror of Raezazel oozed finally onto the bridge. The last few faithful were disappearing into its mass. Haggard knew that the others on the ship were dead. There would be no freedom from Drakaasi. None of them would survive.

Finally, Haggard understood that survival was not enough.

Hundreds of eyes turned to look at him. Haggard didn't know if he could move. It was the most horrible thing he had ever seen, glowing blue flesh and golden blades, rippling with silver.

'Where…' he stuttered, 'where are my friends? Are they dead?'

'Of course,' replied Raezazel in a hundred voices at once.

'Good,' said Haggard. He slammed the butt of the pistol down on the navigation helm.

The command stud rescinded the last coordinates input into the cogitator. The *Hammer of Daemons* reverted back to its previous course: the way to the Promised Land.

Haggard emptied the rest of the gun's ammunition into the navigation helm. The controls exploded in sparks and blue flames. Haggard fell to the deck, slick with the blood of the faithful.

Raezazel the Cunning looked up at the viewscreen. The *Hammer of Daemons* swung around, the stars marching past until the view centred on a glowing red slash in space. It was the warp rift, the gateway to the warp into which Raezazel had promised to deliver souls for Tzeentch.

The daemon's eyes widened in something like fear.

Raezazel threw Haggard aside, but the controls were ruined. Raezazel's realm was the human mind. Machines were just tools, just pieces of metal. He had no way of rewriting the ship's cogitators as he might rewrite the memories of a victim.

Deep inside the warp rift, a great golden eye opened.

The *Hammer of Daemons's* main engines kicked in, propelling the ship towards the rift. It grew larger and larger in the viewscreen, the eye unblinking, transfixing Raezazel where he stood.

'RAEZAZEL,' said a voice that boiled up from the warp. 'YOU PROMISED ME SOULS. YOU PROMISED ME THE FAITHFUL. YOU HAVE FAILED ME.'

For those last few moments, Raezazel screamed, and Haggard laughed.

ALARIC WATCHED FROM the cockpit of the shuttle as the *Hammer of Daemons* suddenly veered off course, main engines flaring. The ship rocketed towards the red slash that Alaric had guessed was the warp rift, the intended destination of Raezazel's flock.

There could be little doubt that everyone on the ship was doomed: Dorvas and the brave men of the Hathran Armoured Cavalry, who had been failed once more by Alaric; Erkhar, whose faith had kept him sane while men like Gearth were losing their souls; and Haggard, the only friend Alaric had really had on Drakaasi.

He tried to grieve for them. He tried to feel the weight of their deaths on him, but he was tired, and he could feel nothing.

Alaric lay back in the grav-seat of the shuttle. The constellations of the Eye of Terror whirled around him in their endless pattern, unconquerable and infinite.

Alaric wanted very much to sleep. He surrendered his mind to the suspended animation membrane that covered his brain, and the stars went dark.

ALARIC STAYED IN suspended animation for seven months.

The catalepsean node in his brain shut down everything except for his breathing and heartbeats. He woke once every several weeks to deplete the shuttle's meagre food and water stash and keep his muscles from atrophying. He was glad when he went back into suspension, because in deep, total sleep he did not dream.

A salvage team trailing an Imperial battlefleet found the distress beacon on Alaric's shuttle. Thinking it was a saviour pod from a larger ship, and that they could ransom the crew inside to the Imperial Navy, they eagerly boarded the shuttle among visions of retiring on the armfuls of credits the Navy was sure to give them for the officers inside. By the time they breached the hull they had become convinced that the occupants were officers, rapidly rising in rank until they expected to see a rear admiral or fleet commissar weeping with joy to see them.

Instead, they got their first look at a real live Space Marine.

Since they had no idea how valuable a Space Marine might be, but were very aware of how dangerous he was, the salvage crew debated whether to cast off and leave the shuttle to drift. The Space Marine's great size suggested that he would eat too much for the salvage ship to be able to make it back to port without running out of supplies. Other crew members were in favour of killing him, since he was no doubt a devout warrior monk hell bent on exterminating evildoers, and none of the crew had particularly spotless records. Alaric put a stop to all this by kicking down the airlock door and telling them that if they did not take him to a location of his choosing, he would kill them. The crew believed him.

His chosen location was the Inquisitorial fortress on Belsimar.

THE GENERAL LUMBERED up onto the peak of the ridge. He had lost many limbs in the past few months, but he still had just enough to drag his insect bulk around. His abdomen was covered in scars, and his mandibles were blunted by enemy armour and bone, but he was alive, and that was more than could be said for any of Drakaasi's lords. They had burned brightly, charging at the head of their armies, and duelling one another in week-long conflicts, but they had burned out first as well.

The old scaephylyd took in the scene around him. Aelazadne stood in the distance, its crystal towers shattered and blackened like the stumps of decaying teeth. In the valleys formed by the undulations of the plain, he could see bands of humans, near-feral, armed with teeth and fingers and the odd stone spear, scrapping with one another.

New champions would be born from this, new heroes of the Dark Gods. They would look upon the collapsed heap of ancient weapons in Vel'Skan and the corpse-mountains of Gorgath, and they would seek to emulate those who had created them. The general, and the scaephylyd nation, had seen it happen before.

For now, there was nothing: no order, no structure, and no power save that which a man could wrench from the bodies of his enemies.

More scaephylyds clambered up the ridge. Many of them were scarred by war too, and all of them had become veterans. It had been a long time since the scaephylyds had marched to war, and before long, when the predatory war bands began to organise themselves again, they would retreat below the earth and take up waiting once more.

Among the scaephylyds were newcomers. Green-skinned and hulking, most of them were brute animals, barely able to hold an axe the right way, but a few of them had enough cunning to lead their fellow creatures, and one, the grizzled one-eared greenskin, had a light in his eyes that suggested he might still understand.

The scaephylyds and greenskins assembled around the general, lowering their weapons in deference. The general waved a forelimb, encompassing the shattered city and the landscape still torn by desperate, endless war.

'Do you see now?' he asked, his intonation of the scaephylyd tongue a momentous rumble. 'Chaos.'

'This place,' said Inquisitor Nyxos, 'used to be a pleasure world.'

Nyxos leaned his old body against the railing of the balcony. He looked out on a rampant forest dappled with dead browns and greys. Colonies of swooping predators fought for scraps in the treetops. The sky was stained, and the rivers flowing down from the distant mountains were the colour of mud.

'You could win a place here with a lifetime of service and a few medals. Lord generals, admirals, that sort of thing. Good hunting, plenty of imported lads and lasses, all very willing. Hot and cold running narcotics. Well worth a couple of centuries in the trenches.' Nyxos turned away from the sight with a smile. 'I suppose the planet didn't like it.'

Alaric did not return his smile. There wasn't anything particularly funny about Belsimar.

The stately pile, half-reclaimed by the forest, had apparently once been the Inquisitorial fortress. All the equipment had been stripped out when the planet decided to turn on its inhabitants, but the mansion still had warrens of cells and storage vaults beneath the handsome exterior. Alaric fancied it looked better now than it had ever done, its garish mosaics fragmented and its overwrought architecture split and dragged down by the forest. Belsimar had been worth watching over once, no doubt because of the temptations of pleasure cults and the dangerous nature of knowledge being brought together by noteworthy people from across the Imperium.

'You picked a hell of a place to turn up, you know,' said Nyxos.

'It was the only place I could think of in the Eye that wasn't under siege,' replied Alaric. 'I'm surprised I remembered anything was here.' Alaric had heard that there was an Inquisitorial facility on Belsimar from an inquisitor he had been assigned to before he had attained the rank of justicar. That same inquisitor was probably elsewhere, trying to fend off the tide of Chaos that was flowing out of the Eye.

'And I'm surprised you're alive.'

'Haulvarn is dead.'

'So is Thane. Dvorn and Visical made it.'

'They're alive?' For the first time in a very long time Alaric felt something like elation. He had thought he was the only one left.

'They made it to a refinery and got out on the last fuel container. Dvorn is assigned to Brother-Captain Stern's Terminator retinue. Visical's under Inquisitor Deskanel around Agripinna. I don't know how they are faring, I'm afraid. Things are rather confused around the Eye.'

'Not so confused that you couldn't find me.'

'Ah, justicar, what are friends for?' Nyxos sat on the stone bench beside Alaric. The room had once been a ballroom, with grand windows opening onto the balcony and its once stunning view. Now chunks of fallen decor and an orchestra pit full of dead leaves were all that remained of its opulence. 'I have read your preliminary report.'

'The full one will be a lot longer.'

'So it will, so it will.' Nyxos looked up at the sound of footsteps on the stairs. 'Ah, Hawkespur.'

The last time Alaric had seen Interrogator Hawkespur, he hadn't been able to tell if she was dying or not. It had evidently been a close thing. The lower half of her face was ruined by pockmarks and chemical burns from the pollution she had inhaled on Chaeroneia, and the front of her throat was taken up by a bulky rebreather unit. She still wore her naval uniform, stripped of its insignia. She was carrying a heavy piece of machinery that looked like it was designed to punch holes in metal.

'It's primed, sir,' she said, her voice stiff and metallic.

'It'll work?' asked Nyxos.

'There were good results with prisoners at Subiaco,' replied Hawkespur.

'Then proceed, interrogator.'

Hawkespur stood behind Alaric. Even with him seated, she had to hold the device at eye level to reach. Clamps fastened around the Collar of Khorne around Alaric's neck. A flash of heat hit the back of Alaric's neck, and the clamps banged shut. Alaric felt pain, and a great pressure on his neck. Metal complained, and then barked as it was sheared through.

The two halves of the Collar of Khorne clanged to the floor.

Alaric gasped. He saw the ghost of Belsimar, the image of a beautiful planet flickering over the dreary landscape. Then it was gone, replaced with a new hyper-awareness. Alaric could feel the echo of Belsimar's sorrow, and the pain of the war in the stars overhead.

'Did it work?' asked Nyxos.

'Yes,' said Alaric, a slight shudder in his voice. 'I am whole again.'

'You will be back to normal in a few days,' said Nyxos. 'Disorientation is normal.' He prodded the remains of the collar with his toe. 'Dispose of this thing,' he said. Hawkespur obliged, picking the halves of the collar up with sanctified tongs and carrying them away.

'I'm glad she's alive,' said Alaric when she was gone. He fingered the callous around his neck where the collar had rubbed away at his skin.

'She would say the same about you,' said Nyxos, 'if she felt that such a thing was appropriate. We had written you off, Alaric, I am sorry to say. When we found out who had raided Sarthis Majoris we feared the worst. I hoped that you had died on that battlefield, Emperor forgive me.'

'Perhaps...' said Alaric faltering, still coping with the return of his psychic awareness, 'perhaps it would not have been such a bad thing.'

'What makes you say that?' asked Nyxos. He did not sound surprised to hear it. 'There are few enough Grey Knights in the galaxy. Why would it benefit from one less?'

'To survive,' said Alaric, 'I did some terrible things. I turned Drakaasi's lords on one another, just like a cultist would to foment rebellion. I consorted with heretics, and aliens. I left a great many people to die to escape, and to get revenge. A Grey Knight would not have done those things. Many times, I wondered if the right thing to do would be to just die, but I... could not. I had to survive. I had to go that far, and even survival was not enough.'

'You fear corruption,' said Nyxos.

'I do. More than anything. I know what fear is now.'

Nyxos smiled again. He was a very old man, probably centuries old, and even by Inquisitorial standards he had done a sterling job of avoiding death. He had probably seen just about every strange and terrible form corruption could take, but a Grey Knight who had fallen was beyond any of that. 'Alaric, there are ways you can be purified. It is not easy, or painless, but it can be done. We have ways.'

'Can I fight as a Grey Knight again?'

'Ah, what an interesting question. There is more than one way for a Grey Knight to serve, and many more for you. You have an imagination, Alaric, dedication, yes, but creativity too. How many Grey Knights could have survived on Drakaasi? Ignoring whether it was right or not, how many could have thought it up in the first place?'

'Not many,' admitted Alaric.

'That is something to be proud of. It is another blade in the Emperor's hand. I dare say my word would get you back into the training halls of Titan, if that is where you can best serve, but matters at the Eye are reaching a dire state and we need more than just soldiers, even Grey Knights.' Nyxos dusted his hands on his long dark robes and stood up. 'Our shuttle leaves in two hours. Say some prayers and forgive yourself for a while. Think about what you can do for your Emperor, instead of what sins you committed in the past. I have some very particular plans for you, Justicar Alaric. You might be surprised just what a man of your skills can achieve. Although no one on Drakaasi would be in any doubt.' Nyxos followed Hawkespur down to the lower floors of the mansion and the shuttle hangar.

Alaric hung his head, feeling the psychic eye inside him blinking in the sudden light. He was glad that it had been shut while he was on Drakaasi. The underlying ugliness of the place might have been too much.

He thought about Haulvarn and Erkhar, and the Hathrans on the *Hammer of Daemons*. He thought about Raezazel, Ebondrake and Arguthrax. He saw Venalitor's face as he fell, the expression turning to horror as he realised he had failed. Thinking about it, reliving it, would not change it.

He clasped his hands in front of him and began to pray.

'I am the Hammer,' he whispered. 'I am the point of His spear, the mail about His fist...'

ABOUT THE AUTHOR

Freelance writer Ben Counter is one of the Black Library's most popular SF authors. An Ancient History graduate and avid miniature painter, he lives near Portsmouth, England.

WARHAMMER
40,000

THE SOUL DRINKERS
OMNIBUS

BEN COUNTER

ISBN 978-1-84416-416-5

WARHAMMER
40,000

THE BLOOD ANGELS
OMNIBUS

Contains
the novels
Deus Encarmine and
Deus Sanguinius

'War-torn tales of loyalty and honour.' – SFX

JAMES SWALLOW

ISBN 978-1-84416-559-9

THE ULTRAMARINES
OMNIBUS

'Great characters, truck loads of intrigue and an amazing sense of pace.' **Enigma**

GRAHAM McNEILL

NIGHTBRINGER • WARRIORS OF ULTRAMAR • DEAD SKY BLACK SUN

ISBN 978-1-84416-403-5